JACK THE LAD AND BLOODY MARY

Joseph Connolly is the bestselling author of *Poor Souls*, *This Is It*, *Stuff*, *Summer Things*, *Winter Breaks*, *S.O.S*, *It Can't Go On*, *The Works* and *Love is Strange*. He has also written several works of non-fiction, including admired biographies of Jerome K. Jerome and P. G. Wodehouse.

JOSEPH CONNOLLY

Jack the Lad and Bloody Mary

ff

faber and faber

First published in 2007
by Faber and Faber Limited
3 Queen Square London WC1N 3AU
This paperback edition published in 2008

Typeset by RefineCatch Limited, Bungay, Suffolk
Printed in England by CPI Bookmarque, Croydon

A CIP record for this book
is available from the British Library

ISBN 978-0-571-23468-4

2 4 6 8 10 9 7 5 3 1

To Steve Cox
(Thanks for Number 10)

What happened

Can I? Can I go on loving the man, now I know that he's a killer? It's the hardest thing, this – of all the things he's done to me, it's this one, oh God yes, this one is just the very hardest to bear. He denied it, my Jackie – denied it to my face. And I just stood there looking at him, while he went on doing it. Sorry, he said – I'm truly sorry, Mary, but I simply can't accommodate you on this one, see? On account of I never so much as even touched the geezer, not even so much as laid a finger on him, see? Wasn't even close to the vicinity in question. So he's wound up dead now, has he? Old Sammy Punch. Well I'm sorry for that too. But you got to know, Mary, there's no how at all it could be down to me now, Mary my love – hand on heart: I swear it to you. Are you getting all of this, Mary? Can you hear me?

But you always know, don't you? When your man, he's done something bad. It's the war, you see – it's the war itself that tells you. After all these years, it gets so you're expecting a disaster the moment you're awake – not the things you read about in the news- paper or hear on the wireless, I don't mean – all the big efforts going on overseas – no, it's the things round here, the things that touch you. And I smelled it off him – even as his big and beautiful bastard eyes were imploring me to believe in all the love and sweetness that used to hang there behind them . . . well I just knew it for sure then, didn't I? My man Jackie, that now he was a killer.

It was Jonathan Leakey who told me, Jonny Midnight, they all call him now – and I used to know why, but all of that, that's got

1

lost in the dust and ages of the war, the war – I'm telling you, it's just ripped us all up, and for years and years. Any little bit of knowledge you think you might have had, any certainties – anything at all, really, that once you could depend on – you lose just the lot, bit by bit, like each one of your old photos dropped singly into a bonfire; it happens to you quickly, that's what's so frightening. Parts of yourself, they're just falling away – half of your stuffing, you see it coming out and then you just leave it all behind you.

When I heard the knock, I thought ah, that'll be Jack, that'll be my Jackie, then. He's timed it well for once, I remember thinking, because I'd got a good strong brew of beef tea on the stove, and it was just warming through quite nicely. *Bandstand* had just finished on the wireless, and I was on the pouffe just by the fireplace, getting some darning done. It's all I ever seem to be doing, nowadays – mending things. Making do and mending, it's become a way of life. It's not like in the old days when he worked for Mr Wisely, but Jackie, he still brings me nylons – I don't ask him where he gets them from. Jonathan Leakey, he's always got some stuff about him too – tinned loganberries it is tonight. And a nice piece of tongue. Well you can't say no – well can you? They're like gold, these things: ordinary people, they just can't get hold of them for love nor money. Not in the normal way.

So Jonny, he says to me Listen to me now, Mary – I've got to tell you, fill you in on how it was. It's not I mean to hurt you nor nothing, sweet Mary – you know that – but you just got to understand how it happened – the truth of the thing, Mary: that's what you just got to know, now. Because all the wrong word'll get back to you, elsewise – they'll be saying it's Jonny Midnight, this, got his stamp on it, this has: who am I kidding? They're saying it now. But they're wrong and you know it – you know it deep down, you know you do, Mary. If I were behind it, if it were anything to do with me, not a soul would even be aware it had occurred. You do know that, don't you Mary? It's not how I work. It's messy, this – it's a bad affair, and it ain't over yet, not by a long way. They won't just let it end, not them, you can stake your all on that. What it was, Mary – Jackie, he got panicked, he got clumsy: I watched him, and he just gone wild. Any of that, you don't want to let it happen to you, but Jackie, well – don't have to tell you, do I Mary my sweet? Ay? You know him well as I do. Better, some respects, I'm not denying. And it was him, it was him all right. How do I know? How come I'm this sure about it? Because it was him what told me, Mary – it was him what give it all to me. And I'll tell you now just what he said. Are you listening to me, Mary? Are you? Pour you a drop of beef tea or something, can I? No? Sure? All right. Well look, then – here's how it went, this is what he told me: his own sweet words.

I were *blazing*, Jonny – that's what he said to me, Mary, after me and the rest of us caught up with him, finally. Tell you – led us a right old chase, your Jackie did. He were real determined – you saw it in his eyes. He was going to get him, Sammy Punch, even if he was to drop down dead in the doing of it. Me and the lads – I'm telling you, Mary, we hadn't been in the motor, we never could've kept up, would've lost sight of him for sure. Nearly killed ourselves, we did, with the bleeding blackout, and all. So when it's all over and I go up to him – well, he were just standing there, not shaking nor nothing – not even out of breath, he was, which I could barely bleeding credit, you want the truth of it, Mary – the running he done. It all came down on him later, all of that did – his heart, then, it were thudding in him like a, I don't know – it were thudding in him hard, that's all I can say. Wheezing like a bellows, he were, both his legs gone right from under him. But when I first got there, he were right easy, you know? Calm as you like. Like it never happened, sort of style. And then he looks at me and, well – you know his eyes, you know how he can do it. I were *blazing*, he says to me – *blazing*,

3

Jonny: you hear me? You hear what I'm saying to you, Jonny? Yeh yeh, I says to him – I hear you, Jackie: I can hear you. So look, you want to tell me what's been going on, then?

Well listen, Jonny, he says – you have to know I didn't want any little part of this. It wasn't my plan, this – you know me, Jonny, I don't go looking for trouble, do I? Ay? But he, well . . . bloody Sammy Punch, he just forced me into it. You know the warnings I given him. I've bent over backwards for that one, I have, tried everything I could to, well – accommodate him, but no. So down the Rose & Crown, I lays it all out for him. It were quiet in there tonight. Gordon Tallyman holding up the bar and knocking them back, moaning on about his Amelia, like what he always do. There was a nice old fug going on, but I don't reckon the chimney can be right because the smoke there, it'd blind you – had to move off. Dawny behind the bar, showing off all she got – I sometimes get to thinking I could go a tumble with that one (and you don't have to go telling Mary all about it). Old Mr Prince in his camel coat and his ruby cufflinks chucking darts at the board, all on his tod. One or two others. Didn't see Squibbs, though. He weren't in. So anyway: Look Sammy, I says, we're not in this for the fun of it, are we? Ay? Not any one of us. Earning a crust at a difficult time, that's all we're doing. Best way we know how. Ay? And he nods, he nods at me, Sammy, and he don't look too happy. I light up a fag and chuck him over the packet. You wanted the documentation, I says to him, and I *gave* you the documentation. You want out your call-up, I sees to it that you get it, don't I? And he starts doing all of these faces like he's a bleeding woman, or something – he's waving his hands at me to sort of shut me up, I suppose – but I told him, I said to him listen to me Sammy my son, we're in the Rose & Crown, remember? It ain't Scotland Yard, is it? Ay? Everyone's got a number going on in here, and none of them's flapping their ears at your little slice of bother, now are they Sammy? Ay? You

4

want to get a grip, you do. So listen – we made a deal, didn't we, the two of us? Fair and square. Eighty quid we said, didn't we Sammy? You was pretty bloody pleased at the time, and well you might be. Eighty quid to save you being shot to bits in bleeding Africa, or somewhere? Cheap, ain't it? Ay? Dirt cheap, I call it. And he says *yeh*, Jackie – I know that, I know that, it's just you got to give me a little more time. *Time*? I says. You want more *time*? I've give you time – I've give you a lot more time than what you deserve, you cheeky scamp. And what if I'd said that to you? Ay? What if, when you come to me begging for the doctor's bleeding certificate – and you was, if you remember Sammy, you was begging, begging me you was, practically down on your knees at me, is what you was. No don't interrupt – you've had your say, I've heard you Sammy, I'm up to here with all you got to say – and it all of it comes down to one big *nothing*. So when you come to me – what I say? Ay? You recall, do you? I said yeh OK, Sammy – see what I can do. And then you said yeh but it's got to be real quick, see Jackie, because I'm up before them come Tuesday. And I said blimey, that is quick – but OK Sammy, seeing as how it's you, I'll do all I can to accommodate you. My words exactly. And then we agreed on sixty – you do recall all of this, do you Sammy? – plus another twenty on the top of it for getting it through that fast. Come back to you now, do it? The detail? And I done it, didn't I Sammy? Went as sweet as you like. And now you're in Civvy Street official like, and I'm out of pocket. Aren't I? Ay? And whichever way you look at it, Sammy, that just ain't right. I got people to see to, Sammy – and that's why you got to see to me. *Now* – I mean right *now*, Sammy, or else I will do you harm. You will definitely be the subject of harm if you don't pay me now. I hope I'm clear. I do hope you're clear about that. And he starts going quivery – his face, it looks like it's melting or something, and he's shaking now, he's shaking – his glass, it clatters his teeth when he's trying to get the Scotch down him. But Jackie, he says – I give you thirty, didn't I? Didn't I Jackie? And I say yeh Sammy, you did: you did give me thirty. Now I don't know what sort of a school you went to, my son, but where I come from, thirty – it ain't eighty, is it? You see what I mean? You see what I'm driving at here, do you Sammy? You do see where all of this is taking us? I'm getting *upset* with you, Sammy: you're really upsetting me now.

And that's when he done it. He just kicks back his chair, and he's out of the pub like a bloody greased whippet. And I'm up and I've cracked into this pair of old biddies by the door and one of them's got her gin and orange all slopped over and down her coat and she's calling out at me like she's some sort of a parrot or something and she's clawing at me too but I shove her right away and I barge straight through the other one as well and I'm slashing at that bleeding black curtain they got at the door and I'm out of there like a bloody flash, I can tell you that, because I'm *blazing* now and I'm pounding down the road and then I'm *after* him. I knew it straight off that he were heading for the railway – you could hear those boots of his clattering a mile off, and he was panicked now too because it were just the very tips of them, the tips of his boots, they just were hitting lightly – he must have been spilling along like an angled blade, one of them for throwing, like he was trying to fly, or something. These blackouts – well, you know it Jonny, don't you? Your nerves, they're always on edge and you get to sense things like a bleeding wild animal – you're just alive and aware of the whiff of something before it's even going off. But anyways, he had to be making for the railway, didn't he really? Not on account of the trains, nah – I don't think he had it in his head, our Sammy, that he could actually go getting on a train to somewhere, no – not that time of night, he wasn't. But where else was he going to be headed? Ay? Down past the Co-op and the terraces and then the dirty little park there what's leading nowhere at all? No. I don't think so. Even given the state of him, he weren't going to be that daft, were he? And all this calculation, all this what I were thinking, it were drumming in my head, see, while all the time I were haring down that pitch-black bloody street, and my eyes, they always open up so wide when I'm on the hunt, when I'm on the chase – they get so hard and cold – and it ain't because I can even see a single bloody thing in front of me, no – it's that it always makes my ears prick up, it makes me hear things better, like I got an aerial or something. And maybe as I just tore along there, maybe I were getting the echo of those boots of his, the tips just touching, or the heels slamming down like crunch on to the cobbles if he were swerving hard into a corner, maybe, or if he ran slap bang into a pillar box or something – could have maybe winded him. And then I hear this *Hoy!* going up – some old geezer, could well have been, and he sounds like he been knocked for six – and *Hoy!* he's going – hoy *you*, I'm hearing now – and so I concentrate real hard on that like a dog what's got the scent of it, and I'm really – I'm telling you – I'm *blazing* now, Jonny, because I know I'm within a grasp of him, I even get to thinking I can hear his breathing – hard, and then him panting like a clapped-out old horse what's heaving up a deadweight. I'm near to the tracks now, just by the steps there to the side of the platform, and I know by the speed and the distance I been going and going I should be down on my knees and hacking up my guts – but I'm not feeling like that, no, I'm not feeling nothing, nothing at all – I just go on winging like a bullet and all I know is, the only thing in my head is I'm going to *get* the bastard. Then I'm stopped dead and I'm blind and shattered. There's this jarring all down one shoulder – I just went careering into into some damn bloody hard great metal sort of a thing, and it's twanging in the air with the power I just was ramming into it, and I couldn't even now begin to tell you what it were – the blackness down by the railway, I'm telling you, it's total, just

7

total. And I'm staggered, I'm reeling – the pain of it now, it makes me want to retch, but I don't go down – I'm spinning around like I'm drunk or something, but I don't go down – and then I'm just crouching low and I try to quieten down my breathing, and I just go on crouching there and rubbing down slowly the bleeding shoulder, and the cold and the silence then, it just wraps itself around me and it's like I don't know where I am and I'm really all alone, and then something inside of me, could even have been my bleeding soul, I feels it kicking up, like just before it could have shut down on me. And still there's all this silence, and I'm nearly sobbing with disappointment because I've *lost* the bastard, he's gone: the bastard, he's got away from me.

And then I hear it. Just this one sort of plocking sort of sound – like mud in a puddle sort of sound, and not too far away. And all the blood inside me, it races up and I feel it's kind of bursting into my head and it sounds a bit crazy but it makes me feel as if it's like a sort of beacon now, and everything, look – it's suddenly got lighter. Still I don't move, though – I got to get a bearing, see – I just got to be sure, because if I go careering off now in just slightly the wrong direction, then he's gone, then he's really gone, and then I've truly had it. I'm straining, I'm really straining hard now – not to breathe, to keep my feet quite still, even though my haunches now, they're near to breaking beneath me, I been skulking down here for that bleeding long. My shoulder, well – it's like it's someone else's shoulder, this great big numb thing, and killing me, it is, hung like a hundredweight all down the side, there. Then I hear just the breath of a breeze – or was it the bastard sighing? Weeping, maybe – I wouldn't put it past him. But still I'm going nowhere – still I got to will myself somehow to keep on crouching down there, like a statue what inside just needs to be screaming. And then I'm thinking I heard it again – just the slightest little hiss, you'd never even be aware, not if you weren't after it. And no – I don't think at all, not for one moment, that it could be a cat, because that little sound, that barely there little whisper in the dark, still I smelt the fear off of it, so there's *no* doubt in my mind: the bastard is close.

Then I got it. A *tsk* – no more, just that, just the ever so slight deepening of that first bit of hissing, and so then I got it. I'm up like lightning, and none of my body is really going for it at all but I say to hell with all that and I'm completely blowing away all of this silence because now it's down to speed, see – that's my only chance now if he's not going to get to them tracks and way across into them trees and then that's the end of him. It's my wide and blind eyes what are guiding me now, and I'm skittering around that corner and then suddenly *yes!* Yes yes! *There!* I hear him whimpering, and I can even feel the flap of the wind off of his coat and he's nearly half-falling down the staircase there and I'm thundering down and after him like a mad and hungry hound now and he's crying out quite openly, and his footsteps are all unsteady and I hear him go down and now he's got to be scrabbling on the ground and I go slamming right into the bastard before I even know that he's grovelling down there around the floor and his arms go up and he's going Oh *please* Jackie – for the love of *God*, Jackie – please please oh Jesus *please* Jackie don't do this to me – we're *friends*, ain't we? *Mates*, Jackie – we're *mates*, God sake – oh Christ *please*, Jackie – I'm begging you – please please *please*, Jackie – anything, I'll do anything you say, Jackie, but oh please God don't! *Don't!* And I'm kneeling on his chest and he's wheezing badly and I roar into the dark where his face has got to be that he's now got to shut his bloody mouth right this bloody minute and just give me, give me the fucking fifty *quid*! And he's babbling and I hit his face and it's all wet with his dribble and his bloody tears and I hit his face and he's not talking no words at me no more and I'm really just raving at him now to just give me give me give me the fucking fifty *quid*. And I don't really know that I'm beating his bloody head against the

9

ground until I suddenly stop doing it and he's all gone quiet and there's sort of a gurgling from out of his throat, and the wet on his face, it's all coming out warm. Well he had it coming, didn't he? Why didn't he just give me the fifty fucking *quid*? So I'm rifling through his pockets now, aren't I? And all I'm thinking is I didn't bloody half destroy myself running after this bastard just in order to be having a late-night *chat*, and that I wish I could bloody *see* something, because I'm heaving all of this junk from out of his jacket and his wallet's a bloody waste of time with just bits of pasteboard – tickets to somewhere he won't be going – and then more shiny bits, could be pictures of the bastard's loved ones: who's to say, and who's to bloody care? And then I get the crinkle, then my fingers is ruffling through paper of the right sort – quite a fair wad if I'm any judge, and I'm having it – I'm having it, mate, and no mistake.

Yeh. Well that's when you and the rest of them turned up, weren't it Jonny? Put the fear of God into me, you lot did, all coming down the stairs in a rush, like that. Thought it were the rozzers. Now I know I can trust you, Jonny – not a word, ay? Not to anyone. And I mean *anyone*, Jonny. All right?

'Someone's got to find out some time, haven't they Jackie?'

'Why? Don't see why. This war – people's getting it all the time. Anyway – Sammy, he'll likely just wake up with a sore head in the morning, ay? Chalk it up, likely as not.'

'Who you kidding, Jackie boy? Ay? Look at him.'

'Can't, can I? Can't see a bloody thing. I only know it's you in front of me, Jonny, on account of your voice.'

'Yeh well – you don't have to look at him. You just know it. I met it before, see? You just know it.'

'So what's the difference? Who bloody cares?'

'You're shaking, Jackie. Voice gone funny.'

'Nothing wrong with my voice. Hurt my bleeding shoulder, that's all. Not shaking. Here – you got a torch?'

'What you want a torch for? Close-up of your handiwork?'

'Don't be clever, Jonny. You got a torch or not?'

'Yeh I have, matter of fact. Here you are, Jackie.'

'Right. Give it me. See what we got here. Christ. You see! Stupid bastard – he had it all the time. Seventy-five nicker, he got here – stupid bastard. He only were into me for fifty. We could've saved all this. All he had to do was accommodate me. Stupid bastard.'

'So how come you're pocketing the lot then, Jackie?'

'Ay? Well I reckon I earned the extra pony, didn't I? All the grief he put me through.'

'Firm, they might not see it like that.'

'Yeh? Well the firm can go and do the other thing then, can't they?'

'Don't do to meddle with them, Jackie. It'll be their money. They're going to be after you for this. And they're bigger than what you are. They won't let it lie – you know that. I hope you know that, Jackie.'

'Yeh well. Twenty-five quid – ain't going to hurt them, is it? Look – I don't want to hang around here no more. Any room in that motor of yours?'

'Where you want to go?'

'Anywhere. Out of here, that's all. And remember now Jonny – you don't say none of this to no one. Clear?'

'Get in the car, Jackie. Just get in the car, ay? You want a fag?'

'Christ yeh,' he says to me. 'Oh yeh by Christ I do.'

⊙

Mary had just been getting on with her darning. She had not so much as glanced at Jonathan Leakey, not even once as he told her all of this. There was the shortest of silences – just the ticking of the clock – as Jonny now shifted in his chair and idly looked about him. He touched each side of his thin black moustache.

'So anyway, like I says to you Mary – that's how it gone. Sorry to be the bearer. But listen – why you go on living this way, ay? You don't mind my asking. I mean I ain't being, you know . . . what I mean to say is I don't want to go running you down nor nothing – not you, Mary, no never – and I mean you make the best of it, I'm not saying that – it's all very cosy and that, very sort of homely – but, well, not much of a room is it? When all's said and done.'

Now she was looking at him.

'It suits us. We like it here. What's wrong with it anyway? We can't all be living like you do, Jonny. And some of us, we maybe don't any more want to. That last place we had, Mr Wisely's place, well – it just didn't suit.'

'But it's still "us", then, is it? After all what I told you?'

'I've only got your word.'

'Come off it, Mary love. You know I put you straight. Else you'd never have heard me out. Shown me the door. You want a fag?'

'No thanks. And what's wrong with this room anyway, Jonny? I can't see anything wrong with it.'

'Mind if I do? Ta. Senior Service. Like hen's teeth, just lately. Lucky I know a bloke. But no – you're getting me all wrong, Mary love. I mean – you done good with what you got, I'm not saying . . . but I mean – what I mean is – you don't have to want for anything, you don't. Not ever. What I mean is, before your Jackie went and blotted his copybook, naughty boy, you must have got a fair little taste of the finer things in life, is all I'm saying. Well – I'd give you anything, Mary. You know that.'

And now she was looking at him hard.

'You mean if I were to play my cards right?'

'Oh come on, Mary love – give a man the benefit! All I'm doing is being nice here, aren't I? Ay? No sense in you getting all like that. Also, you got the kid to think of, haven't you? Little Jeremy, ain't it? Doing all right, is he? Sort him out a good billet, did you? If not, you only got to say.'

'Haven't you got somewhere to go to, Jonny? People to see?'

Jonny snapped on a humourless smile and opened wide his eyes, while conceding the round. His finger and thumb probed the tip of his tongue for an atom of tobacco.

'Yeh yeh – OK, Mary. Point taken. Never let it be said. No offence, I hope? Right then, I'll be off. Leave you the packet, will I? Jackie, he might be in need of them.'

Mary set aside her darning and shrugged her indifference.

'I'll see you to the door.'

'I wasn't waiting for no thanks, but I was neither expecting to be chucked out into the night.'

'Oh Jonny – who's chucking? You're a big boy now. You're not afraid of the dark.'

'You're a real little peach, you are. You know that? When you give us a little smile like that, it fair lights up the whole of London. No blackout when you're around, gel.'

'Goodbye, Jonny. And . . . I am grateful . . . I think.'

'Yeh well. Just bear it in mind though, ay Mary love? Anything you ever want, anything I can ever give you – you just get in touch, ay? Night or day. Jonny Midnight, he won't never let you down. You got my word.'

Mary shut her eyes as she nodded him away, and softly closed the door behind him. Then she let her forehead touch the dark varnished jamb as her lips became hard and drew away from her teeth and formed into the rictus of sadness and deep-down unease that she had held back for ever; and her stomach was aching as the sobbing began.

And later, when Jackie came home for his tea, it was almost as if she had dreamed the nightmare. Jackie – he was just so like Jackie in every single way that Mary became dizzy, and doubted her senses. She watched him as he took off his boots and set them close to the fire and then folded back the hearthrug, the way he always did. He liked the feel of the lino beneath his stockinged feet. She placed the tray on the three-legged table beside him and watched him still as he set to frowning, and roving around the plate with the prongs of a wary fork.

'What is it?'

'Fritters.'

'Don't look like fritters . . .'

'Well it is. Corn beef. Don't turn your nose up.'

'Not. Only asking.'

'Well it's fritters.'

'Yeh, you said. You not having any?'

'I've had. Where've you been, Jackie?'

'Me? Been? What – today, you mean? Oh – here and there. Here and there. What've you been up to, Mary my love?'

'Oh. Nothing much. Bit of darning. Jonathan Leakey – he came over earlier. Told me some things.'

And still there was nothing. He went on shovelling the fritters into his mouth, and chewing them hard: no movement at all at the back of his eyes.

'Oh yeh? Jonathan *Leakey*, is it now? Don't we call him Jonny Midnight no more, then? He too posh for all that lark, is he?'

'Did you hear me, Jackie? I said he told me some things.'

'Yeh, I heard. What sort of things?'

Mary crouched down beside him. She was stirring his tea.

'Bad things, Jackie. Very bad things. And you know what they are, don't you?'

'Me? I don't. I don't know what you're on about, girl. What – old Jonny's been a bit naughty, has he? Not the first time.'

'Not Jonny – *you*, Jackie. God sake stop playing about.'

And then he turned to her, and his eyes were beseeching.

'Look now, Mary love. Look at me. I don't know how many ways I can rightly say this to you, but listen to me – all right? I don't know nothing. I ain't done nothing bad. And if I had I'd tell you, wouldn't I? Ay? I'd tell you, wouldn't I, Mary love? How could I keep it from you?'

Mary shook her head in near despair. 'Sammy Punch . . .' is all she said.

'Sammy Punch? What about him? Ain't seen him around for a bit, now you come to mention. He owes me a few bob, he does. Ought to look him up.'

Mary just stared at him.

'Jackie. Please. Stop. He's *dead* – you *know* he's dead. You *did* it! I still can't believe you could *do* such a thing . . . !'

Jackie laid down his fork, and gripped her by the arms. The look on his face was urgent, now, and she felt its intensity.

'You're having me on. Sammy Punch – dead? And what – you think *I* did it? You're out of your mind. Where'd it happen, then? When was all this?'

Mary wrenched herself away from him and wept in frustration, dashing away the tears with tight-clenched knuckles and a bewildered anger.

'Oh Jackie stop *doing* this to me! You know where it happened! Down by the railway. You *did* it! You *did* it!'

Jackie's eyes had narrowed into near-invisibility.

'Jonny said that about me, then he's a bloody liar and I'll have him for it, I can bloody tell you that much. Now you listen to me. I'm sorry. I'm truly sorry, Mary, but I simply can't accommodate you on this one, see? On account of I never so much as even touched the geezer, not even so much as laid a finger on him, see? Wasn't even close to the vicinity in question. So he's wound up dead now, has he? Old Sammy Punch. Well I'm sorry for that

15

too. But you got to know, Mary, there's no how at all it could be down to me now, Mary my love – hand on heart: I swear it to you. Are you getting all this, Mary? Can you hear me?'

And she just stood there looking at him, while he went on doing it.

◉

He stayed in all evening. Mary had expected – no, she was just positive that the minute he had finished up his big dish of loganberries (she had put on some Carnation, because even now if she was to do a thing, then she liked to do it nicely) Jackie would be up and wrapping one of his mufflers around him, and after the well-meant and customary cheek-peck, he would take himself off (to the Rose & Crown, is where he always said he was going, but God alone knew where it was he got to really; Mary didn't care for pubs, and anyway would never have dreamed of checking up on him, because all she wanted to know these days was less and less and less and never, please God, any single new thing – not that that seemed possible, now). But no. She was wrong. He was going to stay in. And even this, it shook her quite badly because, well look – she did, didn't she? Know this man of hers inside out? Know what he'd do in a given situation, and what he'd run a mile from? Divine when he was lying, and be sure when he was not?

Jackie was giving the fire a poke, and now he folded the *Evening News* quite tightly into quarters, settled down into his armchair and was sucking on a pencil. This means then, thought Mary, that he is going to do the simple crossword – which means in turn that she'd be given little peace to think things out. 'Wild

cat,' he'd be going. 'Four letters. Any ideas have you, Mary?'
And from only the outskirts of where she had yearned to
disappear, she'd sigh and say 'lion'. No, he'd say – sorry not
to be able to accommodate you, but it can't end in no N, I'm
afraid. Puma, she'd utter, but of course it would be no: can't be
puma, girl. Any more ideas then, Mary? Lynx, she'd practically
moan, and wonder out loud why he even attempted them,
these things, if all he did was ask her for the answers. And then
he'd chuckle like a much much older person, as he always did:
helps to pass the time, doesn't it Mary, my love? Helps to pass
the time.

'Capital city,' he called out now. 'Six letters. Any ideas have
you, Mary?'

And he watched her as she went on darning by the light of a
dark wood Tudor galleon in full-blown parchment sail, its little
red and blue flags aflutter – heard her as she suggested to him
London, went on regarding her more and more closely as he
slowly shook his head by way of return and muttered mm, well,
yes it *could* be London, I suppose, but I don't think it can start
with an L, you know. And I wonder what she's thinking now?
Not about my crossword, that's for bleeding sure. Well about
what she was saying to me earlier, of course – what else can I
imagine she'd be thinking? Hasn't gone and slipped her *mind*,
now, has it? No – you can tell it hasn't, for all her trying to look
all normal, like what she is. She's a grand-looking woman,
though, Mary, you know – everybody thinks so. I know that
bloody Jonny Midnight do, for starters – Jesus, sometimes the
way he goes looking at her, it makes me want to deck him on the
spot; don't, though – never do. Various reasons. But I'm telling
you, she looks no different now from the day I first set eyes
on her. Must have been near Christmas time, that dance affair up
the Lyceum – '34 maybe, '35 it could have been. Can't be more
recent, I shouldn't have said. And she were only twenty, you

know – looked a lot younger even then. Loveliest mum around, she was, when little Jeremy come along. She had her hair – and it's all coppery, her hair, lovely hair, got a real glow to it – yeh, she had her hair kind of rolled under at the back, sort of style; there's a name for it, that hairdo, but I'm blowed if I know it. Slim, she was – just the way she is now – and them deep green eyes of hers . . . I tell you, she's a smasher. She's got her legs tucked up beside her on the chair, look, the way she always do of an evening. Reckon when I'm not around she has the wireless on, likely as not, but she knows I never care for it. Never did go for the music she likes – boogie-woogie sort of music, I suppose is what it is: too jazzy for me – and all them comedy programmes everyone's always on about, all these cheeky chappies – well, leave me cold, you want the truth. More laughs at a funeral, you ask me. And as for the news, well forget it. There ain't any real news unless it's round here: that's what news is, whatever's going off around here. What do I care about Japan and the bloody African desert and all the rest of the bloody show, ay? Mugs getting shot at – more fool they. They wanted to be a little bit lively like what I was, didn't they? There's always ways of doing things, getting things done – you just got to find the bloke what'll do it for you, that's all. And at the time I were one of them: I made things happen.

But look at her – just take a look at her, will you? Pretty as a picture, she is, and darning away, darning away. I asked her one time how come she's always darning – how come she's always got darning to do: why do we make so many bleeding holes? She just smiled – smiled the way she do. Yeh. But she weren't smiling tonight though, were she? Well upset, she were – and who can blame her? She reckons I'm a killer, and that's not good. Well is it? Not by any stretch. It ain't good at all. And anyway – if anyone's the killer . . . well – not called Bloody Mary for nothing now, is she? Ay? Yeh well. She got a way of forgetting all of that side of things, when it suits her. Yeh well – leave it alone: I ain't knocking it.

But so far as this evening's going, well, like I say – reckoned I'd stop in, give her a little bit of a treat. Maybe tomorrow I can pick her up half pound of Roses – she likes her bit of chocolate – put a little smile back on to her face. Eddie's always good on the confectionery side of things, and he owes me a couple. So yeh – thought I wouldn't seek out bloody Jonny Midnight, ask him man to man what in hell he thinks his game is. No – leave it a bit, I thought, and think of the lady for once in your life. Because I'm stupid, me, where women is concerned. And yeh, there's some I know what'd just say I'm stupid, and there's an end on it – but they wouldn't be right about that. Man can't be stupid if he wants to get on, not if he wants to survive, he can't. That's true any time, we all know that – but when there's a war on, well – the stupid ones, it's them is always the first to go. True, ain't it? Them's the ones what's going to end up dead. Yeh. Well not me, matey. Not me, my son. God'll have to wait – I'm really very sorry but I just can't accommodate him, not for a good while yet. I'm looking out for myself, you can bet on that. Got to, now. But I'll be all right. You won't catch me being no mug – not like bleeding Sammy Punch, winding up dead, the silly bleeding sod. No – I ain't stupid, and I ain't going to die, neither. Leave all that to the mugs, will we? Yeh – think so. But when it comes to the women – yeh, this is what I were on about – well when it all comes down to the women, then it's something else again, way I reckon it. That's something else altogether, that is. I just like to see them happy, that's all. Put a little smile on their faces. Not a sin, is it? Because when you got a pretty girl what's all happy and smiling, well – we're all going to get the benefit, ain't we? Stands to reason. So yeh – I'll just stop here for the evening, go on smoking these Senior Service (Jonny's, I suppose they got to be) and try and make a cosy little night of it. Try maybe to put a smile back on to that little face of hers – where can be the harm? But listen – just look at her, will you? Like I say – pretty as a picture, darning away, darning away, and thinking her thoughts. Whatever they be. I wonder if I rustle the paper around, she might look up at me and then I can put on that funny old grin of mine and then well who knows? She might even go giving me a smile.

'Berlin,' she said – but she didn't look up.

'Come again, love?'

'The capital city. Berlin, it could be.'

'Oh yeh – forgot about that. Yeh, love, yeh – I think you hit the nail on the head. I reckon you got it. Blimey – not very patriotic, is it? Ay? Sticking Berlin in the bleeding crossword.'

And then she did: she smiled, God bless her.

And she closed her eyes as she did it, hoping that the gesture – and she knew that he longed for it – would allay for now his doubt and suspicion (might even begin to blunt her own vibrant certainty). How on earth can it be that this damn big man of mine, sinner that he is, is still and also so helpless a child? I really did think, when Jeremy was born – I really did believe, you know, that Jackie, he'd leave it all behind him. I said to him – I said to him at the time, I remember it clearly: now you listen to me, Jackie . . . are you listening? Are you? Well look – now I've got a *proper* baby to take care of, haven't I? Someone who really needs me. So there'll be no time to be pandering to you. Which – I know this now – no man wants to hear. And so I suppose he just didn't. Hear it. Despite all his noddings and assurance, he simply refused to listen. Because he can do that, you know – Jackie, he can do that with ease: deny the very reality that stares him in the face. I think, though, at the time, I only half meant it: he'd always be cosseted wouldn't he, really? Because I loved him then with a passion so strong it makes me embarrassed to think it. And then I was truly a mother – it wasn't a bit like all the silly dreams that untried girls are fed about it; promises and lies, that's all you ever get. And then later, of course, another sort of distortion from the old and beaten, the wives and mothers who are either mad-eyed and reeling with all that life has done to them, or else just slump there, round-backed and worn out and broken, each of them sucked quite dry and hollow-eyed, malevolently silent or else eagerly poisoning a young girl's mind with such terrible warnings of a permanent death, long before your demise, that stays within you and lasts for ever.

I enjoyed the whole of it, the time I was carrying Jeremy. It seems now sometimes that before the war, there was really very little that I didn't enjoy, one way or another. Everyone was always so kind to me – asking me when it was due, telling me how healthy I was looking. And I felt it too – I felt so free and proud and so very womanly, now that I was pregnant. I never let on I wasn't married, of course: that would've taken the bloom off right away. But striding along the lit-up streets (oh my goodness: the lit-up streets!) and buying all the lovely things in shops that were crammed to bursting – if you didn't meet others who remembered it too, you'd think that you'd dreamt it all up. Even Jackie, in those days, he was always so terribly caring – before he went off it, of course. He went from constantly asking me if I was sure I was as right as ninepence, and could he now maybe fetch me something, help me in any way . . . ? Yes well, quite rapidly he stopped all that and then all I heard was 'What about me?' and 'I do still *exist* you know, Mary: I ain't become invisible . . . or maybe you forgot.' I thought it was a phase, but it wasn't. He's better now, though, in that respect: since we sent Jeremy away. For his own good. I do hope it is – people say it is, it's what they're always saying, you keep on hearing it on the wireless . . . but then some mothers round here – there's Mrs Hobbs for one, and Sally in the greengrocers – they brought their kiddies back home. Said they'd risk all of Hitler's bombs just so's they could be a family again. I put it to Jackie – I'd made him a really nice fry-up with some Spam I'd been saving and two whole eggs that I'd somehow scrounged up, and there was a rhubarb crumble for afters. I said to him, listen now Jackie, what do you think? Maybe he shouldn't, Jeremy, be out in the country, stuck out there with strangers, not any more. But Jackie, he wouldn't even hear of it – said I was being selfish, and that made me cry. Then he tries to make me feel better and says that we're all right, we are – just us, snug as two bugs in a rug. It gets so you don't know what to do for the best: what can be right, and what is wrong. I used to miss him so very desperately, my sweet little boy. I cried and cried the first night he was gone, and I barely slept for the rest of the month. Now, so much time has gone by . . . and sometimes, you know, a day will pass and I fail to think of him at all. How can it be possible?

And just how I can be thinking all of this . . . I just can't understand it, quite frankly. Here I am, darning away – and there's him, over in his chair with his fags and his crossword . . . The killer now is maybe struggling to nail down the name of an imperial measure, rack his brains for the five-letter breed of domestic pet – wondering, he could be (before he ups and asks me), who in blue blazes could be expected to know what the bleeding capital of Canada might be. Still and all, though, he looks so very handsome, my Jackie. Like he always did.

I'll never forget the day I first met him – and not just for the reason, I don't think – no, I'm sure not – it's not just because for so long after I always used to read and read and read what I'd said about him in my diary (August 16th 1936 – I don't have to look it up). Always, you know – I've always kept a diary, since I was a little girl and I was given one for Christmas, and I'm really very glad to have got into the habit. You forget things, otherwise – even some things that you're sure at the time will be with you for ever, you can forget them too, or else you remember them wrongly. And sometimes even now, you know, I can look back on an entry I made when I was just, oh – couldn't have been twenty, not much more – and I'm reading the excitement I felt about an incident that to me now, well – has completely vanished. Without the plain and stark evidence of my very own hand, I'd swear it had never occurred. Not the day I met Jackie, of course – that'll travel with me wherever I go. Whatever may happen to us now.

It was the hottest summer day, when all you long for is a cooling fountain to bathe your feet, an ice-cream cone and the humming of bees as you stretch yourself out on a new-mown lawn and breathe deep inside you the scent of its freshness. Well there was none of all that, but my goodness it was a scorcher, though. I'd just had my hair cut the shortest it had been, and Sheila, who did it, she put on a much lighter rinse than I'd ever have now. I'll never forget – 11/9 she charged me, and she told me it was cheap; I wasn't too sure about it, to be completely truthful. Anyway, I was in the little park – not the main park, but the little one just up the road – and it was my afternoon off from the laundry (the hardest work I've ever done, that was – if I hadn't been so young, it truly might've killed me). There was this little boy – I can even remember these little knickerbockers he was wearing – and he was sailing a toy boat that he'd maybe put together for himself – it looked to be no more than a hull made out of a cigar box, a bit of a mast of some sort, leaning – might have been a knitting needle, now that I think of it – and for a sail there was a gentleman's handkerchief that had seen better days. It's not much of a pond, the one in the little park – hardly more than a bit of a ditch – but he did get so very upset, this little lad, when his boat, it got all snagged up in the reeds to the side, and there was I on my hands and knees trying to help him to move it, but the blooming little thing was just out of reach of the both of us. And that's when I was aware of a rolled-up brolly repeatedly prodding – the boat was dislodged and then it was bobbing back over to the delighted child. And on the other end of the umbrella, there stood my Jackie, grinning so broadly that at first I thought with a bit of a shiver that he might actually be drunk – it was clear when he spoke that he wasn't, though. I looked up into his eyes, those big brown eyes of his – and that lump of hair at the front, it flopped over his brow (even now, you know, he can never get it to stay down, no matter how much brilliantine he slathers all over it) – I looked up into his eyes, those big brown eyes of his – and his shirtsleeves, they were all rolled up to above the elbow, and they strained so tightly against his muscles (I don't think he can have shaved that morning) – I looked up into his eyes, and I suppose I was lost from that moment onwards. Sounds a bit soppy, when you put it into words – but not then, not then it didn't seem to me soppy, not soppy at all – not when I looked up into his eyes, those big brown eyes of his. It seemed to me to be the most wonderful thing that could possibly have happened on so very splendid a day. I said to him, that was kind of you, but he said nothing back. And then I asked him, why are you carrying an umbrella? The sun is shining, it's terribly hot. Ah yes, he replied (still grinning, he was, and a voice so deep), but what if later it comes on to rain? Which made the two of us laugh, but I think anything would have, quite frankly: we were both of us ready to quite let go. I said to him, I hope you don't mind me saying, but your voice, it sounds just ever so slightly northern – are you? No, he said – Londoner born and bred, I am: my mum's from Seven Sisters, round about. Oh, I said (and why did I go *on*?) – well maybe on your father's side? Perhaps? And he laughed again (lovely sound, rich and low). My father! Christ, that's a good one that is – I don't even know where the bastard *went* to, let alone where he come from! My name's Jackie. What's yours?

I'd never heard a man swearing before; it didn't put me off. I stood in the sunshine, regarding him I hoped a bit coolly in a way I tried to memorise from Veronica Lake in some picture or other, and wishing terribly that I looked like Veronica Lake. In reality, I suppose I just must have been squinting. Bit fresh, aren't you, is what I said to him, as casually as I dared. And he grinned – that grin – and then he came back with Well Miss, better than stale, ay? What's your name, then? And I told him: Mary Gordon.

So. One thing led to another, and all these years later here we now are. It wasn't all plain sailing with Jackie and me, not by a very long chalk. Even before the war, and all the trouble it's brought to us. My mother, she hated him. Said he was common – 'oik' was the word she called him – said he'd bring to me nothing but grief. I defended him with such ferocity that I was frankly astounded. I hadn't even known my feelings for him were quite so full of fire, that much beyond my control, until I heard such ardency hanging in the air, until I saw it hit my mother – hard, and in the face. I said to her that what you mean is he's not stuck-up and mealy-mouthed like all the people you know. She told me I was young, so very young, and that I didn't have the first idea as to what I was meaning. When Jeremy was born, I kept it from her, she found out and practically suffered a seizure. He's a good person, Jackie, I repeatedly told her – despite what you see, no matter what you may think him to be, I know him better, I know him utterly – and my Jackie, I'm telling you: he's a really good person. And even now, you know – well, he's not a *bad* person (and believe me, it's not just love now that's talking). None of us are – we're not bad. It's partly the war, and it's everything else. We're all ripped up. We're not that bad, but we're all of us guilty. I mean to say – look at me. What has become of me? Before the war, all I was called was nice. Everyone thought how terribly nice I was – and I was, they were right, and I still am, God help me, I am nice, I *am* nice. But now I'm the other and dreadful thing too. Bloody Mary is what they now call me – it makes me cringe, just to think it. Jackie, though – he was always judged to be no more than just a bit of a lad, and even now, whatever he's done, that's still, I think, how people would look at it. Because, I suppose, he's still such a charmer – and so he seems to get away with it all.

And here I still sit, darning away, gazing at the loved one, and dazed by murder. Because of all the things he's done to me, it's this one, oh God yes, this one is just the very hardest to bear. And can I? Can I go on loving the man, now I know that he's a killer? Oh dear God. All I wish is what I always wish for, these days: that we could just go back. Go back to then, to before the war, when I always seemed to feel such terrible happiness, and was so ready to embrace true joy. What we none of us could see, I suppose, during all those seemingly sunlit days, was that here among us was the joy itself. And despite all the growing up that each of us has had to cope with – and we go on coping, day by day – we're really little more still than babies in a cradle; the war, it's just rendered us helpless. And here and now has become so frightening. Because it's just like Jonathan Leakey said: after what's happened to poor old Sammy Punch, the firm, they're not just going to leave it, are they? It's not as if it's *over*, or anything. Oh dear God. When did the whole thing happen? How did it all begin . . . ?

Mary's musings were cut into of a sudden by the long and idle moan of the jeering siren. As the tone of it rose, she could sense inside her the electric anxiety of the whole of London, and then as it switched and descended she felt the lowering in the pit of just everyone's stomach as millions of eyelids were collectively cast down as one more massive sigh was hugely expelled and so many weary limbs were summoned up again for yet another struggle. Jackie was up and on his feet, shuffling on his boots and pocketing the Senior Service and a box of matches.

'Come on then, Mary love. Let's be having you.'

'You go, Jackie. I'll be down in a minute.'

'No – come on, Mary. You didn't, the last time. Did you? Ay? Come on – we'll be snug as two bugs in a rug, down there.'

'I'll just check the blackout. Find a magazine. You go, Jackie. I won't be a sec.'

'Well . . . if you're sure you'll come?'

'I'll come. Promise. Off you go, Jackie.'

And there he goes, look – straight out of the door: these days, he always gets nervous in a raid – and I used to too, before it all changed. Now I don't care. I won't go down. I didn't the last time, and I won't tonight. I doubt I'll ever go down there again. This is how you get, after so many years of it. I'll just carry on with this darning and put on the wireless – a bit of lively music, not that it'll blot out even some of the awful and nasal lowing of the siren. And should a bomb come down and hit us directly – well then Jackie will be crushed and buried in the shelter, while I'll be up here, and shattered into pieces. And then that's the end of us – Jack the Lad and Bloody Mary. Oh dear God. When did the whole thing happen? How did it all begin . . . ?

PART ONE

Before the War

5th November 1938

It's one of those days when there isn't enough space to write in everything that's happened! I would have saved some space if I hadn't written that. Or that. Enough. A red letter day! We had the most wonderful fireworks party in Dickie's garden tonight – it was so freezing out there, but the colours and the excitement! Dickie had rockets and catherine wheels (one of them didn't go round and Jackie went up to it with a stick and it fell off on to his boot and exploded! He leapt up into the air and fell into the bushes – I was screaming with laughter, we all were). I ran away from the jumping crackers and Jackie kept on chasing me with bangers because he knows I simply loathe them. I don't think little Jeremy very much liked all the noise (he looked so serious, sitting in his highchair) but he seemed quite fascinated when I lit up a sparkler. Sheila had done sausages and there was beer and celery and a sort of a salad cream dip. I think it was, and then we all had fancy cakes and tea. My hands were practically dropping off from the cold when we finally came inside, but oh! I wouldn't have missed it for worlds. Jackie keeps on looking at me, so I'm going to have to stop. No more space anyway. Wasted most of it.

'What are you scribbling there, Mary my love?'

'Finished now. Only my diary, Jackie. Writing about the wonderful fireworks.'

'Day's not over yet. Thought you only wrote all that up at the end of the day?'

'Well it's nearly ten. I thought we'd be going to bed.'

'Well that's just where you're wrong. Had a word with Dickie, didn't I? Seemed a shame to break everything up, I thought, so I said he should get hisself down the off-licence and then him and Sheila can come over here – keep the party going. Got a bit of ham, or something? Do a few sandwiches.'

'Oh my goodness, Jackie! I had no idea. My hair – I'll have to put it up again. But how terribly exciting! No . . . there's none of the ham left, I'm pretty sure, but I've got lots of tins of things, and plenty of bread. We can get out that Chinese ginger – we've had it for long enough. Oh my goodness – what a day! We mustn't make too much noise, though, because I've only just got Jeremy down.'

Jackie grinned. 'We'll drink in whispers. And there goes the doorbell, if I ain't very much mistaken. Let the revelries commence!'

'My hair! I won't be a jiffy – you let them in, Jackie – and then I'll see to doing us some food. I'm actually pretty full after all those cakes and everything, but I know you men – you're always hungry.'

'Well well well,' said Jackie at the door. 'Dickie and Sheila, as I live and bleeding breathe. This *is* a surprise. Come in, come in.'

'Just passing, you know,' laughed Dickie. 'Here, Jackie old man – give us a hand with these bottles, will you?'

'Blimey, Dickie – clean them out, did you?'

'Oh well you know, old fellow – if a chap's going to do a thing . . .'

'Come on, Sheila – don't hang about. Get yourself into the warm, look. Mary's seeing to her face, or something. She won't be a mo. Now then – give us this day our daily booze, and forgive us our corkscrews!'

'Oh Jackie,' giggled Sheila, 'you are so naughty.'

'What would you be knowing about naughtiness now, Sheila my love? You're going out with a bleeding monk here, ain't you . . . ?'

'I say!' protested Dickie, quite joyously aggrieved. 'Have a care now, Jackie old man.'

'He's no *monk*,' laughed Sheila. 'I'll have a drop of port, if you're asking. Oh there you are, Mary! Thought you'd gone off to bed, or something.'

'Hello again, you two!' Mary greeted the company. 'What was it that person in the film said . . . ?'

'What person?' said Jackie, chucking up his eyes to the ceiling.

'What *film*?' chortled Sheila.

Jackie had on his grin again. 'She's always doing this.' And then his voice went up two octaves as he affected a genteel accent. 'You know that woman – the woman who was in the B-picture at the Gaumont not the last time but the time before? Well she's the dead spit of the girl who sold me them gloves in Swan & Edgar's.' Then his voice dropped down again. 'I'm telling you! She always doing this.'

'Oh shut *up*, Jackie,' squealed Mary. 'I'm not that bad. But anyway you *do* know who I mean – he said it in that film, we only saw it a few weeks ago – 'Long time no see' – and I was going to say it too. It's a joke, you see, because we—'

'Yeh, I get. Because it's *not* a long time, is it? You want to be on the wireless, jokes like that.'

'Oh you really are so *beastly* to me, Jackie! Come on everybody – sit down by the fire and I'll get us some . . . well actually, I don't quite know what we've got in the cupboard, but I'll get us all something. Humphrey Bogart. At the Odeon. The gangster man. It might have been him. Not sure, now . . .'

'Don't listen to her,' Jackie was saying, shaking his head as he poured out for Sheila a very large port and rammed a glass of Bass into Dickie's eager hand. 'I'm telling you – she'll make you go barmy, this one, if you listen to her. Just look what she done to me! That's why I gone so loony.'

'The only thing that makes *you* go loony,' Mary was mock-chastising him, 'is too much draught ale in the Rose & Crown every evening. And don't you go laughing, Dickie – you know you encourage him.'

'That's right,' nodded Jackie. 'It's all Dickie's fault – it's all down to you, Dickie, my terrible ways.'

'Oh I say!' said Dickie, smiling very broadly.

'You leave my Dickie alone!' pouted Sheila.

'As the bishop said to the bleeding actress!'

'Oh *honestly*, Jackie,' Mary deplored. 'You really are too awful. Isn't he Sheila?'

'Too too!' gurgled Sheila, holding out her empty glass, and wagging it at Jackie.

'Right – I'm going to see what I can rustle up,' decided Mary. 'Does anyone want the wireless? We could maybe find something like Victor Silvester.'

'So long as it's not that nigger jazz sort of music,' cautioned Jackie, prising away the crown caps from two more big bottles of Bass. 'Can't abide all that. You don't like all that jazzy tripe, do you Dickie?'

'Not me, old man. Strauss – that's more in my line.'

'And what's "Strauss" when it's at home? We ain't all educated like what you are, you know, Dickie.'

'Oh *God* . . .' moaned Sheila. 'Don't start up on all that malarkey.'

'Well it's true,' insisted Jackie. 'He's only slumming it when he's with the likes of me – ain't that the fact of it, Dickie?'

Dickie took a mouthful of beer and looked away.

'Draw it mild, old man,' he said quite softly.

34

'But it *is* true – ain't it Dickie? I mean – face facts, ay? You'll be a doctor one day. Won't you? Ay? Got to be educated for that.'

'I think . . .' said Sheila, getting up from the sofa – wobbling a bit and narrowing her eyes as she coped with all these sudden and new perspectives. 'I think . . . I'm going to the little girls' room and then I'll help Mary in the kitchen.'

'But *won't* you, Dickie? Ay? You finish all your exams and then, my son, you're an important man. Doctor. And look at me. What am I ever going to amount to? Ay? You tell me that.'

'You're not doing too badly, Jackie old boy . . .'

'Not too badly, no. Not at putting up wallpaper and varnishing floorboards. Not at slapping a bucket of distemper on yet another four bleeding walls – no, not too badly. But it ain't *proper*, is it? It ain't like being a doctor. And you got a *car*, ain't you? Ay? Outside, you got a car. Haven't you? Your Morris.'

Dickie ran a finger around the inside of his collar.

'Only secondhand . . .'

'Yeh maybe – but you *got* it, that's the point. I couldn't run to it, not me, never. I ain't got no rich daddy, do I? Your pop, he didn't scarper, did he? He hung about. Got you an education.'

'Oh come on, old man,' tried Dickie. 'We've done all this. It's not my *fault*, is it? Any of it. Let's just enjoy the evening, hey? Why don't you get yourself another drink in, Jackie?'

'I *am* enjoying the evening. You not enjoying the evening? The girls – they're enjoying the evening, pretty sure. So what's wrong with you now, Dickie, that you ain't enjoying the evening?'

'I didn't say—'

'Yeh? Well it sounded to me like you did.'

Mary came in with a plate of haslet sandwiches and she placed it on the three-legged table next to Jackie.

'What're you boys nattering about? Me and Sheila, I suppose. I've got some tinned peaches and Carnation to follow, anyone's interested . . . Where is Sheila?'

'Bog,' said Jackie.

'Jackie!'

'Sorry – "little girls' room". My mistake. No – Dickie's just been telling me what a common little washout I am, and I been agreeing with him. Dickie – he'd never say bog, would you Dickie? Ay?'

'I say! Now come on now, Jackie old boy. I never said—'

'It's all right,' laughed Mary. 'It's all right, Dickie – I know you'd never say anything like that about Jackie. Ignore him. It's just his chip on his shoulder. Whenever he's had a few, he always gets like this.'

'Yeh yeh,' said Jackie. 'You're right, Mary – he never. He's too much of a gentleman, ain't you Dickie?'

'Oh for heaven's *sake*, Jackie . . . !'

'Much too much of an educated gentleman. Unlike myself.'

'Here, Jackie,' said Mary, pushing the plate at him. 'Eat a sandwich. It'll give your mouth something else to do. Here, Dickie – you have one too. Oh *there* you are, Sheila! Thought you'd got lost.'

'I think . . .' said Sheila uncertainly, as she made her way weavingly back to the sofa and dropped herself into it. 'I think . . . I had one too many sausages, earlier on. Feel a bit queasy.'

'Yeh,' laughed Jackie. 'And maybe them last two bottles of port – maybe they wasn't such a great idea neither, ay Sheila my love?'

'Oh God's *sake*, Jackie,' sighed Sheila. 'I haven't had that much.'

'No?' queried Jackie, holding up the bottle of ruby to the light of the fire. 'Well I tell you we been spilling one hell of a lot of it then, that's all I can say. No but listen – seriously, Dickie. I envy you, that's all I'm saying. That's all I mean. Admire you. Proud of you. Like I'm proud of my little brother, Alfie – he's doing his best, ain't he? Ain't he, Mary?'

'He looks ever so smart in his suit, going off to the office of a morning,' smiled Mary. 'Shall I start fiddling with the wireless, or do we not want it?'

'What line's he in?' asked Dickie. 'Your Alfie.'

'Insurance,' said Jackie, nodding with emphasis. 'He's in insurance, young Alfie is. Only a clerk, mind, but he'll work hisself up – he's a little grafter, Alfie is. He'll do all right. Proud of him. He ain't in a hurry to get his hands all dirty. He won't be mopping his hands with no rag and a bottle of turps at the end of the day. Picking splinters from out his bloody fingers . . .'

A rush of hissing static suddenly filled the room, and as Mary went on twiddling the big brown knobs on the wireless, it was suddenly replaced by an indeterminate howl, and then a snatch of funereal speech referring to the Foreign Secretary in the Commons today.

'Must be some music somewhere . . .'

'And my Jeremy,' went on Jackie – leaning forward with eagerness and warming to the thing, in a way that Mary well recognised. 'My kid – he won't be doing what I do. Not if I can help it. He'll be a gentleman – maybe even a doctor, ay Dickie? Maybe he'll even be a doctor, one day.'

'Can't see why not, old man.'

'That's music!' piped up Sheila. 'Just there – back a bit, Mary – you had something there . . .'

'It was jazzy,' grumbled Jackie. 'Don't like jazz. Can't abide it. Try and find some – what was it? Grouse?'

Dickie chuckled, quite good-humouredly.

'Strauss,' he said.

'Yeh! That's it!' Jackie agreed. 'Strauss. See if you can find us some of them Strauss, will you Mary? Then we can all find out what it is the toffs like listening to, ay? Or Prime Minister – maybe little Jeremy, one day he'll be leading the country. Ay? What about that?'

Whoops and crackles from the wireless were suddenly so raucous that everyone's hands went up to their ears.

'Sorry!' called out Mary. 'Sorry, everybody. I think I'm going to give this up as a very bad job. There – I've turned it off now. It's a shame – usually there's something nice on somewhere . . .'

'What you think, ay Mary?'

'What do I think about what, Jackie?'

'Our little Jeremy. Being the Prime Minister.'

'Yes, Jackie. Very nice. And what – you'll be King then, will you?'

'God help us all!' laughed Sheila. 'Ooh . . . I do feel so queasy, you know.'

'I wouldn't mind it,' said Jackie. 'Being King. Wouldn't mind it at all. Palace – servants kowtowing to you left right and centre. Yeh. Reckon I could cope with it.'

'Carry on dreaming, Jackie,' Sheila was slurring now. 'Mary – you haven't got any Beechams, have you?'

'I'll have a look. Jackie – why don't you offer Dickie a sandwich?'

'Ooh no – not for me, old girl. Well up to the Plimsoll line as it is.'

'What's that?' queried Jackie. 'Them's gym shoes, ain't they?'

'Hm? Oh. See what you mean. But in this context, Jackie old sport, I rather believe it's a naval expression, don't you know.'

'That right? Naval expression. Well there you are. You see what I mean then Mary, don't you? Got to be educated, know a thing like that.'

'Here we go again!' laughed Dickie, rolling up his eyes. 'Look I tell you what, Sheila old girl – no Mary, don't bother hunting out the Beechams. It's actually jolly late, you know. We'll take ourselves off, think that's best. All got work to do in the morning, haven't we?'

'Oh God . . .' groaned Mary. 'Don't remind me. That awful laundry. Gosh, Jackie – you go on and on about how rotten your job is – you should try working in the laundry. Honestly, Dickie

– it's dreadful, really dreadful, I just can't tell you. I wish I was like you, Sheila – nice little hairdressers. Must be lovely, that – having a talent.'

'Some of the people, though,' said Sheila. 'You just want to kill them, sometimes. Not a clue what they want, and they're never ever happy with what you give them.'

'What you up to tomorrow then, Dickie?' Jackie now wanted to know.

'Hm? Oh. Lecture in the morning. Got a paper to write, actually.'

'Yeh? Paper to write, ay? Me, I got to dig out a cesspit up by the Co-op. Says it all really, don't it? Sums it up a treat.'

Dickie was standing and beating at the pockets of his blue flannel blazer.

'Come on then, Sheila old girl. Let's have you on parade.'

'Are you sure, Dickie?' asked Mary. 'You're very welcome to stay, you know, if you'd like to.'

'No no – don't want to overdo our welcome, and all that sort of thing, you know. Come on, Sheila – here, let me give you a hand-up. There. All right? Have you home in two shakes of a lamb's tail.'

'Jackie,' said Mary, getting up from the pouffe and rubbing her thighs. 'Can you get the coats? They're just over by the – yes, just there. Well *golly*, everyone – what an evening we've had! Thanks *so* much for the fireworks, Dickie – they were perfectly spectacular.'

'Glad you liked, old thing. And thanks for the sandwiches and beer. So long then, Jackie old man. Maybe see you in the Rose & Crown tomorrow some time, hey?'

'Yeh, Dickie. Yeh. Here's your coat, look. Come on Sheila – stick your arm in there, there's a good girl. Yeh, Dickie – I'll pop in for a jar after my work, likely as not. And don't worry – I'll wash my hands before I come, make sure you don't catch nothing off of me.'

'Oh *do* shut up, Jackie,' sighed Mary. 'Gosh – I'm suddenly so terribly tired . . .'

'It was the sausage,' whispered Sheila. 'I really do feel quite queasy . . .'

'And another advantage of being in your line,' announced Jackie, quite suddenly, just as Mary had the door open to usher them out, 'is all them nurses, of course. Once you pass your exams – and you will Dickie, flying colours, I've no doubts on that score – well then you got all them pretty little nurses at your beck and call, ain't you?'

'Be quiet now, Jackie,' cautioned Mary.

'He doesn't want any nurses,' said Sheila, quite aggrieved. 'Do you, Dickie?'

Dickie laughed. 'Just you, my love. To soothe the fevered brow, and so forth.'

'All over you, they'll be,' Jackie went on quite excitedly. 'Coming out your ears, them nurses'll be. And pills. You'll have access, won't you? All the drugs. What with that and the nurses, well – you'll be up to your neck in a right bleeding orgy half the time, won't you Dickie old mate?'

'Jackie, stop. Stop now,' Mary was hissing at him. 'Don't mind Jackie, will you? Well look goodbye, the two of you. And thank you again.'

'I think,' said Sheila, 'I might be going to be sick . . .'

'Contra-wossnames!' Jackie was shouting. 'You know – devices.'

'Jackie!' warned Mary, really quite annoyed now.

'No but listen – he'll need them, won't he? All them nurses, high as a bleeding kite. And he'll get them buckshee, I shouldn't wonder. Me and Mary, we never really got the hang of them, did we really Mary? Ay?'

'We'll be off now,' said Dickie, as brightly as he could manage. 'Bye, Mary. Get a bit of a kip in, hey Jackie? Get your head down.'

'Yeh I will, Dickie. I will. But them things – couldn't tell one end from the other, could we really Mary? I wouldn't wear them things, not me.'

'Look,' interjected Mary, very flustered. 'Just go, you two, can you? I'm going to close the door now.'

'So Mary, she had one them metal things stuck up her. You'd know about them, wouldn't you Dickie? Line you're in. They don't look much, but it seems to do the trick. You know – stops the little bastards. So Bob's your uncle, really.'

Sheila had wrapped a hand across her mouth and her eyes were bulging but Mary more or less pushed her out of the flat and urged on Dickie to follow her. She slammed shut the door behind them and with her back hard against it she glared up at Jackie, and her eyes were blazing.

'What in God's name did you think you were *doing*? Hm? Tell me, Jackie – why is it, whenever we're with people, whenever we're all just having a perfectly pleasant time – why do you always have to *do* this? You embarrass people, Jackie – you embarrass *me*. Why can't you just, oh God – *chat*? Like normal people do.'

Jackie's eyes were wide and his palms were before her in a pose of supplication.

'It were only Dickie and Sheila! And anyway – I *were* just chatting. Just chatting – that's all I were doing. I don't know what's got into you.'

'You *weren't* just—! And keep your voice down or you'll go and wake Jeremy. Oh God, Jackie – I'm exhausted. I've had enough. And it doesn't *matter* that it was only Dickie and Sheila. No – I just don't want to go on with this, not tonight. I can't. I'm going to go to bed, all right? I just want to get some sleep.'

'Fine, love. That's just ticketyboo, far as I'm concerned. We'll get ourselves off to bed.'

'No, Jackie – no. You stay here on the settee. I just need to get some sleep. I've got to be up at six.'

'Understood, Mary – understood. You go and get yourself under the covers, and I'll just creep in ever so quietly. You won't even know I'm there.'

'No, Jackie – no. I said no and I mean it.'

Mary turned away and into the bedroom, and she closed the door behind her.

Well fine then, thought Jackie: be like that. I don't know – what's she have to go flying off the handle like that for anyway? Ay? Just chatting, that's all I were doing. Just having a bit of a chat, that's all. Women – I don't know. I reckon they're mostly half mad, way they go on. Don't think straight like what blokes do. Ah well: sod it. What I think I'll do now is, I'll have myself one of them sandwiches before they goes all curly on me, and I reckon I could make room for that last bottle of Bass there – get that supped up, and then in my own sweet time, when I'm good and bleeding ready, I'll go into the bedroom and show her what's what. Telling me what to do! My own house this, ain't it? Telling me what to do! Just because she thinks she's better than what I am – just because her and Dickie Wheat and that bleeding stuck-up mother of hers think I'm just a bit of muck what wants scraping off your bleeding boot . . . well I ain't having it. Not now and not never. Telling me what to do! In my own house and all. No – I ain't having it. Not at all. She earned a slapping, she has, but I'd never raise a hand. I may be no gentleman, but I do know that much. So she's lucky. But still and all, she don't want to go round telling me what to do. Because I just won't stand for it. No I bleeding won't. Not now and not never.

I tell you one thing, though – that were a very tasty little sandwich, that were. And the ale, it settles the stomach, you know – settles it a treat. Better than any of your Beechams

Powders, a nice drop of Bass. So: damp the fire down. Keep my long johns on, I think I will; be freezing in that bleeding bedroom – always bleeding is. And then I'll get myself in there sharpish, is what I reckon I'll do. Show her what's what.

○

My mother – I never saw very much of her at all, in those days, not after Jeremy was born, but whenever I did (and it was never easy, it was never what you could call a pleasurable interlude, nothing like that, because if she, oh – *deigned* to come over to the flat, well then – you could almost hear her sniffing her disgust: she'd close her eyes to make it clear to me. I think, that she was ... I don't know – mournfully masking a severe inner pain, it could very well have been, this charade of hers, or else she simply still had failed to come to terms with what she insisted were my ever so humble surroundings). But whenever I did – see her, I mean – all she said to me ... and this is why, I think, I'd more or less decided that there was really no point in us meeting any more – certainly not in me going round to hers, anyway, because she said this to me every single time now and then despite what I'd determined upon beforehand, I did get upset, and then she got upset, and my dear old Dad, well – he just looked at each one of us in silence, never said a word, and I knew, of course I knew that he was upset too because his wife and daughter, well – we were upset, and he always hated to see it, he must have done, but he could never in any way help us, or anything; he never could, my Dad, not really. So whenever I did actually meet her, try to have a chat with her, try to be light, try to be civil, all she had to talk about was the laundry that I worked

43

in. That and the shame that I'd brought upon the family by having given birth out of wedlock (she never said this – she just called it 'doing *that*'). Which I haven't, actually – caused any shame – because nobody knows. I've never said that I'm married, exactly – it's not the sort of thing I could ever tell lies about, it's much too important, much too sacred in my eyes to ever tell lies about – but, well ... I suppose it's because the two of us live together, Jackie and me, all the locals, all the shop people and the coalman and the milkman and everybody else, they all started calling me Mrs Robertson, you see, and I just never got round to putting them right. That's all. And they've seen the ring, of course. They know it's just a brass one I actually myself had to pick out of the Rufflette heading from the curtains we had up in the scullery because I always used to make a joke of it. Jackie says, I'd tell them – if ever they asked me – that it's only temporary until he can afford to take me up West and together we're going to the very swankiest jewellers in I think it's Bond Street and buy me such a ring that it'll put the Queen of England's to shame. Most people have been nice and friendly about it (even if they don't believe a word) because it's not at all a stuck-up and snobby neighbourhood, and although we none of us around here are truly wanting for anything, there's nobody rich, there's not a lot of money about, and so people, they generally understand, or have the goodness to pretend to. Sally in the greengrocers, though, she got a bit sniffy and she said to me Hm yes I daresay – I don't know about it being the best in England but, well – he could hardly find a worse one now, could he, your Jackie? But I know she didn't mean to be beastly. Of course – he never did say any of all that, all that about Bond Street and the Queen of England; I don't suppose for a moment he's ever thought to give me a ring of any description whatever. It's just a little white lie on my part because, well – you've got to say something, haven't you? You can't just stand there like a lemon. But no – he's never asked me to marry him, never even mentioned it. I did, of course, I mentioned it – once I'd found out that I'd fallen pregnant with Jeremy. And what he said was All in good time, ay love? Let's just see, let's just see. No sense rushing into things, is there? And I didn't say to him in return Well that's as maybe, Jackie, but I don't recall you exercised quite so much caution in rushing in to *this* thing, did you Jackie? No, I didn't say that – because what would be the point? It only would've upset him. Or me. And it's years ago now, so I suppose that's the end of it. But he never walked out on me, like a lot of men would. And we're still together and happy and everything, aren't we, the three of us? A proper little family.

So what I said to mother is – I said to her, look: nobody knows, so where can be the shame? And then I regretted it, I regretted it at once – because she always came back to me with the very same thing. Her face, it went so rigid and she breathed in deeply as if she was about to plunge deep under water and stay there for ages. 'Ah but *I* know,' she'd say to me. '*I* know, Mary – and it's all that a mother can bear.' And then she'd start up with this great string of questions – not to me, but looking about her and into thin air – and they're not the sort of questions she ever wants me to answer. 'Did I fail you when you were a girl? Did your dear father and I ever once hold back in the love we both bestowed upon you? Did we not bring you up to be moral and upstanding?' On and on in that vein for quite a long while, and I just sort of sat there, looking and feeling actually pretty miserable, as a matter of fact. And then she'd lift up her hands and drop them into her lap with an air of finality – as if to say, I suppose it must have been, that what's done is done and we all must daily cope with humilia-tion and despair as best we may and trust our souls to the mercy of the Lord. Except, of course, that there was never anything remotely final about it because the very next time we'd encounter (and whether or not there'll be another such meeting I am quite genuinely undecided, for I am constantly wondering where can be the wisdom in it) – well then she'd start it all again, right from the beginning, item by item, and sparing me nothing. Even if Jeremy was sprawling in my lap, smiling the smile that would surely melt a glacier – still she'd just sit there, my mother, so stern and unmoved. He looks, she once said of Jeremy, exactly like his father. And that, as far as she was concerned, I may only assume, was very much that. (And in this opinion – if valid opinion is what we had here, her glance was that cursory – she is utterly wrong. Jeremy's eyes and nose are mine and mine alone, and if she could but see it, my quite unyielding mother, there is about the lips and jawline something of her own.)

And then she'd get on to the laundry, and this was much harder for me to deal with, actually, because although I'd never dream of letting on, I agreed with her, you see – I had to agree with every word she said. She asked me why I had to demean myself by toiling away in so awful a place, and I didn't really know how I could answer. You see, when Jeremy was born, I said to Jackie that he'd never have to worry, not about Jeremy – not about the baby, he wouldn't, because I was going to be the very best mother the world had ever seen. I'll devote my whole life to him, Jackie – I swear to you I will. Night and day, whatever he needs, his mother will be there. Yeh well, is what he said. Not quite what I'd been expecting, I can hardly deny it, but that in the event appeared to be all he had to say to me: yeh well. It turned out that his work was getting harder to come by, he told me – and I had, I admit, I'd heard a bit of talk, around and about. It wasn't so bad as it had been just a few years ago – oh my goodness, in those days, it was really so awful – there were that many men around here who'd just been laid off and couldn't get

46

another job anywhere, not for months – years for some of them. The hardship was terrible. The looks on everyone's faces – the women, the mothers, you saw a determination, as if all of them had taken a solemn and collective vow to go on slaving for their families and keeping up not appearances but standards, whatever it took and no matter how hard the times. If we came through the Great War, is what a lot of them said, then we can surely come through this. And then you saw fear as the misery deepened; only the very strongest did come through – a lot of them eventually succumbed. They were worn out and beaten, you see, so many of the women, and the menfolk, they just looked on – for what else could they do? – at their increasingly lean and raggedy brood, the deep hot anger inside them – you could see it – it was always ready to break and erupt at the slightest provocation. And often they would turn upon their own – the very ones they had been struggling to keep; sad little children, they just ran away, and so many bruised and battered women, they simply couldn't take it any more. And each of these people was so thoroughly innocent, here was the tragedy: hard-working English men and women, denied the right to continue. It's still so painful, just to think of it. They were terrible times, and I know it. Every day I thank the Lord that now, things can only get better.

But still, when Jeremy was born, there remained a very uncertain future for many of the men round here, so it wasn't Jackie, it wasn't just him – he's never been idle, he's always eager, but the work, well – it just wasn't there. And nor was he unwilling to try out new things. He started out as a painter and decorator – that's what he was when first I knew him – but then after people started cutting back on all the non-essentials (well, you don't think of wallpaper, do you? Not when you don't know where the next hot meal might be coming from) – well then Jackie, he broadened out into all sorts of things,

picking it up as he went along, learning by all of his mistakes –
trial and error is what they call it – and he was the first to
admit it, my Jackie, that back in those days he made errors
aplenty. He was sinking a heavy upright into somebody's back
garden, one time – putting up a new fence – and he thinks what
must have happened was that he hit the gas main – the stench
was that bad – and the whole of the area, it had to be evacuated.
Then he tried his hand at a bit of plumbing and drainage – I
lost count of the number of times that he came back home to
me soaked to the skin or reeking to high heaven, and half his
fingers covered in plasters. He'd take on anything, my Jackie,
but by the time little Jeremy came along – well I don't know
quite why, but it really did look as if he'd run out of options.
So he said to me Look: it'd only be temporary, just for a bit –
it can't last for ever. And I said yes of course I will, Jackie – I'll
look around in the morning, see what I can get. Well – everyone
else, all the young mothers, they were looking too, of course,
and so by the time I got round to it, all the part-time jobs that
I might have chosen – serving in a stationer's, say, or manning
a switchboard, I once thought I could do (because everybody
said I'd certainly got the voice for it) – well there was nothing
like that, nothing at all decent, and so I ended up where a lot
of us did, at the Manor Street Laundry. I'd worked there for
a short while before I met Jackie, because I so badly needed
some money, but I just had to leave – it is terrible work. Your
arms are cooked and raw from heaving these sopping great
deadweights from washers to mangles, and feeding them into
the driers . . . I sometimes was crying with the heat and the
pain – and it was not just tears but sweat as well that constantly
ran down my face. But even the laundry, even that wasn't so
bad as some women had to endure. Phyllis and Dorothy,
I remember – looking after their invalid mum and a simple
brother at the back of the tenements – they had to go to the

Steele's Road Abattoir, and even to this day they can't bring themselves to talk about it: show them a bit of brisket and they nearly pass out on you. They'll cross any road at all to avoid a butcher's window.

So when Jackie wasn't working – and it got to be more and more, he hardly ever had a job on – then he'd stay in the flat and look after the baby, because now I was working full time. Or else Sheila, she'd have Jeremy for a bit in the hairdressers – although once when I called on her to fetch him back home, I found he was playing with curling tongs and scissors and I nearly had a fit. He's all right, Sheila assured me – kids aren't stupid, you know: kids, they're not made of glass – they can look after themselves. This is a thing that mothers never say, because they know it to be wrong.

Anyway, slowly – bit by bit – things began to pick up, so far as Jackie and his work were concerned. The economy – I heard it on the wireless – the economy, it was beginning to pick up too, is what they told us. Neither me nor Jackie could have quite told you what exactly this economy was, but it was picking up, you see, and that was surely the point: that could only be a good thing – and it seemed to be so, because generally speaking, things did appear to be picking up all round. And all the other forms of work that Jackie had laboured to master when there had been very little choice in the matter – well, they went on to stand him in very good stead, because now it was a rare thing when he had to turn a job down, and goodness, I was so very pleased for him, pleased for all of us, really I was. Yeh, he grinned, 'now I'm a proper little Jackie of All Trades: good, ain't it?' (I think he meant it was sincerely good, it's sometimes hard to tell.)

So I said to him well now listen to me then, Jackie – I can't tell you how happy I am because I can be honest with you now – I just *hate* it, working in the laundry, Jackie, I hate it, I hate it, I just can't say to you how much I simply hate it. It'll be so very lovely, being back at home, being back here with Jeremy again, devoting all my life to him, night and day, night and day – now I really can be the very best mother in the world. And Jackie . . . he said to me Yeh well, all in good time, ay love? Let's just see, let's just see: I mean it's not as if we still couldn't do with the few bob you're bringing in now, is it love? Ay? Always use a bit extra, can't we? And also, I got to quite like it, spending a bit of time with the lad of a daytime. So I reckon we don't want to rush into it, not just yet we don't. And anyway – what's all this about devoting your whole life to him? Ay? What about *me*? I do still *exist*, you know . . . Or maybe you forgot.

So I went on with it, working in the laundry. I can't pretend that I wasn't resentful – I even threw a bit of a tantrum, which isn't a thing I'd ever do. I rounded on him, and my face, I can only imagine what it must have looked like. It's not fair! It's not fair! You said it yourself, Jackie, that things were looking up – and you said, you said it would only be temporary, just for a bit, you said. I can't *bear* it there, Jackie – oh please please please don't make me go back there. Please Jackie, don't do it. Because it's really not fair! It's not fair! It's just not *fair* of you, Jackie! And he just looked at me and he said yeh well: life, who ever said it was going to be fair then, ay? Who ever told you that? And why you go believing them?

Well yes. But anyway – all that was *then*. All that was *before*. Because today, well – I suppose this is why I've been thinking about all of the past – because just today, this evening, I've had the most absolutely wonderful surprise! I'd been wrapping a few presents in front of the fire – little Jeremy, he was gurgling beside me and kicking his little feet – because Christmas, you know, it so quickly creeps up on you when you've so much else to think of. Well Christmas, it's still just over a week away – but me, I've already been given just the best present ever! From Jackie, from my man – he just came in and surprised me like I've never ever been surprised in the whole of my life. He came up behind me and stooped over and put his hands over my eyes and he said to me 'Guess who?' – which was really so silly, as I'd just been watching him walking through the door and then coming across the room to me.

'Don't be so silly, Jackie.'

'Nothing silly about it, Mary my love. Because if you don't guess right – if you guess wrong, well then you don't get your present.'

'Don't want a present, Jackie. Nothing I need.'

'Well you'll want this present, Mary, if I'm any judge.'

'Can you take your hands away, Jackie? I want to get on.'

'What you up to, then . . . ? Ah – presents for me, ay?'

'No – no no. These aren't yours. It's just a couple of handkerchiefs for Dickie and a little tippet I saw in the market. It'll go beautifully with Sheila's colouring, the complexion she's got. It's a lovely minky brown. And I've got a bit of a confession to make, Jackie. I got one for myself while I was about it. Rose pink – they were only two-and-three, but I'm not asking for any extra. It's just that it'll go so wonderfully well with my coat – you remember it, Jackie? My good one. The one with the little half-belt and epaulettes. People always say I look ever so smart in it.'

'What're you rabbiting on about? How's my boy been today, ay?'

'Good as gold. Better. Haven't you been even better than gold, little Jeremy? Yes you have! Yes you have! Why don't you sit down in your chair, Jackie? Get a bit of a warm. Just like to finish off this little package, if that's all right with you. Won't take half a mo.'

'Mary. Did you hear me, or what? Maybe you gone deaf.'

'What? What do you mean?'

'I mean—! I come in, and what did I say? Ay? What's the one thing I says to you the moment I step through the door?'

'I've got to get up off the floor, you know. Ooh! My leg's gone all pins and needles . . .'

'I *said*, Mary, that I got you a present, Yes? Remember?'

'Oh Jackie you're being so terribly *silly* tonight – I don't know what's got into you. Except maybe some ale in the Rose & Crown.'

'Ain't been near the Rose & Crown – well, just for a very fast one with Jonathan Leakey and a couple of the others. I ain't never sure I can trust that one, you know Mary – Jonathan Leakey. He says to you one thing, but you always got the feeling that there's some other bleeding thing what's hiding behind it, sort of style – something he ain't exactly coming out with, but it's still kind of . . . oh, I can't put it, what I mean . . .'

'You mean he's implying something else . . . ?'

'*Implying* – that's what I mean. Yeh – that's it. Implying. What would I do without you, ay? My little scholar. Just as well we ain't the both of us pig-ignorant little yahoos, ain't it Mary?'

'Oh *don't*, Jackie – I hate it, I just hate it when you say that sort of thing. You're wonderful – you're wonderful to me, anyway.'

Jackie leaned back in his armchair and felt the quiver of a smile very quickly take light and spread all over the rest of his face.

'Well now you come to mention it, I *have* been pretty wonderful, Mary – just lately I have. Which is how I come to be in a position to be giving you this bleeding present what I been on about, if only you're ever going to listen.'

'Well where is it then? Why don't you keep it for Christmas?'

'Because I got you something else for Christmas, ain't I? And I want to give it you now. Now listen – you remember me talking to you about Mr Plough, do you? Yeh? Mr Plough? Remember?'

'Man you've been working for?'

'Yeh. That's it. Man I been working for. Well I ain't never mentioned it before 'cause I wanted to see how it sort of was going before I ups and says anything. But I been doing a lot of carpentry just lately for Mr Plough – shelves and that, couple new sashes – because he owns a lot of property round here, Mr Plough do – don't know if you knew – he's quite a big man round here you know, Mary, although he don't go putting it about – not like Jonathan Leakey and Mr Prince and some others of them I could talk about. Keeps hisself pretty much to hisself, Mr Plough do. Anyway – long story short, this morning he has me into his office.'

'Oh my goodness, Jackie. What've you done wrong? Is everything all right? You haven't lost your job again?'

Jackie just looked at her, as if he'd been struck.

'You know, I sometimes find it really hard to work out what's *wrong* with you, Mary! I'm telling you a story, telling you I got you this bleeding present, and you want to know if I gone and got laid off!'

'Oh I'm sorry, Jackie – I'm so sorry. It's just that I'm so very anxious, these days. You know – after the last time, and everything.'

'Yeh well,' conceded Jackie, more or less mollified. 'All that – ain't never going to happen again. All that – it's behind us. That's all done with, that is. Because this is it, Mary – this is what I got to tell you: Mr Plough, he says to me listen to me, Jackie – I been watching you, and I like what I see.'

'Oh! Jackie!'

Mary's eyes were shining as she grasped his hands in hers.

'No listen – listen. You ain't heard it. So, he says to me – yes, Jackie my boy – he talks like that – I like what I see. You're a good worker, very . . . um . . . very – what is it? Very, um—'

'Clever?'

'*No* – not clever. No. very . . .'

'Versatile?'

'Spot on. Yeh. You're very *versatile*, he says to me. You can do woodwork, decorating, plumbing – bit of digging. All sorts. And what's more, you put your back into it, not like some of them round here. So what I propose to you, Jackie my man . . .' And Jackie grew animated as he returned the pressure in Mary's fingers. 'And see, Mary – I'm really getting quite, well – excited, I suppose it is, Mary, because whatever he's going to say to me next, well – it ain't going to be *bad*, is it? Not the way he's going on. Whatever he's got for me, I'm reckoning, it's got to be good, yeh?'

Mary was dizzied by the light in his eyes, and the spell he was spinning.

'Tell me, Jackie! What? What did he say?'

'He said . . . he said he wants me to work for him full time – just for him, no one else. He's guaranteeing me five pound a week—'

'Jackie! Jackie! Oh my God, Jackie, I can't *believe* it . . . !'

'—Five pound a week, that's the minimum. And that ain't all. He says to me, I'm going to keep a very close eye on you, Jackie my boy, and if I go on liking what I see, then come the new year – spring it could be, is what he says to me – then I don't see no reason why you shouldn't become a – wait for it, Mary – a *partner*.'

Mary's mouth was open, and Jackie was very contented with the stupefied silence that briefly took over.

'Yeh,' he went on. 'I know. Me. A bleeding partner. Can't hardly believe it.'

Mary was stooping down low now and kissing his hands, her face pulled tight by delight, and spattered by tears that she was smearing away.

'Plus . . .' continued Jackie. 'I got more.'

'More! There can't be. I don't believe it. There can't – there can't be any more. Oh Jackie – I can't tell you—!'

'No listen. This bit's for you. This is your present, Mary – this is what you been deserving. In the light of what I been saying, you come off of the laundry, first thing in the morning. How's about that?'

Mary's face, it crumpled into almost pain, such were the convulsions that all this were causing her.

'Yeh. First thing tomorrow morning, you march in there, my girl, and you tell them what they can do with their poxy little job. All right?'

Mary's eyes beheld him.

'Jackie. Oh Jackie . . . !'

'And plus. I got more.'

Both Jackie and Mary were now quite wild. Mary, suddenly, had no words – she just, in a sort of trance, kept on repeating his name, over and over, again and again.

'What I thought was,' Jackie carried on, with a blitheness he was so unused to, his eyes like wet and shiny stones with two white pinpoints in the firelight. 'What I were thinking was, if he come through, Mr Plough – if in the spring he, you know – still reckons I'm up to the job and he makes me a partner . . . well then, Mary, he told me I could be earning a right little bundle and so what I were thinking was, well – we might start looking around for a – you know, little house. What you think?'

Mary was weeping quite openly and shaking her head with such energy that Jackie was stopped and confused.

'What . . . ?' he checked, searching her face. 'You don't *want* a little house . . . ?'

And then it all just rushed out of her.

'Oh Jackie Jackie Jackie . . . ! Of *course* I want a – oh Jackie, I'm just so – I've never been so happy, not in all my life. You've just given me everything I've always longed for – just to be with you and Jeremy in a house of our own . . . ! Oh Jackie, I love you – I love you so much, I just think I could *die* . . . !'

She threw herself upon him and hugged his neck so tightly and covered it in kisses and she yelped and laughed into his ear.

'Here here! Steady on, girl! I'll be in a wheelchair, you keep this up – and then where will we be, ay?'

Jeremy, then – he sent up a howl and they both looked around, she in some alarm. But all that Mary could see on his face was just laughter and a kind of mad relief, as if he somehow understood it all (no, thought Mary: it's me that's mad). She picked up Jeremy and sat on Jackie's lap, and he held them both close. Then he shifted slightly and set to pulling out a flattened brown paper package from inside his jacket.

'I got this for you, Mary . . .' he said quite softly. 'Something for yourself.'

Mary stared at it, and then she tore off the paper in something like a frenzy, hardly aware of what it was she was doing. And then she simply gazed down at the rose-pink tippet, and wept and wept.

'Shame,' said Jackie quietly, 'that you already got it. I just seed it, you see Mary – and I thought it'd go real nice with, you know – that coat of yours . . .'

Mary was staring at him, and again her eyes were misted and glassy.

'The one with the half-belt . . . ?' she managed to stutter.

Jackie nodded profoundly. 'And them epaulettes on it. Yeh.'

Mary just slowly wagged her head, and then she kissed him, long and deeply.

'Blimey,' said Jackie. 'Blimey, Mary.'

'I love you, Jackie . . .'

'Yeh well. Just glad to be able to accommodate you. You know that.' He dandled his finger at Jeremy's lips, and then he looked up at her. 'It were only two-and-three . . .'

Mary's insides were collapsed by love; she felt so weak and sick and fine.

'I *love* you, Jackie, with all my heart. I always will. I always will. Nothing will ever stop me from loving you, Jackie. For ever and ever: I will always love you.'

⊙

Jonathan Leakey was sighing deeply as he set one foot quite firmly on the thick brass rail that curled around the horseshoe bar. He shook his head as he stared into his Scotch and a splash, and then he made quite a show of clapping his palms to either side of his head – quick to elbow some old and gaudy drunk well out of the way when he stumbled towards him and came just that close to slopping his beer on to Jonathan's boot.

'Christ Almighty, Len – this time of year, it gets so you can't never have a quiet little drink on your tod in your own bleeding local.'

He lit a Senior Service from the butt of his last one – dropped this on to the floor and stepped on it hard, swivelling his foot this way and that. Len was behind the bar, coping his best with the hot and braying swell of men, plucking the ten-shilling note from the hand that was waving it and shouting out All right so what's it going to be then, ay? He chucked over a couple of raised-up eyebrows in Jonathan Leakey's direction, a sort of sympathetic understanding, he could maybe take it as. Got to be nice to the regulars, of course – they're your bread and butter – but me, I just love it, this time of year. Yeh granted, you get worked half to death – that's a given – but at least you've got the chance to turn over a couple of bob while the going's good. Everyone round here, they all say how it's the hub of the community, the Rose & Crown, but some days of a midday dinnertime, well – you could do yourself a favour and lock up shop and go and get your head down for a well-earned kip, but the brewers, well, they just wouldn't stand for it. So all you can do is soldier on. And yeh, I well understand what Jonny might be meaning, but the way I look at it is, you strike while the iron is hot, if you take my meaning: grab the money while they've got it to spend.

'Oh it's you is it, Jackie,' said Jonathan Leakey – aware now of somebody standing beside him. 'Get you one, can I? Christ Almighty – you can't hardly hear yourself think, all this bleeding hoo-ha going on.'

'Let me get *you* one,' said Jackie, slipping down a quid. 'I don't mind it myself. Quite like it a bit lively.'

'Bit flush are we, Jackie old lad? I'll have a Scotch and a splash then, you twisting my arm. Large one, there's a good boy. Well not me, Jackie – no not me. Christmas come around – turns people's minds, far as I can see. Everyone starts behaving different. Everything looking different and all. Breaks your routine – and it don't half cost you. Women – they're the worst. Goes without saying. I reckon it wants banning, bleeding Christmas. Just messes you up, that's all it ever does. Want a fag do you, Jackie boy?'

'Yeh I will. Ta. Wotcha, Len! Pint of the usual, I'll have, and a whisky and wossname for old miseryguts here. And get one in for yourself and all, Len lad. Look like you could do with it.'

'Large one . . .' put in Jonathan Leakey.

'Yeh. Mr Scrooge here, he wants a large one. Drown his sorrows. And you Len, ay? You get yourself in whatever you fancy.'

'Ta, Jackie. You're a scholar and a gentleman.'

'That's a bleeding laugh, that is . . .' muttered Jonathan Leakey.

'You watch your mouth,' said Jackie. 'Bloke goes and buys you a drink, least you can do is keep a civil tongue. Here you go, Jonny – get that down you, my son. Might put a bleeding smile on your face. Aye aye! Here he is, here he is – here's the genius, here he is – Dickie Wheat, the man hisself. Come on, Dickie – let's be having you, fight your way through. What's yours then, ay?'

'What ho, Jackie. Gosh – quite a scrum in here, isn't it? Just a half for me, thanks awfully much.'

'Come on – it's Christmas, ain't it? Where's your Christmas spirit, Dickie?'

'Yes – righty-ho,' agreed Dickie. 'Pint, then. Jolly dee.'

'What're them girls of ours up to then, ay?'

'Oh search me, old man. Whatever they always get up to, I expect. Bit of a mystery, perfectly honest with you. Women and all that sort of thing, you know.'

'You're telling me. Here, Dickie – you know Mr Leakey, do you? Dickie Wheat – Jonathan Leakey. Scrooge to his mates. Christmas, he says to me, it wants banning. Life of the party, ay?'

'How do you do. Mr Leakey. No we don't, um . . . seen you in here I think though, haven't I? Time to time?'

'More than likely, more than likely,' Jonathan Leakey conceded. 'You see that bit of holly they got hanging up there? Berries, they look like they been kippered. Hardly surprising, the fug they got in here. So what you having then, lads? Same again, is it? Here – take a fag, you want one.'

'Blimey, Jonny – you got that one down you sharpish, didn't you?'

Jonathan Leakey shrugged. 'Only way to get through it, ain't it? Bleeding Christmas time. Roll on thirty-nine, that's all I can say.'

'Gosh you know it's dashed extraordinary, isn't it really?' piped up Dickie, looking from one to the other.

Jonathan Leakey regarded him, and Jackie was laughing.

'I got to explain to you, Jonny. Dickie, he ain't like you and me. He's top drawer, our Dickie is. You got to understand it.'

'Oh God's *sake*, Jackie . . . Don't go *on*.'

'No but you is, you is – you know you is, Dickie. You're a toff, that's what you are, and there ain't no mistaking it. Nothing to be ashamed of, is it? Being a toff.'

'I'm not – *ashamed*. I'm not anything. And I'm certainly not a *toff* . . .'

Jonathan Leakey sniffed elaborately.

'*Sound* like a toff . . .' is all he said, pulling on a cigarette he was lighting from his stub.

'See! I told you, Dickie. Anyway look – don't mind us. Come on – drink up. Jonny's offered us another one, which is right nice of the man, ain't it? So get it down you, Dickie my son, before he go and change his mind.'

'Well I'm still all right with this one, thanks all the same. But no listen – what I was saying. Don't you think it's perfectly extraordinary that soon it's, you know – as you said Mr Leakey – 1939 and so on, and then gosh, before we know where we are, we'll all be in the *forties*. Hardly bears thinking about.'

'Only a number,' said Jonathan Leakey. 'That's all it is. You been around long as I have, you get to understand. Week or so, they'll all be doing the Auld Lang Syne, won't they? Stupid fuckers. Welcoming in the bleeding new. Only it ain't new, is it? Never is. It's always the same as the last. Thirty-nine – you won't notice a bleeding bit of difference. It'll be the same as this, you mark my words. Always is. And then this time next year, we'll be propping up the bar, just like now, and someone or other – you most likely, Mr Weak—'

'Wheat it is, actually,' said Dickie, coughing in apology.

'Yeh Wheat – what I said. There you'll be saying Cripes, cor blimey – here we are on the edge of the forties. And I'll be saying to you so bleeding what? Because it'll all be the same. More of the same, that's all it ever is.'

'Now at a *funeral* . . .' Jackie was musing, clapping Jonathan Leakey around the shoulders and inhaling deeply on his latest

60

cigarette, 'I can see that, yeh, you might be just the geezer to add the right bit of tone, you know what I'm saying? But blimey, mate – you don't want to be around you any other bleeding time, do you? Ay? Right face-ache, you are.'

Jonathan Leakey did his shrug. 'Just how it is, that's all. So any of you buying, or what?'

'Oh yes – rather,' put in Dickie. 'What can I get you, Mr Leakey? Same again?'

'Yeh. Scotch and a splash. Call me Jonny, ay?'

'Right-o. Coming up. One Scotch and a splash. I'm Dickie.'

Jonathan Leakey looked at him. 'Yeh,' he said.

'What about you then, Jackie old man? Go another pint, will we?'

'Yeh – go on then. And then I tell you what – after, we better get ourselves back to them girls. All right? I swore on my life we wouldn't be late – she'll have my guts, elsewise. So just one more then, ay? And then we'll take ourselves off.'

'Large one . . .' said Jonathan Leakey. 'All right?'

'Yes indeed,' agreed Dickie, nodding his head and smiling with eagerness. 'Rather. Yes indeed.'

'You know what I reckon we ought to do with him, Dickie? Here mate – watch where you're treading! Get out of it! Bleeding liberty. See that, did you? Bleeding old fucker, careering around . . . dear oh dear. Gawd it's getting loud in here – can you hear me, you lot? Yeh? Now what were I . . . ? Oh yeh – our Mr Leakey here. You know what I reckon, Dickie? I reckon we want to ask him along to our party. Might cheer him up. What you say?'

'Oh rather. Yes indeed. You'd be most terribly welcome, Mr Leakey, I do assure you.'

'Jonny. You call me Jonny, all right? Party, ay? When would all that be going off, then?'

'Well now let me have a think . . .' said Jackie, corrugating his forehead and touching his temple with a finger. 'I mean call

61

me a nutter, but I were thinking, seeing as how it's this time of the year, that we might go and have it at *Christmas*, you stupid bleeding sod! When else we going to have the bleeding party?'

'What? A proper Christmas party? Turkey, and that?'

'The lot. The works. Whole bleeding thing. Tree, and all.'

'Blimey. Can't hardly recall the last time I were at anything of that order . . .'

'So you're on then, are you?'

'Well . . . yeh . . . reckon I am. Yeh. Reckon I could go for that. Ta, Jackie lad. You're a mate. Have another fag.'

'Right then. That's fixed. Yeh I will mate, ta. And, er – I never know, but – you got a missus, have you Jonny? Little woman, is there?'

'Oh yeh . . . ' nodded Jonathan Leakey. 'There's always one of them knocking about the place somewhere. Bring her, will I?'

'Yeh. Bring her along. What's she called, then?'

'I ain't decided, have I? Not yet. Right then lads – that's right good of you. Let's all have a drink then, shall we? Let's get you on to the Scotches, ay? Enough of that swill. Make a bit of a night of it, ay?'

'Cor blimey, Dickie – just you take a look at him. Got a smile on his face, once in his life. Now I seen everything. Well yeh then – all right Jonny, my son. I'll have a short with you – why not, ay? And then we got to be getting ourselves off back to the girls. Yeh, Dickie? Else she'll have my guts, I'm telling you.'

Jonathan Leakey signalled over to Len and laid a five-pound note on to the bar.

'Large ones . . . ' he said. 'And keep them coming, there's a good lad. And give us twenty Senior Service, you got a minute.'

◉

22nd December 1938

Well – it's done. I am now officially an ex-laundress! It felt wonderful when I told Mrs Marsh that I was leaving – she was terribly sniffy about it, the way I just knew she would be. She said I was passing up a good secure job that plenty would be glad of! The things I could have said to her! But I didn't. I felt so sorry for Lorna, though – I think she hates the work there even more than I did, but she's got no choice since her mother died and left her with all her little brothers and sisters to take care of. She's already old before her time, poor Lorna. Bought some pineapple segments for the party in the Co-op – 5/10½d, but it is quite the most enormous tin I have ever seen. I thought my trusty string bag was going to break with the weight of it!

Feeling a bit guilty being at home all day, so I decided to give the whole flat a really good clean – it's so shaming when you see the colour of the water in the bucket! I couldn't reach the really high bits because Jackie's taken the ladder off somewhere – but with a bit of luck we won't be here much longer, so it won't really matter. I'm so terribly happy. Every single day I thank God for each of my blessings. I thought that Jeremy might be coming down with something this morning – looked a bit peaky – but he didn't have a temperature, it was just a false alarm. Just this minute looked in on him again, and he seems as right as rain. Gave him some blackcurrant and sang him a lullaby. I'd die, if anything happened to him.

Sheila was on the settee, slowly turning the pages of the Army & Navy Stores Catalogue, pausing frequently to express her amazement to Mary at either the beauty of this thing or else the unbelievable cost of that one, look – I mean to say when all's said and done it's only a wireless set, isn't it? Even if it is in a fancy cabinet. So how can they possibly justify asking 16½ guineas for it? I mean I know it's a Pye, and Dickie – he says they're tip-top, Pye are, but still, if I had that sort of money burning a hole in my pocket I'd go for this 'radiogramophone', is what they call it – £16.19.6d. That's even a bit cheaper, isn't it? I can never work it out when they put half guineas on to it.

'Well yes,' said Mary, 'but then you've got to buy the gramophone records, haven't you?'

'There's that . . .' conceded Sheila. 'And I expect they're ever so expensive, aren't they? Gramophone records.'

'Expect so. All these sorts of things seem to be.'

'But just imagine, though – being able to put on any tune you fancied, any time of the day. Golly – I don't think I'd ever do anything *else*.'

'Oh but I think that's half the fun of the wireless, though,' said Mary, shuffling over to Sheila the crumpled bag of assorted fruit jellies. 'Not knowing what sort of music is coming up next. It's like a lucky dip.'

'Oh my goodness look at this!' squealed Sheila quite suddenly, the wideness of her eyes compelling attention as she stabbed at the catalogue with a stiffened and incredulous finger. 'They've got a television here – I don't believe it! I can't believe they actually *sell* them – it must be like having your own little Odeon in the corner of the sitting room. Wait – what does it say . . . ? Hang on – let me read it. It's a funny-looking thing, going by the picture. Here listen, Mary – it says it's got the "latest Cossor Giant Cathode Ray Tube". What on earth is that?'

'Sounds like one of H. G. Wells's spaceships, or something. Rather frightening.'

'Oh well I'm sure it must be perfectly *safe*, or they'd hardly be selling it, would they? To the general public. Not in the Army & Navy, anyway. But goodness, I thought it was only the King and people who were allowed to have this sort of thing. Oh look – I'm right because it says here that you get a perfect picture up to twenty miles approx – what's approx? – from Alexandra Palace. Oh . . . *Alexandra* Palace, I see – I thought for a minute I was reading Buckingham Palace – I got all my palaces a bit confused. Oh my *goodness*, Mary – look at this! Look what it costs! 51 guineas! Who could afford that?'

'The King. I think you *are* right. But listen, Sheila – stop looking at all those sorts of things and let's concentrate on the stuff I might actually be getting. Well . . . it won't be very much, as a matter of fact. I had no idea that things like, well – I had my heart set on a really proper three-piece bedroom suite. You know the sort of thing – dressing table where I could put out all my little pots and things, brushes and so on, and a matching wardrobe and one of those lovely wooden headboards that look like the steering wheel bit of those really expensive motor cars. Not the steering wheel, but the bit behind. Have you seen them? You know – Rolls-Royces and things.'

'When have you been in a Rolls-Royce?'

'Well I haven't, obviously. But you see pictures, don't you? Anyway – the prices! I just couldn't believe them. I've never actually owned any furniture. Have you? No – nor me. All the things here, they belong to the landlord. They're not very nice, are they? I mean that sideboard, it's really horrible, I think. I like things that are much more modern. But look – give me the catalogue over here for a minute, will you Sheila. I marked the page. Yes – here we are: bedroom suites. This is the one I loved – I really love this one – just look at it, Sheila. Isn't it beautiful?'

Sheila studied the spread as it was laid out before her.

'Mm – I *suppose* so . . .' she said quite doubtfully. 'But what are all these funny sorts of squiggles all over it?'

'Well it's only a *drawing*, isn't it? You see it's . . . what does it say it is again? Oh yes – figured walnut, that's it. And that's got a really swirly grain in the wood, you see, and then it's polished up so it looks like it's almost glass. Well obviously you can't get all that, can you? Not in a drawing. But it doesn't matter anyway, as it happens, because just look at the prices. £13.17.6d – and that's just for the dressing table. 'Dressing chest' they call it, some reason. There's even something here called a 'millinery cabinet'. Can you imagine it? A figured walnut cabinet for seven pounds five, and just to stick your hats in.'

'I wouldn't need a very big one,' said Sheila, quite ruefully. 'I've only got two hats. If you don't count the cloche that my mother gave me that time. Wouldn't be seen dead in it. She used to wear it in the twenties – I mean I ask you. So what are you going to get then, Mary? If you can't afford the figured walnut.'

'Well . . . they've got quite a lot of whitewood. Jackie said – he knows about varnishes and things like that – and he said he could probably make it all *look* like figured walnut and I'm sure he could because he's ever so clever . . . so I should imagine we'll maybe be thinking along those lines. I mean a whitewood wardrobe – here's one, this is the sort of thing I mean, you see? It's only 78/9d. Well yes, I know that's still a lot of money, but it's hardly in the region of £13.19.6d is it? That's what they want for the walnut one.'

'Yes but listen, Mary. What I don't understand is – how can you go buying all this furniture if you don't actually know where you'll be living? I mean – it might not fit. It mightn't go. And where are you going to put it all in the meantime?'

'Oh we're not actually going to *buy* it. Not yet. We're just sort of looking, you know, for when we're in a position to go ahead with the thing, you see. Jackie's going to get some brochures of all these new houses they're building out at Golders Green.'

'Where on earth is Golders Green? I've never even heard of it.'

'Well no – nor have I. Jackie hadn't either, but apparently it's terribly nice. North London. I've never been, but apparently it's very leafy, lots of green and so on – not like round here – and so they'll all have lovely big gardens, these houses, when they build them. Always wanted a lovely garden. Some streets, they're already there, and Jackie said to me we can get the Tube out one Sunday – because they've got the Tube. And have a look. The incredible thing is, Sheila, that according to Jackie you can put down a deposit of ten pounds, and then it's just eighteen-and-nine a week after that. And you can live in it straight away. Eighteen-and-nine! I mean, the Army & Navy are asking about twenty times that for a figured walnut dressing chest. So something pretty funny's going on. I can't begin to understand it, finance.'

'No – I'm pretty in the dark myself. Dickie – he's always going on at me. Says I spend money like there's no tomorrow. And I don't ever *think* I do, but I must do, I suppose, because I'm always pretty broke, no matter how well I'm doing in the salon. Never seem to have anything to show for it, either . . .'

'Never mind,' laughed Mary. 'Just as soon as Dickie becomes a doctor, you'll be able to buy one of those cathode death rays, or whatever they were.'

And Sheila looked sad and reflective, which Mary hadn't expected at all.

'Mm. Well yes, I suppose so. Doctors, I imagine they do earn quite a lot of money. I suppose they must do . . .'

'So, then . . . ?'

'Well, Mary – who's to say we'll still be together by then? Dickie and me.'

'Oh Sheila! Of *course* you—'

'Well no you don't *know*, do you? No one does. I mean to say, Dickie – he's such a handsome chap, well I think so anyway – and I know Jackie's always going on about it but, well . . . he *is* pretty posh, isn't he, Dickie? And well – who knows? When he's a doctor, it might get so's he's wanting more of a, I don't know – more of a lady, maybe. Someone in Society. And not some little hairdresser . . .'

'Oh don't be so *silly*, Sheila! How ever could you think that? You and Dickie, you're made for each other. Everyone says so. Oh here, Sheila – don't *cry*. What's wrong? There's nothing wrong, is there? Hm? Don't *cry* . . .'

'Sorry . . .' sniffed Sheila, rifling through her handbag. 'Oh bother – I don't seem to have a hankie. Oh – here it is. I've got it. I'm sorry, Mary – I'm just being silly, I expect . . .'

Mary went over to her – put a protective arm around her shoulders as Sheila set to honking her nose into the handkerchief.

'You most certainly *are*. Now come on – pull yourself together. The boys'll be here soon. At least I jolly well hope so – I told Jackie not to be late. I'll just put on the kettle for us, all right? Yes. Oh and Sheila – you simply must look at all the other things they've got in the catalogue. Some of them are perfectly hilarious!'

Sheila looked up, smilingly blinking her utter willingness to be cajoled.

'Really? What sort of things?'

'I'm going to get the tea going. You look at page 309, for starters – I remembered it specially. And then we've got to decide finally who we're having to the party – I can't believe it's only two days. That's the trouble with Christmas – there's never enough time. Still got to get a tree and put up all the decorations, and everything.'

'Oh I'll help you, Mary – I can help you do that. Hang on . . . it's huge, this catalogue, isn't it? . . . page 309 . . . page 309 . . .'

'Well I was *counting* on you actually, Sheila. I'd never have the time to do it all myself. Take another fruit jelly – I know you love them. Look – I'm just going to pop in and see that Jeremy's all right, and then I'll make us both a nice cup of tea, all right?'

'Mm, I do. Love them. Strawberry I like the best. That's definitely my favourite. Right now – here it is: page 309. Oh my goodness, Mary! *Toilet* paper. Just look at them all. I had no idea there was more than one kind . . .'

Mary bustled over, laughing delightedly, because she really did want to be part of the nonsense.

'I know – it's quite amazing. Look at this: "Victoria Thin Perforated Toilet Paper – 7½d." What can the old Queen have thought about that, I wonder! If it existed, in those days. Must have used something, I suppose . . . It's extraordinary it's allowed, if you think about it, you know. I mean, yes – they put the Royal Family on biscuits and chocolates and things, but I mean really!'

'Well I suppose they could argue,' Sheila was reasoning, 'that they didn't at all mean it to be *that* Victoria – you know, that they just meant it to be, well – any old Victoria, really. Like Victoria Huggins, for instance – you know, the rag and bone man's wife. Except that if I'm honest, I should think that she's quite a stranger to toilet paper, that one.'

'Sheila! Honestly!' And all of Mary's fingers were clutching her nose, and her mouth she left agape.

'Well it's true! You're married to a man who's constantly bringing home bales of old newspapers, you're hardly likely to go to the Army & Navy and spend sevenpence-ha'penny on – what is it? "Victoria Thin Perforated Toilet Paper"! Well *are* you?'

'Oh heavens you're *awful*, Sheila – you really are awful. But here – look at this one. This one I love – this is my favourite. "Mikado Japanese Crepe Toilet Paper" – and all that Chinky writing! It's just so ludicrous. And that one costs ninepence.'

Sheila leant forward to read the minuscule print beneath the illustration.

'*Not* perforated, it says. Why's that then? The Japanese, do they use a whole roll of it, do you suppose?'

'At a sitting!' shrieked out Mary, as the two of them convulsed into quite helpless laughter.

'I tell you what, though,' gasped Sheila, recovering just slightly, and dabbing her lower eyelid with a curled-over finger. 'If it's crepe and unperforated, we could maybe make use of it for the Christmas decorations – wind it around into those sort of festoons.'

'And if we got a roll of the Victoria as well – because that one *is* perforated, the Victoria, remember – well then we could tear it all up and make it into paper chains – just so long as nobody *pulled* them . . . !'

'Oh Mary, Mary! That is just so rude . . . !'

'I know – I'm feeling quite flushed . . .'

'Oh *stop*, Mary – please stop it. My sides are just killing me. Go and make the *tea* for heaven's sake, you silly silly woman. Oh God, I'm just aching . . . well go on then, Mary: *tea*. I'm gasping.'

'All right, all right – I'll stop. I promise. I would say I'll make the tea at my own *convenience* – but I won't, I won't. Because I've stopped, you see. There, Sheila: I've stopped. Right – straight face. Look in on Jeremy. And then tea. Goodness. I haven't laughed like that in ages. Make a start on the list, can you Sheila? We can't have too many, but I don't want to leave out anyone we've really *got* to invite.'

'Got to? Like who?'

'Oh – like our landlord, for one. Otherwise he'll only go and complain about the noise and then we'll have to stop – he's just upstairs, you see. Him and his busybody wife. She's a bit awful, actually. I saw her looking at all the letters in the hallway one time, and I'm sure that if I hadn't just suddenly appeared she would have been steaming all of them open. Jackie hates them because they're Jews – he says that it's the Jews that are ruining Europe and that we'll be next on the list.'

'Is all that true, do you suppose?' asked Sheila, rather seriously.

'I really haven't the slightest idea. I'm not quite sure I know where Europe even is, if I'm completely honest, and I'm sure Jackie doesn't either. Well I know where it *is*, but I'm not sure what it means, exactly. The Germans, they don't like them obviously, because that's why they're all coming over here, I'm pretty sure. Because the Germans – I heard it on the wireless . . . well, you hear quite a lot of it, actually, they go on about it quite a good deal. Anyway the Germans, far as I can make out, are being really pretty beastly to all those Jews – and these are Germans, the Jews, which seems a little odd – and so they're packing up what they can, and they're coming over here. Safety's sake.'

'Why here, though?'

'Well yes – that's what Jackie says. He says that Germany is a country with its head screwed on the right way, and if they don't want them, the Jews, then they must know something about them that we're unaware of – and if they're not good enough for Germany, then why should we have them over here? He's got a point, I suppose – but honestly, I just don't know the first thing about it. And Jackie, he also says that if they're arriving here penniless – because that's what we keep on hearing – then how come this Jewboy and his wife can end up being our landlords, and we English who were all born around here – how come we end up paying them all of our hard-earned money in rent? He gets quite worked up about it sometimes – and he's really quite clever, you know, Jackie is – he is really, he knows quite a lot about things, although he didn't go to school very much . . . so he's probably right, I should imagine. What does Dickie think about it all? He must read the papers and everything, doesn't he?'

'We don't really talk about all that sort of thing, you know, Dickie and me. He maybe thinks, I don't know – that I wouldn't understand what he was saying to me, or something. Probably true – I doubt if I would. But he's very down, you know, on any sort of, um – you know, one lot of people ganging up on another, sort of thing. So I don't suppose he approves of the Germans, or anything. I think I've heard him calling them bully boys, or something. At least I think it was the Germans he was talking about . . . it might have been the Labour Party – I get so confused. Oh no – *I* know what it was, it was the trade unions, that's right, that's what it was. They're not German, are they? I don't know an awful lot about it all, you know. I don't think I'd make a terribly good Prime Minister, would I Mary?'

'That job's reserved for Jeremy, according to Jackie. Gosh – my Jeremy, if he just got a good education and grew up to be a fine young man with a decent job and a lovely house and a pretty little wife and one or two children just as a beautiful as he is now . . . well, I'd settle for that, I can tell you. That would be more than enough for me. But wait a minute – listen: talking of Dickie and Jackie, where *are* they, in heaven's name? I *told* him not to be late – I told and told him till I was blue in the face. His tea's been in the oven for . . . oh, it'll be all dried out.'

'I think Dickie said he was meeting him in the Rose & Crown . . . think that's what he said.'

'Oh well if *that's* the case, heaven only knows when we'll see either of them again. Oh goodness me – *men*, I don't know. Why can't they just have the one drink because they're thirsty, and then come home? Still – I don't suppose we should be complaining, either of us, should we really, Sheila? We're luckier than most, you know.'

'Luckier than a lot of them around here anyway,' agreed Sheila. 'You know – I'm going to have just one more fruit jelly, and then I just must stop. Don't let me, Mary – don't let me eat any more of them.'

'Oh – scoff the lot, Sheila. Why not? It's Christmas time, isn't it? No – we *are* lucky, though. At least both of our men – at least the two of them are *going* places, anyway.'

◉

'Where you think you're going then, Dickie old son?'

'Well actually, I'm not too sure as a matter of, ah . . . Looking for the lavatory, you know. Can't seem to, um . . .'

The Rose & Crown was thick with heat and a sort of fog, mirrors as steamed as the frosted glass around them. The packs and walls of all the men, wedged in and backed up, shoulder to shoulder, were flushed with the muted roar of banter, each aware of the care now needed to not go spilling their glasses, jogging the elbow of a stranger: you didn't want any unpleasantness, not when you were out to be rip-roaring, yearning for a rare serenity, yet needing the tug of a sudden wild-mindedness. But unpleasantness, or the threat of it, was always lurking. Each of them had learned at some time or other and in their own way that the mighty canopy of its potential was ever hovering above them: the daintiest of tricks was to keep it well up there – never to allow even just the fringe of it to float down into your vision, and stare you in the face.

'*Lavatory* . . .' scoffed Jonathan Leakey, with a fair bit of edge, as he wagged his head in almost sorrow.

'It's over that way, Dickie – don't you remember? Blimey – you been in there often enough.' Jackie had to more or less bray this into his ear, and even then he may not have been heard. Dickie, grinning his confusion, tottered in the direction. 'Yeh, Jonny – I know what you mean. But like I said – he's posh. He can't help it. He ain't like you and me.'

Jonathan Leakey lowered his Scotch and a splash and now he was looking at Jackie quite levelly.

'Now listen, you . . .' he murmured, deep and darkly.

'Can't hear you, Jonny. Can't hear you, can I?'

'I said *listen*, you . . .'

'Sorry, mate – not hearing a bleeding thing. You want to speak up.'

'I said *listen* to me, you bleeding fucker – what's wrong with you?!'

'Oh all right – got you that time. What's wrong with me? What's wrong with *you*, more like. What's got into you all of a bleeding sudden? Here we are, having a nice little drink . . .'

'Yeh – *my* little drink.'

'No one were wrestling them off of you, Jonny. You was offering. Wasn't you?'

'Yeh. Yeh – no I didn't mean that. But what I do mean Jackie is this. That's the second time you gone and said that to me tonight, and it's wrong. It ain't right. Got it?'

'Got it? Got what? What's wrong, Jonny? What ain't right? What you on about?'

'When you said your mate, the toff – when you said he ain't like us.'

'Well is he? You met him. He only got to open his mouth . . .'

'No Jackie, no. You ain't seeing what I mean.'

'Dear oh Lord. Well you will tell me, won't you? Before one of us drops dead of old age. You got a fag Jonny going, have you?'

'Yeh – help yourself. What I mean is—'

'Got a light?'

'Bloody Jesus, Jackie. You do anything for yourself? Now bleeding *listen*, will you? What I mean is – less of the "us". Got it? We, my son, we ain't an "us". Now I may not be out the top drawer like this mate of yours – I ain't saying I am – but listen to this now Jackie: I ain't like you neither. You and me, we ain't the same. Not even close. Got me? No offence, but you ought to know. We two, we ain't an "us".'

'Right. I see. And by not the same – by us being so bleeding different, you wouldn't be sort of suggesting to me, would you Jonny, that you might in some way be *better* than what I am? That wouldn't, would it Jonny, be what you're meaning?'

'Bleeding exactly what I'm meaning, and you bloody well know it.'

74

'Well now listen to me now, Jonny. If a bloke weren't a mate, he could go taking offence, remark like that. I mean – you say to me "No offence", and then what? I'm supposed to shake you by the hand now, am I? And say to you "Oh no – none taken, son, none taken". When you just good as called me a bit of muck. Well you got to know, Jonny, I just can't accommodate you – you go round saying offensive things to a bloke, then offence, my son, it will be taken. This you got to know.'

'I'm just saying it as it is, that's all.'

'Yeh? Well let's know a little bit more then, shall we? Hang on – where's Len . . . ? Let's get another couple in before he goes ringing that bleeding bell of his. Christ knows where Dickie's got to, silly sod. Yeh now listen, Jonny. We're different, right? That's what you're saying to me. Not like each other. Different. Right?'

'Yeh. Right. Well done, Jackie.'

'Funny, Jonny: funny. Well what's so different, then? I mean yeh – you got better clothes than what I got. You always got a wad on you. Yeh – granted. You got a nice little motor . . .'

'Humber. Nothing little about it.'

'Yeh well never mind about that. What I'm saying is – all that, it's what you *got*, ain't it? That's all it is. It ain't who you are – it's what you got.'

'You know what, Jackie my son? I never had you down for stupid. Thought you was one of the bright ones. Oi! Some bugger's gone and spilled my bloody—! Oh. Oh it's you, is it?'

'Hallo, Dickie. Spilled Jonny's drink, you did. Find it all right, did you? Didn't get locked in your lavatory with all them other little old ladies then, did you? You're just in time, as it happens – Jonny here, he's explaining to me how I'm just some little bit of scum what you wouldn't look twice at, and *him* – he's, well – I don't quite know what he do reckon about hisself, be honest with you, on account he ain't yet got to telling me. But maybe now he will, ay? So where was we, Jonny?'

'Oh leave it, Jackie. I'm sick of it. Where's them drinks then, ay?'

'Yeh. Len – here Len! Good lad. Same again then, ay? Suit you does it, Dickie? Same again?'

'Golly . . .' said Dickie, closing his eyes.

'Reckon your mate's just about had it,' said Jonathan Leakey. 'Let's get out of here, ay? Car's outside – drop you back, you want.'

'Yeh well – I reckon we'll just get these down us, ay? And that'll give you time, Jonny, to tell me what's so bleeding great about yourself.'

'Leave it. I said to leave it.'

Jackie's face was suddenly empurpled as he rammed it up close to Jonathan Leakey's. He would have drawn back his fist much further if the jam of people had given him sway. Dickie had somehow put one of his arms like a barrier between the two of them, and was suddenly cold and sobered.

'Oh now here here, Jackie old chap. Come on now. Come on now.'

Jonathan Leakey's teeth were bared.

'You just got to say the word, Jackie boy. You want it – you can have it.'

And Jackie now was screaming into Jonathan Leakey's face.

'It's just what you *got*! You got nice stuff! It ain't who you is! It's just what you *got*!'

'Look, you miserable little bleeder—!'

'Oh now come on!' tried Dickie.

'Fuck off, you. Listen to me, Jackie, you stupid fuck. What you don't see, and I doubt you ever will – it ain't what I *got*, it's how I *got* it. That's why we're different, Jackie. That's why we always will be, unless you get smart. You're up a ladder with a bucket of whitewash – me, I got people to do what I want. Get it? I *am* what I got because it's how I *got* it.'

Jackie was staring at him, and breathing quite slowly. His muscles relaxed and he shrugged off Dickie, who he hadn't realised until this moment had been gripping his arms very tightly.

'See it now, do you Jackie?'

Jackie swallowed some Scotch and looked thoughtful.

'I do, Jonny. Yeh I do. Here, Dickie – here's your glass.'

'So . . . ?' said Jonathan Leakey. 'No offence then, ay?'

Jackie was nodding, his eyes quite narrow.

'No – yeh right. None taken, Jonny. None taken.'

'Good lad. That's more like the Jackie I know.'

The clanging of the time bell as Len with a joyous energy played merry hell with the dangling clapper had Dickie flinching away quite openly and Jonathan Leakey cursing darkly, his lips just forming the words. Then he looked up.

'Right, lads,' he said. 'That's it. So. Like I say – motor outside, you interested.'

'Gosh,' said Dickie. 'You all right to drive then, are you? I don't think I could get the keys into mine . . .'

'All right to drive? Joking. I drive better when I'm like this. Oils the wheels. So what's it to be? You're only round the corner anyway, ain't you? Coming, Jackie? Yes or no. I got to be off. See a bloke.'

'Yeh Jonny – ta. Come on Dickie, my son. You fit and able-bodied? Nick just one more of your fags, can I Jonny?'

'Dear me, Jackie. Dear oh me . . .'

'I know. Got a light . . . ?'

And Jonathan Leakey was throwing back his head and laughing out loud as if he'd been paid to. His pouchy eyes were moist and blurred as he struggled with a bout of coughing and he clapped his arm around Jackie's two shoulders and hugged him close.

'You're a one, you are. Do you know that Jackie, my son? You truly are a one, you are.'

'Yeh,' said Jackie quite meekly. 'I am, ain't I? I am, I am. I'm a one. That's what I am.'

'Tell you what,' said Jonathan Leakey, raising a finger as if in inspiration. 'This bloke I got to see, yeh? Come along. Might learn something.'

'Oh well now look,' Dickie was protesting quite mildly. 'You go, Jackie – you go by all means, but I really have to, um . . . I do hope you won't think I'm being rude, Mr Leakey, if in view of the, um – well, in view of . . . er. Oh God – I don't really know what I'm talking about, actually . . .'

'That's all right,' said Jonathan Leakey. 'You wasn't invited.'

'Ah!' said a pink-faced Dickie, all understanding – visibly wincing as the terrible bell was clanging again.

'Come on now gents!' Len was calling. 'Let's be having you! Let's all be good gentlemen now!'

'I mean,' conceded Jonathan Leakey, 'you wasn't *not* invited – welcome to come along, course you are. Just that it were Jackie here what I were talking to, see?'

'Yes yes,' said Dickie, rather flustered. 'No. Yes. Course. Course.'

'No no no no no!' yelled out Jackie. 'We're out, ain't we? The three of us making a night of it. We one of us goes, then we all do – ain't that right, Dickie? Ay? Who is this bloke then, Jonny? Anyone I know?'

Jonathan Leakey could barely hold back a smirk as they shuffled along behind the throng, and through the door.

'Not likely. That's my very point, Jackie. You don't mix in the proper circles – present company excepted, of course. No offence, ay Mr Weak?'

'Ah – that's Wheat, actually. No no – none at all, Mr Leakey.'

'Wheat, yeh – what I said. And it's Jonny. All right?'

Dickie, more confused than ever, screwed up his eyes and concentrated now upon nodding quite profoundly, suddenly disinclined to ever speak again. He had been unaware of clambering into the back of the Humber, though now he found himself sprawling all over the seat – and my bally coat, you know, it seems to be caught in the door – conscious now too of the rumble of the motor and of Jackie and Jonathan Leakey in the seats in front. Jackie's just asked Mr Leakey something – or Jonny or whatever it is he wants me to call him – and what I think he said was, because I do honestly, you know, feel just the tiniest bit, well – not quite tip-top, if you know what I mean. I mean to say I simply lost track of the number of Scotches I must have put down me in there. Don't touch it, you know, as a general rule, whisky. Christmas time, of course . . . which this is, naturally enough, and so there you are, really, I suppose. It's all a bit of a puzzle. And God alone knows what time it must be. Well – pub's just shut, hasn't it? Haven't we just left the pub . . . ? So – late, it's fair to say. And weren't we meant to be . . . ? I'm rather sure there's somewhere that Jackie said earlier that we were meant to be . . . I don't know. Doing. Or going to. Anyway. Well we're certainly going somewhere, that much is plain. Voices again. It's Jackie, and what I think he's said is so what are you thinking of doing then, Jonny, come the new year? Fairly sure that's more or less what he said – gist of it anyway, you know. And Jonny, he's just said Well Jackie, what I am thinking of doing then, come the new year, is I am thinking of growing a moustache. And this is obviously an extraordinarily funny thing to say then, is it? This that Mr Leakey has just come out with? Because the two of them are absolutely howling with laughter – I do awfully wish that they'd stop – and the car, it swerved quite badly just a moment ago, I thought – juddered around – or maybe it's me, just lolling about. My hat: don't seem to have it. I only thought of it because Jackie, he's wearing his hat, and Mr Leakey, I'm not sure even that he had one to start with, you know – rather odd in itself, I should have said, going about without a hat. But then he is rather, isn't he? I mean to say,

79

one doesn't want to go around saying things about a chap, but I have to admit to myself that all round he does seem fairly rum, you know. And Jackie – he seems actually to admire the man, in a rather strange sort of a way, unless I've misjudged the whole thing (always a strong possibility – and this evening, a virtual certainty); and as to all that nonsense about – what was it? He is what he's got because it's how he got it . . . ? Can that be right? Well for myself I shouldn't care to enquire at all deeply into how our Mr Leakey 'got it'. Whatever 'it' may be. As I say, quite a puzzle, on the whole. So anyway, no – I can't pretend that I thoroughly warm to the fellow – but then Sheila always says – oh my goodness, Sheila! . . . I'm pretty damn sure, you know, that it was something to do with Sheila that we were meant to be . . . I don't know. Doing. Or going to. Anyway. Well we're certainly not going there, that much is plain. Just glancing out of the window there – got a bit too close, as a matter of fact, and I've just gone and clonked my forehead up against the glass, which is just about all I needed at the moment, quite frankly . . . Anyway, point I'm making – had a, you know, sort of a look out of the window there, and I don't seem to recognise . . . I mean I get the strong feeling that we've travelled a fair way. I could have been in this car for just years, the way I'm feeling. As it is, you know – my coat, it *is* jammed into the door because I sort of rolled across and gave it a bit of a tug just then and I'm not quite sure what happened but there was some kind of noise which didn't seem to me to be altogether healthy, and it's still stuck tight, so I really couldn't tell you what on earth is going on. And no – my hat, it doesn't seem to be here. Don't appear to have it. Unless it's on the floor there – but I tell you, if I start horsing around down there I don't think I'm ever getting up again.

And now what's this? That was my name, wasn't it? Didn't I hear it, someone calling my name? Jackie, presumably. Probably one of his periodic check-ups on my immediate welfare. Always doing it: All right, are we Dickie? Bearing up are we, Dickie old lad? Fit and able-bodied, Dickie my son? Fond, I suppose – I suppose it's fond, his constant concern. The trouble is, I never know quite how to . . . I mean what are you supposed to say when you're constantly being badgered with this sort of thing? I just say tip-top, from morning till night: seems to keep him happy enough. I think I've just said it again, you know – pretty sure it was me who said that. But Sheila, of course – oh yes, oh yes: Sheila, I remember. While I was thinking a while back there about Jonathan, um . . . good God, do you know I can't remember his other, um . . . Lucky? Lackey, is it . . . ? Anyway. When I was saying there you know that I didn't quite respond to him, as it were – well that's just the sort of thing that Sheila is always trying to explain to me. Because she says I'm out of my class, and people can be wary of me and I haven't yet come to grips with the vernacular. So that when Jackie asks me if I'm 'doing good', or whatever sort of nonsense he can so easily come up with, I'm not actually supposed to be struggling to find an answer – tip-top, she says, that's all wrong. What I should be doing instead, if I've gathered all of this correctly – and in the state I'm in now I would severely doubt it – is either to repeat to him exactly whatever he has said to me, or else I should grin like a baboon and affect to hit him on the jaw – all of which just seems so absolutely preposterous to me that I can only assume that she's joking, or something. Anyway, she says – it was your choice to come and live here, so you've got to expect it. If you'd stayed in Mayfair where your family all live, then you'd be among your own and you'd know how to do it. And I didn't say to her well actually my family doesn't *live* in Mayfair, they live in Wiltshire. Because either she wouldn't have understood, or else I think she might have been upset. Leakey. That's the fellow's name. Odd name – but there, at least I remembered it, which is more than he seems able to ever do with mine. Nice to know, though, that there still appear to be one or two of my brain cells I have left unimpaired.

I rather wish I could get off to sleep, you know. But of course I should be aware of all this from my training – I'll never manage it, not now I won't: sleep is just out of the question. Because alcohol, of course, while initially it serves as a, um . . . No, wait a minute. God – if I were taking my finals in the morning, well – I *wouldn't* be taking my finals in the morning because I'd be bound to fail every paper quite spectacularly badly. Completely blanked out. Can't remember a single thing. You dangle a skeleton in front of me now and I'll happily point out to you the skull affair at the top, and from then on you're on your own, chum. But anyway, the general sort of idea with an excess of alcohol is that although one part of you is well nigh shattered, there's another part somewhere that's racing to compensate, it very well might be – needn't at all, though – and the thrust of the upshot is that if you're cannoning around in the rear of a Humber driven by a drunk in the middle of the night and headed towards God only could tell you what sort of a place and your temple is giving you absolute gyp and your blasted coat is jammed into the door and your hat's not stuck on your head where it jolly well ought to be, well then you're just not going to float away into a dreamless slumber, and that's the bally end of it. And particularly not now because these two in the front have started up their howling again and Jackie I'm fairly sure just needed to reassure himself that I was all nice and shipshape and Bristol fashion (Dickie old lad) and I just said to him mm oh yes – tip-top: rather.

I've never actually spoken to anyone, not in any sort of depth, about why I came down here to live and one day, I hope, actually have a practice on the go. I haven't spoken about it because frankly it's nobody's business but my own. That, and of course no one has really asked me. Not in so many words.

For which I am profoundly grateful, of course, because I've never really seen how I could have put it without somehow or other managing to give offence, or else confirming their suspicions that I'm a stuck-up halfwit refugee from the pages of P. G. Wodehouse. Should they ever have heard of good old P.G.W., which I severely doubt. People round here, they don't ever seem to read. Except for Mary, she does a bit – Mary, she's the nearest I know to a recognisable, straightforward and everyday member of society. Sheila, of course. I need her, Sheila – she keeps my feet on the ground. I think that's what she does. She stops me from flying away. God I do feel sick. Are we ever going to get there, wherever we're going? Jackie, now – he's rather different. I mean to say, the two of us – if ever there was really such a thing as chalk and cheese . . . but I did so take to him, you know, from the very first time I met him – in the Rose & Crown, not too surprisingly. When? Must be a year ago, now. I thought that if it was here that I intended to pursue my career, I ought to get to know it – more to the point though, I suppose, that the people, that they could begin to get used to me. Trust me, a bit – although I think that a good deal of them still think of me as some sort of a spy, more than anything. An outsider, certainly. And Jackie, he ribs me, of course – I can't pretend that it doesn't grow wearing, the way he's always ragging me about 'posh' and 'toffs' and all the rest of his perfectly ludicrous imaginings. But I'm sure that his affection is at base sincere, you know. But does he ever wonder how it would be if I were to take him to the Ritz or somewhere and my father was there and maybe one or two of the chaps I was at school with, say, and I kept on joshingly referring to him as an oik, this working-class cockney lout, you've only got to listen to him – but it's not his fault, is it? That he speaks and dresses so perfectly appallingly: that he's just such an *oik*. Well. I don't know which of us he'd slaughter first, quite frankly, and he'd be well within his rights. But what we used to refer to as the lower orders, the lower classes, they seem to think they can say what they like to you these days, and it appears as if they're probably right. I mean to say – I never effectively stand up for myself, well do I? Manners, really. Though it translates as maybe a weakness that they smell off you, and then they make play of it. I really couldn't say.

My father, yes. Well obviously he's got a great deal to do with it, my being here, and so forth. I mean to say I have nothing but the very highest respect for the man, harbour no doubts on that score – but because he is the most eminent physician in his field (as all my fellow students are most horribly aware) I have always known that he could acquire for me a perfect and fashionable practice somewhere quite glorious, but you see I've never wanted it, not that. Nor, of course – and one has to be honest – do I wish to be compared with him, and be found most glaringly wanting. The other factor is the calibre of the patient. Half of the people my father and his colleagues attend to, well – there's absolutely nothing in the world that's wrong with them. Dear boy, he used to say to me – it is the wealthy hypochondriac who enables us to carry on living in the manner to which he has made us accustomed. A quip, of course, but rather too true for my liking. Gosh – around here, it just couldn't be more different. People deny to themselves and everyone around them that they are ever ill at all – even when it is perfectly plain that they are wasting away before your very eyes. A doctor, for most of them, is an unthinkable luxury. People die – it is the way of things – so better to do it quickly, and avoid incurring a doctor's bill. And so many of the women continue to give birth without fail each and every year – I think they see it as stocking up the cupboard, in some rather awful way, with plenty of reserves, so that if one should die, there is always another to take its place. Contraception is seen by the men, I think, as a sort of a slur, even a form of weakness. It is left to the women to wangle a way of clawing back the meagrest portion of their remaining lives, or else quite literally to be worn to death: to die in the process. When Jackie made that wholly ill-timed and very vulgar outburst about the subject – I remember this, yes, because it was bonfire night, I remember that – I was highly surprised because it's never ever something that is discussed around here, along with so very much else. Also, just in passing, it's really quite shocking, you know, if what he said is true – about Mary having been fitted with a device. Most uncommon, and utterly unheard of in my admittedly severely limited experience if you are an unmarried woman, as happens to be Mary's state. Well I don't know – maybe she disguises the fact: their affair, of course. But anyway, what I'm saying in a nutshell, I suppose – and one more reason why I should not come to voice it is that I know how very evangelical it must surely sound – is that if I am to be a doctor (and I have never wished to be anything but) then I should really be practising where it does the most good, even though I shall always be poor from it, I imagine. So if someone were to deign to ask *me* what I was thinking of doing then, Dickie, come the new year, I should say to them that what I am actually thinking of doing then, come the new year, is becoming a doctor. It may not, I daresay, be so conversationally *amusing* as growing a moustache, I have no doubts about that, but it is nonetheless a rather more worthwhile ambition, wouldn't you say? Oh dear. I rather think that was slightly pompous. It's another of the things I must guard against, I suppose, if ever I'm to stay around here and make a good fist of it.

Oh. The car has stopped. And so we're somewhere else, then. I almost feel like I have been asleep, but my mind, I know, it's been racing; the pain in my head is near splitting me in two. Jackie's on the pavement, and pulling at my sleeve. Where on earth in God's name are we? I do so wish I was back in my little room, warm and safe and tucked up in bed.

85

⊙

24th December 1938
I'm writing this terribly late at night – Jackie's asleep, and so
is Jeremy. He doesn't know yet what Christmas is all about,
but I can tell that he senses something. He'll love the little
push-along train that Jackie has got for him – it's beautifully
made in solid wood, and all the different parts are painted
in really bright colours. I got him a teddy bear in the market
and I've put a bit of velvet ribbon around his neck: very
smart. I do so hope that Jackie likes what I've got for
him – we'll find out soon.

Goodness! I've just seen *how* late it is – if I don't get to bed
soon, Santa won't be coming! It excited me, writing that
down. Silly. But I'm going to make sure that Jeremy believes
in Santa for as long as possible, like I did. Jackie and me have
patched things up, but I've told him that if he ever stays out
that late again without even telling me, then there'll be wigs
on the green – I think he knew I meant business. He smelled
terribly of drink and he started touching me you-know-
where. I said I wasn't having any of it – that I'd been worried
sick and had hardly slept a wink. I'm not sure that I believe
that Mr Leakey's car ran out of petrol, but I honestly can't
imagine what else might have happened.

Today we spent doing the tree! Jackie worked only the half
day for Mr Plough (£5 Christmas bonus!) and came home with
this most beautiful Christmas tree, smelling so wonderfully of
the forest. He put it in a barrel we found in the cellar and
filled it up with sawdust. It nearly touches the ceiling – I've
never seen such a big one! (I've got to continue this on the
notes pages of the diary now, because I've run out of space.)

(This is continued from the Christmas Eve page.) We don't have nearly enough ornaments for the tree, but Jackie says he can borrow some from someone. I asked him who would be lending Christmas ornaments on Christmas Day, and he said wait and see. Also tomorrow I've got to collect the goose – and I'm getting some chickens as well so there's enough to go round. There will be sausages too, and a selection of dainties. Sheila's done the pudding (I hope!). Molly downstairs is cooking the chickens because my little oven couldn't cope. And I must remember to iron my dress. It's the green one again, but I bought some bright red Chantilly trimmings at the market that I've put at the throat and cuffs and Jackie says we'll have *two* Christmas trees then! Jackie's doing the drinks – and I told him not just to get beer and whisky but to make sure there are some cordials and sherry and port and lemonade for those as wants it.

Final guest list: the landlord and his wife, Mr and Mrs Stone (worse luck), Molly downstairs (who is hoping her beau can get down from Manchester), Jackie's brother Alfie and maybe his girlfriend – Dickie and Sheila, of course – poor little Lorna from the laundry, if she'll only bring *some* of her brothers and sisters (she practically cried when I invited her). My mother wouldn't come, and Dad – I suppose he wasn't allowed to. It's very sad. And Jackie's asked various people that I don't even know – including Mr Leakey – but he says not to worry because they're all very nice. And Sally in the greengrocers has more or less invited herself, which is Sally all over.

Jolly tired now – and I've run out of space again. Off to bed. It's now gone midnight. Merry Christmas!

'Did you enjoy that, Jackie? I'm not sure that Jeremy did – just look at the funny little face he's putting on! Did you not like that,

Jeremy? Was it horrid? No? You *did* like it . . . ? I think he did like it, Jackie – he's not *un*happy, anyway . . .'

'It's always that way,' said Jackie, pushing back his chair from the flap of a table in the kitchenette. 'Marmite – it takes people different. First time you have it on your bit of toast, you don't know what to make of it, do you? Like me – I never reckoned it, first off. But now – the way I were dipping them soldiers into the egg there? Wouldn't have been nothing without a lick of Marmite. Here Mary – what you grinning about?'

'Oh gosh I'm just so *excited*, Jackie – I know it's silly. Can we do it now? You said we could open them when we'd all had our breakfasts, didn't you Jackie? So let's go in and do it now. Happy Christmas!'

'You said that to me twenty times. *And*,' he smiled, 'I *haven't* yet finished my breakfast.'

'Jackie! Don't do this to me – it's too cruel!'

'Maybe it could be I want another cup of tea . . .'

'I'll *get* you a cup of tea, Jackie. You go and sit by the fire, and I'll bring a nice cup of tea for you, all right?'

'By the fire?' checked Jackie, raising his eyebrows and teasing out the monent. 'That wouldn't be the fire what's next to the biggest Christmas tree in all of London now, would it?'

Mary was laughing delightedly.

'Oh Jackie – you can't be so *beastly* . . .'

'The Christmas tree with all them presents underneath it? That the fire you mean? The one what's next to all of that?'

'Yes, Jackie – yes! Come on – let's do it now.'

Jackie smiled and stood up and kissed her on the cheek.

'Well why didn't you bleeding say so then?'

Mary hugged him and she picked up Jeremy from his high chair and he tottered through the doorway. Jackie was kneeling down on the hearthrug, and he began to finger his way through the small pile of presents that Mary had clustered at the base of the tree. She had covered the barrel the day before in red crepe paper and was annoyed to see that it was already beginning to come away at the corner and all down the edge, look, because of this blessed ugly manila tape that you're supposed to lick and it never ever *sticks*. She took out a hankie and tried licking that and then she started to rub at each gummy corner of Jeremy's mouth.

'He's got more Marmite on his face than in his tummy, I think . . . Oh give me something to open, Jackie. I can't wait any longer. But just put the guard in front of the fire though, will you? I don't want any accidents. And remind me at ten, Jackie – ten sharp. Got to put the goose on.'

'Won't suit you, love – you stay with that little green dress of yours.'

'Oh Jackie! You're impossible! Now enough. Present. Now!'

'Right, then. Here you are. I hope you, you know – like it.'

'Oh no Jackie – not the one from you. I want to save that for last. Give me that one, the one in that funny paper. Over there. It's from Dad.'

Jackie picked up the package, very loosely wrapped in what looked to be shelf liner.

'When did this arrive, then?' he wanted to know.

'Oh it's so *awful* . . .' Mary deplored. 'Mrs Stone, she handed it to me yesterday. Said it had been left on the step. He didn't even ring the bell. I would so love to have seen him . . .'

'Yeh well. It's that mother of yours, ain't it? She's the trouble. Mind you – your fault too, Mary love. You lived with someone like Dickie Wheat, she'd be round here all the time.' And then he laughed. 'Maybe just as well, ay?'

'Don't be mean. It's not her fault. Here – let me open it.'

The stiffish grey paper fell away easily enough, and there was a half-pound box of Cadbury's Milk Tray and a small cream envelope. Mary opened the envelope and unfolded a little slip of paper; a ten-shilling note fluttered away from it. She read the few words, and her eyes glazed over. Mary looked at Jackie in utter wonder and helplessness.

'He says I should look after myself . . . and then he puts, Love You – Dad. And there's a cross . . . !'

'Here here here, Mary love – come over here. Don't you cry, now. Christmas, ain't it? Can't have you crying, Christmas Day.'

Jackie held her as she sobbed just briefly into his shoulder.

'I miss him, you know Jackie. He is my *Dad* . . .'

'Yeh yeh. I know. Never mind, ay? Come on – cheer up.'

Mary pulled back and smiled a crumpled smile, taking Jackie's proffered hankie – dabbing at her eyes now while blinking an apology.

'Look on the bright side,' grinned Jackie. 'I like Milk Tray.'

Mary gasped at his cheek and swiped him with a cushion.

'It's *my* Milk Tray – how dare you!'

'Pack it up – we can't have scenes of violence. Come on – open something else. And let's give something to little Jeremy now, ay?'

Mary nodded joyfully, and the two of them tried to make Jeremy's fingers tug open the wrapping of his teddy bear, and after a bit of that Jackie ripped the paper asunder for him.

'Isn't he *lovely*?' cooed Mary. 'Do you love him, Jeremy? He's your new friend. Isn't he? What shall we call him?'

To Mary's extreme delight, Jeremy squealed and reached out for the little orange bear and held it to his face, still squeaking with surprise and pleasure.

'Oh!' gasped Mary, her happiness complete. 'Oh just look, Jackie, will you? He loves it. He really does love it.'

'Adolf.'

'*What* did you say, Jackie?'

'Adolf. We can call him Adolf. Coming man, he is, what I hear.'

'We will most certainly not. He's completely awful, everything he's doing.'

'Well I don't know . . . Reckon we could maybe do with one or two of him over here. My way of thinking.'

'I don't want to talk about any of that on Christmas Day, thank you very much. We'll call him . . . Fluffy.'

'Fluffy! What sort of a stupid name is that then, for a bear?'

'Well it's a jolly sight better than Adolf!'

Jackie smiled in a sideways manner. 'Not too bad a name. Better than Neville . . .'

'We're not calling him after the Prime Minister either. He's going to be called Fluffy, and that's the end of it. Oh *look*, Jackie . . . he really loves him, he really does. *You* open something now, Jackie – it's your turn. Go on.'

'All right, then. Now let's have a look . . .'

'Not the one in the shiny paper though, Jackie. Not the red and gold one. That's from me. Do you like it, Jackie, the paper? It's proper – I got it in the stationer's. It's not from the market, or anything.'

'It's lovely, love. What Dickie would say's tip-top, that is. Very nice. So, um – I don't open it, then?'

'Not yet. In a bit. When I open yours.'

'Fair enough, I suppose. Well – I've only got one other one here, by the looks of it, so I'll open that, will I? Yeh – right then. Feels all right, this – I reckon I've an idea what this could be. What's it say here? "Cheers old man – joyous Yule, Dickie". Well that's nice of him, ain't it? Now let's see what we got . . . oh yes, very nice. Ay Mary? See? Nice little half bottle of Haig. Keep out the chill, won't it?'

'That's kind of him. Isn't that kind of him, Jackie? And you did – you did get something for him, didn't you? You didn't forget?'

'I did, my love. Got him a hundred Player's.'

Mary looked alarmed. 'But – Dickie, he doesn't smoke. I'm *sure* he doesn't smoke . . .'

Jackie was rueful, and stroking his chin.

'Yeh. I only realised after I got them. Still – he's getting the party off of us, ain't he? Maybe he'll bring them along – find them a good home. No no no – I'm only kidding you, love! I'm only joking. I got him a nice big bottle of Taylor's port. He likes a drop of port, Dickie do. And here – just look at what he wrote. Ay? I mean – who else but Dickie? "Joyous Yule"? Ay? Priceless, he is. My one and only toff. And look, Mary – he got you something and all.'

'Really? Oh how terribly sweet of him. Give it to me, Jackie – I'll open it now. No – you come back over here now Jeremy – don't go crawling away. You come over here with your Mummy and Daddy. It's Christmas Day, isn't it Jeremy? And we're all warm and cosy by the fire. You've got your lovely new friend to play with, haven't you? Jeremy? Haven't you? Here he is. Say hello.'

'Say hello to Adolf.'

'Jackie! It's *Fluffy*, isn't it Jeremy? Yes it is. Yes it is. Don't you take any notice of your silly old Daddy. Here – you hold Fluffy now, Jeremy. Mummy's going to open Uncle Dickie's present, all right? Oh gosh, Jackie – the time! It's not ten yet, is it?'

'You got ages. Here you are, Mary – here's your present from "Uncle Dickie", Gawd help us. I tell you one thing from the feel of it – whatever it is, it ain't a nice little half bottle of Haig, that's for certain.'

'I wonder . . .' wondered Mary, tearing the paper. 'Oh – it's books. Two books. That's nice. Because I do actually quite like to, you know Jackie. Read. It's just that when I was at the laundry – well, you know . . . Jeremy and everything, I just got so tired.'

'I read a book at school,' said Jackie. 'They made me. Don't remember nothing about it. Can't even remember the name of it. And they called themselves teachers . . . !'

'*Great Expectations*. I've heard of that – I've not read it, though. It's Dickens, Jackie – you know: Oliver Twist.'

'Who's he? He an author and all, is he?'

'No! You know – Oliver *Twist*. Please sir, may I have some more . . . ?'

Jackie looked amazed.

'What in Gawd's name you *talking* about, Mary? Have some more *what* . . . ?'

'No no – it's . . . Never mind. Let me see now – what's the other one? Oh. It's modern. *The Code of the Woosters*. What a funny title. By . . . P. G. Wodehouse. Never heard of that one. I wonder what it's like . . . it looks quite childish, going by the cover. Look, Jackie – sort of a cartoon, or something.'

Jackie now was profoundly bored.

'Yeh well – enough about that, ay? These authors – they got it made really, ain't they. When you think about it. Sitting at home all day drumming up a pack of lies, and mugs like Dickie go and pay over good money for it. Ah well – lucky for some. Here – watch it, Mary . . . Jeremy, he's off again. Here – you want a drink or something, do you?'

'Oh God not *this* early – we've only just had breakfast. It's not ten yet is it, Jackie? I mustn't forget.'

'No it's not ten yet – and there's a clock up there, Mary, staring you in the bleeding face. There's something here for you from Sheila, look.'

'Oh how lovely. Oh look, Jackie – Jeremy's getting sleepy, he's closing his eyes. But I can't let him sleep yet because I've got to get him down later for the party, or else it'll be just impossible. Shall we give him his Tee Arr Ay Eye Enn . . . ? Shall we?'

Jackie blinked.

'His what? His tea in a what?'

Mary hissed her impatience.

'No no, his – you *know*. His Tee Arr Ay – *oh*! His *train*. His *train*. What's the matter with you, Jackie? I was spelling it *out*.'

Jackie blinked.

'Why? He can't spell. *I* can't spell . . . !'

And Mary was wagging her head and laughing again.

'Oh *God*, Jackie! Just give me Sheila's present, will you? I just hope it's not more greengage jam, that's all. She makes all this greengage jam and she never knows what to do with it. She gave me just a ton for my birthday and it's nearly all of it still stuck in the cupboard. Look – I'll open this, and you play with Jeremy, Jackie. Open up his train.'

'Um – how are you spelling that, Mary love?'

'Jackie! Oh – I think it's two things in here, you know. No – it's three! What's this . . . ? Oh – she says this one's for Jeremy. That's kind. Don't know why she didn't wrap it up separately, but still . . . oh yes, I've seen these. Look, Jackie – it's bricks. Wooden bricks with the alphabet on.'

'Oh good. You can teach me how to spell.'

'Oh *stop* it, Jackie! Mm – but the trouble with these is that long before they're learning their letters, they're throwing the things all over the place, aren't they? And they're really very solid – feel them. Could kill you, one of these. Mm – I think we'll put them away for when he's older. Now what else is there . . . ? Oh – he *does* like it, doesn't he Jackie? Isn't that a lovely choo-choo, Jeremy?'

'Yeh,' agreed Jackie. 'That's *See Aitch Owe Owe* . . . Anyway, who says he's going to get to play with it? This is my present, this is.'

'The only reason you bought it, I suppose . . .'

'Dead right. So what else has Sheila coughed up for you, then?'

Mary was staring down at the present she had just unwrapped. Her hand flew up to her mouth and her eyes were gleaming with a startled amusement.

'Oh my *goodness*, Jackie – you won't ever believe it!'

'What? Why? What you got?'

'Just look! I can't *believe* it . . . !'

Jackie peered into the tissue, and then he let out a great guffaw that split up into a cackle.

'Well I can tell you one thing for sure, Mary my love – you ain't never going to go short on rose-pink tippets are you, ay? Dear oh me!'

Mary was laughing so much, her eyes still wide in disbelief.

'I suppose she'll say "Oh Mary – I just thought it would go so very well with that coat of yours – you know, the one with the half-belt"—'

'—"and the epaulettes"!' chimed in Jackie. 'Still – least it shows we all got your best interests at heart, I suppose.'

'Mm . . .' said a suddenly sobered Mary. 'What it shows is that everybody knows that old coat of mine *by* heart – that's what it shows.'

'Yeh well – never mind. Next year – next spring, when I'm a partner with Mr Plough, I'll get you a mink. How's that?'

'Oh don't be so *daft*, Jackie. A mink!'

'All right then – *two* minks. Don't want much, do you?'

'Oh do stop *teasing* me all the time, Jackie. Oh – wait a minute. There's this other thing here. Heavy. Oh yes. Of course – had to be. Greengage jam. Another hundredweight, I'm afraid.'

'Maybe stuff the goose with it, ay?'

'Oh my goodness Jackie – the goose! Is it ten yet?'

'You ask me that just one more time and I'll clock you, and no mistake. Here – open what *I* got for you now, Mary. Sorry the paper ain't all fancy like yours. Least it's wrapped though, ay?'

Mary accepted the package with grace and pleasure.

'It's beautiful. It's even got a ribbon on it!'

'Yeh well . . .' muttered Jackie, looking away. 'Found a bit handy . . .'

Her fingers hovered above the bow. She wanted to tear into the package so terribly much, and she wanted to keep it just as it was, and for ever.

'I honestly can't imagine what it could be ... I'm just so excited ... !'

'Yeh well – best news is, it ain't a rose-pink tippet. Go on then, Mary love – let's be having you, there's a good girl.'

Mary threw over to him a quick and conspiratorial little glance, and then she pulled away at the end of the ribbon. A brown corrugated cardboard box was what she discovered, and inside that was a screwed-up bung of yellowing tissue. And it was when she tugged that out and peered inside that she gasped out Oh my—! Oh goodness, Jackie, how very ... ! Is it a ... ?

'Well if you get it out the box you can see what it is, can't you? There – that's it. Like it?'

Mary held up to the firelight a small and heavy bottle, three-quarters filled with something amber. Trailing away from the neck was a powder blue, silken and flexible tube and then a sort of a bulbous egg-shaped thing – a bit like the tiniest rugby ball, is what Mary thought it looked like – and covered in the daintiest crochet; a thick and floppy tassel in the same powder blue was dangling quite gorgeously at its end.

'You ain't saying nothing, Mary. You like it? Something wrong, is there ... ?'

And Mary's eyes were blurred and sparkling again – she flattened her lips, and as her eyelids descended, a single tear was fatly expressed and quickly continued its easy and languorous rolling across her cheek, and down.

'Oh – you *do* like it. Pleased. You see what you do – it were explained to me, this – what you do is, you hold the business end up to your neck, all right? And then you squeeze on the hooter here and the spray, it come out this little hole there, see? Don't have to be your neck – that's the beauty. And it's the proper

96

article. Eau de Parry, is how you say it. That means it's water of Paris, but it ain't like our water, nor nothing. This one pongs. But *good* pong, you know? Try it, Mary. Have a squirt.'

Mary, finally, found some words.

'I've – seen these in the films. Jean Harlow and . . . oh Jackie, this – it's far too good for me. It's just so *beautiful*. It must have cost you an absolute—'

'Never mind about none of that. *Nothing*'s too good for you – and nor for me neither. That's what we got to bear in mind: I'm learning that. Now go on – try it. Go on.'

Mary gingerly held it a little away from her and pressed so lightly on the bulb; a puff of fragrance – it tingled on her throat.

'Oh it's *wonderful*, Jackie. Smell. Smell it. Isn't it wonderful?'

Jackie now nuzzled his nose and lips deep into her neck and inhaled quite deeply.

'I wouldn't change you for a hundred Jean Harlows . . .'

He kissed her, and his hand slid downwards and then it covered her breast. He wasn't that surprised when she quickly pulled away.

'Goodness, Jackie – not now. Jeremy's looking. Don't be silly. I've so much to do – it *must* be nearly ten by now. Oh thank you *so* much for this, Jackie. It's just the most beautiful thing that I've ever owned in the whole of my life. And now open *your* present, Jackie. Oh gosh I hope you like it! Are you all right now, Jeremy? Are you all right, little man . . . ?'

Jackie looked down at the small parcel that Mary had dropped into his lap and he thought, you know – she might've saved all the money and the trouble, going to the stationer's for the classy paper: there ain't hardly none of it here. And then he quite willingly ripped into what there was.

It's funny – I ain't never been bothered one way nor the other, you know, with presents and that. Women, they're different – they go all like kiddies, don't they? You give them something. But me, well – like I say, not too bothered. Not a lot of practice, of course. Never got nothing when I were a kiddy, did I? That's when I should of been give it. I had this mate, Jimmy his name were – had a wooden castle what his dad knocked up for him, and then painted it and all, so's it all looked like it were stone, and that. Little – what are them things? On chains – comes down. Bridge – drawbridge. Yeh. I really fancied that. But my dad, well – shoved off, hadn't he? And my poor old mum – we had enough to eat it were a bleeding miracle. Christmas Day, she never took in no washing; nearest she ever got to a holiday, poor old mare. We had a rabbit most years, Christmas time. Could've been a cat. Anyway – none got left out of the eight of us. Sucking the bones, we was. She been gone a long while, my old mum. She just give up, I reckon. When I seed her all laid out – first time she had a smile on her. Dear oh dear.

Oh my Gawd – what have I been thinking about! Don't know why I went off like that, all of a sudden. Mary, look – she's all nervy. I ain't gone and thanked her for her present on account of I ain't even seed what I got here yet. So I chucks her a smile – that'll tell her I'm dandy – and I look down now and – oh blimey. Oh dear Lord. That is handsome – that I do like. I am fair taken with that. That is a cracker, that is.

'Mary Mary Mary – that is a cracker, that is. I always wanted one of them – and them, you see them in the films and all, don't you? That frog – Charles Boyer, is it? And Bogart. All of them got one of these. Never thought I would – my own cigarette case. Blimey – most the time, I ain't even got me own fags!'

Mary was beaming and pointing at it eagerly.

'Do you see, Jackie? In the corner? Had it done specially.'

Jackie looked down, and there in the corner of the sleek and rhodium-plated cigarette case were the initials, J.R.

'Blimey,' he said. 'Blimey, Mary.'

Mary clapped her hands once and kept them joined in front of her face, as if she were praying. Her eyes above them glowed like embers.

'Open it, Jackie. Open it up.'

Jackie did as he was told – freed the little catch, very nice action – and there inside were not the ten Senior Service or Player's that he had fully expected (not Woodbines, though, not from Mary – she'd never do Woodbines) but instead a chunky cigarette lighter in the same material; and just above the base of it – oh look: J.R.

'I've got the petrol, Jackie, but I didn't know how to put it in. The man in the shop, he wasn't very helpful. But you can do it Jackie, can't you? Is it all right, Jackie . . . ?'

Jackie glanced away and up towards the ceiling. He tried to laugh away this choked-up sensation that was rising in his throat.

'You got me going, you have . . . I gone all funny . . .'

'But you do *like* them, don't you Jackie? They are the proper thing though, aren't they . . . ?'

Jackie laid them down and held her wrists and kissed her mouth.

'I love them, Mary. And I love you. You know that?'

Mary looked down at her hands locked into his and all that she was thinking was that I mustn't start crying again, because it's just too silly.

'I *do* know it, Jackie,' she sniffed. 'It's just that you haven't said it to me. Not for ages.'

'Yeh? Well I'm saying it now. Here – I can't wait to get these into action. I'll be quite the toff. People'll be thinking I'm like Dickie Wheat, I get these out. I tell you what – I wouldn't mind a fag right now. Put it into my head.'

And Mary placed before him – and where did this just come from all of a sudden? – a slim flat box of fifty Senior Service in a blue and silver seasonal sleeve bearing a cameo of a robin on top of a snow-domed pillar box.

Jackie – his eyes filled with wonder – just wagged his head so slowly and leaned across and kissed her again. And then he whispered into her ear:

'And me. I got one more thing for you and all. One more present. You just look over at the tree there.'

'Oh Jackie – nothing more! You've already given me so—!'

And she shuffled over this soft and loose-wrapped parcel, laughing so gaily as she opened it immediately. Her eyes became narrow and her lips were pursed as the flat of her hand was tentatively roaming over a glossy plane of cool and creamy, pale grey silk. She picked up the camisole by its two slender straps, the soft folds falling away as she held it before her.

Jackie's eyes were hard and gleaming as he searched her own for something.

'Try it on,' he said. 'Why don't you? See if it fits.'

Mary's eyes were still so wide as she went on beholding the thing.

'It's . . . it's truly *amazing*, Jackie. I'm just . . . But how did you ever—?'

'Why don't you, Mary? Ay? Try it on . . .'

'Oh not *now* I can't, can I? I can't *now* . . .'

Jackie jerked his head over in Jeremy's direction.

'Look at him. Asleep. Dead to the world, he is.'

Mary glanced across. Her little man was sprawled over the hearthrug and hugging the teddy, his soft upper lip just twitching so slightly. She looked then very briefly to the left and right, as if to make sure that not a single witness was skulking to either side of her – and then with an intake of breath she compressed her lips and the decision was made.

'Well . . .' she said slowly – and her eyes were dancing – 'just very quickly then. It'll have to be quick. You wait here, Jackie – and I'll just slip next door. But just quickly it'll have to be. All right?'

Jackie closed his eyes and nodded to that. When she was gone, he carefully slid a cushion under Jeremy's head – gently ruffled his tousled hair. He thought now of having that first festive cigarette, and then he remembered that his new and very pukka lighter was still uncharged. There were some matches in the kitchenette . . . but no: he'd wait until later. Instead, he slipped out the box of Senior Service from its sleeve and carefully slit with a thumbnail the seal at the front of the box. He flipped up the lid, peeling back and away the silver foil. That waft of sweet aroma made him want one even more, but still he found it easy to resist. His mind, as he slid just ten of these tightly packed and fragrant cylinders beneath the elastic stay inside the cigarette case, was reaching now for other things. And then he was aware of Mary's head, just, craning out at him from behind the bedroom door. A slender and naked arm was signalling to him some sort of a message or other, but all he could do was shrug and raise his eyebrows, smiling at her his utter incomprehension.

'The light, Jackie,' she clarified. 'Switch off the light, and then I'll come in. And do it, you know – carefully.'

'Well well,' he said – making quite a big show of getting up from the floor to do as she had told him. 'You shy?'

Mary looked down, and her loosened hair fell forward and across her eyes.

'It's just otherwise my legs will look ever so podgy in this. And anyway, it's nicer isn't it? With just the fire.'

Jackie ambled over to the corner and slowly eased upwards the dark metal light switch – if you snapped it up too quickly it fizzled and crackled, and according to Mary it once even gave off a sudden and sharp blue spark, and she'd been nervous about the electric ever since. Jackie turned then and held out his arms towards her, but still she stood back – so he walked across to the bedroom door, took her by the hand and gently led her out. Mary looked down, willing her hair to cover more of her face.

'I'm not very good at this . . .' she whispered. 'Sorry, Jackie.'

He took her across to just by the side of the fireplace and one of his palms smoothed away her hair and back from her face, and then it came down to first softly cradle and then lift up her chin, so that he could look into her eyes. She simpered a sweet but still hesitant gratitude. Then Jackie dropped his gaze to the length and flanks of her – the firelight licking pink spatters on to the sheen of the silk and casting her body into soft and rounded mounds, and deep dark beckoning shadows. And his groan which they both heard said that that was enough for him. She whimpered lightly as he hauled her to the floor, and even before her back had hit the mat there his hands were slithering all over the whole of her in a gluttonous compulsion all of their own. He gasped out her name as she whispered for him to be careful – be careful with the camisole, Jackie, and be careful with me when you're doing it. She felt shocked, as ever, when she soon felt the whole of him inside her – always so strange an intrusion, but also a sometimes quite jarring collision with this alien thing high up and inside of her. As usual, she simply bore it, waiting patiently for it to become just numb and then quite nice, when she knew that warmth could begin to flood her. It was then that Jackie would grunt and hiss and slump across her, and once again she was all out of kilter. He had been careful with the light switch, careful with her camisole, but not, she reflected, too careful with her. And after he rolled away and on to his back she would deal with her confusion, and then hold him closely, so much loving it as her blazing cheek would rise and fall with each great heave from within his heart. It was this huge peace that she needed the most, and always she clung to him, to make it all last just a little bit longer. But he had roused himself already from the drowsy place he used to be, and Mary could feel him just stirring – his leg, it seemed to be taut and reaching away from him, and then once more he appeared to relax.

'Think I heard Jeremy . . .' is what he now mumbled.

Mary threw her arm across his chest and held him more tightly, as she snuggled in closer.

'He's fine,' she assured him. 'Just stay with me here. He's perfectly fine. He's asleep.'

I know, thought Jackie – I know he's asleep. I know that, don't I? I just been prodding him with the tip of my toe, and he never so much as budged. Normally all bawling and crotchety, you go and disturb his kip. I really could go with that fag now, I tell you that for nothing. So what else can I do? Because I hate it, this bit, if I'm honest with you. I mean, Mary – she's a lovely girl and I'm bleeding lucky to have her, I know that, I know that – I do know that, yeh. No fool, am I? And just the sight of her there, while back – well I'm telling you, I were that fired up . . . And the feel of her, yeh, all that silk, the heat off of the fire – and the old Eau de Paris, that weren't no waste of money. But we done it now, ain't we? Ay? I mean, yeh – we done it. So that's it, right? So let's all get on to the next thing, why can't we? Well Mary, she don't ever seem to see it like that. She's a bit funny like that, Mary, because it's ever such a palaver just to get her to *start* with it, you know? Always some bleeding reason or other why we shouldn't – wrong time, wrong place, someone's coming round, you name it – but then when I finally gets her on to her back and we *done* it, then she don't ever want to let it go. All bleeding vicey versy, my way of thinking. Like now, see? I want a fag. Do with a drink and all – got a ton of it in the cupboard. Also my arm, it gone all dead. And my back's bleeding killing me and all. But Mary, she'd be happy lying here till the wossname come home. Oh dear. So what can I do now? Oh I know – I can do this:

'Here Mary, love – them tree ornaments you said about, yeh? I better be on to it, you still wanting them . . .'

'Mmmm . . .' went Mary. 'You can get them later.'

Bleeding hell. And I just been shoving at Jeremy again, but he's right out for the count, he is. No help at all. Bleeding hell. Oh yeh! Course! I got it.

'Here, Mary love?'

'Mmmm . . . ?'

'Way gone ten, you know. That goose . . .'

Mary sat up as if electrified, and was gathering her camisole around her.

'What! Oh my *God* Jackie – why didn't you *tell* me? What time is it then? Oh I've got to – oh God – I've got to—!'

And she skittered away in order to do it. Jackie was stretching himself and scratching at his head – careful now to be nowhere close to Jeremy, or else he'd be the one who'd have to take care of the screaming tantrum that would surely be coming. Really should get a bit of a move on, though – fair old load to deal with. But the fire – it's a very nice little blaze we got going there (Mary, she were up at Gawd alone knows what hour, seeing to it – heard her clattering about) and everywhere else in this bleeding little flat, I'm telling you – like the bleeding North Pole. And now I'm on my own, like, it's comfy, just lying in front of it. And also, I'm getting a fair view of all them decorations what Mary and Sheila been killing theirselves over – all I been hearing about. And lying flat on your back, you get to look at it different. There's these strips of coloured paper – you know, that crinkly paper, used to remember the name of it, and there's four of them coming off of the light there in the centre of the ceiling, look, and they sort of twist around like a corkscrew, sort of style, and each of them leads off into a corner. Reckon they must of tacked them into the picture rail. And hanging from the lampshade in the middle we got a paper bell – were last year, I think she got that. It's flat when you start out, and then it opens up like a wossname – sort of expands like a . . . and then you clips the ends in and you got yourself a merry little jingle bell. Concertina – opens out like a concertina:

clever little thing. The tree over there – well, that were down to me (and yeh – them ornaments. Got to sort them out, shortly). Feller in the market – not a regular, only ever catch a sight of him this time of the year. I heard he's a country bloke, and what he does is he grows all these Christmas trees and holly and ivy and that other thing what you kiss under (and I got me some of that as well – stick it up in a minute) and him and his brothers, they get theirselves down to London come December time and cover all the markets. What they make in a couple weeks, it sets them up for the rest of the year, that's what I heard, if you can believe it. Funny, ain't it? All the different sort of graft what people get up to, earn a crust. Because that's what it's about – we're all of us just earning a crust, ain't we? Best way we know. Do brighten up the room, though, all of this. And Gawd knows it could do with it. Jew landlords we got, they done nothing to the property in all the time we been here. This room, it's got a sort of a lumpy wallpaper the colour of tea, and all the woodwork's this real dark brown, bit like gravy of a Sunday. Settee – that's brown and all. I reckon it had a bit of velveteen pile to it, once upon a time: it's all shiny now, where your elbows go. I put a bit of hardboard under the cushions, else your bum'd hit the bleeding floor. Mary knocked out a set of them . . . what are they? on the backs of the seats, on account of my brilliantine. Her mother give her this lacy old table-cloth, before she gone funny, and it had this hole in it, Mary were telling me – why her mother give it her, I shouldn't at all wonder – and so she cuts it up and she made these anti-whatchamacallits for the back of the seats, like I say, and then she says she got enough over for a scrap of something on the table, so she done that – and she's sewing a few beads and all around the edges, because she's a knacky little thing. Fruit bowl's in the middle of that – couple apples, few bananas (I'm partial to a banana). And the fireplace! Dear oh me. When we come here, there were a little gas fire in it, and stuck right next to it were a meter what was twice the size. Well two things: first, that meter, it sucked in money like there weren't no tomorrow, and the fire, it give out no sort of a heat at all. We'd be huddled around it, the pair of us – all our teeth rattling away, wearing mittens as likely as not – and by the time you got a bit of bread even half decent toasted, bleeding thing'd go out – and blimey, you lost the will to go on living. Then it starts popping when you light it, so Mary, she wouldn't go near. Well I'd had enough. I rip it out, give the grate behind a good old sort-out, get the sweep to see to the chimney, and now we got ourselves a proper fire. My line, I get all sorts of off-cuts – there's always something to burn, so everybody's happy. Gives out a very nice heat, and it do look grand. Trouble is, like now – you don't ever want to leave it. Now Mary, she'll be all right in the little kitchen now on account of she'll have the oven on, won't she? But you go into the bedroom, well – bleeding Arctic. We got that many blankets it'd crush you, you wasn't careful. And then when we got to spend a penny down the hall . . . ! Gets froze before it even hits the pan. And that's why I had enough of this place, really. I'm telling you – them houses what they're building out at Golders Green, they're little palaces, I am not joking. First, you ain't got Mr and Mrs bleeding Stone up and down the stairs and eyeing you every bleeding hour of the day. You got your own bathroom with a water heater and all – so no banging on the door when you're going blue with the need to have a wee, and there's some bleeding sod in there having theirself a good old soaping. And they got lovely big gardens. Always fancied a bit of a garden, growing a few veg – runners, caulies, marrow, that style of thing. Couple roses, keep Mary happy; bit of a lawn for the kiddy. Yeh – so that's the plan, anyway; up to me, really. I go on working hard, go on pleasing Mr Plough, and next Christmas – who knows? Could be Lord of the Manor. That's all I'd ever want.

Some people, though – blimey: the way they live, the things they got, you just wouldn't believe it. Like take the other night, yeh? Jonny and Dickie and me. Well look – we'd had a good few, I'm not denying. And there we all was in Jonny's great Humber, bowling along to Gawd knows where. Asked him, Jonny, once or twice. Where we off to then Jonny, I go. See a bloke, he says. That's all he says: see a bloke. Next thing I know, I'm falling out the motor – dragging old Dickie out the back (I reckon he dozed off: looked like he were dead) and the air outside the car, that nearly did for me, I'm telling you. I couldn't say to you where we was, but I can tell you this: it were a far cry from round here, that's for bleeding sure. Lovely area. Could've been where Dickie's lot have got a place, but Dickie, he never said. Lovely wide street, it were – all these houses joined up in a curve with railings in the front with the gold bits on the top. And Dickie, he were going Oh but look Mr Leakey – we can't just . . . what did he say? You know the bleeding funny way what he talks. He said . . . he said Oh but look Mr Leakey – we can't just go *barging* in, you know! What what! Or something. And then he calls it an 'ungodly hour', dear oh dear, and he says they'll all be asleep, whoever it is what lives here – it must be *terribly* late, what what! And Jonny, he says to him Nah – don't go worrying on that score: they won't be asleep (and nor were they, mate). So we clang on the old bell, and some flunkey come along and even now, I can't hardly believe what I seen.

'Jackie! Jackie – are you there?'

That's Mary, calling from the kitchen. I would get up now, make myself a bit active, but I left it a bit late, see, because she's in here now, look – got her little pinny on, fists on her hips, holding a . . . what is it? Oh yeh: wooden spoon. Very womanly she's looking, my way of thinking. Be thinking along other lines, if I hadn't only had her.

'Jackie – what are you just lying there for? I thought you were going to get the—'

'I am, love, I am. Just about to.'

'And there's the drinks, Jackie – you haven't put out all the—'

'Yeh yeh, I know. I know. Just going to do that as well. Right now.'

'Well come on then, for goodness sake. *Aaaaah* . . . Look at little Jeremy. Still fast asleep. I expect we'll have to pay the price though, won't we? Later on. I've got the goose in anyway – it looks lovely. Do hope it's not too fatty. Now listen, Jackie – I'm just popping downstairs to see how Molly's getting on with the chickens, all right? And if you hear the bell, it'll probably be Sheila with the pudding. So listen for it, will you?'

'Righty-o, Mary love. You want me to put Jeremy in his bed, do you? Or maybe just leave him be.'

'Oh . . . leave him, I think. Looks so peaceful. Oh and Jackie – did you borrow those glasses from the Rose & Crown?'

'No – but I'm just about to.'

'Well for goodness sake don't forget or else we'll all be up a gum tree. Right – I'm going to see Molly. Won't be a mo.'

Jackie smiled and waved her away. Yeh – she's right: there's a fair old bit to see to. Times like this, you could do with a few servants, couldn't you? Or a butler – wouldn't that be prime, ay? Like the other night – first time I ever laid eyes on one, a real-life butler: even now, I can't hardly believe what I seen. The door, it were swung right open, and there was this great big hall – you could fit the whole of this flat into that hall and you'd still have room to take in a party of lodgers. All shiny black and white on the floor and them columns up the wall like what you see in the pictures when it's the Roman Empire. And there he were, this butler – tall and thin, he were, great big red conk on him and all dressed up like that bloke in the films what Mary loves so bleeding much – I don't reckon him myself because it's all just dancing about and jazzy music and that, but the woman in them, she's all right – that Ginger Rogers, I don't mind her at all, but like I say, I don't too much reckon the feller. But what I'm saying is, there's this geezer here all got up in his tails and his spats like he's off to see the king, and all what he do is he opens the door for the likes of me.

'Mr Leakey, sir? You are expected. Would you be so good as to step inside?'

'Thank you, Barnstaple,' said Jonathan Leakey, very cordially. 'I don't mind if I do. Parky out here. These is friends of mine. All right?'

'Please, gentlemen. Pray enter. May I relieve you of your coats and hats?'

'You see that's the bally *trouble* . . .' said Dickie, chucking his coat over to Barnstaple in so casual a way that Jackie could never have contemplated. '*Lost* the damn thing. My hat. Somewhere along the line. Still – one less thing for you to deal with, hey? Splendidly warm in here, I must say – Barnstaple, is it . . . ?'

'Indeed, sir: Barnstaple. Mr Leakey, sir, would you and your guests be so good as to follow me? Mr Wisely is in the rose drawing room this evening.'

'Good lad, Barnstaple – you lead the way, ay?' And then in a smirked-out aside, rustled into Jackie's ear: 'Last time I come, I reckon it were the green drawing room what we was in. It's a right laugh, ain't it? You and me, we got a nice little sitting room apiece – Mr Wisely, he got one in every colour of the bleeding rainbow.' And then more seriously: 'You want to sober yourself up a bit, Jackie – pay a bit of attention, ay? Might learn a thing or two, you keep your ears open.'

Barnstaple swept open the double set of doors, sternly announced the arrival of Mr Leakey and friends and by means of an inclination of his head and the most soft and sheltered cough, he indicated to the party that they should each of them be preceding him now and into the room. A man of middling height in a satin and quilted smoking jacket the colour of damsons rose up in one quite fluid movement from a very large and deep-buttoned sofa that was more or less covered, so far as Jackie could make out in the shimmering pinpoints of light from a crystal chandelier, in a stupendous array of the most beautiful women he had ever laid eyes on. The man – moustache he's got, Jackie could now make out, a bit like Clark Gable – ambled with ease towards Jonathan Leakey, took his hand briefly, and then let it go.

'You are most welcome,' he said, in the sort of tone of voice that had Dickie now tearing away his attention from the sofa full of women – because I mean to say, quite splendid and various though the charms of the room undoubtedly are, that particular corner does rather tend to draw the eye, don't you know. I think (is what was running through his mind) that if I can feel anything at all through this accursed veil of stale and clinging alcohol, then it is the most profound and heartfelt relief. I've rather missed it, all this. I mean I'm not going so far as to suggest that I've made a mistake, taken a wrong turning in my chosen path but – well, a leopard and his spots and all that sort of thing, you know. Not that this house is at all like pater's – this is very much new money we're dealing with here – oh yes, very much so. Gleaming furniture straight from Harrods, beautiful leather bindings bought by the yard, you know the sort of thing – somewhat in the manner of our gracious host's speaking voice, I'm rather afraid to say, everything really just a bit too perfect . . . but nevertheless there is an enviable air of calm and plenty that I'm really quite a stranger to, these days, and it is, I have to say, most thoroughly welcome.

'And Jonathan . . .' said the man, revolving his head and concentrating the most extraordinarily warm and really rather dazzling smile on to both Jackie and Dickie in turn. 'You will please introduce me . . . ?'

'Oh blimey – forgive me, please forgive me. I don't know what I done with my manners,' blustered Jonathan Leakey, in so unnatural and deferential a way that Jackie had to blink: ain't never seen him this how before, I ain't – not Mr Jonathan Leakey. So Jackie thought he might step forward, because the sooner all the chat was done with, the sooner he might get a bit closer to this scented little harem we got over there – because just look at all of them now, will you? All whispers and tittering, they is – all looking over and giggly they is – and I reckon I'm near reeling from all the perfume off of them from right over here where I'm standing.

'My name's Jackie Robertson, and this here's Dickie Wheat. Pleased to meet you.'

'I were just on my way to *doing* that,' put in an evidently irritated Jonathan Leakey. 'This' – and he took a deep breath before he made the announcement – 'is Mr *Wisely*, lads. Mr Wisely – well, you know who they are now, don't you? Jackie Robertson, as he says, and that's Dickie Weak, yeh.'

'Nigel Wisely. Charmed. Quite delighted.'

'How do you do, Mr Wisely,' said Dickie. 'And it's *Wheat*, actually, my name.'

'Wheat, yeh,' grunted Jonathan Leakey. 'What I said.'

'Doesn't matter – not at all,' said Dickie magnanimously, quite suddenly a bit hot and cold and really rather ill again. 'But I say! What a perfectly splendid place, and all that sort of thing.'

Mr Wisely smiled his smile – even more radiant still, if Dickie were any judge of the thing.

'It suffices,' he shrugged, with a lot of modesty (yes, thought Dickie: quite a lot). 'But please, gentlemen – won't you do me the honour of sitting? Do tell Barnstaple whatever it is you would care for to drink. And then we really must become properly acquainted, must we not? Do tell me, Jonathan – where have you been hiding these two young gentlemen? Mr Robertson, indulge me if you will. How do you fill your day? Spend your waking hours, hm? Barnstaple – cigars for our guests.'

The seats that Nigel Wisely had bidden them to occupy were set in a half-circle around a very low and cuboid pink-mirrored table just to the side of a velvet-curtained bay. He followed the course of the sidelong glances of his guests, each of them quite unequivocally trained in the direction of the women. More than a glance, maybe – and certainly so in the case of our Mr Jackie Robertson, here – almost a longing, that look, it might be interpreted: how terribly graceless – but then he is so very young, and so utterly untutored. Mr Wheat – he darts across his coral-cheeked and rather furtive peepings as if he is naughtily flicking inky pellets from a ruler in a classroom not that long distant in his boyish and so very English memory. And Jonathan, as usual, is collectively appraising them, my girls, my lovely girls, as if he has been asked in the capacity of a professional to come up with an estimate of their current market worth. Vulgar, oh yes of course, but at least realistic.

'Please, gentlemen,' smiled Nigel Wisely, extending his arms in meek supplication. 'Can you find it within you to forgive me? I have omitted to introduce to you the delightful ladies.'

And just look at young Robertson now – up on his hind legs as if promised a titbit from the hand of his master. Wheat, predictably, is now the scarlet of the cushions, agitated and fidgety, and looking the other way entirely. Jonathan is carelessly sipping a very large whisky – by no means his first, I am in no doubt at all – and now he is rolling between his thumb and forefinger a fine H. Upmann Number One from the silver humidor on Barnstaple's tray. He will sniff it now, the oaf, put it to his ear as if it were a conch shell, and then he will place it behind the ruffled-up handkerchief in his jacket's top pocket and gently pat the whole ensemble, while more or less winking. As he does, habitually. Well well, there it is: business is business, as one must never forget, and Leakey, he's efficient, one must grant him that. And if part of the price is to suffer him periodically, to be seen to play up to – nay, be a party to the flexing of his oh so terribly puny little muscles as he revels and cavorts in so fine a reflected radiance as this one, then so be it, I suppose; for as long, anyway, as I deem it to be politic. And now I see that I must cater to the lusts and whim of this motley assembly.

'Ladies! Do please be so good as to present yourselves to my guests, if you will.'

Well gosh, thought Dickie, who had already half-risen in the full expectation that it was they who would be making the pilgrimage to the enormous sofa, and hardly the other way about. I mean that really takes the jolly old biscuit, you know – clapping your hands like some sort of a pasha, or something, and here they come, look, must be five of them – there are five of them, and see those dresses, how they shimmer as they move – coolly ambling over, the playing of that hint of a smile common to each of them, rather as if they are on the inside of a really cracking and endlessly intricate joke that the rest of us will never be told – and nor, were we, would we have the remotest idea as to even the nature of the thing, and no hope whatever of grasping its essence. I do rather wish, you know, that I didn't still feel so damnably ill and befuddled, because I doubt if I shall ever again in my lifetime find myself in a circumstance even similar to this. Those dresses, you know – and they're here now, the five of them, and even were one blind, the rustle and the scent would have told you that – they are around and above us (I did stand up, but I was alone in that, so I've now sat down again) – but those dresses, you know, they seem to me to be all of them in the form of an almost liquid gold and silver – bronze and steel, fluid columns, as straight as a funnel and hitting the floor. Two of the ladies – one with a chignon, the other with the fairly alarming Eton crop that's going about – are smoking coloured cigarettes in diamante holders – fuchsia and kingfisher, the cigarettes are, with little gold tips only barely discernible: they seem quite challenging, these two, one leg away from them and their hips akimbo. Mr Wisely, he's speaking – saying something to or about them – but still I have to look and absorb it, and I can't be listening to that as well. The other three ladies seem almost demure, in a way that is also a . . . what? Dare of some sort? Can't get any closer than that. Their eyelids look like damaged fruit, overripe grapes that are ready to burst, dark bruised plums, both indigo and maroon – half-veiling eyes that are ice and electric. Long white naked necks and arms, and bony shoulders striped with straps so very very thin, and all that is preventing a rushing and vertical collapse of all this cluster of metallic sheaths into a crumple of glimmer, a handful of spangles about their ankles. The décolletages are lavish, you know, and gently ruched, with more than a hint of small and liberated breasts – nipples, were one to be fanciful, active and eager for their share of the limelight. Well good heavens: that's all *I* can say.

Nigel Wisely rose to his feet, the palms of his hands brushing away from his immaculate trousers nothing whatever.

'Gentlemen – Mr Leakey and myself must briefly retire to attend to one or two tiresome and exceedingly footling little items . . . Barnstaple will see to it that your glasses are refreshed – and now that I have introduced you to these so very charming ladies, I feel sure I can leave you in their capable hands. On any other evening, gentlemen, my house would be completely at your disposal – but I regret, the ladies and myself, we leave for the country directly. So much more pleasant, I always feel, to spend Christmas at the heart of the matter, as it were. Though when I return, Mr Robertson, you really must, you know, as I think I said to you earlier – you really must tell me how it is that you fill your day. Spend your waking hours, hm? Well now.'

With a bow of his head to the assembled company, Nigel Wisely glided away, with Jonathan Leakey padding quickly behind him. Jackie was watching them go through a door at the far end that he hadn't even noticed as he continued to busy himself with gathering together a few more chairs, as he was urging Dickie to expand the circle. While back, it were like I could've passed out, way I were feeling, but I had a couple more now – lovely drop, ever so smooth, couldn't tell you what it were because Barnstaple, he gives you it out of this decanter what looks like it's made out of diamonds. That's just one of the fancy things round here. On the table there, look – all pinky mirror, the table: who would've thought of such a thing? – there's this great big lighter made out of a sort of a green shiny marble, some type, with little brown bits going on in it: heavy as a house brick – one quick snap of it and you're lit up a treat. And the paintings on the walls – pinky walls and all: why it's called the rose drawing room, I ain't an idiot, except for they're paintings, not drawings – and yeh anyway, these paintings on the walls . . . not that I could put my hand on my heart and say I could live with them myself, mind you, because I mean to say, well, how many cows and bunches of flowers can one man take? But yeh, the paintings on the walls, they all got these little brass lights on the top of them – all of these paintings, and I wouldn't want to go counting them – every one of these bleeding paintings got its own little light. Never seen nothing like it in the whole of my life. But look – let's be honest – it ain't the paintings what I'm look-ing at now, because these girls, I am not joking, they want to be in the pictures – and I don't mean the one-and-nines in the stalls, neither. They are film stars, each and every one of them – and this one, this one what I made sure I'm sitting right next to, this one in particular. Can't remember what Mr Wisely said her name were – it could be Amanda . . . or Helen, was it? Helen is she called? Anyway – some bleeding name she got, don't hardly matter. But just *look* at her, will you? I know I am.

'Hallo. Don't know if I said – my name's Jackie, yeh?'

The girl revolved and regarded him. Her purple eyelids descended elaborately and then they rose again in so languorous a manner, so that once again the gooseberry eyes could sparkle entrancingly.

'Jackie . . .' she repeated in a monotone. 'How thoroughly amusing. Barnstaple, my sweet! Will you be the most adorable darling and make me just a teensy one of these utterly divine little cocktails of yours? You're an absolute poppet, Barnstaple.'

'So . . .' pursued Jackie – looking to Dickie for maybe some assistance (but I just heard him come out with Lord's and Oval, so I don't reckon I'll get it: look at them four girls he's sat next to – seem close to death). 'So, ah – what do you do, then, um . . . ?'

The girl threw her head back and howled quite alarmingly in what could be delight – it had Jackie darting his eyes first this way then that, and quickly back to her again.

'*Do*? What do I *do*? Well my darling dearest I do absolutely the very very least that I possibly *can* do, of course. Isn't that what we *all* do, darling? Why, my angel? Do *you* do something? Quaint. *Divinely* interesting.'

Jackie, suddenly, didn't like her quite so much as he did – she maybe takes a bit of getting used to, does she, this one? Not met her type before.

'Well – I'm a painter, you might say.'

The girl's eyes were wide in the way they might be if a child had told her he had just come top in geography.

'A painter! Well. How decadent. Nudes, I imagine. Why you all become painters, isn't it really? Do you have a studio?'

'Studio. No. Oh no – I ain't that sort of a – no, you got me wrong. I'm a—'

'Oh *Barnstaple*, my darling – a million thanks. You're an absolute lifesaver. I haven't the slightest idea what it is he puts into these things, you know, but they truly are heaven, absolute heaven. You really have to try one.'

'Ay? Oh – no ta. Fine with my Scotch. No but listen – when I said I were a . . . well, I don't suppose it sounds very much to you, being a lady and all, but I'm a painter and decorator. Not

116

just that though, Helen – do a bit of woodwork, generally make myself handy, sort of style.'

The girl just blinked at him – once, and rapidly.

'Who in the world is *Helen* . . . ?'

'Ay? Oh sorry – I'm ever so sorry. I thought Mr Wisely said—'

'You thought he said that my name was *Helen*? Well you're wrong, because he *didn't*.'

She shrugged away from him and glared at the ceiling.

'Right. Well look, I'm ever so sorry, like I say. I just thought . . . well which one of you's Helen, then?'

The girl now focused the glare on to him, and him alone.

'*None* of us is called Helen. You really are a very tedious little man. Maybe it's your, oh God – *sweetheart*, should you have such a thing. Maybe *she's* called Helen, conceivably.'

'No. Yes I do, matter of fact. Have one. And she ain't, no – she ain't called Helen.' And then his neck was livid – throbbing cords there, thick with fury. 'She's called *Mary* – and I'll tell you something else and all: she's worth twenty of you lot any bleeding day of the week.'

'Oh well now look if you're going to be *offensive*. Barnstaple . . . ?'

Jackie stood up – shuffled around the knot of his tie.

'No. Don't bother. You don't have to get me chucked out. I'll chuck myself out. So don't worry – I'll be very pleased to accommodate you. Dickie! Hoy – Dickie! You coming? Time to be off, I reckon.'

Dickie's face was flushed and dappled, his eyes uncertain as he tried his best to focus.

'That you, Jackie old man? Off, did you say . . . ?'

'Don't want to outstay our wossname, do we? Ay Dickie?'

'Oh no – right you are, old chap. Well, ladies – it appears as if—' Dickie blew out his cheeks and struggled to his feet (oh my Lord! The floor and the ceiling are doing the damnedest things).

'It rather appears as if, ah . . . well I can't actually recall now, you know, what the devil I was about to say . . .' He glanced down at the ladies, two of whom he just about saw were staring straight ahead of them, while the remaining pair could well be in a coma. 'Well . . . daresay it doesn't matter, what?'

And much to his addled surprise, all of the girls seemed to raise themselves then – though only, as even Dickie could distantly perceive, because Nigel Wisely was once more among them.

'Leaving, gentlemen? So very *soon* . . . ?' he deplored, with elegance.

Jonathan Leakey now stepped in front of Jackie.

'Don't have to go *quite* so soon, Jackie. Mr Wisely and the girls . . . got a little time to spare. Ain't that so, Mr Wisely? Ay girls?'

'No,' said Jackie. 'Nice of you – it's good of you, Mr Wisely. You been nice, really good. Ta very much. But I got to go now. You know how it is, do you? When you just got to go? And listen – you still interested in what it is I do, you ask this lady over here, ay? Couldn't tell you her name – ain't Helen, I do know that. But I reckon you remember it, ay Mr Wisely? More than I did. So yeh, like I say: I'll be off.'

Nigel Wisely's eyes had narrowed into a private amusement.

'Well naturally whatever you say, Mr Robertson – of course, of course. Mr Leakey will be delighted to drive you both home.'

'Ay?' queried Jonathan Leakey.

'Won't you, Jonathan?' said Nigel Wisely, watching him.

Jonathan Leakey shrugged his surrender.

'Yeh,' he sighed. 'Yeh. Course.'

'Excellent,' said Nigel Wisely, with a sidelong smile. 'And you will take particular care of our Mr Wheat here, who I suspect is feeling just somewhat fragile. Now ladies – to your rooms, if you please, for final arrangements. Barnstaple, once you have seen these good people to the door, you might then ask Sharples to bring the car around, yes?'

Barnstaple stiffened and bowed his head in acknowledgement. 'The Bentley, sir?'

Nigel Wisely nodded. 'Mm. Yes – I rather think it'll have to be, don't you? Quite a number of us, after all.' The brilliant smile was back on his face. 'Well now, Mr Robertson – Mr Wheat – I simply can't tell you how great a pleasure this evening has been for me. Mr Robertson, I do hope and trust that we shall meet again, so that you might indulge me in that little chat I alluded to earlier. Yes? Charmed. Well gentlemen – I bid you a good night. And the compliments of the season to you all.'

Nigel Wisely then extended his hand, and after a moment's hesitation Jackie then reached out to grasp it, his forearm just tightening with the shock of the palm, its dimpled creamy softness, and the abrasion of his own upon initial impact.

And then the next thing Jackie could remember was that he was back in the Humber, his forehead plastered hard against the rain-spattered window – his eyes were groggily tracking the wavering course of each of the globules – and his jaw still shivering from the sudden sock of cold that smacked him in the street after all the opulence and warmth in that great big house they had all just left. Jonathan Leakey was fumbling around at the dashboard, feeling about with the flat of his hand and repeatedly prodding forward his ignition key and cursing in an undertone when he couldn't find the hole. Jackie said Whassamatter? Ain't there a light? And Jonathan Leakey, he hissed out at Jackie that Yeh, yeh there's a light, only it don't bleeding work. He got the motor running then, though you could barely hear it over the drone of Dickie's snoring in the back.

'What's the time then, Jonny?'

'You don't want to know it Jackie, believe me. Here, lad.'

Jackie felt a something, a light flat something – box, could be – dropped on to his knees.

'What's this then? So it's that late, is it? Yeh . . . suppose it has to be, really . . . Blimey – you hear old Dickie, do you?'

'Can't hear nothing else, can I? That mate of yours, he's a bleeding liability, you want my opinion. It's a present for you, Jackie. From Mr Wisely. He said for me to give it you.'

'Present, ay? Nah – he's all right, Dickie is. You just got to get used to him, that's all. So what – you do everything what Mr Wisely says for you to do then, do you Jonny? Proper well trained, are you Jonny?'

'Shut your mouth Jackie, there's a good lad. Had enough, one night. You don't want it, I take it back. Tell him you don't fancy it.'

Jackie felt around the surface of the cardboard box.

'What is it, then?'

'Oh Christ just open the fucking thing and then you'll know, won't you? Stupid bleeder. Oh bugger me – I can't remember if we do a left or right here . . .'

'All right all right, Jonny. Keep a hold on it . . . Right – I got the lid off, but I can't see a bleeding thing, can I? Feels all soft and silky . . .'

'Yeh – that'll be on account of it's silk, you—! It'll be for your Mary. I reckon she'll like it – all the ladies does. One of Mr Wisely's lines – top-class lingerie, that style of thing. You want to be grateful. Gets results, that do. Top-class lingerie. Gets results.'

'What he want to give me that for?'

'Christ knows. Reckon he liked you. Wouldn't be the first time.'

'What's that supposed to mean?'

'Oh do shut up, there's a good Jackie. I'm dead on my feet, I am. It means whatever you want it to mean, all right? I reckon . . . you know what I reckon? I reckon we should've took a left, back there. We're well out of our way now, we are. Maybe do a U . . .'

'Well,' said Jackie, slipping back the lid of the box. 'That's right nice of him. I'll give it her for Christmas – put a bit of paper round it. Blimey, though – he got it made, ain't he? Your Mr Wisely.'

'More than you know, son. It's Mr Wisely you want to be thinking about. You're a smart lad, Jackie, and he saw it straight off, like I knew he would. He could do you a lot of good.'

'Yeh? How you mean?'

'You'll find out, I daresay. Fullness of time. Mr Wisely – he don't never forget. Oh yeh . . . I think we're all right now – we're back on the main wossname, look. There soon.'

'He on the level, is he?'

'Gawd help me, Jackie! You can't see the hands in front your face, can you? Ay? Right . . . just nip down here past the dairy and I'll let you out on the corner, all right? And take bleeding Goldilocks with you. Had enough of him, I have. And look, it's not a question, is it Jackie? If he's on the level. Point is – you seen what he got. Ain't you? And that ain't the half of it. Why he got respect, see? Because he is what he's got. Like I was saying to you earlier, yeh? See? See it Jackie, do you?'

'Yeh. I sort of see what you're saying – yeh I do, Jonny, I suppose. Blimey, though – he's going to have hisself a Christmas, ain't he? All them women. Snooty tarts, but still – serve the purpose, ay?'

'No, Jackie, no. They're for decorative purposes only, they are. That, and business. He likes having them around him – pretty things, he likes them about – but that's as far as it goes. I ain't saying no more. Right lad – this is it. Let's be having you. And haul that old dosser out the back. All right, Jackie? You fit? Got your present? Right, then. Christmas Day invitation – that still good?'

'Yeh Jonny – course. Come on Dickie, you bleeding old drunk, you – out you come, there's a good boy. Here, Jonny – tell you one thing!'

'What's that then, Jackie lad?'

'Weren't an evening you're going to forget, were it? Ay?'

'Not likely, no. There's more evenings like that you know, Jackie. And better. Up to you, son. Think about it.'

And Jackie, yeh – of course he knew he'd remember the evening – and yeh, that he'd think about it too. Like now – right now, lying out by the fire, might have been dozing off there a little bit, from the heat of it – I have, haven't I? Been thinking. And one thing I thought was well, he were right there anyway, weren't he? Ay? About the top-class lingerie. Got results.

As Mary backed her way rather awkwardly into the room, coping with something quite huge and unwieldy, Jackie hastily roused himself and was very nearly eager and up on his feet as Mary managed a half-turn and kicked shut the door behind her.

'God it's like an oven in here . . . Oh Jackie I don't *believe* it. You've been lying on the floor all this time! Here – take this from me, can you? Can't see where I'm going . . .'

Jackie stepped forward and found that he was limping – the whole of his thigh and the calf below it seemed dead to him now, like an odd and other part of him, clumsily added as unnecessary ballast.

'No – I weren't, honestly. Well I *were*, yeh – but I had a reason. I thought – blimey, Mary, this *is* heavy, what's in it? Lead weights? No listen, I thought if I go banging around with bottles and all the rest of it, well then little Jeremy, he's going to be bawling his eyes out, ain't he? And I couldn't *leave* him, could I? Well could I? Couldn't take myself off to get the glasses and all the rest of the caper. Not with you not here to keep an eye. But you're back now, see Mary? So I can get it all done. Just put this – what? In the kitchen, will I . . . ?'

Mary was disarmed, as he knew she would be.

'You make it sound as if I've been holding you *up*!' she was hooting, in an attempt at outrage. 'Yes – just on the table. In there.

It's three chickens all in different pans – I thought she was only going to do two. They look lovely – all golden. Molly's very handy, you know – you wouldn't think it to look at her, but she is. Now come on, Jackie – get a move on now for heaven's sake. They'll all *be* here soon – look at the time!'

'Right – I'll go. Oh – just one thing I got to do first.'

'No, Jackie – no. There's nothing you've got to do first – just please go now and get the—'

'No no – won't take a jiff. You just stay where you is – all right Mary love? You just stand there, exactly where you is. All right? Promise you – half a mo, I'll be back. Shut your eyes.'

'Jackie—!'

'No come on – shut your eyes, and count to five, and then I'll be back.'

And Mary was smiling, and now she was closing her eyes.

'Feel so *silly* . . . So much to *do* . . .'

'I can't hear you counting. Go on – up to five.'

'Oh Jackie . . . ! Oh all right, then. One . . . two . . . are you still here? Are you still in the room, Jackie? Oh this is ridiculous – I feel such a lemon, just standing here counting . . . Three . . . Four . . .'

'Right. I'm back. Say five. Go on – say five.'

'Jackie! It's so *silly* . . . !'

'Say five, I would. Else we could be stood here till Boxing Day. Up to you.'

'Oh all *right*, then: *five*. There. Happy now?'

'Very. Open your eyes now, Mary.'

She blinked them open and was aware now of the tickle of leaves, it could be, fluttering across her nose and eyelids – and then Jackie had her tight about the waist and her mouth was crushed by a long hard kiss that softened then, and became so sweet. She gasped for breath as she pulled away, and laughingly batted away the thicket of mistletoe that Jackie still dangled in front of her face.

'Happy Christmas, Mary love.'

Mary's eyes were close to melting, as she shook her head in the same old wonder. How was it that he could always do this to her? Whatever her mood, however much there was for her to do, Jackie could just blow a whistle and change the rules – sometimes instigate another game altogether.

'I love you, Jackie ... Happy Christmas. It is a happy Christmas, isn't it? Now *go*, for heaven's sake, or I'll take my rolling pin to you! I mean it!'

Jackie gave at the knees and threw up his arms, his face now a picture of theatrical alarm.

'No no Mary! Not that! Not the rolling pin! *Anything* but the rolling pin!'

Mary laughed and slapped him away. 'You're impossible. Do you know that? You're just impossible!'

Jackie – laughing too, now – had scurried to the door. He turned abruptly, clicked together his heels in the manner of a Kaiser, and then he bowed deeply from the waist while doffing in deference a splendid hat of his own imagining – that of at least an ambassador, and covered in plumes.

◉

Everything was as ready as Mary could make it – she had banked up the fire and it was crackling brightly and smelling so fine from the armful of pine cones that Jackie had magicked from somewhere, and set amongst the kindling. One of the crepe paper festoons had come adrift from the corner and so Mary had got out and set up the little pair of steps and couldn't find the hammer that she remembered having put away safely somewhere quite different from the usual for a reason now lost to her, and so with a carpet tack firmly sandwiched between her flattened lips, she climbed up the rickety little ladder while keeping a firm hold on to the retwisted garland (because once before it had already floated down and away from her grasp) and doggedly she thumped in the tack with the heel of a bottle of Stone's Ginger Wine, praying the while that it wouldn't explode. The goose and the chickens were proudly displayed at the centre of the table – all ready for Jackie to carve, if ever he came back from wherever to goodness it was he had got to. And yes – it would have been nice, of course it would, to serve the poultry hot and piping from the oven, but really quite impossible if you look at the facilities – but still they'll be nice, they'll still be delicious. That goose, it gave off an enormous amount of fat – nearly two jugs – but when it's solidified, good knobs can be dropped inside the baked potatoes the minute they're done: that, and a scattering of parsley makes for a feast in itself. The sausages were cut and arranged around quarter tomatoes, and the pineapple segments she had attempted to stack – though thoroughly unsuccessfully, she was bound to admit, as they did seem to have this tendency to wilt, and then slither. There was a bowl of Smith's potato crisps, and Mary had gathered all the little blue paper twists of salt to one side, so that people could scatter one or not. A pot full of sprouts was simmering on the stove and there was a heap of bread and butter on a near-undetectably cracked and mended serving plate of the willow design that her mother had told her she might as well have, or else it would go straight into the bin – and radishes in salad cream alongside. Mary had been doubtful about this particular concoction but Sheila had assured her that it tasted a great deal better than it tended to appear – which, looking now at the dish of it, was really just as well. Mary had made Sheila promise her quite faithfully that she and Dickie would be the first to arrive (and there was a space on the table, ready for the pudding) and yet she knew that as soon as the doorbell sounded, she'd be as nervous as a fawn, with an impulse to bolt.

The tree, though, was looking remarkably lovely – Jackie had, he had come back with a boxful of ornaments earlier in the morning, though not at all the sort of thing that Mary had been expecting. They were these tiny chocolate bars wrapped in coloured shiny paper and tied into stacks of three with a bow of silver twine. He got them from the confectioner's, is what he had told her – a new line, he had been given to understand – because the traditional glass and tinsel ornaments that he had been all set to borrow had simply failed to come up to the mark, is what he said to her: not really of the standard, Mary – not by a long way. Whether they had ever existed outside of his own imagination was a question that Mary chose not to go into. But these were better in every way, Jackie had assured her – and she was bound to agree, because as the day wore on, well those with a sweet tooth, they could all get the benefit. Once they were eaten, of course, the little bars of chocolate, then again the tree would look to be a sparse and denuded thing . . . but it's today that's Christmas, after all. It's today that counts. Oh yes and then at the very last moment, Mary had remembered the candles – or remembered, at least, that it had completely flown out of her mind that she had determined to buy some. So out came the pair of steps once more, and there was Mary, high up in the dinginess of the very cramped and cobwebby cupboard in the hallway, blindly groping about upon the dusty shelf above the fusebox for the two emergency candles that she always tried to keep there. They were the colour of dripping and covered in fluff and one of them had about it a noticeable curve, but they were decidedly better than nothing – and once she had rubbed them over with some cardinal red Meltonian polish that just last summer she had bought expressly for the care of the mock lizard courts that went so terribly well with the rather jolly handbag she had so rashly splurged upon in the Bourne & Hollingsworth sale (only to discover that she could hobble no more than a dozen yards in them, before doubling over with a crippling pain) – once she'd made those candles as glossy as cherries, she much less regretted the outlay on the polish. There were miniature candles too, held in silvered pincer jaws that were gripping the more prominent branches of the tree, but she did not know if she dared to light them because quite a number were angled so very precariously that the messy and conceivably perilous outcome was to be perfectly frank a rather foregone conclusion. The bottles of Bass and Guinness, Cyprus sherry, port and ginger wine (because it didn't explode) were all ranked up on the three-legged table, though the glasses from the Rose & Crown had yet to make their appearance – nothing to do, we don't think, do we, with Jackie's protracted absence? Well, he'll turn up soon enough – probably on his way.

And my dress, I'm really quite pleased with. The red Chantilly really does make it come into its own, you know, and I've got the silver locket on, and the bracelet that was my grandmother's. What I have to remember to do just before everybody arrives is to take off this pinny, and maybe spray my hair with a little more Eau de Paris – I can't wait to show it to her, Sheila, my so elegant new atomiser. It will look so well on a figured walnut dressing chest, if one day we can ever run to such a thing. Oh and there weren't nearly enough serviettes – even odd ones – so I cut up some of last year's Christmas wrapping into squares, and I know that it's far from ideal, but I hope that they will do. Jackie said not to bother because nobody ever uses them, serviettes, not these days, but I don't really think that that's the point: you have to have them because they ought to be there – simple as that, really. And anyway – I use them, and so does Dickie. Oh and Jeremy! This is the amusing part of it – he's still fast asleep!

I became a little bit worried at one point a while back, but he hasn't a fever or anything – I've checked him twice – he's just sleeping like a lamb. Heaven knows how long it can last, of course, but fingers crossed in the meantime.

Well, people will be arriving soon – and I do now wish that Jackie, he was back here. And Sheila and Dickie, they promised me they'd be first, and so I wish they'd hurry up about it. And even though I know it'll be them when the doorbell goes, I just feel sure that I'll go all into a flap, because then, at that point, the party has started and – well, I do just so hope that it all goes well, that it all goes nicely. And Jackie . . . he just loved the present I gave him, I just know he did. I mean, whatever he'd been given he would've been pleasant about it, of course he would, but you always know, don't you really? If somebody *truly* likes whatever you've got for them – you can see it in their eyes, and they start to use it immediately or show it around. It's just as well that he likes it, really, because I've been paying for it, you know – the lighter and the case – bit by bit, a little every week, since – ooh goodness, long before Easter. It wasn't easy, with what I was getting from the laundry and Jackie not working, but I'm so terribly glad that I did – of course I am – and it's not as if we ever went without. I always saw to it that Jackie had a proper tea on the table of an evening.

It's a bitter day – freezing out, you can see it on the window, the drizzle when it hits, it crazes into patterns. So there'll be an awful lot of coats to be dealt with when everyone comes, so what I've done – I've laid out a lot of old newspapers all over the bed, so it should be all right, in case they're all damp. And I really can't think now of anything else – I've checked and checked, looked and looked, and I really can't think now of anything else. I just want Jackie to come back. And then Sheila and Dickie to arrive. And even though I know it'll be them when the doorbell goes, I just feel sure that I'll go all into a flap because – oh! My goodness! That's it – that was the doorbell now. And I am – I have done, I've gone all into a flap, just look at me – but because I know it's just Sheila and Dickie, I'm going to right this minute stop being so silly – and so now I'm at the door and I'm going to let them in: and the Christmas party can begin.

Mary must have been staring – goggling, she could even have been – and afterwards she even fancied that her mouth might well have been hanging open as well, at the moment when she heaved open the door and then came face to face with Mr and Mrs Stone. In his thick blue chalk-striped suit, he seemed shorter though much less wiry than usual, Mr Stone – and his greying hair, it shone like glass and the first cloying wave of very recently and assiduously brushed-in brilliantine caused a catch in Mary's throat, and her eyes were stinging her. A high and off-white cellulose collar seemed to be maybe too small and digging in deeply to the side of his neck, where the razored skin seemed so much darker. His wife, hanging well behind him, was tugging at the lace on her sleeve and gazing quite resolutely away at the split and hardened linoleum the length of the corridor.

'We come,' said Mr Stone, quite gutturally and simply, the set of his shoulders expressing a much-practised stoicism, a weary resignation to his fate, whatever it may be. He thrust at Mary a brown paper package, as he wagged his head and sighed.

'Mr Stone, Mrs Stone – how nice to see you. Please do come in – come in, won't you? Happy Christmas! Oh and thank you – thank you so much.'

Mr Stone edged in carefully, as if there warnings of wet paint to all sides of him, and his wife followed on, and still she looked down. He shrugged away the gratitude.

'Is cheap . . .' he said. And then he glanced up at the coloured paper garlands leading away from the light and into each corner. 'You put in nails . . . ?'

'Why don't you sit down, yes? Come on, Mrs Stone. Do sit down by the fire. Can I maybe get you a drink of something?'

Mrs Stone looked over to her husband with hesitation; after a barely there flick of his eyebrow, she duly sat down in the chair that had been indicated. Her eyes, thought Mary, seem to be constantly pleading, and there are dark soft pouches beneath them; she looked to be eternally fatigued – or maybe the sallowness was common to women of her race. Mr Stone stood before the fire and ran the palm of his hand along the surface of the mantelpiece and then he glared at that palm as if it were a criminal. He made no move to pick up the Christmas card that he had dislodged as he did it, and so Mary knelt down and recovered it from the hearthrug and then fairly pointedly propped it back into its place. My God, she thought – these people, they're just so terribly rude – but . . . and I've thought this before . . . I don't think at all it's because they actually *mean* to be, or anything. They're maybe just shy, I don't know. Foreigners – they're so terribly different, aren't they? And of course the language – that's strange to them.

'Would you like a drink, Mr Stone? A glass of beer, maybe.'

Mr Stone now looked about him.

'We early? This right day?'

'Oh no, not really. Yes. No, it's – of course it's the right day! It's Christmas Day, isn't it? Everyone else will be along quite soon. So, um – a beer, then? Yes? And for you, Mrs Stone?'

'Mrs Stone,' said her husband, gravely, 'she not drink. I have beer. Tenk you. Pretty tree. What cost? Much? Why you not open present?'

Mary looked down at the package she had forgotten she was holding.

'Oh yes – of course. I shall open it now. How terribly kind of you.'

The manila paper was soft with creases and multiple use. I really do hope, thought Mary quite anxiously, that Jackie and

Sheila and Dickie – that they do turn up extremely soon, because I'm finding this all rather difficult, to be perfectly frank.

'You like? I have beer. Tenk you.'

Mary looked down at the box of four bath cubes – Parma Violet, it said they were. The cellophane covering was yellowed and cracked, and the torn foil cover of one of the cubes was peppered with a hard and bluish crumbling from within.

'Oh how lovely!' exclaimed Mary – rather too loudly, she thought straight away, as she heard it in the air. 'How very very kind of you both.'

Mr Stone shrugged his shoulders so very elaborately, as if to distance himself completely from any knowledge at all of whatever it was she might be suggesting.

'Is cheap . . .' he said. 'Mind rinse bath very good when after you use. Or pipes go kaput. I have beer. Tenk you.' And then he thrust his hands deep into his trouser pockets and again he was looking up at the ceiling. 'You put in *nails* . . . ?'

And then Jackie burst in, and Sheila and Dickie were laughing and bustling behind him, all of them quite raucous and carrying their various bundles.

'Hallo Mary love!' Jackie hailed her – his eyes already quite glassy, Mary immediately observed, and very much too early in the proceedings for her liking, thank you. 'You remember these two old reprobates, do you? Picked them up in the street – they wouldn't let me alone, so I brung them home. Can we keep them? Can we, Mary love? They won't be no trouble – I'll take them for walkies every morning, quite religious, and they can live on scraps. Let's just hope they're house-trained, ay?'

'Ha ha!' laughed Dickie. 'What-ho Mary, you know. Merry Christmas all round! Sorry we're a bit late. Here – one box assorted glasses, courtesy of Len at the Rose & Crown. He's coming across once he's closed up for the day. Not sure it's even legal for him to be open. Still – absolutely crammed in there at the moment. Said to wish you the compliments of the season and all that sort of rot. I say – what a cracking fire. Make way there – freezing outside, I tell you. Tree looks prime, I must say – see the tree, Sheila old girl? Topping, hey?'

'Oh of course I've *seen* it Dickie, you absolute ass. I was helping with the decorations, wasn't I? I did *tell* you . . .'

'Put your coats in the bedroom, you two,' called out Mary. 'Oh my goodness, Dickie – what on earth has happened to yours? It's all torn at the hem, look – it's all hanging down . . .'

'Oh that . . .' said Dickie, quite sheepishly. 'Not too sure how that can have happened, actually. Still – not to worry. Only an old thing, what? How about a drink then, Jackie? Parched. And my – that food, you know. I'm quite starving, all of a sudden.'

Mr Stone now coughed, quite long and loudly, causing Mary to glance at him with concern.

'Are you quite well, Mr Stone? Is there something I can get you?'

Mr Stone nodded. 'I have beer. Tenk you.'

'Oh heavens! What must you think of me – I'm so terribly sorry. Jackie – pour a glass of beer for Mr Stone, will you? And are you quite sure Mrs Stone won't have anything at all? Not even a cordial? Some ginger wine, maybe – it's named after you! Stone's – yes? No? No. Well if you're both quite sure . . .'

Mr Stone moved over to the table where Jackie was snapping off the caps from three large bottles of Bass. Dickie hovered alongside as Sheila entered into a rushed and whispered conversation with Mary, largely concerning the bulbous enamel basin in her arms, swathed in a knotted tea towel as if it were the victim of the worst attack of toothache. Mr Stone confronted Dickie, and jerked his head in Jackie's direction.

'He live here. You I don't know.'

'No,' said Dickie, very affably. 'Well my name's Dickie Wheat. Dickie, don't you know. Merry Christmas! Jolly good to meet you. And you are . . . ?'

'And I am Mr Stone.'

'Er . . . right. Jolly dee. Well now look, Mr Stone – you get around this bottle of Bass, and you'll be a better man for it, what? Cheers, old chap. Oh and Mary, old girl – thanks awfully for the port. That'll hit the spot and no mistake. Where's little Jeremy? Not sold him, have you?'

'Oh and for the *books*, Dickie. I just can't wait to get into them. No – oh gosh he's still asleep. Jackie? Did you know? Jeremy – he's actually still asleep. Simply can't last. Oh – that's the bell! Jackie – be an angel, would you? Oh my *goodness*, Sheila – why didn't you *tell* me? I've still got my pinny on! Oh and you must come and see what Jackie got me for Christmas – it's just too wonderful.'

'Was the tippet all right for you, Mary? I just thought it'd go so terribly well with your—'

'I know! The one with the half-belt. And it does – it's perfect. How clever you are, Sheila. And the jam! Yum yum. Oh look – look who it is! Hallo again Molly – what a lovely dress! Is it new? That colour, it really does suit you. You remember Sheila, don't you? Sheila – you remember Molly from downstairs? Yes of course you do. She did the chickens – don't they look marvellous? Molly was hoping that her young man from Manchester might be able to make it down, but it's the *trains*, apparently . . .'

'Mm,' put in Molly, smiling wryly, 'that's what *he* says, anyway. Maybe just couldn't face the sight of me . . . !'

'Oh don't be so *silly*, Molly. Honestly! He adores you – you know he adores you. Now listen – I'm going to leave you two now, if that's all right. I'll just get your gorgeous pudding on the table, Sheila – I saved a bit of holly for the top. And then I think we might start offering some food around, don't you?'

Mary made her way to the kitchenette, both her arms wrapped around the pudding. She paused on her way to give Jackie a very quick peck on the cheek and whisper to him in the way of a conspirator: You are all right, aren't you Jackie love? And his big brown eyes were turned full upon her as he kissed her back and said of course I'm all right, why shouldn't I be all right and mmm, I tell you what – you don't half smell good, girl. And then suddenly she was waylaid by a flurry of pink and even quite rather red-faced party guests who all now seemed to be arriving at once, bellowing their greetings and setting down packages and then – all the while slapping shoulders and calling out yet more hellos – making a beeline for the hostess, the fire, or Jackie with the drinks. There's Sally from the greengrocers – that dress, emerald, and a sort of shantung, you might call it: I saw one just like it in the market, on the Romany stall; a size too small for her, I'd say, but then she's always been aware, Sally, shall we say, of her figure – likes to show it off. But give her her due, thought Mary quite guiltily, she really has done them proud, look, with this quite wonderful basket of fruit that she's waving in front of me: honey-coloured wicker, and all sorts of different green and red and yellow shiny apples – and I even see the tuft of a genuine pineapple, oh my goodness I can hardly believe it: and what a pretty bow. And so I'll have to put this pudding down just anywhere for the time being and say a hello and kiss-kiss with Sally – and oh look! Where's Jackie? I just must wave to Jackie. He's not looking this way – he's giving Molly a glass of sherry, I think it is – but I must just get his attention because look! Oh look who's here – it's his brother Alfie, haven't seen him for ages, and quite a pretty girl he's brought along, if you go for the peroxide look, which I know is catching on, so I really mustn't be beastly about it; and anyway, I'm sure she's very nice.

'Alfie! Over here. Oh *hello*, Alfie – how lovely to see you. Merry Christmas! Merry Christmas!'

'Hallo, Mary love,' grinned Alfie. 'And a merry Christmas to you, I'm sure. Gawd it's parky out there, I am not joking. Mary – this is Jeanie. Jeanie – this is Mary – she's the one what puts up with that no-good brother of mine. Where is he anyway? Oh I see him – over by the booze, now there's a surprise!'

'Oh you don't change, do you Alfie?' chided Mary. 'Now give me your coats, you two. Hallo, Jeanie – give me your coat, will you? Then you can get a warm by the fire. Alfie – you go over and say hallo to Jackie – he's been talking about nothing else but you coming over for days on end. I'll look after Jeanie, don't you worry. Get you a drink, Jeanie? Come and sit by the fire. Have you known Alfie long? He's a lovely lad, isn't he? I've always thought so.'

'Here – steady on, Mary!' laughed Alfie. 'I am still *here*, you know. Oh and here, Mary – Christmas present.'

Mary put down the basket of fruit (weighs a ton, and I don't quite know now where I left the pudding . . . must be somewhere about, I suppose) and then she grasped the dark blue thick and hard-covered volume that Alfie was holding out to her. She turned it over in her hands. The spine was rounded and a soft brown leather, and the edges of the pages were all aswirl with maroon and mustard marbling, flecked with spatters of green.

'It's a ledger,' clarified Alfie. 'I won't pretend but I got it at a reduction from work. It's very good quality – used by all the top firms, you know. I thought – you being the businessy one, Mary, the one what keeps everything in order, I shouldn't wonder – I thought it might, I don't know . . . come in useful, sort of thing.'

A quick hot roar of laughter rose like a wave from somewhere quite close to the fireplace – Dickie had Sally's feathered beret perched quite jauntily to the side of his head and he was curling a hank of Sheila's loosened hair – she was laughing rather merrily as she bent to her task – across his upper lip and allowing it to dangle, asking anyone around to guess who he was. Sally was laughing herself into a bit of a state, so far as Mary could see, but it wasn't *that* funny, surely . . . ? She is holding out her port glass to Jackie again, though, and we haven't even eaten yet . . . Festive spirit, is what they call it.

'It's *perfect*, Alfie – just what I needed. What a very thoughtful boy you are. Now go on – go and see Jackie. Go on. Now, Jeanie – we've got sherry and port – ginger wine and cordials, lemonade . . . beer, if you'd like it.'

And then Mary got such a shock and she flinched away as suddenly a quite deep voice was droning in her ear. She distantly was aware of Dickie now squawking out No no no – I'm Charles the First, you ass!

'Mrs Robertson – please do forgive. We ain't never met, but Jackie – he might have mentioned my name in passing, Jonathan Leakey. Pleased to meet you. And this, dear madam, I have taken the liberty of bringing along with me, as I thought it might add to the general gaiety of the occasion, as you might call it. Get the joint jumping, as the Americans express it. Where do you keep your electrical socket?'

Mary just gaped at the man (how black his hair is – how very pale, the grey of his suit; purple stones in his cufflinks, as he raises a hand to finger the dark cluster of prickles above his upper lip). Jeanie now was glancing about, and wondering what she might do.

'Mr Leakey, I – yes of course, I do know of you. But what is this . . . ?'

She glanced down at the large, rounded and highly polished wooden casket on the carpet, by his feet. It reminded her rather of a sewing machine case, but the grain and the glossy finish were so very superior. Do you know . . . it might even be figured walnut, the veneer.

'It is what I believe is termed a turntable, Mrs Robertson.'

'Oh – Mary, please. Do call me Mary. I'm sorry Mr Leakey, but—'

'Jonathan. My name is Jonathan. Jonny, should you prefer.'

'—Jonathan. But I don't quite understand what you mean . . . ?'

'It plays recordings of music, Mary. A selection of which I have had the foresight to of brung with me.'

Mary's eyes were gleaming with delight.

'Oh! Music! A gramophone! Oh how *wonderful*, Mr Leakey. I was going to put on the wireless later, but they only ever have carols and so on at Christmas time, don't they? And though I do rather like the odd carol, I must say they become a little, well – tedious, don't they? After a while, I mean to say. It isn't carols you have brought, is it Mr Leakey? Jonathan? It's not just Christmas carols?'

And then a cry went up from Jackie and Alfie (their arms were entwined about each other's waists, and Mary was so very pleased to see it) and Dickie was waving Sally's hat around his head and in the direction of the doorway. It was a purple-faced Len from the Rose & Crown, with two – no, it's three – rather beery-looking men, to Mary's way of thinking, trailing in behind him and grinning all around them.

'Greetings to all my regulars!' shouted out Len. 'And all you irregulars too!'

He wove his way through the tight-knit throng, a bottle of cherry brandy held high above his head, and a large cardboard carton tucked beneath his mighty arm (as Mary now saw it to be).

'That's Len,' explained Mary, turning back to Jonathan Leakey. 'From the Rose & Crown.'

'Ah yes – we are well acquainted, me and Len.'

'Oh – oh yes, of course you must be. But Mr Leakey – Jonathan. Your gramophone records – please do tell me!'

'Well why don't you see for yourself – yes, Mary? I'll just lay them out here for you, will I? Floor seems to be the only space. There's a fair little selection – and not a carol among them, think you'll find.'

The hubbub around her was now quite forgotten as Mary stooped down and started eagerly sifting among the stack of records. The sleeves were largely the brown of so much that was made of paper, it seemed to her, these days, but she set now to scrutinising the dull silver lettering on the black and blue and blood-coloured labels at the records' centres.

'Oh!' she squealed – glancing up in such girlish pleasure to a clearly very gratified Jonathan Leakey. 'Ambrose! I do love Ambrose and his orchestra – I always turn up the volume knob when he's on the wireless. "The Clouds Will Soon Roll By" . . . don't know if I know that one or not – I expect I'd have to hear it. "Cheek To Cheek" – oh yes, I certainly do know that one! That's Fred Astaire, isn't it? Seen the picture. Wonderful. Oh Mr Leakey! Jonathan, I mean – I'm so terribly grateful to you. It's just what the party needed, this. And there are about a dozen records here, by the looks of it. Goodness!'

Jonathan Leakey nodded. 'Around the dozen mark, yes. And they're double-sided. Have you spotted the Al Bowlly? "You Couldn't Be Cuter"?'

'Oh!' gasped Mary, clapping together her hands. 'That's one of my absolute favourites!'

'And so very appropriate for your fair self, if I may say so, Mary.'

Mary was caught by that, and she coloured immediately. In a much lower and more serious voice, she said quite slowly:

'Well really, Mr Leakey. I don't think that was at all called for.'

Jonathan Leakey was alive with apology.

'A thousand wossnames, my dear Mary. Pardons. I do hope you will grant me—?'

And Mary smiled – just too thrilled with all this music to care that much, if she was honest.

'Oh yes – quite forgotten, I do assure you.'

'Excellent,' grinned Jonathan Leakey. 'So tell me then, Mary: where do you keep your electrical socket?'

'But don't you just wind them up, these things? And is there no horn? Shouldn't there be a big horn?'

'You are looking here at the very latest appliance, dear lady. As supplied to His Majesty the King. I am not joking.'

The shadow of Mr Stone was suddenly cast over Mary, still squatting on the mat.

'You plug in, this?' he said.

Mary nodded. 'We did intend to, yes. We're just about to.'

'Why I put in meter. You got shilling?'

Mary laughed. 'I *think* so, Mr Stone – yes thank you.'

'I can lend shilling.' And then he raised an admonishing finger. 'But want back!'

'No no – I do assure you,' giggled Mary. 'We have a shilling. Now please do excuse me. Why don't you ask Jackie for another glass of beer?'

Mary turned away and was laughing with Jonathan Leakey over the antics of Mr Stone, when Jackie and Alfie nearly stumbled right into her (they still had their arms about one another and seemed so very boyish, to Mary).

'Here, Mary love – hallo Jonny, good you could make it – listen Mary, there's this young gel over there by the door, yeh? Got a pack of kids with her. Looks ever so lost. What you think?'

Mary jabbed her head left and right in between the jostle of bobbling people, and her heart gave a kick that was followed by sadness as she glimpsed them clinging to the doorframe. Poor little Lorna from the laundry – cleaner and much less ruddy than ever she'd seen her before, she'd little white bows at the ends of her plaits – and these sets of frightened eyes peering out from around and behind her. Mary quickly turned with a word of apology to Jonathan Leakey – could you go and ask Jackie to plug in the machine, and do then please play a record of your own choice, and I promise you I shan't be too long; Jonathan Leakey said he'd be happy to do exactly as she asked – that her wish was his wossname, and that she could rely upon that.

Mary edged a path sideways through all of the people – my goodness, I can't believe how full the room is now! – indicated to a somewhat forlorn and abandoned Jeanie the whereabouts of Alfie and Jackie, noted in passing that Len and his acolytes had all of them so very surely graduated in the direction of Molly, and now formed an eager circle around her, three of them proffering their packets of Player's (always a magnet for men, is Molly – I've often observed it), and then she was at the door and gently approaching Lorna with outstretched arms, the smile on her face as reassuring as she could make it. It was as if she was taking particular care not to alarm a trembling stray, allaying its fears before it fluttered in fright, and bolted. But Lorna was the first to speak.

'Look, Mary – it were right nice of you to ask me and all, but I can see you've got a houseful and you won't want to be doing with the likes of us so we'll just take ourselves away and no more need be said about it. I got for you this bag of fruit jellies because I know how well you like them.'

And Mary actually had then to take Lorna by the shoulder as she hastily turned to leave, and gathered with a gesture the party of siblings about her; Mary was forced to use both hands now just to turn her back around and face her.

'What are you *talking* about, Lorna? I'm so *pleased* that you've come, and you mustn't even think of leaving. I've got a mountain of food and everything, and if you and your family don't help me get rid of it all then I shall be most terribly offended. And thank you very much for the jellies – you know my weakness, don't you? Now won't you tell me who everybody is? Your hair – the plaits, they look *wonderful*, Lorna – and such a pretty frock.'

Lorna smiled her relief and sincere appreciation: she seemed now to be letting out for the first time in a long time just so very much pent-up breath.

'Thank you, Mary – you're always so very kind to me. Well now look then – if you're sure . . . ? Well this is Imogen. Imogen is the oldest after me – she's just nearly fifteen now. Say hello to Mary, Imogen.'

She was a slight thing, thought Mary – great black eyes, and so pretty a face if only she'd smile. She could be anything really from twelve years old to approaching fifty, so young and very worried did she look.

'Hello, Imogen – I'm very pleased to meet you. And you've got a lovely frock too, haven't you? I do like gingham. Did you make it yourself?'

Imogen bit her lip and gazed at all the people in the room and winced just slightly as Jackie started up his bawling from somewhere that the time had come to carve the goose!

'It were Lorna's . . .' she eventually said – so softly that Mary would have been straining to hear her at the best of times, but amongst all of this great hullabaloo . . . well honestly! 'And I changed it to fit me . . .'

A small boy was clinging to the skirt of that frock – sucking the thumb of one hand, while the other was placed quite protectively across the shoulder of an even smaller boy. He looked up to Mary with some hesitation, and then he piped up:

'Please miss – when can we eat the mountain of food what you want to be rid of . . . ?'

And as Lorna went through all the business of being shocked and embarrassed by such a display, and said that she was sorry, so sorry, and that no mind at all should be paid to our Timmy, Mary laughed quite delightedly and leant down to hold him by the shoulders as she assured him very happily that as Jackie had said, that very moment has just arrived, Master Timmy, and you must hold my hand now right this instant, young man, and accompany me to the table, if you would be so kind. This he seemed pleased to do, and Lorna and Imogen and the other little boy were content to pad along behind, as if they had been trained to.

'Ah – Miss Mary,' blustered Len, as they all squeezed through the bluish smoke-haze of the beerily glistening knot of Molly's admirers. 'I been holding on to this box since I come through the door – and now I can present it to you. And a merry Christmas, if I may say so.'

'Oh – thank you, thank you – merry Christmas, Mister Len. Come on, Timmy – let's see what's inside it, shall we?'

Timmy did not need to be encouraged any more than that. He threw off the lid of the box, and then just stared into it.

'Oh!' said Mary, genuinely gratified. 'Crackers! Oh how perfect! It's the one thing I didn't get you know, Len, because . . . well quite frankly because they were so jolly expensive! You really shouldn't have, you know. But I'm ever so grateful.'

And Jackie's voice had once more risen and was filling the room.

'Right ho, ladies and gents! Line up, if you please – no shoving at the back, mind. We have a feast now for your delectation . . . think that's the bleeding word . . .' he put in in a jocular undertone, bowing in due acknowledgement at the ensuing roar of approval. 'We got chicken – roast chicken, yum yum yum – and sausages and taters and . . . well everything really, ladies and gents. Oh – and there's a goose and all, but I wouldn't be too sure about that because Mary, she cooked that, so you never know, do you really?'

Amid the calls of mock-chiding and the general jeering, Mary blew out her cheeks and turned her face both this way and that and she beamed in pleasure and stamped her foot so that everyone could have a chance of witnessing all this bogus outrage.

'He's a one,' laughed Len. 'You got a right one there with Jackie and no mistake, Mary. No but listen, them crackers, they come from the brewery – gratis, sort of style. And I thought, well

– why go wasting them on a load of old boozers down the Rose & Crown when I could be wasting them on a load of old boozers up here!'

'Less of the "old" and the "boozers" if you don't mind, Len!' hooted Mary, batting away with a flapping hand any more of his nonsense. 'Well look now, Timmy. Crackers! What do you think of that?'

He had barely taken his eyes off the rank of red and green crêpe paper-covered crackers since he had opened the box. He fingered one of the stuck-on coloured scraps, depicting Santa on his sleigh. His eyes, it seemed to Mary, had doubled in size as he raised them to ask her:

'What *are* they . . . ?'

Mary was all ready to laugh again, but then she was touched and her face was checked in the middle of the impulse.

'Come with me,' she said. 'Take the box and take my hand, and come with me.'

The table now was very much the centre of activity: Sheila rushed up to tell Mary that the goose, it was just so perfect – moist and tender and so very full of flavour, she said it was – and Dickie, whose straining mouth was crammed full of something or other – he merely widened his eyes in appreciation, while signalling a double thumbs-up. Mary introduced a now quite startled Timmy to first of all Jackie ('How do, young feller!') and then to Sheila – who smiled quite peremptorily (she's never been at ease, Sheila, not with children, Mary just had to acknowledge) and then she confided to Mary in a confidential rush that she was that worried about the pudding now because to be perfectly honest, you know, I feel that it might just be a little on the dry side, you see, and what if there isn't enough to go round? Sally – brandishing a half-eaten sausage in a boisterous attempt to attract the attention of Jackie – still joshing around with Alfie and Jeanie – so that he might just put a drop more port into this glass of hers, if he would be so good – Sally said that she couldn't help but overhear that, Sheila, pardon me I'm sure for doing so, but if there wasn't enough pudding then there was plenty of fruit – and had Mary had the time to notice, by the by, that all them apples, she had polished each one of them personally?

Mary assembled for Timmy a brimming plateful of food – a little bit of everything, and then an extra piece of chicken because he had bolted down the first so extraordinarily quickly, it must clearly be his favourite. Mary then added a heap to Lorna's plate and Imogen's plate, because the portions they had allowed themselves were so terribly meagre – and the very youngest boy, whose name was Little Davy (he had whispered it into Mary's ear and made her promise that this was to be just their secret, and that she mustn't ever tell anyone else in the whole wide world – and his intensity, and the tickle of the whisper, they brought her near to tears) – Little Davy, he had been eating his way through the bag of fruit jellies that Mary had set down on the table, and she had to very quickly assure an outraged Lorna that it was perfectly all right, no truly, and maybe now he'd like a drumstick, yes? And Jackie, she called across to him – see to everyone's drinks now, will you, because I've got to go and take care of the baked potatoes (they should have been done before). Oh hallo again, Mr Stone – are you enjoying the party? Have you got enough to eat, and everything? And Mrs Stone – she's all right, I hope? Hasn't moved, has she? Still just sitting by the fire, I see.

'Goose good. Is not cheap. Mrs Stone, not eat animal. I give her tomato and yellow fruit.'

'Yellow fruit? Oh – you mean the pineapple. What – you mean she's just had a tomato and a pineapple segment?'

'And lemonade. She happy.'

Mary and Mr Stone then both glanced across at her, sitting by the fire and looking down intently at her two white hands clutching an empty plate.

'Not *look* happy . . .' conceded Mr Stone. 'Since must leave Germany . . . not look happy.'

Mary nodded. 'It must have been so awful for you – just forced out, like that.'

Mr Stone shook his head. 'Not talk.'

Mary touched his arm, and with a quick sympathetic smile, she said she was sorry to break away but she just must see now to the baked potatoes (they should have been done before). Why don't you, Mr Stone, go and pull a cracker with that little boy over there? See him? He's called Timmy, and it would please him very much – and you will help yourself to another drink, won't you Mr Stone?

'I have beer. Tenk you. Cracker. Not cheap . . .'

It was when Mary was back in the kitchenette, and smarming quite generous knifefuls of goose fat into the burst-open and steaming-hot baked potatoes that she heard at first just the great and glorious roar of wonder and approval, and only when it had slightly died down did the wonderful music begin to get through to her, and she immediately then let go of the knife, forgot the potatoes, and wiping the flats of her hands down the front of her pinny, she skipped back out and into the throng and was immediately and so utterly thrilled by the sound of 'You Couldn't Be Cuter', Al Bowlly singing it so much more richly than at any time she had ever heard him on the wireless. Gosh – it's so loud! It's just as well we invited Mr and Mrs Stone along, isn't it really? Or else there'd be the dickens to pay, now. And already – oh my golly, just look at the two of them! – Len had taken Molly by the hand and they were sort of I suppose you could call it dancing now in a space that had magically cleared – and Alfie and Jeanie, they're both there too now, doing a sort of American jiggy style of a step, is what that is (because Mary, she'd seen a photo montage of all those movements in *Picture Post* barely more than a month ago). All the men from the pub and Dickie now too were clustering around the sleek and

gleaming gramophone, praising a very proud Jonathan Leakey
for the total wonder of it all, Mary could only imagine, and all
clearly eager to know more about it. Jonathan Leakey was
stroking the brilliantly glossy cabinet, inhaling deeply a Senior
Service, and happy to indulge them – although his eye, in
common with those of the rest of them, Mary could hardly stop
herself from observing, would keep on sliding sideways to the
vision of Molly, her hips now wagging really quite sinuously,
much to the red-faced and bloated delight of Len, who had himself now given up any pretence of dancing – he seemed more
than content to just stand to the side now and clap quite eagerly,
egging her on with his bulbous eyes. Mary had never seen Molly
in this way before – it was all something of a revelation to her.

'I say!' shouted Dickie to Jonathan Leakey over the din of the
machine. 'This is really quite the most splendid thing, I must say.
Often thought I wanted one. Dashed expensive, I daresay. Come
down soon I suppose, though. This sort of thing, it generally
does. Oh – record over, old man. Listen to everyone – they want
more music, Jonny. Oh – hallo Jackie, old fellow. This is a bit of a
corker, wouldn't you say? This gramophone caper.'

'Come on Jonny!' urged Jackie now, clapping Jonathan Leakey
about the shoulders. 'Slap on another record then, there's a good
lad. Keep the party going, ay? But none of that jazzy stuff. Keep
it light, that's the ticket. Here lads – got you another beer. Cheers,
ay? Having a good time, are you? Have to lay in a few more
though, I reckon . . . anywhere open, you think?'

Jonathan Leakey had carefully lowered another record on
to the turntable, and after all the hissing and just a bit of crackle,
there came a great yell of pleasure from all over the room as Fred
Astaire was blithely telling them all that Anything Goes.

'I thought of that one, Jackie. Why I just nipped out – looked
like you needed a few reinforcements. Got a couple crates in the
back of the Humber, you inclined to go and fetch them up.'

'You're a good 'un, Jonny!' cried Jackie, slapping his back again. 'That were the only thing what were bothering me – us running out of wallop. Come all on your own then, did you? Can't say I blame her, whoever she is. But it's a good little party though, ay?'

'Tip-top,' enthused Dickie. 'Utterly tip-top, I'd say.'

Jonathan Leakey shook his head. 'Tip-top . . . dear oh dear. What a toff. No but it is, Jackie – cracking, this is. There were some woman I were going to bring along, yeh – couldn't be bothered to ask her, when it come to it. But talking of that – who's the lady? One over there.'

'What?' checked Jackie. 'Oh – what, her with the bum? Yeh – she's all right she is, ain't she? That's Molly, that is. Lives downstairs.'

Jonathan Leakey eyed her narrowly, and nodded very slowly.

'Handy . . .' he said. 'For some.'

'Now now now,' Jackie mock-admonished him. 'You forget yourself, Jonny: I'm spoken for, I am.'

'Yeh. It looked like it round at Mr Wisely's, didn't it? Eyes on stalks, they was.'

Jackie looked about him quickly.

'You just shush about that now, Jonny. What you thinking of?'

Jonathan Leakey chuckled quite softly.

'Oh yeh – and talking about that night . . .' he said, pulling out something quite crumpled from the inside of his jacket and presenting it formally to a rather surprised Dickie. 'Yours, I fancy.'

'Mine? Oh – oh I say! It's my jolly old hat. Oh I say – top-hole. Where was it, old man? In the car, was it? Thought it had to be. Well thanks an awful lot – jolly decent of you.'

'My pleasure, Mr Weak.'

Dickie's grin was caught and frozen.

'No now look – let's just get this straight, shall we? Once and for all. Firstly – I'm not a *toff*. And secondly – it's *Wheat*. All right? Dickie *Wheat*.'

Jonathan Leakey gazed at him, amused.

'I know. I don't know why you keep on *doing* that. Wheat – what I said.'

'Here – shut up you two. Take a look at this, then. Jonny – you want a fag, do you?'

'Blimey Jackie – that's a first, that is: you giving me a fag.'

And then, with an exaggerated flourish, Jackie had snapped open in front of Jonathan Leakey's face his brand-new cigarette case, and Jonathan Leakey simply raised his eyebrows by way of acknowledgement – and then he leant down as Jackie attended to the end of the cigarette with a click of his lighter.

'Santa been good to you,' said Jonathan Leakey, exhaling a plume of blue with an audible sigh. 'Initials and all. Nice to see you're beginning to appreciate the better things in life. Aye aye – you got a visitor, Jackie.'

Jackie glanced around in the direction of Jonathan Leakey's nod of the head, and there was that little puny-looking girl, the one who'd been hanging around the door, back then. Just standing there staring at me, she is now, and wringing her fingers: looks a bit worried, do she?

'Help you, can I?' asked Jackie, pulling a generous swig from the bottle of Bass (set my glass down a while back, blowed if I know where). 'Get you something?'

'I'm ever so sorry to trouble you, mister,' stuttered out Lorna, apparently tortured, even to speak. 'I would've said to Mary, but I think she must of gone to the toilet or something, pardon my language.'

Jackie, raising an eyebrow, glanced from Dickie to Jonathan Leakey, and then looked back at Lorna.

'Yeh . . . ?'

'Well there's crying coming from the room. You can't hear it unless you're real close up. I think it must be your Jeremy.'

Jackie clapped the heel of his hand hard to his forehead.

'Blimey – litle Jeremy. Clean forgot about the little sod. I'd best go and—'

'It's just,' cut in Lorna, her hands still writhing – Dickie was no expert, but it looked to him as if she was almost attempting to tug out each knuckle from its connecting joint: haven't often encountered social anxiety on this sort of scale (although I suspect that round here it could well be endemic). 'It's just – my sister Imogen – she's ever so good with the little 'uns, and if you was happy about it – well maybe she could maybe . . .'

It was only then that Jackie spotted her, half behind her sister Lorna – her shoulders were shrivelled within themselves and her eyes cast resolutely downwards: it was as if she was willing her own invisibility.

'Well . . .' considered Jackie. 'Yeh. That would be lovely, if you're sure . . .'

Imogen turned immediately and went to the bedroom door – opened it just barely, and then she had slipped inside and closed it behind her.

Mary then appeared quite suddenly from somewhere, and Lorna rushed over to tell her the news. Mary – she seemed to be saying something or other back to her, Jackie couldn't be sure, because over where he was still standing Jonathan Leakey had just put another record on to the turntable, see – bit too jazzy, this one, for my liking – and there's a little kid all around my legs now, Timmy he says his name is, and he's wagging a cracker at me and he says will I pull it with him, only he gets to keep for hisself whatever's inside of it – cheeky little bleeder, ain't he? You got to love them, though; reckon I would've been just the same when I were a lad – but me, them days, never had nothing I could call my own. Christmas crackers? Never heard of them. So yeh – I'm bending down to him now, and I got to jam my fag into the corner of my mouth, let the ferret see the rabbit (only got one eye on the job though, because the smoke, it ain't half playing merry gyp with the other one, I'm telling you) and now I got the end of the cracker all crumpled and tight in my hand – and look at him, will you? Look at little Master Timmy here – both hands on his end, hauling away like he's dragging at a carthorse, red in the face he is – and whoop! There – that got it, nice little snap and he's near fell over, this little kid here – but he's righted hisself now and he's down on his hands and knees, look, and sorting through all the bits of cracker and his face as he come up with . . . I don't know, looks like a little tin whistle, sort of a thing – he's all smiles, look, and now he's only tooting on the bloody thing, fit to bust – going to drive me nuts, that is, what with the jazzy music going thirteen to the dozen in my other ear. But it's nice though, ain't it? Way it just takes a little thing like that to make a kid so bleeding happy: it's nice, that.

Mary was beside him then – ruffling Timmy's hair as he skipped about, blowing into his whistle.

'My, that's a wonderful thing that you've got there, isn't it Timmy? Yes it is. Now listen – if you go over to Auntie Sheila at the table . . . do you see her? Lady with the blue dress and – oh my goodness, Jackie – do you see? Look at her! What is that she's got on her head? A little clown hat, or something – where on earth did that come from? Well listen, Timmy, you go over to that lady over there and she'll give you a great big bowl of pudding. Would you like that? Yes – I thought you would. And she might even pull another cracker with you. Oh gosh *look* at him, Jackie – I've never seen anyone move so quickly! It's lovely, isn't it, having all these children here. It makes it so much more . . . I don't know – Christmassy, really. And you know I've just been in to see Jeremy – and that little Imogen girl, she's only fifteen you know, but she's, well – perfect with him. Quite perfect. Got him smiling and laughing, playing with all his toys. I expect she's been a mother all her life, poor little thing. Never been allowed to be a child herself.'

'Good to know though, ain't it?' said Jackie. 'Might be useful, you ever want a break. I expect you like this song, do you . . . ? Yeh – thought you might. Too jazzy for my liking. Take it off Jonny, there's a good boy. What else you got?'

'Have you had food and everything, Jackie? If you want some of Sheila's pudding I'd get over there quite quickly, if I were you. It's going fast – and it's awfully good, I must say. I had just the tiniest mouthful, and would you believe it – I got the sixpence! I gave it back to Sheila and told her to slip it into Timmy's portion, poor little mite: I doubt he's ever had a sixpence to himself. It's going so well, isn't it Jackie? The party. It's going really really well, I think.'

Jackie was about to take another big swig out of his bottle of Bass, but then he shook it, held it up to the light, and set it down with a sigh. Reckon I'll get myself down to Jonny's Humber in a minute – fetch up the rest of it. He nudged Mary sharply as he made a very great show of getting out his cigarette case, flipping it open and carefully extracting a Senior Service in the exaggerated manner that he thought a toff might do it, with two quite stiff and pernickety fingers. He pointed out to her his initials on the lighter and the arch of his eyebrows told a delightedly laughing Mary, who hung on his shoulder now, to take a very good butcher's at that, then. He touched the flame to the cigarette's end, sucked down a lungful, and exhaled the shaft of blue with slow and quite luxurious deliberation. Feeling very contented now, he leant his back against the wall, his narrowed and smoke-stung eyes set to roaming around the scene before him. Mary now, she's drifted off to have another little natter with Sheila, shouldn't be surprised – and look, she's a good little hostess, that one, because she's gone over to the fireside – touched that miserable old bastard Stone on the shoulder, offering to get the two of them something or other, I should think she's doing. Looking at that wife of his, it's maybe no wonder he's never got a smile on him – make you want to pray for death, that one would, ugly old cow. What I can't still understand is what they want to come over here for. Why can't they stay in their own bleeding country? Mary says it's because if they hadn't got out when they did, then they'd be chucked out or even killed, she says, but I just can't see it. I mean – they're *Germans*, ain't they? So bleeding stay in Germany, why don't you? We got enough Jew capitalists in London, screwing the likes of me – we don't need to go shipping in more of the bastards just because their own country's gone and kicked them out. And he gets to buy this house – that's the bit I can't stomach – and here I am slaving my guts out paying him rent: no, whichever way you look at it, it just can't, that – it just can't be right. Englishman's home his castle? Do me a favour. Not nowadays, it ain't – not when you're paying out money to some bleeding foreign Jew-boy what can't even speak to you proper. Still – sod him. What else we got here . . . ? What else is going on in this merry little festive scene? Jonny, he just gone and stuck another bottle of Bass in my hand – and I bless him for it: must've been down to his car, then – he's a good lad, Jonny, you get to know him. Got this great cigar stuck into his face, at the minute. Reckon it's the one what he got off of Mr Wisely, that time. It's a right laugh though, ain't it? When he and Dickie gets together. It's like a music hall act – you can't barely credit it, they're so bleeding different. And there's old Dickie now, look – arms above his head, his glass of beer swaying around and slopping down his sleeve, and he thinks he's dancing, do he? Jumping about – and he ain't at all in time with this record we got on now, couldn't tell you what it is. Not too jazzy, though – not too bad. Singer keeps on saying Okay Toots, far as I can make out. Okay Toots, I ask you. Them Americans, they're everywhere now. In the pictures, in the papers – everywhere you look. Okay Toots. What's toots? Ay? What little Timmy do on his whistle, that's all I know. Hanging about Molly from downstairs, Dickie is now – but them old sods from the Rose & Crown (only know two of them, and then just to nod to – don't know why Len brung them over) – they're doing their all not to let him get a look in. Every time she go for a fag – and she is, give her her due, she's a very fair little looker, that Molly – there's all these lighters and Swan Vestas coming out at her. Dear oh dear – don't think Dickie's got a hope with that lot – and if Sheila catches a sight of him, he'll be in for it good and proper, tell you that. And here comes Jonny – Jonny's moving in on her now – circling around her like a cat, he is – stroking them few bristles up on his lip: looks like he going ahead with the tache idea, then. Might suit him, hard to say. There's Len – he's over with Sheila at the moment – and what's he up to? Pouring the cherry brandy what he brung all over her bit of pudding – she's looking not sure about it, but she bungs a spoonful in her mouth now – and yeh! Oh yeh! Big grin, look – she likes that all right, our Sheila. Look at that Timmy lad! Got his little brother on his knee, he has – and he's stuffing . . . what are they? Into his face. Oh yeh – it's them little packets of chocolate off of the tree (and I do, time to time, have to do that, don't I? With Mary. Little white lies – it's kinder, see, in the long run. You like to spare them what you can). So yeh – hadn't been promised the loan of anything at all, had I? Like what she said – who'd be lending Christmas tree ornaments on Christmas Day? She ain't no fool. But I go into the tobacconist – weren't expecting him to be open, if I'm honest – because that box of fags what Mary got me, well, won't last no time, and you never do know, not at Christmas time, when you're ever going to get hold of anything again, you see, because all the shops, they ain't normal are they? And he do a little line on the confectionery side, old geezer in there, and then I see them – all these little stacks of chocolate, all done up and festive, they was. Got them ever so cheap – and he, he were right pleased to get them off of his hands, you could easy tell that: thought he were going to be stuck with them, so he more or less give them away. Well – won't last too long the way's Timmy's going it, look – it's one for his brother and two for him, far as I can make out. Mouth all covered in brown, it is – he'll be sick as a dog later on, shouldn't be surprised. Still – what Christmas is about really, ain't it? Feeling a bit woozy myself – lost track of how many of them Basses I got down me. But look – Boxing Day tomorrow: sleep it off.

What I'm going to do – I'm going to get myself over to the corner there and have a chat with that little brother of mine – looks ever so smart, he do, that suit he got. Proud of him, I tell you. One of us had to do good, didn't we? And I ain't really spoke to this girl of his, Jeanie. So yeh – don't see too much of him, do I? So I reckon I'll have a word, now I got the chance. Give a big cough, is what I think I'll have to do when I come up to them – having a right little canoodle, they is: proper pair of lovebirds. All grown up now, Alfie is – good job in an office, nice little girlfriend: real man, he turned into.

'Hallo Mary love – I'm just off to have a word with Alfie. You all right, are you? What was that song all about then? What's a toot?'

'Mm – Alfie looks like he might be quite busy to me,' smiled Mary. 'Oh I'm *completely* all right, Jackie. This is the best party ever! And I do so love you, Jackie. And it's not a *toot*, silly – it's *toots*. You know – it's an expression they have. Like darling, or something. Deary – something like that. Harry Roy and his orchestra, that was. Oh Lorna! Lorna – come over here. Sheila's got just one more bit of pudding left, and I know you haven't had any. Come on – come over here, don't be shy.'

Right little wonder, Mary is – always seeing to everyone but herself. I got a real treasure there with Mary, you know – and I won't never let her go. (If it means darling or deary, why can't they bleeding say so? What do they want to go and say toots for?)

'Now then, Alfie – let's be having you. Straighten up now, lad – you ain't married yet, you know. Look lively. What's this brute doing to you Jeanie, ay? Not even under the mistletoe . . .'

Jeanie laughed very lightly as she put a hand on Alfie's shoulder and pulled herself away from him. She patted her hair, smoothed her hands down the length of her dress – nice dress, blue and white stripes – and then her little varnished pinkie nail came up to the corner of her mouth which she pursed quite briefly, dabbed there twice, and then she let it alone. Blushing, she attempted to appear demure, but was really far too flushed and contented for any of that.

'It's a lovely party, Jackie,' she said quite happily.

'Told you,' put in Alfie. 'I said it would be. My brother Jackie – if he puts on a party, then he puts on a party – ay Jackie mate?'

'Yeh well,' smiled Jackie, 'you do what you can, don't you? So listen – you two been seen to all right, have you? Plenty of scoff? Kept your whistles wet, yeh? Get yourself another one, Alfie lad – my mate Jonny, he just gone and heaved us up another couple crates. No? You sure? Well it's there when you want it. So tell me then, Jeanie love – what you get up to when you ain't hanging around this young villain here then, ay?'

'Well – I'm training to be a shorthand typist, as a matter of fact. Ooh – I love this song. I love this one, Alfie – Whistling In The Dark, I think it's called. And what do you *mean*, Jackie? *Villain?* My Alfie's no villain – he's a good boy, he is. Aren't you, Alfie? No but I was working in Huntley & Palmers, but I couldn't stick it any more. It got so's when I got home and put my feet up with a nice cup of tea, I just couldn't stand the sight of a digestive.'

Jackie laughed. 'Took the biscuit, that job, did it? Yeh – all right, all right: stale one. Get it? No? Please yourself. No but well I reckon you're best off with your typing, Jeanie love – oi, watch where you're going, you! Oh Gawd it's Len – lumbering about like a bleeding elephant, he is. Carry on like that in the Rose & Crown and he'd have you out on your ear. Aye aye – look at him now. See him? I know what he's up to. Here – watch this, Alfie. This'll be a laugh, this will. See? See he's gone up to old Sally there. She's from the greengrocers, she is. Big girl, ain't she? If you know what I mean. No disrespect nor nothing, Jeanie. And yeh – thought so. Look where he's taking her – right under the old mistletoe! Go on then, Len! Go on, boy! Yeh – that's it. A right big smoochy one he just plonked on her . . . and look at Sally, will you? She don't mind a bit. Well well well. That'd be the greengrocers, see. Knows all about fresh.'

Alfie and Jeanie were laughing at that – and looking at each other quite longingly again. Mary had weaved her way up to them, and then she was tugging sharply at Jackie's sleeve.

'Jackie – can you come over and sort something out? It's those men – the ones that Len brought along. Molly – I think she's quite upset.'

He'd just caught sight now of Molly and the knot of them over there in the corner, and already he was squeezing his way through, Mary holding his hand and tagging on behind. Whoopsy . . . dear oh me: felt just a little bit wobbly there, I did – eyes went funny: reckon it's the heat. Fire's still blazing away, look, and there's quite a fair few of us, you know, crammed into this room. Yeh: reckon it's the heat what's got to me.

'Now then – what's all going on here then, ay? Someone annoying you, Molly love?'

'Didn't mean no harm . . .' slurred one of the men – collar abandoned and up on one side, a lump of hair over his brow – squinting to the left of Jackie's shoulder. 'Entering the party spirit, like.'

Molly was dabbing at her mascara with a little lacy handkerchief that came away smudged, and damp.

'It's all right, Jackie. I just think I'll go back downstairs now, if you don't mind. Sorry Mary – bit tired anyway. Think I'll just go back down now . . .'

'Oh are you *sure*, Molly – it's not too late yet, you know,' said Mary, putting an arm around her shoulder. 'Do something, Jackie . . .'

'You don't have to go nowhere,' said Jackie. And then he addressed the shifting wreckage of this sheepish cluster of men. 'Now look – I don't properly know you lot—'

'I'm Reg,' said the one who had spoken earlier. 'There's Dave here, and this is Arnold. We didn't mean nothing, Jackie. Lovely party . . .'

Reg – Jackie could see it – was frightened of him, and this made him a bit more assertive than otherwise he could in all honesty have been bothered to be.

'Yeh? Well listen, Reg. Listen to me Dave and Arnold. I'm right glad you liked the party what I never even bleeding invited you to – and now you gone and upset a lady, see? And I'm not having it. So what I suggest, gents, is that you get yourself down them stairs – sort of right now, if you take my meaning. Else a few of us'll have something to say. All right?'

Reg was nodding and putting down his glass.

'All right, Jackie – all right. We didn't mean no offence. Don't want no trouble. We'll be off. Yeh – course we will. Come on, lads – let's be getting away. Sorry, um – Mary, is it? Yeh. Well – sorry, ay?'

The three of them shuffled away, and Jackie kept an eye on them until they were out of the door. Then he was jolted off balance as Dickie more or less fell into the back of him, his rolling eyes just barely contained in a face now looking as if it had been braised.

'Whoop! Sorry, old man. Oh dear me. What was all that about, hey? I say listen, Jackie dear chap. Jonathan Leakey – he's just come up with the most topping idea, don't you know. God it's hot in here. Come over – come over and hear what he's got to say. Topping idea – quite wizard.'

'You go, Jackie,' said Mary. 'I'll just stay here and take care of Molly.'

'Oh no,' protested Molly – sniffing bravely and perking herself up. 'You don't have to take care of me, honestly Mary. I'm quite fine now. Sorry, Jackie – and thank you for – Feel so silly, I do.'

Jackie just patted her cheek, and then he turned and reeled away with both his arms about a staggering Dickie.

Mary got Molly to sit, and tried to get her to sip a little cherry brandy.

'What happened, Molly? What did they say?'

'Oh – it was nothing, I suppose. It wasn't what they said, really – it was just . . . me, I was worried about. Who I am.'

'Who you are? Whatever can you mean, Molly? Oh – *ow* . . . !'

Molly looked up in concern and saw Mary's whole face pulled tight and so in the grip of something, as the fingers of one hand were probing her midriff.

'What is it, Mary? Are you all right? Oh my goodness —!'

But Mary's closed eyes had relaxed a bit now, and her face – though still uncertain – was coping with a smile of easy reassurance.

'Mm . . . yes, it's all right now. I get it more and more, though. It's this – *thing* I've got inside of me. I shouldn't really be talking about it. But I don't think it can be right, you know. It's always – there. I can never forget that it's there. And then sometimes it . . . well. Never mind. Too boring for words. I'm perfectly all right now. Now tell me, Molly – what did they do to you, those horrible beery men?'

'You sure? You sure you're all right, Mary? Well . . . oh – nothing. Nothing at all, really. They just – they said would I like to go to a drinking club they know. Soho, I think they said. Don't even know where that is. A drinking club! I don't even drink – all I've had is a sherry and a ginger wine. Should've just walked away, but I didn't like to. And then one of them, can't remember which – Arnold, it could have been – he sort of looked at me in a certain *way*, if you know what I . . . But the thing is, Mary – why did they ask me? Why did they think I would go with them? I don't, do I? I don't look like that sort of a girl? Do I?'

Molly's eyes were imploring, her fingers bunched so tensely.

'Oh of *course* you don't, Molly. They were drunk, that's all. Couldn't even see straight.'

Molly's wet eyes had risen up to face her, and a rounded tear began to roll.

'Should I not have danced, do you think? Was that a bad thing to do? But I love to dance, you see Mary. It's a thing I love to do . . .'

Mary closed her eyes and shook her head and took hold of Molly's white and tightened fists.

'There's nothing wrong with *dancing*. And you dance very well, Molly – I was watching you. It's just . . . men. They see things . . . differently. And they were very horrid anyway, and utterly drunk, and I don't even know why they were here in the first place – so you must just put them completely out of your mind and – oh! Listen! It's You Couldn't Be Cuter again. Oh it's my favourite, this one. Come on, Molly – dance with *me*. No come on – let's dance. I'd really like to.'

And Mary led a pathetically grateful and simpering Molly into the tiny scrap of space in front of the gramophone, and the two of them began to move their feet, at first quite tentatively, and then with this growing awareness of fun and assurance that burst into a gale of joy and abandon that had Jonathan Leakey now up on his feet and quite openly applauding – and Mary was so happy again as Molly just threw back her head and laughed and laughed and laughed while Mary kept spinning her around in an ever-increasing circle as Sheila and Len and Sally and even little Lorna gathered about and clapped them on.

'That's what you want to see!' shouted Jonathan Leakey to Jackie, over all this din around him. 'People enjoying theirselves. That's what you want to see at a party, ay Jackie? So come on – what you think of the idea? Cracker, ay?'

Jackie was nodding with enthusiasm and tapping his feet to You Couldn't Be Cuter while swigging away from a bottle of Bass – and this caused quite a cascade of ale from out of the side of his mouth there, look, but he handled that deftly by righting his head and setting down the bottle and passing the back of his hand once and quickly and then again across his mouth.

'Yeh, Jonny – like it a lot. But you sure we'll all fit in?'

'Well – it ain't no charabang. But we're all right for six of us. Seven at a pinch . . . us lot and Mary, course . . . that Molly girl, maybe . . .'

'Seven, ay? I'll have a word with Mary, see what she reckons. You're right you know, Dickie – it *is* bleeding hot in here. Think I got to just sit down for a bit. Blimey, look at the sight of that table – what a wreck, ay? Yeh – just sit down a bit, I reckon. But here – there's your car and all, ain't there Dickie? Not just Jonny's Humber, is it?'

Dickie, his back quite flat against the wall – his head just boiling and his fingers so suddenly cold now, they felt, as if they were bonding with the glass that he just about managed to dangle from them – closed his eyes in defiance to that.

'No can do, Jackie old son. If I were to drive anywhere, I'd kill the lot of us, I am not joking. Don't know how Mr Leakey does it, to be frank with you. Jonny, I mean. Jonny. Think I need some air . . .'

Jonathan Leakey smiled. 'You get to pace it, when you're a bit older, son. Don't never know when you're going to be needing to get away quick from something, if you know what I'm saying.

Always you got to be ready. Without a motor, well – could be the end of you. Oh look, Jackie – your lady friend's come calling again.'

Jackie looked up from the chair he was slumped in and just about made out the face of that skinny little girl – what was her name . . . ?

'I just wanted to say thank you ever so much,' stuttered out Lorna. 'I never had so much fun – not in all my life. But I ought to be getting my brothers and sister now. It's time we was going. I'd say it to Mary – but look at her! She'll be dancing for ever!'

Jackie cocked an eye over to Mary and Molly who were still gyrating around there and waving their arms and cackling like a couple of loonies, seemed like to Jackie.

'No listen, Dawn – you can't go yet because we're all of us off on a little trip, My friends and me are – and you're invited, see?'

'Oh no please – honestly. I couldn't go nowhere.'

'Yeh you can – look, here's Mary. She'll tell you. Mary – come over here, girl. We got a plan. Come and listen. Yeh you're right, Dickie – bit of air, that's what we all need . . .'

'I can't come anywhere,' insisted Lorna. 'You wouldn't want me.'

'Yeh you *can*,' Jackie was drawling. 'And we *do* want you, Dawn, course we do – don't we Mary?'

'I don't know what you're talking about Jackie, do I? And this is Lorna – her name's Lorna, not Dawn.'

'Yeh?' checked Jackie. 'Well why didn't she say so then? Anyway – never mind that. What we're going to do – we're all of us going to get into Jonny's little motor car and tool off and look at all the lights up West. How's about that?'

Mary looked at Lorna, and their eyes in an instant were fused by delight. Mary clapped her hands, and Lorna, she just stood there and looked so dazed.

'Humber . . .' muttered Jonathan Leakey. 'Nothing little about it . . .'

'Oh I think that's just a *wonderful* idea,' Mary was enthusing – and then her face just gently clouded. 'Oh but Jackie – we can't, can we? Jeremy. What about Jeremy? We can't go and leave him.'

Jackie nodded. 'Yeh. Course. Jeremy. Forgot about that. Not like the old days, is it Mary? Come and go as we pleased . . .'

'Oh no but listen,' said Lorna quite suddenly – and Mary, Jackie, Jonny and even Dickie were looking at her now, because the directness and animation in her voice were both quite new to all of them. 'It'll be all right. Come – come and look.'

And with no further word, Lorna quite excitedly set off for the bedroom – Mary hauling Jackie to his feet and somehow or other managing to get them both over there. Lorna was gently easing open the door, and after a quick glance over to Mary, she peeked inside. Then she beckoned to the two of them – Mary and Jackie – to come and take a look. Jackie, thought Mary, is not at all up to this – so I'll just prop him over here for the minute (I would signal over to Dickie to come and give me a bit of help, but just look at him, will you? In an even worse state, still flat against the wall. Where's Sheila got to . . . ? Oh there she is – over by the fireplace, talking to Mr Stone). Right then – I'll just sort of crane my neck around Lorna, and . . . *aaah*! Oh just look! What a little picture. Jeremy is fast asleep across the bed, his nose just nuzzling the muzzle of his teddy, and so is Imogen, her arm about him. On the other side are Timmy and Little Davy, their pale and peaky faces caked with chocolate, and flecked by saliva, the cradle of Timmy's fingers still loosely clutching all the booty from the crackers – the whistle and a little wooden pop-gun, a couple of balloons and heaven only knew what else it was he'd got there.

'They'll be all right,' said Lorna quite earnestly. 'If you just maybe could write a little note, so's Imogen ain't feared if she wake up later. Do you have a bit of milk, maybe, you could leave out for them? It's Little Davy – it quiets him, if he's troubled.' She maybe saw the flicker of hesitation dart into Mary's eyes, and so Lorna rushed on now to reassure her: 'Honest, Mary – Imogen, she's a wonder with the little 'uns. She won't never let you down.' And then she turned to face her, and her voice dropped lower and it became so intense. 'Please, Mary – *please*. Say yes. I ain't never seen them. I heard about them so many times, the lights up West – but never in my life have I seed them. So please do, Mary. Say yes.'

Mary was touched by how piteous Lorna's pleading had suddenly become, and on impulse she hugged her tight and told her that of *course* they could go, and that she knew quite well that Jeremy would be perfectly all right in the care of Imogen who did, she had to admit, appear to be an absolute natural for all this sort of thing. Well the whoop of joy that Lorna gave out then had her immediately clamping both her hands across her mouth as Mary was flapping agitated fingers and hissing at her to *shush* for heaven's sake or else she'd wake up the lot of them and then they'd all be up a gum tree. Lorna was wide-eyed with the simple need to obey, and nodding her immediate understanding she slowly and noiselessly closed the bedroom door and then turned away from it with a new and happy face.

'Oh Jackie,' Mary was cooing, 'you should have seen him. All tucked up and fast asleep, he is – and he's still cuddling Fluffy – isn't that sweet?'

'Cuddling what? Here, Jonny – we're on for the trip. Get your skates on, ay? I just got to sort out who's coming. He's cuddling what?'

'Well Sheila and Dickie,' said Mary. 'They've got to come, obviously. Fluffy, his teddy – have you forgotten already? And Molly, she could do with it, I expect – blow away the cobwebs. What about Alfie and Jeanie, though?'

'Too many. We can't be no more than the seven of us, unless someone wants to go up on the roof. I wouldn't worry about them two, though – I got a feeling they'll think of something they can be getting on with. What – we called the teddy Fluffy, did we? Can't recall that . . .'

'Mm, all right then – I'll go and talk to Sheila. You come with me – yes? Well *I* did – I called him Fluffy. You said it was stupid.'

'Well it is stupid – Fluffy. Cat's name, that is.'

'Who says it's a cat's name? It could be a dormouse's name or a puppy's name – it could be anything's name, Fluffy.'

'Excuse me, you two,' put in Jonathan Leakey. 'You think this could maybe wait for another time, do you? Only it'd be nice to see these lights before it's dawn and they go and turn the bleeding things off, if you know what I mean.'

Mary laughed, and covered her nose with her fingers.

'Sorry, Jonathan. Come on, Jackie – let's go and see Sheila. And so you managed to get some more petrol then, did you? For the car?'

Jonathan Leakey was looking rather puzzled.

'Petrol? Didn't need no petrol . . .'

'Yeh well,' interjected Jackie quite rapidly. 'Never mind all that – come on, we'll go and talk to Sheila. Jonny – be a good lad and go and see to old Dickie – see he ain't gone and died on us, ay? Right then – get your coat on Dawn, there's a good girl.'

'It's *Lorna*,' admonished Mary. 'Her name's Lorna – what's wrong with you?'

'Least I didn't call her Fluffy . . .' muttered Jackie. 'What's Sheila nattering on to that bleeding Jew-boy Stone for? He ain't got nothing to say for hisself. Can't even speak the King's bleeding English. And what's he still here for anyway? Why don't he get back to his hovel? And bring that face-ache of a wife with him.'

'Oh don't be so horrible, Jackie,' deplored Mary. 'He's not doing you any harm.'

'He do me harm to the tune of one pound two-and-nine a week, money-grubbing bugger that he is . . . !'

There was an edge to his voice now, and Mary – catching it immediately – glanced up at him as she felt inside her the flutter of alarm. Sometimes – quite often, really, and usually towards the end of an evening when he'd had maybe just more than a few, my Jackie, he can suddenly flare up – just like that, and over nothing at all, more often than not. Or he'll maybe start talking about something he shouldn't, and then someone will end up embarrassed or hurt. Me, usually – others, sometimes. Never him, though – until maybe the next morning when I lay it all before him, and listen again to all the remorse. Other times he denies it, or says he doesn't remember – which could easily be true. His face now though, it's become less rigid, not so red – the gleam in his eyes is fading, thank God. And what's this now . . . ? Oh it's Lorna: she's looking a bit anxious, and she keeps on pulling at my sleeve.

'The coats, Mary. They're all in the bedroom . . .'

'Oh my God, Jackie – the coats. What are we going to do?'

'Well,' thought Jackie, scratching his head (and blimey I do feel low – reckon I'll need a quick one, before the off), 'we're going in a car, ain't we? Maybe we don't need no coats.'

Lorna wrapped her arms about herself, as if in preparation for the shivering to come.

'Oh of *course* we'll need coats,' insisted Mary. 'It's absolutely freezing out there. Lorna – you'll have to go in and terribly carefully pull out everybody's coats and hats. All right? Think you can do it?'

Lorna nodded with eagerness. 'I'm sure I can, Mary.'

Jackie chuckled as Lorna ducked back into the bedroom, leaving the door very slightly ajar, and he and Mary made their way now to the fireplace.

'That one – she's that keen to go up West, reckon she'd move a herd of elephants, if she had to. Hiya, Len! What – you off then, are you?'

Len had wandered over with his arm around Sally, and was nodding with energy.

'Reckon I will, yeh Jackie. Been a lovely party. Wouldn't have missed it for all the tea in wossname. Best Christmas what I can recall.'

'Had a lovely time,' put in Sally. And then she signalled to Mary to come away and hear a whispered aside, just as Jackie was lobbing a laddishly knowing and archly raised eyebrow over in Len's direction – and Len fielded it deftly, nudged Jackie in the ribs and then gave out a throatily lascivious cackle.

'No listen – what I said to him, Mary,' rushed out Sally, 'was that yes, I'd be happy to accept his kind invitation to the back room in the Rose & Crown and drink a pink gin with him, seeing as how it's Christmas, and then I'd have to be getting myself home for my beauty sleep, see? And that's what I will do too, Mary. He got any other ideas, well – then he's in for a big surprise, that's all I can say.'

'Well all right then, Sally – but look after yourself, won't you?'

Sally gave her a theatrical wink.

'What you think? I were born yesterday? I've handled better men than him in my time, I can tell you that, my girl.'

Mary laughed. 'All right, Sally. Night then, Len – thanks ever so much for coming. And for the crackers – they were a godsend.'

'Only too pleased to be of service, madam,' pronounced Len, bowing from the waist. 'Come on then, Sally – let's get a nice drop of Gordon's down you, ay? Keep out the winter chill.'

Jackie slapped his back and pointed out to him the growing heap of coats and hats over on the floor there look, just outside the bedroom – as Lorna was sneaking out with another one to add to the pile.

'See you tomorrow – ay Len? Hair of the dog, shouldn't wonder. Wouldn't mind one right now, if I'm honest. Alfie! Over here, my son. Come on – come over here. Yeh. Now listen, Alfie – few of us setting off in the motor. Up West, sort of style – only there ain't enough room for—'

'Oh no, Jackie. Don't you worry about Jeanie and me. We're just off anyway. We'll be all right.'

'I *know* you'll be all right, you mucky little brother, you. Go on then – off you go, lad. Ever so good to see you, Alfie my son. Let's not leave it so long the next time, ay?'

'Had a great time, Jackie – we both did. That Mary – she's a lot better than what a bloke like you deserves. Champion, ain't she?'

'You're telling me, Alfie old lad. I don't know I'm born, with that one. I'm Jack the Lad, I am. And your Jeanie – she's all right and all, she is. Dead spit for that other Jean, ay? You know. So what – you get her in the Selfridge's sale, did you? Harlow – that's it.'

'Matter of fact, I met her at this course what I'm doing. Did I say? Learning French, I am.'

'You're having me on! Blimey – you go on this rate, next Christmas you'll be the blooming Prime Minister. French, ay? Oo la la – if you'll pardon my French.'

'Oh Jackie, oh Jackie! You don't get no better, do you?'

'Too old, son,' laughed Jackie. 'Set in my ways, see? Go on then, Alfie – me and Mary, we got to round up Sheila and Dickie now.'

The fire – well yeh, damped down a fair bit, but the heat what's still coming off of it, I'm telling you, it'd cook you, you wasn't careful. How the Stones and Sheila been sticking it for all this time I do not know. Air – that's what I need. Bit of fresh air: my head now, it's near to killing me.

'All right then, Sheila? Mary told you, has she? What we're up to? Yeh, good. Well listen, love – go and get Dickie crated up then, will you? Coats are all over by the door, look.'

Mary held on to Jackie's arm as she said quite carefully:

'Mr and Mrs Stone are just going back upstairs – isn't that what you were saying, Mr Stone? I expect you're both quite tired now . . .'

Mr Stone rose slowly from his chair and with so careful a deliberation, he set down his glass on the three-legged table. His wife now glanced up at him, ready to rise at any bidden moment.

'Tired . . .' sighed Mr Stone. 'Not tired . . . no different. Not sleep.' He jerked his head abruptly in Mrs Stone's direction. 'She – she sleep. Me – no. Is the way. So tomorrow – you take out *nails*, yes?'

Mary felt the stiffening in Jackie's upper arm, and she held on to it more tightly.

'Ay?' he said. 'What you say? *Nails*? What you on about?'

'Leave it, Jackie,' said Mary quickly. 'It's nothing – it's just how I pinned up the decorations, that's all. We've already talked about it.'

'Oh I *see*,' said Jackie more loudly, marvelling at his new understanding. 'So that's it, is it? End of the party – you've had yourself a nice old warm by the fire, you and your missus, ay Mr Stone? Couple glasses of ale, I daresay. Bit of goose. Nice slice of pudding. And what you got to say to us now, on Christmas bleeding Day – is mind you take out the bleeding *nails*.'

Jackie had coloured, and Mary now was holding him back – smiling with reassurance to Mr Stone and nudging Jackie briefly when he refused to catch her eye.

'Don't be silly, Jackie. Mr Stone – he's already thanked us – haven't you, Mr Stone?'

Mr Stone raised up his dipped eyes to meet her: they were filled with muted pain and an unspeakable regret.

'I tenk you . . . I not tenk you: what different? So – you go out, you come in quiet. Is rule.'

And Mary closed her eyes and winced now at the coming inevitability – she was powerless as Jackie pulled away sharply and brushed her to the side. His eyes were bulging and his forefinger was stabbing the air with force and repeatedly in front of the man's face.

'Now you just listen to me, Mr Stone – or Herr Stein, or whatever your bleeding name is. We got to pay rent to you, and I don't know why. You leave your country, and you think you can come over here and start lording it over the English. Well you're *wrong*, mate. You're a foreigner, and don't you forget it.'

Mary was flustered – she glanced over to Dickie, yes – where's Dickie? He's always so good at calming him down. Oh but my God – just look at him, will you? Sheila – she's fanning his face with one hand and with the other she's trying her best to cram an arm into his coat: he hardly seems aware of either process. Jackie – he's breathing so heavily now, still glaring, and waiting, I'm sure, for just any sort of reaction at all from Mr Stone, and it's that now that I am so very eager to avoid.

'Come on, Jackie – Jonathan, I think he's maybe waiting in the car. Let's go down now, yes? Come on – I'll get your coat.'

She knew it was hopeless, though, as she saw Mr Stone preparing to speak. The tone was low and mournful.

'Forget . . .? You want I forget I foreigner? Never I forget. Every place I foreigner. I not *leave* my country. Germany – she leave *me* . . .'

'Yeh?' shot back Jackie, stepping even closer to him. 'Well they must've had a *reason*. They don't want you – why you come here? Ay? What – you think *we* want you?'

Mr Stone now bowed his head and shook it very slowly, extending a hand towards his wife.

'No. Come please – we go. No – not think you want us.'

169

'*No,*' spat Jackie. 'Right. Because we don't. Our Prime Minister, Mr Chamberlain – you heard of him, have you? Our Prime Minister, he signed a thing, right? A wossname. Paper. With your Mr Hitler. So we're safe. He may have it in for the Czechs, but us, we're all right. It's you lot what stirred it up. You hadn't gone upsetting Hitler, then you wouldn't be here. It's you he wants to be at war with, not us. But you're getting us into *danger*. People is worried, and it's all on your account.'

Mr Stone raised his eyes, and as Mary saw them fill with tears, the light leached out of them; she thought she had never seen so deep a sadness. And can you be rigid, and also trembling?

'You . . .' he said, so softly. 'You . . . such stupid man.'

Then Mary had to immediately insert herself between the two of them, as she signalled quite frantically to Sheila to get over here now – right this second, oh please Sheila look at me! As Jackie's hands were reaching across her and grappling with the air, she grabbed them by the wrists and tried to tug them down, nearly weeping with frustration as she heard again the baleful sound of Mr Stone behind her:

'You think you *safe*? You see *Spain*, what happen?'

Jackie had allowed himself to be gripped by Mary, but his face now was dark red and livid and mottled pale at the side of his throat.

'I don't bleeding *care* about Spain, do I? *Or* the Czechs. Or bleeding *you*. It's England what I care about – and yeh, we *are* safe. And if we want to make sure of it, then what we should do, what this government should be doing, is packing all you lot back home where you come from. Sort out your own problems, and leave us alone.'

Sheila was here now, and so was Molly – each of them startled by the odour of this thrillingly new disturbance that was filling the room. By way of a series of improvised darted glances and energetic gestures, Mary managed to get Sheila to for God's sake make Mr and Mrs Stone go over to the door because I've got to now continue to smile up appeasement into Jackie's face – and Molly, glimpsing Mary, hesitantly took her lead and attempted to do the same. Jackie was breathing deep and slowly as if in conscientious recovery, following a quite strenuous exertion. He continued to stare into the space where Mr Stone had been standing, and then – so suddenly that Mary's mind was reeling again as she was thrown off guard – he spun around and staggered his focus over to the door and roared out lustily at the departing Mr Stone.

'It's *you* what's stupid! Don't you go calling me—! It's you! You're the one. If anyone around here's stupid, well then it's bleeding *you*, ain't it? Ay? Ain't it? Ay? Answer me! *Ain't* it . . . ?!'

Sheila quickly closed the door after Mr and Mrs Stone – leaned against the panels as she looked across to Mary, raising her eyebrows as she puffed out her cheeks. Mary still was slowly stroking Jackie's arm – up and then down, long and even strokes, as if she were now willing his pulse and heartbeat to be lulled and calm and assume the rhythm. Molly was sorting through the coats and Lorna appeared with a small glass of milk in her hand – she extended to Mary a note of some sort, and was seemingly quite unfazed by anything at all she might have heard or seen. Mary glanced down at the tottering capital letters that tiptoed their unsteady way across the paper: 'IMOGEN. GONN. THEN CUM BACK. LORNA'. Mary remembered and understood, and then Sheila rapidly bundled Dickie away as he lumbered over as if newly half-aware of maybe something now, having been drifting in and out of a troubled sleep. What's wrong, he wanted to know. Something up is there, old thing? No, Dickie – nothing. It's all right. Buck up – we'll go downstairs now, yes? Lorna bounded after them and Molly followed on, as Mary guided an urgently muttering and now very heavy-footed

Jackie towards the door. She raised his hand and kissed it, and she smiled up into his eyes.

'Come on now, Jackie love,' she softly whispered. 'We're off to see the lights.'

◉

As any woman will tell you, I expect – the trouble with Boxing Day is all the Christmas clearing up! The amount of dishes to be washed, I just couldn't believe it (some of them are Molly's – I'll have to bring them down to her). But standing in the kitchen all of the morning, boiling up kettles and my hands and arms all red and sore, I was put in mind of the laundry again – and that made me count my blessings, I can tell you. Because anything, any job you've got to do – believe me, it's nothing, nothing at all when you compare it to the laundry. It's probably, you know, because it was maybe too close to the fire . . . it's the tree that I'm thinking about now, because just in the space of a night and a morning, well – all the needles have dropped, they're just all over the mat; it's like a new-mown lawn down there and the tree itself, well – looking very sorry for itself, poor little thing, so very thin and rather brown, with just a few glass ornaments hanging on it now, because all those little parcels of chocolate, you know – every single one was eaten up. Not *entirely* by Timmy and Little Davy, I very much hope – else they will be two rather green and sick young men this morning, I shouldn't wonder. I know *I* didn't eat any, anyway . . . There was quite a pile of shiny wrappings, though – all neatly folded and around the chair that Mrs Stone was sitting in for the whole of the evening. Maybe that's all she did, poor woman – sit on her own in front of a roasting fire, not talking, not taking any food or drink, and swallowing chocolates before they melted in her fingers. I haven't seen them since, or anything, Mr and Mrs Stone. I thought earlier I might give a knock on their door, but then I didn't know what I could say to them, really. Better leave it alone on the whole, I thought. Could be that I won't be talking to either one of them again for ages, now (well – talk to *Mr* Stone, at least, because she, well, she never does). Unless I happen to pass him on the staircase, or out by the bins. The truth is that I've been just a little bit concerned all the morning that Mr Stone, well – that he might go and tell us to leave, or something. Because they do round here, landlords. Don't give you notice, or anything – they just say they want you out, and then when you come back from work or wherever it is you've been, all your things are in suitcases and dumped out in the street. It happened to the Glossops in the next street but one, over by the Green. They were only a week in arrears – Anne Glossop, she had pleaded with the man, but no: out on the doorstep, whatever few things they were left with, after all the pawning, because he's been in and out of work, Mr Glossop, for months and months now. And poor Anne's clothes, they were just thrown there, loose and flapping, and it came on to rain before someone could run and tell her to come and take them in. Well, I've always made sure that Mr Stone's rent is paid on time – I do like to keep things regular, I couldn't abide any sort of a debt hanging over me – but well, after all that Jackie said to him . . . and I put it to Jackie, when he did eventually roll out of bed, way past the time he usually has his dinner of a midday, when he's not out working. Jackie, I said to him – he'd wandered into the kitchen, scratching at all the bristles on his face and his pyjamas gaping open in the way I've told him not to, and he says he's going to help me with all the washing up. Sweet of him, because I could see he was feeling very much the worse for wear (and how Dickie must have been, I just

173

couldn't imagine – thought I'd maybe pop over and have a cup of tea with Sheila, a bit later on: find out if she got him up to his room all right. Oh no – of course, I'm forgetting: we dropped him off, didn't we? Dickie – in the car, and then we took Sheila home afterwards. My goodness what a night we had! It was that late by the time we got back). Anyway – there was Jackie, one eye still closed – how he always is, the morning after – and offering to help me with all the washing up. But he maybe could have been counting on my remembering the last time I let him do any such thing, and there was my good china butter dish in pieces on the floor. So no thank you, I said to him. You go and play with Jeremy and I'll bring you in some tea, do a bit of toast. And Jeremy! Goodness me. When we got in, I suppose I was still a little bit anxious about him – he's never really out of my mind, wherever I am or whatever I'm doing – but there he was, bolt upright in the bed, and biting on Fluffy's ears, if you please. And those building bricks, the ones with the letters on that Sheila had got for him . . . well I was sure I'd put them safely out of his reach, somewhere or other, but whether I did or whether I didn't, Jeremy, he had surely got hold of them anyway, and there they all were, strewn across the floor. And here's the funny bit – Imogen, his little minder, she was fast asleep (had to shake her such a lot to get her to wake up; I said to Lorna that they could stay, the children, but no, she wouldn't even hear of it – because Timmy and Little Davy too, they were all in dreamland, little lambs). Anyway – never mind any of that for now – it's Jackie I was meaning, and all that unpleasantness with Mr Stone.

'What you mean? Unpleasantness? Good party, I thought. You put sugar in the tea, have you Mary love?'

'Yes it was, Jackie. It was – it was the best party ever. But I mean at the end. Just before we all went off in the car. Two spoons. Stir it – it's just that you haven't stirred it in, have you?'

'I remember us going off in the car, course I do . . . But I don't recall nothing else – not about any "unpleasantness", anyway. Think you're imagining it. Here – toss us over one of them apples from the basket, ay? Do with that.'

'Are you sure, Jackie? An apple? Could be upsetting to your stomach, you know, after all you put away last night.'

'Me? Only had a couple beers. Was *Christmas*, you know. But yeh – reckon you're right. Maybe not an apple. When's this toast making an appearance, then? Come on Mary – get your skates on, there's a good girl.'

So I left it there, really. No point digging it all up again, was there? Let's just hope that Mr Stone feels the same way – because I know that the plan is to leave here next year, if all goes well with Jackie and Mr Plough . . . but we certainly couldn't go now, not now we couldn't. And it's ever so difficult to find somewhere, you know. So like I say – let's just hope, shall we? That he didn't take offence. The awful thing was, though – I did get the feeling that he'd heard it before – maybe they all have – a rant of that sort, or something like it, and very possibly a good deal worse. Jackie – it upset him too, of course, but for a different reason. Even later, when we were out on the town and having ourselves, oh – just such a whale of a time, he still kept on murmuring to me that whatever he may or may not be, he certainly wasn't stupid, that was for sure, and he wasn't going to take an insult like that from a . . . well, I won't say what he called him, Mr Stone . . . but Jackie was utterly determined that no one could be allowed to say such a thing, because it was a dirty lie and exactly the sort of poison that people like that had been putting about in Germany, and probably the reason why they were so eager to be rid of them. Well of course it is true that my Jackie, he's very far from stupid – it might surprise a lot of people, but he can be very wise indeed, as maybe only I can know. But I would be the first to admit, though, that he's not – how can I say it? Very well informed about the world situation.

He doesn't read a paper – sometimes I bring home the *Evening News*, but apart from the odd puzzle, he'll never even look at it. I've not seen him listen to the news on the wireless. He wilfully – I think this is what it must be – he wilfully just doesn't want to know. It was surprising, actually, to hear him even mention the Czechs; I didn't know that he was even aware of this annexation, or whatever they call it. He's never spoken to me about such a thing, and nor the Spanish war. And when he talked of the worry – and that danger that he referred to – can he really be a party to them? Maybe he's like the rest of us – secretly concerned, and never ever daring to think it. I don't know. He's never said.

So anyway, Jackie – he got himself away, soon after. Played with Jeremy on the rug for a while, in front of the fire – he's ever so good with him, endlessly patient . . . and I've noticed, whenever they're together, it's as if little Jeremy – he's really straining to understand, to do whatever it is that Jackie is trying to teach him – little furrows on his brow . . . and his lips, he sort of pouts them out into the sweetest rosebud. And Jackie – well like today, for instance, with the building bricks (a very good present, they've turned out to be – and I'll make a point later of thanking Sheila properly). There he was on the floor, stacking them up in alphabetical order and pronouncing each of the letters as he did so – and all the time, his eyes, Jackie's eyes – he wasn't looking at the bricks, you know, but he kept on watching Jeremy so very intently, maybe to gauge his reactions, I couldn't really tell you. And Jeremy, he was really concentrating hard – didn't reach out and knock over the pile, as I thought he would. He just watched it rise until it began to wobble – Jackie had got it right up to about M or N – and then he got quite a shock, I think, when they all tumbled down. And after that, Jackie got ready to go out – said he wouldn't be long, said he'd be back quite soon – and I didn't ask him where he was going, because I just assumed that it would have to be the Rose & Crown (though how he could even dream of facing another drink after all he put away last night . . . ! I had just a couple of sherries – three small ones, maybe – and it's all I can do to even look at the bottle. But there – men, they're different). I didn't begrudge him the time – it's so very seldom that he gets a day to himself (because tomorrow, bright and early, he'll have to be back and working for Mr Plough – got to seem eager, hasn't he? Particularly now). And anyway, I still had such an awful lot of clearing up to get done – and then I thought that after, I could wrap up Jeremy, nice and warm – rain's stopped, thank goodness – and take him down the road and have a little natter with Sheila, because she's bound to have all the gossip about Sally and Len by now, and even last night when we dropped her off I could see that she was bursting with eagerness to talk to me about how terribly well Molly and Jonathan Leakey had seemed to be getting on. So I'd just put the roasting pan in to soak in the basin for when I came back (the gallons of hot water I have got through this morning – sevenpence into the meter already, and still I'm nowhere near done yet) and then I just froze over completely when suddenly the doorbell went. Oh my God! That was my first thought. Oh my God, I thought – there's only one person that can possibly be: Mr Stone, who will simply stand there wordless, holding out to me a manila envelope, and then as he turns to leave I shall jab my thumb underneath the flap and jaggedly tear it asunder and call out to him to not just walk away but to stay and tell me to my face what it is that is in the envelope and still he won't turn back and nor has he met my eyes and by now I am staring at the paper which orders us to be out of the flat within twenty-four hours! All of this, it raced through my mind in maybe no more than a second – and I found that I had been chewing on the corner of the dishcloth. And then I thought – oh no, it can't be him, of course it can't be him, because that bell, the bell that's just rung, that's the street bell, not the flat bell, so it couldn't possibly, could it? Be Mr Stone . . . so who on earth is it?

Sheila, I suppose – she maybe couldn't wait. And by now I had anyway run down the stairs and was halfway across the hall and already my arm was out and reaching for the door and all I really registered as I turned the knob on the lock to let in whoever it was who might be calling was that the bulk of shadow on the other side of the frosted glass panels could never be Sheila, and going by just the trilby alone, it really had to be a man.

He looked apologetic and on the point of bolting, as he always, always did, Mary had never known why.

'Oh *Dad*!' she exclaimed. 'Oh my goodness, what a—! Oh come in, please come in – you must be freezing.'

Mary's father doffed his hat, and his thin and silvery hair was caught in the flurry of a breeze. Without yet looking at her, he reached up a hand to flatten it down.

'Don't want to intrude, Mary love. Can always go, if you're busy . . . ?'

'Oh goodness *sake*, Dad. Come in – come in. I'm just so pleased to see you. It's such a surprise. Is . . . ?'

Mary's father shook his head briefly as he entered the hall.

'No. She's not. Bit of a chill, she's got. Thought it best if she didn't venture out.'

Mary nodded. 'I understand, Dad. Well look – come upstairs. Get a warm by the fire. Jeremy – he'll be so delighted. Can't remember the last time he saw you.'

Mary's father smiled as he shifted the bulk of brown paper parcels that were under his arm, and plodded up the staircase after Mary.

'Little scamp . . .' he said. 'And, um . . . ?'

'Jackie? He's out. You've got us all to yourself. Come on in, Dad. Jeremy . . . ? Jeremy . . . ? Look who it is! It's your Grandad, isn't it? Say hello. Say "Hello Grandad". Come on. Oh look at him, Dad – he's all shy. Come on, Jeremy – it's Grandad, isn't it? You remember Grandad, don't you . . . ?'

Mary's father gazed down at the boy, and with pantomime eyes he mummed a silent greeting.

'He'll come round,' he said. 'Here, Mary – take these packages from me, will you? Nice and warm, I must say. Sit here, will I?'

Mary took the parcels from her father, and set them down on the table.

'What are they, Dad? Here – give me your coat, that's it. You've already given me a present, haven't you? You don't want to go spending all your money, do you? Hey? Here – you sit right down here, right close to the fire. Oh God – that tree! Looks so sorry for itself. You should have been here yesterday, Dad – it was looking lovely, then. We had ever such a good party – I'm so sorry that you and . . . that you couldn't come to it, Dad.'

Mary's father settled himself into the armchair and spread out his fingers in a gesture of helplessness. His eyes were wide as if to say to her Well look now Mary, you know how it is – and Mary, she nodded, because she did, of course: well of course she did.

'There's not much there – toy for the lad. Dundee cake. Few sweeties . . .'

'Oh Dad – you're so kind. You're such a good man.'

Mary knelt on the floor beside him, took his hand in hers and stroked his knuckles, looked so fondly at the creased and papery skin, deckled in brown.

'Now now,' he said in an admonitory tone. His eyes then softened and he patted her wrist. 'So – what's this young man been up to then, ay? Building a house? Is that it, Jeremy? Building a house with all these bricks? Is that what you're about? He's a cheeky monkey, that one. Aren't you lad, ay? Cheeky monkey you are, and no mistake. Yes you are.'

Jeremy drizzled out laughter and held up to his grandfather his upside-down teddy bear.

'Oh Dad look! He wants to show you his new little friend. His name's Fluffy. Isn't it, Jeremy? Yes it is. Fluffy.'

'Fluffy, ay? Funny name for a bear, isn't it?'

'Oh goodness don't *you* start now, Dad. That's what Jackie said.'

Mary's father nodded, fingering the limbs of the teddy bear.

'All right, is he? Your Jackie? No – problems, or anything?'

'Oh no Dad – why did you say that? Oh no – we're wonderful. Never better. I've got just so much to tell you about everything. Don't know where to begin. Tea! Let me get you a nice cup of tea, yes? And maybe a slice of the Dundee cake. Is it the usual one, Dad? The one we always used to get?'

'Oh yes. None better. Not to my knowledge. So – you had a good Christmas, did you Mary love? I'm very pleased to hear it. Here – open up that package there – no, yes – that one, yes. Playmate in there for little Fluffy, if I'm not mistaken.'

Mary tried unknotting the string, but she just had to go into the kitchen for scissors and cut it in the end. And then she unfolded from the paper a lanky and grinning gollywog – so smart in his tails and red and blue striped trousers, his cream buttoned spats and bright yellow waistcoat, and a big and indigo white spotted dicky bow. Jeremy's eyes were alight and he yelled out his excitement as he tottered over to Mary to grab hold immediately of its thicket of jet-black hair.

'Oh Jeremy isn't he *beautiful*! What a beautiful golly. Say thank you to your Grandad for the beautiful gollywog, Jeremy.'

And Mary was more pleased than she could say when Jeremy went over straight away and willingly to his Grandad's side and said to him Fankoo Ganda – and then Mary's father hoisted up both him and the gollywog high on his knee and Jeremy, quite unprompted, kissed him on the cheek. Mary went over to the chair and stooping down awkwardly, she somehow managed to embrace all three of them.

'Do you love your new golly, Jeremy? Oh Dad – you really shouldn't have, it must have been so expensive. Thank you so much. What shall we call him, Jeremy? Shall we call him Golly? Is that his name? Say hello to Golly.'

And Jeremy hit the golly twice on the head and then he hugged and kissed him and started shouting out *goggy goggy goggy goggy* . . . ! On and on, as if he'd never stop – and Mary was clapping with delight, and her eyes were shining.

'Well . . .' said her father, with a good degree of satisfaction. 'That doesn't seem to have gone down too badly, does it? Now, Mary – did I hear you mention tea a while back, or was I dreaming maybe?'

'Oh gosh yes! Right, Dad – sorry, I'll do it now. You'll be safe then, will you? With Jeremy and Golly?'

'And Fluffy,' chuckled Mary's father. 'Don't you go forgetting Fluffy.'

Mary touched his shoulder. 'Thank you, Daddy,' she said quite quietly. And she turned abruptly, sniffed just once, and went off quickly to make the tea.

I don't suppose, she thought, as she swirled around a teapotful of boiling water and then tipped it away into the sink, that Dad, he can really have had much of a Christmas. The meal itself will have been sort of all right: chicken, I expect, with carrots and sprouts and roast potatoes – that's what we always used to have, anyway, and my mother, she isn't a great one for change. But what else can Dad have done to while away the day? Because they never really had any friends, not properly – not as a couple, at least. Dad, he knew a good few fellows at Dillon & Baldwin's – until he retired, anyway . . . and then they either fell away or else my mother made good and sure that they never called again. And my father, he was no sort of a drinker, never smoked – he was the only man I ever saw when I was growing up who didn't – but he always cared for an hour or two in the pub, of a weekend; it wasn't the ale – I'm sure it was just for the fug and clamour that you get in these places, and a bit of a chinwag with one or two of his mates. But my mother, she made it increasingly clear to him that she didn't at all care for it – he went more rarely then, until she became quite shrill, and soon after that he stopped it altogether. But still he's always kept himself busy; he missed the engineering business – I knew that on the day he retired (it was in his eyes, he looked just so amazed when he walked through the door, and so very confused the following morning when he had just nowhere to go). But for a biggish sort of a man, he's always been very good with the fiddlier little things, rather surprisingly, and so he's always kept his hand in by mending clocks and watches for people, sometimes remaking a broken part in his funny little shed at the back of the garden. I've seen him dismantle an alarm clock that was in perfect working order – lay out all the bits on an oilcloth, wipe each of them down with such fastidious care, apply a little oil, and then put it all back together again; I asked him why he did it, and he looked at me and smiled his smile and gave the nickel casing of the clock a final buff and polish, and told me that it helps to pass the time. Always rereading his beloved Dickens books, of course (must remember to tell him that Dickie gave me one of them, I can't recall the title now) – and then there's the wireless, his more or less constant companion in the evenings, after he's had his tea. So I've answered myself, haven't I really? That is how he will have got through Christmas Day. And he will have given my mother the Yardley gift set that she always expected (there were always three or four of them quite intact and carefully stacked in the bottom of the wardrobe, because although she loved the fragrance – the toilet water and the bath oil – she thought it extravagant to use them at will). And a box of Roses, he always gave her too (violet creams if he'd been lucky on the pools) and then he'd refund to her whatever she'd spent on a new Christmas outfit (usually a costume from Marshall & Snelgrove) though the time to actually wear it never seemed to come. And she gave him Brylcreem, which he didn't wear – why his hair was always flying about in the slightest draught, and why she always bought him Brylcreem, because it annoyed her so. Admittedly he's not the easiest person to buy for; she once gave him – birthday, I think – the latest J. B. Priestley – he read the first twenty pages or so, and then he laid it aside: he's good, he said – I'm not saying he's not good, but when all's said and done, he's not a patch on Dickens now, is he? And then he'd go back again to *Nicholas Nickleby*.

So maybe if I tell him all about *my* Christmas – it might make him feel as if he'd had one too. I will – I'll tell him about the party . . . well, that won't take long, I suppose . . . and then I'll tell him . . . oh *I* know what I'll tell him – I'll tell him about later, when we all of us went off in the car and up to the West End – yes, that's what I'll do. Remind him, maybe, of when he used to do that sort of thing, of when he was younger, if he ever did (and if he ever was). I'll tell him everything in detail – right from the moment I first set eyes on Jonathan Leakey's beautiful Humber, glistening under the street lamp – covered, it was, in all these pearly raindrops, lit up and shivering. I had expected it to be black, of course, the car, I don't know why – maybe I always do expect cars to be black because they nearly always are, aren't they? But this, it was the loveliest deep and cherry red, so long and swooping and elegant, with all these silver metal stripes going the length of the running boards – those huge chrome headlamps, they seemed more like searchlights. The leather – it was all so slithery as we scrambled inside, and the smell, it reminded me of something – I think it was when you walk through the handbag section in the big department stores like Whiteley's or Swan & Edgar. There was an awful squeeze – I was in the front between Jonathan Leakey and Jackie, and first of all Molly had found herself wedged in tight next to Dickie in the back, but she wanted to swap places with Sheila because Dickie,

she said, he kept on lolling all over her. So they all got out again
– and Dickie, oh dear me, he was reeling all over the place by this
time, not too sure he was even aware of what was going on – and
then Sheila and Jackie somehow bundled him back in, and his
face was jammed so hard against the side window and then
Sheila piled in to make sure it stayed there, and Molly followed
on behind. That still left Lorna, of course – and Jackie said well
look, she's such a little slip of a thing, I reckon we can fit Lorna
in the glove compartment – and he even went and opened it, the
fool, to take a look! Then he shook his head so terribly sorrow-
fully (he can be such an actor, my Jackie, if the audience is there)
and he said no, sorry, no room – there's gloves in there. What an
ass! In the end she managed to cram herself into the back with
the rest of them, Lorna, some way or other, and her legs were all
sideways and half over Molly who was asked if she was comfy
and replied that it was a whole lot better than Dickie, anyway.
And Jackie was right – Lorna didn't seem to mind the discom-
fort a scrap: she was going to see the lights and that was that, so
far as she was concerned.

'Right then,' called out Jonathan Leakey, firing the ignition.
'We all fit and happy, are we? That's the style – off we go, then.'

Mary, Sheila and Lorna gave out a whoop as the car pulled
away from the pavement – and Lorna's was the loudest of all.

'All aboard the Number 46,' called out Jackie. 'Have your
tuppences at the ready, ladies and gents, for when the conductor
come round. So listen, Jonny – you know the way there then,
yeh?'

Jonathan Leakey inhaled the Senior Service that Jackie had just
lit for him and placed between his lips.

'Back of my hand . . .' said Jonathan Leakey, one eye closed
and the side of his face screwed away against the smoke.

'What time is it?' piped up Sheila from deep in the back. 'Oh
Dickie – put your tongue away, God's sake.'

'Who cares?' hooted Jackie. 'Christmas, ain't it? Time don't mean nothing.'

'No – what I really meant was,' Sheila was at pains to clarify, 'how long do you think it'll take us to get there? Ages since I've been up West. Can't remember how far it is.'

'Well . . .' opined Jonathan Leakey. 'Won't be no traffic at all till we get up close. And then we don't mind, do we? Because we want to go slow, else we don't see nothing at all, you see.'

'I'm so excited . . .' Lorna breathed so very quietly that most of the party missed it completely.

'So I reckon . . .' went on Jonathan Leakey, 'quarter of an hour ought to do it, give or take. Here, Jackie – reach us out that bag there, look – under the seat where your feet are, see it? And then pull that handle back above your head. You twists it over to the left, yeh? And then you give it a pull.'

Jackie was craning with one hand feeling around in the space beneath the bench seat.

'Mind out the way Mary love, there's a good girl. Oh yeh – I got it. Oh lovely, Jonny – well done, my son. Look at this, Dickie! Dickie? You still alive, are you?'

'Barely . . .' grunted Sheila. 'Look at him, will you? One minute he's as red as a beetroot, and then he's looking like a bedsheet.'

'He can't be ill,' Jackie called back to her. 'He's a doctor, ain't he? Or as good as. Anyway – our chauffeur here, Mr Jonathan Leakey Esquire of this parish – he very kindly furnished us with a little flattie of Haig, look.'

'Oh God's sake,' deplored Sheila. 'Don't go offering him any more – he's pickled as it is.'

'Yeh well – if we step out the car, bit later on, he'll want a drop of something warming inside of him. Stands to reason.'

Jackie had been fiddling with the capsule around the neck of the half bottle of Haig, and now he gripped the stopper and eased it out, took a good pull and passed it over to Jonathan

Leakey. And give him his due, thought Jackie – Jonny, he takes one hand off the wheel, gets a hold of the bottle, brings it up to his mouth, throat banging away like a piston there for a good couple of glugs, and not for a second does he take his eyes off the road in front: mark of a pro, that is – mark of a pro.

'Now tell me again, Jonny – what was that about a handle? Oh yeh – what, this handle yeh? Right I – what do I do? Oh yeh, I give it a turn – right, done that.'

'Oh Jackie!' squealed Mary. 'Your knee's in my face. Be careful!'

'Shush a minute, Mary. Important business here. And then I just pull on it, do I? Oh no – I got you. I slides it back. Yeh. Oh blimey – look at that, will you? Look at this, everybody – we got ourselves a skylight!'

The rush of icy air that suddenly filled the car had Lorna tugging her thin little coat about her, Molly yelling out to shut it for heaven's sake because it was so utterly freezing, and Dickie sort of coming to life with a few quite high-pitched noises of his own.

'You'll thank me,' said Jonathan Leakey, 'once we get close up.'

Mary turned aside from the tang of smoke from Jackie's and Jonathan Leakey's cigarettes – tried to not be knocked by Jackie's elbow as he raised up the bottle of Haig again. The tip of her nose was just touching the cold of the windowpane, and she saw through the spinning droplets of rain and her own grey reflection the glistening and slate-like streets, fast-looming and then scudding away behind her, the navy blue of the briefly glimpsed voids at the ends of terraces, almost molten – and then the way a street lamp could make the kerbstones look like so many slabs of wetly gnawed-on cork, pitted and rugged. A blinking Belisha Beacon would instantly set a shop window on fire, and then in a moment it was doused. Still in the gaps between curtains on the upper floors, you could make out the warmth of light, the flicker and shift of festive activity. Behind every single one of these windows, Mary reflected, a different Christmas had taken its course – and here in this car is mine.

'Now then!' called out Jonathan Leakey, hauling the Humber around quite a tight corner – straightening her up again with practised ease and the lightest of touches on the wheel. 'Have a little look at this lot, then.'

Molly had quickly to shield her face as Lorna scrambled across in her unstoppable eagerness to see what it was he was meaning, Mr Leakey, and she squealed like a puppy as she did so.

'Oh! Oh Mary – look at this! Look at this, will you!'

Mary was already looking – how could she fail to? – as the Humber eased its way towards Oxford Circus – many more cars now, and coming from all directions – and high above the lit-up windows of D. H. Evans and John Lewis (and that one with all the twinkling Christmas trees the whole long length of the façade, I think that must have been Debenham & Freebody) there were ropes of soft white lights, elegant in curves, and gently swaying between the lampposts they were strung from.

'Prime . . .' said Jackie quietly, nodding to the left and right of him. 'Proper prime, that is.'

'Not seen nothing yet,' said a very self-satisfied Jonathan Leakey. 'You just wait till I make this turn here and we get into Regent Street. Oh yeh – fair old queue of cars now, look. Thought there might be. So who wants to up periscopes then, ay? Who's going to stick their head up and out the wossname?'

Lorna ignored, or maybe she didn't even hear them, Jackie's barked-out protestations as she kneed him in the back of the head in her so very wide-eyed and now quite frantic determination to trample over anyone it took so that she could ease her shoulders up and through the rooflight – and Mary was quite startled and held her hands over her ears now as Lorna shrieked out so suddenly at the smack of iciness that stung her face, and the sheer bright and gaudy dazzle of an endless swagged and triumphant corridor of lit-up stars and snowflakes and trumpets and bells, curving on and away against a midnight sky and bespattering the slow lines of cars with dancing spangles of white and colours.

'Dickie!' urged Sheila, pummelling his shoulder. 'God's sake wake up, you stupid man. Look out of the window, not down on the ground – what's wrong with you? Yes – that's right. Look that way – see? Can you see it? I'll hold your face up for you, all right Dickie? You just look. Oh honestly, Mary – he's quite impossible. But I must say, all this – it looks really quite wonderful, doesn't it? Oh! Look at that – did you see that, Mary? The angel? Did you see it?'

Mary had – and she was suddenly quite transported by the whole blazing sight of all those lights above and around: just as she knew her heart was rising within her, she got a hold of Jackie's arm, and hugged it tightly.

'Oh Jackie – isn't it marvellous, all of this? It's just so perfect . . .'

Jackie nodded. ' 'Tis, Mary love, and no mistake. Here, mind my arm – spilling the Scotch, look. Hey Molly – you gone very quiet. You getting all this, are you?'

'All right are you, Molly?' called out Mary (she tried to turn around, but it was too much of a squeeze).

'Oh – yes,' Molly rushed to assure them. 'I'm just speechless, that's all. I never thought it would be so . . . !' And then she laughed, as more of Lorna's yelps and squawks of delight floated down from above. 'I don't think Lorna will ever recover! But God – she must be so frozen up there.'

'No look,' interjected Jonathan Leakey. 'You're all in for another little treat in just half a mo. See, interesting thing about Regent Street is, it ain't straight. See? So you don't know what's down the other end until you just get the car round this little curve, see? Like what we're just about to do, matter of fact. Then you get your Piccadilly Circus. Full doings. Just coming up now.

Don't know what young Lorna's going to make of it. Could kill her, she don't get a grip.'

And then quite suddenly, amid the cacophonous blare of so many motor horns, it came all upon them in an engulfing rush. Mary intook her breath sharply as the whole of the windscreen before her was immediately filled by the vast and twinkling vista of a swinging pendulum on maybe some titanic cuckoo clock that was surmounted by the slogan Guinness Time, spelled out and glittering in a thousand coloured lights. Advertisements for Bovril and Player's and so many other such familiar names were sparkling on and off and spinning in circles, and Lorna – now nearly running on the spot in the back of the car and drumming her fists so madly up on the roof – was suddenly swimming with an instant giddiness as she felt as sure as she had ever done that all the lights were moving now, and heading towards her. The traffic had come to a virtual standstill, the noises of all the cars barely inching forward like a constantly discordant orchestra as a lone and grandly moustachioed policeman in a mackintosh cape with an imperious palm would hold back this lane, and beckon on with urgency another transection, the stripes on the cuffs pulled over his sleeves glowing pale with a phosphorescent green – so surprisingly visible amid this much spectacular colour. Sheila tapped Mary on the shoulder repeatedly and with a quite painful energy as she jabbed another finger in the direction of a purple-faced and shirt-sleeved young man at the apex of Eros, holding on to the bow and waving around a black-and-white flag . . . and oh my goodness, it's a skull and crossbones! But how terribly strange! There is a tiny news cinema just over there, look, so tightly sandwiched between a neon-lit tea house and a jeweller's window as bright with gold as a broken-open treasure chest, disgorging its contents – and from the cinema now there streamed a huddle of gossiping people, as more were pushing to cram inside, and the piercing scream of the

189

policeman's whistle was overlaid at once by the bovine drone and then sharp trumpeting of all these horns, and Lorna now became so utterly overwhelmed by the teeming bustle, so much swarming movement and the laughter all around her. One man in a staved-in bowler wove his way in dainty and uneven steps towards the car, the blue balloon on a string in his hand hovering above him and bobbing against the roof. He tried to focus upon Lorna in the dazzle, and then he blew her a chord on the little tin bugle in the corner of his mouth that he then gnashed down on, hard. Jonathan Leakey – who had been glancing about him at the state of the bottleneck – happened upon a gap just a little way along and he made for it immediately, edging the car forward and swinging it left and into a side street, and Lorna – still aloft – was plunged into a comparative darkness, after the crackle and blaze of all behind them.

'We can park her a little way along,' said Jonathan Leakey – inching the Humber with expert care through the narrow tunnel between the parallel lines of stationary cars, all of them drunkenly askew with two of their wheels humped up on to the pavement. 'Then we'll have ourselves a little stroll about, anyone game.'

He rammed closed the skylight before they left the car in Brewer Street, and then he directed the party along the length of Glasshouse Street, and back into the shock of Piccadilly. Jackie was holding up Dickie, much to Sheila's relief (because you know the weight of him – and just look, will you? His legs are boneless) and she hurried to catch up Mary and Molly, who had linked their arms and were chatting excitedly. Lorna had skittered on ahead of all of them, quite careless of where she might be headed. By the time they remustered in Piccadilly Circus, there swilled all around them a stew of indecipherable sounds and echoes, combining to be enormous. Mary was suddenly struck by the waft of roasting from the chestnut seller's blackened brazier – the molten lick of orange at its heart – and she knew at once that she was starving. Jackie propped up Dickie on to Jonathan Leakey, and set to handing around the hot and fragrant fivepenny bags: they were received with greed and pleasure into stiffened fingers, white with cold. Mary was doing her best to ignore the bites of pain when feeling slowly seeped back into those fingertips of hers as she picked away bits of incinerated shell, so eager was she to taste the boiling sweetness of the chestnut inside.

'You not eating, Molly? They're the most delicious thing I've ever had.'

'I just want to hold the bag for a minute – my hands are so cold. I should have brought gloves – but I didn't know, did I? We were going out. What shall we do now? Where are we going?'

Everyone's faces save that of Jackie (too busy forcing a chestnut between Dickie's wet and yammering lips: there were even some words coming out of him now – he was wakening up) – they were each of them turned towards Jonathan Leakey. He amusedly surveyed them glowing in the lights, their cheeks endlessly dappled with revolving colour, and then he announced quite loudly – to surmount the roar of the devil's jazzband now at full tilt from the horns of jammed and boxed-in motorists:

'I am very glad you asked that question. Follow me, if you will. Jackie and Sheila – if you'll take care of our friend Mr Weak, here . . . Mary, my dear, you will see that young Lorna, she don't get lost in the crowd . . . and Miss Molly, if I may make so bold, might care to accompany my humble self – and on we go to a very select establishment within my ken, hard by Trafalgar.' He half-bowed and extended to Molly the crook of his arm. 'May I . . . ?'

Molly simpered – glanced over to Mary, and took it gladly. All of them were quite startled when Dickie very suddenly began to sing at full throttle God Rest Ye Merry Gentlemen – more lustily now, and at the very top of his croaked and fractured voice – and then he abruptly broke off to swing around his arms in an all-encompassing and generous gesture of embrace.

'My friends! My friends! What very heaven this is. Lead on! Lead me where you will.' And then he spun around to Jonathan Leakey – nearly lost his balance, but a steadying arm from Jackie soon had him to rights. 'And it's *Wheat*, you bastard . . . ! But never mind, never mind – couldn't matter less, is what I say.'

Sheila now laughed out her delight at Dickie's at least partial return to a form of sentience, and she took his arm as they all moved off – weaving their way through the cars and happy people under the leadership of Jonathan Leakey and Molly to the fore. They edged their way past a chattering mob that clustered outside the Criterion and then straggled into Haymarket – Lorna having to quickly avert her face from the sight of a doubled-over reveller elaborately spewing while being joyously encouraged by a peroxided lady with crimson eyelids and a beauty spot large on her ash-white face: she called him Harry Boy, struck his shoulder blades repeatedly with a sequinned clutch bag and assured him with gusto that it was better out than in.

The crowds had thinned away now and it was suddenly quite quiet and darkish as they all made their way down the full length of Haymarket – Dickie, he was singing again and waving his arms, but it was quite beyond Mary to identify the song. She saw, though, that Jackie had passed over to Dickie the half bottle of whisky which, well – it can't be a good idea, can it now really? Lorna had taken to skipping, just like a child in the park, her white-ribboned plaits swirling around her – she was asking everyone in turn whether they had had quite enough chestnuts because if they did not feel they could force down themselves another and maybe had one or two left in their crumpled paper bags, then Lorna for one would not at all mind relieving them of the burden of still having to carry the thing, but they must please not even begin to think of her as in any way forward or rude.

Sheila had graduated to Mary's side, quite sure that Jackie alone could easily deal with the Dickie situation: his apparent recovery was really quite dramatic – due to the cold night air or maybe the chestnuts, who was to say?

'The walking warms you up a bit, doesn't it Mary? Hope we're not going too far, though – not in these shoes.'

Mary pulled her beret down lower on to her forehead – eagerly linked arms with Sheila and folded her hand over hers.

'Just look at Lorna,' she said quite fondly. 'Skipping along. I'm so pleased I asked her. I can't imagine what sort of a Christmas she would have had otherwise. And that sister of hers, you know – Imogen . . . did you meet her? Little Imogen? Very sweet – so docile. Well anyway, she's quite a treasure. Without her, well – I couldn't be here, could I? It's so lovely, you know, to feel free like this again. Before Jeremy came along, we used to do this sort of thing all the time, Jackie and me. We'd go to a Lyons', or the pictures – or just for a walk, or a drink somewhere. Never had to plan it, that was the thing. But there – that's parenthood, I suppose. You suddenly have to be so terribly grown-up about everything – and of course you don't always want to be. That's the trouble.'

Sheila strode along, arm in arm with Mary, and seemed to be studying the plume of her breath as it was briefly held in the cold night air.

'I'd love it,' she said, quite shortly. 'To be you. To be a mother. I'd love it.'

Mary stopped and turned to revolve Sheila to face her.

'You've never said that to me before, Sheila. You've never ever said that. When did you decide that?'

Sheila laughed quite lightly, relinked her arm with Mary's, and the two walked on.

'Oh – it's not a sudden thing. I've always thought that. When I was little, I used to pretend that Susan – she was the youngest of us – I used to pretend that instead of my sister, she was really my baby. I used to do everything for her, you know. It got so that if my mother came anywhere near to Susan, I became really quite cross. Jealous, I suppose I was really. And it never left me. I need someone to look after, you see. Always have done.'

'Well I think that's a perfectly sweet story, Sheila. And what's happened to Susan? You've never mentioned her. Are you still very close?'

'And that's why, you see Mary . . . much as I do love old Dickie, silly ass that he is, I can't really think that he's truly the one, you know. I mean I know he's got a glittering future, and all the rest of it – and he's kind, he's a very kind man, Dickie, well in many ways he is. But . . . I don't really see him as a husband and father so much as, well – the little thing to take care of. Why I'm with him, it could be. Don't know.'

A cry came up from someone in front – might have been Jackie, too dim to see – and Mary and Sheila scuttled along to catch up with the rest of them. They turned the corner and saw straight away why Jackie, Dickie, Lorna and Molly were just staring ahead of them, and upwards. There was a spotlit Lord Nelson atop his dizzyingly tall and noble column – and the sight of his profile, quite stark against so very black a sky, well . . . all you could do was gape at it, really; and then sort of giggle with an unnameable glee. The fountains too in the Square were lit and gushing – and also white from floodlights was that big domed building with all the pillars along the front – Mary couldn't have sworn to it, but she rather thought it might be a museum or a gallery of some sort.

'Why is he?' asked Jackie – to Dickie primarily, or anyone else who cared to answer. 'Up there? This Nelson geezer. What they stick him up there for?'

'Well old man,' said Dickie – still gazing up at the admiral, and swaying only slightly. 'Greatest Sea Lord, wasn't he? Battle of

Trafalgar, mainly. Other things too, of course. Saved England from the Froggies. Napoleon and all that sort of nonsense.'

'Yeh? Blimey. I never even knew there were a battle round here.'

'No no,' Dickie rushed to correct him. 'Not here – here is named after it, you see. Trafalgar. The real Trafalgar – where the sea battle was, you know – well that was, um . . . well that was somewhere else entirely. Abroad, fairly obviously . . .'

'Yeh? Well good old Nelson then, that's all I can say. Won't try it on with us again, will they? Ay? The Froggies. You know what? I heard they eat snails, the Froggies does. What you going to do with a country like that? My Alfie – he's learning to talk it, French. Don't know why.'

Lorna's face was wrinkled in disgust.

'Oh they *can't* do! Snails? Oh no – oh no: they can't do.'

'Oh yes they bleeding does,' insisted Jackie. 'Ain't I right, Dickie? Don't them Froggies eat snails of a dinnertime? And frogs – why they call them Froggies, I suppose.'

Dickie nodded. 'Delicious, I believe. Rather them than me. No danger of them being at war with us again, though. They're on our side, these days. It's other countries that are a bit of a nui- sance. I say, Jonathan – getting rather chilly just standing about, don't you know!'

Jonathan Leakey stepped forward, his arm still linked into Molly's.

'Follow me please, ladies and gents. A rare treat – and just around the corner. This way, if you please.'

He led them across the Square and into St Martin's Lane – took a sharp right just after the church, and there was an alley – dark, and a little bit frightening at first, it looked like to Mary's eye, but there was a warm and inviting glimmer at its very end, and it was towards that light that Jonathan Leakey now seemed to be taking them.

'You all right, Sheila?' checked Mary. 'My goodness – what an adventure all this is turning out to be. You all right, Sheila? You've gone awfully quiet.'

Sheila seemed to be consciously tugging herself out of a reverie, and back to where she belonged – here, and at Mary's side.

'Oh no – yes yes. I'm fine. Perfectly. Of course I am.'

And then she stopped quite abruptly and detached herself from Mary and stood right in front of her. Her eyes were hard and dark as she said quite woodenly:

'She died. Susan. She died when she was still so little.'

As Mary's eyes crinkled into sympathy, Sheila laughed and batted it all away with an impatient little wave of her fingers.

'Silly. I'm just being silly. Come on – let's catch them up. We don't want to get lost – not round here we don't, do we? They're getting on terribly well though, aren't they? Jonathan and Molly. Quite a picture, they seem to be. Ow! Oh my gosh you know, Mary – these shoes of mine, they really are giving me gyp, now.'

'Well ...' considered Mary. 'I suppose that Mr Leakey – Jonathan – he's quite a charming sort of man, in a rather odd sort of a way. I mean if you go for that sort of thing, of course ... Are you sure you're all right now, Sheila?'

'Mm – well Molly seems to, anyway. Go for that sort of thing. Yes I *told* you, Mary – I'm perfectly well. Apart from these shoes. It was just a silly moment, that's all. Oh! Oh look – oh Mary – just look at *this* now, for heaven's sake!'

Jackie and Dickie – and he did, you know, Dickie, he seemed now to be just about perfectly well again, if you can possibly believe it – they were already jostling among the knot of eager and seemingly good-tempered people around this rather large and cream-painted caravan affair – propped on brick piles, and with two great open flaps jacked up on arms the length of its flank, and these served well as both roof and counter to the tired and hungry masses that were clustered all about it. The light and warmth, the fug of haze from within, they seemed to have the allure of a beacon, and all were drawn towards it. There were highly decorated and crenellated boards leaning to the side of it and hung from hooks that proclaimed in a cluttered variety of richly coloured Victorian typefaces reminiscent of the circus and the fairground, that Messrs J. P. Cockerell & Sons Ltd had been the exclusive purveyors of comestibles to the gentry since the year of Our Lord eighteen hundred and thirty-seven, and that their pigeon pies and pease pudding stood alone as the most supreme quality – their soups and saveloys without peer or comparison within the Empire and beyond. For ninepence there were chops or eels with mash and liquor – a shilling would buy you a cut off the joint, with a ladleful of boiled cabbage and bacon; tea and cocoa were tuppence a pint and all minerals just three farthings more, and a penny of that reclaimable on the bottle. There was even a crest in maroon and gold, resplendent over the wide open window where three very hot and perspiring men were constant and busy with frying and carving and passing out piled-up plates of piping food to greedily outstretched hands, the women on tiptoe in their efforts to reach them. The cartouche surmounting this coat of arms – not quite the Royal one, Mary observed – proclaimed the establishment in enamel and leaf to be By Appointment to All Crowned Heads of the Civilised World, and proud suppliers to the Aristocracy of England.

'Well!' laughed Mary, urging Sheila on to join the rest of them, milling around. 'Who could resist? Come on – I'm starving again. I've never been sure, you know, quite what a saveloy is – but I think I'm going to have one. And tea. Oh how wonderful.'

Jackie came towards them, then – a brimming pair of huge white china mugs gripped tight in either of his fists, steaming as if they could burst into flame.

'Tea up!' he announced with a grin. 'Here, Mary – get a hold on one of these. There you go, Sheila – nice mug of tea for you. But listen – give him his due, old Jonny, ay? Knows his London, don't he? Me – born here, lived here all my life, and I never even knowed there was such goings-on as this. Fancy a bit of a bite, do you Mary love? Far as what I can make out, the King hisself comes down here for his supper. He ain't around tonight though, else I would've noticed. Oh no – course! Christmas, ain't it? They all go up to Scotland, don't they? Yeh – shame. Otherwise I could of stood him a mug of tea, had a bit of a natter.'

'Oh Jackie you're so *ridiculous*, sometimes!' laughed Mary. 'God I'm just dying for this tea – too hot to drink, though. Don't want to burn my tongue. Who's that, Jackie . . . ? Who's Dickie talking to over there? Do you know him, Sheila?'

'Don't *think* so . . .' doubted Sheila, peering over to the far side of the van. 'But I always think men, when they're dressed like that, they look all exactly the same, don't they? Whoever he is, he does look ever so posh, doesn't he?' She glanced across to Lorna who was gazing over intently at Dickie and this rather elegant gentleman – he didn't seem to be even remotely chilly in just his white tie and tailcoat, a cream-fringed silk evening scarf crossed over lightly around his neck – and nor did the very lovely young lady beside him, so tall and slender, although she did have what could have been a chinchilla stole shrugged loosely over her long and sparkling gown; the big white china mug looked so very out of place as she clutched it in both of her tiny little hands, a shaft of light from the van setting afire her bright red fingernails. Lorna was blinking now, as if to be sure that it wasn't a mirage. 'Here, dear,' Sheila encouraged her. 'Take your tea from Jackie, there's a good girl. What are you staring at, Lorna?'

Lorna now seemed to remember that there were other people around.

'Oh – sorry,' she gulped. 'It's just – that gentleman. He looks just like the actor Cary Grant – have you heard of him?' Her eyes were huge now, and she seemed quite desperate to convey to Sheila every scrap of information that was at her disposal. 'He was on the cover of *Picturegoer* with Mae West and my friend what showed it to me, she said he were the handsomest man in the whole wide world and I thought he were too and I said that when I were older and all my brothers and my sister was older as well then I'd go on the boat to Hollywood in America and meet him and then we'd get married and I'd be Mrs Grant and she said, my friend said, Florrie her name is, she said no – no Lorna, you can't do that because I'm going to – I already decided to go to Hollywood in America and meet him and marry him and everything and it's my *Picturegoer*, ain't it? But do you think he's come here? Do you, Sheila? You tell me, Mary – do you think it's really him, come over for Christmas? Maybe he's filming a picture. Do you think it's really him? Mr Grant?'

Mary was so amused by this, and her eyes were dipped down into such fond sympathy with Lorna's breathless condition – Mary, she'd been just like that herself, and not so long ago: Ronald Colman and Errol Flynn – oh yes and Clark Gable, they were my favourites; but you sort of get out of all that kind of nonsense, somehow, when you've a man of your own to take care of – and when you're a mother, of course (and I do so hope that he's all right, my Jeremy, with little Imogen – I mean I'm sure he will be, but still, you know, it's never too far from your mind . . . even on an evening such as this, it never quite leaves you).

'Oh Lorna – I do doubt very much if it is actually him. But we'll be able to ask Dickie now, won't we? Here he comes – he'll tell us all about him. Drink your tea now Lorna, else it'll be cold.'

'I really do urge you good people,' Dickie was chortling, as he strode towards them, spreading wide his arms as if he were

Santa himself, 'to do yourselves a very large favour and devour a chunk of their steak and kidney – quite the best in its class, I'd say.'

'Thought you said you wasn't hungry,' Jackie reminded him – shaking the half bottle of Haig to the side of his ear, and then offering it neck-first to Dickie.

'Well I wasn't,' admitted Dickie, holding out his mug of tea to receive a slug of Scotch. 'But goodness – the aromas over there, I am telling you . . .'

'Mm,' agreed Mary. 'I do think I might have that saveloy, you know. Whatever a saveloy is . . . But listen, Dickie – what we all want to know is how you came to be chatting away with Mr Cary Grant.'

Dickie seemed to be dumbstruck – looked to Jackie, who was grinning and wagging his head as he looked down at his feet which he had begun now to stamp up and down to fend off a growing numbness. He spun a glowing cigarette end into the grille of a drain.

'The bloke . . .' he nudged him. 'The geezer what you was talking to. Ladies here, they want to know who he were. Because if he's a famous Hollywood film star – Lorna here, she going to march right over there and drown the lady in one of the fountains, see, and then she going to marry him – ain't that the truth, Lorna love?'

Mary put an arm around Lorna and clucked her reassurance as Lorna, quite scarlet, glanced away and downwards.

'Oh *him*,' Dickie now understood. 'Oh good Lord no – no no, he's no film star, no not a bit. No – most extraordinary coincidence. I was at school with the chap, as a matter of fact. Well – I was his fag, actually. Seems a bit rum, now . . .'

Jackie gaped at him. 'You was his *what*?'

Dickie looked up sharply as if caught by torchlight in the midst of a crime.

'Oh – nothing. Just a word we . . . No no. No – I was at school with him, that's the up and down of it. Nothing Hollywood about Davenport – English as they come.'

'Oh how very disappointing,' deplored Mary. 'So sorry, Lorna – not Cary Grant after all. So what does he do then, Dickie, if he's not a film star? He's most terribly handsome.'

Dickie drew a blank.

'Do . . . ? Well, um . . . doesn't do anything, really. Not to speak of. He's a *Davenport*, you see.' And then – realising quite quickly that no one actually did see – he continued in his well-meaning effort to make things clearer. 'Well it's just that families of that sort, you know . . . they don't really do anything in the sense that we, um . . . They just sort of *are*, really. I mean I expect he rides – shoots, and so forth . . . Think he's handsome, do you? Can't say I see it myself . . .'

Jackie looked to Mary for guidance – and she laughed when she saw on his face such total incomprehension.

'Oh Dickie . . .' she smiled. 'You really are awfully different from all of us, aren't you? But we love you very much – don't we Sheila? Don't we Jackie? Yes we do – there you are. But you really must tell me – where was this school of yours? You've never mentioned it before, where you went to school.'

Dickie was flustered, and he looked about him and he gulped his tea.

'Molly and Mr Leakey seem to be very deep in conversation, don't they? What? Over there. Oh . . . you know, Mary. Just a school – just a school somewhere. Too dull to talk about, frankly. Look – are you chaps getting any grub or aren't you? Because otherwise, you know, I think we maybe ought to be making a move. I'm more or less freezing to the pavement, don't know about you.'

'Reckon you're right,' said Jackie. 'What you say, Mary? Have a saveloy another time, ay?'

Sheila was nodding to that. 'I do feel rather tired you know, all of a sudden – I expect it's the excitement.'

'I suppose you're right . . .' Mary concurred. 'I don't know about Lorna, though. I don't think she'll ever want to sleep again – will you, Lorna?'

Lorna smiled, quite sheepishly. 'I've never had such a time . . .' she whispered excitedly.

'Right then,' concluded Jackie. 'Settled. I'll just go and round up Romeo and Juliet over there – because we're all a bit stuck elsewhere, ain't we? Without our chauffeur. Jonny! Hey – Jonny! What's wrong with him? He don't hear me . . .'

'Well don't *shout*, Jackie,' Mary hissed at him, glancing about her. 'Don't go shouting the length of the street. Go and *talk* to him, heaven's sake . . .'

Jackie formed his hands into a funnel around his mouth.

'Jonny!! *Jonny!!* Over here, look! Yeh – come on, come on. Yeh . . . he heard me that time. That's it. They're coming over now, look.'

Jackie tapped out a Senior Service from his new cigarette case, lit it with his lighter – and when he caught sight of Mary still glaring and holding the pose of great indignation, he tossed her a wink and she melted completely.

'Well my friends,' said Jonathan Leakey, ambling towards them, his arm still tightly linked with Molly's – and she was looking up at his profile, Mary could hardly stop herself from noticing, in the sort of admiration that borders upon rapture. 'I can't tempt you to the menu here then? Telling you – Simpsons and the Savoy just up the street, ten times the price and the quality's barely a fraction. No? You quite sure? Very well then – we'll get to the car round the back way. Not so scenic as how we come, but hell of a lot quicker, now it's so nippy. Right then, ladies and gents – best foot forward.'

Just then, and so surprisingly – because the canopy of sky above and around them was still that clear and the colour of coral – it came on to rain in such sudden gobbets, as if it were fighting an airlock or blockage, so nervous and sporadic was each of the bursts. A wind whipped up from nowhere too, and that had all of them turning up collars and holding down hats and spattering away as quickly as they could manage, the occasional mustering cry from Jonathan Leakey some way to the fore, urging them to close up the gaps and to keep him in sight. Molly was gasping and laughing so terribly much as she hurtled along that her throat kept on catching, and she'd raise up her face and was bathed in the rain. Jonathan Leakey did not catch a word of what she said when she squealed at him as the pinpoints of rain, they were so very tingly when they spangled her tongue – he just grinned at her broadly and hugged her with one arm more tightly about her waist as the two of them clatteringly splattered along – weaving very suddenly into darkened side streets and veering at speed around the more troublesome puddles in shining cobbled alleyways. Sheila was yelling at Mary to not for heaven's sake leave her behind because she'd be bound to get lost and she couldn't, not in these shoes, she just couldn't keep up, and no I *can't* Mary, can I? Take them off, because these stockings, they're my only good pair, and they're already so covered in splashes and streaks and I can't go risking a ladder as well. Jackie was howling like an owl and repeatedly patting his hoot-shaped mouth with a spade of flattened fingers so that the noise came out now like a Red Indian on the warpath and Mary was just running full pelt alongside of him, laughing and scudding him with the side of her handbag – calling out to Sheila to hurry up for goodness sake. Dickie was chanting away the endless Glorias and other assorted highlights from Ding Dong Merrily On High, occasionally whooping like a diving submarine, and Lorna – who had swept off her hat as the first raindrops fell – was just dancing along, and so terribly lightly, like a frolicsome gazelle in a new and dewy meadow.

And then somehow – and Mary had thought that they'd just never get there – they all of them, and more or less at once, fetched up at the side of the glistening Humber. Sheila was hobbling quite badly and cursing her shoes and all this blessed weather as Jonathan Leakey fumbled around with a great fob of keys. Everyone then piled into the motor car, much as before – and Lorna had this time to be more or less dragged into the back, so much still did she seem to need all the lights and the coldness, the ceaseless rain that still went on coursing in rivulets over her radiant face, and had rendered her plaits into two dark and sopping lengths of heavy dripping rope. Mary's thought now was – oh, I do so hope that all those leather seats in Jonathan Leakey's beautiful car are not going to be ruined, because you can just hear the rainwater plopping down from everybody's hat brims – and Lorna, you could wring her out, half-drowned little thing, and have enough water to fill up a bathtub. Oh my goodness, though – what a Christmas Day, and what a Christmas night! I'll just never forget it – not for as long as I live: I shall remember this, and for always.

◉

As, of course, I am remembering it now . . . it was only last night, after all; and yet already it seems to me to be, I don't know – a complete and separate thing, a little gem from long ago. I'll bring my Dad in his tea now – and by the sounds of things, he and Jeremy are certainly getting Sheila's full moneysworth out of that little set of building bricks. I don't know, now, if I'll tell him all the ins and outs of what we did . . . he doesn't know the people, you see, my Dad, so it wouldn't mean a very great deal to him, would it really? You maybe just had to be there.

'Here you are, Dad. Nice cup of tea. Sugar's already in. And we've ginger biscuits, if you'd like. Fancy a few, do you Dad? I can do a sandwich? Hm? Chicken, I think . . . or there's always cheese. And there's cake – there's your cake, of course. How does that strike you, Dad? Nice piece of cake?'

Mary's father was half lying on the rug now, with his back propped up against the three-legged table and Jeremy sprawled all over his legs; between them they seemed to have built a sort of a windbreak, I suppose you could call it, and Golly and Fluffy were nestled inside. He ruffled Jeremy's hair, easing him away to the side. It seemed to be quite an effort for him to raise himself up so that he could hold on to the side of the armchair and drop himself back into it, with just the one exhalation. He reached up both his hands to take good hold of the cup and saucer. Seeing the two of them like this, you know – it's started me wondering whether Dad, whether he ever played with me in a similar kind of a way, on a different rug in another house. I certainly can't recall such a thing – he always seemed to be out and working, according to my mother. It might have been different, maybe, if I'd been a boy; I never asked why I was an only child. I don't think that Dad did either.

'Just the tea, Mary love. Do me capital. I'm still bloated from yesterday, you want the truth. Your mother, she did me proud. Chicken, we had. Sprouts and carrots. Potatoes, course . . .'

Mary smiled as she crouched at his feet, idly piling up the bricks into a haphazard stack as Jeremy passed them over to her, one by one, the windbreak now a scattered ruin.

'Isn't this the moment, Dad, where you're meant to tell me that she sends her love . . . ?'

Her father drank some tea and looked about him, and then down towards his grandson.

'My, though,' he said. 'He's come on, hasn't he? Since last I saw him. Leaps and bounds, I'd say. Leaps and bounds.'

Mary concealed her hurt, and carried on talking.

'Went up West last night, Dad. Jackie and a few friends of ours. It was lovely.'

Mary's father nodded, as he slowly stirred his tea.

'I've heard it's quite a sight, this time of the year. Not been. But just look at that young man there, will you? Leaps and bounds . . . what a little scamp.'

It's difficult to know, really, how much my Dad has changed over all the years. He's the same person, I think – older, of course . . . it was a little bit shocking actually, a minute or so back there, seeing the way he clambered up into the armchair. He always used to be so very agile – a great one for walking, swore by shanks's pony, didn't often take the bus, even to work. I don't know his age, not exactly. Sixty-five? Older? Not seventy – he can't be that. He did get married late in life, I do know that. I'm not very good with people's ages – I hate it if ever anyone asks me to guess or anything, because you never want to offend, do you? And it's even harder when they're old . . . it sounds awful, I suppose, but when they're old, it doesn't really seem to matter, the exact number of years that they've been on the earth. They're old – and that's that, in a way: they have just become this other and distant thing that the rest of us call old. They've crossed the divide, if you like. A bit why children, I think, often take to them so immediately – it's rather as if they are a completely different breed from the rest of us, like ponies or hamsters or nuns, or something.

'Well anyway . . . It was lovely.'

And then, so suddenly, Mary was empty of things she could say to the man. It had happened before, this. She was always so very pleased to see him, but once she had offered him tea and got him settled and he'd played a little with Jeremy, there was just nothing in the world left to talk about. It's the great divide, you see – once one person has crossed it, there's so little ground in between.

'Have you seen the gramophone, Dad? See it? Over there on the floor. Isn't it grand? It's not ours, or anything. Friend of

Jackie's, he lent it to us for the party. There's some wonderful records. Would you like to hear it, Dad? Shall I put a record on for you? I expect you're a bit like Jackie – nothing too jazzy, is what he says. You're the same, are you? But there are some really pretty songs if you'd like to hear them, Dad.'

Mary's father set down his cup and saucer on the three-legged table, as he slowly shook his head and smiled his regret.

'Not on my account, Mary love. Get to my age, you value a bit of peace. But it's a fine-looking instrument, that's for sure. I was thinking – that must have set you back a pretty penny.'

'Mm, yes – well as I say, it isn't ours, more's the pity.'

And I had said to Jonathan Leakey when he dropped us back last night in his beautiful Humber – and oh my goodness, when I looked at the clock I just couldn't believe it – I said to him Oh Jonathan, the gramophone, do you want to come upstairs and collect it? And he said Oh no hurry at all, Mary my dear – you get the benefit, ay? Think of the loan of it as my little Christmas present, why don't you? And then afterwards, just as he was leaving, he said something so perfectly strange: he said Oh yeh, talking of Christmas presents, I hope and trust that that very fine little silk camisole went down well with you? And then he assured me that it was – what did he say? Top of the range, I think. And I must have been confused at the time – as well as just so very desperately tired – and so I just sort of said Oh yes, very nice – lovely, it is. It was only after and in bed that I got to thinking how very odd it was that he even was aware that Jackie had given me such a thing, let alone that he should have been so rude as to have just brought it up, like that. And then I thought, well – the only way he could have known is if Jackie had spoken to him about it, and I must say that the thought of that made me go quite cold. I mean to say – it's so personal, so intimate a thing . . . how could he go discussing it with a man in a pub? I may be silly, but I found it disturbing – and still I haven't quite decided, you know, whether or not to put it to Jackie, ask him for an explanation.

'So, Dad . . .' said Mary now, as casually as she could. Jeremy – he's getting a bit tired, look. You can always tell because he starts to rub his eyes and he becomes really quite impatient with whatever it is that he's doing: I've had to stop him twice now from throwing those bricks about. And now that I've said 'So, Dad . . .', what do I follow it up with? Because I have – I have completely and utterly run out of anything to say to the man. And that disturbs me too.

'So, Dad . . . any plans for the new year? Made your resolutions?'

And Mary now was even more disturbed than ever as whatever colour there had been in her father's lean and sunken cheeks now so suddenly seemed to be leached away, and his face became quite set and as serious as she remembered it could sometimes be.

'Well . . .' he said so quietly. 'Not too sure we want to go thinking very much at all, so far as next year is concerned. One thing and another . . .'

'Oh . . . !' exclaimed Mary, quite shocked. How odd though, is what she was thinking: even at my age and a mother myself, the sight of a parent of mine who is this uneasy, it is just so totally alarming.

'Best left alone,' her father concluded. 'And me – I'd better be getting myself off. Thanks for the tea then, Mary love.'

Minutes ago, if she was honest, she would have rushed headlong at this chance of his leaving – not because she wanted to be rid of him, exactly, but simply because she had felt so wholly drained of anything more. But suddenly it had become of the utmost importance to keep him here, to keep him here with her and her son, her father – to keep him here and make him tell her whatever it was that had troubled him so that she could laugh it all away and assure him that any fears he might be harbouring were utterly groundless and then he would be so very relieved and then

208

Mary, she could stamp down hard on all of her own, and kill them – and then (who knew?) she might even be able to breathe again.

'Oh no please, Dad – don't go. Don't go yet – we never see nearly enough of you. Please stay – I'll make us some more tea, yes? Or – I know! Would you like a glass of beer? I'm sure there's some left. Should have offered it earlier – it's just that I never think.'

'You sure, Mary love? Taken up a lot of your time . . .'

'No no – yes of course I'm sure, Daddy. Here – you stay there, and I'll get you some beer to drink, yes? Still Christmas after all, isn't it?'

'Well . . . I wouldn't say no to a drop of beer, if you're sure your Jackie wouldn't mind . . . ?'

'Oh *goodness*, Dad – he'd be *insisting* on it, if he was here, of course he would. You just wait – I'll be back in a jiffy. Oh look – Jeremy's gone to sleep. I thought he looked tired. Well he'll be fine down there – nice and warm in front of the fire. You just stay there and get comfortable, Dad – all right? And I'll bring you a nice bottle of Bass.'

Well right then, thought Mary, as she clattered around in the kitchen drawer in search of the blessed bottle opener which she remembered perfectly well putting back in here it couldn't be more than an hour ago. Well right then, I've made him stay – oh here it is, I've got it now – so I have to ask him. I maybe don't want him to answer, but I've done it now – and I have to ask him.

'Here you are, Dad. I don't think I've poured it out terribly well – all a bit frothy. But there's more in the bottle when you want it. All right? Nice? Good. So, Dad . . . why do you say that? All what you said. About next year, and everything.'

Mary was back on the hearthrug, hugging her knees and looking up at her father, she hoped not over-anxiously. She watched him sip his beer.

'Mm. Good drop, very. Always dependable, Bass is. You know where you are with a bottle of Bass.'

'I'm glad you like it. So, Daddy . . . ?'

'Well, Mary love . . . I'm no politician . . . don't pretend to know the powers that be, how their minds are working. But you've got a wireless, haven't you Mary? You see what's in the papers, do you? Have to make your own mind up.'

'But – *we're* safe, aren't we? I mean I know it's awful for Czechoslovakia and the other places round there, can't remember what they're called. And it's beastly for the Jews, of course. But – well . . . *we're* safe, aren't we? Aren't we, Daddy?'

Mary's father set down his glass and spread out wide the fingers of both his hands.

'Oh – I expect so. All things being equal. I will take the rest of that bottle then, Mary, if it doesn't inconvenience you . . .'

Mary rushed up to fetch it: she poured it slowly into his glass. So there we have it, then: I asked him if we were safe, and he says he expects so. All things being equal. Whatever that may mean. And anyway they're not, are they? Equal. Nothing and nobody can ever be equal – and that's always the trouble.

'But it's *definite*, isn't it? That we're safe? Because Mr Chamberlain, well – we've signed a treaty, haven't we? England. Is it a treaty? Well we've signed *something*, anyway, with this Hitler person, so that means we've *got* to be safe, doesn't it? Otherwise what's the point of signing it? This thing. What's wrong, Dad . . . ? Why are you looking like that?'

'Well . . . it's just that, people can sign things sometimes and, well . . . just a signature, isn't it? When all's said and done. No more than writing on a piece of paper. They're not Englishmen, you see. Your foreigner, he doesn't think like we do. In particular the Hun. You never know what he's thinking next – and he's not going to tell you, either. Still – best leave it all to the experts, hey?'

'But you don't really think there could be a . . . ? I mean it *couldn't*, could it Daddy? Actually become . . . ?'

'Well . . . we hope not. I doubt it will – no, of course it won't. But they are digging trenches, aren't they? Hyde Park and other places. Not for daffodils, is it? These gas masks they're giving out: not a pretty sight. National Service, that's back with us . . .'

Mary's eyes were bright, and she had to talk very quickly now because all of this, it had to be stopped because she couldn't really bear it, all of this – and now there rose up within her the flame of fury: she was very angry with him indeed, her father, for not just telling her that it was all just a storm in a teacup and that everything would be well, you just see if it won't.

'But it's *voluntary*, isn't it?' she gabbled excitedly. 'It's not like they're conscripting people, or anything. It's just these young men who quite fancy the idea, that's all it is. It's all *voluntary*, isn't it?'

' 'Tis, oh yes. It's all voluntary. But then you see it always is. That's always the way, right at the beginning.'

Mary now was startled, and she struck up more shrilly.

'The beginning! What do you mean the beginning? The beginning of what? There isn't a beginning. You don't know what you're talking about. There's not going to be anything, so how can there be a beginning? I don't know why I even brought it up – I thought you'd know, but you don't. You don't at all. You simply just don't know what you're talking about. So there's no point going on.'

'No reason to lose your temper, Mary my dear. I wasn't the one who was talking – it was you. But one thing you ought to remember . . . you ought to remember, Mary, that me: I've been here before.'

Mary stared at him – and just had to stop all the bluster, then: a relief, in truth, for whatever she was feeling (so hard to say – such a tangle of things) it was far from the feistiness that she had more or less determined to exhibit. She breathed out quite slowly and lightly rested her chin upon the domes of her drawn-up knees, her arms wrapped protectively about her legs, as if she might lose them.

'I know . . .' she said, in a very small voice.

Mary's father nodded, as if there was nothing further to say upon the matter. He smoothed his palms along his thighs, easing himself forward in the chair, eyes alert and ready to make a move.

'Don't go yet, Dad. Please. Stay a bit longer. Talk to me.'

And there was such supplication in her voice – the whine of need, cut by urgency – that Mary's father was stopped where he was, in a sort of confusion.

'Best all left alone, you know . . .' he said to her, quietly.

'Or maybe it isn't. You've never ever mentioned it. Not to me. Were you actually . . . ? God, you know, Daddy – I'm just realising, it's really quite a shock . . . I don't know anything about you. Do I? What you've done, how you've spent your life. All I've ever known is . . . well, that you married my mother and that you're my father. That's all. That's all I've ever known about you.'

Mary's father was shifting uneasily, now – not at all content with this danger of intimacy.

'All you needed to know,' he said quite gruffly. 'All that concerned you.'

'But the Great War,' Mary persisted – not at all really wanting to, but very vexingly driven, it would appear, by something inside that just wouldn't be quelled, however much the rest of her was yearning even now for the balm of uncaring, the warm bliss of ignorance. 'You were – in it, were you? Sounds so stupid . . . I just don't *know*, you see? But something so very huge as that, so very important – how can it be that you've never even mentioned it?'

She watched him now as he sighed – sat back in the armchair, accepting of a sort of defeat and resignation, as if under the lights and relentlessness of intense interrogation, each of his feints and prevarications had one by one been rumbled and exposed, the gauze of subterfuge torn away raggedly and opening out into the light of day this shifting mulch of all that he had failed to conceal. It was only then that Mary realised how very much older he looked to her now than the image of her father that she carried within her. The moustache – once so very luxuriant, auburn, even reddish in the sunlight, and just very slightly turned up at its pointed ends . . . it now was more brittle and hard and gunmetal grey, just a patch of scrubby growth, any jauntiness gone from it. The folds of skin beneath his eyes drew them down into an air of melancholy and almost regret, even if the light of a smile just flickered within them. His ears seemed larger – flat and fleshy – and each with a thicket of ugly hair. While he was living his life – of which I know nothing – my father, along the way, became an old man.

'It didn't . . . *do* . . .' he said, eventually, and with extraordinary reluctance, as if each of his words was a tortured extraction. 'We never did, none of us did. Talk about it. It was something that was past. It was the future, that's what we were all told was the important thing. That's what we were told, yes . . . can't say it seemed to turn out that way. Still . . .'

His eyes flicked over to Mary, to see if she was following, to see if she was anxious. And then he suddenly was hunching forward, one finger jabbing angrily into the palm of his hand.

'What they never told us, though – and we never thought it, either – is that all of it . . . the whole damn business wouldn't make a difference. Well – I knew a good few lads who it did make a difference to. Cut down, they were, and barely twenty years of age. I was amazed, when I saw it. We were all of us, that – amazed, every one of us, walking around dazed, most all of the time. Weren't soldiers, you see – none of us were. There was a baker's boy, and a carpenter . . . one I remember, don't recall his name, though . . . worked in a funeral parlour. Got a lot of ribbing over that. Come to the right place, they all said to him – you'll make your fortune over here, you will. There was lots of jokes like that – jokes that weren't funny. Made us laugh, though. Else you'd go mad, you didn't laugh. Me – I wasn't anything, really. Just a worker – so I was ideal for them, wasn't I? Just another one of the millions. But I wasn't that young, of course – not much shy of forty I was, by this time. And earlier, Mary – when we were talking about conscription, you recall? Well – that's how it was, at the beginning. Kitchener, he got his hundreds of thousands of volunteers at the drop of a hat. So eager, they all were. Not me, though. Oh no. I didn't want to go to war. I never wanted to be a soldier. I just wanted to be an engineer – all I ever did want. Never wanted to go abroad – least of all to fight in a war. And then I was not long married to your mother – I didn't even think of volunteering. Few of my mates did, though – you couldn't hold them back, not at the beginning. And then . . . well, they were saying it would all be over by Christmas, that's what the experts were saying. Yes well. We used to say – ho yes, but they never told us *which* Christmas, did they? Anyway – needed more men, didn't they? And it wasn't so easy, second time around. And that's when the call-up started. It was the younger ones they wanted first – and then a bit later, well . . . anyone at all, really. That's when they got me. Never forget – stared at the letter, stood in the hallway just staring at that letter, read it over and over, read it a thousand times. Couldn't hardly believe it. True, though. And then before you knew it, well – saying goodbye to the wife and then to my Mum . . . my Dad, he was already gone by this time, wore himself out, I reckon. And two of my brothers, they were already in uniform – the other one, Jimmy, he was still just a little lad, thank the Lord, so he was safe and out of it. And my Mum, your Gran, dear old soul, she says to me now listen Raymond, first thing you do when you get to France is you find out where Samuel and Michael are – that's my two brothers – and you make sure you give them this parcel. I said I would. Remember it clear as day. Had in it socks and scarves she'd knitted for them. When I got over, over the Channel, I laughed. I looked at what was in front of me, and I laughed. Gave the socks to a young bloke I'd met on the crossing over, kept the scarves for myself. Never did see them, throughout the whole of the war, Samuel and Michael. No. Never did. Not throughout the whole of the war.'

He sat back abruptly then – gazing about him as if in astonishment at the shock of this voice all around him, talking so quickly, and filling the room.

'You all right, Dad . . . ?' Mary whispered with hesitation, hardly daring to breathe as her mind continued to tiptoe into this alien and vibrant territory. 'Get you something . . . ?'

She was reeling with all that she had heard, and she had to know more, all of it – she had to know everything. Most fantastic of all was the mention of his mother – who I never knew, I don't even know if she's alive – and her addressing him as Raymond: my mother, she always called him Ricky, if she called him anything at all – how on earth could this be? And the brothers, Samuel and Michael – my uncles, then. Never before have I heard their names. And there was another and younger one called Jimmy . . .

'No no . . .' sighed Mary's father, passing a shaky hand across his brow – glancing down to Jeremy, still curled up on the rug, and breathing so softly. 'No no – nothing at all, thank you Mary. Well anyway . . . there it is. The rest of it, you don't really need to hear. No one does. Best we just live in the present, hey? And hope that the next future, well . . . that it just takes care of itself. Because we're powerless, all of us, you see. Always were – always will be. So what I think we should all do now, Mary, is just enjoy what's left of this Christmas, and then . . . oh yes, oh good God yes – Christmas . . . that's a memory that'll never leave me. That very first Christmas out there. Freezing, it was. And all the banter in the trenches . . . you can imagine the sort of thing: call this Christmas? Blimey – where's the turkey, then? Where's the goose? All that. It was bully beef as it always was, but there was a bit of chocolate, I recall . . . tin of tobacco . . . I was a smoker in those days – the lungs, they can't take it any more . . . and a tot of something good and warming, yes. And then we heard it . . . couldn't believe it at first – all looking at one another, we were, as if we were going mad, or something. But no – it was right enough. From way across over No Man's Land, from the German trenches, they'd started singing Silent Night, if you can imagine it. "Silent Night . . . Holy Night . . ." they were going. And there was this Welshman in our regiment, fancied himself as a bit of a singer – well, they all of them do, Welshmen – and he starts joining in, and then we're all doing it. We're all in that freezing cold trench singing Silent Night with the ruddy Germans! Never forget it. And then one of them, one of the Boche – he takes a real risk, he does – you could see him standing up on the parapet and he's clapping and waving about his arms, and then we hear him calling out; "Happy Christmas!" he's going. "Happy Christmas, Tommy!" And all in English, as well. I thought one of our officers, he'll have him – have him picked off straight away, he will. But no – that was the miracle of it. Not a single shot. No noise at all. That was the big shock, really . . . the noise, we'd got so used to the noise, that all this silence all of a sudden, it made you go funny inside. And then I heard a bird. It's like I can hear it now. There was this little bird, somewhere about – singing its heart out. Don't remember when last I heard it. And then one or two of the lads, they start climbing up the ladder – sticking their heads over the top. And our Lieutenant –

I remember him, yes – Jefferson, his name was, his last week on earth did he but know it, poor devil – he was shouting out orders and waving his revolver about, telling everyone to get down – but they never listened, they went right over the top, and I did too – I followed them over. I was that frightened – and I didn't really know what I was up to. But I went over, and all I saw was this icy mud and broken-down stumps of trees and all these Germans way over there, and coming towards us. I walked right over to their barbed wire – there was a lot of us now – and this German, young boy, could've been half my age, all blond he was – he came right up to me and he put his hand out and I shook it, I shook his hand, and he offered me a cigarette – English, I couldn't not notice, Woodbines, God knew where he got them – and I gave him a bit of my chocolate ration, and then he ups and he says to me "Do you know the Old Kent Road . . . ?" Here I am on a Christmas morning on a battlefield in the middle of France, and this young German soldier – and I'm smoking his fag – he wants to know if I know the Old Kent Road . . . And I tell him yes I do, matter of fact, and he says he likes it there, and it's where his auntie lives. I ask you. Over to the side a bit, a few of the lads were kicking around a football with the Hun, couldn't barely credit it. And then . . . after a bit, there were whistles blowing and all sorts from the German trenches, and I looked back at our position and I see that Jefferson, Lieutenant Jefferson, he was waving a flag about, so I look at Karl – Karl his name was – and we both shake hands again, and we turn about, the two of us, and we go back to our trenches. I just sat there a bit, talking to my mates. Come on to rain, but the ground, it was too hard with all the cold to make more mud, so that was one good thing about it. And then the sky, it was split with thunder – but it wasn't weather, oh no it wasn't that – it was the thunder of shelling again, the noise and the screaming lights, they were all of them back again, and our heads were well down,

I can tell you – and Karl, he must have been doing the same. Could've been frightened to death, because he was only a young lad, like I say. That bombardment . . . it kept up from both sides for the whole of the rest of the day, and well on into the night. You couldn't even think, with the noise. And the rain, it got really bad, and all the mud was all around us again and, well . . . that was Christmas Day. That's the one I recall. Couldn't really forget it, could you? It was a little miracle, what happened that day. Yes. A little miracle.'

He seemed to be caught in a dream for a good long while as he continued to sit there, and now in silence; then he looked over to Mary – he breathed in sharply and his eyes were concerned by what they saw there: tears were rolling freely down the length of her face, quivering at the tips of her nose and chin, and dripping off on to her hands.

'Here now – here, Mary. I didn't mean to distress you . . . I should never have opened my mouth. You see it can do no good, can it? It's no good to anyone, raking it all up again.'

Mary shook her head rapidly – her face looked maybe fierce, but her meaning was to absolve him of all responsibility, although she doubted that he saw it that way; she patted his hand and smiled up her sympathy into his face – more than that, really: a sort of collaboration. He seemed to her now to be more astounded than anything, so far as she could make out.

'And . . .' she stuttered uncertainly, 'Samuel and Michael? Your brothers?'

Mary's father looked down at his intertwined fingers, and inclined his head.

'No . . .' he sighed. 'I'm afraid not. They never came out the other side. So very many didn't, you know. Me, I suppose I was one of the lucky ones – three years, near to the day, and nary a scratch to show for it. Didn't feel it at the time, lucky though. Don't suppose I've felt it since, come to that. Anyway. Look,

Mary – let's lay it all to one side now, will we? I'm going to get going. Your mother, she'll be wondering.'

'And yes but – *your* mother. What about *your* mother?'

'Oh – dead, of course. Long dead. She got the telegram, you know, about Michael, and then less than a month after they tell her that Samuel, he was missing, presumed killed in action. I didn't get to know myself till, oh – maybe months after. Hard time – that was a hard time for me, that was. Still at the front – not being able to offer her . . . well, anything at all. There was nothing I could do. I wrote to her a lot – she was about the only one I ever did write to, the only one I had. Well – your mother, of course: dropped her a line, time to time. But dear old Mum – she never even got the most of them. And after Armistice Day, maybe a fortnight on, she died in her sleep. Quiet, like.'

'Oh. I'm so sorry. And the youngest? Jimmy? Is he—? Was he—?'

'Ah – little Jimmy. No – far as I know he's alive and well, young Jimmy is. Met some Australian lads, he did – they must have done a good job of selling him their country because that's where he went – oh, very long ago now. Sent me a card once, seemed to be doing very nicely. Tried to get me to go with him at the time, but I said no – I wouldn't have been happy there. Too flaming hot, for one thing. And anyway, it's round here, isn't it? It's round here I belong. Course, you do get to wondering how it would've been . . . Come Boxing Day, I'd not be here by the fireside – I'd be by the seaside, shouldn't wonder, because it's all back to front, you know, the weather over there.'

'That's quite a thought . . . And my mother. How did you meet her? When did you?'

'Ooh, Mary love! All these questions! Enough is enough now, don't you think? Well . . . I just sort of met her, you know, the way you do. Social of some sort. Can't hardly recall. We wed – you came along, and I worked. That's my life, really. That's all of it. Now come on, Mary – get my hat and coat, there's a good girl. And go easy, else you'll have a bawling young man there, if the last time was anything to go by.'

Mary unfolded herself and rose to her feet – smiling at him again before she went off to fetch his coat. He was standing by the time she returned – yawning extravagantly, and raising his arms above his head. Makes you dozy, he said – the fire, and a glass of beer. When I have a bit of spare cash to myself, she suddenly thought, I'm going to get him a new hat, my Dad. Because this one – just look at it. There's a tide mark, a much darker charcoal than the rest of it – all wavy over the line of the hatband, and a little mouldy right at the point, the front of the crown, where he pinches it between his fingers before he puts it on to his head – and then he pulls down the brim and to the side, with a sort of a snap. I've never ever seen him wear another – although my mother told me once that he's got a brand-new black one in tissue at the top of the wardrobe; she said she didn't know what he was keeping it for – maybe to be buried in.

As Mary wrapped his maroon and grey muffler around his neck and helped him to ease on the gabardine overcoat, she was really quite surprised when he started up his talking again, because already this afternoon he had said to her more than all the other times in her life put together.

'I think it's a shame, you know Mary, that you didn't do similar.'

She was immediately confused, as her eyes maybe told him.

'You know – do what me and your mother did. Meet – get wed. I thought it was what everyone did. But you, you had little Jeremy there – and I'm not saying anything, he's a cracking little lad, I'm not saying anything – and well, we stood by you, didn't we? Your mother and me. Through all that.'

'Well, Dad – you did, anyway. You did.'

'Yes well – she was very troubled, your mother. Still is. Worried for your reputation. You know how it is – people talking, and the like. But see – I sort of assumed, I suppose, that once you were – well, caught short, shall we call it, well then you and Jackie – and he's all right, Jackie, I'm not saying anything – but I always more or less assumed, you see Mary, that you'd both be eager to do the right thing. But it's years now isn't it, Mary love? And still there's no wedding bells. It's why your mother is the way she is. It'd bring her round, a wedding would. So what I can't understand is why you don't. I mean to say – you love him, don't you? Jackie? And I've got a few bob, you know – put aside, like.'

And while her rapidly moving lips were so very ready to comply with a gaudy abundance of platitudes – of *course* she loved Jackie, and yes I do see why my mother is upset by it all, of course I do, and it's just that we're all so very happy together, the three of us Daddy, and everyone we know just assumes that we are a married couple and you see we've just never got around to formalising the union, that's all it is – but who knows? It could happen so easily, and any time at all . . . yes, even as she was hearing her strings of words filling the air and hanging there stalely in the face of her good and stoic father, so desperate to understand, her mind was energetic in its pursuit and dissection of all the usual questions that she only could put to herself alone (and more and more often, as time went by).

When all of her idle reassurances had finally ceased, Mary's father nodded slowly and seemed quite expressionless as he took his hat from her, pinched the point of the crown between his fingers, and put it on his head. Mary was subduing a conflict of emotions, watching him as he pulled down the brim and to the side, with a sort of a snap (the glitter of pain still alive in his eyes).

'Give my love to Mother if you think it's appropriate, Dad. And thank you so much for the presents and everything. And the talk. It meant so much to me.'

'Right then, Mary love. Well you've always been one to know your own mind. Regards to Jackie, hey? Sorry to have missed him. And he's all right then, is he? No problems at all?'

This time Mary just shook her head briefly, and kissed him on the cheek. She walked down the stairs with him and stood in the cold of the street, waving him away until he turned a corner. One of his feet . . . as he plodded away, Mary noticed that one of his feet – and she had never observed it before, so maybe this was a recent thing, and she was ashamed that she couldn't have told you – but one of his feet, it came down just more heavily than the other one did, and the roll of it slightly tipped him with each of his steps, the hint of heaviness to just one side. It made it seem from the rear as if he was humbled and resigned to quite rhythmically putting to an unseen presence a series of maybe rather delicate questions, and receiving only silence for all his pains. Mary felt a pang inside her that drew itself out and became such an aching – a sweet and yet convulsing remorse for all that she and anyone else had ever forced him to endure, and so great a regret that she could do nothing to spare him this eternal hurt that he must carry about him, crouched and unforgiving, upon his shoulder. Then she shivered, closed the door and ran back up the stairs to be warm and safe in the flat with Jeremy.

He was still fast asleep on the rug where she had left him. Mary took her father's cup and saucer along with the beer glass into the kitchenette, where she set them down on the draining board. And then she was quite surprised to be pouring out for herself a mid-afternoon measure of ginger wine – a thing she'd never do (and it wasn't even a drink that she particularly cared for). She sat down in the armchair still dented and warm from her father's impression, and looking into the dull, now, and barely alive embers in the fire grate, she slowly sipped the ginger wine. And then she had a little touch more, thinking yes, I really don't at all care for it, you know, this ginger wine. Sheila does – she likes it, and it had seemed to go down not too badly with Molly as well, but it's not wholly for me, not quite to my taste. In truth, I don't really have a favourite – sherry, time to time, a glass of cider on a hot summer's day . . . beer and spirits I can't abide. But it's not at all drinks that I'm thinking about, really – that's no more than a floating curtain, a gauzy little wisp of a thing, barely filtering the glare of what is confronting me now.

Because *I* had – I had assumed that too. What Dad said. Because there had never been any doubt in my mind that Jackie, that he was the man for me. And here was not the outcome of experience, for I had none. I only ever knew two boys before I met Jackie in the park, that day. There was Simon, the son of one of my mother's neighbours – he worked in the dairy just lifting churns, so far as I could see; people called him Simple Simon, and it wasn't just on account of his name, I don't think, because he did seem to be, a bit. Never quite with you, if you know what I mean. We went to the Gaumont and we saw some awful cowboy film or other – his choice, needless to say – and during the Movietone news he put his hand on my knee and I picked it up immediately between my thumb and forefinger and placed it very deliberately on the arm of the seat; it was rather as if I had happened upon a tattered piece of litter, and had fastidiously deposited it in the nearest and most suitable receptacle. And then there was Emil – his father was French and terribly rich, my mother would keep on telling me, in wholesale food, or something strange. He was a handsome young man, Emil, and one evening when we had known each other for a month or more, I let him kiss me properly and I rather enjoyed it, I have to admit. We saw each other a few times after that, but he became extremely difficult to control, Emil, following the kiss we had shared. Sometimes, in that Austin he had, it was for all the world like wrestling with an octopus – it was all so very physically wearing, keeping him off me, quite apart from just utterly dispiriting. I was still, I suppose, officially going out with him – and then I met Jackie and, well . . . that was that, so far as Emil was concerned, I'm rather afraid. And Emil, he said he was desolate – he said that life for him now would be but a hollow sham, were I not to be a part of it. I told him to stop this minute being so perfectly ridiculous, and he damned me for an unfeeling and cold-hearted Englishwoman and demanded to know from heaven on high what I was made of, that I could treat him so cruelly. Hardly a week went by, and then he was seen by all and sundry stepping out with the widowed owner of the Sealey Road Chop House, and I must say he did look so much more calm and content than ever he had done with me at his side.

But Jackie, well – it was all so different. He began to sweet-talk me, of course, but in truth he didn't have to. I was his, really, fom the moment I laid eyes on him. And so we made love – and God, although it's always over so terribly quickly, it was still so very sweet to me, just having him there and inside of me – but nonetheless it was a perfect shock when the curse that month, it just didn't come. Jackie, he brushed it aside – until he couldn't, of course. And I was frightened – I thought that now he maybe wouldn't want me any more, that he'd just go off and leave me as my mother had always warned me that all men do. Well, of course that didn't happen, and it made me love him all the more. But yes – I had assumed that too, what Dad said. That after a bit, and while I was still pregnant, that we'd go and get married, Jackie and me. I wouldn't have minded a registry office – it didn't have to be in a church, or anything, although I knew that that was what my mother had always set her heart on (and me too, in a way – I had too, when I was younger: I always thought that that would be the way). But like Dad says – it's years now, isn't it? And still he's never asked me. I said it to him once – long ago, and in a very roundabout manner: he didn't rise to it, not even a bit. It could have been him being so clever as to appear to be stupid – it could have been one of those times. Or maybe, since the crisis had passed, it has simply just never occurred to him, I really couldn't say. But I had assumed – I always had. And I am still hoping. Sounds maybe silly, I suppose, but if I am honest, it is the one thing in the world that I most desire – to be married to Jackie, and in the eyes of God.

So there. And just to think, though – that throughout the Great War . . . and they say it's the war to end all wars, don't they? So for all its horror, there's comfort in that, at least . . . but throughout its endless duration, I was just like Jeremy is now, look – asleep and oblivious of all that is happening. So hard to believe. But I'm not, you know, a great thinker. It quite shocks me to realise that I don't ever seem to have thought about anything at all. I mean I'm not a stupid person, although I know my education – I am well aware – it was very ordinary, and really quite brief . . . but I have maybe deluded myself as the years have passed into imagining that I know and understand things – because I'm a bit of a reader, maybe, or because, I suppose, if I'm honest, I do not often, if ever, encounter the need to, well – rise to a challenge in conversation, say, or delve into a matter, analyse anything . . . and I have become complacent. I do not enquire. I mean to say, if I had been bothered at any point in the past to just sit down on my own for two minutes and won-der about my father's life, then I surely must have divined that it was extremely likely that he, in common with the bulk of British manhood, had served his country as a soldier at arms. And yet I never did – and I never asked, and neither he nor my mother had ever so much as mentioned it. I suppose that with-out ever putting it into words, I assumed that my father had met my mother, that I came along, and then he worked: that that was his life – just as he said – and that all the silent older people, they were not entitled to a history of disappointment and desire, ambition or vitality. How very shallow and selfish we all can be. And do you know . . . I truly do so much dislike this ginger wine that I'm going to stop drinking it, right this instant; I can pour what's left of it back into the bottle – because just to flush it away, that would be wrong, somehow: I just know I couldn't do it.

That was the door. That was the door downstairs in the hallway. That'll be Jackie then, back from wherever he's been. I'd better get rid of this glass – and I'd better look lively, put a smile on my face to welcome him home, that's what I'll do. I would have expected the flat door to have opened by now – because he bounds up the stairs, Jackie does, three at a time he takes them – so I wonder what it is that can be keeping him. It *was* the door I heard . . . I'm sure it was. Living somewhere for a while, you get to know all the very individual sounds that a house can create – sometimes, it seems, quite independently of human interference. The creak of the floorboards by the fireplace, the boom and shudder of that Ascot heater, the fizz of the light switch in the bedroom – the tinkle that the glasses in the cupboard always make whenever a bus rumbles by: I could hear recordings of them all on a desert island, and I'd identify every one of them. Ah! Yes – I was right, it was the door, because now I hear him right outside . . . and here he is now, back at home, red-faced and maybe not too happy, by the look of him – but I'm standing up, and I've kissed him now.

'Hello, Jackie love. All right? You just missed my Dad. He sends his . . . Look at this – look at the golly he brought over for Jeremy. Isn't he smart? Still asleep, look – don't wake him.'

Jackie ran his hand through his hair and idly glanced over to more or less where it was that Mary had been pointing.

'Mm? Oh yeh – nice, very nice. Um – wouldn't mind a bit of a lie-down, if I'm honest with you Mary. Get a little kip in before suppertime, that's all right with you.'

'Oh – yes of course, Jackie. I think that's a very good idea. You enjoy what holiday's left to you. Do you want anything?

Tea? Shall I make you some tea? I expect you've had beer, though . . .'

Jackie was looking about him, his eyes alert in a weary face; it was as if he suspected strangers of lurking behind the curtains, or something.

'You all right are you, Jackie . . . ?'

Jackie looked at her sharply.

'Yeh. Yeh – yeh, course I am.'

Mary nodded to his reassurance.

'No – problems at all, are there Jackie?'

And then, thank the Lord – because Mary would confess to feeling just a little uneasy – Jackie's face was transformed in an instant by that warm and roguish smile that he knew she so loved – and he winked at her then and touched her lightly just under the chin.

'Problems? Nah. Not for us, Mary love. Problems? Nah.'

And he shook his head with energy at the very idea.

◉

Jackie was feeling bilious, if anyone wanted to know. He was wincing even at the watery gleaming of mute winter light that was crazing the grime of the outside of the windowpane as he drew the thin curtains against it. He eased himself on to the bed and lay on his back, keeping very still there, his two palms and interwoven fingers forming an inadequate cradle for the bulk of his head that was seeming now a shade too large, too tender and lagged within, his brow just palpitating coldly. His eyelids closed, as he tried to work it out.

It were that last pint what I shouldn't of had. First one, well – you want that, don't you? Clear your head. Because I don't mind telling you, earlier on this morning – what with Mary banging around in the kitchen the way she was doing, well . . . my head, oh dear oh dear – and the old tum as well, I weren't too happy. Little Jeremy – when there was all the doings with his building bricks on the floor, there – he ups and give out one of his little yelps and I'm not kidding you, my son: like someone gone and shoved the poker right through my ears and out the other side. So what I reckoned I'd do is get myself down the Rose & Crown – I knowed that Len'd be there – help out his regulars, sort of style – and Jonny and all, shouldn't wonder, and maybe a couple of the other lads. Didn't know about Dickie, though: sobered up nicely at one point he did, but blimey – time we drop him off he were roaring again. So I reckoned, well – come midday dinnertime, he either going to need all the doctoring he can give hisself, or else he's stone dead, mate – and then it won't be so much the hair of the dog as a bleeding wake we got on our hands. So like I say, the first pint, well – that's more a medicine, times like this, than an actual drink – it's something you just got to get down you. Then you're a little bit better – got the other eye open, you take my meaning, and well – you sort of get a taste for it then, don't you? Next one or two – slip down like mother's milk, they does. And before you can say Jack Wossname, you're all having a good old natter – nice little drink with your mates – and it's like the Christmas party again, like it all still going. So there he were, old Jonny – like I thought he'd be, propping up the bar, and blimey – don't he look a picture. I mean he were smart last night, but here he is now in a brand-new suit, looks like – stripes, it got: shine on his shoes'd blind you. Me, I ain't even wearing no tie – just the muffler stuck in my coat. And scratching away at my chin like I am, I'm reminded I ain't gone and shaved neither. Ah well – still the Christmas holidays, ain't it? See to all that palaver in the morning.

'How you do it, Jonny? Ay? Fresh as paint, you look. I hadn't seed it with my own eyes, well – I wouldn't never credit it, you been out half the night. Vampire – that it, Jonny? You drink the blood of virgins, do you? Keep you young? Talking of which – how's old Molly getting on then, ay?'

'Keep a civil tongue, there's a good lad Jackie,' said Jonathan Leakey, his eyes quite careful to conceal their secrets. 'Don't do to go casting aspersions against the good name of a lady.'

'Weren't the *lady* I were casting wossnames about, were it Jonny? Here Len – you tell me how *you* got on, then. We won't get nothing out of Jonny.'

Len was laughing as he polished up a pint pot with a swift and practised flourish of his cloth – fist wrapped tight inside it, two swabs inside to the left and two to the right followed by a good and rapid buffing up the sides and around the rim.

'Nor me, Jackie lad. What I will say is that Sally and me, we partook of a merry conversation, discussed the world situation – put it to rights, like. Pooh-poohed all them clowns in Downing Street, and sank the best part of a bottle of gin – I am not joking. Taking her up the Kardomah, Wednesday.'

'I am *proud* of you, Len!' laughed Jackie – reaching across the bar to slap him on the back. 'And one thing with that Sally, ay? Won't never go short, will you? Ay? All them peaches and melons . . .'

'Now now, Jackie,' admonished Len. 'Keep it nice, ay? Keep it nice.' And then he smirked, despite his efforts not to. 'Know what you mean, though – she's a big girl, Sally, there's no denying – but sweet-natured with it, if you know what I'm meaning.'

'I *do*, Len – I *do*, my son. See, Jonny? Len – he don't mind, do he? Filling us in a bit. So how come you're all silent, then? Bit of a frost, were it? Rumble you, did she? Flea in the ear was it, Jonny? Get us in another couple, Len – there's a good man. Nip for yourself and all, ay?'

'Just shows what you know,' sniffed Jonathan Leakey. 'No more ale for me, Len. Can't take the volume. Give us a large

Scotch, ay? All right Jackie – I'll pay for this lot. No – we got on very nicely, as it happens, Molly and me. Taking her to meet Mr Wisely, come the weekend. Be back down in London by then.'

'Yeh?' checked Jackie. 'What you doing that for? And no it's all right, Len – I'll get these, these is mine. I mean, what – don't you want her for yourself? And anyway – thought you told me that Mr Wisely—'

'Yeh – yeh I did. But like I says to you, he likes them around him. So when I see a pretty thing what might appeal, well . . . always like to do a favour for a mate, don't you?'

Jackie nodded, and then he set to supping his new pint, not really minding too much one way or the other.

'He's a bit of a funny one though, ain't he? Your Mr Wisely.'

'Singular, Jackie, I think you'll find the word is. You don't want to forget him, though. Mark my words – he'll do you a bit of good.'

'Yeh – you keep saying. Good, like in what? What sort of good can he do me? What makes you think he want to, anyway?'

'Took an instant shine to you, Jackie lad – seen it a mile off. Ever you want a job, he's the man to go to. Cheers, Jackie: your very good health.'

'Yeh – cheers, Jonny: cheers. I got a job. Don't need no job.'

'Yeh I know, Jackie, I know – but I mean a *proper* job. No offence.'

Jackie slammed down his glass and turned to face him.

'You do this, don't you Jonny? Ay? You says things to me and you know right well I'm going to get the bleeding hump, and then you gives me all of this "no offence" lark of yours. I mean – what you're doing, what you're doing Jonny, whether you know it or not – and you maybe do – you're writing me off, that's what you're doing. You're saying – no no, you just shut up and listen now Jonny, no good you barging in again while I'm still bleeding talking, is it? What you're saying is whatever

230

it is I does, it ain't nothing at all next to all the caper you get up to – and as for the big great god on high Mr bleeding *Wisely*, well – I ain't fit to get down on my knees and tie up his wossnames, am I?'

'I never said that, Jackie. I never. All I mean—'

'Yeh – all you mean is that I'm just a bit of muck, that's all you're meaning, Jonny. And I ain't. See?'

'Course, Jackie – course. I know you ain't. Course I know that.'

'Yeh well – don't go forgetting it. I got a good job, I have. And next year, it going to get even better, see? Partner, that's what I'm going to be. And earning good money and all. Maybe it ain't much compared to you – pocket change to Mr Wisely, I've no doubt at all – but it's a lot for me and Mary and I'm going to make sure I get it, get that job, and get us a better life and all.'

'Commendable, Jackie. Highly commendable. Len – man's just earnt hisself a very large Scotch. Yeh, and stick another one in there, will you Len? One for yourself, ay? No but listen, Jackie – that's exactly what I'm meaning, ain't it? Course you want a better life for you and Mary and that little nipper you got. Nice little lad, what I hear. So yeh – course you do. And all I'm saying is, you listen to me and go and see the man – no listen, hear me out – you just go and see him, right? And you can get all of that and better, and a bleeding sight quicker and all. I heard you're going to be sniffing round one of them new little houses they're throwing up round north London. Well – mortgage, Jackie: don't come cheap. And it's every week, mind. Can't be chucking all your cash about in the Rose & Crown no more. Things'll be tight. And then little Jerry starts growing up . . .'

'Jeremy his name is, you want to know.'

'Yeh – Jeremy. What I said. He starts growing up, well – going to need a lot of money, ain't it? And who knows? Another one come along, well – don't need to spell it out, do I?'

'Yeh well I thought of all that, ain't I? I ain't stupid. Everyone round here seems to think I'm stupid, or something – well I ain't. Now my little brother Alfie . . . well, granted, he's the brains in the family – yeh, give you that. He's the one what stuck at his schooling, reading books and that. Nice little office job he got – proper pension lined up . . . even learning how to speak French, he is now. Now *I* think that's a waste of time – never going to France, is we? But he's right to do it because he wants to make more of hisself, and that's always right, ain't it? Got to be, every time. And yeh I *know*, Jonny – you don't have to go butting in to tell it me again – I *know* that's what you been saying, but see – I'm doing it my way, ain't I? I work with my hands – it's the only way I know. And I got good at it. And I'm going to get even better, see? And I'll be well able to afford that mortgage and . . . yeh, I'm going to have to cut down a bit, here and there. In here mainly, I suppose, yeh . . . but still, I'm going to make it work, see? Mary and Jeremy – and myself and all – we'll all get the benefit. He's going to have a real good life, that lad of mine – better than what I ever got, that's for bleeding sure. Big success, he's going to be – a proper swell. Worth ten of your Mr Wiselys any bleeding day of the week. Listen to me: next year – you mark it, Jonny: next year – come 1939, yeh? I *will* do well. And if I'm wrong, I'm wrong. But I won't be. You'll see.'

'All you got to do is go and *see* the man, Jackie . . . Can't hurt, can it? Little talk.'

Jackie simply regarded him.

'You been listening to a single bleeding word I been saying? Have you? I reckon that Scotch you keep on sinking over there, it's done for your brain it has, Jonny. You just ain't taking it in, is you?'

'Yeh – taking it in. Have to be dead and buried, wouldn't you? Not to be taking it in – Gawd knows you're on about it enough, ain't you Jackie? Ay? Oh my good Gawd – oh blimey . . . ! Look what's just fell through the door. Your very dear friend Mr Weak, if I ain't mistaken. Dear oh dear – what do he look like?'

Jackie turned away and towards the door – and he had to laugh out loud at the sight of him: white as a wossname, he is – looking like he just taken a tumble off of the roof, or something.

'Oi Dickie! Over here, you terrible person you! What a wreck, as I live and breathe. Here, Jonny – why you go on calling him Weak, when you know full well that his bleeding name's Wheat? Ay?'

Jonathan Leakey shrugged his indifference.

'Wheat, yeh. What I said. Don't know what you're talking about. Anyway – whatever his bleeding name is, it looks like we got to get him in a belter, and pronto. He don't get a drink under his belt a bit sharpish, he's going to pass out on the floor. And Len, he don't like that – do you Len? Rose & Crown ankle-deep in dead people – bad for trade, ain't it Len?'

Len was chuckling as he pulled a pint.

'I've seen worse,' he said. 'Morning after, ain't it? Well – after-noon, in his case. That's Christmas for you – only natural. Ale he'll be wanting is it, Jackie? Or a little nip, you reckon?'

'Let the lad hisself make up his own mind, ay? Here he is. Well well well Dickie. Made it, then? Good lad. Now then – what you having, ay?'

'Please, Jackie old man . . .' said Dickie so tremulously. 'I can just about take all the hearty banter, don't you know – yes, I believe I can . . . but I beg and implore you, Jackie – please do not even contemplate slapping me about the back or shoulders because I most sincerely believe that should you do so, I shall simply fragment. Greetings, Jonathan. Do I find you well?'

Jonathan Leakey gurgled his amusement into his glass of Scotch.

'You find me a bleeding sight better than yourself, by the looks of it – that's for bleeding sure. Have a whisky – sort you out no time flat. Len – tot of gold for the lad, ay?'

Dickie leaned heavily against the bar, his eyes softly flickering as he passed a hesitant hand across his pinkish forehead, where strands of his hair were clinging stickily.

'Most kind, Jonathan. I thank you. Much appreciated, I do assure you.'

Jonathan Leakey rolled up his eyes and nodded robotically.

'He don't get no better, do he . . . ? Here, Jackie – you been smoking my fags just one after the bleeding other, you know that?'

'Oh blimey – I clean forgot. I got my case, ain't I? I just ain't used to carrying them about, let alone in a case. Sorry, Jonny – here you go, you have one of mine. Prime, ain't it? Lovely little cigarette case, that is. And the lighter – works first time every time, it do. My Mary – she give me them. Oh – told you, did I? Yeh well. Here – how come you don't never smoke then, Dickie? Always meant to ask.'

'Oh . . . down to my medical training, I suppose it is partly. Terribly bad for you, you know. A lot of people say it's harmless, but I can't see how it can be. Filthy stuff really, tobacco. Do you know, about fifty years ago, not much more I don't think – oh no, it was less actually, much less. Turn of the century, probably. Anyway, at Eton – you know, the school – every boy was forced to smoke a cigarette before morning roll call. Good for the tubes, is what they told them. And rather interestingly . . . um – something wrong, Jonathan, is there? Said something, have I . . . ?'

'Oh no no *no* . . . !' yawned out Jonathan Leakey, with exaggerated swagger. 'No no – not at all. All very *interesting*, I must say . . .'

'Oh. Well. I'm sorry if I'm being tedious. I'll just drink my drink and shut up then, shall I?'

'No no – come on now!' laughed Jackie. 'Don't go getting all female on us Dickie. You finish what you was saying, and then you can get us in another one, ay?'

'Mm. Well – it was nothing, really. Just the observation that very few of the Eton intake at the time went on to become smokers in later life, you see. Because they were made to do it at school. Basic psychology, I suppose it is. Same again then is it, gentlemen?'

And then a new and rather menacing voice from behind him cut through all that and still was hanging quite jaggedly in the air:

'Yap yap yap – what a fucking racket . . . !'

Jackie revolved immediately he heard it – raised up his chin and assumed an attitude of defiance. Jonathan Leakey glanced over with a degree of curiosity, and Dickie was still trying quite doggedly to properly focus – to locate the actual source of the remark.

'Accommodate you in some way, can I?' said Jackie, quite coldly. And yeh – I sort of do, recognise him, this geezer. Seed him in here, time to time – not what you'd call a regular, mind: wouldn't know him to talk to. So what's he reckon he's up to then? Bleeding cheek, I call it.

The man had big shoulders made huge by a thick woollen navy coat in the reefer style, a dark blue cap pulled down low over his wide and bony forehead. He shifted only slightly, as if newly awakening.

'Weren't talking to you. It's the toff I were talking to.'

'Yeh?' bristled Jackie – his glass back down on the bar, his hands just loosely clenched now, and down at his sides. 'Well you can talk to me instead, you got something to say.'

'It's all right, Jackie . . .' said a doubtful Dickie, consciously striving to dampen his alarm while at the same time so terribly aware that however he would approach this, whichever way it was he set about it, it would not be right, and the outcome bad. 'I don't mind talking to the chap – rude though he is . . .'

The big man turned to face him.

'I ain't a "chap". I ain't, for your information sonny, a bleeding "chap". All right? I've heard you before in here. I come in for a quiet little drink, and all the time I'm hearing this bleeding squawking what's all that ever come out of you. You so high and mighty – you such a toff – why you come in here? What you doing in a boozer with the likes of us? Ay? Having a bit of a laugh, are you? Think it's funny, do you? Drinking with men what have to *work* for a bloody living!'

Jackie stepped forward and glared into his face.

'Now you listen to me, friend—'

'What's the matter? Toff mate of yours can't speak for hisself? What are you then? His little nursemaid?'

Jackie was scarlet, and seething within. He could feel a hand on his arm – Jonny, shouldn't wonder – warning him, it was, and urging caution. Well all right then: I'll give it a go.

'Like I were saying. We can do this two ways. You say you're sorry for causing offence to Mr Wheat here, and we all have a nice little drink together and forget about the whole thing, yeh? Or—'

'Or what? Things going to get nasty, are they? I wouldn't advise it, chum. Mop you up, no trouble. And as for your Mr whatever-you-called-him – Weak, is it? Him I can spit out in bits.'

Jackie turned away from him slowly, his eyebrows raised up to Dickie and Jonathan Leakey – this, and the spread of his out-stretched arms urging the two of them to behold and marvel at the bravado of the man. And then a lightning pirouette that the big man behind him could never have seen coming, and his fist lashed out once to the centre of his face – and up now came the left, jabbing repeatedly into his red and roaring jaws. Len now was running away down the length of the bar and around the horseshoe end, so very eager to reach these men and stop all this – but Jackie now was just so simply amazed that this big man before him had barely even flinched under this quite ceaseless bombardment of blows to the face – and there was his very last thought before the man ended everything by raising up a mighty arm, and then he brought down with power the heel of his fist on to the very crown of Jackie's skull, as if he were wielding a tremendous gavel, and determined upon an end to uproar. Jackie could see only black and stars and then a dazzle of splintered colours as his legs just folded – gave beneath him so very completely – and he dropped down to the floor like a redundant chimney stack, imploded at its core. Len and two others now, they had the man by his arms and they were quite gently though insistently shuffling him away and over towards the door, Len keeping up all the while his much-practised, rushed and hushed-up litany of calming reassurance in the manner of a cleric possessed, rapt in his involvement with a perpetual cycle of prayer and devotion. The man – still so calm and seemingly untroubled by any sort of injury – was explaining to Len as he allowed himself to be escorted away that he was a reasonable man, did he see, and that all he wanted to do now was to finish off his drink in silence and in peace, and then Len was gabbling out a conspiratorial assurance that the next time he came in, then he could do just that, of course he could, and that a drink of his choosing would be on the house, and that on Len's word the man could depend. He waved him away off down the street and wiped over his face with a sopping beer cloth that had hung from his apron, so very relieved that the man had not just upped and killed him, nor rendered his pub into matchwood and ashes. By the time Len got himself back to where Jackie still lay slumped on the ground like a sack of clinker, a narrow-eyed Dickie was kneeling over him and with probing and professional fingers, sifting through the thickets of his hair.

'There's no contusion . . .' he was idly musing. 'No cut, or anything – can't even feel a bump, rather oddly. How are you feeling, Jackie old man? Hear me all right, can you?'

Jackie was groggily protesting his complete and utter fitness and trying to struggle back up to his feet, in the face of no co-operation from legs gone to rubber.

'Lesson Number One,' said Jonathan Leakey, lighting up a Senior Service. 'Don't never get involved. Thought you would've known that, Jackie.'

'Honestly, Jackie,' chipped in Dickie, still peering down at his head. 'I could've handled it myself.' And this immediately struck him as quite as laughably ridiculous as everyone else had considered it too, though each of them, at least, had had the goodness not to say so. 'Here, old man – let's get you up now, shall we? Lend a hand, chaps . . . that's it – nearly, nearly . . . there we are! Now you just sit down here for a little bit, Jackie. Soon have you doing the Gay Gordons, and all that sort of rot.'

'Large brandy called for, I think Len,' grunted Jonathan Leakey – and Len, nodding rapidly, went back around the bar to fetch it, assuring the little knots of mutely curious drinkers that the pantomime's done with, gentlemen, and everything now is hunky-dory.

Jackie was sitting wide-legged on a bentwood chair, his head hung low and his arms very loosely at his sides.

'Bleeding hell . . .' is what he managed to come out with. 'What a bleeding fist! Ain't never met nothing like it. Were like one of them sledgehammers – what you hit the wossname at the fair with – you know: banging the bell.'

'Yeh well,' said Jonathan Leakey, 'he certainly banged your bell for you, that's for bleeding sure. Reckon you'll give him a fairly wide berth, ay Jackie? You see him in here again. Ah – brandy. Very good, Len. And what're you having, Jackie? No no – only joking. Here you are, lad – you get that down you, ay? Right as rain, you'll be. Cures all sorts, nice drop of three-star.'

Jackie took the glass and tasted the brandy – and then he knocked back the whole of it. Wiping his mouth with the back of his hand, he murmured slowly, and with a gathering menace:

'I see him in here again . . . or anywhere else, come to that . . . I'll bleeding murder the fucking bastard.'

'Yeh?' chuckled Jonathan Leakey. 'Well you want to make sure you got the Coldstream Guards with you, then. Or maybe you could get the loan of a tank . . .'

'Don't need no tank!' retorted Jackie, quite angrily. 'I just got to be prepared, that's all.'

Dickie coughed. 'No lasting damage, old man . . .'

'Not the point. Is it? Not the bleeding point. I'll have him – you bleeding see if I don't.'

'Nah,' said Jonathan Leakey, dismissively. 'You ain't the murdering type, Jackie. Ain't in you. Believe me. I know one or two what is . . . and you? Well – you just ain't it, Jackie boy. And anyway – you don't want to go harbouring grudges. Life's too short for all that sort of caper. You go harbouring a grudge every time a geezer go and cross you, well – turn you bitter, wouldn't it? Spend the rest of your life just sorting it out.'

'Yeh? So what you reckon then, Jonny? "No offence"? That it?'

Jonathan Leakey grinned at him like a collaborator.

'Yeh. Something like that. Come on, lads – enough of all this. Set us up another round, ay Len?'

'Right you are, Jonny,' Len agreed. 'And these is on the house, boys. You all right now, are you Jackie?'

'Never better, Len old mate. Never better.'

And he was standing now, and Dickie was very relieved indeed to see him up and behaving much in the way that he always did. He made very quickly for the glass of Scotch that Len had just set before him, because he was feeling just a little bit on the shaky side himself, if you want God's truth on the matter.

'Here lads,' said Len, dumping a large glass jar of pickled onions on to the bar. 'Solids. Do you a power, they will. Mop it all up.'

Jackie appeared thoughtful as he leaned against the bar, slowly exhaling a much-needed lungful of good old Senior Service – he had drawn on the cigarette so long and fiercely that the smoulder had rapidly crackled, and he felt the heat of it so close to his fingers. Then he fished a pickled onion out of the jar with the slotted spoon that was chained around its neck.

'Yeh – you say all that about smoking being bad for you, Dickie,' he said to him – easily resuming the conversational style, quite as if their bar-room chatter had suffered no interruption whatever. 'But what about all the booze you put away, then? That can't be doing the body a favour now, can it? Stands to reason.'

'Yeh,' agreed Jonathan Leakey. 'Good point, Jackie. How about that then, Doctor?'

Dickie nodded – wagging his empty glass and signalling over to Len.

'Well quite,' he said. 'Nail on the head, old man. I don't think I could do without it though, tell you the truth. I know you probably both don't really think that I, you know – *do* much, sort of thing – but I'm telling you, all these bloody textbooks I'm having to read . . . sometimes I wake up and it's dawn, you know – all the little birdies tweeting away there – and I'm still at the desk, slumped over all these books. I didn't have a snort or two – God, I'd be a nervous wreck, telling you. Even worse than I am now, if you can believe such a thing.'

'Yeh well . . .' allowed Jonathan Leakey. 'Couple drinks – never did no one no harm.'

'And did they do that and all at that school, then?' asked Jackie, spooning out another pickled onion as he registered the mirror of blank expressions on Dickie's and Jonathan's faces. 'At that Eton. Did they ram a tot of rum or something down the kids' necks, did they? Thought it'd do them a bit of good?'

Dickie laughed. 'No no – they didn't go quite that far. Don't think so, anyway . . .'

'My Mum . . .' ruminated Jonathan Leakey. 'She give me gin, I were a nipper. All the women did, round our way. Said it were the only way they got any peace. You can see their point. Noisy little bleeders, kids is.'

'Let's hear it for Santa Claus!' laughed Jackie – spluttering as he said it through the first mouthful of one of the fresh Scotches that Len had just poured out for them.

'But it *is* a bad thing,' said Dickie, more seriously. 'The drink. And it's not just what it does to your constitution and the jolly old brain cells, you know – well of course you know. Don't have to tell you chaps, do I? It's when one is in one's cups, as it were . . . well, one can get up to all sorts of shenanigans, can't one? And live to regret them.'

Jonathan Leakey's face assumed the masquerade of utter sobriety.

'Oh one *can* – one certainly *can*. Can't one Jackie, what what?'

'Yes all *right*, Jonathan,' said Dickie, quite testily. 'I really do wish, you know, that we could all just simply accept that our speech patterns, well – *vary*, shall we say, and just leave it at that. I don't make fun of the way *you* speak, do I? Your accent, and so forth . . .'

'Nothing wrong with my accent,' said Jonathan Leakey, defensively.

'No well anyway,' Dickie hastened along, 'we're not talking about that now, are we? We were talking about drink, and what it can do to you.'

'Talking of which,' put in Jackie. 'Stand another one, can we?'

'Ooh . . .' doubted Dickie. 'I really shouldn't have said so, Jackie old stick. Well – maybe just the one more then, hey? No but listen – like take Sheila, for instance. Just last evening. Very good example.'

'Sheila?' laughed Jackie. 'Dear oh dear – what she been up to? Yeh – she did have a few, I suppose. Here we go, Len – same again then, ay?'

'Is there, Jackie?' queried a still aggrieved Jonathan Leakey. 'My accent – nothing wrong with it, is there?'

'God . . . !' said an exasperated Dickie. 'I didn't say there *was*, did I Jonathan? No but Jackie, you're absolutely spot-on – because yes, she did have a few, didn't she? Sheila. And round about lunchtime today – just before I came over here, matter of fact – I popped round, you know, just to see that everything was all tickety-boo, sort of thing – and well my goodness! Good Lord! She's got this real shiner – looks like she went ten rounds in the ring.'

'Sheila?' checked Jackie. 'Blimey. What happened, then?'

'Maybe,' smiled Jonathan Leakey, 'she ran into your chum with the dynamite fist, Jackie . . .'

'Yeh – shut up Jonny, there's a good boy. So tell us, Dickie – what happened to old Sheila then, ay? You know – they're all right, them onions is. You want to try one. Get a taste for them once you had a few.'

'Mmm . . .' demurred Dickie. 'Don't think I will, thanks all the same. But no – that's just the point I'm making, Jackie old sport. She can't remember – complete blank, you see. Far as she knows, she dropped me off – well you know that, you were all in the car at the time. She dropped me off, she says, and then she remembers you driving her home, Jonathan, and then she went straight up to bed, she says. Next thing she knows, she gets up this morning, goes into the bathroom and bingo! One very black eye, if you please. Extraordinary. But obviously, you see, such a thing could never have happened if she'd been strictly sober. My point, you see.'

Jackie was nodding to that.

'Yeh. I see. So what you reckon then? Walk into a door, did she?'

'Could be. Fell out of bed, maybe. Anything, really. Had a look at it – appears a lot worse than it actually is. Put something on it for her. It'll go down, day or two. Hell of a colour at the moment though. I must say. Poor old Sheila. But it rather makes you think though, doesn't it? That sort of thing.'

Well yeh it do, that sort of thing. And other things and all. And that's just what I'm up to right now, as it happens – lying on my bed with my eyes tight shut, thinking over this and that, and trying to take no notice of the pain in my bleeding head and this ache I got right down in the gut. I reckon I just stay still for a bit, it'll all sort itself out – and then Mary'll do me a nice tea and I'll be right as ninepence. Can't say I fancy nothing to eat nor drink at the present, mind – but give us half an hour and I reckon I'll be champion. Because I can, you know – think. There's a lot of people what don't maybe believe I can, but I can, I'm telling you. I ain't book-learned, and there's lots of things what go right over my head, I ain't denying – but when some lousy little Jew-boy like that bastard Stone from upstairs – when some bleeding foreigner ups and calls me stupid, well ... he wants to be learned a lesson, he do. Because I *do* remember, course I do – never mind what I were telling Mary about it. Yeh. So when I come home – just a little while back there, when I come in from Jonny and Dickie and my little bit of bother in the Rose & Crown, there he is in the hall, sneaky little bastard. Just standing there, he is, like a bleeding vulture or something. Herr Stein. Weaselly face – all wrinkled it is – great big conk on him, shifty little Jew-boy eyes. No wonder they wanted shot of them, the Krauts. What I still don't understand is what they had to come here for. And that's all I said, weren't it? Nothing wrong in that – it's if you *didn't* think that, it's then you'd be stupid. Right stupid you'd be then, you didn't think that. Stands to reason. So there he is anyway, stood like a statue and just eyeing me, he is. And I were in the mood, I'm telling you – if he'd started up with his calling me stupid again, I tell you this – I would've had his head off, and no messing about. But nah. Turns out he wants to make his peace. Lot of things was said, he's going – and they're all best forgotten, is what he's telling me. Water under the bridge, sort of style. And I looks at him, and I don't know . . . I'm almost feeling sorry for the miserable little sod – all humble, he is, and weedy like. He don't apologise, mind – and I don't neither. But I sort of nods, as if I'm sort of saying Yeh all right then, have it your own way – if it makes you happy then I can accommodate you, yeh why not. Because also, if I was stupid, I would've dotted his i's for him, wouldn't I? And then what? Me and Mary and Jeremy, we're out on the bleeding street, that's what. Because they can do that, them bastards, without so much as a by your wossname, the bastards. Leave, yeh. Without so much as that. But soon as I can, we're out of this rat-hole, I'm telling you. Nice little three-bedroom house – semi-detached is what they call them – up Golders Green way. There's a heath nearby, someone were telling me. Decent air. Bit of a garden for the kid to play in. Prime, that'll be. There is the bleeding mortgage side of it, though – and for all I were banging on about to Jonny in the pub there, I ain't too happy about it: not too sure. I mean it works out on paper, yeh – I done my sums – but it's everything else what's eating away at me. Because life, well – and you'd have to be real stupid, wouldn't you? Not to know this – life, it don't never work out, do it? Like it do on paper. Because paper's one thing, see, and life's another. And it's all well and good me saying I ain't going to be shouting out for another round down the Rose & Crown – but I know me, don't I? And I reckon that no matter how important it is for me to be hanging on to what money I got, it's exactly what I will be doing. Because it's me, ain't it? That's who I am. That's what I does. And then when we're living in the house, the three of us – well, there won't be no Rose & Crown, will there? We'd be miles out. So there's all that to think about. Not too happy about it: not too sure. One of the troubles, you know, when you get couple days off – there's too much time to drink and think in. I get back to working for Mr Plough come tomorrow morning, and I reckon I'll be a sight better off. Keep yourself busy, that's the ticket. Else you'd go barmy with it all.

Now wait a minute . . . what am I doing now – lying in a meadow, all of a bleeding sudden? All the tall grass around and about – and them flowers, look: yellow flowers, swaying away, this way and that. Sky's red, which you don't see a lot. Red like a pillar box, is what I'm meaning – looks all wet, like it just been painted – and you don't, do you? See that a lot. A blood-red sky what's just been painted . . . And there's noise, now – like a lot of drummers or something, it sounds like . . . hundreds of drummers, banging away . . . and there's a little black line now up there, look – a jagged line what's splitting up the sky – and yeh, it's all torn up now and it's gold and boiling in the underneath – and that drumming now – my head, it flown out like a parachute and now it's caving in, and I want to put my hands up, wrap them round my ears – but my arms, they ain't having none of it – just lying there, they is, a good couple of yards off, in all that bright blue water, floating away from me, they is – just floating off and bobbing about. And there's a great roaring coming from somewhere now – and this great big angry face, it's pouring out of the sky and there's fire in its mouth and the flame, it's so bloody hot and it's licking out and down at me now and I reckon it's the Devil hisself what's trying to burn me – and I need my arms again to shield my face from Old Nick's bonfire because it started to melt, I can feel it melting, but they're way over there on the horizon now – waving at me, look – my arms is waving me goodbye. And the grass – it's falling away from under me – I'm going down, I'm sinking – I'm being swallowed up – and now there's screaming, there's

245

high-pitched screaming what's cutting me in two and I'm plummeting away down now and it's only when I get to hear Mary's voice – it'll be all right now, look, because it's my Mary talking and she saying that it's all right, it's all right, and that you mustn't go crying now – don't cry Jeremy, because your Daddy, he's having a little rest and he's just next door and if you go on crying like that, then you're going to disturb him, and you don't want to do that, do you Jeremy? No you don't, no you don't . . . so you just hush now, and we'll go in and see him, shall we . . . ?

'You all right, Jackie? You're sweating. Not got a fever, have you . . . ?'

Jackie sat upright and wiped off his forehead with the palm of his hand – and he looked at it then, the whole of his hand: the way it linked up with his arm and attached itself to his shoulder. And she's right, Mary – I am, I'm sweating like an animal. Reckon I must just have dropped off there, for a minute or two. Yeh. So what I'll do is, I'll smile at her a bit – Jeremy too, give him a bit of a smile – let them both know it's all all right. That no one must cry because it's all all right, now. Dear God, though – but I do feel queer. Reckon it must have been them onions.

○

1st January 1939

A brand-new year, and the very last of the decade! This is the ledger that Alfie gave me for Christmas – very smart! – so I've got lots of space to write. It will be more of a journal than a diary I've decided, except that I won't be writing every day – just when there's something important to say. It's a quarter past six in the morning – I'll have to wake Jackie in about half

an hour, make his breakfast, get him off to work. We didn't go
to bed till nearly two o'clock, but I feel quite fresh. How
Jackie's going to be is quite another matter! Len was doing a
lock-in at the Rose & Crown last night and Jackie wanted to go
but I said oh no please, Jackie – I don't like pubs and we can't
ask Imogen to come over so late and it would be much nicer
anyway if we just saw the New Year in all cosily at home. So
he just dropped in there earlier for an hour or two, and he and
Dickie came back in good time with a crate of ale, a bottle of
whisky and one of sherry, and then Sheila came over as well. I
wore my blue shantung and put on some Eau de Paris. We had
a rare old time – Sheila was laughing at what's left of the
Christmas tree, all brown and withered, but I said we had to
keep it up until Twelfth Night and she asked my why and of
course I hadn't a clue why, had I? But I'll keep it anyway – bit
superstitious. Her awful black eye is looking much less swollen
now, but still I knew better than to mention it, she's that
embarrassed. I'd done some sausages, and then Molly came up
with a lovely tomato salad and a nice piece of Cheddar and
said she hoped I didn't mind but she's said that Jonathan
Leakey could pop in a bit later. He arrived just after twelve had
struck when Jackie and Dickie were still playing the giddy goat
– he said he was 'first-footing', which I'd never heard of –
he said it was a Scotch tradition. I must say I never had
Mr Leakey down as Scotch, but there you are. Jackie said he'd
always think of him now as 'Jonny Midnight'! The big
excitement was that he'd brought a new record – The Lambeth
Walk! So there we all were, trying to do the dance and getting
into the most hopeless muddle – and the shouts of 'Oi!' were
getting louder and louder and I begged the men to be quieter
for the sake of little Jeremy, fast asleep in his bed like an angel.
I was worried about Mr Stone upstairs as well, but I didn't say
so. And then Jonathan said something extraordinary – I could

247

keep the gramophone, he said! New Year present. Well of course I protested that I could do no such thing, but he was most insistent – and if the truth be told I had been dreading having to give it up! I play the records when I'm doing the dusting and the washing up and the hours just sail by – and I think that Jeremy might be developing a musical ear – he always seems to be listening so very intently. He must be rather rich, Mr Leakey, with his Humber and giving away gramophones like that. We all talked about the coming year, of course – but I forbade everybody to say anything that wasn't good and hopeful, and no mention at all of Germany or anything of that kind. Molly said her New Year resolution was to give up cake and biscuits, but I don't know why – she has a wonderful figure as it is (Sheila and I are horribly jealous). Dickie said that in the light of all the studying he had to do, he was going to give up work! He was joking, of course. It's next year – *this* year, I mean (have to get used to it), that he qualifies as a doctor. Just imagine! I've never known a doctor, except to go to. And Jackie said he was just simply going to give up! The reverse is true, I am pleased to say. He's working ever so hard – so fingers crossed for spring, when Mr Plough said he'd consider him for a partnership. Jackie's got his heart set on it – and so have I now because at the weekend he took me out to Golders Green to see our new house! Well – not exactly, because they're not built yet – but there was this Show House, so you could see how they would be. I was surprised – quite olde worlde. Probably not the right description, but it reminded me a bit of where Shakespeare was born – I had it on a calendar once. I thought it would be all white and curved like a boat in the style they call 'moderne' (don't know why there is an 'e' on the end). I read about it in one of Sheila's magazines in the salon. But Jackie hates those – too jazzy, he says. My favourite bit was the stained-glass panel in the front door – a green galleon with red sails on a bright blue sea. The brochure says you can also have rambling roses in pink and crimson or what they call a 'radiant sunset' in two sorts of orange and a golden yellow! I think Jackie would think that too jazzy as well, by the sound of it. I think we'll stay with the galleon. And *inside* the house – oh my goodness! A lovely bathroom with a checked floor and its own water heater. Tiled fireplaces – quite the latest thing, the man said – in the sitting room and the main bedroom. And the kitchen! A stove with two ovens and four gas rings! A machine that washes clothes – and a proper larder you can walk into. Even an electric refrigerator! We wouldn't have all these things, of course, but it was lovely to see them. They'd done the garden beautifully – a rockery and crazy paving and a little rustic arch with a seat in it. I can just see myself there in the summer, doing my sewing, and Jeremy playing on the lawn. And there's a garage as well – Jackie said it wouldn't be big enough for his Rolls-Royce, and where would he put the Boogatty (not sure how you spell it). I sometimes wonder if he'll ever grow up. I've got to go and wake him now.

Eight o'clock. Jackie's gone to work – looking a bit groggy, and I don't wonder at it. I don't know where these men put it all, the beer and so on. Saw he had a good big breakfast, though – plenty of bacon and eggs. Jeremy at the moment is making an awful mess of his face with his Marmite soldiers, and so I've just got time to finish this terribly long entry before I tackle an absolute mountain of washing up. And although it's freezing outside, I'll have to open all the windows and get rid of all this stale cigarette smoke. It was a good year on the whole, 1938. Jackie got work, I gave up the awful laundry, and Jeremy has come on leaps and bounds. That's what poor old Dad said about him. It's understandable why he's concerned about the world situation, remembering the war as he does, but I don't think it'll come to anything. How can there be a war? It's only twenty years since the last one. The Prime Minister isn't a fool, is he? Why would he sign a treaty with Germany if he wasn't going to make jolly sure that they stuck to the terms of it? 'Peace for our time' – that's what he said, and I bless him for it. I don't know much about it, and I'm pleased really. I always leave the cinema now when the Pathe news or Movietone comes on – it spoils the picture. Well – I've filled nearly four whole pages of this ledger, but it is a special day. My only New Year resolution – and I haven't told Jackie, I'm just going to have it done, I've decided – is to finally cut off my hair and get one of these neat little perms that you see in the magazines. Molly's got one now (Sheila did it for her) and it's very fetching. She said I'd find it easier to cope with the gas mask. Nothing was further from my mind. *Two* resolutions, actually – I'm going to get this *thing* taken out of me.

So welcome 1939! Let's all hope for health and prosperity.

○

'This . . .' sighed Sheila, 'is perfect. It's just perfect. I've never known it so lovely, this early in the year. Can't recall it – can you, Mary? Being in the park, and we're not even into Easter? You want to try this, Mary – and you, Molly. Ever so cooling.'

Mary laughed and shook her head at the sight of Sheila on the grass, her two feet splashing up and down at the edge of the pond, to the evident anger of a solitary duck circling at a distance – and glaring, it looked like to Mary. But Sheila, though! She'd unrolled her stockings and peeled them off just as calm as you like. She doesn't care, Sheila, what anyone thinks. I could never be so brazen, to do such a thing.

'Come here, Jeremy,' she called out to him. 'Don't run off now – I've told you before. Just stay where I can see you, there's a good boy.'

'He is enjoying himself, isn't he?' said Molly, sitting on the bench alongside with her ankles crossed and looking rather graceful – her very elegant turquoise frock, Mary couldn't help observing, fluttering so fetchingly about her calves, as the faintest of breezes played around the hem. Such cheekbones, and so terribly slender: she really is, you know, Molly – a natural beauty.

'Mm . . .' agreed Mary. 'First bit of sunshine he's seen in ages, poor little mite. Oh . . . this is *so* lovely – and aren't you pleased, Sheila, it was your half-day today? You wouldn't want to be washing heads in this weather, would you?'

Sheila squinted away from the sun, one cupped hand forming a visor over her eyes so that she could turn to face Mary, the better to emphasise what it was that she now had to say.

'Or *any* day. I tell you, Mary – I'm just so utterly fed up with working. Two pins, I'd give it all up tomorrow. I just have to meet a rich and handsome prince like Wallis Simpson did. I used to enjoy it – used to look forward to going in every single morning, I did . . . but now I just dread it. Same old thing . . . and all the chemicals, they're doing my hands no end of harm, you know. Look at them, will you? All red and chapped. Pains me even to see them. And having to talk to all these women – they've got nothing to say, not one of them, but they'll never stop with all their talking. Just tell me how wonderful or dreadful their husbands are and where they're going on their holidays. As if I care. And particularly that Jenny Rumbold – you know her, don't you Mary? I'd have brought a towel if I'd known I'd be going paddling . . .'

'Don't *think* I do . . .' said Mary, doubtfully. 'Jessie Rumbold . . . ?'

'No – not Jessie, Jenny. Works in Farthingales, at the cheese counter. They say she's sweet on the general manager. Nice for some.'

'Jeremy . . . ! Here, Jeremy – don't go wandering off. Here's your ball – you want your ball?'

'I'll roll it to him, Mary,' said Molly, standing up and smoothing down the panels of her dress.

'Oh thank you, Molly. I'm telling you – this age, they're just everywhere at once. Can't take your eyes off them for a single second. Oh yes I think I do know who you mean, Sheila. Fair-skinned – plumpish girl, is she?'

'Plump is generous: fat, I'd say. Fair-skinned . . . yes I suppose so. And she *was* fair-haired. Now she's got a henna rinse. I advised against it – does nothing for her. This colour, actually – see it? It's still under my fingernails. Oh heavens, I do hate so much what I have to do. Oh to be a lady of leisure, like you two! I must say I am very much taken with that frock you're wearing, Molly. Silk, is it? Must be, going by the look of it.'

'It is lovely, Molly,' agreed Mary. 'I was just thinking the same. Not seen it before, have I? New, is it?'

Molly was crouching down now, throwing wide an arm in an attempt to garner in the rubber ball that Jeremy had just flung wide to her.

'Oh – newish, I suppose,' she said quite carelessly. 'He'll be bowling at Lord's, this one, before you know it, Mary.'

'And,' pursued Sheila, 'it is silk, is it?'

'Mm? Oh – yes, I suppose it is. I didn't ask.'

'Mm,' said Sheila, her head held sideways to better reappraise the frock before her. 'I'd say it had to be, the way it just falls like that. Wouldn't you say, Mary? Couldn't be anything but.'

'Oh *look* . . .' said Molly, suddenly flustered and turning to Sheila. 'Can't we just stop talking about my dress for a moment? It's just a dress, Sheila, and I honestly couldn't tell you what it's made out of. Just a dress, that's all. Let's sit and enjoy the sunshine, shall we?'

Sheila raised her eyebrows as her lips compressed, and she passed the glance over to Mary alone, whose eyes flicked up momentarily as she briefly shrugged – and then looked down, and away. But she was very surprised when Molly, for whom she had been perfectly prepared to drop all further mention of the subject, suddenly continued in a rush – quite testy, she sounded, and maybe rather determined now to set a few things straight.

'Because I'm getting just a little bit fed up of all this! Actually. If you want to know the truth. Bit fed up of it. All right?'

This tersely expressed sentiment had Mary truly mystified. She gazed over to Sheila, who going by the look in her eyes, seemed more to understand what Molly was meaning.

Sheila looked haughty. 'I don't know what you mean, I'm sure.'

'Oh yes you do,' Molly rounded on her. 'It's not the first time, is it Sheila? All this 'lady of leisure' business and talking about my clothes, and how terribly expensive they are. All it is – and it's really none of your concern, but maybe if you know you'll just stop going on about it—!'

'Molly . . .' said Mary – with solicitude, yes, and a growing bewilderment. 'Why whatever is it? Why are you becoming so terribly upset? Sheila didn't say anything – did you, Sheila? Jeremy – here now please. Just stay next to me, there's a good boy . . .'

'Oh yes she did,' huffed Molly.

'I didn't,' put in Sheila very quickly. 'Mary's my witness. I said nothing at all – all I said was how very pretty your dress was looking. Of course if it's a crime all of a sudden to compliment a young lady upon her attire . . .'

'Oh *stop* it, Sheila,' said Molly dismissively, and quite exasperated. 'Well all right – maybe you didn't actually *say* anything, but you really might as well have done. It's what you're always *implying*.'

Sheila looked at Molly very thoughtfully.

'Do you know what, Molly dear?' she said quite slowly, and at her very most sweetly conciliatory. 'I really do think that you might have gone a little bit dippy. Losing your reason, you know.'

'Oh Sheila . . . !' deplored Mary. 'How can you say such a thing?'

'Well! spluttered an outraged Sheila. 'She's as good as accused me of – well I don't know *what* she's accused me of, to be perfectly frank with you. I was just sitting here, enjoying the sunshine and a little bit of a paddle, and suddenly I'm the victim of all of this malarkey. Honestly, dear – as I say, I think you've gone a little bit dippy.'

'Oh shut *up*, Sheila,' squealed Molly. 'I have *not*, as you put it, gone a little bit – God! *Dippy*. Look: listen to me. Yes I do – I step out with Jonathan, Mr Leakey, from time to time – very infrequently, I may say—'

'Oh Molly . . . !' whispered Mary with urgency. 'You don't have to tell us this . . . you don't have to explain . . .'

'But that's just what I want to *say*. There's nothing *to* tell – nothing to explain. We go out – sometimes to the pictures – and then he drives me home. He has introduced me to a real gentleman by the name of Nigel Wisely – doesn't live round here – and Mr Wisely, he's promised he can find me work. Dancing. You know, Mary – it's all I've ever wanted to do.'

'Mm,' agreed Mary, nodding at her happily. 'You've often said it. Well how wonderful for you, Molly.'

'Well – it hasn't happened yet. But he did promise. And . . . he's in the garment business, I think. He seems to be in quite a few different sorts of businesses, actually . . . and he's given me a few samples, he says they are, so that when I go for auditions I'll stand out from the crowd. And I said well I don't mind borrowing them, if you insist, but I must give them back to you afterwards. And that's all it is. I swear that's all it is – and I just could burst into tears when I think of what you, Sheila, can be imagining I'm doing—!'

'I . . . !' protested an aggrieved and wide-eyed Sheila. 'I'm not imagining a thing! I don't know what you can mean.'

'Yes you are. Yes you do. But you're wrong. I'm not like that – I never was and I never will be. And you should know that.' And then her pretty face crumpled and she shook her head in annoyance at all that, and began to rummage impatiently in her handbag for a handkerchief. 'I just want you . . . to know that . . .'

And Mary moved quickly across to her and put an arm around her shoulders.

'Don't go upsetting yourself, Molly. We neither of us thought anything – honestly we didn't. Did we, Sheila? Oh and Sheila – keep an eye on Jeremy, can you?'

'I'm watching him,' said Sheila. 'He's quite all right – happy as Larry, he is. And yes of course, Molly – I believe whatever you tell me.'

Molly looked up from her handkerchief, sniffing blearily and blinking with hope.

'Do you . . . ? Really? It's so important to me that you do. That both of you do. And the only reason I'm a 'lady of leisure' as you call it, Sheila, is because I haven't yet got any work. I do *want* to work – and that's why I'm waiting for Mr Wisely to honour his promise to me. Which I know he will do because he is a very educated and high-class gentleman.'

'I see, dear,' said Sheila. 'Yes dear – I see. Well let's just all wait for that then, shall we? Of course there's lots of work about nowadays, isn't there? In the meantime. Helping the country out, and all that sort of thing. Red Cross – not paid, I don't think, but there it is. My Dickie, you know – did I tell you this, Mary? He's gone and volunteered for ARP. Air Raid . . . Something.

I said to him – oh you are such a crazy person, Dickie, I said to him. Two months – just two months it is until your final exams now – what on earth do you want to go dressing up in a helmet for and staying out half the night? Wouldn't listen to me – stubborn streak, Dickie. Says to me it's the right thing to do. Your Jackie – he's no fool, is he? Wouldn't catch him wasting his time with all of that, would you?'

Both Sheila and Molly now glanced quickly at one another – each of them immediately and strikingly aware of how very much affected Mary had become. She looked so very grave as her arms were reaching outwards to take a hold of Jeremy by his shoulders, and draw him towards her. She closed her eyes as she lowered her lips into the tousle of his hair, nuzzling his head with the whole of her face as she grasped him to her quite worryingly tightly. Sheila reached out a tentative hand, and laid it upon Mary's shoulder.

'You'll squeeze the little man to death, you go on like that . . .' she said quite mildly. 'What is it, Mary? What's wrong? Something I said? Hm? I really do seem to be putting my foot into it quite properly today, don't I? Don't I? Hm? What's wrong, Mary? Tell me. What is it? What is it that's bothering you?'

Well, thought Mary, as she raised her head and simpered a watery sort of reassurance over to Sheila: fair question – what is it, then? What is it that's bothering me? Oh – so much, so very very much, and I just can't seem to hide it any more. Because I have – I've been putting it all away – burying it deeply – for really so terribly long now, all these fears, all the unease. But what, though, is it? What exactly is it that is bothering me? Well: where to begin? I think it came to a sort of a head just maybe only a fortnight ago – when the rest of Czechoslovakia was taken over by the Germans. Everyone suddenly was speaking so gloomily (goodness – you should have heard them on the wireless) and I heard Poland being mentioned, I don't understand why, and it was no good asking Jackie because he just says it's all Tory baloney and you don't want to pay it any heed. I might have asked my Dad, but I was in just too much dread that he might have told me, explained it all to me in such a way that there could no longer be any room at all for doubt or supposition – because although I had within me a deep bad feeling over all of this growing upheaval, still my ignorance and hope – battered though that was – seemed so much preferable, so very much better than any form of certainty. It's Jackie I envy – so long as he's making good money with Mr Plough and he's got the Rose & Crown to go to and his dinner and tea set before him, then he's just Jack the Lad, isn't he? Or maybe he's only seeming that way for my sake, I really couldn't tell you. He doesn't talk about anything, you see – not anything of that sort, anyway – and I don't either, now. Nor do I buy the *Evening News* any more, because it's all just so terribly serious, page after page of it – even the odd cartoon, which I always like, even they were suddenly all about shelters and gas masks and ARP and every other sort of horrible thing you can possibly imagine. And it was that – it was just Sheila a while back mentioning the ARP, it was that, I suppose, that did for me. I only recently found out that it stood for Air Raid Precautions, and I'm afraid that I rather went to pieces. Air raid! Bombs from planes – it just couldn't be possible. Well could it? Just not possible. And yet here were all these people like Dickie queueing up to do their bit, as they put it on the wireless – and all sorts of young men hurrying off to join the army. It's almost as if they *want* it to happen, or something. How can they? How can they look at the children – their own children, or any children really – and actually contemplate any such horror? Even all the people who remember the Great War, fought in it – like my Dad, people like him – they're not happy, of course – they're not happy, no they're not, but I can't for the life of me detect in them any sort of outrage: sad and regretful they

257

may be – but there's a resignation in the air, a sorrowful bowing to the coming inevitability – and I just simply can't accept that. Can't. Won't. It's just too terrible. And what on earth has it all got to do with *us*, that's what I can't understand. I mean – Czechoslovakia, Poland – I don't even know where these places *are* . . . !

'Mary . . . ?' Sheila was insisting, her eyes still full of gentle inquiry. 'What is it? What is it, Mary dear? What's troubling you? Tell your Auntie Sheila.'

Mary looked up suddenly into the dazzle of the sun, and boldly displayed her very brightest smile.

'Oh goodness *nothing*, Sheila – it's nothing at all. Just me being very silly. Sorry. Sorry, Molly. Time of month, I expect. Ought to be getting back, really . . . Jackie'll be home soon and he'll be wanting his tea. You should see the mountains he gets through – but he does work very hard, you know: it's a very long day he puts in. And look at Jeremy – I think he's getting a bit tired . . .'

And that was another thing that had been bothering me greatly: the thought . . . no, even the tiniest possibility that Jackie could be leaving me. And not even in the sense of going out of London, but just for nights on end if he too went off and joined this wretched ARP, like Dickie seems to have done. And this time I just had to voice it: this I just couldn't keep in. He looked at me . . . when I told him what it was I was fearing, he just stood there staring at me as if I had taken leave of all my senses.

'*Me*? You remember who you're talking to, do you Mary love? This is Jackie. Remember me? What – *me*? Join up? Got to be joking. I got a job, ain't I? Got a nice little job and I ain't about to mess it up. Me as a bleeding soldier . . . ? That's a bleeding laugh, that is. And as for all the rest of the caper – walking about half the night looking out for things what ain't bleeding occurring . . . ! Want their heads tested, them blokes do. Mug's game, that's what that is. And me, Mary – look at me when I'm talking to you – me, Mary: I ain't no mug, see? So stop looking so bleeding gloomy and go and get the kettle on, ay? There's a good girl.'

And in remembering that much, at least, Mary could once again continue her enjoyment of the sun on her limbs as she gathered up Jeremy and all his scattered toys, while in the face of his strenuous opposition to anything of the sort, she tried to still his flailing arms and slip on to him the little sky-blue linen coatee that she had made up in the winter from a Butterick pattern and the saveable bulk of a soup-stained tablecloth that her mother had one day just more or less thrown at her.

'Leave him, Mary,' urged Sheila. 'Don't make him if he doesn't want to. It's so warm – he doesn't really need it.'

Mary happily acknowledged that Sheila was quite right about this. The sun was glinting white and dancing sparkles on the surface of the pond, and the blaze of crocuses all about them – they seemed to be lit from within. It's a lovely little park, this is: never really looked at it before. (Not long, I suppose, before they dig it all up for their wretched trenches.)

'Here,' said Molly, passing it over. 'You've forgotten his spinning top.'

'Oh gosh *thank* you, Molly,' Mary was gushing, as she crammed that too into the bulging string bag. 'All sorts of hell to pay if I'd left his top behind.'

Sheila now was dabbing at her feet with a tiny handkerchief embroidered at the corners with pink and lemon rosebuds.

'Don't really need a towel . . .' she was musing, quite idly. 'The sun's so warm. Wouldn't have bothered with my girdle, if I'd known.'

'Oh honestly, Sheila,' Mary chided her. 'You couldn't possibly go out without your girdle! Where do you get all these ideas?'

'I expect it comes from living alone and being an independent woman – working for myself, worse luck,' Sheila answered her with a brief and throwaway little laugh which she tacked on lightly, when she had finished. And then, more seriously, she at once resumed: 'I do so envy you Mary, you know. Being looked after, the way you are. Having people to care for – properly, I mean.'

Both Mary and Molly turned to regard her – in Mary's case, trying to glean from her expression any sort of inkling into how casual or profound she was meaning this to be. Sheila's slightly gingery hair had frizzed a bit in the sun, and her small blue eyes were glinting. The freckles that covered the bridge of her nose seemed a little bit browner now – and suddenly, within the click of this snapshot vision of her, Mary looked down into depth and saw in Sheila the presence of sagacity, momentarily betrayed by so rounded and girlish a face. She was going to speak – she felt her lips fluttering on the verge of uttering words that her brain was still so very far from forming, but already Sheila was wagging her head as if to forestall all interruption – and now and straight away she was talking again.

'And you Molly, of course – well of course I envy *you*. Expect every woman does. You must be quite used to it.'

Molly seemed stung – as if she had just been accused of a thing so very out of the way that she never could even have contemplated.

'Oh yes you are,' Sheila insisted. 'You just must be, looking the way you do. I go on diets, time to time. And still I'm as fat as a pig. I just look like a pig, that's all. I'd die – I'd simply die to have a figure like yours you know, Molly. There's no girdle on earth that could ever help me. And your hair – like silk, and always just so. Mine, now – I've no doubt that it looks like a gollywog.'

'Oh for goodness *sake*, Sheila,' said Mary – uncertain as to quite how much laughter to suggest in her voice, and plumping in the end for nearly none.

Sheila shrugged. 'It's true,' she stated, quite matter-of-factly. 'First hint of drizzle, bit of wind, touch of sun, and no matter what I put on it – and believe me, both of you, I've sometimes stayed on into the night in that salon of mine, trying out every single one of all the shampoos and setters and conditioners that I've got . . . and still it just looks like a gollywog. I'm a pale and freckled roly-poly gollywog.'

Both Mary and Molly just had to laugh now – but still Sheila was denying them the right to interject by way of closed eyes and tight lips, and then the most peremptory single shiver of her frizzy head of hair.

'That's me, and there's no arguing about it. But listen, girls – one thing I would like to get out in the open before we all go home, and it's this. You remember, Molly – when we had that stupid little tiff just earlier? And you said that I thought you were, well . . . a certain kind of woman? Well I didn't, Molly. I know I said I didn't at the time, but I don't actually think that you believed me. Well that was not my thought – it never is my thought, it's simply not what I assume of people. And here's what I mean – this is what I want to say. Dickie and me – yes? I know we've been stepping out for quite a while now – and that we often turn up to this and that together, and we leave at the same time and so on. Well – it's not at all how it maybe might appear. I've never ever gone beyond a kiss with Dickie. Little bit of a cuddle in the pictures, maybe. But no more. I wouldn't ever. And I don't know if you knew, but now you do. Anyway. That's all I've got to say. Poor Dickie – sometimes feel quite sorry for him. But I don't see how he can *really* mind because, well – just look at me: I'm a pig.'

Sheila smiled quite sunnily then – and seeing that neither of them seemed at all sure as to what they might possibly say next (Mary was repeatedly and unnecessarily combing Jeremy's hair, and Molly – her eyes cast downwards – was irritating a non-existent blemish on her perfect downy forearm) Sheila then went on to conclude her little oration in rather a gayer and more jocular form:

'And so although I am consciously saving myself, it is not really for a rich and handsome prince. Because I thought at the time, you know, that King Edward and that American Simpson woman – I thought it the most perfect romance. But looking at them now, well . . . he really is the most awful drink of water, isn't he though? And as for her – well all I can say is I'd rather be a pig than a horse, any day of the week.'

Mary, so relieved by the lighter touch, laughed inordinately at Sheila's outrageousness – and as the three of them and little Jeremy wended their way along the winding footpath and towards the gate, all that now was storming her brain was Oh my God in Heaven: Molly and Sheila, so much purity and decorum between them: what on earth, at base, must they really think of *me*?

☉

Just had haircut, and I ain't too happy. Ain't the haircut – I always have the same thing done, don't I? Nice and short to the back and sides, keep it clean. Think he's an Eyetie, bloke what do it for me – don't ask because I don't bleeding care, to be honest with you. It's just that, yeh – you takes off your collar and tie, and he'll put a towel around your neck, Tony – his name's Tony . . . some feller once, he were telling me he don't spell it Tony, and I says to him well there's only the one way of spelling Tony what I know: reckon he were talking through his wossname. Mind you – foreigners, they gets up to all sorts with the language, don't they?

Least they could do, seems to me – they come over here, least they could do is get a hold of someone what can learn them the bleeding language: what's wrong with them all? But I ain't bothered with none of that – what gets my goat is all them little hairs what go down your back no matter which way you playing it. Drives me round the bend, that do. Been annoying me, it has, all bleeding day at work – that, yeh, and how many other things. Not too happy, just at the present, you want the honest truth. And them bleeding little hairs . . . ! Even now, just sitting quiet, I am, in the corner of this room what I'm doing up – nice mug of tea I got, just lit myself up a fag – and even now, them little bastard hairs all over my bleeding back, they got me scratching away like I'm a bleeding chimp at a tea party, or something. Still – generally takes a bath of a Saturday evening, so that'll sort it out, I daresay: Mary, she'll give us a bit of a scrub-up.

I'm completely tired out, you want the whole of it. Dead on my feet half the time, I am. Other night, Rose & Crown – old Dickie were on about some old load of rubbish or other and I never even take in a bleeding word of it, near dozing off I were – and it weren't the first time. Part of it is I been putting in so many hours way up over my usual, and Mr Plough, oh yeh – he's happy enough all right. Very good work Jackie, he's going, very nice indeed – keep it up, keep it up. Yeh well – I mean, fair enough, I'm getting paid for all the work what I'm doing, yeh yeh, fair enough – but never mind 'keep it up', because at this rate I'm telling you, it's falling over what I'll be doing, and no mistake. What I want to know is – when do he reckon spring is? Ay? I mean – last year, when we was talking, he says to me yeh Jackie boy, come spring I'll be looking to you, won't I? That partnership, well – I were led to thinking it were as good as in the bag else I never would've gone and said it to Mary, not elsewise I wouldn't. And he don't say he's changed his mind nor nothing – ain't nothing like that. But he don't say nothing at all, that's what I'm noticing. 'Keep it up' is what he says to me. Yeh well. And see – March, that's gone, and we're nearly out the backside of April and all. Now seems to me, May – well May, that's the very last of them, ain't it? You can't go saying June, that June is spring, can you? Nah – summer, June is. Known for it. So I'm looking at four weeks, I reckon, and then I'll know if I'm in or I'm out. And in the meantime I got to go on killing myself, I reckon – working all hours like a bleeding horse – because if I goes slacking off now, well: reckon I had it.

Done myself a bit of good Tuesday, though. Maybe: still in two minds. But Mr Plough – he were well impressed, I could see that much on him. See, what it was, I were down the basement – it's this big five-floor house what we're doing up, old sort of a house it is, hundred years maybe . . . pong in the basement, could be a thousand. Anyway, I were down there having a look at the brickwork – not too bad as it happens, considering all the damp what we got – and I sees this sort of paper packet under a broken old table, half on its side there. And I don't know what it were made me go for it – there was rubbish all about, so I can't tell you what it were about this particular lump of paper what draws me over to it . . . but anyway, I were peeling it open – pretty wet, the paper were – and inside, strike me down dead if there ain't this bloody great wodge of cash, all in them big white folded-up fivers. Didn't even know what they was at first – how many times I clapped eyes on one of them? – and then when I knows what I got here, I start easing them out, like – gentle, because I don't want to go tearing them, do I? And I do a quick count up, and what we got here is sixty-five quid. Couldn't hardly believe it. Blimey, I thought, I got to slave my guts out for nigh on a quarter of a year to get my hands on this sort of money – and here it all is, just lying in front of me. And I sat back, got out my cigarette case, tipped out a Woodbine – it's bleeding Woodbines I'm on now because I'm meant to be cutting down on the spending, Gawd help me – and I flames it up with the old lighter, see, and I'm just sitting back and having a bit of a riffle through all of these folded-up fivers. Sixty-five quid's worth. That'd buy me a fair few Senior Service, that would – or never mind that, I could run to Sobranie or Passing Clouds or one of them. And then I thought – this'll please Mary no end, this will. Put an end to the mortgage worry for a good little time, we ever get this bleeding house out Golders Green. And also, she got this catalogue, great big fat thing it is – Army & Navy Stores, if you please – and night after night she going to me Oh look at this Jackie – ain't it lovely? And I says yes to her – and then she pointing out some other thing and she going That would go lovely, wouldn't it Jackie? And I says to her it would do, Mary love, you're dead right about that, course you are Mary. There's Lloyd Loom and there's Ewbank . . . I don't even know what she's talking about, what these bleeding things even is, but she been going on about them for so bleeding long, all the names, they gone and stuck in my brain. Kelvinator – that's another one. So anyway, I'm sitting down there, thinking all of that, and then I hear someone on the staircase and I stand up real sharpish and the packet, I got that stuffed behind my back – and then there's Mr Plough now stood in front of me and he's saying Oh there you are Jackie, been looking all over, so what's the extent of the trouble down here then? Reckon we can fix it ourselves, do you? Or do we maybe need to bring in a specialist firm? And I says to him Well Mr Plough – it's pretty bad in parts, I ain't denying, but we get a proper drill and a mixer down here and I reckon me and a couple of the lads, we can make a fair little job of it, you want my opinion – oh and also Mr Plough, you might want to take charge of this little lot what I just found down on the floor there, look. And I'm passing him over the packet before I even know what in blue bleeding blazes it is I'm playing at. And he takes it off of me, Mr Plough – has a little look inside and he gives a sort of a whistle, as well he bleeding might. Well well, he goes – the things you do come across in derelict buildings: I'll see this safe to the authorities, rest assured on that score Jackie, and I commend you, he says, for doing the right thing. Yeh well . . . whole of the rest of the day, my heart – it just ain't in it, is it? The work what I'm doing. Because I just can't get it out my mind, can I? I only come in to sixty-five pound, and two minutes later I gives it away. And then I got to thinking – who's these 'authorities' then, what he's going to get it to safe, Mr Plough? Ay? It's him what owns the house, ain't it? There ain't no bleeding 'authorities', is there? He going to collar the bleeding lot, and already he's as rich as the blooming King hisself. And Mary, she can kiss goodbye to her Lloyd Loom and her Ewbank, whatever in Jesus name them bleeding things is – and me, I'm back on the Woodbines and I never even come off of them! End of the day, Mr Plough, he come up to me and he says I won't forget it, what you done Jackie boy: there's not many in your place what would've done what you just done (no, I were thinking: too right. You'd have to be a certified fucking loony to go and do what I just done) – and then he give me a little envelope, he do, and I thanks him for that, and when he gone off I tears it open and what I got is four half-crowns. Ten bob, he give me. And I give him sixty-five quid. Dear oh me. Still – it were time for knocking off, so I goes down the Rose & Crown and old Dickie were in there – and I tell him, I tell him what had just occurred, and he says he's right proud of me on account of it's this sort of thing what makes Britain great. Yeh? I go to him. Yeh? What – a poor old bugger like me making a rich old bastard like Plough even bleeding richer? Yeh – you could be right: that's what's been making Britain great for about five hundred bleeding years, but it never done the likes of me no good though, did it? And nor it won't, neither – not till we get a Labour government in, it won't: string up all the bleeding Tories. And oh *Lord*, Dickie's going – you don't want to talk about *politics*, do you? Old chap, what what – the way he go. And I says no I bleeding don't, son – what I want is to exchange one of these big silver half-crowns here with my good friend Len, and see how much ale and Scotch it'll bring us – because *that*, my dear old mate, *that* is what makes Britain great, or it do in my eyes any road. So we had a fair old time, Dickie and me – and he says, what I should be (and I learned this – he told me slow a couple times, and I learned it) is *philosophic*, that's what I should be, and that means I got to take it on the chin, far as I can make out: see it as ten bob up and not as sixty-four pound ten down, sort of style. And I says yeh, I think I can accommodate you on that on account of there ain't a lot of bleeding choice, is there? And still, I reckoned – Mary, she'd be able to get something or other, wouldn't she? Off of the Army & Navy for seven-and-six. Yeh – trouble was, time I get home, it's down to one-and-nine. Which I never give her because, well – insulting, ain't it? You give someone one-and-nine. So I never mentioned none of it to her. Bestway, I reckon.

And it were that night, the Tuesday it were, that were when Dickie, he tell me all about this ARP caper he's got hisself into. Said to him he's barmy. Going to be a doctor come the summer, ain't you? Ay? And here you is getting all excited about your little tin helmet and freezing your balls off of a night-time, sitting around a pile of sandbags.

'Well obviously, Jackie old sport, there isn't a great deal one can actually accomplish at the present time, as it were – but it's all awfully good training, don't you know. For when the real thing comes along. I've already learned to use a stirrup pump, great fun – although strictly that's the FPO's responsibility, but all of us we sort of muck in, you know. Early days, and all that sort of thing. All a bit new to it.'

'What the fuck you talking about? What's a syrup thing? What's all this FO's . . . ?'

'Pump. It's a stirrup pump. FPO – Fire Protection Officer. As I say, it's their baby really, the stirrup pump. Basically, it's just this gadget that you stick in a bucket of water and then you just sort of, well – pump away, sort of thing. Everyone ought to have them, you see. Well if not the pump, then certainly the bucket of water. But my main concern will be making sure that the blackout's observed. Bound to be one. Total blackout, shouldn't wonder. Heard that the relevant government department – can't think who it'd be – they're churning out all the material and so forth like absolute billy-o. One can't help thinking, you know, that the powers that be know a jolly sight more than they're letting on.'

'Nah. Won't never come to that. Wasting your time, you are. Either way – waste of time. No war – you look a proper charlie, don't you? And if it do – if it do come to it, which it won't, well then you ain't going to be winning it, is you? With your bleeding bucket of water and your wossname doodah. Waste of time – won't never come to it.'

'Well . . . I was listening to the wireless the other day, and according to Mr Churchill—'

'*Dah!* What's he know? What's he know about anything at all, Mr bleeding Churchill? Old hasbeen, he is – that's what everyone says about him. Warmonger, that's all he is. Every time he stands up, he gets shouted at. And he's old – silly old sod, that's what he is. Trying to live all the past glories of the last lot, that's all it is. Forget about him, tell you that.'

'Mm – well, that *used* to be how people were thinking, I grant you. But just lately, well . . . and after all this Czechoslovakia business—'

'Oh blimey – I hear that word just one more time I reckon I'll spew, is what I'll do. Who bloody cares about it? Why people keep going on about it? It's *us* we want to be caring about – and that means no war, don't it? Stands to reason. We want to be safe, then we stay well out of it. You get in a fight – whatever reason – you going to get hurt.'

'Well *you* did, Jackie old fruit. Remember? Just before Christmas – pretty much just about where you're standing right this minute. That's *exactly* what you did.'

'What you on about? Tell you what, Dickie – we'll break into just one more of these half-crowns, yeh? And then I got to be getting myself off.'

'Well just the one then, if you insist old chap. I mean that big fellow – don't you remember? Can't have forgotten, surely. You went in to bat for me, old boy, and got a sore head for your trouble. Could've left me to my own devices, couldn't you Jackie? But you didn't. And I rather think that's going to be our position, you know, if there's any sort of trouble about Poland. Got to be done, really. The English way.'

'Not the same thing. Different, Dickie. You're a *mate*. Don't give tuppence about bleeding Poland, do I?'

'Ah but the principle holds good, Jackie. It's the principle, you see.'

'*Wrong*, Dickie – all wrong. And that's what the government don't see neither. You don't never do nothing for a bleeding *principle* – you do it for a reason what an ordinary bloke like me can *understand*. Else you got a load of frightened and chattery people what don't know what in Christ's name's going on – just like what you got now. People's going crazy with all the not knowing. And what good's it doing them, ay? None. No good at all. What we wants to hear – I'll tell you, will I Dickie? What'd put the smile back on everyone's faces? That bleeding Chamberlain, he stands up in the House of Wossname and he says right, now: you listen to me, you lot. We're all right, we are – we got an Empire. And we ain't about to slash it away up against no wall. So all them bleeding foreigners, they can do what they bleeding well like – but us, we're sitting tight, mate:

we ain't going into no war on account of a load of people we ain't never even heard of. They can't look after their own little poxy countries, well that's their lookout. But us – we can. We're the Island Race, we is. Like that bloke we saw up the column Christmas time – yeh Dickie? And that's the way we're going to keep it, come hell or high water. Nelson, yeh. Tell you, Dickie – he gets hisself on the wireless, old Chamberlain, and he come out with that little lot, there'd be cheering and dancing in the streets, you mark my words. Never mind you and your bleeding blackout – there'd be fireworks, my son: fireworks.'

Yeh: that's what I said to him. Can't recall if he come back to me with anything after, old Dickie – don't matter too much one way or t'other. Chalk and cheese, me and Dickie you know – fond of the bleeder, though: something about him. But oh dear me – his attitude, it couldn't be further away from our dear old chum Mr Jonathan Leakey. Two minds I am about Jonny. There's times I reckon we see right eye to eye, the pair of us – but then he gets to telling me *no*, Jackie, we ain't a pair, we ain't alike: we're different, you and me. And I see it when he says it, course I does: plain as the nose on your wossname. Way we live, miles apart. And I been thinking a bit on what he says about . . . now I think I got this straight, but let's just go slow, ay? What he says is, if this is right – it ain't what you got, it's how you got it – and then you *become* what you got. Or something like that. Sometimes I sees it, other times I reckon it's like one of them riddles what you got as a kid, can't recall one just now as a for instance, but it's like one of them things where first off it's a right old puzzle to you, and next thing you know it's all as clear as daylight. He's a stirrer though, Jonny. Don't think he's too fond of people being happy in theirself – he don't mind them being happy, but he wants it to be happy in the same way what he is. And he'll needle you, he will – goading, like. I don't bother saying to him no more that I'm all right, I am – content with my little lot – because then he'll start up about why does I want to settle for a little lot when I can have a big lot, no questions asked. And nor I don't ask him how, because then he'd bleeding tell me. Course, just now I'd be a bloody sight more content with my little lot if that bugger Plough would just come through with the goods what he been dangling in front of me: then I'd be set – that'd do me, then. And Jonny, I don't know – he's maybe picked it up, that I don't talk so much about this bleeding partnership like what I used to . . . yeh, because he can do that, Jonny – sense things, know what's going on, sniff out the lie of the land: see in the dark, Jonny can. Jonny Midnight. Like just the other evening: well into his stride, he were – smelling blood, for all I could tell you.

'We'll just have the one more than, ay Jackie? Then I got to be off. Got a man to see. You can get them in leather now, you know – think I even seed them in suede, now I come to think of it. Your Mary, she's a knacky little thing, have them sewed on for you in two shakes of a donkey's tail, she would.'

'What the bleeding hell you talking about, Jonny? Sometimes, as real as I'm standing here now, I'd swear to wossname that you gone simple.'

'Patches, mate. Your *elbows*, Jackie – ain't you spotted it? Gone shiny, they have – one of them's all frayed, look. Maybe you want to see to it. Maybe your Mr Plough – that the geezer's name? Plough? Your governor? Yeh, thought it were – maybe he'd reckon you was more partner material if you got yourself up a bit more smarter, ay? No offence, Jackie lad.'

'No, Jonny – like usual. But yeh . . . Mary, she were saying something about it the other day and all. Not too fussed myself, but yeh – take your meaning. She were telling me, Mary, she seed this advertisement in one of them magazines what Sheila keep giving her. Round Clerkenwell, place you can get a suit for one pound five. They maybe does instalments. Course – won't be in your league, Jonny.'

'I should bloody well say it won't! Bleeding cheek. Won't tell you, Jackie, these whistles of mine, what they set me back: bring tears to your eyes. But you want quality – you got to pay for it. Way of the world. Now a twenty-five-bob suit, Jackie – what's that going to look like?'

'Well . . . it'll be all right, I reckon . . .'

'It *might* be all right – oh yes granted. It *could* be all right, I'm not saying. But right or wrong, Jackie, what it'll look like is a twenty-five-bob suit. You get my meaning? See – someone what don't know a bleeding thing about nothing, they might take a look at you and say oh yeh – there's Jackie, new suit, very smart. But someone who knows what's what – someone what's got an iota, well . . . all he going to see in front of him is a twenty-five-bob suit, and the person what's inside it, well – pretty much invisible, you want the truth. And that is not the point, is it? Ay? You get a new suit, you want to stand out from the crowd. Don't you? Ay? Else what's it bleeding for? Now – you turn up in your twenty-five-bob suit, all stiff as a board and baggy round the bum, I shouldn't wonder, and what people see – people what count, mind – what they see is someone what's struggling with the one-and-a-tanner a week it's likely costing them. And *struggling*, Jackie, is what you don't want to be seen doing. Not never. See? Whatever's going on – whatever's going wrong – to the outside world, it got to look *easy*. Get it? You make people feel that everything's easy, they're going to have faith in you. Trust your judgement. They'll want to be close to you, Jackie, so that they can take it easy and all.'

'Bit like you, ay Jonny? Bit like you.'

'No, Jackie – wrong. A *lot* like me. Very wholly like me, as a matter of fact. You listen: you learn. Now – you temporarily embarrassed, that's perfectly understandable. Commitments – I can appreciate that. All you got to know is a bloke what knows a bloke who would be only too happy to help you out of this predicament. And if you was lucky enough to know such a bloke what knows the bloke who's the man to know . . . well then, Jackie: all you got to do is say the word. See? Simple as that. Just you tip me the wink, Jackie old lad, and all your grafting days is behind you. Milk and honey, son. What's wrong? Don't you want some?'

And yeh of course it got me thinking – would for anyone, wouldn't it? Just like he meant it for. Because I ain't a fool – I know what he's up to, Jonny: he sow a seed, is what he do – water it, time to time, and then he just sits back and waits for the flower to come up. Blimey though – I couldn't tell you why he's always so dead keen for me to go and see you-know-who, the Lord God Almighty Mr Wisely. Can't see it's any skin off of his nose. But talking of him, Mr Wisely – when Jonny said that about an end to grafting, I found myself looking down at my hands, I did – all the little nicks from the plane and the chisel, that dead lard skin on my thumbs, the chewed-up nails with the distemper underneath, the great big red and bony hulk of them, like they been battered and boiled and hung out to dry. And when I shook his hand that night – that bleeding funny night, when we was all of us round at Mr Wisely's . . . well, I say *shook* his hand, I never, not really – would've seemed wrong, somehow, to actually take a hold of the thing and give it a good pumping. I just sort of touched the palm of it, really – fingers just there, and then they was gone – and I'm telling you, aside from Jeremy's little bum, I ain't never in my life ever felt a thing what was quite so bleeding soft. I am not kidding you – it were like that little feather puff what's in Mary's compact. So: an end to grafting? Well yeh – sometimes, there's some times, yeh, I wouldn't say no. But I try to sort of laugh it off with Jonny – I says to him yeh, Jonny, but if I weren't grafting, what else would I be doing, ay? Because it's all I know – down on my knees and banging away: what else am I good for, ay? Laughing it off, just making a bit of conversation, sort of style, that's what I were doing . . . but Jonny, well, I don't

273

think he were taken in for a single bleeding moment – no, not Jonny: no, not him. On to it straight off, he were – like a butcher's dog with a cut of brisket.

'Well that's why you want to go and see him, ain't it Jackie? That's what talk is for – you says something, he says something, and then you each of you gets to know what you're all talking about, don't you? Not for me to say, of course, what it is Mr Wisely's got on his mind. And that's why I says it to you, Jackie mate. Go and see him – why don't you? What's to lose, ay? Only a chat, when all's said and done. And oh yeh – a word to the wise, Jackie old lad. I was in your shoes, I'd make it sooner rather than later. You don't want to go and see a man when you ain't got no choice in the matter, see? Puts you in a weaker position. Now at the moment, Jackie, you got this job of yours, whatever it's worth. But you got it, that's the point. Now what I hear, well . . . building trade, in for a little bit of trouble. Bit of a shake-up. Way things is going. That's what I hear, anyway. That's the word.'

'What you mean, way things is going? You talking daft. Business is good – no slackening off, far as I'm aware.'

'It ain't the business, Jackie boy – it's the world. It's all down to what's going on in the world. Aware, are you? That there's this little war just around the corner?'

'Oh Christ, not you as well, Jonny. There ain't going to be no bleeding war – how many times I got to keep on saying it? Even the Tories – even the fucking Tories ain't so stupid as to get us into all that. All they're trying to do—'

'I wouldn't be too sure of that Jackie, what I hear.'

'Listen. Just listen. All they're trying to do – the government, right? Is make Germany believe that they'll go to war, see? Now Germany, she ain't no mug neither, is she? All very well marching into all these poxy little countries what no one's never heard of, and they puts up their hands and lets the Krauts walk all over them. Not going to take on Britain though, are they? Ay? What – with our navy, and all? Our Army? Air Force? They wouldn't dare. We'd crush them just like that, and don't they know it.'

'Well – you could be right. I ain't saying you're wrong. But that's not how the government's looking at it, see? What's going to happen is, all essential supplies – wood, metal, paint, brick, you name it – it's all going to be stockpiled, ain't it? And all the new doings what's being turned out, well – that's going on the pile and all. So you see, Jackie boy – your Mr Plough, he may have the jobs to do, but he ain't going to have the materials to do them with, that's the point. And also, there's talk of a ban coming in – a ban on all non-essential use of all of the wossname. So there could come a time not too distant when you're not only breaking your back, Jackie, but you'd be breaking the law of the land on the top of it. And I were you, I'd check on this little house you got your eye on. What I heard, there's no more going to be built. That's what I heard. Looks like you missed the boat, son.'

Well all of this were news to me – and I'm swiped by it, I don't mind telling you. I never heard nothing about none of all this before – but then be fair, I wouldn't of, would I? Packed in all the papers and the wireless months back, I did – couldn't stand it no more, the way they was always going on. And Mary, she don't know nothing – or if she do, she ain't letting on. But this here, if it's true – and it will be, I bloody suppose, because if there's one thing about Jonny, he's always well informed (got to be, as he keeps on bleeding telling me) . . . well, what I'm meaning is, if all this is on the level, then I'm hit from all sides, ain't I? Can't go on in my trade, better myself, become a partner, get my hands on a bit more money and then buy us all this nice little house – all I ever wanted, weren't it? – on account of there ain't going to be no trade, and there ain't going to be no bleeding house neither. Very nice. And all down to this scaremongering government what we're stuck with: oh yes – very nice. And it could be even worse than that because this morning, well . . . I had another run-in, didn't I, with that bleeding Jew-boy Stone. It's people like him what's caused all this. They hadn't rubbed up Hitler all the wrong way, then maybe he wouldn't have gone marching into all them other places like he done and messing up my job and doing for my future. Just as well I didn't know the length and breadth of it when I met him on the stairs – else I would've tipped him over the wossname, sure as eggs is eggs. What he had to say to me this time, in his bloody stupid foreign accent – what he were on about this time, if you can believe it . . . banisters, banister rail, yeh – would've tipped him right over, I would . . . what he were moaning on about were the doormat, you want to know. Yeh – not kidding: the bleeding doormat, I ask you. What's wrong, I go to him – how've I hurt your sodding doormat, you miserable little bleeder.

'No cause you rude, Mr Robertson. I say most polite.'

'Yeh yeh – you say most polite. Bleeding hell. So it's covered in muck – it's a muddy day out there, see? That's what a bleeding doormat's for, ain't it? Ay? Or maybe they don't have them where you come from, that it? Live in a tent, did you? In your Germany?'

'My homeland . . . had big beautiful house. They took.'

'Well you want to fight back, don't you? What you made of? I had a big beautiful house, ain't no one's going to take it off of me, that's for bleeding sure.'

'And muck – all up stair. My wife – she must clean. Is not right.'

'Yeh well – maybe you ought to do something for all the money I gives you. What else she got to do anyway? Your missus. Any time I seen her, she just staring at the bloody wall. Do her good, get a bit active.'

'You most rude man.'

'Yeh I know – and you say most polite. We done this one. I tell you one thing, mate – you want rude? Here's rude. Now I don't

276

know how much English you got, but when I tells you to fuck off, like what I'm about to do, then you can run off up the library and look it up in a dictionary, you don't know what it means. All right? Now then: fuck *off*, son. There: said it now.'

And blimey – he gone all purple in the face as if he were going to go up like them mountains they got abroad, when all the doings go blowing out the top and cause all sorts – and what he says to me, and I'm picking around for the few words I can make out, is that he ain't at this point going to evict me on account of Mary and the kiddy, but that the very next time I 'not say polite' to him, silly bleeder, then I am out on my ear, and no questions asked. Yeh. That were pretty much the gist of it. And I know I shouldn't do it – I know I shouldn't, but it's just the bleeding sight of him, miserable weedy little bugger in his cardigan, all hunched-up and whispery, and his bloody stupid foreign accent, bleeding Jew-boy that he is – there's something goes snap, just like that. Something inside of me, I just hears it go snap, and that's me finished and I'm off. Yeh well . . . light of what Jonny's telling me now, I reckon I got to go very easy with Mr bleeding Stone from now on, don't I? Else we'll all of us be up shit creek, right royally.

So I'm all a bit confused . . . I mean I'm always pretty tired these days anyway, all the work I'm doing, and after a couple jars with Jonny, well – I could just curl up like a pussycat and have myself a good old doze on the mat. But now there's all of this new stuff I got to be thinking about and I don't want it, to be frank with you – I don't want much to think about nothing, I never does, but in particular I don't want it to be new: can't be doing with new – it's hard to get your mind round it, and it unsettles all the old stuff what you reckoned you did know like the back of your wossname, only now you don't know it at all because when you took your eye off of it for just a minute back there, it all gone and changed, didn't it? And what you end up

277

knowing is bleeding nothing. And Jonny – he ain't about to let up neither – still going, he is. He got more of it:

'See, Jackie – what you don't seem to be realising is, there's going to be changes – big changes, like of which you ain't never imagined in all your bleeding life, and right across all the classes and all. That's a turn-up in itself. Largely, of course, it's still going to fall to the poor little bastard what don't know the time of day – yessir, he'll go, to whatever they tell him, and he won't be lasting two minutes, poor sod. Cannon fodder, that's what they called it in the last war.'

'Yeh – and it *was* the last war and all. Remember? War to end all wars? Because we learned the lesson, didn't we? What makes you so bleeding sure, Jonny? Ay? Why you keep on saying it's going to be war?'

'Well Jackie – no offence, but I reckon you'd have to be dumb, deaf and blind not to know what's coming down now, son. Like I say – no offence. But this time it's going to be a people's war. What I heard.'

'Yeh? And what they use the last time, then? Bleeding giraffes?'

'Yeh yeh – very funny, Jackie. Highly amusing. No – what I mean to say is, there ain't no one's going to escape. Women, children – old folk. Aristos. Bleeding lot. And it's up to us, Jackie, to be prepared, see? We don't want to be one of the mugs what get caught out. And we got an advantage, see? We know there's going to be a war – no, don't interrupt me, Jackie boy, let me say my piece . . . all right then – just to keep you happy, let's say there is a very strong *likelihood* . . . all right? Better? Right then – a very strong *likelihood* that there's going to be a war . . . but we don't know when, see? We don't know when. Now – lot of people, it's this what's driving them barmy, see? The not knowing when. And it's them what's almost longing for it to happen tomorrow morning, so they can just knuckle down and get on with it. But that's daft, that is – that is to lose all sight of the advantage we got. Because every day of peace, Jackie boy, is a bonus. See? Time. Time to prepare, that is. Time to sort ourselves out. Like Mr Wisely done. Whatever happens, he'll be on Easy Street, like what he always is: he made bleeding sure of it. And like what I'm doing. And that's what you should be doing and all, Jackie lad. You go on denying it, you go on sticking your head in the wossname and you're going to be one of them, mate – the mugs what get caught out. And that ain't you, is it Jackie? Ay? One thing you ain't, and that's a mug. Am I right?'

'That's for certain. I ain't stupid . . .'

'That's it – you ain't. Course you ain't. And you got to start behaving as if you ain't. Else I'm telling you, Jackie – you won't know what's bleeding hit you, my son.'

So I chews that over for a bit – I know there's sense in it some-where, deep down, blowed if I know where – and I'm trying to think well all right then – there ain't going to be no war, I know there ain't going to be no war, but let's just say, will we, just for the sake of it, that a war do come along, well then yeh – I can see Jonny's meaning: got to be ready, haven't you? Got to have in your mind what it is *you* want to be doing about it, and not just get pushed around and wherever the bastards want you. So yeh – I'm with him so far as that goes . . . but I tell you, for the life of me I can't think of a single bleeding way I can go about it. I mean, yeh, be prepared, that's all well and good – but how? Ay? What you do? How you set about it, then? Couldn't tell you, son. Not a clue. So I got to ask him, don't I? Got to get Jonny to tell me.

'Well, Jackie – there's various ways, course there are. Depends on your situation, don't it? But you, lad – you are most definitely vulnerable. Now there's voluntary conscription, right? Yeh well – that's a bit like saying there's going to be voluntary income tax that is, if you know what I'm saying. Once we get stuck in, there ain't going to be no bleeding voluntary about it, son. Now – if you're an old geezer, all the old blokes what was in the last lot, well they're reasonably safe, I'd say. At the outset, anyway. Kids'll be well away, much as they can be – evacuation, that's what they're talking about . . . can't see how it's going to work myself, but still – nothing to do with me. Bit to do with you though, ain't it Jackie lad? Ay? Another thing you got to be thinking. Married men, big families, reckon they'll go light on them to start with – only to start with, mind – and then there's what they call the key professionals and trades, what they'll have to keep behind. Shipbuilders. Farmers, course. Police, more's the pity. You get the idea. Now where does that leave you? Ay? Up to your neck in it, son – that's where you'll be. Young, single – because they go legal, see? And in legal, you're single and that's all there is to it. Fit, you look to me and all. Well – stands to reason, don't it Jackie boy? Army, it's got its beady little eye on you, and no mistake. Fancy the idea, do you? Marching up and down like a clockwork wossname, nice little khaki suit on you – off to war with a gun on your shoulder? Like the idea do you, Jackie?'

'They'll never get me in no bloody army . . . right mug's game, that is.'

'*Right*, my son. You're right on the money there, mate. But what I'm saying, Jackie – you don't do something about it in the time you got left to you, and that's exactly what's going to happen: you'll be called up, and you'll be in. And that means you'll be one of the mugs. Got it?'

I'm not liking it. I am not liking this conversation – no, not one little bit. He's got a way with him, Jonny has – way with words, makes it all seem so bleeding real, he do. Like he's almost got me believing there *is* going to be a bloody war now, and two minutes ago I were convinced there bleeding wasn't. I get so confused, that's the trouble with me.

'So . . . for the sake of argument then, Jonny . . . just say all of this was about to happen, just like you say . . . what's a bloke going to do then, ay? To get out of it. What can I do, Jonny? Ay?'

'Now that's more like it, Jackie lad. Beginning to see a bit of sense now, ain't you? First wise thing you asked me, that is.'

'Yeh. Well. So? What I do? Tell me.'

'Well, Jackie – and you really is a bit slow on the take-up, no offence – but in a nutshell, what you do, Jackie my friend, is you take yourself off and you go and see Mr Wisely. See? Simple as that. He'll know what's best – he always do. And like I said to you, Jackie – took a real shine to you, he did. He'll sort you out, no bother. And once you done that, what I reckon you ought to do then is forget all about your Mr Plough and going up a ladder and digging bleeding holes and whatever other caper you get up to – what I reckon you should do is book yourself a nice little holiday – get away for a bit, take Mary and the kid. Make it soon and all, Jackie. It ain't a time to be hanging about.'

'It's Mary's birthday in the summer . . . not too far off. I ain't never took her on no holiday . . .'

'Well there you are then. Perfect. Love you for that, she will: love you for it.'

Yeh well . . . wouldn't mind if she did, to be honest with you: love me for it. Because I been going a bit shy on all that side of things, just lately. Something else what's been on my mind. I mean to be fair to her, it ain't always her fault. Quite a few months now I been so bleeding done in when I get home of an evening, all I'm up for is a plate of something hot inside of me, pint or two down the Rose & Crown, and then out like a light until the next thing I know it's the bleeding morning again, and she's dragging me out the bed and little Jeremy, he'll be sitting on my head and pulling at my hair and what I got to do then is I got to get myself up and go back and work for bleeding Mr Plough. Other times, I'm feeling a bit frisky and I says to her – here, Mary love, what say you put on a squirt of your Eau de Paris and slip into that little camisole what I got for you, how about that for an idea then, ay? And once or twice way back she gone for it, I'm not denying, but more likely than not it's either she's dead on her feet, she says to me, or else she got the curse on her or there's all the bleeding ironing to see to or she promised to have a natter with Sheila. One time, we's just getting down to it, all tucked up nice of a night-time, and then bleeding little Jeremy starts up all of his rumpus, don't he? Like he knows, or something. And never mind that I says to her oh leave him, leave it Mary, he'll cry hisself out and then he'll get back to sleep – no no, you can forget all of that – she's in there, ain't she? Like a bolt shot out a crossbow – so fast and slippy she is, I can't never even grab a hold of her and drag her back and tell her what's what. It's months since we done it, I reckon: months and months. And anyway, yeh – next thing I know it's the morning again – and there she is, hauling me out the bed on account of I got to get myself up and go back and work for bleeding Mr Plough again. And it's only now I twig – courtesy of Jonathan Leakey – why it is he said nothing to me about it, our partnership and all. Not a bleeding dicky bird. Knew, didn't he, the writing were on the wall. Knew all along there weren't never going to be no bloody partnership, and still he had me slaving my guts out so's I'd impress him and all – and fuck me if I ain't just give him my sixty-five quid in exchange for ten fucking bob. Yeh well – soon put a stop to all that malarkey, I can tell you that much. And here – I'm just thinking . . . I took her on a holiday, neither of us'd be so bleeding tired, and there'd be a lot more hours in the day, wouldn't there? So maybe, yeh, if I done that, it might be the way Jonny said, ay? And she'd love me for it.

And in the meantime, here I still is – just sitting in the corner of this room what I'm doing up, that sweet smell sawdust got, that's all about me. My tea – that's gone cold, because I never paid it no mind. And I did, you know – I did fix up the damp in that basement, fixed it up quite nice: ain't going to last a thousand years, but I reckon it's as good as what the pros would've done it, and never mind all the fancy prices they're going to be charging you. See? Catch that, did you? Still doing it, ain't I? Thinking like a partner would be thinking. Thinking like I got a stake in it. And I ain't. Truth is, there ain't nothing I got a stake in. And I just sit here, don't I? Smoking a fag – a young, fit, single bloke I am, and what that makes me, according to Jonny, is definitely bleeding vulnerable. Very nice. And them little hairs ... ! All still crawling down my back, they is: driving me wild. And my face now – when I get all the bristles back, this time of an evening – I'm clawing away at that and all, it's so bleeding itchy. Talking of that ... blimey O'Reilly. Do you know what Jonny were telling me? About Mr Wisely? Won't never forget it. Them women what he got – haughty lot and no mistake, but you ain't never in your life seen nothing so beautiful – them women, Jonny were telling me, they takes it in turns – and he swore he weren't making it up – to shave him. He sits in his leather chair there, and one of them'll give his face a good old soaping, and then with this solid silver cutthroat, she'll give him the closest shave ever, and don't never disturb that little pencil moustache what he got. Can you imagine? I ain't never before heard of such a thing in all my born days. And I won't never forget it neither.

29th August 1939
Well here it is again: my birthday. And this time I'm a quarter of a century old! Sounds ancient, but I must say I don't feel any different, apart from this bit of sickness I get when I've just

eaten – nerves, I expect. So much for the physical – but oh, my mind! Everything has been happening so terribly quickly, one thing after another, although Jackie keeps telling me that it's all good – he still doesn't think there will be a war, and I refuse to think it too, but we seem to be just about the only ones left, now. But if someone had told me on my last birthday that this time I would be writing my diary in a Hastings boarding house (Jackie's gone walking somewhere) with Jeremy still in London with Sheila and little Imogen – that we don't have anywhere settled to live and everyone you talk to with the one single topic of conversation (war war war!), well I just wouldn't have believed them. But it is so – these are the facts. When Jackie first suggested a couple of days at the seaside, I was thrilled of course – we've never been anywhere, Jackie and me. And it is very nice here – the air is lovely, and Mrs Crane who we're staying with does a very good meat supper and our room is spotlessly clean. But of course I wanted to bring Jeremy, couldn't even think of leaving him, but Jackie said I wouldn't get the benefit if we brought him along and Sheila said she'd be only too pleased to take him for the couple of days, and when Lorna got to hear of it she told me that Imogen was dying to see Jeremy again, thought of him as her own little baby, which is so terribly sweet, and of course I know that between the two of them Jeremy will be perfectly well, but still I find it so very strange to be without him. I never have been before. Jackie says it's like a second honeymoon we're having, and I didn't like to say that we never had a first. It seems to have slipped his mind that we aren't actually married – the only reason, in truth, that I am relieved that we are not now going to be living in a house in Golders Green. I got the feeling that an unmarried mother would not be too welcome out there – it's much more strait-laced than where we're used to. I was disappointed at first, of course (Jackie explained about the shortage of building materials, and so on), but I quickly forgot about all that in the light of (1) Jackie losing his employ with Mr Plough (for the same reason, apparently – this shortage) and (2) Mr Stone telling us we had to leave the flat. I must admit I panicked – how could Jackie think of us going on a holiday with all these terrible things going on? He says they're not terrible, and I so much want to believe him. He says that by the time we go back (tomorrow morning, 9 o'clock train – it's been nice here but I can't wait, quite honestly, to see Jeremy again) he'll have a new job and somewhere much better for us to live. This to me sounds less of a plan and more of a conjuring trick, but I held my peace. I only knew that we had to leave the flat from Mr Stone, Jackie never said – and Molly, oh goodness, she's still so upset. He was ever so apologetic, Mr Stone, and he didn't say exactly why he was doing this to us, but knowing how Jackie has been behaving just lately – all the things he has to say about foreigners and everything – I can more or less understand it, I suppose. He gets it all confused, that's the trouble. I sometimes think he imagines the Jewish refugees and the Nazis to be one and the same, but I just can't bring myself to discuss it. Too too depressing.

He has been very amorous, Jackie – barely let me alone. Says we haven't been intimate for nearly six months, which is nonsense. Sometimes I think he had so much ale he didn't remember. He gave me a black silk nightie for my birthday – it's getting to be a habit. I just hope he didn't talk about it to Jonathan Leakey.

If my worries about Jackie's work and where we're going to live weren't enough, there's everything that Sheila's been saying to me for the past month and more. She became so fed up with the hairdressing that she applied to the council for some job to do with the 'effort', it's called – and I must admit I didn't think she had it in her. She felt she had to be doing something useful, particularly now that Dickie has qualified as a doctor (we're all so proud of him – Jackie went wild when he heard the news). I said to her at the time that all these volunteers for these various posts that seem to be springing up in all directions – they're going to look a bit silly when all this talk of war just fizzles out and comes to nothing. Anyway, they offered her something to do with ambulances which she didn't fancy and something else to do with aircraft which I actually believe she thought too terrifying for words. Eventually she became an Assistant Evacuation Officer – and I'm not sure I want to write any more about this, but I must. She says that if it comes to it, she'll be able to make sure that Jeremy is placed in a comfortable billet. Oh that phrase! 'Placed in a comfortable billet'! My Jeremy! I said that if Jeremy goes anywhere, then I go with him – and Jackie then said no to that, and I was so shocked, so very shocked. He said he'd want Jeremy to be safe, of course he would (if it comes to it, which it won't), but he'd need me at home to look after him. Which of course I am happy to do – I hate the thought of being without either one of them, because looking after them is all that I am for, really. Anyway – can't. Can't write any more about that. Home tomorrow – wherever home might be. We shall have to see. About everything, really.

I was looking at the two books that Dickie gave me for Christmas (seems so long ago now) but I can't really concentrate on either one. Dickens – he seems to have so little to do with everything that's going on now. And that other one – P. G. Somebody. Awful I can't remember. Wood something. Anyway – I could see why Dickie would like it, but honestly – all these posh silly asses. I can't see they have any relevance at all. It's meant to be funny, but I haven't laughed. This could be just me, of course – the way I'm feeling.

Yesterday, in the old part of Hastings – very appealing, lots of winding lanes and little shops – I bought an electric torch and a battery, and then I found myself going back later and buying another one. And all because I'd read somewhere that there was going to be a shortage! All this anxiety, it's a form of contagion. I'm not going to write in this ledger again until everything's much more settled.

As Dickie cut the engine of the Morris, Jackie swivelled around in the passenger seat and clapped his hands once, and sharply.

'Right then, Mary love – close your eyes, there's a good girl now.'

'Oh Jackie I can't – how can I? I'll fall over if I close my eyes . . .'

'I'll look after you, Mary,' laughed Sheila beside her. 'I won't let you trip. Oh my goodness – you're so *lucky*. Looks lovely from the outside.'

'Jolly decent building,' agreed Dickie. 'And not too far at all from your old stamping ground, hey?'

'Yeh,' nodded Jackie. 'I asked for that specific. Too far from the old Rose & Crown and I reckon I could lose my head. So come on then – out you get, Mary – see to her will you, Sheila? And mind what I say – eyes tight shut, all right? No little peeks.'

Mary giggled indulgently and closed her eyes and with a probing toe felt her way down to the kerbstone, Sheila holding on to her arm and shuffling out behind her – Mary felt Dickie, now, taking her by the hand and she laughed as she heard him encourage her with an Upsy-daisy, old girl, that's the style.

'Now the good news is,' said Jackie, 'we's on the ground floor, yeh? So there's only the one step up to the front door, all right? And then it's just off the hall. Right then – best foot forward.'

Dickie, for one, was quite startled as Jackie threw wide to them the door of the flat.

'By Jove!' he exclaimed. 'Well I must say, Jackie – this is a bit of a surprise, what? Not at all what you'd expect, going by the age of the building. Well well well – very swish, I must say. Très chic!'

'Can I look now . . . ?' piped up Mary, as Jackie took hold of her shoulders and guided her to the centre of the sitting room.

'Ooooh . . . !' sighed Sheila, with longing. 'Oh it's heaven – it's very heaven, this is.'

'Oh God's sake Jackie let me *look* . . . !' Mary implored him. 'I can't *stand* it any more . . . !'

'What you reckon, Sheila?' queried Jackie, quite archly. 'Let her look, will we? What you say, Dickie? Ready for a bit of tray sheek, is she? Whatever the bleeding hell that is . . .'

'I think,' chortled Dickie, 'that we really ought to put the poor old thing out of her misery, don't you know. Decent thing, Jackie old man.'

'Yeh – could be sound, that: could be sound. All right then, Mary my love – get them peepers open.'

So Mary did that, gingerly, as everyone watched her – in Sheila's case with gleeful and practically uncontainable anticipation – as she gazed about her, her eyes just huge and her mouth hanging open, quite without words. She shook her head in happy disbelief.

'Corking, what?' Dickie urged her. 'Utterly ripping, I'd say.'

'Do you love it, Mary?' Sheila rushed in now. 'Isn't it just too too wonderful? I'd die – oh I'd just die to be living in a flat like this.'

Jackie thought he'd say nothing, just for the time being: let it sink in with her – light up a Senior Service and have a gander at the toe of my boot, bit coy like, while it has a mooch about the fringes of the rug there . . .

Mary appeared to be still in the grip of a trance of some sort, her neck revolving as if on a ratchet like an alert and curious bird, her eyelids descending as if they were the shutter in a camera – rising then, and clearing the lens as each new snapshot was taken and stored. Soon her vision was swooping up and around and then down again, so greedy was she now to devour it all at once – the sweep of all these flat and perfect stark-white walls, the way they just curve up into the ceiling like that with no hint at all of cornicing or a picture rail to distract the eye or interrupt the line. The corners of the chimney breast, they're rounded as well – and oh my goodness, the fireplace! Have you ever seen such a thing? A black and glossy mantel, and it must be a gas fire, it looks like, set into what appears to be a sheet of glass in pale and milky turquoise-green, and edged in fluted chrome panels. The floor is parquet and very highly polished – mats and rugs here and there, each of them with these rather odd and asymmetric, is it . . . ? Asymmetric, I think, geometrical patterns – segments of circles and intersecting bars in the same pale green with charcoal, ochre and a dark rusty red. There's a small plump sofa and two deep matching armchairs – they're covered in what Mary knew very well from the Army & Navy Stores catalogue to be something called Rexine, but you'd swear it was leather, deep maroon and piped in white. Next to one of the chairs stood a low and circular side table made entirely of shiny polished steel with a plate glass top – and upon it is a heavy black telephone. A telephone – oh my goodness me . . . and there's the dearest little dining table and four black straight-backed chairs . . . a standard lamp with a globular shade . . . a splendidly veneered sort of bureau affair . . . goodness goodness – Dickie's right, oh heavens he is . . . this is chic, très chic, that's what Charles Boyer would call it – it's *moderne*, that's what this is, and I utterly, utterly adore it.

'Jackie . . . !' she eventually breathed – and he darted across to her in an agony of relief, so sick of subtlety, and determined now to be the pilot at the helm of the fully guided tour, replete with all manner of thoroughly informed commentary, as well as his own brand of gusto.

'I think . . .' he announced, with a sweep of his arm – his other hand working hard and failing to extricate himself from a near frenetic Mary, hanging on to his neck and covering it in kisses – 'that it would be safe to assume that the lady of the house approves of all this what she are seeing! Now come on, Mary love, pull yourself together – messing up my hair, look. Come on – you ain't seen the half of it yet. Follow me if you will, ladies and gents. Bedroom next.'

'But oh *Jackie*,' gushed a breathless Mary, her eyes as glossy as glass, each cheek pointed up with a smudge of deep pinkness. 'Jackie Jackie Jackie . . . all this . . . it must cost an absolute . . . ! I mean, how can we—?'

'Hush hush hush – never mind all of that. Blimey – I don't know: you try to please the woman, and all she give you is grief! Come on, love – don't you want to see the bedroom? And there's a separate room for Jeremy and all, always assuming he's . . . well, he got his own room anyway. Only small, mind – but ever so well got up. Now – bedroom, yeh?'

Mary nodded eagerly. 'But Jackie – all this, I didn't think you liked it, all of this. Too jazzy, I thought you'd think.'

'Oh do come *on*, Mary,' Sheila was yearning. 'Stop gabbling and let's go and see the bedroom, heaven's sake. Can't wait – I don't know how you can.'

'Yeh but no – she got a point,' Jackie allowed her, expansively. 'Didn't use to care for all of this caper, all the modern stuff – but when I seed it, well, different thing altogether. Like it – like it a lot. But I'm sorry, Sheila – looks like she don't want to see the bedroom after all, so I got to disappoint you, I'm afraid . . .'

'Oh *Jackie*!' squealed Mary delightedly, hugging his arm. 'Of *course* I do – of *course* I want to see it. Come on – which way? This door? Here?'

'No – that's just a cupboard, that one, far as I can recall. Only been here the once – not too sure myself, tell you the truth. Have a little look . . . yeh, yeh – cupboard, that is. Quite handy – knick-knacks and that: soon have it filled, I daresay. No – this is the door. Little passage, see, and then we got the bedroom, the kitchen, the bathroom – cor blimey, just wait till you clap eyes on the bathroom, dear oh dear. Reckon we'll save that one for last, ay? And then there's the little room I were talking about. And oh yeh – because we's on the ground floor here, we got the cellar and all. Exclusive. What is a boon, I can tell you – be needing that when the . . . well, just a good thing to have, ain't it? Really. Cellar. Now come on – here we are: bedroom. What you think? Ay? What you think? Like it, do you? All right, is it?'

Mary could hear Sheila's very sharp intake of breath as she was barging aside Dickie and jostling between her and Jackie's shoulders, so very eager to see all this for herself. Or maybe it was Mary's own hiss of breath that she had been hearing – either way, all she could do was just stand there, feeling quite winded. Sheila uttered a whoop of joy as finally she managed to muscle her way through, and now all of the chatter just simply fell out of her, and there was no sign at all that she ever would end it.

'Oh *look*, Mary – oh *look* at it, won't you? It's just so exactly what you always wanted! It's just – isn't it, Mary? Exactly what you saw in the catalogue. It's all in that wood that you love so much – and oh my, Mary, a sateen coverlet, and all these little cushions . . . a dressing table, with the mirrors and everything . . . oh it's heaven, it's very heaven – it's like a Fred Astaire film, just like one. Smaller, yes – but otherwise it's just like one, isn't it Dickie? Oh Dickie – now that you're a doctor and everything, do you think you could get a flat like this one? Do you, Dickie? Oh but Mary you must be just so . . . ! Oh my goodness – there's *another* telephone – do you see it, Mary? A white telephone – I've never in my life seen a telephone in white ... well except in a Fred Astaire film, of course, and pictures like that ... at least you *assume* they're white, don't you? I suppose they could be yellow or pink or any other sort of pastel colour, really – but I rather think they *are* white, don't you Dickie? Oh Jackie – how very clever you are, how very marvellous to have ... Oh and look! Little lights on each side of the bed ... !'

'Yeh,' said Jackie quickly – nip in sharpish, I reckon I ought to, else she'll be on till doomsday. 'And Mary – see the chair, did you? Like it? Know what it is?'

Mary nodded dumbly, from amid a deep swaddling of so much utter bliss.

'Lloyd Loom ...' she sighed. 'You remembered ...'

'Yeh,' nodded Jackie with enthusiasm (oh this is prime, this is – I am well enjoying all of this, I am). 'And that ain't all. Take a look in the wardrobe. Go on. Yeh – go on. Just give the little knob there a bit of a twist. Like the wardrobe, do you? Figured walnut, that is. Top-class. No go on – don't be nervous, girl. Just open the door of the wardrobe – see what we got inside, ay?'

Mary floated over the pale pink carpet and did as she was told. The door yawned open and she was straight away assailed by the smell of the cigar box that her father had once given to her so very long ago, and beneath all the pencils and erasers that she kept inside it were the three tightly folded and so often pored-over little pencil-written notes from Bobby Markham that he had blushingly passed to her during that one quite dizzying geography lesson, proclaiming his undying love to the seven-year-old Mary, whom he described as an angel, what falled from heaven. And the sight of what was in the wardrobe made all the emotion just too much now for her to bear any more. She was racked by sobbing, and a shocked and very confused Jackie now rushed to her side and just stood there.

'What's up? Ay? You being stupid, are you? What's wrong, girl – ay?'

Dickie coughed. 'All a bit much for her, I'd say. Needs a bit of a sit-down, maybe.'

'Hear that, Mary? Doctor says you want a bit of a sit-down. Just as well we got the old Lloyd Loom just handy here, ay?'

'What *is* it, Mary?' asked Sheila, rather puzzled. 'You're *not* upset, are you? You *can't* be . . .'

Mary shook her head with energy as she snuffled into her handkerchief that she had hurriedly tugged out from the sleeve of her cardigan.

'Just being so silly. It was the sight of the Ewbank in there . . . I'm just so . . . It's like Sheila says – it's just everything I've ever wanted.'

And then she turned to Jackie with a new and wary urgency, as if realising with a flush of horror and a kick to the stomach that she had omitted to attend to an overwhelming duty of the utmost importance.

'Jackie! This . . . all this . . . it is *ours*, isn't it? I mean – it's not a joke, or anything? There hasn't been a dreadful *mistake*, has there . . . ?'

'Nah nah *nah* . . . !' chimed Jackie, on a descending scale of indulgent consolation. 'No mistake here, girl. What we got here – this is the real thing. And it's all for you.'

Mary just gazed at him – and then quite suddenly her neck was thickening and there was the jet of alarm in both of her eyes.

'Bathroom . . . !' she managed to splutter out.

'Yeh yeh – later, ay? Said we'd leave that till—'

Mary shook her head insistently, and shoving aside Sheila she made for the door – signalling quite frantically to Jackie that he must show her now, this second, which door she should go through – and when he just continued to stand there, arms by his sides, staring full at her (Sheila and Dickie still goggling at each other in a state of apparent bewilderment) she turned away from them and hauled open the first door to hand and there was a box room and now another cupboard, and only as the sweat and lightheadedness were causing her to come so close to swooning did she drag open a third door and stumble her way inside, very dimly aware of a flash of mirrors and the peach sheen of porcelain as she made for the basin and all that Jackie was aware of as he reached the doorway was the convulsive and guttural retching, the ensuing heavy and disparate splatter and then a series of more awful jerks and heaves and a stench that would have you reeling.

'Bleeding hell! Dickie! Get in here, my son. Professional duties called for. Mary just gone and christened the new bathroom, look. Colours maybe didn't agree with her. All right are you, girl?'

Dickie was dabbing at her mouth with the clean white handkerchief that he had just flapped out from his jacket breast pocket and cooing to her there there there, old thing – you'll be right as ninepence in no time at all. Sheila was clucking around and tutting as Jackie filled a beaker from the tap. In between noises that sounded as if they came up from somewhere profound and rumbling – seemingly stranded between utter vanquishment and a deep and earthy rapture – Mary was struggling to string together some words.

'Oh *God* . . .' she was softly bleating. 'So much *mess* . . . oh God I'm so sorry, Jackie – all this awful *mess* . . .'

'Oh *Mary*,' hushed Sheila, 'don't you go worrying about that – I'll have it all cleaned up in two shakes of a lamb's tail, course I will.'

'No no,' said Jackie. 'Don't you go bothering with none of that, Sheila. Tell you what – you and Dickie run her back, ay? Got a few things I got to see to anyway. She all right, ain't she Dickie . . . ?'

'I'm fine . . .' said Mary. 'I'm completely fine, honestly . . . I just feel so awful about all this *mess* . . .' And she did now feel quite a good deal stronger. Now that the terrible and insistent pulsations of nausea were through and out of her, all she could think of was the mess and her own unquenchable embarrassment: what on earth could have come over her? Whatever it was, it had been quite unstoppable.

'Good wheeze,' agreed Dickie. 'Come on, old fruit – Doctor Dickie will whizz you back in his ambulance. Bit of a lie-down, ay? Your fault, Jackie old man – surprise a woman with all this sort of rot and what do you expect? Course she's going to have the vapours, so to speak. Only natural. Anyway Mary – topping billet, what? Bet you can't wait to get back here. Never get rid of Sheila, you know, once you're living in all this splendour.'

'Come on you lot,' urged Jackie, marshalling them away. 'Stink in here'd kill you . . .'

On her way back through the sitting room, Mary – still apologising, and more and more fulsomely to absolutely anyone who would even pretend to be listening to her – she paused to finger appreciatively the thickly lined and silky-seeming curtains, hefting the weight of them.

'Lovely . . .' she whispered to Jackie. 'Oh – and what's this stuff behind them? This sort of . . . ?'

'Oh yeh,' acknowledged Jackie. 'That's, um – blackout, that is. Got to have it – law, now. Won't never need it, but there it is.'

'Oh . . .' said Mary, quite hollowly. And now she was peering through the window into the small back yard.

'Nice little space,' she said quite simply, 'for Jeremy to play in . . . I hope he's all right with Imogen. I'm sure he will be. What's all that metal, Jackie? All those piles of metal sheets . . . ?'

'Blimey – she don't miss nothing, do she? Oh you don't want to worry about all that stuff, Mary. Just something I got to put together later on. Help earn my keep.'

Dickie was glancing over Mary's shoulder.

'Oh yes,' he said. 'Andersons, aren't they? Lucky to have them, from all I hear.'

'Oh *God* . . .' moaned Mary, so very dejectedly.

'Yeh right,' said Jackie rather testily. 'Thank you oh so *much*, Dickie, for your learned comments. Now come on – you all get yourselves off, ay? Give a man a bit of room to swing a cat.'

Jackie stood at the door and waved away the car until it reached the junction and turned the corner. Then he lit himself a Senior Service and came back into the house. Blimey, he was thinking, inhaling deeply: what a time I had, just lately. What with one thing and the other . . . I never really thought, not really I never, that it'd all come out so nice as it's done. Because that weren't the way it were looking a week back, I can tell you that. There were this one morning there – Mary, she wakes me up and she's going Come on Jackie, else you'll be late for work. And it just hit me between the eyes: what am I still going in for, day after day – heaving this for Mr Plough, sawing that chunk of timber for Mr Plough, climbing up ladders and going down the drains, and all for Mr Plough, what still ain't let on to me what might be occurring and just what ain't. And he's in a real big hurry, all of a sudden, to get all the houses dickied up and on the market. 'There'll be people needing these before very long, Jackie my lad: we could be in a seller's market, we could.' And that's when I said well that's all well and good, mate – but there ain't no 'we' about it, are there? Ay? I been putting in all the slog – and you're all set to get the benefit. Now way I reckon it is, come last spring, you should of did what you said you was going to do, and now I'd be a proper partner – and yeh: then I'd be in a seller's market and all, wouldn't I Mr Plough? Ay? As it is, I ain't. So what do I do now then? Mr Plough? Apart from a bleeding grafter – what the hell am I? Ay? Answer. Go on. Bleeding *answer* me, Mr Plough.

'Now now now, Jackie my boy – don't go getting like that. No call, is there? Times is hard – you read the papers. Changing world, Jackie. Look – when I said all that about a partnership, I meant it, course I did – meant every word of it, I did. You're a fine worker, Jackie, and you're an honest one and all, as you proved to me on more than the one occasion. But you see, Jackie – I'm a builder, aren't I? Ay? I'm a builder and a developer and a landlord and, well – I'm a bit of an entrepreneur, I suppose you might say, not to put too fine a point on it . . .'

'Yeh yeh. Get on with it. Never mind what you is – I said what am *I*?'

'Well I'm coming to that, aren't I Jackie? That's what I'm getting round to. Now see, because of the government's edicts, I can't lay my hands on the raw material. Now ask yourself, Jackie: what good's a builder, a developer, call me what you will, if he can't lay his hands on the raw material? See my predicament. So what I got to do is, I got to *consolidate*, that's what I got to do. With me?'

'Yeh. No. No I ain't – what's consolidate? What's it got to do with me?'

'Consolidate, Jackie. I mean I got to bring my existing assets up to the mark – capitalise on the maximum rental available in this very uncertain market we got. While the going's good, so to speak. Because God alone knows what's about to be unleashed on all of us now. Could be soon, I won't have a brick left standing.'

'Nah. Rubbish, that is. Won't be like that. But look – you still ain't answered me, Mr Plough. I keeps on asking you, and you keeps on talking but you ain't bleeding answering me, is you? Ay?'

'Well forgive me, Jackie, but I was toiling under the impression that I had, if maybe a bit obliquely, answered you most generously.'

'Talk plain, can't you? Because I'm getting right riled, now.'

'Well all right, Jackie: fair enough. You got a right to be told plain – I just never liked to do it, that's all. The fact's this: I ain't got the materials, then I don't need the workers, do I? Can't be paying people to be sitting around now, can I? You can understand that, can't you Jackie?'

'Yeh. I see. I see. So what you're saying is – I'm out, then. Never mind partner – I'm just out on my ear. That it?'

'Well, I wouldn't have . . . but yeh, in a nutshell. I'm rather afraid that is it Jackie, yeh. I mean – I'll see you all right, and everything. But yeh: that's the up and down of it, I'm sorry to say.'

'Oh you're sorry to say, is you? Well how sorry you think I am, then? Ay? You reckon I'm sorry and all, do you? Near killed myself for you, I have – and all because I thought I were bettering myself, working my way up to having a hold on something I could call my own – what I ain't never had, not never in my life. And what about Mary now, ay? And I got a kid – you recall that do you, Mr Plough? What's my kid going to do then, ay? With a father out of work.'

'Oh God's sake, Jackie – you'll find work, course you will. Strong upstanding lad such as yourself – people be falling over theirselves.'

'Yeh? What people they, then? I don't see no queue of people, do you Mr Plough? Can't see all these people what you're on about, all of them so bleeding eager to get their hands on me. It's all I can do, this – grafting. If you ain't hiring, then no one else is neither. So where do that leave me then, ay?'

'Well, Jackie . . . Well – here's a bit to tide you over, anyway. Three weeks' money, there is there. Not bound to give it you, you know – but I'm doing it because I want to. Well so long then, Jackie – and no hard feelings, ay?'

'I see. You're giving it me because you want to. Goodness of your heart, sort of style. Well ain't that nice. Fifteen quid. I got a family and no job and you stick fifteen quid in my face.'

'Well like I say, Jackie – I'm not bound to give you a penny. You take that attitude and I'm very happy to take the fifteen pound back off you.'

'Yeh? Well have this off of me instead, Mr Plough!'

And I just turned and decked him. Never even planned to do it – the fist just came up into his face, sort of style, and he fall over like I shot him with a gun. He's holding his nose and there's blood all over and down his shirt and he's roaring at me now to give him back his money else he'll have the law on to me, I should see if he don't. Well I just walk out the door, then. Ain't no more to say. Except I do – I calls back to him Well so long then, Mr Plough – and no hard feelings, ay? The bleeding bastard. Yeh. So anyway – that were the end of that.

And still it were only just on eleven in the morning – can't recall when last I found myself just kicking about, that time of day. Well yeh I can – course I can: last bleeding time I were out of work. Just ten minutes into it, and I recalled all the misery. See – when you're grafting, you're always fancying an hour or two to just put your feet up, bit of extra kip of a morning. But when you don't got no work, it kills you, it do – worms its way into you like rust in a tin can – just mooching about, nothing to do, nowhere to go: you sees it in the eyes of every bloke what you run into, because they're all of them – every sodding man jack of them – they're all in the same bleeding boat, ain't they? Why else they going to be sitting in the park, staring like a dead man at the bleeding pond? Or leaning against a lamppost outside of the tobacconist's – hoping some flash sod'll toss them a fag. And when you been at it a long while, even a half-decent chucked away dog-end'll do you. It's just how it gets. Or slamming out the house when you only just been there a couple minutes because the missus says she got enough to do with all the kids and the housework without having to cope with a bleeding man about her feet, getting in the way of it. So what happens is – and it's always the way – you end up at Len's. You got a few bob, you has a drink or two; if you're down and out, you can only hope to God that there's someone just a little bit better off than yourself to take pity on the thirst inside of you, and send you over a half. And that's what happened to me, well of course it did. I walked about the streets a bit, shaking my fist, time to time, and blowing on my knuckles (must have hit him hard, the bastard), and then I just thought oh sod all of this – I've had it with all this walking about: I'll just get myself round the Rose & Crown.

Len had only just unbolted the doors by the time he got there – the lights weren't turned on and it was definitely on the chilly side, Jackie just had to notice, despite the sun beyond the frosted windows.

'Early bird, ain't you Jackie? Truant, is it?'

'Yeh, Len, yeh. Bit of time off. Blimey – out of practice. What's a man drink, this time of a morning?'

'Cup of tea, if you're anything like me. Got the kettle on, Jackie, you fancy it. Drop a tot of rum in, keep the chill off. What you say?'

'Sounds prime, Len. Yeh, ta.'

'Best get it inside you while we got it, ay? Word is from the brewery, they don't know what they'll be able to get hold of, now on. Nor when. Scotch is going to be gold, they reckon. Plus the government, they're going to slap another great tax on it, what I hear. As if we ain't got enough on our plates, they want to deny the working man his little glass of pleasure – not to say take the bread from out of my mouth. Bad times, Jackie – telling you. Still – expect we'll be seeing you in uniform before long then, will we Jackie lad?'

'Joking, Len. Last thing I'd do, that'd be. Mug's game.'

'Yeh. That's what Alfie said you'd say.'

'Alfie? What – my Alfie, you mean? My little brother? What –

he been in, has he? He never said. I hope he were behaving hisself.'

'Him? Oh yeh – yeh yeh. Course. Yeh, course he were. He's a good boy.'

'The best, Len. Only the very best. What was you talking about, then?'

'Oh nothing, Jackie – nothing really, you know. You maybe best let him tell you hisself. I'll just get the tea going.'

'Tell me what hisself? What you on about? Something I should know, is there?'

'No no. Well – yeh, but it ain't none of my affair, is it? Like I say – he'll get round to telling you hisself, daresay. Fullness of time. Get the tea, I will.'

'No – wait, hang on there Len. What's going on? What he been saying? Come on Len – you can tell me. I'm his brother, Christ sake.'

'Yeh I know, Jackie – I know. I just ain't sure I want to . . . look, I'll just get the tea and we'll have a nice tot of rum in it, ay?'

'Sod the tea, Len. What's up?'

'Well, Jackie . . . it's just that . . . well – he got hisself signed on, ain't he? Army, like. Volunteered. What can I say to you?'

And Len was looking anywhere now except into Jackie's hard and stricken eyes.

'He . . . done . . . *what*?!'

'Yeh well . . .' said Len, looking down and away. 'Never wanted to be the one, did I? Don't know why I went and opened my bleeding trap. But there it is, Jackie. Would've found out sooner or later, wouldn't you? Ay? He said you wouldn't be pleased about it.'

Jackie slammed down his fist on to the counter; the eyes were dull now, and his lips set grimly.

'Right. I'm off to see him. Sort this out straight off.'

'Yeh – hold your horses, Jackie. He ain't here. Buggered off for training, Gawd knows where. Reckon you got to take it, son. He been and gone and done it. What I think it is, he wanted you to have a couple days to get a bit used to the idea – then he'll be in touch, course he will. And anyway, Jackie – no listen, let me finish up here before you go ranting off again – army, these days: cushy number, what I hear. Piece of cake. And you said it yourself, Jackie – it's what you're always saying, ain't it? Ain't going to come to nothing. So why not let the government do his laundry and his meals for a bit, ay? And pay him into the bargain. About time they give something back, you ask me.'

Jackie was nodding slowly – his face less taut and his eyes just flickering.

'One way of looking at it . . .'

'That's more the style, Jackie lad. Tell you – younger man, I'd do it myself. Don't you worry, son – he's on Easy Street, Alfie is.'

'Yeh. Yeh – probably right. All them lads – out of uniform again come Christmas time. Once they realise what bleeding fools they all been. Here – Len?'

'Yeh Jackie? What can I do for you, son?'

'*Tea* is what you can bleeding well do for me – and don't go forgetting that tot of rum neither. Then I got to get myself off. Talk to Mary. One or two things I got to talk to Mary about.'

Yeh well – time I gets to see her, turns out there's another thing and all what I got to talk to her about, don't there? One thing and another, it weren't shaping up into a good day at all. I get back the house, put my key in the lock and give the door a shove and it goes clanging into some bleeding thing or other and I can't get it to open all the way and then there's that bleeding Mr Stone calling out to me to hang on for a minute and I hear him banging around there and then he opens the door and his deaf and mute Old Dutch, she's here look – hands and knees, floor all wet and shiny, and there's this great big grey bucket – what I reckon the door's been slamming into.

'Not expect, this time day,' grunted Mr Stone. 'My wife. She clean your mess.'

'Yeh? Well that's nice for her, ain't it? Give her something to keep her mind on, ay? All right are you, Mrs Stone? Don't get up on my account, will you? No – no answer. Don't say nothing. Never do, do she? Move the bucket out the road, there's a good girl.'

'Please wait floor dry.'

'Sorry, Mr Stone – can't accommodate you there. I ain't waiting for no bleeding floor to dry. I'm going upstairs now – I live here, case you forgot. No? You ain't moving it? Right then – I'll do it myself.'

And Jackie crouched down to the steaming galvanised bucket and was halfway to reaching for the handle when he suddenly thought oh fuck all this to hell and back – what the bleeding hell do I think I'm up to? And then he straightened himself and gave the bucket the most powerful kick he could possibly manage and although the pain in his foot had already begun to glow, still it was utterly eclipsed by the sheer tug of delight that was juddering all over him as Mrs Stone howled and staggered to her feet and ran from the hall and Mr Stone was roaring as the bucket glanced off his knee and clattered away and now he's shouting in German and waving his fist, his trousers drenched as he just stood there in his seeping slippers amid the lake of soapy water that fled away under the doors – Jackie was engulfed by the hug of true pleasure, before all the misgivings began to niggle, and then assailed him. He splattered his way over to the staircase in as nonchalant a manner as he could decently muster, shadowed by shame as another sort of unease was now growing within him. Just as he had placed his foot upon the first of the stairs, Mr Stone rushed towards him and grabbed a hold of his arm and still he was raving at him with all these horrible and throaty noises and although Jackie now regretted his impetuosity, if not all the vibrant glory of its spectacular effect, he now just blacked out again and was suddenly furious. He slapped away the man's hand and as Mr Stone sought to restrain him again, well – he just turned and decked him. Never even planned to do it – the fist just came up into his face, sort of style, and he fell over like Jackie had shot him with a gun. And he went a bit quiet. Jackie nearly leant down to him – a terrible sight he was, look: sprawling askew in the wash of grey water, his thin white hair in a tousle of madness, and then all the blood on his face ... But now Mr Stone was shouting again – still defiant, in the face of the state of him.

'Now you go! You out this house by tonight! Hear? You take wife and baby and you *go*. And Gott help them.'

Jackie's first instinct was to help the man up – try a bit of salvage, maybe. And then the anger took him.

'Yeh? Yeh? Well you just listen to this: I wouldn't stay here, mate – wouldn't stay in this bleeding fleapit if you paid me. Got it? Bleeding hell-hole, this is. We'll be well out of it. And as for my wife – well she *ain't* my wife, see? We're living i
n sin is what we're doing – and under your poxy roof. So why not go and tell your bleeding ugly and miserable old woman that little lot then, ay? Go on – get out my sight, you bleeding Jew-boy!'

And Jackie stamped up the stairs three at a time, his mind in a dazzle of confusion – and the coldness of fear was leaking into it now because that old bastard Stone, I wouldn't put it past him to call the bleeding cops – and what am I going to tell Mary? Now on top of all else I got to hit her with. And blimey O'Reilly – what the fuck's going to become of me?

Tell you one thing – I were right relieved when I got up to the flat and found that Mary and Jeremy, they wasn't neither of them there. Well – stood to reason, really: she would've heard all the racket and come down pronto, wouldn't she? And stopped me – course she would. So where the bloody hell is she then? Could've stopped me, she could, only she been here. All right for her, ain't it? Ay? Strolling in the park, shouldn't wonder. She don't have to get out there and deal with the likes of Plough and Stone, do she? And she ain't got a brother what's just gone and enlisted in the British fucking army – can't wait, can he, to go off and get hisself killed. Not that it'll be like that . . . but what if it bleeding is? Ay? He ain't thought it through, that's the trouble. He should've come to me. Why didn't he come to me? We could've sat down, little drink, man to man, get it sorted out. Except all I would've done is just turned and decked him, I expect. Seems lately what I does. And I regrets it – yeh, course I do, I do, yeh. I mean the both of them had it coming a long time, Plough and Stone, but still and all – they're only old geezers, ain't they? And it ain't what I should be doing. And Mary, well . . . I can't come out and tell her straight, can I? That I spent a good part of the day giving a wallop to a pair of old blokes what couldn't hurt a fly. No – she wouldn't care for it, not a bit she wouldn't. So what I'll have to do is I'll have to go careful. Put it in such a way . . . yeh yeh, but no matter how I goes and puts it, the truth of the matter is, when it all comes down to it . . . well the facts is plain, ain't they? Staring me in the face. I got no job, and we don't none of us got nowhere to live. And Alfie's all set to be a bleeding hero. Nice. So what I reckon is, I got to listen to what old Jonny were telling me – that's what I got to do now. And that's what I'm going to do, right this minute – because let's face it, there ain't no time to hang about. So I got the address here – Jonny, he give it me – and so what I'm going to do is just give the old knuckles a bit of a rinse off (all skinned and gone red, they is) and then I'm going to get myself off and see Mr Wisely.

○

'Do you have an appointment, sir?'

Jackie had been interrupted in a very critical scrutiny of his own pale reflection in the black high gloss of the double front doors, while the sun winked gold from the ram's-head knocker – and he had hefted this and brought it down twice (it was as heavy as a crowbar). And then, as he waited, his attention was held by the glancing shards of his face and clothes, fractured and distorted by the raised and fielded panels in the great big jet doors, and he thought to himself – You know what, Jackie lad? You looking a bit on the scruffy side, you ask me. It could be maybe just the surroundings what make me feel that way, yeh it could, it could easily – because round here, this area, I'm telling you, it's like you see in the pictures with that posh geezer, what's his name? Very posh and what what. It ain't like nothing you thought could ever be for real. Take a fair old while to open the door though, don't they? Mind you – got to walk a bleeding mile just to get to it.

'Sir? Do you have an appointment?'

'Do I got a what?'

'Are you expected, sir?'

'Um – no, no I ain't. Expected, exactly. No. But maybe you remember, do you? I were here a few month back, with Jonathan Leakey. Yeh? No? Just before Christmas, it were. Don't recall your name, I'm afraid though. Mine's Jackie – Jackie Robertson. How d'you do.'

'Barnstaple, sir. However as you do not have an appointment, I regret to inform you that the master is not at home.'

'Oh. Right, I see. Popped out a minute, has he? Well maybe I could hang about a bit. Long, will he be? You reckon?'

'I regret, sir, that that would be quite impossible. However, sir, should you care to make an appointment through the customary channels . . .'

'Through the what? Look – never mind all that, Barnstaple. That right? Barnstaple? Yeh. Right then – when he come in, you just tell Mr Wisely that Jackie wants a little natter with him. All right? Urgent, like.'

And then there was a voice that he recognised from somewhere behind and maybe to the left of Barnstaple's shoulders; Barnstaple coughed discreetly into the cup of his hand, and deftly stepped to one side.

'It's quite all right, Barnstaple,' Nigel Wisely assured him – bowing to Jackie and ushering him across the threshhold with a sweep of his arm. 'I shall of course be perfectly delighted to receive Mr Robertson. Mr Robertson – Jackie, if I may – please won't you be so good as to enter? How kind of you to come. Barnstaple will take your hat.'

Jackie nodded to that, tugged off his old trilby and jerked it sideways and quite forcibly into Barnstaple's shrinking fingers. Passing him by and into the hall, Jackie hissed at him out of the side of his mouth: Thought you said he weren't in? A lie, son, that is. Barnstaple lowered his eyelids and appeared to be inhaling deeply some novel aroma – and one which, he made plain by the raising up and then aversion of his head, could hardly be further from his taste.

'Come, Jackie,' said Nigel Wisely, placing an arm about his shoulders and guiding him across the gleaming black-and-white chequerboard floor and through one of the many doors leading off it. 'It would require an era to fully comprehend all the code and conventions as to whether or not a body is or is not at home. I do assure you, Barnstaple was in no way directly misleading you. It is the form, do you see? No more than simply the form. You will possibly join me in an aperitif of some sort? I generally take a glass of champagne around this hour.'

Niven, thought Jackie, as he looked at and remembered all of Nigel Wisely's face, and in particular that trimly structured pencil moustache. Yeh, that's the bloke what I were meaning. Posh one in the pictures. Somebody Niven. And just look at that moustache of Mr Wisely's – dead ringer, that is. And what's more, it's shaved around, by women. Just think of that. I have, a lot. David, that's the geezer.

'So tell me, Jackie – comfortable, are you? That chair quite suits you, does it? Excellent. Excellent. Ah – Barnstaple. Champagne – excellent, excellent. Mr Robertson will be pleased to take a glass. Thank you, Barnstaple. Now then, Jackie – any other trifle I might possibly furnish you with? Do just say the word, won't you. A selection of canapés? Cigar, conceivably?'

'No no – reckon I'm all right, ta very much Mr Wisely.' He took a big swig from the thin and shallow bowl of his small champagne glass. 'What they put in this stuff then? Make it go all bubbles like that.'

'Stardust from the gods, is how it always seems to me. A divine sprinkling. But come now Jackie – I hardly owe the pleasure of your company to a sudden urge upon your part to discuss with me the finer points of oenology, surely?'

'Ay? No. No. Right. No see – Jonny, Mr Leakey, he says you wanted to see me. Well no – weren't quite you wanted to see me, but if I ever, you know – sort of thought I ought to, er . . . Well, truth is Mr Wisely – I'm in a bit of a hole, one thing and another. And er . . . well, if I could be of any use to you at all . . . I mean, I'm quite handy. Good with my hands, like. Wouldn't rook you, nor nothing.'

Nigel Wisely eyed him narrowly. And then he smiled.

'You require employment. That the nub of it? Well all you had to do was say so, dear boy. And I am sure in my conviction that you are being most thoroughly modest with regard to the compass of your talents. And I always have room for a person with talents.'

'Well see – thing is, Mr Wisely . . . I don't want you getting no wrong ideas about me. I ain't – isn't, *aren't*, I aren't very, like what you said – talented. No schooling to speak of. I ain't like my brother Alfie, nor nothing. Oh blimey – Alfie, yeh. Well no – I won't get into all that. All I mean to say is, Mr Wisely, I'm a reliable grafter. Work hard. Honest. And that's it. There's no more.'

Nigel Wisely was drawing upon a cigar whose tip he had been thoughtfully cutting as Jackie had been speaking. He expelled quite luxuriously an indigo plume of languorous smoke, removed the cigar from his mouth, and then two perfectly manicured fingernails incisively picked away just the one fleck of tobacco from the tip of his tongue. Then he eased back fully into the depths of his armchair, and so settled was he in his appearance that he might have been on the verge now of launching into a narration, a long and elegantly rambling tale, one with so many engaging twists and turns, such absorbing asides and digressions, that night might die during the telling of it, and dawn could surely break before its joyous end.

'Well now. Attend to me, Jackie. I shall speak, yes? I shall speak, tell you of my surmisings. I shall attempt to outline your current situation – oh but please, should I err or be guilty of omission, do me the goodness of waiting until I am done, whereupon I shall urge you, oh but naturally, to supplement any deficiencies in the narrative, and correct each one of my misplaced assumptions. Clear? No? Well – just wait until I finish, and then you may speak. Yes? Excellent. Now it is evident to me, Jackie, from your own admission, that you have lost your job. However, in the light of the fact that I am fully versed in the nature of your employ to date – courtesy, I have to say, of the estimable Mr Leakey, who really is a veritable godsend, do you know, when it comes to the imparting of information. So, as I say – because I am aware of the nature of your work, I cast no aspersion upon the terms of its recent invalidation. Or, to put it plain to you, I fully understand that your services were dispensed with as a result of no malfeasance upon your part, but simply due to the fact that during these most parlous days in which we now find ourselves so very deeply plunged, all is far from well. The lack of building supplies to the trade, to take a pertinent instance – it is not the only field where very big changes are afoot. Tumultuous changes, I must say to you: make no mistake about it. Everyday life, my dear Jackie – or such we call it – is on the verge of ceasing, for the long and foreseeable future. What some may term a coming disaster, however, I myself choose to see as the very grandest opportunity. That said – all sorts of fellows, such as your very good self – fellows who imagined themselves to be in sound, worthy and permanent employment, now I am afraid they are finding to their cost that all such confidence was severely misplaced. Many, of course, will have no choice whatever in the matter. Many – a very great number – will be recruited into the services, to serve King and country. And now I shall interrupt this little monologue of mine in order to put to you, Jackie, a simple and quite direct question – your response to which, I have to say, will have the effect of colouring highly the complexion of our subsequent discussion. Should, indeed, there be any more at all which we have to say unto one another. And so – to the question. I shall not ask you whether you have considered enlisting . . . and ah yes, I see very well by your expression that I was perfectly correct in this one surmise, at least: you are indeed not the man to contemplate so risible a folly. However, Jackie – were you to be summoned . . . and within a very short time, you know, this is, for a man of your youth, evident – well, vigour, shall we call it? – and general calibre, a virtual inevitability . . . what form, pray, would your reaction take, do you imagine? Now, Jackie, you may speak.'

Jackie set down with care upon the table the very empty champagne glass, whose stem he had been relentlessly twiddling, his eyebrows deeply furrowed into a desperate resolve, so very determined was he to pick out the thrust and gist from so much more that he was shamefully conscious of having missed entirely.

'If you're asking me, Mr Wisely . . . what I'd do if I get call-up papers . . . that it? Yeh. Right then – well in that case I can tell you exactly what I'd do – I'd tear them up into little pieces, that's what I'd do. Spit on them and stamp on them hard. I'd tell them right where they can stick their bleeding call-up papers, that's what I'd do. Because one thing you do got to know about me, Mr Wisely – whatever I am, and I don't say I'm much, but whatever I am, I ain't no mug, see? And nor I didn't think my Alfie were – that's my kid brother, that is, Mr Wisely. But I don't want to go troubling you with all of that, because it ain't your concern. But he did – he went and volunteered he did, the stupid little bleeder. And I'm that scared he's going to go and get hisself killed, I am. And there ain't nothing I can do about it. But I can see to me – I can do that. And yeh – that's my answer to you, Mr Wisely. Sorry if I been going on. Oh no wait – one more thing I got to say. It ain't I ain't patriotic. I love England, love it I do. Best country in the world – stands to reason. But you want to live in it, don't you? Country what you love. Raise your kids in it. What you don't want to do is go off and die somewhere bleeding else. Am I right? And them politicians – all them politicians, and I don't care what bleeding party they're none of them from, because when it come down to it, they're all the bleeding same. Ain't they? Ay? When all's said and done, they're all of them – every last man jack of them, they're all the bleeding same. And that Churchill – he been going on about it so bleeding long, why don't they put him in the bleeding army? Ay? See how he likes it. Yeh, go on – put a tin hat on him and let the bloody Kraut take a potshot. Yeh but he knows he's safe, don't he? Because he's a politician – and also he's bleeding old, ain't he? It's only young ones they want – it's the young ones what's going to die. Like my Alfie, Lord love him. God damn them all, the buggers – I'd have the lot of them, I would. Yeh!'

Jackie now found himself hunched so far forward in his chair that he teetered upon its edge, and he felt himself shaking. He was surprised to find the empty champagne glass back in his fingers, and he still seemed to be intent upon wringing its neck. He put on a nervous half-smile – shrugged away the remains of his intensity.

'Anyway. That's what I think. And like I say – sorry if I been going on. Um, any chance, is there Mr Wisely – drop more of this stuff?'

Nigel Wisely was beaming at him with great satisfaction. He rose from his chair and crossed over easily to the console table where the bottle of champagne was slantingly at rest in its silver bucket. He lifted it out by the lips of its neck and ambled over to where Jackie was sitting back now, and seemingly more at his ease. Laying a hand upon his shoulder, Nigel Wisely leaned across him and poured more champagne. He deposited the bottle on the table next to Jackie, and very glancingly stroked his cheek, once and lightly, and had strolled back over to his chair even before Jackie had registered the touch.

'I rather knew, Jackie, that I hadn't misjudged you. There was something about you, you know – and I vouchsafed my instinct to friend Leakey, which he doubtless conveyed to you in some fashion or another. I knew you were a man I could deal with, Jackie. Trust. To do my bidding. In return, but naturally, for suitable – and, I rather think you will find, not ungenerous – recompense. So now, Jackie: to business, yes? You're absolutely sure, are you, that you won't take a cigar? Ah no – I see you have your cigarettes there – and my, what a handsome case, if I may make so bold. Now you will help yourself to more champagne, won't you dear boy? As and when the whim might take you. Good. Excellent. Very well, then – here is what I propose. My idea is that you will be employed in something of a, well – what shall we say? A roving capacity. In that your brief is yet to be made clear to the two of us, you see. Dependent upon the circumstances – as, I regret to say, we all of us are, and never more particularly than nowadays, I fear. Initially, I should like to take advantage of your existing skills. Earlier, my dear Jackie, you very modestly sought to disabuse me of my unshakeable belief in your talents. You will be very surprised, I fancy, when in the fullness of time, these latent talents emerge. Talents of which as yet you are wholly unaware. Rather exciting in itself, no? What form they might actually assume, of course, will yet again be more than somewhat dependent upon the coming circumstances as they reveal themselves to us all. But for the nonce, during this aggravatingly unsettling little limbo in which we each of us find ourselves, I should like you to attend to one or two small duties that are thoroughly within your line. The erection of a number of these rather preposterous little bomb shelters that the government has decreed – more, I feel, in order to salve what is remaining of their tattered consciences, rather than to protect the citizen, but no matter. They are seen to be doing something, at least, and so, I suppose, must we be. There are four small provisos that I must impose upon anyone who works for me, Jackie – I maybe should, in all politeness, have mentioned them earlier. I do insist upon my key employees – and key, Jackie, do please believe me, is what you are destined to become – I do, as I say, insist upon their living in one of my own properties. It pleases me to know of everyone's whereabouts, you see. Ah – I can tell by this new light that has sprung into your, if you will permit, extremely expressive and rather heart-warming eyes, Jackie, that such a proposal is not entirely unwelcome. I have an extensive portfolio – I fancy you would care to remain within the area to which you are accustomed? Quite so. I have the very house in mind – one of the flats will suit you very well, I feel. You and your . . . lady. For I am told that you are currently cohabiting with a highly personable partner who goes by the name of Mary? Exactly. Now, our mutual friend Mr Leakey will be attending to all of the details – he is, you know, exceptionally adept at dealing with them, details. He will supply you with the address, keys, advance you a sum of money on account, and generally respond to what questions you may have. Determine the style of furnishings you may have in mind. I should do so myself, dear boy – attend to you – but alas I shall be leaving the country shortly. Your timing in coming to see me this very afternoon is, I must say, exemplary. Prescient, one could say. Was it instinct? Kismet? Call it what you will. I admit that it would be fanciful to suggest that I anticipated your calling, but certainly I was unsurprised to see you. I say I am leaving the country – this is not in the emigrant sense, I hasten to assure you. I have several interests abroad – Switzerland, one or two other not unpleasant places – though I shall return to London whenever I deem it . . . oh, do you know, I was about to say "safe". What sort of a craven thing does this mark me down for? "Fit", let us say: when I deem it fitting.'

Nigel Wisely rose from his chair, and a somewhat dizzied Jackie immediately followed suit – walking towards the door at the bidding of Mr Wisely's arm and the easy encouragement in the dazzle of his smile. It was only in the hall that he remembered.

'Um – yeh, thanks. Thank you for all of that, Mr Wisely. Ever so much. It's just that – provisos, yeh? You said something about . . . ?'

Nigel Wisely smote his brow with the flat of his palm, in as histrionic a manner as he considered appropriate.

'Ah! My mind, you see – completely slipped from me. The remaining three provisos. Well do not concern yourself, Jackie – I am quite sure that none of them will inconvenience you unduly. The first is driving – do you drive a motor car, Jackie? I thought not. Well this will be essential, you see. Fear not. Friend Leakey will attend to it all – instruction, and so forth. Man of your evident intellect and application – work of moments, I should have said. And then your own motor car, of course. Secondly – and I know you won't take this in any way amiss – there is the question of attire. One's appearance, you know. You will in effect be representing me, do you see? And consequently there are certain standards, yes? To be upheld. Once again, our Mr Leakey will attend to all of that – tailor, bootmaker and so on. Ah – I can see that none of this displeases you. Excellent. So you are happy then, Jackie, to accept my employ? No reservations of any sort at all . . . ?'

Jackie just stood there in a daze of disbelief: he simply shook his head.

'Good good good – quite excellent. Now your future accommodation is not quite prepared – a few days are all that are needed. And then it must be accoutred according to your doubtless flawless taste, as I said to you earlier. I would suggest that you and . . . Mary, is it? Yes, Mary. That you and Mary take yourselves off somewhere rather pretty for a while. Our English summer is smiling fondly upon us. Oh and yes – the fourth thing, Jackie. A trifle, but I am sure you will understand. In the flat you will be provided with, I cannot support the presence of pets – oh, and neither children. There now – that's the whole of it. So – let's just reclaim your hat from the clutches of Barnstaple, shall we? And then you can be away.'

Jackie stood stock-still in the hall, the blazing from the chandelier causing him to squint. He stared at a modern painting in a heavy gilt and rococo frame (it looked as if some kid had been let loose with the distemper, or a monkey maybe).

'Um. Thing is, Mr Wisely . . . maybe better I tell you now: I got a son.'

'Oh but yes of course I know *that*, dear boy – of course I do. I know all about you, Jackie – it's my business to know, and particularly now that you have accepted the conditions of my employ. But you know, the way things are, he'd be much better off well out of harm's way. Your duty, really: as a father. Wouldn't you agree? They are saying, you know, that such a thing will in any case soon become obligatory. Any day now. That is what they are saying. I really would urge you to take her away, you know – Mary, isn't it? Mary, yes quite. As I have suggested. Just the two of you – whatever could be nicer? And then you'll both have a chance to get used to the idea, you see? It's amazing, you know – astounds me constantly – what habits we simply fall into, and how terribly easily they all may be broken. Ah – my dear!' exclaimed Nigel Wisely suddenly – raising his hand in greeting to an exquisitely dressed and coiffured young woman who was drifting down the staircase, noiselessly and with extreme composure. Jackie – his mind aflame and dancing – was nonetheless aware of the deep silver blue of her eyelids, the smacked pink of her cheeks and the cherry-red lustre of those two plump lips as they all of them were glimpsed amid a blur beneath the mesh of a brief black veil and the brim of a close-fitting hat that sported a turquoise plume. (Reckon I seen this one before – but I don't think it's that haughty one what I were talking to, whatever she were called.)

'Mr Robertson is just leaving. Dommage. When, that is, he can drag his attention away from this painting here, with which once more he appears to be fixated – now that the initial frisson, my dear girl, of your all-conquering loveliness has momentarily subsided. You care for modern art, do you Jackie? You like the picture?'

Jackie was still trying to get straight in his head all that Mr Wisely had told him – knowing he must speak up, coping with a dizziness that was maybe from all of that fizzy drink he'd put inside of him – saw off the bottle, no problem at all – and also the scent of the woman which was near pulsating, and coming towards him in waves. And now he had to say, did he, whether or not he liked the picture. Well did he? He couldn't have told you. Were it not in a frame and stuck on the wall, he wouldn't even have identified it as being a picture at all. It was all just messed-up blobs and lines . . . and an eye, is it? And there looked to be a bit of newspaper plastered on to it – that can't be right, can it?

'It's . . . all right,' he said with reluctance – quite devoid of further reaction as Nigel Wisely intook his breath and brought both of his hands together sharply into a clap, as if Jackie had just come from successfully achieving a pair of double somersaults and a forward roll.

'Splendid – splendid. Did you hear that, my dear girl? Mr Robertson adjudges the painting to be "all right", and who shall gainsay him? Now, Jackie – ah, here is your hat, so we needn't trouble Barnstaple after all. And don't at all concern yourself, will you, in respect of all your goods and chattels. Mr Leakey will see that they are all conveyed to your new abode – your gramophone, and so forth, which I am told is much appreciated.'

And from amid the tumult of just everything, Jackie was taken by that.

'Gramophone? How you know about that?'

'Oh! My little gift, you know. Did Mr Leakey not mention the fact? How terribly naughty of him. Or shall we be kind and call it remiss? No matter – only a humble gramophone, after all. So then Jackie – I bid you adieu. I just know that we are headed for a long and very happy – not to say mutually lucrative – association. More, dear boy – we are destined to be the very closest of *friends*.'

They were at the door now, the woman still behind Mr Wisely, and so very near – her long white hand flat upon his shoulder, the red japanned nails glinting in the lamplight and causing Jackie to wonder whether just such a hand as this – no: this hand, this hand – had soaped the man's face with a badger brush, her lips just open as she slid the cutthroat the length of his jawline. Nigel Wisely now grasped Jackie's hand with both of his own, and although the warmth and softness assailed him once more, it was the fleeting brush of the fabric at his sleeve that was truly shocking – just so very fine, and like nothing else he had ever known.

'One last word,' said Nigel Wisely, leaning into the crook of Jackie's neck and whispering now to him quite conspiratorially. 'You mentioned earlier this little business concerning your brother – Alfie, I believe? Yes. Well now listen to me, Jackie – should he come to his senses and regret the impetuosity of his actions, I might be able to be instrumental in his extrication. There are always ways. On the other hand, should he still feel committed to his pledge, then possibly a circumstance might be engineered whereby at least he is subject to no danger. You will, won't you, keep me informed.'

Jackie felt and nearly tasted the sweetness of Nigel Wisely's breath upon his cheek, smelt the scent on his neck. Although there was something or other clamouring urgently amongst all the welter of his thinking, still he was overwhelmed by a dumb relief and a swell of deep gratitude. He simply nodded. And just before he turned away and into the sunshine, Jackie turned again to face the man.

'So . . . you know there will be war, then? There's no doubt?'

Nigel Wisely smiled quite fondly, and briskly shook his head.

'None whatever, I'm afraid. No doubt at all.'

'Mm . . . yeh. I *knew* that. I knew that all along. That's the bloody thing – I always knew that. Right from the start of all the talk: I knew it, I knew it.'

And then he seemed buoyed up, and filled with a new resolve.

'Right, then: that's it. Well thank you. Thank you very much,

Mr Wisely. And have no fear – because I *will* accommodate you. I can promise you that.'

Yeh I can: too right, mate. And in my book, a promise is a promise. Blimey, though – I can't hardly believe it, what's just gone and occurred. I mean, tell you the truth – when I got myself round to Mr Wisely's, even as I were banging on the door, I never had no idea of what I were after, or nothing, nor what it were he could give me. And when that stuck-up old geezer, what's his name – Barnstaple, yeh that's it, bleeding Barnstaple. And what's he got to be so bleeding stuck-up about, that's what I'd like to know. Bleeding flunkey, that's all he is – just there, ain't he, to do whatever Mr Wisely tells him to do. And yet he's carrying on like he's Lord Muck or something. Well – can't have no respect, can you? Bloke like that. Anyways, what I'm saying is – when he says to me Nah mate, shove off, boss ain't here . . . well I weren't too surprised. I would've left a message, sort of style, and maybe not thought of it again. But now look at what I got! I got a job – and from what he were saying to me, Mr Wisely, it sounds like it won't be just grafting, neither – but I still can't think what else I can do, to be honest with you. And I did tell the man, didn't I? But look: Mr Wisely – no fool, is he? Ay? I mean you only got to listen to the way what he talks. And all his money, well – don't get to be like that, do you? Not if you's a fool. So if he reckons I got talents, well – he's going to be right, ain't he? Stands to reason. Because I don't think he's never wrong, not about nothing, far as I can tell. Jonathan Leakey, he said that to me one time, and I know what he were going on about now. And also – a flat! A bleeding flat! And I just gone and told the Jew-boy where to stick his ratty rooms and now I got me a new flat! Just like that. And how do you suppose I'll be getting there, then? To-ing and fro-ing, sort of style. I'll tell you, my son – in my bleeding motor car, that's how! Because I'm getting one of them and all. Blimey – I don't know why I never went to see him,

319

Mr Wisely, when Jonny first said I ought to. He's like Santa Claus, he is, Mr Wisely. And then what he said about Alfie just at the end, there. I can't tell you how much that means to me. And Len were right – he will, Alfie, he will come round, see me about it, drop me a card or something, and then I can tell him: put it to him fair and square. You want out, Alfie – I can get it for you. Prime. Because he's my little brother, see, and I don't want him to go and get hisself killed. Because I knew, didn't I? Always bleeding knew there'd be a war. Just kept on saying there wouldn't be, but I knew, course I knew: I ain't no mug.

Reckon now I'll get myself back down the Rose & Crown. Put a proper drink inside of me – because I'm telling you, that champagne of Mr Wisely's, well . . . I don't know why all the toffs think it's so bleeding special. Tastes like pop, and a bottle goes nowhere. Then after, it makes you feel all funny – it just ain't like a proper drink. Ain't normal. But nothing is – not round Mr Wisely's. Like hisself – I mean, I didn't never know there could be a bloke the like of that, I mean for real, and not in the flicks. Even Dickie – he's a toff, no mistake, but he ain't never in the league of Mr Wisely now, is he?

I'm going to do what Mr Wisely said. About the holiday. Makes sense, you think about it. Ain't got nowhere to live, just for now, but I do got that bastard Plough's fifteen miserable fucking quid, so I reckon it's all ideal, really. And it's her birthday coming up – give her a bit of a treat, ay? Because she been peaky lately, Mary, there's no denying. Says she's queasy, and she wants to sit down. Well – that ain't my Mary: like an ox, she is, best part of the time. And it'd be no sort of a break at all, would it, if she still got to be tending to the kid night and day – well would it? No point going. Only thinking of her. And Sheila, she's always saying it, ain't she? How she'd love to have him and all – and there's that other little kid, ain't there? That Lorna's sister, yeh – that Imogen. So between the two of them they'll have it all sorted out, I've no doubt at all. Because yeh – it'll pain me, I'm not saying it won't pain me, but it do look like it, don't it? Like he going to be sent off somewhere – for his own good though, ain't it? It's all for his benefit. So Mary, she going to have to start to get used to the idea, ain't she? Whether she likes it or not. Like Mr Wisely said.

And I'm just thinking back to that woman, now. That painted-up woman what was hanging all over him, the way she was. It put me in mind of the fact that me and Mary, well – it ain't like we're nothing no more, in that respect. Ain't been able to tell her what's what in, ooh blimey . . . got to be six months, if you can believe it. Yeh – reckon it is. We ain't done it since bleeding Christmas, and I couldn't tell you why. Always some bleeding reason she got. Well – Jeremy out the way, we can put all that to rights. And I'm walking through the park now, I am – and what I reckon I'll do, just before I duck into the Rose & Crown and have myself a Scotch, maybe – what I reckon is, I'll just sit on this bench for a mo, and see what it is inside of this little packet what Mr Wisely slipped me just as he were holding my hand, like. He winked when he give it me – bit of a shock, that were: ain't never seed him winking before. So let's have a little look . . . oh yeh, very nice, very tasteful. She'll like that, my Mary will – can't make out what it is (well I ain't going to be waving it about in the middle of the park now, am I?) but it's black and it's silky and it's just the job, I reckon, what with her birthday coming up, and this little holiday what I got planned. She'd maybe put some of that blue on her eyelids – get a lipstick what's got a bit more blood to it than the one what she uses.

Blimey – I got it now. That woman – that woman round at Mr Wisely's, there were that much make-up on her, and the veil and all, I never twig. But that's how I come to know her: I knew she were familiar. It's her from downstairs, ain't it? Yeh – telling you: that were Molly.

1st September 1939

You can tell now, on the wireless, by the sound of the
announcer's voice, the tone he takes, that what he's about to
say is not going to be good. I cannot remember, actually, when
I heard them use any other sort of voice, now. You hear 'This is
the BBC Home Service', and you almost feel you have to stand
to attention or something, and your stomach rather sinks.
Maybe if they had women broadcasters it wouldn't always
seem so terribly doom-laden. But doom-laden it is, I'm afraid.

Note: Entries from now on are going to be covered in
crossings-out (or maybe I should be using a pencil?). Dickie
told me about this kind of survey they're doing called Mass
Observation. Some department or office, I'm not clear, wants
people to write down their everyday observations and send
them in. But they won't want me, I told him – I'm just so
ordinary and I can't write properly and anyway I don't think I
actually do observe a great deal. Dickie said that that's exactly
what they do want, which seems very odd I must say. Anyway,
I've decided to take a stab at it and write as well as I can, and
send it in regularly. They say they'll read them and file them,
which I doubt. And I also doubt that in fifty or a hundred
years' time anyone will be the remotest bit interested to read all
these ramblings by an utter nobody called Mary Gordon (not
even Mary Robertson – what will they think of that?). But the
main reason I'm going to do it – for now, anyway – is that it
will force me to write in this ledger more frequently than I
have been. Then I can emend it and so forth, copy it out neatly
and send it in. It looks as if I shall have the time to do this, alas.
Until something else comes along, as I imagine it will.

So here we go: today, the awful voices on the wireless told us that Germany had invaded Poland – aeroplanes, bombs and everything. And we have a pact with Poland, although no one I know seems to understand why. Well it doesn't look to be a happy situation, is all I can say for the time being. No doubt I will write more about the matter at a later date.

As to life on a personal level (which is what the people at MO are after, apparently) – well, I could write a book, really. The new flat is just so perfect, it makes me want to cry. Dickie helped us bring all our things round from the old place. Molly, she's left too – simply because we did, apparently. I think she said she was going to live in the West End, but that we must go on knowing one another. I asked if this is because of a dancing job, but she said no. Mrs Stone was quite tearful – she said goodbye to me, the first word I have ever heard her utter. Anyway, this flat is of course just so much better in every way. Jackie says that it's part of his wages in this new job he's got now, which is just amazing, frankly – I've never heard of such a thing. It was offered to him by a friend of Jonathan Leakey's, and so Jackie gave in his notice to Mr Plough (so that's the end of the partnership idea. I asked him if this was wise, and he said it was, very, because his new boss, who is called Mr Wisely – I can't remember his first name at the moment, but I will find it out for future entries – is streets ahead in every way). He hasn't actually said what his new job is, exactly, but he has been putting up these rather fearsome corrugated iron little tunnel things in the garden – Anderson shelters they are called, I don't know why – and that has involved a fair deal of digging, so he has been kept rather busy. Jonathan Leakey says that Jackie is destined for great things (but still just digging holes so far: I didn't say this). And he has taken to calling him 'Jack the Lad', which Jackie seems to like but I don't, I don't at all, for some reason. It is, though, I know, how a lot of people see him. But this is the only side they see, isn't it? When he's cracking jokes, and so on. For me, of course, it's different. Jonathan is teaching Jackie how to drive a motor car. Jackie never mentions this and so I presume he's not very good, otherwise I'd never hear the end of it.

And now it's time for some confessions. I have been doing some rather odd things, lately. Buying all sorts of stuff that we don't really need, and putting it away (there are so many cupboards in the kitchen, it's just blissful). And the things I do normally buy – the usual things, tea, sugar, biscuits, tinned things – I have been getting more and more of. This is called hoarding, and I know it's silly and I feel it's wrong, but there: this is how I have been behaving. Even more extraordinary – when I was sorting through a box of oddments that we had brought over from the flat, I found an old Senior Service carton – the large one which I bought for Jackie last Christmas to go with the case and the lighter – and I thought that I'd keep it to put a few bits and bobs in. And when I opened it there were still two cigarettes inside – and without even thinking. I lit one up! I was halfway through smoking it (my first ever!) and not only could I not decide whether or not I liked it, but I was still amazed that I had done any such thing. And then I lit the other one! It made me feel a bit better, actually – calmed down my stomach, settled my head. And the tins of mandarin oranges that I'd bought to store – I've had two of those already (just spooning them out of the tin) and I felt so guilty that I rushed back to the shop where I had bought them for some replacements, and they had completely sold out, with no further prospect of more. And that made me feel even more guilty for having eaten them – and then it made me panic and wish I had bought a dozen of just everything when still I had the chance.

We still haven't heard a word from Alfie. I was so terribly

upset when Jackie told me he had joined the army – I just couldn't believe it. And I was so surprised that Jackie wasn't simply beside himself with anger or concern. But he says I shouldn't worry, and that Alfie will be all right. I suppose he only says this because he doesn't want to worry me – and of course because he still believes there will be no trouble (I can't write the word, I just can't. Isn't it funny?).

But I have filled pages now (it's a lovely day – feel quite bad about being indoors. Jackie should be home soon) and still I haven't written about the only thing that really touches me. The reason I am not in the park is that it seems so silly if you're on your own. Jeremy – my dear sweet innocent child – is with Sheila again this afternoon. And Imogen is there as well. Sheila says that it's good he gets used to being elsewhere. She does not say how bad it is for *me* when he is elsewhere – but there, I know she is acting for the best. She says that if it comes to it – and all the Evacuation Officers, she told me, have been placed on standby – that she will ensure that everything goes smoothly. But how can the removal of one's child, one's life, ever be smooth, for God's sake? Lorna has placed Timmy and Little Davy with her as well. Imogen, of course, was adamant that she was no longer a child – and indeed she does seem far more adult than many women twice her age. Sheila has made me promise to pack a bag for him. And I must label the cardboard box that contains his gas mask, which he must carry at all times, along with the rest of us. Oh God. Sheila said that she had been issued with a large sort of luggage tag that she herself must wear around her neck. When she asked why, they told her that it was for identification purposes, in case of injury. And Sheila – she really is so very outspoken – she said but if I am blown up, what makes you think that the label will survive? It made me laugh, but not very much.

Anyway, the reason I am going on and on is because I am

trying to put off the business of packing the bag. All his laundered clothes. And Fluffy and Golly. I simply can't bear the thought of us ever being apart. It is so very wrong, like losing a limb, if not one's very heart.

I am not at all sure about this perm. It never quite lies the way it ought to. Sheila says I should grow it out a bit and then she can redo it with larger and softer waves, and that will solve the problem. I feel slightly queer now – been sitting too long. I would smoke a cigarette, but I don't think there are any. I'll take some Epsom Salts instead. I can hear Jackie kicking at the back door. He hasn't yet worked out how the double lock works, and it's really very simple.

'Blimey, Jackie – what a mess, what a bleeding mess. Just look at the state of you, son.'

'Yeh well. Like to see what you look like, Jonny, you been digging bloody holes all the bleeding day.'

'Pro tem, my son. Purely pro tem. Your suits'll be ready from Harry the Stitch, week or two. Then we'll see a whole new Jackie, ay? Jack the Lad you'll be then, old mate. Cock of the walk, and no mistake.'

'Yeh and what? I'll be digging holes in a brand-new whistle then, will I?'

'The digging holes is just something what come up. What's wrong with you? You don't think Mr Wisely has a look at you and he says to hisself – you know what? I reckon he's just the boy to get them holes dug. Mr Wisely, he got plenty of muscle, son, I can tell you that much. Don't need you for that. All it is is just to keep you a bit busy until the real work come along, that's all. Want another drink, do you?'

'What you think? And when's that, then? The work. What'll I be doing? Ay? Because he never said, and you ain't neither, Jonny.'

'Yeh well you see if times was normal I could tell you, course I could – tell you like a shot, times was normal. But they ain't. Don't have to draw a picture, do I? Even myself – don't know what I'm doing from one day to the next. See, what Mr Wisely reckons – and I ain't never known him wrong – he reckons that once this bleeding war is official . . . and I don't know about you, Jackie, but I wish they'd hurry up and bleeding make their minds up if we're going to hammer the Boche or we ain't, because all this hanging about, it don't do your nerves a shred of good. And plus I can't stand every Tom, Dick and Wossname bending my ear about it all the time. "I don't reckon we'll go to war . . ." "What you talking about? All over by Christmas . . ." On and bleeding on they go: get right up my fuck-ing nose, I'm telling you. Anyway – bugger all that. Want a fag?'

'Them's funny-looking things, ain't they? What are them then, Jonny?'

'Them's Turkish, son. Top-class, they is.'

'Yeh? Stink something chronic, they does. Reckon I'll stop with a Senior Service.'

'Got to get used to it, son. Finer things in life. Poised, you is. That's what Mr Wisely reckons. He reckons you's poised.'

'What – like for a nosedive, you mean?'

'Don't be funny, Jackie. No listen – that's what I were saying, weren't it? I can't tell you *exact* what you'll be up to, on account of Mr Wisely, he playing a bit of a waiting game, see? He reckons that this war what we got on our hands – and he for one ain't never been in any doubt at all that we got one coming, no doubt at all, Mr Wisely.'

'No. Me neither. Coming, all right. Have another one, will we? For the road, sort of style?'

'Yeh, why not. Might make you drive a bit better – Gawd alone knows it couldn't make you no worse. What's wrong with you anyway? Ay? Thought you'd take to it like a duck to wossname.'

'It's them bleeding gears. I'm all right with everything else.'

'Except for the reversing.'

'Yeh – all right, except for the reversing, grant you that. But it's them bleeding gears what get me. Fucking things . . .'

'Yeh well – perseverance, ay? Have you winning the Grand Pricks, we will. You sure you don't want one of these? Taste ever so sweet.'

'Well – go on then. Anything once, ay? Anyway – go on, Jonny. You was saying.'

'I were? What were I saying? Oh yeh – about Mr Wisely, yeh yeh. Well see – thing is, he reckons that come this war, there going to be all sorts of new opportunities for an entrepreneur. Fields of endeavour, that's what he said to me: fields of endeavour what we ain't even thought about, can't even imagine them, till the time come. But see, what Mr Wisely does is, he looks for loopholes, gaps in the market. Supply and demand. People'll want things they don't even know they'll be wanting yet, and Mr Wisely – he'll give them to them. At a price, course. And that and all – the price. It'll depend on market forces, see? Then there's going to be burdens on people, ain't there? Things they want shot of. And Mr Wisely, he'll remove them. Gentle, like – that's his way. And us – we're the agents, if you want. The facilitators. That's a word, ain't it? Ay? Facilitators. One to get your mouth round, that is. Like take a for instance: Mr Wisely . . . one more Scotch shall we have? Yeh? Yeh. Can't harm. So like I say – Mr Wisely, he tells me you wouldn't be so keen if the King of England wants you for his army . . . ?'

'I'd ram it up their throat.'

'Yeh right. So you see, should such a misfortune befall you, Jackie boy . . . and it's "down", I would've said. Ain't it? Ay? Ram it *down* their throat, not up. Never mind. Anyway – you get your call-up and Mr Wisely, mark my words, will make sure that they change their minds. Won't ram it down their throat – not his style. But you won't be bothered, I can promise you that. And nor me. The contacts he got, you wouldn't believe. Now for you, for us, he do this as a favour – kindness of his heart, like. But you ain't the only one, Jackie boy, what'll want out of this caper, not by a long chalk. So there's business to be done. And that's just one way, see, how we'll be helping to give people what they wants. Nice way of making a living, really – giving people what they wants: smiles all round – what could be better? Facilitators, that's what we'll be. Yeh. Nice. So what you think?'

'What? About being a – one of them. What you said?'

'Nah, you dozy pudden. The fag. Sweet or not?'

'Oh. Yeh – not too bad at all, it is. Once you get the taste.'

'Yeh well. Life in a nutshell, son. There's all sorts out there, mate. Just waiting. We don't know what yet – and first off, we may not like the idea, may not go for the look of the thing. New, see? Ain't never met it before. But yeh – once you get the *taste* . . . well then you're on Easy Street, ain't you? Ay? No looking back then. You got to trust Mr Wisely, and you got to trust me as well. You'll be Jack the Lad, you will. Look at me – go on. Yeh – little smile you got on you there. Like the idea, don't you? Course you do. Jack the Lad you'll be, my son. And how bad you reckon that can be?'

⊙

3rd September 1939
A short entry. We listened to Mr Chamberlain on the wireless this morning. He said that as a consequence of Germany not doing something or other they were meant to, we're now at war. I can't speak. And then the siren went off and Jeremy

had already gone on a train with Sheila and Timmy and Little Davy and hundreds of other poor little mites, and I don't even know where. It was very early and we all went to Waterloo and I cried so much and I waved until I thought my arm would drop off. All the mothers were the same. And when the siren went, I could only think of Jeremy on a train and I started to cry again. Jackie and me went down to the cellar – he was making jokes and I asked him to stop but he wouldn't. He seemed excited – maybe just nervous. It was a false alarm, anyway. The sound of it, though, was so horrid. We'll be hearing it a lot, I've no doubt.

As it's Sunday, I went to church. Can't remember the last time. It was packed out. I didn't listen to what the vicar said, I just thought of Jeremy. The smell of him – it's still on my fingers. On the way out, everyone was very quiet. It was so warm and sunny. I bought a packet of ten Craven A on the way home. I thought they might help me, and they have just a little. And then I bumped into my Dad. He just looked at me, didn't speak, and I hugged him and I started to cry again.

I'm pregnant, of course. I've known it for ages – didn't want to admit it. How will I cope now? In a war. I'm crying again – it's awful. All my writing has blurred and smudged – the tears are dropping even now. Sheila promised she would telephone as soon as everyone is settled. She left me a parcel – it was greengage jam. I cannot write any more. My heart is breaking.

PART TWO

During the War

'Way I see it,' Sally was hooting with high indignation – the muscle of her opinion considerably bolstered as it always was when she straddled her own home turf, the mildewed haven of her greengrocer's shop with its softly yielding wooden-planked floor bearing the deadweight of so many thick jute sacks spilling out potatoes and jammed with turnips – the drapes of threadbare raffia grass coddling the russet apples and the last of the satsumas. When she stood defiant behind her counter, by the wad of string-handled brown paper carriers dangling from a nail – wielding the scoop of her mighty scales or hurling silver and coppers into the dented and rusting Oxo tin that doubled as a till – here she was invincible, defying even Mary and Sheila to so much as think of gainsaying her, should they summon the cheek. 'Way I see it is, I'm the only one of them not at it. I put you in an extra couple of sprouts there, Mary, because I know that you and Jackie are fond of them.' And then she broke off to hector an elderly man, hefting an orange in each of his hands. 'Now then grandad – don't go fondling my fruit till it's safely bought and paid for, ay?' In a hissed-out aside for Mary's ears alone, Sally confided in her then that it was the old 'uns who were the worst – always mauling about the merchandise, they were, as if they were suspicious of there being something under the skin altogether other than what you'd expect. And kids – you got to watch the kids like a hawk: one of them gets you chatting about the state of their old gran's bunions, and next thing you know his mate's off down the street with a pound of pippins stuffed up his jersey.

Sheila, meanwhile, was musing over a cucumber.

'I'm going to buy one of these – lovely in sandwiches with a bit of salmon paste. You ever tried that, Mary? I'd buy two, but they don't ever keep . . .'

'That's what I'm saying,' rushed in Sally. 'That's why I can't do it – not that I would, mind, because I think it's downright immoral, taking advantage of the situation. But I'm the only one, I can tell you. All of the others, the length of this street – they're all at it, every single one of them. Well you must both have seen it yourselves. Even in the Co-op, the tea I buy – it's up by a ha'penny a quarter in just the last fortnight. That's the Red Label – Green Label's gone up tuppence. Now how can they justify it, you tell me that. Oh yes – they'll say to you it's shortages and blockades in the Channel, oh yes, they'll tell you all of that, but I'm willing to bet my old mum's dentures on the fact that all that tea, they've had it piled up in their warehouse for months, they have, months and months – years, most likely. Profiteering, that's what it is. Plain and simple. Now me – I'm in perishables. Can't go stockpiling tomatoes, can I? And it's like you just said, Sheila – those cucumbers didn't go soggy on you, then you'd collar a couple of them, wouldn't you? And by the same token, if I don't sell the lot of them before they *do* go all soggy, well – my loss then, isn't it? Can't do anything about it. Certainly can't put up the prices. Not that I would, as I say. That's the damnation of perishables. A pallet of Fray Bentos, you're laughing really, aren't you? Like that old miser Hawkins on Goldmore Road. Yes – you know who I mean. Beastly little man. He's got tinned beans and peas, noodles, suet, syrup – he's got all sorts, Hawkins has, and not a week passes by when there isn't a ha'penny on here, a penny on there. Profiteering, it is – but he's got queues, hasn't he? He'll be doubling his prices, I've no doubt, and still the customers will come. Immoral, that's what it is.'

'Even more so,' said Mary. 'As soon as people see higher prices, they associate it with rarity and then they go and buy even more. It's that that creates the shortage. Vicious circle, you see. It's all these rumours going around, that's the trouble. I really do think we're not told enough, you know. The government, they don't make things clear, and so all the gossips get to work and then you hear one thing and then you hear another – and then they're all saying oh no, that's all nonsense, you mustn't go believing any of that, and then they go and tell you something else entirely. But you see if it's true – that after Christmas they're going to bring in all this rationing and so on that everyone's talking about, well then it's really no wonder, is it? That everyone's stocking up while they can. I mean . . . I'm doing it a bit myself, if I'm honest. I know it's not right and it's probably unnecessary but, well – you don't want to be caught out, do you? What I *do* think is most awfully wrong is that apparently all these really wealthy people from, oh – you know, Mayfair and so on – have you heard this? True, apparently. They're all going to the poorer areas in their Rolls-Royces and what have you, and buying up absolutely everything they can lay their hands on, whatever the cost. Whole shops, sometimes. Wicked, that is – but what can you do? Why they're bringing in rationing, I suppose. Sally, you don't still have any of those prunes at all, do you? I've got quite a taste for them. I have them with porridge. Sheila thinks it's disgusting, but I rather like it.'

' 'Tis disgusting,' said Sheila promptly. 'Even to think of it – turns my stomach. But you know, Mary's right really, Sally – not the rich people, I don't mean them – but ordinary folk like us, you can't really blame them, can you? Stocking up. I see it with all the mothers I have to deal with. They're that worried that their children won't be getting enough to eat when they go off to wherever they're going that they send them away with great boxes of stuff, and they mostly can't afford it, you know. I do have to wonder how much of it actually gets eaten by the children themselves . . . Oh but Mary look – I can see you're all getting anxious again. I didn't mean that the children go without, or anything. Nearly every single one of the billets I've been involved with, well – they're homes from home, really. And if there's a farm, there's all sorts of food, of course. Much better off than if they were in London. And your Jeremy – how many times do I have to tell you? Honestly, Sally – it's heaven where he is. Lovely people. Beautiful house.'

'Mm well,' sniffed Sally. 'Not what happened to my two. That's why I'm having them back.'

Both Mary and Sheila looked at one another in total surprise.

'*Your* two, Sally . . . ?' gasped Mary. 'Why what do you mean? I had no idea at all that you—'

'Oh yes,' sighed Sally. 'Not babies, of course – nearly sixteen they are now. Twins. Two boys. The fruit of my seven-week marriage. Not like you see in the pictures, I can assure you. How is it that you can fall in love with a man, wed him, and seven weeks later you want to murder him with your own two bare hands? Well there – water under the bridge. They don't live in London, John and Robert – that's their names. Strapping young lads, they are. That's why you've never seen them. When they were babies I had them fostered, for right or wrong. Apprenticed in Reading, they are now: bootmaking. Were, anyway. Well – we're always going to need boots, aren't we? That's what I told them. But I wanted them to be well away from it, you know, so I packed them off with one of your lot, Sheila – one of the Evacuation Officers who I must say I didn't take to, not one little bit. Schoolteacher, she was – reminded me of my own. Nary a smile about her. Anyway, my John, he got a postcard to me saying it was like Fagin's den, where they'd been billeted. Starving hungry and living in a kennel, far as I could make out. Well – I wasn't having that, was I? But their firm in Reading, you see – taken over for war work, of course, so no room any more for a pair of apprentices who aren't yet up to muster. So back here they'll have to be. Wednesday, I'm going for them – my half-day, all the time I've got. And if they've been badly treated, I'll have the law out. Don't ask me where I'm going to put them. Well, tell you the truth, my Len – he's been ever so good about it: said he'd make them up a nice little cosy nook in the cellar at the Rose & Crown. Says he can use a couple of strong boys for the barrels, and that. It might be he's just being kind – because he is, you know, Len. Kind man. Ever so thoughtful in himself. And as to the bombs, well – there aren't any, are there? Got us all worked up, frightened the life out of us, they did, with this bloody blackout, pardon my French – and all the shelters and the gas masks and what have you . . . and then what? Nothing. Not a dicky bird. Wouldn't even know there was a war on, would you? Except for all the inconvenience. I reckon the papers got it right, for once: a right phoney war this is, and no mistake. Over before you know it, shouldn't wonder. And all this upheaval . . .'

And the moment they were back in the flat, Mary was flushed and agitated and put it to her directly – as Sheila had just known that she would, from the light that had sprung into her eyes the moment that Sally had brought up the subject.

'Well why can't you? You're the Evacuation Officer – you can arrange it, you've got the authorisation to do it, so do it. You said you'd do anything for Jeremy and me, so do it. Do it now. Don't say you won't – just *do* it, Sheila, what's wrong with you? Oh God I'm just *beside* myself . . . !'

'Oh heaven's sake calm down, Mary. Look at you – all trembling, you are – face all blotchy. Sit yourself down, and I'll make you a nice—'

'Don't want. Don't want one. Don't want a nice cup of tea. I want my son back. *Now*, Sheila – I've got to have him back. I'll go mad if I don't see him.'

'I'm not saying I *won't*, Mary. I'm not saying that. I'm just suggesting to you that it's all a bit premature – that's all I'm saying. He's only been there, hasn't he, just a few weeks, and—'

'Eight weeks. Two months he's been gone. I simply can't bear it . . .'

'It can't be eight weeks, Mary. I only—'

'Well it's *nearly* eight weeks. Or seven weeks. Six! What's the difference? I died on the first *day*, Sheila, and I've been dying ever since. And you heard Sally, didn't you?'

'Oh – *Sally* . . . !'

'Yes – Sally! Good sense, she was talking. And she's not the only one either who's bringing back her children. There are lots of them doing it. We all acted too hastily. We all got panicked. There aren't going to *be* any bombs, are there? If Hitler was going to bomb us he would've done it by now, wouldn't he? What's he waiting for? Jackie doesn't think there's going to be any bombs. All hot air, he says it is.'

'Yes I know, Mary, but what if you're wrong? We none of us know for sure, do we? And whatever you believe, it's Jeremy I'm thinking of. He's just got settled – he's really happy where he is, Mary, honestly he is. I wouldn't say it to you if it wasn't true, now would I? You know I wouldn't. But you start chopping and changing, well – poor little mite, won't know where he is, will he? All be at sixes and sevens. And what if the raids *do* start up? Plenty saying they will. That Churchill, for a start. People maybe should have listened to him a whole lot sooner than they did.'

'Oh God, *Churchill*! I don't want to talk about—! I'm not *interested* in Churchill, I'm only interested in—'

'In Jeremy. I know. Listen to me, Mary – it's Jeremy I'm talking about. If you bring him back now and then the bombs start falling on London – well what are you going to do then? Hm? And it's not just the bombs we're talking about, is it? What about an invasion? You've heard the talk. London sky going black with hordes of German parachutists, that's what some are saying now. I know there's all sorts of wild rumours, Mary – a new one every day, it sometimes seems – but you have to be prepared for the fact that one of them might turn out to be true. And so what, Mary? What will you do? Keep him here in danger because you want to be near him? Or pack him back off again? And who knows where, this time? Won't be able to pick and choose, you know, not when the air raids start, you won't. There'll be a stampede – and even I won't be able to help you then. It'll be every child for himself – any port in a storm. But he's safe now, Mary – safe and happy. They're really lovely people, Mary – very caring. Best leave him be. You know it's right. Don't you? Don't you, Mary? I know it's hard for you, but . . . and what about Jackie, hey? What does he say? He'll agree with me, I bet he will.'

Mary looked away abruptly. Yes, she thought, with considerable bitterness – and I bet he will too: that's the terrible trouble. Or part of it, anyway. Because there is so much else. So much more to think of – and time, oh dear God: even though it always seems these days to be hanging about one's shoulders like an eternal pall, it is, of course, very sneakily getting on with what it always does: counting down, and running out on me. Because every day, you know, I'm just so perfectly amazed that Jackie hasn't noticed – hasn't said a thing. I mean I know he's all taken up with this new job of his (and it's funny, but since this rather ridiculous war has been declared, I don't think that I've ever seen him happier) – but still you would imagine, wouldn't you, that beyond his saying to me that I look a bit peaky or that I ought to take a lie-down . . . he really is so thoroughly unobservant. I mean – are all men like that? I suppose they must be. I had always been assuming, of course, that he would have divined my condition, told me he was pleased (even if it was a lie – because you never know, do you really, quite how, with men, they might consider this sort of thing), and then I would in a rather simpering manner own up to the truth of the matter and that we should then both take it from there. But clearly it isn't going to be like that, and rather soon, I think, the state of me is going to be very apparent to everybody. I already feel like one of those barrage balloons that you see high up, sometimes, when the sky's clear, but even Sheila – although she's given me some funny looks from time to time (and especially when I'm eating those prunes with my porridge) – but even she has not apparently tumbled to the rather obvious solution as to why I'm always so tired and jittery and nauseous. She attributes it to the war; she must think me a very nervous Nellie indeed. And in the meanwhile, the way I'm strapping myself into these ever-tighter girdles, well – can't be good for either one of us, can it really? It can't go on. Going to have to do something about it, and rather soon. Oh dear . . . and it's all my fault, of course – and Jackie, he will point this out, because when I had that monstrous device extracted from so very deep within me (this, the woman said, so clinically, will hurt you: and she was right, it did, so very very much) – I of course didn't tell him, because what would have been the point, in fact? He was never going to use one of those, what are they . . . prophylactics? Well was he? So what on earth did I imagine would happen? How was this consequence to be avoided? Well I don't know – trusted to luck, I suppose. I just couldn't have borne another day with that thing inside me, that's all I

340

knew; and after the pain (it lasted for nearly a week) the relief then was immeasurable – I felt so free within myself, as if I had reclaimed my own body, after such a long time. I can't see – because of course I've thought about it – why he *wouldn't* be pleased, Jackie. Plenty of space in this lovely new flat – and money, that doesn't seem to be a problem at all (Mr Wisely is clearly a very generous employer; Jackie is well reimbursed for whatever on earth it is he gets up to from morning till night, because he's never really told me, not in so many words: it seems to be nothing you could put a finger on).

It's the child I already have, though, that's the anguish I cannot conquer. I need him, need to be with him – I can barely remember the way he smells (when he's just woken, when I've just bathed him, and when he's fast asleep and in my arms). It's the other thing I've just got to talk to Jackie about, got to. He does love Jeremy, I know he does, but it is extraordinary to me how very quickly and utterly he has adapted to living without him. He's safe, in good hands, he tells me – just like Sheila does. And I know that – well, I know it as far as one ever can. Because if your child is away from you, even for an hour, all the doubts and fears, they crawl all over you, and then they invade. The wonderful thing, though, about my condition (and at first I didn't realise, or I would have acted sooner) is that now I too can be an evacuee, and so Jeremy and I can be together again – and Sheila, she'll arrange it, I'm sure she will. But in the meanwhile, though, I *do* believe he is being cared for – but even that: it galls me. I find it unbearable that some other woman, somewhere else and far away, is doing with Jeremy all the tender little things that should be mine, and mine alone. And in return, she revels in the light of his eyes, a gurgle of laughter, the caress of those sweet fingers. Of course I could not stand to think that he was less than doted on and cared for, wherever he may be, but his absence and the very cherishing of another – those good hands – they come so close to sending me mad.

☉

'Aye aye, Jackie boy! Sit yourself down, lad – have a drink, yeh? Looking very dapper, I must say.'

'Ta, Jonny – don't mind if I do. Quick one though, ay? Yeh – he come up the business, didn't he? With the whistles. Bleeding freezing out there, ain't it?'

'Harry the Stitch? Won't never let you down, son. There you are, Jackie – get that down you: that'll keep the chill out your bones. So listen, this war what we got, then – treating you all right, is it?'

'Yeh yeh – mustn't grumble. Gawd, though – it's a right laugh really, ain't it? Life ain't never been so good. Not for me, any rate.'

'Only just begun, son. Telling you – good times just around the corner. So you're happy are you, Jackie? Not missing it too much, then? Being up a ladder or down on your hands and knees?'

'Not *too* much, nah. Christ – don't know how I stuck it so long, God's honest truth. Here, talking of that – funny thing. My old boss – Plough, yeh?'

'Plough, yeh . . . sort of rings a bell. See you're on the Turkish now then, ay Jackie? Finer things in life.'

'Got a bit of a taste for them, I ain't denying. Not too fond first thing of a morning, I got to say. That hacking up of your guts, it's best left to a Senior Service, my way of thinking. No but listen – that old money-grubbing bastard Plough, yeh?'

'Yeh yeh. What about him? Fancy another in there, do you?'

342

'Yeh – go on. I'll get in the next one, ay? Yeh well – Plough, he only got hisself dead, didn't he? Like a doornail he is, silly sod.'

'Yeh? What – knock him off, did you Jackie?'

'Don't be funny. No – it'll make you laugh, this will Jonny. Got hit by a tram, didn't he? It's a right joke, ain't it? Because you know how they don't make no noise, your trams? Well – come the blackout, he's crossing the road and boom! That's the end of Danny Plough. Got to laugh, ain't you?'

'Casualty of war. Brings a tear, don't it? Telling you – this blackout, it's going to kill more of us than Hitler's bleeding Luftwaffe, they ever get up off of their arses and start doing all the business.'

'It don't make the driving easy, that's for bleeding sure. Sometimes, you're going that slow, you be better off walking.'

'They're going to bring in something to cover the headlights with next – that's the next bleeding thing. So all you got is slits.'

'Yeh – I heard that. And petrol and all. Going to hit the petrol's what I heard. That's going to queer us, ain't it?'

'Joking. Ain't you learned nothing yet? Ay? About Mr Wisely? They can do what they fucking well like about the petrol, won't touch us. He'll see to it. Like what he do. Easy Street, son. Like I told you. But see – we ain't rightly got going yet. Marking time, in a sense is all we're doing. Lot of people, they still reckon the war could be over in a couple months. Reckon Hitler's bluffing. Now Mr Wisely, he ain't of that opinion, but still he keeping his cards right close to his chest, you take my meaning. That's why we're still just doing the rents and buying up stuff – marking time, keeping our hands in. But once it's clear we're in for the full long doings – like if they dump that walking disaster what they call Chamberlain and the government gets a good old shake-up – well then, son, the world is our wossname. Then we really get cracking. Our oyster, yeh. Right then, Jackie lad – I got to be off. See a bloke.'

'Yeh – me too, Jonny. Two rents and one debt I got to call in. Then I'm seeing old Dickie, later on. Never cared for them, you know – not my cup of tea.'

'What you on about now then, Jackie? You silly old sod.'

'Oysters. When you said, back there. Slimy bugger, your oyster is. Best off with twopennorth of cod, my way of thinking. Right then, Jonny – love you and leave you, ay?'

'Yeh yeh – ta-ta then, Jackie lad. Be sure and give my love to the good doctor, ay? Stopping in Civvy Street then, is he?'

'Yeh, reckon he is. One of the things what I'm talking to him about, matter of fact. Might have more to tell you, later on.'

'Yeh? Can't hardly wait. Right then, Jackie – what say we have a little rondayvoo back here at, what? Six suit you? Seven better, is it?'

'Yeh – let's say seven, safe side. Right then. Got to see a bloke.'

'You and me both, Jackie. You and me both.'

So I done all that. And one of the blokes what I were down to get the rent off of, I never twig till I got there: only my old barber, weren't it? Italian Toni (spells it with a 'i' at the end he do, some reason, silly bastard). So anyway, he pays up, sweet as you like, and while I'm there I thought to myself, well – might as well get me a bit of a trim, ay? And I says to him tell you what, Toni old son – leave it just a bit more thick, like, over the lugholes, will you? And not so shaved up the back. More the style now, I reckon, looking about me (better sort of class). Don't want to look like no erk, do I? Some kid what's been called up, or something. So he do that, Toni, makes a real nice job of it – puts a touch of some sort of pong on, not too bad, and then he says to me, how about a nice close shave, ay? How's that sound? Hot towels, cutthroat, the works. And I goes to him yeh go on then, why not ay? And after he done, it feel all lovely I got to say: smooth as a baby's wossname. Been a whole lot better if it were one of Mr Wisely's painted-up floozies what was doing the business, I ain't saying – but give him his due, Toni, he's a right pro at what he do. Then he's slapping some old juice all over my face and blimey, it don't half hurt: I were close to dotting his i's for him, and then it come over all lovely, it did – all warm and lovely, it were. Ain't never had that before. And something else I ain't had before neither: I were thinking to myself right then, what with the shave and all the doings, reckon I'm in for, what? Four bob? Five, maybe? Yeh – give the poor old bugger five, why not? So I'm jangling about there with my pocket of silver, and Toni, he say to me oh no Mr Robertson, is quite okay, he goes, in that funny sort of up-and-down accent what he got. Is on the house, he's saying – and give my sincere regards to Mr Wisely next time you see him, is what he saying to me. And I says well right then, Toni old lad: will do. And ta, ay?

And the other rent and all: no problems there. Never is. They seem very eager, they do, to push the money into my hands – smiling, they all are, and nodding up and down like they was puppets, or something. Well – suits me: I don't want no trouble. But I got just a little bit of it, didn't I? When it come to the debt what I had to call in. Some bloke in a crummy little room down Clerkenwell – woman there, banging around with the dishes behind a raggedy curtain. All agitated, the geezer were, so I knew straight off that he didn't have the money. It's this war, he goes to me – we had to send the kiddies away and we wanted them to be all respectable like, so we gets them all these new clothes and new suitcases and blimey – can't hardly remember all the words what was falling out of him. Yeh, I says – but that ain't no concern of mine now, is it? Ay? I mean you can see my position here, can't you mate? (It were Jonny taught me all the lingo, how you put it over to the punter.) If you could just give me a bit more time, he's saying to me then, and I come back with oh dear me no, my son, I'm afraid I just can't accommodate you on that one, you see, on account of time, mate, is what you just run out of, see? And then he looks at me, all imploring like, and his missus behind the curtain, she gone all quiet, she has – forgot about her dishes and just listening, I reckon. And then he says please listen to me, sir – sir he's calling me, what I don't mind – I just this week lost my job: laid me off, they did, and without so much as a brass farthing, and I got a weak lung. And I thought oh blimey, the bastards – because I been here, ain't I? Ain't no fun, ain't no fun at all when you're out of work. Bad enough, ain't it? Living in a rat-hole and your kids all gone – and a weak wossname, he got – without the bastards laying you off into the bleeding bargain. So I says to him well listen to me, mate – how much you got? And he breathes out like he been bursting to up till now, and he ram a couple quid and a pocketful of odds and ends into my hands, and there's maybe, what? Two pound eight there, in total. All right then, I says to him – but next time, mind, I'm going to have to have the lot. And he's thanking me, he is, and he's pumping my arm up and down and he's practically weeping now, like I just give him a present, or something. And then the wife, she come out from behind the curtain – and blimey, she *is* weeping, look, and she gets a hold of my hands and she's going thank you thank you thank you thirteen to the bleeding dozen and she keeps a hold of my hands like I'm the bleeding Pope or something, and I looks at her and blimey – her eyes all sunk in her face, they is, hardly no meat on her bones to speak of, lift her up in one hand, you could. So what I does – and I know it ain't professional, this, and Jonny, he'd have me for it, yeh I know he would – but I give the bloke back his eight bob or whatever, and then I gets myself out of there right sharpish or else they'd be down on the floor, the both of them, and kissing my boots, I shouldn't wonder.

And just before I got myself round to Dickie's (and I were hoping he were going to be in a lot better nick than he were the last bleeding time I seen him, dear oh dear) I thought hang on,

I'll just motor over and have a word with – because I got this spanking new Riley now, and well pleased with it, I am: dark green, she is, and very pacy – yeh, so as I says, thought I might just have another quick word with Jeanie, Alfie's girl, because he's still ever so much on my mind, that one is – and dear oh Lord, the trouble I had with him. When first he come round to see me, it were Mary what answered the door, and next thing I know she's sticking her head in the room and then she says to me Prepare yourself, Jackie, for a bit of a surprise (told me later, she did, that Alfie, he'd been that rattled, he'd said to her What sort of a mood he in? Because if you reckon, Mary, that this ain't a good time then what I'll do is I'll make myself scarce – come back another day. I tried to get out of her how she'd answered that one, but she never told me, not direct. Reckon it were a case of now being as good a time as any, sort of style). And then there he were, stood in front of me – nervy little smile on him, and his hands all twisting about this stupid blooming cap what they give him – because he were only in uniform, weren't he? Head to toe in khaki, he were, like someone upped and tipped a hundredweight of dung on him. Dear oh dear.

'Not too upset with me, I hope Jackie . . . ?'

'Not a question, is it? Not a question of me being upset, it's a question of how come you lost your bleeding *mind*, that's what it's a question of, Alfie my lad. How come, is the question, how come one minute I got a clever little younger brother what's going places and learning French and he's off to his office of a morning and all got up like a proper little gent, and then the minute I takes my eyes off of him, then suddenly he's dumping all his brains in the River bleeding Thames, and next thing you know he's a bleeding *mug*. Because that's what you are, Alfie, and don't you go doubting it. All you lads what run to the colours – mugs, every last man jack of you. And what – no don't interrupt, you just hear me out, son. And yeh – so what: proud

347

of yourself, is you? Ay? Think you done a clever thing, do you? Want to go off to some foreign place and fight their battles for them? That's a bright thing, is it? What you done?'

'I just thought – it were the right thing. Honest truth, Jackie – I didn't think at all. Didn't have to. Just done it. And no – I don't regret it. Feels all right. Ready, I am.'

'Yeh? *Yeh?* You're ready, are you? Ready for what? Ay? What you ready for? Ready to do what some old toff in brass goes and tells you to do, that it? Here you – Private Robertson, you go over that hill and get yourself shot to bleeding bits. And you says Oh yes sir, I will sir, three bags bleeding full sir. Because I'm ready, I am. I'm bleeding *ready* – you silly bloody sod, Alfie. What you *done*, son? Ay? What you bleeding *done*?'

'Come on, Jackie . . . don't be like that . . .'

'Don't be like that? Don't be like that, he says to me. How you bleeding want me to be then, ay? Pat on the back? That what you want? Well you ain't going to get it, son – not from me. And it's all right, Mary – you don't have to hang about like you's some sort of a referee, or something. I ain't about to deck him – although he bleeding earned hisself a slapping, I'm not saying. Go and make us a pot of tea, there's a good girl. Me and Alfie, we're going to have a little talk. Civilised, like. Man to man, ay? Cards on the table. Come and sit yourself down, Alfie. Something I got to say to you. Maybe you don't fancy no tea. I got a drop of Scotch, you interested.'

'No ta, Jackie. Tea'll be lovely.'

'Not when you're on duty, ay?'

'Don't be daft. I ain't on duty, am I? Just come over to see you. We're all of us just hanging about, at the present. No one knows what's going off. But it's real cushy, Jackie – honest it is. There's no hardship.'

'Not now there ain't. Not yet. See listen, Alfie – there's some what's saying, yeh – come Christmas, all this'll be over. Finished.

Now if that's true, all well and good. You get your senses back, set fire to that poxy uniform, and we's all back home where we started. Nice. And it can't be comfy, that uniform. Like it's made out of blankets . . '

'Bit itchy, I got to say. Not too bad.'

'Yeh well. But see – what if it don't? Ay? Blow over. What if Hitler means it? Ay? Goes the distance. Well then you, my son, is going to be practising your French a whole lot sooner than you think. Because them Froggies – Jerry walks into France, they won't last two minutes, them Froggies. Be up to us, won't it? The Tommy. The bleeding Tommy. And that's *you*, ain't it? Ay? And that's why I'm worried. I didn't like to say it, not when Mary were hanging about, but I don't want to see you killed, Alfie – you's my little kid brother and I loves you, you bastard. And I got to know you's safe. No no – it's no good talking, I know what you're going to say. You're going to tell me that you got no intention of getting yourself killed – that you can handle yourself, that you're going to be as right as ninepence and come back a bleeding general with a chest full of medals. Yeh well. Could be. But every one of you, Alfie, every last bleeding one of you, they're all thinking the same, ain't they? Ay? Not me, mate – Boche won't get me. Because I'm invincible, I am – and yeh, I got God on my side. All that tosh. Well Jerry – he's saying the same bleeding thing and all. So what, then? Ay? You're *all* going to be all right, are you? Nice little tea party, and then back home – that it? It's a *war*, son. Maybe you forgot. And in a war, people, they get killed – it's what happens. Famous for it. And the first to get killed is you lot, the poor old bloody Tommy. Why you think they're calling up millions of the buggers, ay? Because they know they're going to need them, that's why. Well they can do what they like – it's you what I'm concerning myself with. Other sods – they can do what they like. Now listen – no, you listen, you can have your say in a minute. I got a proposition for you, Alfie. Now not many people gets a second chance, they do something stupid. But that's what I got for you, Alfie lad – a second chance. A chance to get wise, my son. Listen – you want out of this bleeding army, I can fix it, no questions asked. I can accommodate you. Know a bloke, don't I? And there won't be no shame in it, nor nothing. You had a little think, and you come to your senses. Something to be admired, that is. So what you say? Ay? You just tip me the wink, son, and it's as good as done.'

Yeh well. Weren't having it, were he? Just about held hisself back from laughing in my face, he did, the cheeky little sod. Tells me he reckons the war's going to be lasting six, seven months at the outside – that his insurance company's going to hold his job for him, and that Jeanie, she's behind him all the way – all in favour she is, he's telling me. So I thought to myself well right, then – have to have a word with that one, won't I? Have to do that right away. And then I says to Alfie well then listen, my son, you won't take my offer of a release – and you're a charlie not to, you got to know that: there's many what'd give their right arm to get out of this little lot, I'm telling you. But never mind: leave that. What about you stay in this wonderful army of yours, yeh? But you do all your soldiering in London – now how's that sound? Prime, ay? Keep all the family together, sort of style. Because I can do that and all – and you'd have to be one of them lunatics in the bleeding asylum not to jump at this one, now wouldn't you Alfie old lad? Ay? Stands to reason, that do. But nah, if you can believe it. Take his chances, he says he will, same as the rest of them. And he thanks me, he do – he just gone and shoved all what I got to say to him right back down my bleeding throat, and then he go and thank me for it, stupid little bleeder. Well what can you do? Ay? Done my best, didn't I? Put it to him whichever way I could, and he ain't having none of it. So I thought right, then – only one hope left to me, and that's this

Jeanie ain't it? So I got myself round there. Turns out she's on my side – just was saying to Alfie, she were, that she thought he'd gone and done the right thing. Inside she were churning, she says to me – but he seemed so dead set on it, she couldn't stand to see him put down. So she goes and tells him she's behind him. And I can't tell you how bleeding stupid I thought that were; told her, though. You say to him he being a mug, and he might listen to you, girl. Because you love him, don't you? And she says to me she do. Well then – we got to unite on this one, stand firm. See? Tell him what you really think about it – have a good go at him. She will, she says. I will, she's going – because I couldn't stand to lose him. Yeh well, I says – telling him it were a real keen idea to go and join the bloody army – pretty good way of losing him, weren't it? Seems to me. And she gets all weepy on me then (her heart's in the right place, I reckon – it's just that maybe she ain't too bright, our Jeanie) and she promise me she going to tell him. Have it out, like. So that's why I'm going round now – find out how it gone.

'Oh goodness it's you, Jackie,' Jeanie sighed quite resignedly, as she opened the front door a little wider. 'I'm getting the full complement this afternoon, aren't I?'

And Jackie didn't at all know what on earth she was on about, so he sort of half-smiled at her as he eased his way into the hall (because she still hadn't opened the door all the way – maybe fearful, is she, of granting access to the horde of marauders what I got at my back: she can be a bit of a funny one, Jeanie – nervy, she is. You don't want to go stirring her up).

'Oh Jackie,' said Mary, as he entered the room. 'I was just off – wasn't I, Jeanie? Just leaving, I was, when we heard the bell.'

'Blimey, Mary,' said Jackie, quite surprised. 'You never said you was coming over here. Could've run you in the motor.'

'Hadn't planned to,' said Mary simply, with a shake of her head. 'Spur-of-the-moment thing, really. I just wanted to see that

351

Jeanie was, well – all right, and everything. Expect that's why you're here too.'

'No. Well yeh, I suppose. Doing all right, are you Jeanie? Yeh – that's the style. No but look – you talk to Alfie, did you? Got him to see sense?'

Jeanie glanced over to Mary in a hopeless sort of way and sat down heavily on to the sofa, shaking her head.

'He seems adamant . . .' said Mary, softly and with regret. 'I'm sorry, Jackie – he just won't listen, apparently. But I do understand why he's doing it. I was trying to make Jeanie feel a bit better about the whole thing. Not doing too well though, am I Jeanie?'

'Oh so *what*, then?' demanded an angered Jackie. 'You're *pleased* he's gone and joined up then, are you? Happy for him to go off, are you?'

'I didn't say that, Jackie. Did I? I just said I understood *why*, that's all. Of course I don't want him to go. Don't want any of them to go. Still can't believe it's all happening . . .'

Jeanie was looking up at Jackie imploringly.

'Isn't there *anything* you can do, Jackie? I tried everything I could think of, but he just wouldn't listen to me. I told him I hated the idea – told him I didn't want him to leave me. And I don't. I really don't. I get so scared on my own. If you hadn't been here, Mary, I doubt I would've answered the door just now, you know. It's got so I'm scared of just everything. I was on the Tube last night, and I've never been so frightened in all my life. You just can't see anything, nothing at all. The blackout, it's just so total and I get so scared. And someone was touching me and I nearly screamed and when I got out at our station I didn't know any more which way I should turn and it got so that when I turned left, I didn't know if it was the right thing to do and I've lived here for more than a year. It took me over half an hour to get here from the station. Half an hour! It's only a two-minute walk. And soon I've got to put up all the blackout again and it's like I'm living in a dungeon – and the other night this awful warden, he kept shouting up at me to put a light out, but they were, they were all out except for the one in here and I was sure that the blackout was tight and I had to go out into the street to see what was happening and it was so absolutely freezing that night – and there was, there was a bit of a chink of light showing through – but only a chink, it was the tiniest thing, honestly it was, Mary—!'

'Jeanie – be calm,' hushed Mary. 'Try and be calm.'

'I am calm. I'm perfectly calm. Oh God – I'm not, am I? I don't remember what being calm is even *like*. But it was this horrid warden and he was such a bully, and when I turned back to the house I'd gone and locked the door on myself and I was only wearing a blouse and a skirt and I was freezing to death out there and he didn't care, he didn't care a bit – he was just shouting at me to get inside and cover up the light and if Mr Thomas upstairs hadn't been at home I don't know what I would've done.'

Her eyes were wild now as she looked at Jackie, and then to Mary.

'And I got back upstairs and I thought I was going to die with the cold and the gas had gone out because I'd forgotten to put in a shilling and I climbed up on to the table and pulled at these blessed curtains and then all the blackout – oh God I couldn't believe it – it all just fell down and I screamed and I fell too, I fell right off the table and I was sitting on the floor just there and I started to cry because I was just so *alone* – and that warden outside, he was going mad now and shouting and shouting and blowing on a whistle, and so I turned out the light and I just sat there on the floor, in the cold and in the dark. Stayed there all night . . .'

Mary was next to her now, and trying to console her as best she could. She looked up at Jackie quite helplessly, but all he did was roll up his eyes and glance at his watch. Mary held on to Jeanie's shoulders as she started to sob.

'I hate it, Mary . . . I just so hate it all. And it looks like I'm going to have to do war work and I can't, I don't want to. I've got a job. I just want to do my own job – why can't they just leave me alone to get on with my *own* job? And when I saw Alfie in his uniform . . . I just nearly died – it wasn't my Alfie any more, just some soldier, standing in the room. He should be wearing a lovely suit like you are, Jackie. And I think . . . you know what I think, Mary? I think that wherever they send him, he'll be a lot better off than the rest of us. It's London that's in danger. I heard they're going to drop disease bombs! Can you imagine? We'll all get these terrible diseases and die! And I got a ration card today, and I don't know how to fill it in – I don't even know what it *means*. I can't bear it, all this. I can't be alone. I just can't. And he said he loved me – he swore he did, Alfie – but how can he? How can he really love me if he left me all alone? Oh *please*, Jackie, do something. Make him stay – make him stay with me. *Please* . . . !'

Jackie shook his head curtly.

'Tried, didn't I? Offered him the lot. On a plate it was for him. Didn't want to know. Reckon there's no more any of us can do now. It's up to him. Not a kid no more, is he? So anyway listen, Jeanie – I got to be off. See a bloke. You all right are you, Mary? Run you back? Looking a bit peaky, I'd say . . .'

'Oh no – I'm fine. Honestly. I'll just stay on a bit longer, Jackie. Make us both a cup of something. Have you got any Bovril, Jeanie? Just the job, day like this. You go, Jackie. I'll see you back at home then, will I? Or will you be late again? Quite like a little chat, Jackie.'

'Couldn't rightly say, Mary love. Not planning to be late, no. But you never know, do you? What might come up.'

Well I had to say that, didn't I? Because what were coming up next were Dickie, weren't it? And I didn't know yet how he'd be.

And I were keen to be out of there, you want the truth. That Jeanie – she weren't talking about Alfie at all, were she? It were all about her being on her tod. So what I reckon, she cares for him, Alfie – oh yeh she do, plain as day, that is – but it ain't nothing like the love what she got for herself. Some people, they're like that. Could be she going a bit dippy – I'm seeing it all over from all sorts. Gawd knows what it's going to be like when this here phoney war gets to be the real bleeding thing. And did you hear her with her 'disease bombs', were it? Dear oh dear. What she reckon it'll be then? German measles? Yeh well – I'll just let her get on with it, now: she ain't no use to me. And as to this brother of mine, well – looks like he just got to learn it the hard way, don't it? Can't say I'm surprised, if I'm honest. We're all of us the same, us Robertsons is: stubborn as pigs.

So who's the next bleeding cripple on the list I got to see to? Oh yeh: Dickie. Always tried to time it, I used to, for when he's all done with his wossname . . . what they call it? Oh yeh – his surgery, that's it. But it don't never seem to end now, and it's his own bleeding fault. Too soft-hearted, Dickie is, that's the trouble with that one. Can't turn no one away, can he? I says to him the last time – Look, listen to me Dickie, I says to him: it's way an hour past when you're down to lock up shop now, ain't it? Ay? So do it, son – just shut the bleeding door, else you'll be here the rest of the night, won't you? Tending to these bleeders. Ay? Stands to reason. But nah – he ain't having none of it, old Dickie. Wouldn't be right, he says: they come to see a doctor, you can't go turning them away. Gentleman, you see: be the death of him. And now I go over and it's the same old rigmarole. I tell you this, though – don't hardly know how he can bear it, cooped up all the time in this little hole what he got. Barely more than a cupboard, it is – and painted this green like what you might sick up of a Saturday night on the toot. Piles of papers all over, bottles and jars and gadgets, and this bleeding little gas fire over there what wouldn't even heat you up a cup of tea. Ain't no wonder he's always such a bleeding misery these days, our doctor chum.

'Come on Dickie, let's be having you! You can't be healing the sick no more, you know. Time for a drink, it is.'

'Ha!' spat Dickie, quite bitterly. 'That's really quite funny, that is. Come on in, Jackie. Shut the door. How many more of them are there out there?'

'Bout a bleeding hundred.'

Dickie groaned and closed his eyes. Then he rallied a bit and tugged open the bottom drawer of his desk, pointing the neck of a bottle of Scotch in Jackie's direction, and raising an enquiring eyebrow.

'Yeh – go on then, I don't mind a nip. You into that bottle a bit, ain't you?'

Dickie nodded quite glumly as he poured a good measure into a calibrated Pyrex beaker and slid it across the desk and over to Jackie. Then he put the bottle to his lips and took down a great big pull of the stuff.

'Pretty much all day long it seems to be now, old man. Only this that keeps me going. That and a couple of these little pink pills that I've found to be fairly effective. Never really appreciated, I suppose, quite how long the hours were going to be. Don't really sleep any more – not, you know, properly, I mean to say. In a bed, and so forth. Just sort of doze in my chair, you know. Or on the couch. Drop more, old man? Don't worry – got another bottle.'

'But what – you the only doctor in London, are you? What's wrong with all these people anyway? Look healthy enough to me.'

'Mm. They are, mostly. Except for the ones that are so beyond all help, it just isn't true. Extraordinary that some of them even have the strength to get here. Decades of malnutrition, breathing in God alone knows what at all these terrible places they're forced to work in until they drop. I just give them something to ease the pain. Sleep, if they can afford to. Or maybe just to feel a little bit happy, for once in their lives. A lot of malingerers as well, of course. Well – the men, anyway. Wanting to get out of this or that. Army, largely.'

'Yeh? And what you do? What you give them?'

'Oh – clean bill of health, if I'm feeling a bit of a bastard. Otherwise a pill or two – note for a couple of days. And then they come back, of course. Can't win, really. Round and round, you know. Day in, day out. Rather wearing.'

Jackie leaned forward and poured himself a bit more whisky while Dickie – yawning profusely, his mouth like a cavern – began to fool around with the capsule of a brand-new bottle, newly spirited from somewhere. There was something in Jackie's voice when he urged him to listen very closely – something quite intense and urgent, it is, but to be completely honest with you I'm just so completely damned tired that I might have misconstrued it utterly. Still – have a slug of Scotch, hey? And do my best to listen very closely to whatever the man has to tell me.

'See, Dickie – what you maybe don't know you even got, mate, is power. Power, son. You got the power to change people's lives, you have. You said it yourself – nice little tablet, take theirselves out of theirselves, few days off work, well – power, that is. And what's more, you can do bigger things, can't you? Like say officially declare that some geezer or other's unfit for the military, sort of style. Can't you? Ay?'

'Well . . . in extreme cases I suppose I could, yes. Never really considered it . . .'

'No well now's the time you want to be considering it, Dickie old mate. Because if there's one thing what I learned from working for Mr Wisely, it's this: you provide a service what people is hankering after, then you got them queueing up, son. Like what you already have got, only it ain't doing you a bit of good, is it?

Look at you, Dickie – dead on your feet, you is. People here, they pays you in tanners, shouldn't wonder. And you, son – all you's getting is older.'

Dickie drank some Scotch and sighed.

'Yes well – nature of it, I suppose. Just the way it is.'

'Yeh but it don't have to be that way, is what I'm saying to you. You supply what the people wants, and the people – believe you me, because I seed it, I seed it happen – the people, they're willing to pay.'

'Pay, Jackie . . . ? How do you mean, old sport? Can't go charging these people – they haven't got a bean, that's the whole point.'

'You'd be surprised, Dickie. I were, when first I seed it. They say they got nothing, oh yeh they say that. But you go and dangle in front of their greedy little noses some little thing what they're really after, and hey presto mate: all of a sudden they got the money, don't they?'

'Oooh . . . I doubt that, old man. Not round here. Drop more?'

'Don't doubt – telling you, I seed it. Yeh go on – bung in another one. Blimey – look at that: three fags I gone and had, while I just been sitting here. Weren't even aware of lighting up the last couple: dear oh dear. See, what I'm saying to you, Dickie, is we all of us owe it to ourselves to get in a bit of life before one way or another, it's us for the chopper, mate. And way things are, well . . . could be any time, couldn't it? Ay? I mean it's coming, ain't it? Just a question of when.'

Dickie shuddered and stared at Jackie with baleful eyes.

'Oh God don't, Jackie. Can't think about it. Half, you know, why I work these hours. Mostly why I drink all the time. Too gone to think. Truth is, old man – I mean, sounds rather wet and so forth to come right out and say it, sort of thing . . . but you know, well – I'm *scared*, is the truth of the matter, Jackie old chum. Yes I am. Said it, now. All the time, really. Scared silly. It's rather surprised me – didn't expect it. When I volunteered for ARP – do you remember? Last year? Before war was declared, of course. Well – quite enjoyed it, bit of a lark, you know. But now, oh God – wouldn't consider it. I mean, I couldn't anyway, of course, not with all the work I have to do here, but even if I could, even if it were possible, well – wouldn't consider it. Because air raids, well – they're going to happen, aren't they? As you said, it's simply a matter of when. And I'm dreading it, Jackie – absolutely dreading it. So much so that . . . well, there's a chap called Davenport – you probably won't remember, but I ran into him that time, last Christmas, Christmas Day it was – do you remember? Around Trafalgar Square? The steak and kidney place.'

'Oh yeh. The film star.'

'Well – not, of course, but yes – that's the chap. Well do you know, he's just been commissioned. Captain in the Coldstream. Got in touch with me – asked me how I'd like to be the MO for the regiment. Thought it might be fun, he said, for us both to get together again – because at school I was his . . . oh, well, anyway. Thought it might be fun, he said. Well – abroad, tending to the wounded, not a lot of fun, in truth – but I did sort of consider it, you know, because at least then, well – I wouldn't be in London, just waiting like a sitting duck. But then I thought – oh God, all the shelling at the front, I just couldn't take it. Go to pieces. Just so scared, you see? About everything, pretty much. Shaming. What a business. Anyway – there it is, Jackie old stick. Don't ever say to anyone what I'm feeling, you know. Quite embarrassed, really. Should've kept quiet.'

'Wrong, Dickie: wrong. You want to get it out in the open – and I'm a mate, ain't I? Where you going to be, you can't talk to a mate?'

'Well that's kind of you, Jackie: very generous. But you see the point is, I may not have the choice. I mean, doctors – well, reserved occupation, obviously . . . but they're going to need them out there, aren't they? More and more. So if I'm called up . . .'

And that's when Jackie pounced: he had done with padding around the thing. Dickie's fear had opened up to him a thrilling possibility, and now he was sure he could clinch it. He stood over Dickie, and placed his palms so gently on to his shoulders. Jackie's face was compelling attention.

'If, Dickie, you is called up, well then I – and don't ask no questions, not just yet – but I, Dickie my son, can get you uncalled-up. Just like that. Well – not me personal, like – but I know a bloke what can. And that's how it's all going to work from now on, Dickie. The wheels of war, son. People is going to be trading what they got. And you want to be a part of it, Dickie. You don't want to be one of the mugs what gets left out. Well do you? Course you don't. And you, son – you have a lot to trade. You help a bloke out, bloke's going to help you back. That's how it's going to be. Believe me. Think about it, Dickie. You don't have to say nothing to me now. Just think about it. Promise me you'll do that. You will? Good lad. That's the style. You just have yourself a little bit of a think – because I swear to you, Dickie: you *can* be accommodated.'

◉

1st January 1940
I was all alone at midnight – first time I can remember. Jackie said he wasn't going to be back to see in the New Year, and he wasn't. He still isn't, and it's just gone nine in the morning, at time of writing. After what happened, I didn't expect anything else. And anyway, he's often out late now because he says there are certain parts of this cursed job of his that are best done 'after hours', is what he calls it. All very strange. It

was last New Year that Jackie started calling Jonathan Leakey Jonny Midnight, because of all the first-footing business and so on. Now it's because he's always out in the dead of night, presumably, and Jackie is sometimes with him. It's odd how things have turned out. But he seems very happy, Jackie – happier than he was a year ago, anyway, working for poor Mr Plough. I wish I was. But he's not happy at this moment, I would guess. Wherever he is.

It doesn't do, I've learned, to keep on comparing then with now. If I think back to last Christmas – not the miserable thing that I've somehow just got through, but the one before – well then it could break my heart. The party we had, and then the lights on all over London. And Jeremy, here with me. You see – I've gone all weepy now. It doesn't do. It's not that we went without at Christmas – quite the reverse. Jackie brought home things the like of which I've never seen before, but it just wasn't the same. Well how could it be? Sheila was in Sussex, I think it is (she's still there), with yet more of her evacuees. Some of them, she says, are quite verminous. In their new houses, they have to have their heads shaved and all their clothes are burnt. It makes you wonder how the poor little mites have survived this far. And Dickie was on twenty-four-hour call, so we didn't see him. They're such separate beings, just lately, Sheila and Dickie. She's always busy and elsewhere, and he's like a walking corpse, sometimes. Circumstances, I suppose. Molly is out of London with Jackie's boss, Mr Wisely. She says she sees him as a father, and that I mustn't think badly of her. I tried to ask her gently why she imagined he was being so very kind to her – because my goodness, you should see her now: like a film star. She didn't answer me, though. Not really.

I don't think I have ever experienced a winter as cold as this one. Banks of snow – a lot of buses not operating, and coal impossible to get. I feel very guilty, though, because none of this seems to affect us at all. I was filling in my ration card the other day – sugar, bacon, butter and ham are going to be very thin on the ground, they say – and Jackie told me to tear it up because I wouldn't be needing it. I asked him why and he just came out with one of these maddening and meaningless phrases that he uses habitually, now. 'Wheels within wheels' – 'Ask no questions, be told no lies'. It's as if I'm on the outside of whatever is going on. Despite the cold, though, if there is moonlight I always go out. Just to take a walk at night and actually be able to see your own feet! Not to be bumping into lampposts all the time. We never really appreciated all the light when we had it. Hardly noticed it was there. Sally in the greengrocers – still very sweet on Len, she seems to be – she says that when the moon is out, that is the most dangerous time, that that is when the bombers will come because she heard from a customer who works for the War Office, she says, that the Thames is then lit like a silver ribbon, and all the blackouts in the world can't save us. Well, the aeroplanes, they're still to come. Edinburgh has had bombs already – some bridge they were after, apparently. Jackie says that London is the safest place to be because it's the best protected. Jeanie doesn't see it like that – still quite petrified. I do worry about her. She's turned down all the war work they've offered her, but she's serving now in Marshall & Snelgrove, which seems to be all right for the time being. No news of Alfie, so we must just assume that he's safe. I was discussing war work with Jackie, and he said I wouldn't have to do any. He doesn't seem to realise that I might *want* to. Everyone else is doing something, and I've got all the time in the world now. Anyway, I've applied to be an ambulance driver. I can't drive, of course, but they teach you very quickly, the lady was saying (amazing really – women driving). Haven't told Jackie. And he keeps on bringing the most extraordinary things home – things we never had or even saw before the war – grouse and pheasant at the weekend, and the most awful blue cheese – stank to high heaven. Jackie said it was a delicacy, and I told him he was welcome to it. But still I'm busy hoarding – tinned ham and batteries and sewing thread, things like that. It makes me feel safer, somehow. It used to, anyway.

Lorna and Imogen, they want to be Land Girls. You have to be young and fit for that sort of work. After the laundry, Lorna will find it a treat. Poor little Imogen – she menstruated for the very first time this month (I think she may be younger than I was told she was) and she nearly was crazed with fear. I went over as soon as I heard and tried to calm her. She thought that she had sinned, and that she was dying.

Some of his own people tried to assassinate Hitler, but they didn't succeed. One has to wonder how 1940 would be looking if the evil man were dead. I try to forget it all, but it's so hard for all of us. Many brave faces and lots of jokes, but the strain, the suspense, it's beginning to tell. I think that maybe when the bombs do fall, people might actually even relax a little bit. Until, of course, we experience the terrible damage that they will surely inflict. How awful to be sitting in your own home, and just waiting for it to be flattened. There's talk of forming a home army of veterans and youngsters, and I just know that my Dad will want to be a part of that. I haven't seen him for a while. I gave him three tins of peaches and three of tongue (Jackie had just brought home a mountain) but he would only take just one of each no matter how hard I insisted. I do hope he's all right, because he's only got his tiny pension. How my mother is coping, I simply don't know: still no contact. The wireless helps me a lot – it helps us all. 'Big-Hearted Arthur' on Bandwagon. Tommy Handley. It's so amazing when you hear yourself laughing. I'll need it more and more.

So – 1940, then. And the main reason I dread it, of course, has nothing to do with Hitler's bombs, and not even with the absence of Jeremy (a thing I thought I'd never write). It came to the point when I thought I just had to tell Jackie about the baby. Not the baby – I mustn't think of it as a baby. It is a condition. A state. That's how I just have to think of it, or else I might just go mad. I've been much less sick lately – I might even be feeling on top of the world, if everything else weren't just so dreadful. The main reason I hadn't told him before is that if all this – if evacuation were still going to be in place next summer – if the threat becomes real, in other words – then I would have to go. As well. And I knew he wouldn't have it, not my Jackie. And then I thought I just can't keep it a secret any longer – and last night, before he went out, he was becoming quite amorous (it was the whisky, as usual now) and I thought I'd tell him then. The next bit I've got to write quickly, or I won't get through it. I told him. His face said nothing to me. He asked me when it was due, and I told him that as well. Then silence. Got very nervous. Then he said no, that's not possible. How can I write this? He remains convinced that we were not intimate at that time. I said that of course we were and he had been drunk and didn't remember. He said no, it was not possible. I said it *is* possible – it is a fact: those are the dates. And then he said well then it isn't mine. I cried. I screamed. I'm still crying now. Get rid of it, he said. I screamed. I cried. Get rid of it, he said. So that, now, is what I have to face. And when the bombs are falling, I just won't mind.

Sheila was idly stirring her tea while just nibbling at a biscuit rather in the manner of a mouse or hamster, is what Mary concluded after not too much thought about it – and she did ask her why, yes she did, because that was the thing about Sheila – they had now, the both of them, been through just so very much together that she honestly did think that she could ask her simply anything, so why then be reticent over the gnawing of a biscuit?

'Well it's a silly thing, Mary, and I expect it's terribly vain of me and it must look quite ridiculous, I suppose . . . and that's rather odd in itself, you know, because my vanity, well – that side of it hadn't even dawned upon me . . . but the simple truth is that if I ever eat a biscuit like a normal human being, I don't know why it is but I always end up with lipstick on my teeth. Doesn't happen with anything else, just biscuits. Strange. And it's only me, I know that – I mean you, Mary, I've watched you. You eat them perfectly normally, and not a trace afterwards. On your teeth. Lipstick, I mean. When I'm alone, I simply don't bother. Just eat the thing. And probably two more afterwards as well. But in public, well – you don't want to be getting out your hankie, do you? And rubbing at your teeth.'

Mary smiled and shook her head.

'Well I did ask . . .' she practically sighed. 'How funny you are.'

And Sheila sat forward and seized upon that.

'Well *laugh* then, for heaven's sake! Laugh, if it's funny. God, Mary – I don't remember the last time I heard you laughing. Oh heavens – you can't let it get you down, you know. You mustn't. We're all of us in the same boat, aren't we? Hm?'

Mary sighed and slid away from her yet one more cup of lukewarm tea that she knew even as she had poured it that she would not drink.

'Now we are. Soon will be, anyway. Same boat as Europe. Now that Holland and Belgium have gone. Everybody says that France won't last too long. And then it's us, isn't it? We're next. All these people with their phoney war – they won't have to wait much longer. Will they?'

Sheila was crouching down beside Mary now, her hand in hers, as she looked up in distress at the endless tears just coursing over and down Mary's cheeks, quivering on her chin before they dropped off. And Sheila knew that although all this about Holland and so on was extremely upsetting and that the threat of, oh – heaven knew what, was creeping ever closer, that it was not the fear of encroaching war and the raining bombs that had withered her Mary, made her shrivel within herself and become so sad and sensitive a thing.

'Mary . . .' she whispered. 'It's done, isn't it? Hm? I know it was horrible. It was horrible for me too – but yes of course I know, in a very different way. But it's over, isn't it? No going back. It's done. You've got to move forward, Mary, or else it'll kill you. It's done, Mary: it's done.'

Blank-eyed, Mary nodded; she wiped her face with the flat of her fingers – a virtually reflex and now near-habitual action – as with her other hand she shuffled out a Craven A from the packet of twenty on the table before her. Sheila struck and held out a match and Mary inflected her head towards it. Drawing deeply on the cigarette, she sat back and sighed again, the brief and tight smile of intended reassurance not really even coming close to conviction, not to Sheila's eyes.

'You're right . . .' said Mary, so softly. 'You're right, of course you are: it's done.'

Yes – but the manner of its doing, it is the cruel and awful memory of this that continues to rend me asunder, even after how many months now? We were still in the grip of that terrible winter – there'd never been one colder, is what the papers were saying – and Sheila and I had had to trudge through the drifts and then the slush, all the way there. The buses weren't running, and you never see a taxi, not in those parts you don't. Sheila, she had spent how many days, poor thing, begging and beseeching me not to go through with it. During my occasional calm and more lucid moments, Sheila always seemed to be far more distressed than I was, or than I must have appeared to be, anyway, and I'm rather afraid that I shouted at her, scolded her for her lack of feeling, although I knew that even as I did it, it wasn't that at all.

'Mary, you can't – you mustn't. It's a crime. It's a sin. It's the most awful thing, Mary – and it's so terribly dangerous too, that's what I've heard. People, women can die, Mary. Oh please, in the name of God, Mary – please, I beg you: don't do this.'

Mary winced as she felt just that little kick inside of her – winced again and with a different sort of pain at the sheer sweet memory of it, before rapidly deciding that she had wholly imagined the entire silly circumstance, and that here was no more than a recurrent dyspepsia.

'I've told you, Sheila. I've told and told you, haven't I? Thousand times. It's the last thing in the world I want. I simply can't believe that I have to. But I do. You should see it, Sheila, the look in his eyes. The accusation. Anger. Sometimes something like even – disgust. It is the only way I can even hope to expunge it. The only way.'

'But Mary you're innocent! Pure! How could Jackie suspect *you* of all people of going behind his back and —! Oh, it's just so unthinkable. Let me talk to him, Mary – make him see reason.'

'I've told you this too, haven't I Sheila? If he thought anyone knew, I think he might kill me. It is not me or the problem he is thinking of. It is his honour. He feels . . . God, it's so mad . . . but he feels – besmirched, is maybe the word. Don't know. He simply will not accept the truth. But I think if I do this – carry out his instruction – he might not look at me that way any more. Be Jackie again. I have to try. Because I love him, you see . . .'

Sheila was despairing.

'But I told you, Mary – *I'll* look after the . . . I'll take it. I'd love to have it, you know I would. Take ever such good care, I would.

It's just what I've always wanted. Let me fetch you somewhere, Mary, for the duration, and—'

'Oh Sheila. We've done all this. Again and again. I'm so tired . . .'

'But just hear me out, Mary. Just one more time. I can arrange a most wonderful billet for you somewhere really really nice. Somewhere lovely in the country – or seaside, if you prefer. Would you like the seaside, Mary? Just for the length of your term. And then you can come back as if—'

'You know he won't let me go. I have to be here. For him.'

'But he must be made to *see* . . . !' Sheila screamed at Mary now – standing and quivering and tugging wildly at her hair in a new desperation. 'He's ordering you to kill his own—!'

'Don't say it! Don't, I beg you, say the word. It's more than I can bear!'

Mary now was just sobbing quite piteously – before wheeling upon Sheila and screaming right back at her:

'You talk as if I don't *know*! You think I don't *know* that this is the very worst thing I shall ever commit in the whole of my life? I *know* it's a crime, it's a sin – it's everything dreadful. And it's my body – how do you think that makes me feel, Sheila? It's my body, my mind, and my—! And yet if I don't, I'll lose him – and I have to think of Jeremy, my family, and the man I love. And I don't even know if things will ever be the same again. I don't see how they can. He's *wrong*, Jackie – I know he's wrong, and he's making me do an evil thing that I shall never get over. I shall always know, Sheila, that I am an innocent in this, and yet I must bear for ever the guilt of what he is forcing me to do. Do not once more tell me what it is I am doing, and nor must you ask me not to. I am decided. It must be done. And it must be done soon, or else I'll just – oh God, lose all reason.'

Sheila had been weeping throughout nearly the whole of this, and Mary was crying again too as the two of them lay huddled on the floor, together and adrift, rawly buffeted by so turbulent a thing.

The morning had been agreed upon a long time ago now, and Mary was up and about simply hours too early – eager to appear so bright and normal for Jackie at his breakfast (noncommittal, coldly withdrawn – quite as usual, nowadays) and then when he had left for work, dressing rapidly and staring at her reflection long and quizzically before snatching off this houndstooth jacket and then the bluebottle two-piece and starting all over again. How smart should one appear, in fact, for such a thing? Was one to affect that one had arrived for some altogether other reason? That one simply had been passing? And who, in fact, apart from Mary herself, cared exactly? The address where Sheila was taking her meant nothing at all to Mary: thank the heavens that Sheila was seeing to it all – although she had, of course, been thoroughly appalled by the route that Mary had chosen to take.

'But Mary – listen to me, Mary. Dickie will know of a proper clinic. Somewhere at least clean and well-run. They do this sort of thing in the evenings. I've heard about them. About fifty guineas usually, I'm afraid – but Jackie, he certainly doesn't seem to be short of money, these days.'

And yet once more, Mary felt she had to let Sheila down quite lightly, trying to explain to both of them, really, why what she had suggested just could not be the way.

'You see, Sheila – the rather awful part of this . . . well, it's all of it awful, of course it is . . . but it's Jackie's demeanour, that's what I'm talking about. Since he just said to me . . . oh God – get *rid* of it . . . they were his words . . . he has somehow made it plain to me – blank stares, this wilful and sort of on–off inability to hear a word I'm saying – that he wants to know nothing more. Rather in the way that . . . he expects the flat to be clean and tidy when he gets back from work, his tea on the table and so on, but does not at all wish ever to be regaled with housewifely tales of dusters and polish, nor of shopping and the peeling of vegetables. He seems to need, I think, just the certainty that while he has been else-where, some or other unpleasantness has been swiftly carried out, subject to his – decree, almost . . . and then and only then, he might just re-emerge. I really do think, then – I have to – that it will all be just as if nothing at all has happened. And so you see I can't possibly ask him for money – it would jar, or else he would choose not to hear me. And I have none, practically none of my own. I think, you know Sheila, that quite a lot of men must be like that. See that you have everything you need – clothes, food, comfort, the odd little treat . . . but they never actually give you any money. Not as such. Because that would give you a degree of control, wouldn't it? And it's that, I think, they don't terribly like.'

'But Mary . . . I don't have that sort of cash. What are we to do?'

'Find somewhere cheaper, I suppose. They must exist.'

'Oh well they do, they do – of course they do. But you couldn't possibly, Mary. You could never go to one of those. I wouldn't let you.'

Mary looked at Sheila levelly, retaining within her as well as she could the bellied wall of fear and revulsion that was threatening to split and erupt.

'No other way,' she said quite leadenly. 'And once it's over, it will hardly matter, will it? All things pass. We must just look to the end.'

And so Sheila had canvassed her colleagues in the Evacuation Unit, never ceasing to be so very amazed by the worldliness of some of them, and maybe slightly envious of their matter-of-fact attitudes, the easy breeziness with which they really quite gaily imparted such grim information.

And now the morning had come – and for Sheila, anyway, it was not before time (barely a wink she'd had, the night before) – and at her urging, Mary was swaddled inside her very heaviest coat (she had, as an afterthought, added a rose-pink tippet) and be blowed to whatever she had on underneath. It's bitter out there, Mary, Arctic, she had told her – and it's not, is it, as if we're going to tea at Whiteley's? They were both quite startled when Sheila pulled open the front door ('You're really sure now, Mary? We can always stay and think it out again . . . ?') to see a couple of apparently rather nervous-seeming young men on the doorstep – one of them, his eyebrows set into urgency, stilled in his quest to locate the doorbell.

'Ah . . .' he said – and he and his mate set to glancing back the way they had come, and then with watchful swivelled eyes, to the right and left of them. 'Mr Robertson in, is he? Jackie, we were told his name was.'

'Missed him, I'm afraid,' regretted Mary, smiling immediately and automatically polite. 'If you come back around five, you might be lucky. Six, safe side, I should think. Would you like to leave a message at all?'

The man seemed damned by the news. His back was bowed as he gave the thick tweed cap in his hands one last good wringing before ramming it back on his head and tugging down decisively at its peak.

'Five it is, then,' he said with determination. He flicked the shoulder of his partner, and with lowered eyes they turned away and darted down the nearest alley.

'Well,' said Sheila. 'Not very forthcoming, were they? What was all that about, do you suppose? They both looked as if they were wearing someone else's clothes . . . Are you all right, Mary? Ready, are you?'

Mary locked the door behind them, her face quite shocked by the smack and bite of the cold, now that she was out and quite in the grip of it.

'They come, from time to time,' said Mary idly, setting her shoulders for the ordeal to come. 'Not those two particularly, I don't mean, but men just like them, often in pairs. I mentioned it to Jackie once. He said they were soldiers who had become detached from their regiments or billets or something, and that he was going to help them become reunited. Honestly, Sheila – I don't know the half of what Jackie's engaged in, I really don't. This Mr Wisely he works for, well – it's impossible to say exactly what he does, quite frankly. Just about everything, it seems to me. We'll get a taxi, Sheila, if we see one. I've brought extra money for that.'

But they didn't see one for the entire duration of their long and frozen journey (neither had really expected to) and although they spoke very little at the outset, Mary was surprised to find that each of her senses was as sharp as a pin, her powers of instinctive observation close to overwhelming. Everything she gazed upon as they slipped and skittered on through the glazing puddles and slaps of slush, and huddled so deeply within their coats, was now springing out at her, bright and newly – her eyes felt assaulted, as if they had never before settled upon such as a lamppost, a carthorse, a little corner shop. The whole of her felt so very throbbingly alive, the intensity of her awareness serving even to blunt a cold and thin slice of dread, to shield her from the bitter inaptness of any such sensation. And they were wrong, you know – quite wrong, all of those people who kept on saying that the war so far had made no difference, how fake it was, how phoney, and that soon it would all of it be over. The differences were everywhere for all to see – if only they had the eyes for it, as Mary did, this stark and freezing morning. And they were deep etched too, the shifts, each one of the transfigurations; already they were set and stable and quite familiar, this very air of indestructibility, maybe, rendering them invisible to not just the wilfully blind, but to absolutely everyone save the persistent prober, or one who, smarmed with a need for punishment, felt compelled to be gluttonously confronted by only the very worst of it, the better equipped to shudder away from those who could brazenly luxuriate in what comforts there are left to us. But like the ravages of time upon the face of a beauty – such sunkenness and discoloration, the mean-lined shrinkage, this pall of dullness, the closing in and the shutting down – Mary knew that all about her now was wholly irreversible, the sole potential remaining being merely that of a worsening state, the impossible crumbling of so deep a foundation, and then just the glistening slide into a soupy malaise, in the thick of which one might only bravely flounder while trusting in God to keep one bobbing and hopeful while others about – some serene and others roaring – just gurgled, before they slid under.

Sheila is speaking to me, though the sheer rapidity (nervousness, of course, and the chattering of teeth) makes it sound like I imagine the rattle of a woodpecker – not, at least, intelligible. What this must be, I suppose, is keeping my spirits up, dearest Sheila, as all the while and oddly, my spirits are anyway quite determined to soar. This will not last. When we get there, where we are going, the brick inside will be remembered, and floor me. But just for now, the eyes within my so cold face feel bright and hard like sparkling diamonds and all about me seems so new, and yet just, of course, as it simply had to be. That corner shop, little shop there – so plain, and just like a thousand others then, is it? It is – they are all the same now, but each one of them has suffered a hundred changes over so long a succession of blacked-out nights when even a prying madman, up and looking for it, would still of course be blind. The unlit sign for Wills's Gold Flake, seemingly resentful and steeped in neglect, the open one-pound dummy boxes of composition chocolates, aslant on doilies, the real confection nowhere to be seen. Shutters always half drawn down over all of the windows, the quicker to secure when the siren goes up – and what glass there is visible criss-crossed into triangles with a buff-coloured tape to deflect or contain the wrath of implosion. And inside on shelves, the gaily-labelled and glass-stoppered jars of milk gums and humbugs, butterscotch, fudge and paradise fruits, aniseed balls and peppermint lumps – all with just a shadowy dusting and the few cracked fragments, all that is remaining of sweets that once were brimming. The hand-chalked sign reading 'Sorry – No Cigarettes' ever at the ready, and always the permanent request for old packets to be returned, and silver paper too. Sagging blankets of balding raffia grass are robbed of peaches and limes – more space now for earth-clodded potatoes, yellowish stunted cabbages and uncertain pyramids of hard and worm-drilled cookers. Hastily drawn up cardboard placards advertising the number of necessary coupons for whatever might remain – the only indication ever of something truly good in store, the long and determined straggle of women, two-deep and the length of the street, each of them stolid and fidgety, eyes bright with eagerness to fill their wicker baskets with whatever it might be that they have here. And yet this is now how all the shops appear, and hence each one of them is unremarkable, and therefore quite the same: no change at all.

'You haven't been listening, Mary, have you? Not to a single word.'

'I have – of course I have, Sheila.'

'Might as well be talking to myself. I don't think it's too much further now. My feet are frozen solid. The fleece in these bootees, they said it was meant for Eskimos – that's what was written on the box. Well may God help them, that's all I can say.'

Mary sighed, as she scuttled along. Her misplaced elation, if such it had been – all its stinging pinpoints were suddenly dulled.

'Everything seems so terribly drab.'

'Mm,' sniffed Sheila. 'Well it would. Now listen to me, Mary dear – unless I've managed to get us both quite ridiculously lost, it's just at the end of the next street, I'm fairly sure. Now Mary – we haven't really talked much, have we? About how this is going to be, I mean.'

'No point, is there? Talking. Just got to be done.'

'Yes I know that, Mary – I know that, of course I do. It's just that, well – I don't know what you might have heard about these people, but . . . well the thing is, Mary – yes, this is the street, we're all right: just two minutes now, Mary. But the thing is, you see, you might've heard tell of these old ladies who put you in a hot bath and give you gin and syrup of figs and cod liver oil and heaven knows what else. Well I asked around a bit, you see, and by all accounts it's perfect nonsense, all that. The bath can burn you, the gin, it just makes you tipsy, and as for the rest of it, well . . . I mean I'm no expert and I don't pretend to be, but we *know*, don't we, what those other things, what they do to you. It's well advertised. Not even treating the proper orifice, are they?'

'Oh *Sheila* . . .' hushed Mary – because even now, on the very doorstep of where she was about to undergo only God alone knew what, still she was embarrassed by any such talk.

'Well all I'm saying, Mary,' said Sheila, as she bent quite low and squinted at each in turn of the raggedy row of faded names alongside a battery of doorbells, 'all I'm saying is, I didn't think you'd care for having to go through all of this rigmarole a *second* time – because that's what happens, apparently, if you go to these terrible women. So you see . . . this, at least – it will *work*. You see? At least you know it will *work* . . .'

And only now, and for the very first time, Mary was profoundly frightened. Sheila, catching the stab of her expression, hugged her arm tightly and hoped so much that her brave and encouraging smile would in Mary's eyes anyway serve at least to detract from the flowing eruption of pent-up tears that now she could no longer control. The door then opened – just a few inches, but the vista of ochre and grimy passageway receding into an umbrous distance seemed even more cold than the air outside. Sheila was mumbling some noises and maybe names to an extraordinarily small and hunched-over woman, who then opened the door wider and bade them come in. The hall, as Mary had divined, was so very wintry and hard and overhung by a pall of boiling – clothes or potatoes – though none of its attendant heat. She could then so easily have turned and bolted – but instead, she doggedly followed an equally reluctant Sheila, and now they were climbing the bare-boarded staircase, and to Mary's ears each one of their steps on every sprung and hollow tread was resounding like thunder. On the very top floor of this tall and once, it must have been, Mary idly supposed, really rather a grand and stuccoed terraced house, the waft of damp and maybe worse was quite suddenly overpowering, and just before Sheila, at the behest of the shrunken little woman, bustled her in to a cramped and stuffy room, Mary caught sight of a blossoming of fungus clustered in malignant clouds around the dark brown wainscot. The room was small and made oppressive by both the gloom and quantity of overscaled furniture and ornament from some draped-over and long-ago time, the bulk and mass of it not so much arranged as somehow wedged in and abutted. No fewer than three great and bulbous two-tiered sideboards, each as black, thought Mary, as an unforgiven sin, heavily carved and looking more like ancestral coffins, newly disinterred. A gate-legged table with two square musty cloths aslant and overlaid as a pair of intersecting diamonds, one a green velour, faded at the rim into spectre grey, the other a slate and reddish tapestry depicting something rural, its border made to drag unevenly by the trimming of a good many soft and dusted-over bobbles, at apparently random intervals. The room was poorly lit by a pair of gas mantles, their hissing so clear – and while these could hardly account for the swaddling heat, they were maybe responsible for some of the giddiness Mary now was feeling. She sat down uneasily on a straight-backed dining chair, and did no more than look down at her intertwined fingers. Before Sheila could even launch into her bolstering prattle – the first sort of nonsense that might have sprung to her lips – the door then swung open again, and into the room there ambled a woman who quite took her breath away – and look: even Mary, she too just appeared to be gazing in wonder. Even had she sauntered on to so shabby a scene duly recreated in a Hollywood picture, still it might have seemed a little overdone – for here among them now in the low-lit dinginess was Rita Hayworth – or no, Mary quickly reconsidered: more Bette Davis, this one is (something to do with the deliberate swagger, her practised and general disdain for anyone around her – while still not yet appearing to even have registered the presence of either Mary or Sheila). She hitched her skirt and easily perched upon the corner of the ugly table, carelessly crossing her legs – and Sheila, right there and at that very moment, would happily have bartered all she possessed for just those sheer silk stockings and perfect and peach-coloured alligator shoes (for the long fur stole that cosseted the girl's throat and trailed away for seemingly yards, she simply would have lain down and died). The neat and gleaming handbag exactly matched the shoes – and from it the girl now drew out her compact and snapped it open. Her mouth formed an O as her eyelashes were lowered into a happy and frank appraisal of her circular reflection, and with a gold-cased lipstick she touched quite briefly each corner and then the cupid's bow of her exquisitely made-up mouth. Both Mary and Sheila were startled when suddenly she spoke.

'First time for you is it, dearie?'

Mary, speechless, opened her mouth.

'Mm,' concluded the girl, dropping back the compact into her bag, and snibbing it shut. 'Thought as much. Well – nothing to it, really.'

Mary tried a smile, and simply nodded. She had expected either an American drawl or else the quick clipped chirrup of a debutante; the girl, though, had utterly confounded the splendour of her appearance by sounding rather more like Sally in the greengrocers. Any further reflection on Mary's part was immediately and quite shockingly curtailed by the screaming shrillness of an electric bell that actually had Sheila starting up and whimpering. The girl had now lit a cigarette, making Mary want one. Her lemon-gloved hand held it in a holder.

'That'll be you, dearie,' she said, quite kindly. 'Don't worry, ay? Over in two shakes.'

A door in the corner had opened a crack, and Mary rose, hugging her coat about her – with the impatient batting of a hand forbidding Sheila to even so much as think of following her. As she opened wide the door, stepped into another room, and then quite softly closed it behind her, all Mary could wonder was how she had failed to remember to light up and smoke at least ten Craven A, in very rapid succession – for then she might feel calmer? The room was dark – thick and seemingly immutable blackout board obliterating the window, with just one cream and elbowed lamp, its glaring cowl directed on to what seemed for all the world to be a very large tea trolley, draped in a wrinkled sheet. Mary's throat was dry with fear as she peered about her, her body made up of a thousand pulses, each one thudding out its message of alarm. The silence was total – and just at the second when Mary had decided that she must now turn and immediately recapture the safety of Sheila and even the miserable light and stultifying heat of the hideous room behind her, so did yet another door briefly open and shut, and then she was no longer alone. The voice that now told her to remove her lower garments, if she would be so good, and to lie upon the trolley – it just stopped her heart within her. She had not been expecting a man: had not even considered the possibility. She closed her eyes and gnawed at her lower lip, vowing to say nothing throughout. There was no screen to hide behind, so far as she could see, and so closing her eyes once more – and really tightly, so as to distort her whole face – she complied with the man's wishes, and clutching about her just a brand-new slip, she clambered up on to the trolley and lay there. She saw just red through her clamped-shut eyelids and felt on her face the warmth from the lamp. He must then, she hoped, have washed his hands in the other room, must he? For she heard no gurgle from any tap in here – and now there was the shock of a fleshy hand, laid flat across her stomach. His voice, when he spoke again, was furrily persuasive and yet thoroughly detached from any sort of caring. He cantered through all of his practised phrases as easily and unthinkingly as a bus conductor – room for just one inside (haven't you got anything smaller?).

'Now I'm going to give you an injection. Won't hurt much. Won't help much either, I'm afraid, but still, it's something. Had a few drinks, have you? Beforehand? No? Pity. Some girls do. No matter. Now what I do then, that *will* hurt, of course – sorry, but there's nothing to be done. Grin and bear it, ay? Jolly good. You've brought the money, have you? Ah yes. Good good. Count it later. Right then – well we haven't got all day, have we? Might as well get cracking.'

The needle was not too disturbing, but still as a reflex Mary very nearly opened her eyes – but she addressed herself very sternly on the matter, insisting that she would, of course, get through all this, of course she would, but maybe only if she carried away with her no visual evidence of its ever having occurred. Her hands lay flat at her sides, and she thought she might use them somehow, by way of distraction. She set to flexing her fingers as if she were typing, notching up another character with each of the glancing descents, and concentrating hard upon recalling all the vagaries of the QWERTY keyboard from when she sometimes did the invoices in the office at the laundry. And there are two hands now that bend up her knees, and then they are pulling them apart.

The pain, when it came, was just sudden and searing, so white-hot and shocking that Mary screamed her terrible amazement from so very deep inside her and her eyes were wide and scoping the disjointedly jagged angles of the room as her head was rocking from side to side. A hand now, clamping down over her mouth as the pain became denser, more blunt and congested, before thin and icy shards of a hard pale agony pierced through all of that, and she tried now to fight her way upwards, out from under the strength of this arm that was tight and heavy across her chest – her voice just hoarse and weak as she gasped in her desperation to shriek out over all of the man's staccato instructions for her to lay still right now and stop being so very bloody *stupid*. And then, suspended on a plateau of dizziness and near delirium, she felt as if all her insides had suddenly departed, as if in essence she could no longer be existing – and then the cutting of a more invasive pain and her wild and whipping head and face were grimy and awash with sweat and tears as she fought down her screams and gulped in some air to save her from smothering. And then she was just left, so wet and stranded, the weight of her washed up on to an abandoned beach, her weighted limbs floundering for a grip of any sort and coping so badly with a deep and throbbing ache that numbed and speared her and now was as big as she was, and spreading even further, filling up the room. Then the swivel of her eyes was brought down into focus and she saw the man's face, and he was smiling. The glass in his spectacles seemed perfectly clear – two bright, round and sparkling frames for the easy insolence of his eyes beyond them. His recent exertions had caused a heavy hank of thin and dead hair to peel itself away from the brilliantine slick across the shine of his skull, and lollop down lankly over one of his ears like some threadbare and pitiful trophy from so very unworthy a hunt.

'You girls. Really. Shouldn't do it, should you? If you can't bear the price, you don't want to go committing the deed. Well there. You're all done. Put yourself together as quickly as you can, would you? People waiting, you know.'

He eased aside a galvanised pail with the toe of his boot.

Mary was weeping quietly – sobbing convulsively when she tried to sit up: the cramp of pain and then the sight of her skewed-around, sopping and blood-red slip combining to bring her to the point of unconsciousness.

'By rights,' said the man – as he licked the pad of his index finger and started to riffle through her little wad of money – 'I should be charging you extra for the sheet. But we'll let it lie, shall we? Get dressed now, will you? There's a good girl.'

Mary stood bow-legged at the centre of the room, consumed and blackened by misery, swabbing at herself with a towel that he had tossed to her, the tears still stingingly seeping and rolling down her face, although her weeping now was making no noise.

'It's the state of the nation's morals, you see,' he continued quite airily, slipping the banknotes into his trouser pocket. 'Couple of years ago, a man such as I, barely a living to be made. But now, with this war, well . . . lack of morals, you see. Despite all the talk of Empire, country's lost its pride, you ask me. And as for all you girls, well . . . never thought, have you, of just finding the one good man and sticking by him? Lot easier, I should have said. Save you all this unpleasantness. All ready now? Good good. Now you see these tablets I'm giving you? Three a day, one after each meal. Got that? I doubt they'll do you any good, but still. Can't harm, hey? And you'll need sanitary towels and so forth, first few days. Well then. All done.'

Just before Mary turned to go, she watched the man reach for a large green apple from a brimming bowlful, dig his two thumbs deep into the cleft at its stalk, and crackingly wrench it asunder: he had broken it clean in two. And through the crunched-up half of it, he spluttered out bits as his spectacles flashed white, just once in the lamplight.

'Well Happy New Year, then. Send in the next one, would you? That's right.'

Sheila was weeping as much as she had been, it looked like to Mary, as she tried her very best not to lurch or stagger as she inched her way towards her: Sheila's hankie, look – it was useless and wrung. The glamorous woman strode past Mary and into the room, casting over to her a glance which although not intended to be unkind, Mary thought, had nonetheless made her feel that on top of all the rest of it, she had still somehow managed to let the side down badly. Sheila cradled Mary's shoulders and whispered to her an unending stream of calming and incomprehensible things, as they tentatively negotiated every one of the treads on the endless downward flight. It took simply for ever, as well as two half-crowns, for Sheila to persuade that so very small and malevolent woman to telephone for a taxi, but eventually she did it – and it was only when the two of them were safe and so grateful against the chill of its plump upholstery that Sheila even ventured to speak to Mary in any way coherently.

'Oh my poor dear . . . oh look, you're all bloody, Mary. Was it quite unspeakable? I'm so very very sorry. When I heard you scream, I thought I should die. All men. They're all of them vile. The things they do.'

Mary sighed, glancing incuriously at more drab houses in other bleak streets, as they scudded by her.

'Unspeakable . . . yes. Not all men though surely, Sheila . . .'

'Well *him*, anyway. Just imagine doing it. And your Jackie. Putting you through all this . . .'

Mary knew that she didn't at all know how to respond to that, and so instead she simpered consolingly and patted Sheila's hand. The pain inside her was at once quite detached, and yet still so close to unbearable.

'At least you've got Dickie.'

Sheila sniffed and shook her head.

'Don't you be going by appearances. He's no better. Just a man, same as all of them. Doctor or no doctor.'

'Oh no, Sheila. Dickie? Surely not.'

'Oh yes, very much so. Do you remember, Mary, last Christmas? Not this awful one that's just gone by, I don't mean – but the one before? When we all of us went out, that time?'

Mary nodded sadly.

'I do. Oh heavens yes. Bliss.'

'Yes well. You remember that shiner I ended up with? Well then.'

Mary turned to look at her.

'Sheila. You don't mean—?'

'Of course I do. Who else? So besotted with him I was that I let him put it about that I'd been so very tiddly that I'd fallen out of bed, or some such rot, and clocked myself right in the eye. It had happened before when he was drunk. A lot of men hit their women, I know they do, but still it doesn't make it right. Begged me never to say. And I, like a fool, did whatever he wanted. We do that, Mary. We women. We shouldn't. But we do. And what do you end up with, for all your pains? A drunken man and a fist in your face. And it was Boxing Day too: you've got to laugh, really . . . Oh but listen to me! Here I am, wittering on about nothing at all – and here's you, poor Mary . . . oh my dear girl. It must just have been, oh – unspeakable.'

Mary nodded, and seemed very far away now from the dark inside of the shuddering taxi, its axles wheezing and moaning at each great lump or dip in the road.

'Unspeakable . . . yes. Never have I been party to such a thing . . .'

And then she revolved quite suddenly, her hands so clawingly eager to capture both of Sheila's. Her eyes were wide in their wild determination to convey to Sheila the very shock of the moment.

'He dug in both his thumbs . . .' she gasped in disbelief. 'Good and deep. And then he just wrenched it asunder . . . He broke it clean in two!'

And now, all these months later, on this bright and pretty springlike day, I suppose I can practically run to even raising a smile, you know, at just the recollection of Sheila's white and quite horror-stricken face as I said that to her. At the time, of course – drugged and in pain and utterly bound up as I was in so many other things, it did not so much as even cross my mind as to what on earth the poor dear could be imagining. But I cannot smile at any of the rest of it. There is no woman alive who should be made to suffer in the way I did – and even then to be lectured by so parasitic a butcher. And therefore I have decided: I am to rally round. I am to pull myself together. I am to do good in this war. Not by driving an ambulance, no, and nor by orchestrating any paper drives or the collection of jam jars or aluminium pots. No, my ambition now is grander. I am going to ease the lot of the afflicted woman: I am going to save her.

☉

'Truth is, son,' Jackie was confiding in the frightened young man standing beside him at the bar, and who was forever glancing back to the door he had recently slid through, 'it all depends on what you got. Like so much else, ay Jonny? First we discuss the price, and then we can do you the service. Like a shop, really. Much the same idea.'

Jonathan Leakey lit a cigarette, and offered the pack. 'Yeh,' he said. 'Like a shop, it is.'

'I'll stick with my Turkish, ta Jonny,' said Jackie, slipping out his cigarette case. 'Here, son – what's your name again? Try one of these. Prime, they is.'

'Dan . . .' whispered the man, accepting into jittery fingers a creamy oval cigarette, and inclining his head towards the lighter held out to him by Jonathan Leakey.

'New, that is, ain't it Jackie?'

'What?' checked Jackie, looking about him. 'Oh yeh – my fag case, you mean. Yeh. Nice, ay? Gold. Dunhill. Top of the range. Smart. My old one, well – weren't really the business, were it? Not no more.'

Jonathan Leakey chuckled indulgently, cocking his eyebrow and jerking a thumb in Jackie's direction.

'You want to watch this one, Danny boy. Have the shirt off your back. Jack the Lad, he is, and no mistake. Nah nah – don't look so scared now Danny – only joking. Our Jackie – straight as they come, he is. Like me – I am too. Ain't that right, Jackie? Yeh. See? He's nodding. Straight, we is. We does what we says. You pay – we deliver. Facilitators. What could be sweeter than that?'

Dan was nodding reflectively as he gulped his ale.

'Do you mind awfully if I don't actually smoke this? Terrible waste – so sorry. It's just that I find it a little bit—'

'That's all right, son. They take a bit of getting used to, I ain't denying. And there's plenty more where that come from, so don't you go fretting yourself. Here, Jonny – bung him over a Senior Service, there's a good lad. How old you, Dan? You don't mind my asking.'

'Oh – no. Not at all. Nineteen. Nearly. The thing is, Mr Robertson, I don't have that much money, and—'

'Nineteen. Criminal really, ain't it? Just out of nappies and they chucks a gun at them, tell them to go and get theirselves killed in the name of King and country. Want stringing up, them bleeding politicians does.'

'Anyway, Dan,' put in Jonathan Leakey, 'you come to the right place. You're in good hands now. Jackie'll fill you in, won't you Jackie?'

'Certainly will. See, lad – when you walks out the army without so much as a by your leave, like what you done, well – they don't take kindly, see? They're looking for you. Not just you, I don't mean – you ain't the only one, not by a very long chalk. Thousands of you out there – and who can blame you, ay? Not a mug, is you? Soon as I claps eyes on you, Dan, I thought to myself, aye aye – he's no mug, not this one ain't.'

Dan was hesitant, and then he decided to speak.

'I didn't . . . intend to walk out. Desert. Wasn't planned, or anything. It's just that . . . when they told us we were going over to France, well – I'd heard all these terrible things, you know. How it was out there. And I just said to my chum William – we were at school together, matter of fact – I just said to him, well look, I don't know about you, but I've just got to get out of this. Can't face it. And he was all for it, you know – at first he was. But then when the time came, well – he just couldn't go through with it. Can't blame him. Wished me well. Feel rather bad, really . . . Just leaving all the lads. Hope they're all right.'

'Point is,' said Jackie, clapping his shoulder, 'you're all right. Ain't you? Ay? Now, let's us have a little chat about how we're going to make sure that you *stays* all right. Yeh? Good. Now here's the options. Listen careful. Listening? Right, then. Because what you got to know, Dan, is that up or down, I *can* accommodate you. Now – top of the range is, we get your papers at the War Office mislaid. No record then, see, of you ever having joined up. Trouble is, takes a bit of time – and meanwhile, them MPs is after you, see? Also, they still got track of you in the Ministry of Labour. Another way is, we fit you up with new papers altogether. Passport, identity card, the works. Expensive, I ain't denying – but they'll never get you then, on account of you's someone else, see? But the problem with that one is, they're then going to call up this new geezer, ain't they? And then you're back where you started. So what we has to get you then is your green form – Class IV Unfit, they calls it. That's to say, a doctor says there's all sorts wrong with you, and the army, they ain't interested. Another way – and this is the one what I reckon might suit you – is the doctor says you got amnesia. Know the word, do you? It means you got no memory of walking out. Medical condition, see? Now, if you's caught, that'll get you off, bit of luck, the original charge of desertion, but then, the buggers, they're going to want you back, ain't they? So what the doc do in the meantime is, he teach you how to be an epileptic. How to throw a fit, see? Froth a bit. Thrash about. Well – discharge come like lightning, then. And they won't bother you no more. Favourite, that is.'

Dan was uncertain. 'That sounds . . . very good. I suppose. And, er – they'd be convinced, would they? By that?'

'Well – depends how good an actor you is, don't it? I reckon you'd be prime. Just you think of the alternative. Concentrates the mind, it do. But before you gets to liking it too much, I got to tell you – it do cost. The doc. Paperwork. Jonny and me. All got to be squared, see? Lot of people, lot of risk, lot of time.'

'Yes, of course. Um – how much?'

'There's cheaper ways, I ain't denying. But if it's peace of mind you're after, well . . .'

'Yes – I see that. So, um – how much exactly, then?'

'Well yeh – good question. What you reckon, Jonny? I don't know about you, but I fair took a liking to the lad. Reckon we could do him a right good price.'

Jonathan Leakey sipped his Scotch and a splash.

'Too soft-natured you is, Jackie. Be the death of all of us, giving it away, like you do.'

'Only for very special customers though, Jonny. Like our friend Dan here. I want to help you, Dan.'

'Well . . .' stuttered Dan. 'That's good. And I'm very grateful, of course I am. But um – how much, exactly, is this going to cost me?'

Jackie slammed down the palms of his hands hard on to the bar, and looked intensely into his eyes.

'For you, I'm going to do it for three hundred quid.'

Dan was shocked rigid, and his mouth just hung there.

'Three . . . *hundred* . . . ! Oh my God – look I'm terribly sorry, but I – there's no possibility. I just haven't got anything *like*—'

'Yeh well. That's a problem, that is. There's one more way – much cheaper. You may not care for it, though . . .'

'How – how much is that? What is it?'

'Well see – what it is is, you commit a crime. No listen. Little crime. Like you heaves a brick through a window, sort of style. Or nick something out of Woolworth's. Petty sort of a thing.'

'And . . . how does that . . . ?'

'Well see, you get sent down. Borstal, your case. Three months, shouldn't wonder. Then the army, they don't want you no more. Tainted goods, see? Fifty quid, I can set it all up.'

Panic and a growing despair were visible in his eyes as Dan took a further gulp of beer, and slopped a little over his chin.

'Fifty. Well I suppose I've got fifty, just about . . .'

'Yeh,' nodded Jackie. 'Trouble is, Dan – Borstal, well. Nice young feller such as yourself. Public school, if I'm any judge. Am

I right? Yeh, thought so. Not the sort you're used to, see? Rough. Then there's the birch, of course – savage, by all accounts. You might not come out the other side, you want me to put it you straight. Then you got a record, course . . .'

Dan was now openly frightened. His eyes were beseeching in turn both Jackie and Jonathan Leakey.

'Now the doctor way,' continued Jackie, thoroughly at his ease, 'you pretending to be nuts, more or less – well that one's guaranteed. No unpleasantness. Cast-iron documents. We even throws in a nice new whistle – that's a suit – pair of boots, collar and tie, smart little trilby. All set up for a brand-new life, is what you'll be then. And what's more important, son,' – and Jackie, with his eyes, compelled Dan to look at him – 'is you'll be able to *live* it.'

Jonathan Leakey, observing the trembling in the young man's hands, signalled to Len for a round of Scotches.

'You want to listen to the man, Dan,' he said. 'What's three hundred quid, ay? When it give you back your life.'

Dan was staring down at his feet, his eyes alive with calculation.

'My sister . . . she's in London. She came into a legacy when she was twenty-one . . .'

Jackie and Jonathan were covered in smiles.

'Well there you *are* then, son,' Jackie regaled him. 'End of your little problem. She'd want to help out her little brother, wouldn't she? Only natural. Don't want to see you being killed, do she?'

'No . . . no of course not . . .'

'No. And nor banged up in the clink, neither. And not pulled in for no court martial. No – not that sister of yours wouldn't. Len's got a telephone in the back room, look. Why don't you ring her? Give her a nice little surprise, ay? What's her name?'

'Hm? Oh – Lavinia. I could just give her a ring, I suppose . . .'

'Got to, haven't you? Owe it to yourself. And I tell you what I'm going to do for you, Dan – and Jonny here, he going to have my guts for this, I'm telling you – but what I'm going to do for you, Dan – because you're in a hole, I can see that, and I really want to help you out. I said, didn't I, that I were going to accommodate you? So what I'm going to do is, I'm going to do the whole caboodle for two hundred and fifty. How's about that?'

'Really . . . ?' gasped Dan, just daring to hope.

'You will,' warned Jonathan Leakey. 'You'll be the death of us all, Jackie my lad. Way you go on.'

'Told you, Jonny – took a shine to the young lad, I did. *And,*' continued Jackie, quite seamlessly, 'I'm going to throw in a second pair of boots. Then there aren't nowhere you can't go. Now be honest to me, Dan – can I say fairer? Can I?'

Dan was smiling, and shaking with relief.

'Indeed not,' he said. 'Honestly, Mr Robertson, I just can't tell you how terribly grateful I am. To both of you. For all your help.'

'Take it as read, my son. And it's Jackie – call me Jackie. Now then – clink your glass with Jonny and me. That's the style. And now you get on that blower to your Lavinia, ay? Lovely name, ain't it Jonny? Ay? Class, that is, name like that. Got pennies have you, Dan? For the telephone?'

Dan was jingling the change in his pocket as he drained his whisky, coughing just a bit, and then Len came over and ushered him into the back.

Jonathan Leakey was wagging his head in wonder.

'I got to give it to you, Jackie lad – you're a real pro, you are. Mr Wisely, he were dead right about you, and no mistake. I wish I had a film of what you just done. Masterclass, that's what that were. We ain't never got more than two hundred out of that – not once, not never. What you got is flair, son. Flair.'

Jackie smiled, and lit a Turkish.

'See the lighter, Jonny? That's Dunhill and all. Gold. But nah – it ain't flair, whatever flair is, when it's at home. What it is is art, son.' Jackie raised his glass, and winked. 'Yeh, mate – that's what it is: art.'

◉

'Oh God it's *you*, Jackie – Christ Almighty, I do really wish you wouldn't just come barging in like that,' spluttered a clearly flustered Dickie, hauling back into view now the bottle of whisky he had rushed to conceal the moment his surgery door had been flung wide open.

'Nursey out there said it'd be all right,' smiled Jackie, sitting down heavily on to a rickety chair and propping up his feet on a dented metal litter bin. 'And anyway – we got no secrets, you and me, have we Dickie? Bit early, though, for a snorter, ain't it? Even for you.'

'She's not a nurse, she's an assistant. Want a drink then, do you?'

'Well whatever she is, she ain't half bad, my way of thinking. Ever been tempted, have you? Don't reckon she'd put up too much of a struggle. Yeh, go on – I'll keep you company. Just a little one. Blimey – you do look rough, son.'

'My father telephoned me from Folkestone. Four o'clock this morning.'

Jackie laughed as he reached for the paper beaker of whisky.

'Oh dear oh me! Of all the things you could've come out with, Dickie old mate, that one I were not expecting, I got to admit.'

'Yes well. Completely out of the blue, of course. Been up ever since.'

'Drinking?'

Dickie nodded glumly. 'Oh God yes, drinking. What else? See, thing is – I feel awfully bad about letting him down. Turned him down flat, you see. I could hear how disappointed he was – although of course he didn't actually *say* anything. Never has to, the pater.'

'Um – sorry, Dickie, if I'm seeming a little bit dense this morning. But in layman's terms – what the bleeding fuck you on about?'

'Hm? Oh yes. Sorry. Haven't filled you in, have I? Well it appears there's something on. We'll hear about it on the wireless later, I should imagine. Or maybe not till tomorrow or the next day. Security, and so on. But apparently anyone with a boat – motor boat, you know – has been told to go to Folkestone. Big rescue going on. All our chaps over in France, you know. BEF. They need any boat going.'

'Yeh? What – little tiddly boats, you mean? Tugs, and that? And your old man, he got what? Luxury yacht, is it?'

'Oh no. No no. Decent little cruiser, no more than that. Six berths. Nothing grand. Used to love it when I was a lad, though.'

'Hang on – did you say BEF? British Expeditionary whatsit? My Alfie – he's in that lot. What's going on, then?'

'Well – I don't know very much. All that the pater was told was that all our boys are sort of stranded on the beaches. Jerry's moving in, and they've got to get them off pretty pronto. All hands to the pump, sort of thing.'

'Bleeding hell. I hope he's all right ... Blimey. So your pop – he's over there now then, is he?'

'Should think so. Took my uncle with him. Wanted me to go. Turned him down flat. Feel awful. Mind you,' tacked on Dickie, holding out his shivery arms, 'what good would I have been? Look at me. State of me. Shakes. That's not why I said no, though. The very thought of it just terrified me, frankly. All the way across the Channel, dead of night. No lights. Enemy aircraft. Terrifying. Oh God. Feel awful.'

'It's all the bloody Frogs' fault, this. They hadn't caved in like a bleeding pack of cards, then the bloody Jerries wouldn't be so bloody close, would they? They'll be after us now, you bet they will. And there's my stupid little kid brother caught up in it all. I would've gone. I would've gone over in a boat – save my Alfie.'

'Yes well,' said Dickie miserably. 'You're made of sterner stuff, Jackie. I never knew how much of a coward I was. Well you don't, do you? Until you're tested. Why I turned down old Davenport. Why I took your offer of exemption. Leapt at it, didn't I? I'm nothing but a coward. That's all I am.'

'No no no, Dickie. What you is is not a *mug*. You're safe at home – what's wrong with that? Ay? And you're a doctor, ain't you? You're helping people. We need you, don't we?'

'Oh God. I don't know if I'm helping anyone. God, you know – the other day, in the street . . . no. No. I can't tell you. I can't even think about it.'

'No go on, Dickie. You can tell me. Tell me anything, you can. You know that. Come on – out with it, old lad. What you done?'

'It's what I *didn't* do – that's what's haunting me. Never forgive myself. It was the other morning, Tuesday could have been. Just strolling down the road, you know. Well – just been into the Rose & Crown, matter of fact. Top up. And this chap, comes out of the stationer's and just keels over. Right in front of me. So I dashed along, of course, and he was in a hell of a state, poor blighter – gasping for breath, clutching his chest. It's his eyes I'll never forget . . .'

'So what were wrong with him? What you do?'

'Oh – murdered him, more or less. Undid his collar . . . and then my mind just blanked out on me. It's meant to all come back to you, all your training, moment like this. Well not with me. Nothing. Thought it might be a coronary, stroke maybe. Couldn't think what to do. People gathering around, you know. I sort of felt his chest a bit. Couldn't remember if I should sit him up or leave him lying there. He was clawing at me – panting, quite desperate. Someone said they'd called an ambulance. I'd just about decided to thump his chest, or something – and some other man, he'd knelt down too. To help, I suppose – I must have looked that useless. Anyway. Ambulance came, but he was dead by then. Everyone said that I'd done what I could. They were very consoling. I think if they'd known I was a doctor, they might have lynched me on the spot. Maybe some of them *did* know me . . . Don't think I recognised anyone, though. Oh God. I'm just so utterly useless. All I do here is just dish out pills. Sometimes I don't even know what the half of them are. I'm telling you, Jackie – if I had to retake my final exams, well . . . I just couldn't remember the first thing. Complete blank.'

'Hmm . . . ' went Jackie, just a little bit shaken. 'You maybe want to ease up on the Scotch a bit, Dickie.'

'No, Jackie, no. I need to give it up altogether – it's killing me. But I can't. Can't do it. Can't even get out of bed in the morning without a jolt of something. I was going to ask you to stop bringing it round, because I could never afford it, these black market prices they're charging. But I never have asked you, have I? I'd die without it – and it's killing me. Irony, that is, you know. And Susan – that's my assistant outside, her name's Susan, I don't know if you know – she's an assistant, not a nurse – I did, matter of fact, approach her one evening. Since you mention it. She looked very attractive, and I sort of . . . I don't know – put my arm around her, sort of thing. I was pretty gone at the time, I have to tell you. Made to kiss her, pretty sure.'

'Yeh? And?'

'Well and nothing. She just removed my hand and she said to me "Doctor, you're drunk". Which I was, of course. Usually am. That's the trouble, really. Sheila – she wants nothing to do with me, these days. Can't say I blame her. I've actually thought, you know – and please don't laugh, Jackie – I've actually thought of seeing a doctor.'

'Well you got to admit, Dickie – it is a little bit funny. Look – don't let none of it get you down. That bloke in the street, well – he were going to die anyway, weren't he? Weren't nothing no one could have done about that. Sheila, well – lovely girl, I ain't denying, but she's only a *woman*, ain't she? Ay? When all's said and done. Plenty of fish, mate. Pebbles on the beach. I can set you up, you fancy it. Like Windmill girls, some of them I know. And your old man on his boat, well – he'll either make it or he won't. You being there – wouldn't make no difference, would it? And you do, Dickie – you do plenty of good, you do. All these young fellers you're helping out. Saving their lives, you is. Oh yeh – while I think of it, Dickie – you got that latest batch for me, have you? Take them now, if you got them.'

Dickie nodded slowly from deep inside of wherever he had found himself so recently plunged.

'Green forms? Yes – they're there in that envelope, look. Seven, wasn't it?'

'Prime, Dickie. And there'll be a young lad coming to see you about teatime, that suits you. Dan, his name is. Nice sort of feller he is. Toff like you. Wants to be an epileptic.'

'Another one? They're going to get suspicious, you know. Bound to. The number of epileptics I've diagnosed . . .'

'No they won't. And if they does, well – we'll move on. There's always another way. Always some other way of doing things. You want the cash, do you? Or the Scotch, like usual?'

'Oh . . . might as well be the Scotch, I suppose. Money would end up the same way anyway.'

'Righto then, son. I'll drop you round a case tonight – after blackout, ay? Well – got to love you and leave you, Dickie old mate. Got a bloke to see. Then I got to find out about Alfie's mob. And listen – cheer up, ay?'

'Yes. Yes you're right. I'll try to. Cheerio then, Jackie.'

Jackie had his hand on the doorknob when Dickie very suddenly got up from his chair and lurched over towards him. He was clutching Jackie by the arm, and he stared at him imploringly.

'Oh God though, Jackie. It's the eyes. His eyes. I'll just never be able to forget them.'

As he clattered his way down the stairs and through the green and chilly waiting room jammed with people steeped in sorrow, Jackie was thinking it out: got to keep an eye on Dickie, I have. No good to me, is he, if he start fouling up on the forms. Getting careless, and that. Because I seen this before once, when I were in the building game. Can't remember the sod's name – Tommy, it could have been. Well, we all of us like a drink, I ain't denying, but this Tommy, if that were his name, well – took a hold, didn't it? Late for work. Moaning about his headaches. One day – circular saw we had going at the time – lopped his hand off, didn't he? Silly sod. Well – not a lot of call, is there? One-handed builder. Pretty much drank hisself to death after that. So yeh – have to keep an eye. One thing he said though, old Dickie, that did strike a bit of a chord. About – what did he say? Not knowing how brave you was until you was faced with a situation? Something like that. Well what I says to him about the boat – how I would've gone over, save my brother Alfie? Well I wouldn't. I just know I wouldn't. Alfie or no Alfie, there ain't nothing on earth would get me on to one of them boats. Way I reckon it, we got enough heroes as it is. And they're mugs, the lot of them. I don't know that it was, now I come to think it . . . Tommy, that geezer's name. Still a silly sod though, whatever he were called.

Harry the Stitch, that's where I's off to now. Other day, when I had a couple glasses with old Jonny Midnight, he had on him this new suit, see, what I really took a fancy to. Real dark blue, it were – first off, you'd think it were black, but then when it sort of catch the light, you see it got all of these stripes up and down it, but they're still all this real dark blue, and it got a bit of a shine to it into the bargain. Nice and sharp. So I reckon I'm going to have myself a bit of that, because I just got these shoes, genuine snakeskin – cost me a ration card and half a case of gin, but I reckon they was worth it. Beautiful workmanship. Go lovely with the stripey blue, they will. And I noticed – you got on a decent whistle with all the bits and bobs, and people, they makes way for you, look up to you – tip you the wink, sort of style, which is what I always wanted. And nowadays, well – ain't a lot of clobber about, and a lot of folk, they's looking right on the ratty side, you ask me. Ain't got the coupons, is what they'll tell you – because they don't like to let on that they don't got the money neither. But what I says is: you ain't got cash and coupons? Well *get* them, my son – you go out and get them, like what I done. Or else you go where you don't need neither – a favour here, a little drink there, a word to the wise and Bob's your uncle, you got a bit of gumption. And then after Harry the Stitch – and he's a lovely old geezer Harry is, you know. Jew-boy, of course, but he got a real nice nature, Harry has. He ain't like some of them. He ain't like that miserable old bastard Stone or Stein or whatever the miserable little bastard wanted to call hisself. Telling you – I ever run into that one again and there'll be trouble. Rue the day, he will. Miserable little bastard. Anyway – once I seen Harry, I got a little matter of rent arrears with a shopkeeper (shouldn't take too long) and then I got an appointment with the man hisself, Mr Nigel Wisely. Bung him over all of Dickie's green forms – because he like to see them before they becomes all official. 'Can't be over-diligent', is what he says, means careful, and he's dead right about that one. You always got to be sure – no loose ends. Start getting careless, and it'll be the death of you. Taught me that, he did. Very classy gentleman is Mr Wisely. But it's his brains what have made him the man he are today. And it's that what he sees in me, I know it for a fact. He knows I ain't no mug, and he respect me for it. Oh yes he do. Only one what ever has, now I come to think of it. He don't care that I never had no learning – don't make me feel like I's stupid because I don't always got my nose in a book, or something. And he asks my opinion – listens to the answer. And he knows stuff like what I can't hardly imagine. Not just stuff in books, I don't mean, but all about life, and that: what makes people tick. Like take the last time we was having a natter. Nice glass of French champagne (quite got to like it). He got his cigar, me with my Turkish. Got all the business doings out the road, and then he says to me, how's the flat Jackie? Still like it? And I says to him it's prime, Mr Wisely, tip-top (I got that off of Dickie, but it's funny, he don't never say it no more). And then Mr Wisely, he says he were only asking on account of it seems I ain't there so much lately. At home. And I says well yeh, but I got things to see to, ain't I? And he says oh yes of course – but still, Jackie, nothing troubling you at all? And I knew he meant Mary, course I did, and anyone else ups and starts picking about in my private life, well – soon going to wish he hadn't, ain't he? But with Mr Wisely, it's all different. He cares, see? And he listens to what I says. So I let him have it. Whole lot of it. Because I been bottling it up for a long time now – months, it is – and it felt right good, once I were started, to get it all out in the open. So I tells him about Mary being knocked up, and what I told her to go and do about it, and how she been funny ever since. Because women does – they gets that way. Come over all queer. So yeh – I ain't at home as much as I were.

'But you are, I hope, aware, Jackie, that I have at my disposal highly reliable people who could very efficiently and easily have cleared away your little problem?'

'Yeh. Well no – I didn't know about that side of it, to be honest with you, Mr Wisely, but yeh, I knowed you would've helped me out. But see, thing is – I don't know if I can sort of say this like how I were thinking at the time – but I didn't want nothing to do with it. I didn't want to know. It had to be her what done it. I just wanted to know it were done, and not how or when it were happening. Maybe makes no sense . . .'

'On the contrary, Jackie. I understand completely. But tell me, dear boy – your Mary's seducer. Wouldn't you like him to be found? We do have ways, you know. As a matter of fact, Jackie, I am somewhat surprised at you. I should have thought that by this time, a man of your determination, with all your resources, well . . . a question of honour, after all . . . ?'

'Yeh. I know what you mean. You mean why didn't I tear the city apart until I got him. Well there is a reason for that, Mr Wisely.'

'That being . . .'

Jackie reached over to the gleaming silver bucket, and in a very practised fashion lifted out the streaming bottle, swaddled its neck with a thick linen napkin, and refreshed his glass – Mr Wisely declining by the lifting of a finger.

'Well see . . . he don't exist. There were no bloke. My Mary, she'd never do that to me, and I know it. She's the best, she is. I never in my life met anyone so good as Mary. Tell you frankly, Mr Wisely – if I thought she crossed me, there wouldn't have been no calm and cosy little chats. She'd be in a box. No doubt about it.'

Nigel Wisely gazed at the indigo smoke from his fine cigar, as it hung in the air.

'So then, Jackie . . . forgive my appearing obtuse, but why then did you deem it necessary to terminate the pregnancy? You can afford a larger family . . . if you considered your flat to be insufficiently spacious, then I am sure we could have—'

'Nah. Nah – ain't nothing to do with money or the flat. Sorry to have butt in and that, Mr Wisely. It's just that . . . if she'd gone ahead and had the bleeding thing – pardon my wossname – well then she'd have been off, wouldn't she? Because I know her, you see. I know how my Mary gets to thinking. She'd never have a baby and stay in London – and not now, that's for certain, not now we're going to get a pounding. So she and the kid, they would've been off. Maybe join up with my Jeremy, I wouldn't put it past her. Either way, I would've been left. And I don't like it, being alone. And I know, yeh, there's other women, but they ain't my Mary, see? I loves her, is what it is. So it was for her own good, really. But . . . I don't think she see it like that. She been real quiet ever since. It ain't like it were. Bothers me, yeh. But I had to do it. You see that, don't you Mr Wisely? Else she be gone.'

Nigel Wisely nodded, his expression quite impassive.

'What a really very singular fellow you are, to be sure. Now tell me – is there anything within our power to alleviate the situation? Tempt her to rally round, as it were? I have not personally undergone the honour of having met your Mary, it is true – a pleasure not too much longer deferred, I trust – but ladies, well . . . they are generally susceptible to the finer things, in my admittedly somewhat oblique experience.'

'Mary, she's different. Anyway, I tried all that. Chocolates. New gramophone records. More silk stockings than she got the drawers for. I were down Bond Street one time – got her this little titfer with a bleeding great feather sticking out the top. Paid retail, nearly killed me. She ain't never even put it on her head.'

'Mm. Well you must keep plying her. I've no doubt at all that eventually you will break through to her. She's bound to be upset in the short term, of course she is. Only natural, after all. But you really must see to it that the quality of your home environment is properly restored, Jackie dear boy. You are a general at the forefront of my troops in the midst of our own little war, you see.

And the general must be kept happy. We will all of us require an even greater determination as the war continues. Our services will be eternally requested, of that I have no doubt, but already I am detecting – and I do not speak here solely of the authorities, but amongst the masses in general – an ever-growing sense of resentment. What used to be applauded as a money-making enterprise is now condemned as no more than profiteering, racketeering, select whichever term you find the less offensive. People will come to perceive us as at the very best a necessary evil, I am afraid. We shall not be popular. And therefore our vigilance must be utterly constant. We do not wish, do we, to be stabbed in the back? Quite so. This is why I am eager, Jackie, for you to have no distraction from the task in hand. So you will persevere, will you not dear boy? And be so good as to inform me of the outcome? Excellent. Now I must keep you from business no longer. A further glass of champagne, perhaps, before you take your leave. Oh but I was very nearly forgetting – how thoroughly remiss of me. In view of your current – and I am wholly sure, my dear boy, utterly transient – marital . . . disharmony, shall we call it, I must take the liberty of offering to you a little bit of company, the opportunity for a well-earned release from the trammels of the world. You are important to me, Jackie – do always know this. And I simply cannot bear for even an instant to see you any less than most thoroughly content. Barnstaple will conduct you.'

Jackie glanced over to the door which had silently opened, and there stood Barnstaple, unwavering and expressionless in the way he always had been, conceivably since birth, and summoned here now as if on an ethereal whim. Mr Wisely had made such an offer before, and Jackie had always declined. Initially because even the thought of such a thing, so brazenly arranged, had made him almost laugh, and later because it made him in some unspecified manner very frightened. Once or twice he had genuinely even had a bloke to see, a situation that wouldn't keep, and so could cite the interests of the business as his need to be away. On this particular afternoon, however, there was nothing that could be said to be pressing, and he couldn't, if he was honest, remember the last time when any sort of intimacy with Mary had appeared to be even the remotest possibility. So quiet, she always was: like she ain't really there. And Mr Wisely's stable of women, well, let's face it, we were after all talking, as Jackie had one time put it to Dickie, of la cream de the cream, and no bones about it.

Jackie shook Mr Wisely by the hand – trying to react not at all to the roguish raising of the man's eyebrow – and followed Barnstaple into the hall and then up the soft and thickly carpeted treads of the serpentine staircase. The corridor on the upper floor was rigidly lined with boldly cased and pedimented doorways, punctuated in the spaces in between by an ochre marble Tuscan pillar, each of them surmounted by creamy and impassive busts of not just ancient gods but classical youths, Elizabethans in ruffs and even the occasional eminent Victorian with upholstered Dundrearies, blank-eyed and immortal in their sullenness and rectitude. So silent was the single-file progress of Barnstaple and then Jackie along the sweep of the passage – the puff of the carpet serving to threaten a spring to each of their paces – that Jackie was giddied by the unsettling sensation of being just at the point of floating, and with every one of his steps now he dug in his heels, the better to anchor him down and baffle the danger of his vaulting clean away. And suddenly he was stopped, standing square outside a door, Barnstaple having been spirited away now in not even so much as a whiff of smoke. Jackie, in a little bit of a daze from maybe the champagne, and not at all aware of whatever it might be now that it seemed he was letting himself in for, firmly turned the handle and quite cautiously stepped into the room. It was just how Jackie supposed he might have imagined a bedroom in this always overwhelming house would really have to be. The walls were covered in a dusty lilac silk, densely panelled with dullish gold and rococo mouldings, the daintily ornate and occasional furniture seemingly constructed out of similar stuff, the tied-back lavishly thick and fluted drapes at the window like a softer and colonnaded rendering of the silk-clad buttresses that were flanking it. A very large bed was set into so very deep an alcove and was elaborately canopied in an identical manner, the tent of fabric gorgeously topped by a corona alive with black japanned sunbursts and a gilded fleur-de-lys. A heavy carved mantel in the French style contained a log fire scattered with pine cones that lit the oxblood marble slips, veined in coral, and next to each of the pleasingly sated and sumptuous bergère chairs, squat and bow-legged – littered at random, here and there – stood a little tiered and galleried rose-wood side table, their marquetry tops quite covered by an artful cluster of small enamel boxes, a set of crystal bells, a motley gathering of gold and silver thimbles. Jackie neither saw nor was aware of one single jot of just any of this. He could only stare at the woman there, reclining on a chaise.

'Well well well . . .' is what he said eventually. 'We meet again, ay? How our paths do cross.'

Molly sat up and quite primly adjusted the long silk hem of her gown. Her voice was just a whisper.

'Don't think badly of me, Jackie. I couldn't bear it if you do.'

Jackie sighed like a tried and patient parent as he ambled over, sprawling in a bergère chair beside her.

'What you doing here, Molly love? Ay? I mean – we all come on a bit over the last few months, I ain't denying. But blimey, Molly – thought you said you was a dancer. Well you got to admit – this is a bleeding merry dance you got for yourself here, and no mistake. Mind you – I got to give it you, you do look prime. I mean, you was always a looker, Molly, we all of us always knowed that, didn't we? Ay? But the way you got yourself up now . . . well. A-one, girl: A-one.'

And this, Jackie saw, as he openly appraised her (it's like I'm sat opposite of that Rita Hayworth, matey), did not at all seem to please her. Her brow became set as if in the grips of really quite a tussle with a teasing problem. She slid up and down the length of her finger a ring with a faceted stone the colour of meths.

'I did . . .' she said so softly – Jackie had to hunch himself forward to make out what she was on about. 'I did. Did want to be a dancer – still do. All I've ever wanted. And Mr Wisely, he said . . . well, it doesn't matter what he said. Not now. Because it isn't going to happen. All the shows are closed anyway. For the duration. Even Covent Garden.'

'Windmill,' said Jackie. 'That ain't closed.'

Molly nodded glumly. 'I know. That's what Mr Wisely said.'

'Oh yeh. I see. And what – didn't fancy it, ay? I can see it may not appeal to all and sundry. And you reckon this is a better sort of a caper then, do you?'

'I know what you're thinking, Jackie, but it's not like that. Or it hasn't been up till now, anyway. Mr Wisely, he's offered to introduce me to, oh – scores of gentlemen it must be, I suppose. But I've always resisted. And he's very nice about it, I must say. But I think his patience is wearing a little thin, now . . . I do get very well looked after, you see. Well – you can see, can't you?'

Molly looked at Jackie with a new sincerity and a need for him now to quite understand her.

'I asked for it to be you, Jackie, because . . . well, at least I know you. Does that sound mad? But you see, Jackie – I know how you feel about Mary and everything, and so I thought – I thought we could just talk, maybe. The two of us. And oh God, Jackie – you won't ever, will you? You won't ever tell Mary about . . . oh about just any little bit of this, will you? Promise me, Jackie. Swear to me you won't. I'd just die if she knew. If anyone knew.'

'One thing you got to know about me, Molly, and it's this: I don't go squealing to nobody about nothing. Not never.'

Molly lowered her eyelids, and nodded her gratitude.

'So you know the code. Is that why they call you Jack the Lad then, Jackie?'

Jackie tightened his lips into a humourless acknowledgement of that one.

'No, Molly. No, it ain't. So look – what, um . . . what you reckon you want to talk about, ay?'

'Well . . .' said Molly, more brightly, extending the palms of her hands in order to demonstrate her openness to all manner of possibility. 'Well – what have you been up to lately? How about that?'

Jackie laughed, and shook his head.

'No, Molly. I don't think so. I don't think that'll do at all, do you?'

'No,' she agreed quite miserably. 'No. I suppose not.'

Jackie was watching the swell of a tear as it oozed its way from under the lush and blackened thicket of her eyelashes. On an impulse, he moved over to her, knelt down quickly and caught it on the joint of his finger, just as it was poised upon tumbling – to roll away and down over the creamy curve of her cheek and meander on to the jammy sweetness of those red and perfect lips. Molly and Jackie were both so surprised when he leant down to kiss her. He just tasted it briefly, and then drew back an inch, his hesitant eyes searching in hers for just any sort of inkling into what was occurring. Then his mouth came back down on to hers and he held her close by a rope of her hair entwined around his hand – shocked by both the softness of her skin and the deep and giddy scent of it. His quite brutal desire was all now he was aware of – her little breathy gasps of maybe protest, could be alarm, perhaps collaboration (who quite frankly could even care?), were urging him on as his hands continued to convey to the concentrated sparkle of his red and dancing mind every single one of the sharp electric moments of silk and then her skin, the flank of warmth giving way then to a severe and plunging heat among the rising mounds and hidden clefts, all now newly revealed. His urgency then was total, and the hard and juddering thuds of his body were jolting them both. The roar he gave out was from so deep within him, and then he fell back and down on to the floor, as if he had been kicked there. All he could hear through the scarlet of his ears was the low and steady thump of his own big heart, swelling within him and then subsiding; and now very faintly the rustling of lace, the great broad swish of heavy silk – he could easily imagine her elegantly shaped and red-painted fingernails hurriedly attempting the sorry semblance of a return to decorum. Her breath was catching in her throat, but he was standing and had rammed down his shirt-tails and tugged back together the rest of his clothes by the time all the sobbing had started – he was over by the door when the wrack of her tears and then the howling made it sound as if she were being held by the arms and violently shaken, in maybe a quest for information.

'Is *that* why then, Jackie . . . ?' she blurtingly wailed to him, just as he was making to slip out quickly. 'Is that it? Why they call you Jack the Lad . . . ?!'

He turned, and then coolly regarded her. Her challenging and yet so very weakly imploring eyes were just white and accusing lights amid a mess of mascara, the smarming of lipstick high up on her cheek, an ugly half-smile. There was blood as far down as her ankles. Jackie lowered his eyes and shook his head as he turned to go.

'No, Molly. No, it ain't.'

◉

This very day she had decided, and so for tonight when he came home had made a really special effort. Because it was useless, Mary simply had now to acknowledge, continuing to wallow in her sullen grief, in all this shrunken resentment. A wrong had been done her, oh yes this was true, but since this war began, how many wrongs have there been? I am hardly alone. And now I am committed to doing some good. So I can no longer continue in the way I have been behaving lately: it is up to me to inspire some hope in others – no, better than that, to alleviate anxiety, banish pain, and restore all human dignity . . . so yes, what faith would they have in me? If they see me downtrodden, and on the brim of despair? And all of this, it must begin at home. A bright and happy home – I have been cleaning it, polishing it, all afternoon – is a positive beginning. And Jackie, despite everything, he does, you know, deserve better. Love him, after all. Don't I? So tonight I'm cooking him some of the steak he keeps on bringing home (I don't know where he gets it; I mention it to no one. Everyone around here, they're desperate for just a rasher of bacon. Mostly I simply throw it away, and the waste of it, it spears me to my heart. But what else can I do? He brings back so much of just everything, and I can't even give it away because the first thing people would want to know is how on earth I came to have it, and I simply couldn't tell them. And then word will get round, as word always does, and the last thing I want is for Jackie to get into trouble). So anyway, the steak's all prepared, the vegetables peeled, and I've just poured out a whisky for him. There are flowers – dahlias, I think they are: Sally says she doesn't know when it will be that she sees them again. And now I light a Craven A and wait for his return – and in no time there's his key in the door, but even from the way I hear him close it, and certainly as I see just the set of his shoulders as he walks into the room, I know that this evening my Jackie is in the very worst mood ever, and it will be all I can do to get through to him, to break this deadly impasse.

'Here you are, Jackie. Nice drink for you. Expect you could do with it. I'll just get your tea going, will I? Sit yourself down, then. Did you see the flowers, Jackie? Do you like them?'

Jackie slumped into his armchair, took a deep pull at the Scotch, and stared morosely at the jug of flowers. Then he looked at Mary, quite narrowly. What's all this, then? What's all this with her being little Miss Perky, all of a sudden? Great big loony smile on her, look, and more yap than I had in weeks. What's going on? Ay? What's bleeding going on? Whatever it is, I don't care, do I? Fed up with bleeding everything, I am.

'What's wrong, Jackie? What is it? Have you had a bad day?'

Have I had a bad day. Why I got to answer bloody stupid questions? Why I got to look at her bloody stupid flowers? Ay? What I'm going to do – and I wish to Christ she'd take that fucking grin off of her face – what I'm going to do is, I'm going to give her a taste of her own wossname. Bit of the old cold shoulder. She been doing it to me for long enough. What's that there on the floor . . . ? Oh – bit of glass. Must have fallen out my turn-up.

'Yeh I *have* had a bleeding bad day, since you bleeding ask,' he suddenly rasped out at her, quite surprising himself not so much by the rawness of his tone but by having spoken at all, having just decided to clam right up and let her bleeding get on with it. 'There ain't no one what can tell me what's been bleeding happening over in France. A lot of them boats, they're all back here now, but I been asking all around and they're ain't a single sod in London what can tell me how it gone. I give them all of Alfie's details – all the numbers, all the bits, and all they says is I'll be told in due course. *Yeh*, I says to the bastard. *Yeh*, I goes at him – and I'll be coming round to dot your i's, son, in due bleeding course, so you just fuck off out of it.'

'Oh Jackie – I'm sure he'll be all right. I know it's terribly worrying, not knowing and everything. But there's thousands of them, aren't there? It's bound to take time. But I just know he'll be all right, I just know he will. And you heard Mr Churchill on the wireless, didn't you? That speech he made a week or two ago. Victory at all costs, he said. Very inspiring. We'll get back at the Germans, you see if we don't.'

'Oh *yeh* – very bleeding inspiring, I have no doubt. But them *costs* – all this victory at all *costs* . . . it's my Alfie, ain't it? He's the cost. Just nothing to them, these soldiers. And that were not all he said in his bloody speech, were it? He says he's nothing to offer us except blood and guts or whatever he said, the bastard.'

'No it wasn't that, Jackie. I wrote it down. I can still remember it. What he said was, "I have nothing to offer but blood, toil, tears and sweat." That's what he said.'

'Yeh? Well I don't know about you, love, but I don't call that much of an offer, do you? I could take it or leave it, me. And if that's what he saying to us now, then Gawd help us when the Hun start coming at us across the Channel. What's he going to be offering us then, bloody Winston Churchill? Bullet in the back of the head, most likely. Anyway – I don't care about all that. Don't care about none of it. I just want to know my Alfie's back in Blighty and safe and sound. That's all I want to know.'

Yeh it is. And I don't want no more chat, neither. Because I've had it with chat. That old bastard Schmidt – he thought he could chat his way out and all, didn't he? Well I soon put him to rights. Bleeding bastard – who's he think he is? Ay? You go round his shop after the money what he owe you, and there he is, all smiles, offering you a cup of bleeding tea and expecting what, when he tell me he don't got the money? Pat on the head? Bag of bleeding sweeties?

'Look, Mr Schmidt. Money's due. I don't want no tea, and I don't want no chat. Just give me the money, yeh? And then I'm gone.'

'But Jackie, you will please let me explain the situation—'

'Ain't interested in no situation. And less of the Jackie – it's Mr Robertson to you. I don't go calling you Otto, do I?'

Mr Schmidt now shifted with unease in his chair, a roaming mote of uncertainty alive in his eye, betraying a new concern.

'Well fine, of course. Mr Robertson, if you prefer it. Although always I have called you Jackie. And Otto . . . that's not my name.'

'Don't *care*, do I? If it's your bleeding name. I'm wasting my time, stood here. Didn't come on no social call. Just give me the bloody money, what's wrong with you?'

'Listen to me, I beg you. Please, Mr Robertson – just let me say a few words. The nature of this business – imported goods. I've had no supplies. And – there has been trouble with gangs. You see that glass case? Vandals, they do this to me.'

Jackie glanced over to a mahogany-framed display case, all that was left of the glass being little gritty jagged fragments protruding at the rim.

'You should've told us,' said Jackie. 'Pay a little extra and we can make sure they don't trouble you no more.'

'These are not the usual. It's not just extortion. They – they think, because of my name, that I am a German. But I am from Vienna. Look what has become of my country! Lived in London most of my life. But they threaten to kill me. I have few goods, and now they spread bad word about my shop.'

Jackie sniffed, and he wandered over to the twin of the display case, this one intact and plentifully stocked with all sorts of brightly coloured foreign rubbish, to Jackie's eyes, that he didn't care for the look of, not one little bit.

'Listen to me, Schmidt. You maybe ain't been listening. I don't care if you're a Kraut or if you ain't. I don't care about your bleeding "goods". And you don't pay me to keep them away, then I don't care about your gang of thugs neither. Now listen – I'm going to say this, nice and slow, just one more bleeding time. Give. Me. The. *Money . . . !'*

Mr Schmidt was up now, and agitated. His big moon face was glazed with sweat as he moved quite hurriedly to the counter, and fished around behind it.

'Never before have you behaved this way . . .' he said quietly. 'Here, Mr Robertson. Money. Take it.'

'Well that's how I'm behaving now,' grunted Jackie ungraciously, snatching the notes, his fingers riffling the lightweight wad in a practised manner. As his eyes came up and levelled with those of Mr Schmidt, the big man shuddered as if he were caught in the swirl of a sudden icy blast, and he pawed at the counter as one might the arm of a compatriot, begging assistance.

Jackie's eyes now were dull with anger, and his words were spat out through the clench of his teeth.

'What the bleeding hell you take me for? I've had enough of this. There's eighteen quid here. Eighteen. You're down for thirty, son, and you bleeding well know it. Now either you give me the money, or else for the rest of your days you going to bleeding wish you had done. Up to you.'

Mr Schmidt came towards him, his eyes now dipped in supplication, his fleshy hands spread wide to express his passive and utter dependence upon any mercy that Jackie could show him.

'Next week, Jackie. I swear it. I sell something. Next week. Please. I beg of you.'

Jackie for an instant glanced away, as if arrested by a snatch of distant music, or the hailing of a fellow. Then he wheeled back round and with all the rage and confusion that this day had packed into him, he drove his boot into the glass-fronted case and he heard the anguished wailing of Mr Schmidt just faintly above the explosion of the glass, and then its splintered tinkling. And now Jackie was grinding his heel into all the scattered gew-gaws and crunching up the glass and pounding it down.

Mr Schmidt had fled across to the counter, his terrified eyes never leaving Jackie as his shivery and useless big hands continued to scrabble underneath the shelf there, and then they came up with a fan of pound notes which he rushed across the room and into Jackie's hands. Then he stood before him, head bowed, abject and panting like a flogged and broken horse. Jackie, more calmly, counted the money. And then his eye was focused upon the floor.

'You dropped one,' he said.

Mr Schmidt turned around sharply, as if alerted to danger. He scurried away and picked up the pound note from among all the shards of glass, and piously handed it over to Jackie, as if it were a sacrificial tribute. Jackie just watched him do it, his face expressing his total contempt. He then went over to the counter and lifted out the old cigar box there, scooping out the few remaining pounds.

'And I'll have this on account, as well.'

'But Jackie – please, please, I implore you. My wife. My sons. It's all the money I have left in the world . . . !'

Jackie now took him by the lapels and spoke to him hard, and right up tight into his face.

'I don't – *care*. See? Do you understand? And you ever call me Jackie again – just one more bleeding time, and that wife of yours are going to be a widow. Got it?'

And then he released the appalled and frightened man, who held his heart and shook his head repeatedly as if stunned and in pain over a recent bereavement.

'I'll be back next week,' said Jackie at the door, really rather affably now. 'And if you ain't been burned out by then, I'll want the money – less what I took on account, of course. We ain't robbers. We just take what's our due, see? And if you ain't got it, I'll close you down. Take that to mean what you want it to mean, Otto. And that's it. Chat over.'

Mr Schmidt just wrung his hands as his mouth was yammering noises. And then he whispered in wonder, as if to the vision of a ghost:

'My name . . . it is not Otto. It is Franz . . .'

Jackie now paused at the doorway and cocked his head to one side, as if he were evaluating the catchiness of some new jingle.

'Franz, ay? Nah. Nah – don't like it. I'll go on calling you Otto. Suits you better. Well, like my dear old friend Jonny Midnight would say – no offence, ay? Now be polite. Say goodbye, Mr Robertson . . .'

Mr Schmidt stared down at the ground, and was weeping softly.

'Goodbye . . .' he managed to husk out. 'Mr Robertson . . .'

And Jackie winked. 'Very nice,' he said. 'Now be good, won't you?'

Yeh well – that's how it gone. And if I'm honest with you, I felt right good just after I left him. Only time I did, all the bleeding day. Felt all full of sort of fresh air, like I were down Southend or something. Little bit of a flutter in the old tum, if you know what I'm saying. More than what I ever felt with that one Molly, anyway. She didn't ought to of done that to me – I don't know how she could. I feel right bad about it – dirty, I feel. She made me dirty. Because of all the things I done, I ain't never before gone and crossed my Mary. Not saying I ain't never been tempted – I'm only a bloke, when all's said and done. But I never. And that Molly, she wants a lesson, she do. Doing what she done. She wants a good sorting out, that one . . . Except she ain't hardly worth the bother. Ain't none of them is, tarts like that.

But by the time I got myself round the Rose & Crown, I were boiling again. And I thought, I know – if old Jonny's in here, he'll calm me down, tell me how it ain't worth the candle. Yeh, but he ain't. There's Gordon Tallyman, look (and I thought for a good long while that that were his proper name, sort of style, but it ain't, it's just what he do). And he were moaning on about his Amelia, like what he always is. Why he don't just get shot of her, I couldn't tell you. Len once, he says to me it's because he love her really, is what he says to me. Yeh? I goes. Well he got a bloody funny way of showing it – seems to want her dead, half the time. Yeh well, says Len – mind works in funny ways. And I says to him yeh, if you're a bleeding loony, maybe it do. But far as I can see it, you loves a woman or you hates her: ain't no two ways about it. Stands to reason, that do. So anyway, yeh, Gordon – he were in. Sammy Punch, oily little bleeder. Couldn't tell you what it is he reckons he into lately. Sees hisself as a Nigel Wisely, he do, and I can't tell you what a laugh that is: not fit to wipe his boots, Sammy Punch ain't. One of these days, won't be long – he'll be coming to us for a bit of help, few quid, you see if he don't. Then we'll see him in his true colours, won't we? Little nobody, that's Sammy Punch. Now Mr Prince – and he were in there and all – he's out of a different drawer. Still not nowhere close to Mr Wisely's class, of course (well who are? Let's face it), but still, he got a few things going what you got to respect. Always got these great big ruby cufflinks on him, Mr Prince has – and Jonny, he always say to me oh yeh, and if them's real rubies, then my name's bleeding Goebbels. But you don't never know, not with Mr Prince. He can come on a bit flash, I ain't denying, but still he keep his cards right up close to his chest. Careless talk costs lives – swears by that one, he do. He's down in the murky end, though. Sees to people what have got in the way, if you know what I mean. One time he says to me, Mr Prince, that although he won't never shirk from attending to business, he ain't no bully boy. 'I don't go using rusty pliers on nobody,' he says to me. And I goes oh no, Mr Prince – what, *clean* pliers, is they? We had a good old laugh over that one.

'So what you been up to then, ay Jackie? What I hear, you're Jack the Lad nowadays. That right? Maybe you want to come and work for me. Get you in a drink, will I?'

'Scotch would be nice. Nah – ta and all that, Mr Prince, but I reckon I'm all right where I am.'

And then there were this geezer banging on the bar, just as Dawny brought us over our drinks. Hoy! he were going: thought you said you didn't got no whisky: how come you serving them whisky then, if you don't got none? All that. And Dawny – she new, she is: big girl, all you need really – she look up at Mr Prince, wondering what to do, like. And Mr Prince, all smiles, he walk over to this geezer, and he has a little word. Well – you should of seed his face! Out of there like a jack rabbit, he were. So you see what I mean about Mr Prince: you got to give the man respect.

'Likes of us, Jackie – we're going to be real busy soon. Expect your Mr Wisely, he told you all that. Smart case, Jackie lad – doing well for yourself.'

Jackie briefly stroked his gold cigarette case before snapping it shut and slipping it away. He gulped his whisky.

'Not so bad. But we's always busy, we is.'

'Oh yeh I know. But you see – once the bombs come over good and proper – which are going to be right soon, you mark my words – well then the blackout, that'll be Hitler's little present to the likes of us. I mean, it been right handy already, I'm not saying it ain't, but once there's all that lark going on, well – cover a multitude, won't it? Cover a multitude. And when that siren go up, well – be like a hooter in a factory, game we're in. Be like a call to work, won't it? Here – these any good to you, are they?'

Jackie looked down at the ribboned box of chocolates that Mr Prince had whipped out of his coat.

'Got bales of them, to be honest with you, Mr Prince. But it were right nice of you to offer.'

'Yeh well. Here – I know. Our young Dawny, she'll have them – won't you Dawny, ay?'

'Ooh Mr Prince,' giggled Dawny. 'I wouldn't say no.'

'No,' cackled Mr Prince, 'I *bet* you wouldn't, and all – ay, Jackie? All right, ain't she? Our Dawny. Come on then, love – you come over here and get your chocolates. Present from your uncle, ay? Now just bend down a bit further so's we can see what you're made of, there's a good girl.'

Dawny obligingly stooped low over the bar, still giggling away as she played with the low-cut scoop of her blouse and bounced around her breasts for a bit.

'Oh ta ever so much, Mr Prince. I'm partial to a chocolate, I am. Are they soft-centred, do you know? I love a nice cream.'

'They *are*, my love,' conceded Mr Prince. 'For myself, I prefer the hard-hearted kind. Hear that, Jackie? Hard-hearted kind. Here – what's wrong with you then, Jack the Lad? You ain't all jokey like you used to be. What's up with you?'

'I couldn't tell you, Mr Prince, if I'm honest with you. Maybe it's . . . I don't know. Maybe it's just that it ain't so funny no more.'

◉

4th June 1940
Copied out another chunk of this so-called 'diary' and sent it off to Mass Observation. It strikes me that I don't actually observe very much, but it doesn't really matter as no one is ever going to read it, I do know that. Still, I like to write it, it helps me, so I may as well go on sending it in.

Everything is just so topsy-turvy at the moment. That makes it all sound as if it's a bit of a game, but it isn't at all. The really best news is that we've heard that Alfie has been confirmed as one of the soldiers who have successfully made the crossing from France. Apparently the boats had been taking them off for days before they said anything about it on the wireless, and hundreds of thousands of our boys have been rescued. No details yet about where Alfie is, exactly – they're all in camps and so on all over the coast, apparently, but Jackie says he'll find him tomorrow, and if not tomorrow then certainly by the end of the week. I cannot bear to think of the soldiers who were left there and killed. The wireless said nothing about them, but there had to be some. Len told Sally that one of his friends had taken a boat over – tiny thing, apparently, only room for two or three people – and the scenes were just terrible, with German planes dive-bombing and shooting repeatedly and no sign at all of the RAF, is what he said, though I can hardly believe that. Sheila told me that Dickie's father and uncle had gone over, and Dickie had pleaded with them to be allowed to go too, but there just wasn't the space, apparently. Well, such is the way of God, because they haven't come back yet and poor Dickie is very upset. They might be safe, of course, but that's always the trouble with this war – it's just so difficult to get any proper information. People lie awake at night and try to imagine every possibility, and in the end you just drive yourself mad with it all.

Sheila's engaged in another great wave of evacuation. All the mothers who had so far held back or brought them home again are now quite determined to get their children out of London and into safety. Jeremy is billeted quite near the coast – Norfolk, I think, but they're always so very vague – but Sheila has promised to move him somewhere very rural and inland, so that he'll be well away from all the bombers. More upheaval for the poor little man, but there it is. She had just about arranged for me to visit him, but all these plans are ruined now. Heaven knows when I'll see him again. It is awful, you know, but when first he left me, I simply could not believe that some other woman, some woman I'd never laid eyes upon, was tucking him up in bed at night with Fluffy and Golly, brushing his teeth, ironing his clothes – taking him to school, or wherever they take them when they're very young. I used to toss and turn and bite my pillow at the sheer cruel impossibility of such a robbery. But now I just calmly regard it as a situation about which I can do nothing at all. More and more people, I've noticed – there, that's an observation – are bowing to the prevailing winds. We have all maybe ranted and wept enough, and now we must deal with the reality, for however long it takes. Until victory is ours, as Mr Churchill says. Anyway, Sheila has promised to keep me informed, as far as she can. And goodness – as if she hasn't enough on her plate, she's just gone and taken in a couple of stray cats and she's called them Romeo and Vincent! Romeo, she says, because he's the nearest she'll ever come to the grand romance of her dreams, and Vincent, after her father. And Muggins here has said she'll look after them while she's away, which I don't actually mind too much. Bit of company, really. They seem very happy with the steak I feed them – I just hope they don't tell all of their friends!

Yesterday, my Dad came round. It was so lovely to see him again, because it's been quite a time. I think he mainly came over to show off his uniform – because they didn't have them at first, but now they have begun to arrive (still no guns, though). The Local Defence Volunteers is what they call them (bit of a mouthful) and after Eden made his request for men to come forward they were inundated, apparently. A million men and boys – as young as seventeen, some of them, and up to the age of my Dad, however old he is. He seemed younger, if anything, than at any time I can remember him. They meet every evening in the church hall, he told me, and although he didn't say so, I could see that he is so very pleased to be *helping*. It's important for all of us. Although he asked me why Jackie wasn't in the services, and this time all I said was I didn't know. Well I made a great fuss of him and gave him armfuls of things to take away. Cigarettes and whisky for him and his platoon, and some stockings and chocolates that he could give to my mother. He didn't want to take these, I could see, and I maybe should not have insisted. The chocolates and stockings I tripped over on the doorstep the following morning. They had been roughly wrapped in the *Daily Express* and were quite ruined by the rain in the night. I cried when I read what my mother had written on an old envelope, gummed on with paper tape to the wet and collapsing package. 'I don't take things from spivs'. Just that, and nothing else. And then I got angry and made to tear it up, but I didn't. It's one of those things that I shall keep for ever, though I can't understand why.

I've just made myself some tea and lit a Craven A – I seem to be smoking more than even Jackie does, these days – because now I am going to write about the really important thing: what *I* am doing to help in this war. I never did tell Jackie that I enrolled as an ambulance driver – he's been out so much, I think he hardly noticed anything. But much to my shame, I couldn't do it. I tried and tried – and other women were managing it perfectly well, but no matter how patient the instructors and how many times I went through it all, I simply could not learn how to drive them. It was so frustrating because it was all I had wanted to do, and I couldn't. It was clear I would never be a safe and dependable driver, and one of the older women there, Agnes, she asked me if I had ever considered nursing as an alternative. Well I hadn't, and I told her so – but then while we were talking I had to suddenly sit down, and she became concerned. I had nearly fainted which still happened quite a lot even months after that terrible man had done what he did to me. The whole of my insides seemed to be up in revolt. She coaxed it out of me, Agnes, the whole sorry story, and she said that she had heard of this before, and that no young woman should ever be put through such a thing. And so it was Agnes, I suppose, who made me go back to my idea. She said she knew a very old woman (I actually think that it's Agnes's mother, though I've never cared to ask) who knew everything there was to know, and that I should go and see her. And a bit later I did. And she is extraordinary – Florrie, she's called, in this attic room in Bethnal Green. Barely any teeth and so terribly thin, but a good and kind soul, I knew it immediately. She told me all about a woman's bits, and that was certainly an eye opener. She gave me some rather strange books to read – Romany, one of them is, which I now know means gypsy. And she taught me to brew the most evil-smelling concoctions you can imagine (although the ingredients are actually surprisingly straightforward – it isn't as if it's a witch's cauldron). Agnes says that she meets young girls almost every day, when she's doing the rounds in her ambulance, all of them desperate for assistance. So many of them didn't even know they could ever become pregnant, largely because the boy they were with had assured them that it was impossible. They are often good girls, Agnes says, whose heads have been turned by the day-to-day existence we are all of us forced to endure. They are not sinners, they are just young and frightened girls and all they need is help and reassurance. Which I know to be true. And tomorrow, I am performing my first operation.

So give him his due, Jonny Midnight, he rallies all the lads, don't he? And there they all is, up and down the south coast – been there since the crack of dawn, banging on the doors of all the army camps, driving the brass mad, they is – and I'm there too, and I do mean business, as I think by now they's all well aware. Been at it all the morning, and I'm fair done in. Some of them places, they ain't got nothing in writing – they's in a right old flap, dead on their feet the most of them, women doing the teas, bods out the War Office. We got thousands of soldiers here, is what they tells you, and most of them's without papers: it's impossible to say. And even all keyed up like what I am and thinking of my Alfie, I got to admit, my ears, they does prick up at that. No papers, ay . . . ? Well they'll be wanting them then, won't they? And not necessarily the same ones what they started out with: telling you – bleeding gold mine here, ripe for the picking. But I boot that out my brain, and I sticks to the job in hand: finding my Alfie, and getting him out. Because look, by now, what he been through, even him – even Alfie ain't so bleeding stupid as to want to be going in for no second round of it, is he? So all he got to do is say the word, and I got my little brother back. Maybe we could work together, ay? Side by side, a real little team: prime, we'd be, the both of us. And Mr Wisely, I think he'd like that, I think he'd like that a lot. Alfie, he might want a bit of persuading, I ain't denying – but if Jack the Lad in bleeding person can't go bringing him round, well then ask yourself, go on, just ask yourself: who bleeding can? Yeh – but first off, I got to find him, don't I? And it ain't going to be easy, looks of things.

I'm in . . . where am I? Can't even tell you. Started off in Folkestone – nice run down in the Riley, it were, opened her up a bit; hardly nothing on the roads – well, they ain't got the petrol, see? And that were no good – barely no one there at all. Then it's Dover, and outside of there they set up all these tents and that in a field. Huge, it is. So I goes there, and that's where they tell me they don't know who they got, and I says to them well I'll have a look then – I know my own brother's face, don't I? I'll just go and have a look, see if he's here. And that's when they starts telling me oh no, son, you can't be doing that, else we'd have all sorts down here doing the same. And I looks at him, this geezer – like a ferret, he is, shifty little bastard with his twitchy moustache – and then I looks about me, left and right like, and I says to him real slow, but look at it, mate – there *ain't* all sorts, is there? Ay? I'm the only bleeding one, so don't give me none of that. And then he get all smarmy on me, he do – telling you, asking for a shiner, he were, and any other time or place he would've got it and all – and he says to me, listen to me sir: how many men you reckon we got here? And I says to the fucker it don't matter – I'll have a butcher's at their faces, and then I'll find him. Yes sir, he come back – but how many faces you think you'll have to look at? And I were angry now – could've decked him, there and then. I don't *know*, do I? I goes. Five hundred? More? And then he do a smile like a bleeding nancy vicar, or something. We have, he says, in excess of one hundred thousand men here: you do, don't you sir, see the extent of the situation . . . ? Well blimey. I were that shook by it. Hundred thousand! And there's more, loads of them, all over southern England. He asked me why I didn't just go home, and wait in due course to be notified. I asked him why he didn't just fuck off and die and wait in due course to be eaten by maggots.

Well, this ain't turning out so easy as I hoped. Come two o'clock, I'm in a phone box and I'm ringing up Jonny. He says to me – you heard from Victor, has you? No, I says – I ain't heard from no Victor, who's bleeding Victor when he's at home? Turns out he one of Jonny's boys, ain't never met the man. Anyway, this Victor, he been looking for me. Last Jonny heard, he were in Folkestone. Yeh well, I goes – and I got to speak quick Jonny now, because I ain't got no more bleeding pennies – you tell him, next time he ring you, I'm in a boozer in Dover called the . . . what the fuck's it called . . . ? White Yacht. Got that? White Yacht, Dover. I'll stay put and he can find me, got it? Got it . . . ? Well – I hope he bleeding got it, because it cut off then, didn't it? The bleeding phone. So let's just hope he got it.

And that's where I been sitting – must be hour and a half I been stuck in this dingy bleeding hole. Paraffin lamp they got, if you can believe it. Scotch, I says. Barman, he laugh. Couple old codgers in the corner – look like they been sat there since Armistice Day – they have a laugh and all. Yeh all right, I goes – ale, then. More bleeding laughing. I'm feeling like Max Miller, I am – regular comedian. Well what *have* you got then? Meant to be a bleeding boozer, ain't it? He says to me they got cider, local cider. Right then, I says – give me your local bleeding cider and be bleeding quick about it. He give it me in a metal mug – looks like he washed his feet in it and never bothered with taking off his socks, neither: all bits in it, look. Try this on down the Rose & Crown and they'd have your guts, I am not kidding. So yeh – I been sipping this muck for got to be hour and a bleeding half now – must've got through eight or nine Turkish – and I'm thinking this is a right waste of time. What I'll do is, I'll get myself to London – see if Mr Wisely can't put the old elbow on to some bleeder in Whitehall, get a bit of a result. So I'm just up and leaving, and then the door come open and there's this big bloke here, panting like a Norse and looking about him.

'You Victor?'

He nods, catching his breath.

'Thought I'd never find the bleeding place, Jackie.'

'Well you has. So? What's up?'

'It's your Alfie, Jackie. I got him. Tent hospital, not three mile up the road.'

'Yeh? Sure? Sure it's him? Let's get going. Take my car – you can direct me. Hospital? You sure it's him, yeh? You seen him? What's wrong with him?'

'Nah, Jackie. Ain't seen him. But I see his papers right enough.

He's there all right. Wouldn't let me in to him because I weren't family, like.'

'Right, son. Good enough. We's off.'

Jackie reversed the Riley into a clanging bin, so jittery and eager was he to be out of this forecourt and away on to the road. And then he was spitting out curses as he fumbled the change of gear. He had to veer away at speed from the main street now, the wing just clipping the great tangled coils of rusting barbed wire that were strung across its width, and he cut across the corner of a field to get around it. Victor warned him to keep to the roads or else they'd get bogged down, and Jackie told him to button his lip and just tell him the bleeding direction.

The clouds were clustered low and the windscreen prickled with a grey gauze of rain, and then big droplets that rolled on down. Jackie flipped on the wipers and kept her at seventy, flinging the car late and suddenly into the bends of the road.

'You sure this is right? Thought you said it were close.'

'We got to get on to the upland, downland, whatever it is they call it. I reckon you take the next right and we'll be seeing all the tents. Can't be far.'

Jackie stared grimly at the road ahead, braking hard at the flash of the right-hand turn-off that the Riley had just roared by. He jerked the car into reverse, and heaved it into the curve.

'*There*,' said Victor, with relief and a little satisfaction. 'See it?'

Jackie took it down to thirty-five as the car set to juddering over the tussocks of an unmade road. He quickly scanned the ranks of cream and khaki tents in the green of the vale below them and made for the one with the steepest pitch that was flying the flag.

As soon as he stepped inside, Jackie knew that this whole set-up was of quite a different order to anything he had seen before. There was an air of serious calm and brisk efficiency. Orderlies were to-ing and fro-ing with set expressions, and a nurse looked up attentively from a desk piled high with thick buff folders and stapled time-sheets, as he beat away the tent flap that had been clinging to his coat.

'Good afternoon, sir. How may I help you?'

'It's my brother. You got him. Alfie, his name is. How you expect people to find this place? Stuck out here. Look – here's all his bits, his rank, his number, all of that – Robertson, see . . . ? Is he all right? What's wrong with him?'

The nurse was scanning the papers, and nodding.

'Private Alfred John Robertson, BEF. Yes, I recall. We do have him here. And you are the brother, did you say? I'm afraid I shall require verification of that, Mr Robertson.'

And Jackie didn't let fly at her – march on through, bawl at her that he wasn't wasting no more time with the oily rag, and where's the bleeding engineer? Did none of that, didn't even think it. He quietly placed his identity card on to the table and chewed on his lip as he waited.

'Right,' said the nurse. 'Well that seems to be quite in order. And you'd like to see him, I suppose?'

And still he was subdued. Didn't deride her – didn't roar into her face Oh *no*, course not nursey – don't want to *see* him, does I? I just come ninety mile from London for a little bit of a bleeding *spin*, didn't I . . . ?

'Yes,' he said. 'If that's all right.'

The nurse smiled at him brightly.

'I'm sure it will be. I'l just pop along and have a very quick word with the doctor, and then I'll see he's not sleeping or anything, your brother. You must have been very concerned. I'm sorry you found us so difficult to locate. We must be, I suppose. We did so want to inform all of the relatives but, well – as you can see . . . it's been quite a week for all of us.'

'Yes. I do see that. Course. Thank you, nurse.'

'Sister. Shan't be a jiffy.'

'But why's he in a hospital? He all right, ain't he? Not too bad?'

The Sister smiled, and touched his arm.

'Won't be a mo,' she said lightly, and she rustled away.

Jackie raised his eyebrows, curled his fingers loosely and examined his nails. And then he cleared his throat.

'All right, Jackie . . . ?'

Jackie started and spun around like a culprit.

'Didn't know you was here,' he grunted. 'Go and wait for me in the car, ay Victor? There's a good lad.'

Victor touched the brim of his hat, nodded briefly, and barged his way out of the tent. When Jackie turned back, the Sister was there, and next to her stood a willowy young doctor with sandy hair and a smeared white coat that was rather too small for him. He wore like tattered colours the battle-weary air of a man who had been through it, but still was up and game for a last and rousing hurrah.

'How do you do, Mr Robertson. Doctor Moon. So you've come to see your brother, I understand.'

'Yeh. He all right is he, doc? What's up with him?'

'He's in remarkably good spirits. Just the tent next door, as a matter of fact. Take you through, shall I? Thank you, Sister – that will be all. Just follow me, Mr Robertson, if you'll be so good. All a bit rough and ready here, I'm afraid. Rather caught unawares. Well we all were, of course. Here we are – just step in here, would you? God – this rain. All we need, isn't it really?'

It had not occurred to Jackie, so eager to reach Alfie now that at last he'd got this close to him, to even consider what else he might first encounter, as he ducked in out of the rain and under the tent flap that Doctor Moon had swept back for him. The rows of low-slung trestle beds began immediately – he had already stumbled into one as he adjusted to the gloom – and although it was cold in there, the air was heavy with age-old breath, and then the weight of fatigue.

'Had to rather pack them in, I'm afraid,' said the doctor, quietly. 'Down the other end, your brother. Follow me, would you. Compared with some of them, you know, he's got off fairly lightly.'

Jackie was dazed by the sight before him. Row upon row of these narrow and rickety cots, the jammed-in bulk of the bigger lads causing the belly of the canvas sling to graze the beaten earth below them, where the loose-laid druggets had been dragged aside. Many of the mounds beneath the grey and khaki blankets had been seemingly just dumped there by the sackful and were as still as the dead, while others were shifting – some with an almost luxurious ease as if adrift in a warm lagoon, one or two close by very much more agitatedly, struggling constantly to be out of themselves and away from all this, or else to at least lay claim to a condition whereby a bargain might be struck that would afford them a moment away from the grip of it, offer them the glimpse of escape from all they were going through. One young soldier – hardly more than a raggedy boy, he looked like to Jackie – wore a heavy gauze and padded bandage across the whole of the right side of his face, the seeping redness wet and glazed, his one blue visible eye dancing with astonishment. Jackie tried to be blind and went on following the doctor, weaving his way through the pale and crooked lane between the eternal sprawl of all these beds. Here was a soldier with days of brittle beard skimming the pouches beneath his eyes, and these were wracked and twisted and looked so sore from his perpetual weeping; he fingered a photograph as if it were Braille, and his whole big head was wagging from side to side, so wounded or bewildered by whatever force had caused him now to be so marooned, cast away from all he understood.

It was only when Jackie had shunted into the back of Doctor Moon that he realised his eyes now were both tight shut. He swallowed briefly and willed himself to open them, because he knew that this awful procession was finally over and that before him there must now be his Alfie. The doctor stood aside and Jackie just yelped with delight at the sight that was narrowly afforded by so squinting an approach, which was all he had dared. Here's Alfie, look – quite the cheeky chappie he is, sitting up in his bed, his back propped up by what could have been a couple of well-stuffed kitbags and reading the bleeding paper – quite as if he was a toff or something in a posh hotel, and waiting of a morning for his tea and kippers.

'Blimey, Jackie! What you doing here? Last person in the world. My, it's good to see you, Jackie. Come and sit down beside me, there's a good lad. Bit tight, ain't it? I'll shift up a bit. How'd you find me, Jackie? Mary all right, is she? And Jeanie? My heavens, but it's good to see you.'

'Alfie, you little bleeder. I been that worried about you, you silly little sod. What you doing in here, then? Looks like a right old skive, my eyes. Here, doc – reckon you can turf this one out, for starters. Dear oh dear – what a performance. Never seen nothing like it in all my born days.'

Jackie ruffled Alfie's hair, and was grinning so hard that it hurt his face.

'Mm. Well,' adjudged Doctor Moon, rather measuredly. 'I think a day or two longer here, certainly, and then we'll move him to a proper hospital – London you live, isn't it? If I can find a bed, God knows it's so difficult these days. And then after a few more weeks we'll soon have him fit and up on his . . . well. You know.'

The lad in the adjacent crib was rhythmically moaning.

'What you on about, doc?' hooted Jackie. 'Boy's right as rain – you only got to look at him. Ain't you, Alfie? Ay? Tell the doc. Go on – tell him.'

Alfie looked up at the doctor, and then down at his hands. His lip was quivering as he began to talk quite tentatively.

'Well – see, thing is Jackie. There's a bit of a – problem, like.'

'Problem? What sort of a problem? Whatever it is, son, we'll sort it out. Have no fear – Jackie's here. What's the problem, son? Come on – out with it. What's up, ay?'

But even through the bluster, Jackie's heart was quaking. His eyes flicked up to the doctor, who was glancing away.

'Well look,' said the doctor, coughing discreetly into his fist and clearly quite eager now to be back on the move. 'I'll just leave you two, all right? Have a little chat. Sister will find me, Mr Robertson, if there's anything you, um . . . You know – want, or anything. All right? Jolly good.'

Jackie was eyeing the retreat of Doctor Moon as he threaded his way back through all of the beds, watched him pausing here and there to touch an arm or shoulder, cock his head and crouch down low to hear a hoarsely whispered supplication – wink and nod in equal measure to the hopeful and the stunned. And then as the doctor ducked low and slipped out of the tent, Jackie now forced back his attention to Alfie, lying there. His face was set as he looked at the lad, and all he did was just slightly raise an eyebrow.

'It's my leg, Jackie . . .' Alfie barely breathed.

Jackie briefly swept his eyes over the length of the bed, and then back up to Alfie.

'Leg? What's up with your leg? Legs can be fixed. Blimey, Alfie – here I were thinking it were your guts, or something.'

'Yeh well . . .' sighed Alfie. 'See – thing is . . . now don't go getting yourself upset or nothing, Jackie, will you? Ay? Promise me. It ain't so bad really. Honest it ain't. It's just that, well – my left leg, see . . .'

Jackie was spitting with fear and impatience.

'Yeh? Well? Left leg. Yeh? Well what about your bleeding left leg? Ay?'

'Well see – it ain't there no more. Is what it is. Sorry, Jackie . . .'

Jackie was stony-faced and rigid, his splayed-out fingers shivering at his sides.

'Ain't there ... ? What you mean it ain't bleeding—! Ain't there! Of *course* it's bleeding—! What you *saying* to me, Alfie? What you bleeding *saying*?'

Alfie dropped his eyes and tightened his mouth and swept aside the blanket that had covered him.

Jackie's eyes were hard and trained on Alfie's face, as if he were staring him down – he was willing his belligerent fury into forcing the boy into concession, making him stop all of this, and right now – to look away and laugh, to break the spell. But it was Jackie's eyes now that flickered and slid with hurt into a seemingly inevitable sadness, and with a final and vain imploring glance at Alfie's stark and helpless face, Jackie abruptly switched his gaze to lower down the bed, when he breathed in sharply and both of his hands flew up to his mouth.

Alfie was weeping, the frill of his lips quite useless as they did their feeble best to cope with the rush, a welter of words.

'Ain't so bad, Jackie. Is it? Ain't so ... only below the knee, see? Ain't so bad. Is it?'

And then he clutched at Jackie's sleeve, his small wet eyes so childlike, and beseeching him.

'Tell me, Jackie! Please God Jackie tell me it ain't so bad ... !'

And then briskly, Jackie snapped right out of it, the shock and grief that had held him, for now came the call from his poor little brother, so very young a boy, maimed and just lying there – and by Christ I'm going to help him, you can fucking bet on it, make them butchers pay for this, you just see if I bloody well don't.

'Right, Alfie,' he said, gruff and tight-lipped, bending low and getting him around the shoulders, the better to hoick him up and into his arms. 'Now you listen to me, son. We're getting you out of here. All right? Now don't argue. Here's your coat, lad – just get that over you, all right? Now I got a car outside, and I'll have you back in London in no time. My word on it, Alfie. Out of this bleeding dump. Get you some proper attention, all right?'

Alfie just nodded dumbly as he half shrugged on his greatcoat, and then lay limp in Jackie's arms. As Jackie brushed past him, the moaning boy in the crib alongside reached out a weak and heavy arm, and Jackie kicked that aside as he set to staggering down the rackety line, in and around this endless littering of slumped and mad and shattered men, none of them at heart a soldier, each one of them spoiled now for not just that, but anything. Jackie banged his shin into a metal box and he gasped and lurched with the pain, but still he hung on with a grim resolve to his sweet and precious cargo – he doggedly stumped on further, keeping a determined eye upon the flap in the tent which he just rammed the two of them through and out of, blinking in the rain now and his feet drunk and giddy in the slurry of grass and bog there, his arms so close to breaking, he could feel it, and he licked and shook away the ceaseless downpour as he scanned the distance for the green of his Riley – he yearned for the kick and then hum of its motor, he needed the wheels to propel him away from this terrible evidence of a war in progress. And now he saw it – there was the car – and that man Victor, he was running towards them, the pound of his feet sending up a splattering of rain and silt to either side as he kept on coming – and now there was that bloody nurse woman, look, skittering towards them, calling out in alarm, her arms out stiffly in front of her as if to reach them, and now behind her the doctor was coming, barking out commands immediately lost in the wind and the pouring rain. Victor had got to them, Jackie near to collapsing as he shrugged the dripping deadweight of a cold and frightened Alfie into the big man's outstretched arms, and now the two of them tottered and slithered their way on up the slime of the greasy and downtrodden hillocks and towards the gleam of the Riley – and Jackie now, he had the rear door hanging open, and Victor was humping and shuffling the bulk of Alfie in and over the leather, and then Doctor Moon had Jackie by the arm and he pulled him roughly around and bellowed into his face that he simply could not *do* this and that he was endangering the patient and that the police had been called and all of that was just *enough* for Jackie, that was more than he was going to take, you bastard butcher, and so he punched out wildly at this bloody clinging doctor and that nurse woman, she was here now and yelping and tugging at the door of the car and Jackie was sliding so badly in the mud now and the sheer sopping weight of his coat and shoes was dragging him down and then through his frantic and blinking eyes as he dashed away all the running water from his face, he glimpsed to the side now a pair of MPs, their white dome helmets slick and glistening – there were truncheons in their hands and so that was really that, as far as Jackie was concerned. He hacked out at the doctor who fell down on to his knees, and screaming over to Victor to get the engine up and running he quickly checked the distance of the fast-approaching policemen and now in his hand was a slim and heavy sliver of tortoiseshell and silver, and the nurse was shrieking and the doctor backed away, his arms akimbo in a gesture of truce, for Jackie now had pressed down on the slide and an eight-inch blade flashed white in the light as he thrust it forward into the air, jabbing with menace as he backed his way towards the car, the doctor and the two MPs wary and motionless while the rain cascaded down and ran off their faces as they shouted threats and warnings as Jackie rapidly scrambled into the passenger seat and Victor had the car in roaring motion before even he could slam shut the door. The wheels were slewing to the left and dragging in the mire, but Victor continued to gun it hard and with a surge and lift that a breathless Jackie, bleeding silent tears, believed would overturn them, the car drove forwards and spun off the downland and on to the grip of the road beyond. All that could be heard as the tall and mourning trees were whipped away from either side of them was the tick-tock clunk of the wipers and the steady plop of water from the mangle of their clothes – the rasp in Victor's throat, Alfie's startled gasping, and the beat of Jackie's heart, as the car bore down on Dover.

⊙

I've been preparing it now for quite a time, Jeremy's room that he's never seen. All of his things I've put in the basement, and even that was so strange an experience. When I saw and touched the little lemon coatee that I just couldn't resist in Marshall & Snelgrove – and Jeremy, he barely had it for a season before he outgrew it completely . . . when I saw and touched it, I felt myself quite close to breaking, and yet, rather curiously, as if this would be impossible because I was already broken in two, and had been now for just ages. So what I didn't do, I suppose, what I pulled myself back from was fragmentation. We have a photograph of him wearing it, the little lemon coatee – looks just grey in the picture, as everything does – and the smile on his face would light up your heart. Goodness knows how big he's grown now. Sheila, I keep on giving her bales of new clothes to send up to him in Norfolk, I think it's Norfolk, and she begs me to stop. He could open a shop, is what she tells me. Anyway. But other things – other things of Jeremy's . . . do you know, I simply couldn't remember them at all. Is that awful? There's a set of skittles, quite new, a nigger-brown balaclava and a little toy dog, could be maybe a Scottie, though it's likely just the tartan collar that makes me think so. Well now, each one of these things I must surely at some stage have gone out and bought for him (and now, I suppose, not one such article could be had in England – unless you're Jackie, of course, or someone like him) – and yet I have no recall. Is that awful? We must at least once, Jeremy and I, have rolled the ball towards the skittles. There has to have been an occasion when I buttoned his dimpled face, tight and cosy, into the balaclava. And the Scottie, if Scottie it is, I will have grasped by its scruff and waddled it along the floor, saying woof-woof repeatedly, and urging Jeremy to copy me, or laugh, or reach out for it. And yet I can remember no such instances. I have drawn no conclusions from any of this. I don't really want to, and I anyway doubt if I'm capable.

But the room is clear now, that was the point of the whole operation. There's a paraffin heater in the corner that does not smell nearly so badly as some of them I've had in the past. The light bulb over the bed is a strong one, but the green glass shade makes it not too overpowering; still, though, I'll be well able to see what I'm doing. And on Agnes's advice – she really has been wonderful, so encouraging, I maybe would have taken fear and backed away from it, but Agnes has always been there to remind me of the good I shall be doing. And yes – on her advice, I have covered the bed with a rubber sheet. Well – it isn't strictly a sheet (they, in common with everything else, are simply not to be had, and I couldn't, could I, ask Jackie to bring me home, oh – not more steak, no more nylons, and I have my fill of chocolates, dearest . . . but if you happen to come across a heavy rubber sheet . . . ? No: I don't think so). So what I have here is more oilskin, I suppose – so not rubber, and nor a sheet: an offcut from some sort of temporary shelter, I can only imagine. Brand-new, though, and smelling powerfully, but Agnes tells me I'll soon get used to it. I've got a couple of burners for heating the concoctions, and a small array of – oh God: instruments. Very simple, most of them adapted from other things entirely, but still quite menacing, I can hardly deny. Agnes says that it is a virtual certainty that I shall never actually require them – or seldom, at least – but it is as well to have them by my side. She says I will need a great deal of hot water, though she has never explained to me why. But she's going to be here beside me for the first one – to hold my hand is what she said to me, kindly – so I daresay it will be all right. Lots of cloths . . . and some buckets with lids. Yes I know – it can make you weak to even think it, but one must simply remain quite firmly focused upon the outcome: the saving of a young girl's future, the alleviation of her predicament, the easing of pain and the maintenance, so far as such a thing in the circumstance is possible, of her dignity and pride. None of this will make it pleasant. But which of us, in this war, can be out for amusement? There is so much suffering, and all that is coming is more.

I have been sitting here, waiting, for nearly an hour, smoking endlessly my Craven A. It is not that anyone is late, it is just that I have been pent-up and prepared for so very long – I have checked and rechecked every little thing a thousand times, and so all there is to do now is wait. And still I start so violently when suddenly the doorbell rings.

'Here we are,' said Agnes brightly, tugging away from her a green chiffon scarf while shepherding in the girl beside her. 'All safe and sound. This is Mary, Jennifer – this is the lady I've been telling you about, yes? There, that's right – Mary will take your coat. That's it, that's it. There's a good girl, Jennifer.'

Mary was smiling so desperately hard, willing the girl to at least raise her head and just look at her. She seemed so terribly slight and pale, and her brow was hung defiantly low, the flop of hair across it her last and sole defence. Mary ushered the two of them inside, and closed the door behind them. She was about to ask them whether they had had any trouble at all in finding the house, was about to deplore the eternal drizzle and the lowering sky, was now on the verge of inviting them to share their views on the glory or otherwise of the Dunkirk evacuation – was even prepared to decry as a collaborator the paucity of the ration, although she was a stranger to any such thing. And she didn't.

'Tea . . . ? Would you like . . . ? Can I get you . . . ? Maybe . . . ?'

Agnes glanced at the hunched-up girl, her back against the wall. A shake of the head was just about discernible. Agnes then looked over to Mary, her eyebrows raised and her lips compressed – intending to convey to her. Mary supposed, that you could hardly really blame the poor little wretch – well could you, really?

'I think . . .' said Agnes, 'I think it might be just as well if we got down to brass tacks. Soonest broached, soonest over – yes? Come along then, Jennifer. Don't be afraid. You're in very good hands. Come along now, dear. In here, is it Mary?'

Mary nodded quickly and pushed open the door. The room, which she had earlier decided with some satisfaction looked clean and professional and not too austere, now gaped right back at her and seemed as bereft of heart as the loneliest place, and as threatening as a chasm. Jennifer flinched, but Agnes had her firmly.

'Now you just slip off your things, Jennifer. That's right. And I'll get a kettle going. There we are.'

Jennifer, resigned and yet seemingly quite horrified, did as she was told as if held by a henchman at gunpoint. Mary smoothed the white sheet that lay stretched across the oilskin and was already quite perfectly smooth. Agnes stepped over to one of the burners, struck a match and touched the gas under the very large kettle, its two great handles bound in strips of towelling, according to her direction. She sniffed the brew that was simmering alongside.

'Very good, Mary,' she said approvingly. 'Looks just right. It's hard to do it so there aren't these little bits all floating about, but apart from that it's very good. Very good indeed. Now you come over here, Jennifer, that's right – don't be afraid, no one's going to bite you. That's it. Now just hop up on to the bed, there's a good girl. There. Comfy? Now you just sip this cup, all right? It's not too bad – you can hold on to your nose, if it helps. There. Not too hot, is it? No, I didn't think so. Good. Now when you're done, you just have a little rest on the bed and then we'll see how we're all doing, all right? Yes. That's a good girl.'

And Mary was quite startled when Jennifer looked up from the earthenware cup, where she had been held in thrall by its deep brown depths, and the clear crystal blue of her eyes was both shocking, and beautiful. My God, thought Mary, she can't be more than – what? – fifteen, this pale and puny little girl before me. And then there was a hesitant flicker across those bright blue eyes, and her lips now – thin, and almost grey – were seemingly poised to speak.

'I am,' is what she said. And then she took a tentative and exploratory sip of the concoction, her mouth quickly twisting away from it.

'You must drink it all now, Jennifer,' cautioned Agnes, firmly but still very gently. 'And what do you mean, dear? "I am". What can you mean by that, hm?'

'Good girl . . .' whispered Jennifer, her blue eyes misting over into a liquid melting. 'I am.'

Mary nearly swooned with the pang of pain that speared her.

'Of *course* you are,' she rushed to assure her. 'Oh of *course* – of *course* . . .'

'Drink up, Jennifer,' Agnes urged her.

The girl, though, was still looking up at Mary, as if seeking the answer to a riddle.

'I don't know how I come to be here. Thought I were just sickening for something. Don't understand. It's Agnes here as says I fallen with child. Is that right, miss?'

Mary could no longer bear the imploring pierce nor the fright and challenge in those sapphire eyes, and she glanced over helplessly to Agnes, who was nodding energetically.

'There's no doubt there, I'm afraid dear,' she clucked away. 'But that's why we're all of us here, isn't it? Yes? To make it all right again.'

'But miss,' persisted Jennifer, full into Mary's blank and defenceless face. 'I can't see how it's right. How can I be going to have me a baby if I ain't even got myself wed?'

Mary just shook her head and willed herself to keep a steady grip now, not to cry, not to embrace this bewildered child (because then I would be useless).

'Finished your drink, dear?' asked Agnes. 'Nearly. Just one last drop – there's a good girl. That's it. Now I'll just take this cup away from you, and you have a little bit of a lie-down, that's the way, and then we'll see if you need another little cupful or not.'

The girl quite fearfully eased herself down, as if a bed of nails could be lying in wait.

'Don't think I could take no more of that . . .' she said quite faintly.

'More than likely won't need to,' Agnes reassured her, bright and brisk again, while beckoning Mary over into the corner. Mary, feeling quite honestly rather superfluous, smiled briefly at Jennifer – whose eyes had closed now as she lay back on the bed – and then hurried over to Agnes who stood now by the tightly curtained window, and hard by the burners.

'I'm worried she's so skinny,' whispered Agnes. 'You don't ever know, you see, until they get their things off. Tiny bones, you see. Tiny bones.'

Mary nodded, understanding nothing of this.

'So it's unfortunate,' Agnes continued confidingly, 'with this being your very first one, and everything. But sometimes with the very young, it all happens in no time. Or the brew, it might be needing a little bit of help. You just never know. But let's just see for now, shall we? No point, is there? Jumping the gun. You all right, dear? Look a bit peaky . . .'

Mary smiled, she hoped quite bravely, and quickly glanced over to the bed.

'Is she asleep . . . ?'

Agnes sniffed. 'Could have dozed off. That'll be the rum in it. But we'll know soon enough when it all begins to take its course, if I so may put it. Don't worry, dear. One way or another, it'll soon all be over.'

Mary performed another of her smiles, knowing it was much less brave than the one before – and then she yelped in shock at the hacked-out rasp of Jennifer's convulsion. Agnes quickly snatched up some towels and bustled over to the bed as Mary held back quite fearfully. But she did then run across when Agnes called her and Jennifer now was making more of these terrible noises, struggling to sit up as Agnes forced back her shoulders with all of her strength. Mary had forgotten, completely forgotten everything Agnes had ever told her she must do and just stood there and gaped at her beseechingly. Jennifer's face was white and astonished and her stomach was bucking quite wildly and then she shrieked and Mary heard a gurgled rumbling just before a welter of blood was expelled from the girl, seeming almost like a vast and livid bubble, molten gel for just the second before it poured in pools on to the floor, either side of the bed. Jennifer gasped and fought for breath and seemed so confused as to why all her insides should be ganging up and rebelling and refusing to remain within her, and Mary now – responding finally to Agnes's quite frantic gesturing – pressed down hard on Jennifer's belly with the pad of a towel, and the girl seemed more easy or else more exhausted, and she slumped back down on to the pillows and Agnes released her grip on her and proceeded to coo an endless series of soothing noises, as she dabbed at the sweat on her cheeks. Mary stared down at her own two hands, red to the wrists, and was aware of her shoe, sliding and sticky.

'All over . . .' whispered Agnes, to Jennifer or Mary, or even to herself. 'The worst of it, it's over.'

She peeled away the stuck-on strands of Jennifer's hair from her pale and glassy forehead, and laid a cool flannel there. And then, to Mary's very fretful amazement, Agnes calmly collected her hat and coat and handbag, and made for the door.

'What are you doing . . . ?' Mary managed to stutter out. 'Where are you going? You can't leave me . . . ! Don't go. Not now.'

Agnes turned at the door and smiled at her.

'I think it's best I do, dear. You'll have to learn to cope. Just remember everything Florrie and me's taught you. I'll pop round in the morning, see you're all right.'

Mary opened her mouth in protest, but Agnes had slipped through the door and was gone. Jennifer suddenly was stirring now, moaning gently, and Mary did her best to comfort her, stroking each of her closed and empurpled eyelids with the pad of her finger and the lightest of touches. The girl was shifting almost languorously now, as if tipsily delighted by a titillating dream. Her legs were flung wide, and it oozed out easily, dripping dark blood and lying there. And before the young girl could be fully aware, Mary knew that she had to now dispose of this thing, and so twisting her head as far over her shoulder as she could possibly force it to go, so as to be wholly sure of seeing nothing at all, she picked up a towel and groped about and felt both the slime and the tenderness through all of that and stumbled away blindly in search of a bucket. She kicked it out from under and had to put down her so very light and clammy burden in order to take off the lid, fury with herself at not having attended to all of this earlier warring amid her boiling face with what was at first little more than a simple disgust, a physical revulsion, but now was blunted and had shaded into remorse, an aching of regret that it had to be. She felt as if she herself had been the victim of a recent evisceration. When she stood and turned around, she saw the staggered path she had taken, thinly delineated across the floor by a spattered trail of blackening blood. Jennifer was sleeping . . .? Mary gasped and her throat was caught by panic, and she rushed to fumble with the girl's lank wrist and find her pulse and she couldn't find it, she couldn't find it, and then she found it and yes, yes, yes – there was a steady throbbing, it was all all right. Jennifer was sleeping.

Mary elaborately tiptoed out of the room, and as soon as she was behind the other side of the door, she breathed out heavily as even in the corridor she proceeded to peel away from her every single thing she had been wearing. In the bathroom, she shrugged on a candlewick robe and turned on the bath taps. Then she went quickly into the kitchen and crouched down low at the cupboard beneath the sink and pulled out of there one of the stiff brown paper carrier bags that Jackie kept on bringing home, brimming with steak, and she took this with her as she went back to the bathroom and dropped all of her clothes and particularly those shoes into the carrier bag, and then she knotted the string handles firmly. Of course she knew that she could not dispose of her clothing on each and every occasion, but for this time anyway, she was sure that she never wanted to see them again. Before her bath, she slipped in again to check on Jennifer, who had not stirred – but oh my God, the scarred and awful sight of the place! An abattoir scene of the crime – which, she reflected, she was now, of course, just fresh from committing. Mary yearned to wake up Jennifer, urge her to bathe so that she could get all the mess cleaned up, but she knew from Agnes that the longer the sleep the better she would eventually feel, and so she let her lie. And there couldn't, Mary believed, have been very much pain – just at the beginning, yes, but it had not been at all like the stark brutality that had been done to her. And so yes . . . I shall continue in this, my calling: so long as there is a demand, I shall only live to meet it.

Mary would have lingered longer in the bath – she had littered it heavily with lavender crystals – but she was conscious and increasingly anxious of all the work now that had to be done so that everything could be normal again for when Jackie came home. Jennifer, mercifully, was lazily waking when Mary popped back in to see her, and she helped to ease her out of the bed and asked her how she was feeling, but Jennifer didn't reply.

Mary left her in the bathroom with plenty of towels and then grimly turned her attention to swiftly and urgently swabbing down the room amid a hurtle of industry and the meaty clatter of the galvanised pans. She ground the mophead into the grille to the side of the bucket, twisting it about to rid it of its redness, and then she poured from the kettle yet another great pan of boiling water – all the mopping up being its only purpose, Mary now could see. The heat of the water and the smell of carbolic were making Mary feel a good deal better, as she strove to obliterate all of the evidence. Jennifer called her before she got to the area just by the window, so Mary let her mop drop down on to the floor and undoing her pinny, she went into the corridor where she was surprised to see Jennifer completely dressed and even with make-up, and seemingly eager to leave. All her shyness had returned to her now, and she would not look at Mary as she fumbled in her handbag.

'Thing is,' she said so softly. 'Agnes – she never said. So I don't know how much. Only . . . I ain't got very much . . .'

Mary was shocked and guilty, her hand darting out to cover over Jennifer's, to stop it right there in its tracks.

'No no,' insisted Mary. 'Oh no. I thought that was clear. There was never any question of . . . No no. Nothing. Nothing at all. I want to *help*, you see . . .'

Now the girl raised up her head, her face so happy with surprise, her blue eyes dazzling.

'What . . . nothing? No money at all? You sure?'

'Yes. Quite. So long as you're all right. That's all I want.'

'Blimey . . .' said Jennifer, with wonder. 'Nobody never give me nothing before . . .'

'Yes well,' said a flustered Mary, wringing her hands. 'I'm sorry it had to be this.'

Mary walked her to the door. She had turned down the offer of a cup of beef tea, and no, she wouldn't take a biscuit.

'Thing is . . .' said Jennifer, just before she left. 'I got this friend, see. Maude, her name is. She got the same trouble as what I had . . .'

'Well tell her,' urged Mary. 'Tell her to come and see me. Agnes has my telephone number. Tell her to make an appointment, and I promise you I'll help her.'

'And . . .' hesitated Jennifer. 'And . . . would that be free and all . . . ? Pardon me for asking, I'm sure.'

Mary smiled. 'Yes, Jennifer. Quite free.'

'Coo. You're a real lady, you is, miss.'

'Mary. Call me Mary.'

'Right-o then – I will. And I'll tell Maude. Thank you. Thank you for what you done.'

'Well – try to be more careful next time, yes?'

Jennifer looked at her in open puzzlement.

'What you mean . . . ?'

'Well – you know. If you're with a boy . . . ?'

Jennifer looked at her blankly and shook her head.

'You don't know? No – I suppose you don't. I'll tell Agnes to help you there. You get in touch with Agnes, yes?'

'Okey-dokey. Well I'll be off then. And ta ever so much. I'm sorry for the mess. I'm sorry it were all of it so very bloody, Mary.'

Mary just slightly winced, and then she smiled, touched Jennifer lightly on the sleeve of her coat, and quietly closed the door behind her. The time had not yet come for any thinking – there was still the cleaning up to be finished, so let's just get on with it, shall we? And when Mary got back to what she could not now nor ever again call Jeremy's room, she stood stock-still and screamed in horror at the sight of the sinewy cats. Romeo was licking the floor just over by the window, and Vincent was pawing at the lid of the galvanised bucket. They squealed as she rushed at them with the mop, and she shooed them both out of the room. Dizzy with shock, she completed the mopping of the room and stripped off the streaked and bloodied sheet from the bed and set to scrubbing the oilskin with a scourer. And the sheet, I'm throwing that away too – and the bucket, the whole bucket, it just has to go. I'll buy more in the morning, if only I can find them, but I simply can't keep these things, not this time I can't.

Her hands were raw and floury by the time all the washing was finally done. She trussed up the sheet into a newspaper and dropped it into the outside bin and the bucket she tied up with string, and that went in on the top. And then all of the towels, wrapped in more papers. Madness, yes, but there it is. Then Mary went back to the bathroom and again turned on the bath taps and scattered in all that was left of the lavender crystals and she turned around to the basin and was convulsively sick, her throat quite agonisingly racked by each of her eruptions. Just like, she reflected later, immersed to her chin in the hot and fragrant water, the very first time I ever entered this flat, and I did not yet know of my pregnancy. Well there.

Later, when Jackie should have been home, Mary, in a navy pleated frock and purple-beaded slippers, smoked a Craven A

444

and nestled into an armchair, willing herself to be at peace. The smell of blood was still about her though, like a stale and captured cough. And then she jumped up at the sight of the carrier bag with all of her clothes in it and she quickly snatched it up and slipped out of the back door and into the yard and she lifted the lid of the bin and crammed into it the brown and bulging bag which she now saw in passing had printed across it in black the garlanded head of an ox and the legend 'High Class Family Butcher', which wasn't, actually, in the least bit amusing.

☉

The whole of London, I'm telling you – it fair gone mad, it has. There's all sorts going off, and for the likes of me and Jonny Midnight, it come out something like a gold mine, just like Mr Wisely says it were going to (and I ain't seen too much of him, just lately – Jonny, he says he's out the city, somewhere safe, and who's going to blame him, ay? Got interests to protect, ain't he?). It were soon after all this Dunkirk lark when it all come down. For months we had it now. And my Alfie, it were just as well I got him out that rat-hole like I done. I ain't saying it were planned, nor nothing – when I snatches him, it were all of it on the spur of the wossname, I ain't denying, but I reckon my hand were guided, is what I reckon – my guardian angel, you want to put it like that. Because the Jerries, they started hitting all the coast down there real hard, soon after – Dover, Folkestone, even all them seaside places what you've had a nice fish supper in and a wafer on the pier, like – they all gets it too. I wouldn't be surprised to hear that a lot of them young lads what made it back from France in all them little boats, they gets all patched up and kitted out again in dear old Blighty, and the next thing you know they're blown to kingdom come by a bleeding Jerry bomb. Yeh well – you ain't going to hear about that on the wireless, is you? Ay? You get old Churchill droning on about never had many so few, or whatever the old bastard were coming out with this time around – when all the planes was buzzing over us like flies, there – oh yeh, you get all that. And how many of our boys we got off of Dunkirk, in one piece or otherwise (and no, I can't get myself into all that again – I start up on all that side of things, well – I ain't going to be able to concentrate, am I? On my job) . . . yeh, but like I'm saying – what they *doesn't* tell you is how many of the poor little bleeders was shot to bits when they was up to their necks in water, and waiting for a ship to come across. Because people, well – they don't want to know, do they? They just keep hearing how we's hammering the Boche and all the rest of it, and there ain't none of them what gets to wondering well hang about a bit – we's doing so well, how come we keep on sending out more and more lads, then? How come we got to rip up the park railings, turn them into a bleeding Spitfire (and I don't reckon that can be right, neither – I may be no expert, but what? A cast-iron fighter? I don't reckon it). And how come – and this is it, really, this is really the thing – how come London's now getting pounded on a near nightly basis, if we got the Hun on the run? Ay? Don't make sense, do it? I tell you one thing it done, though – we all of us hate the Germans good and proper nowadays, we does. Because up till now, you'd hear them – the posher ones, the milksops, all your nancy boys and the women in the queues – they'd all be going on about how your average Jerry soldier's just a frightened young lad like what ours is. He didn't never *ask* to be in no war, they'd be telling you. He never wanted to leave his job, his family, his home town. Yeh well – there ain't none of that now. They hate them. They hate every bleeding one of them. I heard one old biddy the other morning, and she were going the reason they're called German is because they's a breeding ground for *germs*, see – and if they lands here, if they come over in their parachutes and all the rest of it, they won't need no bombs and bullets, on account of we'll all drop dead of the plague the first whiff we get of them. Well – God help any Kraut parachutist what *do* make it, that's all I can say: tear him limb from limb, they will. And Hitler, they'd burn him at the stake, no danger about that – and I suppose it'd be Jonny and me what'd be selling tickets (and the most of them dud 'uns). As for me – yeh, I'd put a bullet between his eyes, Hitler, course I would, but I'd do the same for Churchill and all. And the bleeding generals – Monty, all them. If it weren't for them, we wouldn't be in all this bloody mess, would we? Ay? And my Alfie . . . yeh well. I got to face all that soon enough, I know that, I do know that. But for now, I got to concentrate. On my job. Because with all the air raids, well – opportunities, see? I reckon Mr Wisely, he's a bit of a genius, you ask me. He seed it all perfect, how it were going to be. Maybe it's him they want up Downing Street, and not this bleeding Winnie; I know where I'd stuff his fucking cigar. And that's another thing – all these mugs what seem to think he's God Almighty, they don't get bothered that he got a best Cuban always rammed in his boat while they'd sell their own granny for a packet of Weights. Nah – because it's still them and us, see? He's a toff, so he gets a cigar. We're all rubbish, so what we get is blown to fucking pieces. And I don't know where he buys them, Churchill, his bleeding cigars – but I bet I could get them for him cheaper.

But I tell you, the things we got going at the moment, well – I can't hardly believe it myself. Jonny and me, we's at it round the clock, we is. All the lads as well – too much work to handle. We're still doing all the deserters and the call-ups, of course – old Dickie, you come round to see him of an evening and there he is up to his eyes in all his medical books, look, ferreting out some new disease we can bung them down for. Epilepsy – had its day. He reckons we milked that one dry – reckons you can't have all these hundreds of twenty-year-olds all at the same time having a fit on the floor. One option we got now is queer. They reckon you're one of them, they steers well clear. Don't get you out of war work, mind, but we's only charging them seventy-five, so you can't expect jam on it. We get the odd officer and all on the skive – baby lieutenants, we call them – toff kids, hardly out of nappies. If they bring their service revolver with them, they get a nice little discount: growing market in them – goes without saying. Petrol were good for a while – army supplies mostly, we was selling. But now you ain't hardly allowed to go nowhere at all, so it's pretty much over, that one. Plenty more, though. Ration books we been buying up from all the poor old buggers what ain't got the money for even the few little bits of grub they's allowed, and never mind the clobber. You got to laugh – half the stuff on the ration, bit of butter, rasher of bacon, chop if you're lucky, they ain't never had it in their lives. Ready market for the coupons, though, with them as got a few bob. Jonny got this printer up Aldershot now – he can knock them off a treat, them coupons, so all the poor buggers we was buying them off of, they selling private now – and best of British, that's what I say. There's a lot of business going on down the shelters – Tube, and that. Jonny's got a team of dips going – plain and simple. People, they're mugs ain't they? They goes down the Tube when the siren go up, and what you reckon they take with them? Sandwich, yeh – nice Thermos of tea, I ain't arguing. But what else? Yeh – you got it. Everything they don't want blown up in their house. Blimey – one night, I goes round to Jonny's when his boys come home, and you wouldn't hardly credit it. Fob watches, diamond rings, rolls of oncers: mugs, the lot of them. And gambling, that's good down the Tube. Some of it's simple – the old three-card routine, the ball under the cup. Amazes me, it really do. What do people think? That this bloke in his chalk-stripe and his two-tone shoes and his cufflinks and his little Errol Flynn moustache – he going to *lose*, is he? Going to be giving away money to a pack of drifters and housewives? Very likely. Still though – queuing up, they is, to lay down whatever they got. Mugs. And the other thing what they don't seem to get is that when you got a couple streets-worth of people down the shelter, well – that's a lot of empty houses then, ain't it? So the boys, they's in and out of them like nobody's business. Police? Not really, nah. See, the most of the proper mob, your professionals – all in the army, ain't they? Or one of the others – navy, what have you. So the coppers we got on the streets nowadays, well – don't know the first thing, do they? They's either taking shelter theirselves or else they're too stupid to see what's going off right under their bleeding noses. Or they doesn't want to – them's the brighter ones. You shove them a couple quid, they're somewhere else entirely. Mind you, I ain't saying it's all easy pickings for the lads – they got to be out there grafting away with all the bleeding bombs dropping down like billy-o. Building gets blown out, these boys got to be first on the scene. We got a good few ARP geezers and all, what's wise enough to see reason. But I got to say, they's a tougher nut to crack, they is. Older people, see – got values, straight as a die. But there'll always be a couple of them, won't there? Ay? What might pick up a pony from us and then very carelessly leave their little white helmets lying about. Because they're gold, them are. You turn up anywhere in a raid and you got one of them things on your bonce, well then you are in, my son, and no questions asked. So our lads'll be loading up furniture and wirelesses and bedsteads and that – you'd be amazed at the demand – on account of official, like, they's saving them from looters! Joke, really – like I say, you got to laugh. Shops is even better, of course: shops is always favourite. The one what we always talk about, Jonny and me, is the wholesale tobacconist up Spitalfields. Couple of the lads outside – all dickied up as ARPs – and we not only got half a million fags out of it (didn't take no time to shift them, neither – never do) but we even trolleys out the bleeding safe – up on to the van, and away. Telling you – it's evenings the likes of that one what makes it good to be alive.

What else? Ooh blimey – I could go on all night. We does a fair little bit of protection – businesses what else'd be one of our targets (so one way or the other, you got them really). There's some minding – tarts of a night-time and conchies what don't want to get sliced – because all of them as has lost a loved one over in France or wherever, they get right riled up with the conchies, they does. We been round the posh addresses up West – it's Jonny and me, this caper, on account of we got the whistles, we got the gold cigarette cases, we got the diamond stuck in our ties – and we signs them up for a very select place in one of these real deep hush-hush underground shelters, bunkers, like what Churchill scurry off to, first sign of danger. They can't get the money into your hands fast enough, them toffs can't. Course, there ain't no bunkers – clear as day, less you was stupid. Then we'll go into a restaurant, time to time – not the British Restaurants, the government ones, because mostly they're too scared to step out of line. But others – and sometimes the big hotels what everyone's heard of, you'd be well surprised – they're all of them selling meals for more than the five bob or whatever it are you're allowed to charge. And there's always a nice bit of rump or a orange, maybe, for them as flash at them a bit of a wad. And then, see, you takes the top bloke over to one side, quiet like, and you shows him all your badges and your documents – because what you is that day is an official inspector, see, out there to make sure that none of this sort of caper's going on. Well – you should see their faces: proper little picture. But still you got to be all stern, like, even though you's fit to bursting out with laughter at how jittery they all now got. Ho yus, you's going – I can have you shut down, son. Huge fine. Maybe even the jug – who can say? Then you give a little hint that there might just be a way to get out of a whole lot of unpleasantness, that we just might see our way to accommodating them . . . the light go on in their eyes, and they's yours. Out come all the loot again – peeling off the fivers, they is, like they's waiting for you to up and say when. And they's all over you with the gratitude – telling you to call in any time you likes for a slap-up feed, French champagne, you bleeding name it, and all on the house, our compliments: *sir*. And more often than not, we takes them up on that – and round about afters time, you gently remind them that this blind eye what you got, it seems to be regaining a little bit of vision, if they know what you mean: only blurry at the moment, yeh – but I reckon it wants shutting down permanent – don't you? Never so friendly the second time, but they do see reason.

We got a ambulance and a couple hearses. Amazing the doors they opens wide to you. The NAAFI's always a fair source of supply – I ain't never met up with no NAAFI what ain't got one bent person behind the counter: you just got to sniff out which of them it is – ain't difficult. And the ambulance, see – very handy (we got the uniforms and all, of course: we ain't amateurs). Covered-over stretcher, bells all clanging away, ain't no one going to stop you. Hearses, well – even better, ain't they? Stands to reason. You got a coffin jam full of Scotch or parachute silk (the ladies, they do love that) and you ain't going to have no copper meddling with you, is you? Matter of respect. Sometimes, you don't know what you going to get. One bombed-out warehouse one time, we got about three or four gross of little empty bottles. Leave it, Jonny said – let's get out of here. But I says to him no, hang on – have a butcher's at the labels. And he goes yeh, Yardley's – so? And I says trust me Jonny, ay? So we loads them up into the van and we's away. Telling you – two days later, we cleared the lot. Yardley's cologne – like gold dust. Sold it to all the little corner shops, didn't we? Gawd alone knows what the lads went and filled them up with – some things best left alone, ay?

How much more you want? I ain't barely scratched the surface of it. Crime. Yeh – well it is crime, I ain't denying. But you don't want to go condemning it willy-nilly, like. Because you see what you got to understand is, we's all of us at it, every man jack of us, one way or another. Now granted, us – we're the pros, we go about it businesslike, I ain't arguing with you. But like take them little corner shops what I were just on about, yeh? You know why they gone and took all this dud cologne off of us? Tell you why. Because if they hadn't, the shop down the road would've. And then they'd be out of pocket. Dog eat dog, are what it is. And talking of that, you get these people what says they doesn't mind a bit of bacon or a nice bowl of stew, but they could never kill a living thing. Yeh? Oh yeh? *Really?* You lock them in a room for a week, and then you bung them in a puppy or something. They'd have it by the throat and in the oven with a bit of parsley before you can say Jack Robinson. And if there weren't no oven they'd have the bugger raw, fur and all. Not ideal, not by a long way – but what I'm saying is, you learn to adapt because you got to. People's at it every day – fiddle on the rations, sausage under the counter, packet of fags bought round the back of a boozer, fare-dodge on the railway, having a swift word with a well-placed mate so's he can sort you out a little favour. None of them was at it before the war, course they wasn't – but only because they didn't *have* to, that's the truth of it. You ain't no thief, you says to yourself – but if you starving, that loaf of bread you will nick, son – mark my words. So all I'm saying is, up and down, you don't want to be so quick as to wossname. Got it? We none of us know what he is until he's up against it, see? Me, I learned it early on. So – crime? Yeh, OK. But the real crime is, it's all so bleeding easy. I ain't saying I'm complaining, nor nothing, but if you want to stop and get all moral like for just half a mo, well – way it all is now, it just ain't right. But it suits me. Suits me grand. And do I worry about ever getting nabbed? Course. We all does. Keeps us on our toes – you can't never go getting slack, nor too clever, not in this game. But listen to this: fortnight back, bloke in the papers convicted of clubbing a feller to death: after his wallet, he were. What did he get? Three year. Three year, all tucked up safe and sound in Dartmoor or somewhere, most likely eating better than in all his born days. Week later, some other geezer got banged inside for three month. Know what he done? Do you? Kill you, this will. He were smoking too *bright*. No, I ain't kidding – I seen it in the papers. During the blackout he come out with his fag, poor little sod, and the copper run him in on account of he were puffing it too *bright*. Well. See what I mean? The whole of London – fair gone mad, it has. But I don't mind. I love it. I'm Jack the Lad, I am. Keeps my mind off of the war.

●

12th October 1940
The bombing now, it's just so terrible – so much worse than anyone expected. Night after night the planes come over, sometimes even in the day – the chill of the siren, it's something no one ever talks about, but you feel it, you feel just ill when you hear it, and then there's the drone of the planes overhead. The noise is like just the one gigantic and drowsy bumble bee that is constantly hovering, and just above you, but it must be simply hundreds of planes, hundreds and hundreds of them. Then there are noises like the jumping crackers we used to have on Bonfire Night – little

453

squibs, they sound like, but it's all the ack-ack guns – and one of the girls I attended to yesterday, she works at an emplacement somewhere on the docks and she told me that the noise of them when you're right up close, it splits your head. And I did have to raise my voice to her – she could be going deaf. Twin foetuses, she had. Twins.

Sheila is back in London. She says she prefers the bombs to the boredom of the countryside – but heavens, I'd give just anything for one night's sleep that wasn't shattered by having to scurry back down into the basement when the awful siren goes up again. And if they don't come, still you're just lying there, waiting. And I'm so often alone. Jackie, he's out more and more, and always at the most dangerous times. I never know if I'll see him alive again. He says not to worry because he's indestructible. Maybe he's right. I'm not though, and I know it. I dread going out in the morning now because the landscape, everywhere you thought you knew, it keeps on changing. Just the other day, the terraces near the Co-op, it looked like the whole of the front wall of all these houses just fell away into the street and what's left is like an open doll's house, with curtains fluttering and pictures on the wall, but nearly all the floors gone. And now you can see the park beyond. It's just terrible to think of all those deaths and the plight of the survivors, if any. Jackie says I mustn't get sentimental or it'll kill me.

Sheila saw Jeremy and he's doing wonderfully, she says, and that soon I'll be able to visit. I begged her to take a photograph of him, and then I begged her not to. I said to her she can always come and shelter in my basement if she wants to. I've decided it's better than the Anderson – it's certainly a lot more comfortable, and warmer. Of course, if we get a direct hit, the whole house will bury me – but then I don't suppose a tin hut just a few yards off would offer any more protection. She shares Dickie's shelter, if she's with him at the time. I think she feels sorry for him. Terribly often he's drunk, she says, and then she hates it because he doesn't know what he's doing, but he's got no one else, she says. Since his father was killed in his boat (four crossings he made before they were hit, according to Sheila – Dickie talks about it all the time) his mother has gone very strange and now is in Scotland where they've got a place, apparently. Dickie's Anderson always fills up with water if it rains, and so Sheila brings the wellingtons, and Dickie the whisky. And she sometimes takes along Romeo and Vincent in a fisherman's creel. I've told her what I do, now. I didn't for ages because I simply could not know in what way she would react. At first she wouldn't believe me, and so I unlocked the room and showed her. Talking of which, Jackie has never remarked upon the fact that the door is always locked. He maybe has never tried the handle, or maybe he just doesn't care. She was shocked, I think – who wouldn't be? – but she quite quickly rallied round when I explained to her all the good I was doing. Also, I had to ask her for help. At first there were no more than a few girls, but word must quickly have got round, I suppose, and now I am engulfed. None of them believes that I'll take no money. It is terrible to think that there are so many girls who need me. I always take care to never pry into their circumstance, but one of them not too long ago told me that a soldier on leave who she had never met before had persuaded her that by tomorrow the two of them could well be dead, and so what was there to lose? When she found out later that she was pregnant – she could not recall whether the soldier had ever told her his name – she says she wished she *had* died, instead of having to live on in so much shame, and what nice boy would want her now, just eighteen and pregnant? And then, she said, someone told her about Bloody Mary. I was speechless, and I think she saw it. 'But miss,' she

455

said, 'it weren't meant in no bad way.' Since then I have
heard the name many times. It seems to be now what I have
become.

Sheila of course agreed to help me – she's such a friend, I
am so very fond of her. I have a very tight system these days,
but I needed someone to answer the door and arrange
appointments, make the beef tea (it's very restorative) and
generally attend to everything except for the operation itself,
when I like to be alone – and it puts the girls more at their
ease. I now have an electric machine for washing the sheets
and towels, which is half of the battle, frankly. I casually asked
Jackie one day if he knew of such a thing, and the very next
morning he had it installed. He didn't ask me why I wanted it.
Sheila can't be here all the time, of course, but it's so much
easier when she is – and I'm so glad of the company. I pay her
in steak for her cats, chocolates, nylons – all the usual plunder.
She says I take on too many cases, and of course she's right
about that. What with the workload and the ruined nights
and the often quite emotional scenes that I am forced to cope
with, I mostly feel dead on my feet. A blessing in one way –
sometimes during a raid, I'm barely aware. I still always make
a point, though, of having Jackie's tea on the table of an
evening. And, when he doesn't arrive, throwing it away. Last
night – he was here, for once – he fell asleep fully dressed on
the bed. I undid his bootlaces and loosened his braces and tie,
and then I eased off his jacket, and it weighed a ton. I didn't at
all want to be looking in his pockets, but I found myself doing
it all the same. His wallet was stuffed with cash, as usual, and
there was this curious and rather pretty little thing in silver
and pearl, it looked like. It had a button which I pressed and a
blade shot right out of the thing – I got the shock of my life
and nearly dropped it on the floor. I have never before seen
such an article, and I have no idea why he has it.

456

Now that the bombing is so severe, everyone is talking of invasion again, and my dear old Dad, he's on full alert, and clearly pleased to be so (it's called the Home Guard now, they've renamed it). I asked about my mother, as I always do, and at first he would say nothing. Eventually I got out of him that she's taking the raids very badly – stays in the shelter all the time, night and day. He brings out her meals to her on a tray and she reads the Bible constantly, which as far as I know she has never before so much as glanced at. I said I would go and see her, and he said – best not. I offered to send her some chocolate and some books and anything else I could think of, and try to persuade her to come out of there. And he said – best not. So I won't.

So far tonight the siren hasn't sounded. I'll try to get some sleep before it does. Seven girls are coming tomorrow, into the care of Bloody Mary.

Tonight Alfie, I told him – tonight, the two of us, we's going to be bandits. He liked that word, like I knowed he would. Same as when I said we was a right pair of rascals – laugh like a drain, he did. But right back when we started on it, he reckoned it were all a game of cowboys and Indians, the great big kid, but I says to him no, son – we's all cowboys, it just we got goodies and baddies, black hats and white ones, but don't go asking me to tell you which is which because, well – there ain't no black and white no more: it all gone hazy.

At the start of it I had to put it over to Alfie like it were all a bit of an adventure, else he'd never have went for it. Not that he had a lot of choice, poor little bugger, hobbling about the way he do. And Mr Wisely and all, he took a fair bit of convincing, I ain't denying. My organisation is not in the habit of employing lame ducks, is what he were saying to me – and I tell you, I were that raw, I'd only just come from kidnapping the boy and getting him round to Dickie's, because I'm telling you – after that drive back all the way from Dover with that other one, what's his name, in the Riley, my little Alfie, he were in a terrible state, poor little kid, and me, I were hardly no better. So I were that raw, I'm telling you – it been anyone else other than Mr Wisely, I would've decked him on the spot, saying that. As it was, I had to swallow it down and go on being nice to the man, but it were hard, I'm telling you that. Got him to see reason in the end, mind. Said I'd keep him under my wing, my Alfie, give him my word he'd be no trouble. Victor, yeh that's right. I'd only just come from me and Victor heaving the poor little sod up to Dickie's, and the girl he got outside there, Susan is it, she says to me I'm awfully sorry Mr Robertson, she says, but people is waiting and Dr Wheat, he got a patient with him already. Darling, I says to her (we's all dripping wet we is, Alfie's just got his sopping pyjamas on him and there's blood, look, all down what's left of the poor little bugger's leg – I'd had that Churchill in the room at the time, he would of got strung up from the bleeding rafters, I'm telling you – we was all just stood there, Victor and me and Alfie slung between the two of us) – and Darling, I says, you just tell the people to fuck off, there's a good girl. And the patient in with Dr Wheat, you can tell him to fuck off and all. And no, love – don't go giving me none of that, or else you're going to buy yourself the sort of trouble that believe me, you don't really need in your life, you got me? Yeh? Good girl. Well *do* it then – and then you can bloody well fuck off as well. Cheeky bitch, she were.

So we crashes into Dickie's little hovel just as little nursey, she bundling out some mad old cow what's maundering on about her corns, or something (she maybe wants sawing off her leg, ay? That'll do it for her) and I'm roaring out to him – Dickie, you better be sober, mate, because this is Alfie, this is my Alfie I got here, this is my lttle kid brother, and they mashed him up, the bleeding bloody army, they left him all in bits – and he hurting, look, you just got to look at his eyes, all screwed up they is, so what you waiting for? Ay? Clear all that caper off of the couch and come on Victor, give us a bit of help – no good is it? Just loafing about – come on, let's get him up there. Well, Dickie? Give him something. He hurting. And what's with all this blood? Ay? Well go *on*, for Christ's sake – *do* something, what's bloody wrong with you?

'All right, Jackie – just keep calm, you know. Hello, Alfie. Been in the wars, hey? Oh God – sorry Jackie. Right, now we'll have to cut off the leg of, um – these pyjamas, all right?'

'I'll do that,' said Jackie, shouldering Dickie out of the way. 'You go and get him a pill or something. You all right are you, Alfie? Soon stop the hurt, you hang on there, son.'

Jackie flicked open his pearl-handled knife and slit away the blood-sodden pyjama leg, which just hung down. And then he gasped, and was shocked by the tears that sprang out of his eyes at the sight of the pale and rounded bony knee, and nothing else at all.

'It's the sutures,' said Dickie. 'Looks like he's been jolted around a bit. Steady on, old man. Soon see to this.'

Jackie was trying to get the tablet Dickie had given him under Alfie's lips – he was forcing it through the tightly clenched teeth.

'Here, Alfie – drop of water. Get it down you, ay? Do you a power, that will. Now listen, Dickie – you sure you know what you doing? How much you had? Smell like a bloody distillery, you do. You just remember, son – this ain't just one of the mugs. This is Alfie – this is my Alfie we got here, my little kid brother, and don't you bloody forget it. This pill ain't no good – it ain't doing nothing, what's wrong with you Dickie? What sort of a bleeding doctor is you? Ay? He *hurting* – he ain't saying nothing but I know he hurting, you just got to look at him.'

'Just hold this towel here, Jackie. No – just here. That's it. I'll give him an injection. He won't feel a thing after that – promise you, old man.'

'Yeh? Well *do* it then – don't stand there talking about it, do it for Christ's sake. All right, Alfie? All right? Soon have you in the land of nod, son, don't you worry about that. Come on, Dickie! What's bleeding keeping you? Here, Victor – you hold this cloth on his forehead, he all sweating, look. And don't go pressing hard.'

Dickie swiftly administered the injection, and Jackie was entranced by the sight of all the pain and tension sliding away from Alfie's face, and then came the hint of a dreamy smile (look at him – you'd swear he were no more than ten year old, the poor little crippled bleeder). As Dickie attended to Alfie's stitches, Jackie, suddenly exhausted, slumped into the old swivel chair, yellowing kapok poking from the tatters of the Rexine seat.

'Which drawer?'

'Top left,' said Dickie. 'Pour one for me too, will you Jackie old man?'

'No I bleeding won't. You can have one when you's done. Here, Victor – drop of Scotch. You earned it, son. Couldn't have done it without you. Blimey – look at the state of this suit, will you? My boots is caked. What a bleeding performance . . . And where's my hat? Reckon I lost it . . .'

Jackie drew on a Turkish so long and deeply that nearly the length of it down to his fingers was glowing hard and orange before it withered into ash. After a while, Dickie proclaimed himself done. He'd discarded Alfie's pyjamas and slipped a dull green sort of smock across him: he was sleeping, his face so serene.

'Tell you what,' said Victor suddenly, as Dickie sat down and grabbed at the bottle. 'You two – you'll want to talk, yeh? I'll just slip down to the motor, Jackie. And you want to go some place after, I'll drive you round there. How's that sound?'

And Jackie had to admit that it sounded very fair, very fair it sounded: he felt beaten by clubs, and he needed more Scotch. And Victor was right about the rest of it too – I do want a little word with Dickie here, and yeh, there is a couple faces I got to see, then. Jeanie, for one – she got to know. He been babbling about her best part of an hour, he has, little Alfie – nearly all the way up from Dover. And then there's Mr Wisely – because Alfie, I got to get him sorted out now, ain't I? Because I been thinking about that – all the way up in the car I been thinking about that. I mean yeh, I can just have him to stay – Mary, she'd take Trojan care of him, no fear there, but see . . . I knows my Alfie, he wouldn't care for it. Just hanging around, like, and being a dependant. And me, I understand that – for myself, I couldn't have it neither. Well the army – they'll only be after him for the paperwork side. All what he is now is no more than a loose end: it's just he ain't been signed for. After that, they won't want to know about him: he ain't fit. He ain't A-one. He ain't in no condition to get hisself all shot to death. And you can forget his old job in the insurance – none of that's on now, not no more it ain't. And then there's Jeanie, ain't there? He'll need to be bringing in a few bob, and he won't want it to be no hand-out, neither. So way I sees it, he got to get his self-respect back. We'll get him the best new leg we can get him, I tell you that. I ain't having him stumping about on no bit of log like some old pirate in a bleeding pantomime. We'll go up Harley Street, get him the best. Then he'll want to be out of all that khaki rubbish for good and all: I'll take him up and see Harry the Stitch, he'll see to him grand. But first off, I got to square it with Mr Wisely, yeh I do know that. And even with the regard the man got for me, it ain't going to be no piece of cake. But it got to be done. Because it's family.

461

'Look, Jackie – I really would love to chat to you, old thing – but my patients, you know . . .'

Jackie shook his head. 'Nah, son. You ain't got none. Not today.'

'Really? Are you sure, old fellow? Highly unusual. Oh. Well. I'll just go and have a word with—'

'What? Your Susan, is it? Nah. She gone. It's a half-holiday all round, Dickie old son. Just you and me. So you can relax, see? Grateful what you done for my Alfie. Have another vat of whisky.'

'Oh God, Jackie – it was nothing at all. Poor old chap, hey? This war, I don't know. All these young fellows. I'm awfully sorry, Jackie . . .'

'Yeh well. Not your fault. I'll see him all right, don't you worry. Go on, Dickie – have another. You knows you wants to.'

Dickie nodded as he poured from the bottle.

'Always want to. That's the trouble. But I'm doing my best, you know. Cut down a bit. After I heard about the pater, of course . . . well, practically drowned in it, then. Bad choice of word . . .'

'Oh yeh. Yeh, Dickie – sorry. I meant to mention . . .'

'Mm, well. Nothing much to say about it, really. Never is, is there? Times like that. Uncle, too. They both were lost. Can't tell you the state the mater's in, poor old thing. Had a chum of mine give her the once-over. Bit deranged, apparently. Might pull out of it. Might not. Who knows? Who knows anything any more, hey Jackie?'

'You're right there, son. You're right there. Still – look on the bright side, ay? Least you never went with them. On the boat. Ay?'

'Suppose so. Don't know. Yes. I suppose so. Sheila, you know – she's been awfully good about the whole thing. I really don't deserve her, way I've carried on. Could be she just feels sorry for me, of course. But one has to think it's more than

462

that, doesn't one? One just has to. Hard to bear, otherwise. We have some really rather jolly times, you know, the two of us, in the old Anderson of an evening. Quite cosy, unless it's been raining. Tried everything to keep the bally rain out of it but, well – useless at all that sort of thing.'

'You should've said, Dickie. I'll fetch you a bloke round.'

'Really? Oh well I must say that would be really awfully, um . . . thank you, Jackie. Thanks. But it's jolly in there, just the pair of us. She brings sandwiches. Sometimes, though – gosh, I shouldn't say it, because she's really such an awfully kind soul, you know – but sometimes, she brings them and they're all crammed full of that greengage jam she keeps on making. Well, one doesn't like to say anything, you know, but I tell you quite frankly, Jackie – just a little of that, well – it really does go rather a long way, you know.'

And Jackie laughed, which came as something of a relief, what with one thing and another.

'Dear oh dear, Dickie. You don't get no better, does you? Fancy a Turkish? Oh no course – you don't. Watching your health. Well here, son – have another drop.'

'Mmm . . .' demurred Dickie, looking at the bottle ruefully. 'You see that's the trouble. I'm all right at the moment – only had a few today. Six or seven. Couple more, possibly. But all quite in control, you know? Now if you and I sit here for much longer and see off the rest of this bottle, all that I'll do is open up another, you see? And that'll go as well. That's one of the troubles with being in the shelter – and it's awfully difficult, what with Sheila being around, but, well – it's just so terribly dull, isn't it? With these night-long raids. I mean to say, well – what else is there to *do*?'

'Well pardon me for mentioning it, Dickie, but I would have said that a bloke and a lady, all tucked up snug as two bugs in a rug with a bottle of Scotch and half a ton of greengage sandwiches – well, no telling what they might get up to, ay? Knock your Romeo and Juliet into a cocked bleeding hat.'

'Ah . . .' said Dickie, giving a little cough and looking suddenly quite serious. 'Well now yes it's funny you should come to mention that, Jackie old chap. But, er – truth is, we don't actually go in for all that sort of thing. Never have, no. Well there you are. She told me rather early on, you know, that she wasn't that sort of girl – and what it all rather boils down to, I suppose, is that by Jove it, um – surely does appear as though she isn't. Probably my fault, I expect. Not quite a film star, am I?'

'Oh dear oh dear oh dear, Dickie. Now you listen to me, son. What you got to do – and pronto and all . . . blimey, no wonder you drinks so much – must be climbing the wall, you must. No listen, what you has to do is, you has to gently coax her, see, into seeing the error of her ways. There's a war on, you got to remind her. Listen to it Sheila, you got to say to her. Hear all that? Know what all that is, do you? That's bombs, that is. Bombs, Sheila, what Jerry are aiming right square at us two. And one day, well – they could get lucky, couldn't they? Ay? And where's that leave us, then – apart from six bleeding feet under? More, most likely, you take a direct hit. It leave us *unfulfilled*. Yeh. That's the word. Blimey – I hit it spot on, there. *Unfulfilled*. And then you be nice to her, see? And nature – you mark my words, son, because I been there – nature will take its course. You rest assured.'

Dickie was blinking at him hopefully.

'Really? You really do think that, do you Jackie? Well. Well I never did.'

'No I know, son. That's the bleeding problem, ain't it?'

Jackie stood up and yawned extravagantly, his arms reaching out for the ceiling.

'Blimey, I'm fair done in, I am. And Christ, just look at the state of me – mud all over. So listen, Dickie . . . Alfie, he going to be . . . ?'

464

'Oh yes. He'll sleep on for a good while yet, and then he'll be fine. Well, you know . . . relatively speaking. I'll stay here with him, you don't have to worry on that score. Of course, long run, he'll need a good deal of help. You know – to adjust, sort of thing . . .'

'Yeh well. He'll get it. All the help in the world. Right then, Dickie – I'm off. And don't go drinking so much you forget you got a patient on your hands, all right? I got to see a couple people. Then I reckon I could do with a bit of a kip myself. Knocked, I am. See you in the morning then, ay?'

'Yes yes. Absolutely, old thing, I'll be here, have no fear. And if there's a raid – will be, I suppose – there's a couple of fellows downstairs and we'll have him in the shelter so he'll be perfectly safe, Jackie old man. And um . . . all that sort of rot you were going on about earlier, you know. About Sheila, and so forth. You really do think, then, do you . . . ?'

Jackie smiled and clapped him about the shoulders.

'Get it done, lad. For England, ay?'

I were still chuckling away to myself when I got back into the motor alongside of Victor, there. Could've been hysteric, if that's the word I'm meaning, because I weren't happy, no I bleeding weren't. So yeh anyway, he get me round to Jeanie's, Victor, and I were only thinking you know I don't have no idea, that Jeanie, what she do, what she get up to of a day time, never troubled to ask her, so whatever it is, it could be she out and doing it. But nah – she were there.

'Oh it's you, Jackie. This is a surprise. Come in, won't you? Oh my heavens – just look at you! What a mess you're in. I've never seen you turned out less than perfectly, not you Jackie. What have you been doing? Where's your hat?'

Jackie looked down at the beggarly state of him, and shrugged it all away.

'Yeh – what I come to see you about, matter of fact Jeanie.'

'I can't offer you anything, I'm afraid Jackie. I've nothing at all.'

'Yeh. No. Don't matter. Don't want nothing. Listen, Jeanie—'

'Only I might have a custard cream. I was saving them, there's only two, but I don't mind you having one, Jackie.'

'Yeh. No. Don't want no custard cream. Listen—'

'Ooh – are those Turkish, those cigarettes?'

'Yeh. You want one? Here you go. No listen to me, Jeanie—'

'Mm – lovely. Haven't seen one of these since before the war.'

'You want some, I'll get you some. Now shut up and bleeding *listen* to me, will you? It's about Alfie.'

'Alfie? Where is he? Is he all right?'

'Yeh. Well no – not exactly. He's here. Back home. London. But thing is, Jeanie – I don't know how I should tell it to you, but—'

'Where's he come from? Was he overseas?'

'Of course he were overseas. France, weren't it. BEF. Dunkirk, yeh? No? What – you don't know?'

'I don't. I don't ever listen. I can't stand it. What's BF?'

'BEF. British – look, never mind what it is. Don't matter. Point is, Alfie were in France, right? And now he back here. But see, he ain't quite like he were before, on account of—'

'What do you mean? What's wrong with him? Has he gone mad, do you mean?'

'No! Ain't gone *mad* . . . why would he have gone *mad*, for Christ's bleeding sake?'

'You hear about them, soldiers. They lose their minds.'

'Yeh well he ain't. What it is is, he lost his leg. Half of it. Yeh.'

Jeanie just stared at him.

'Yeh,' said Jackie again, looking down at his hands. 'It's a shock. It's a real bad thing. I ain't got over it myself. But them's the facts of the matter, Jeanie. And what it is, he going to need a lot of care, see? Now I can get you moved in somewhere on the ground floor, so he won't have no stairs to worry about, and I'll see you got everything you need and all that, and then we . . . what's wrong? Ay? What's up with you, girl? What you keep shaking your head for? Tell me what's going on with you. Well go on! Don't just sit there, shaking your bleeding head all of the time.'

Jeanie looked up at him, and Jackie had been ready for sadness and tears but there was none of that at all. All he saw there was a kind of horror. And then she was shaking her head again.

'No, Jackie. No no. I'm sorry. But no.'

'No? What you mean "no"? No what?'

'Can't. Have him here. Look after him. Not what I want.'

Jackie lowered his cigarette into an ashtray, and looked at her levelly.

'Not what you want . . . It ain't what you *want*, is that what you're telling me? And what – having half a leg, it's what he *do* want, is it?'

'I'm *sorry*, Jackie – it's just that I'd be no good at all in a situation like that. I mean I nearly faint if someone just cuts their finger – I just couldn't stand it. It's . . . disgusting.'

Jackie nodded slowly.

'I see, Jeanie. Right. Now let's us get this all squared up, will we? Alfie, he been fighting the war and he lost his leg, and it ain't what you want on account of it's *disgusting*. That it?'

'Oh Jackie – that makes me sound so—'

'Yeh, it do. Because you *is* so, ain't you? Ay? That boy, that little kid brother of mine, he ain't stopped talking about you, Jeanie, since I pick him up. It's all "How's Jeanie, Jackie?" and "How's Jeanie been keeping?" and "I just can't wait to be back with my Jeanie, Jackie"—'

'Oh God . . .'

'Never mind *God*. You just leave God bleeding out of it, girl. And you're saying what to me now? Ay? That you don't want nothing to do with him no more? That it, is it Jeanie?'

Jeanie was kneeling beside him now, sobbing away as she looked up at him imploringly.

'Oh please don't think badly of me, Jackie! I'll . . . see him, of course I'll see him, if that's what you want, but . . . well I just *couldn't*, Jackie. Can't explain. I just couldn't be with a man like that. I need a big strong man, Jackie. It's what I've always needed. Someone like you, Jackie – someone with substance. Someone who can look after me, take care of me, give me all the things that I've always wanted. Look at me, Jackie – look around you. I've been living like this for it seems like eternity. I can't – look *after* someone. I need someone to look after me. Be nice to me. And then . . . I can be nice to him. You do see that, don't you Jackie? Don't you. Hmm?'

And she only stroking my arm now, and she giving me that look what she giving me, and I seed it before, that look. It's all big-eyed and innocent on the one side, and then there's a little bit of naughty going on, if you's out to catch it. Some of the tarts I collects off of, they give me that look, time to time, when they's shy in their payments. Don't never work, though. Not with me.

Jackie stubbed out his cigarette and rose to his feet, automatically brushing off with his fingers a fragment of ash from his hard and corrugated, mud-logged trousers.

'I see. Very well then, Jeanie. Well I'll be off now, then.'

Jeanie was standing now too, looking wary and puzzled. She touched his arm.

'And . . . that's it then, is it Jackie?'

'Oh yeh. That's it. You made yourself very plain, Jeanie. So I'll say goodbye now, all right?'

'But Jackie – I don't mind just *seeing* him. Like I said to you, Jackie – I will *see* him . . .'

Jackie smiled at her, as he opened the door and stood there.

'No, Jeanie. You won't. Not never. Believe me.'

And whatever the look on her face was now, Jackie could only enjoy it as he clattered down the stairs and back into the Riley.

'Victor . . .' he said, almost wistfully. 'There's a lady up there, second floor, name of Jeanie.'

'Yeh?' grunted Victor, shifting in his seat. 'So what?'

'I'll tell you so what, son. Word is, she needing a big strong man. Someone with . . . now what were it she says to me . . . ? Oh yeh – substance, that were it. Now I looks at you, Victor, and I sees just such a bloke. See? So what's going to happen now is, I takes the car back home, get these bleeding clothes off of me, and you son, what I want you to do is, you get yourself up there, second floor, and you show that lady just what it is a big strong man can do. Ay? Be big, Victor – and be strong. Got it?'

Victor nodded curtly, and eased his bulk out of the car. Jackie turned the ignition key and leaned over to the window for a final word.

'Name of Jeanie. Second Floor. I'll give her *disgusting* . . .' he said – and then he pulled the car away, fast.

◉

And all the way over to Mr Wisely's, I were thinking now what's this then, ay? What the bleeding hell is it what's going on at home? Ay? What's Mary been up to, what I don't know about? Something's bleeding going on, I can tell you that, on account of Mary – she ain't no good as a liar. Ain't got the knack. So when I come in and sees Sheila there, I didn't think nothing of it. Perfectly frank with you, I ain't never there of a day time – nor of a night time neither, often as not – so I couldn't tell you nothing about what's going off at the flat, most the time.

Sheila – far as I knew it, she could be round there every day. Not too surprising, really. When you're just a little homebody like what Mary are, well – you want a bit of company, don't you? Cup of tea and a natter. Only natural. Mind you, if that were my life I'd be halfway round the bend by now – but women, well, don't take too much to keep them happy, do it? Nice bit of steak, couple pair of fifteen-deniers, assortment of soft centres and your average cutie, well – eating out your hand, sweet as you like. So anyway, yeh – it weren't that Sheila were there what were odd, it were just that she were acting all shifty, like. I just come through the door, and it were like she wanted me right back out of it again.

'All right are you, Sheila? Ain't seen you in a bit. Hear you and Dickie's all as snug as two bugs in a rug again, ay? Nice. You seem a bit jumpy, Sheila. All right, are you?'

'What are you doing here, Jackie? What do you want?'

'What am I doing here? Well pardon me if I got this all around my neck, but I had this idea at the back of my head that this is where I bleeding *live*. What you mean – what am I *doing* here?'

'Oh – yes, sorry Jackie. I didn't mean . . . it's just that, well – we never ever see you, do we? Not at this time of day, anyway.'

'Yeh well – as you may have spotted, I got a little messy. Quick wash and brush-up, change of duds, and I'll be off. Where's Mary, then?'

'Oh, Mary, she's um – busy, Jackie. At the moment. So you'll be wanting the bathroom, will you?'

'Now let me think . . . washing, soap, water . . . yeh Sheila, I reckon you hit it on the head there, girl. *Course* I'll be wanting the bleeding bathroom – what you on about?'

'Oh, it's just that I think Mary, she's maybe in there at the moment.'

'Yeh? Well is she or ain't she? Plus, I got a bit of news. Not good news, but it got to be said.'

'Bad news? Oh dear – it's not your Alfie, is it?'

'Is, matter of fact. No no – don't go getting all . . . he ain't *dead*, or nothing. But he got a – injury. You can hear it when I tell it to Mary.'

'She's in the bathroom, I'm pretty sure. I'll just go and see.'

'Don't trouble yourself, Sheila. I can see for myself, can't I?'

'No no. It's no trouble. Back in a jiff. There's some custard creams on the table, Jackie.'

'Yeh. No. Don't want no custard cream. What is it with you women and your custard bleeding creams? Right – I'm off to have a wash. No, Sheila, I don't want to chat no more, no offence. I'm tired and I'm dirty and I got to see a bloke, all right?'

Sheila just sighed and dropped her arms to her sides as she saw she couldn't stop him, and Jackie made a show of stepping around her and then made quickly for the figured walnut wardrobe in the bedroom, pulling out the nigger-brown herringbone three-piece, a fresh white shirt and collar, the tie with the little green and yellow paisley design, and then he topped off the bundle with his umber and cream two-tone brogues. The hat would have to be one of those he'd never much cared for that hung in the hall (bleeding annoying I lost that fedora, somewhere in the bloody wilds, because I were right fond of it: bloke I got it off of, he said it were part of a parcel for Harrods).

Jackie was just at the door of the bathroom when Mary stepped out of little Jeremy's room, wiping her hands on a small white towel. And then she locked the door behind her.

'Jackie,' she said lightly. 'I thought I heard you. Goodness, what a mess you're in. Oh heavens, Jackie – is it Alfie? Is he—?'

'Yeh yeh. He all right, I got him back. He over with Dickie. Thing is, Mary, he um – well, there ain't no two ways about it, he lost his leg, poor little bugger. Half of it, any road.'

Mary's eyes were filled with alarm and then a mute compassion, as she brought up the towel to her face.

471

'Here,' said Jackie. 'What you done to yourself?'

'Hm? Oh – it's nothing. Opening a tin. Little nick. Nothing. But listen, Jackie – I'll have to go over and tell Jeanie.'

'Nah. I done that. She knows. Let me see your hand. Where you cut it?'

'Oh I told you, Jackie – it's nothing at all. But I really think I should go and see her anyway, you know. She'll be so upset.'

'Well she gone away, is the truth of it. Country, somewhere – I didn't ask. You sure you're all right, girl?'

'Positive. Gone away . . . ? How terribly odd. Oh well. If you're sure . . . Going to wash now, are you Jackie?'

'Yeh. All right with you, is it? Sheila, she didn't care for the idea.'

'Of course it's all right. What a silly thing to say. Oh my poor Jackie – you must be feeling terrible about Alfie. When can he come home? Will we have him here? Oh I'd *love* to, Jackie . . .'

Jackie's eyes dipped in fondness.

'Yeh. I knows you would. That's because you're one of the good 'uns, Mary. You always was. Why you locked that door?'

'Oh. It's a surprise for you. Didn't expect you back, did I? Don't want you spoiling it. You go off and wash up now, Jackie. And if you're not in this evening, promise me you'll shelter somewhere safe. There's bound to be another heavy raid tonight. It's a bomber's moon. Promise.'

So I says yeh to that, get myself all cleaned up, and then I were off in the car to see Mr Wisely. Sheila, she were pleased to see the back of me, that were for sure. And all the way over – because I got here now, look: just park the old motor and square myself up for another little run-in with bleeding old Barnstaple – all the way over here I been asking myself: what's Mary been up to, what I don't know about? Ay? She never got no surprise – and her hand weren't cut, neither. She ain't no good as a liar – ain't got the knack. So what's going on then, ay? That's what I'd like to know. Yeh well – sort it all out later. Business to see to.

'Your timing, dear boy, is as ever most fortuitous. One hour earlier and I should still have been partaking of a perfectly delightful little supper at the Savoy Hotel. Beluga, a fricassée of chicken, the most divinely scrumptious Pauillac and a really rather heavenly apricot soufflé. They are very ingenious, you know – they circumvent the tiresome five-shilling rule by the levying of a three-pound cover charge. Highly enterprising. One must applaud it. And, my dear Jackie, had you arrived just one hour *later*, then you would have found me flown once more from this increasingly dark and wounded city. Doubly fortuitous, I might say, as there were a couple of little matters that I had hoped to raise with you. You will take champagne . . . ?'

'Yeh – ta, thank you, Mr Wisely. Had hell of a day, matter of fact.'

'So sorry to hear it. Let us hope your brief time here will in some measure compensate. Always delighted by your company, dear boy, though to what, pray, on this occasion do I owe the considerable pleasure?'

'Ay? You mean why am I here? Yeh. Well see – it's my brother, Mr Wisely.'

'Ah. The warrior. The fighting man.'

'Yeh. Well he done his fighting, and he come back with half his leg off.'

'Dear dear. One would say that half a leg is better than none, but this is hardly the case. The upper half, conceivably, one might shed without too much of a care, but alas it is never the way of the thing. And it is the extremities, of course, that exert all pedal power. The inconvenience is great. I am most sorry for your brother, and indeed for you, Jackie.'

'Yeh. Thank you, Mr Wisely. Thing is – I'd like to be working with him. He's a good lad – bright, he'll pick it up quick. And he'll need to be working, see Mr Wisely. For his wossname.'

'Keep . . . ?'

'No. The other thing. His, blimey – what is it?'

'Self-esteem . . . ?'

'Yeh. You got it. Nail on the head. So I were thinking – and he won't be no bother, I'll look after him and all that. But I'd be really happy, Mr Wisely, if you could take him on, like.'

Nigel Wisely pursed his lips and formed his hands into a tentative arch, the pads of his slim fingers just touching.

'My organisation is not in the habit,' he said quite slowly, 'of employing lame ducks.'

Jackie chewed his lip, and swallowed hard.

'I know what you saying, Mr Wisely, but he'd be with me, see? I'll see he's all right. Won't give him no job what needs—'

'Legwork . . . ?'

Jackie nodded, not caring for any part of this interview.

'Well I must be frank with you, Jackie my dear boy. I am not quite convinced that there is the latitude, you see. The leeway for more potential error. This brings me to the other little matters to which I earlier alluded. Your drop last week, Jackie – it seemed to me a trifle . . . shall we say on the light side?'

Of all the things that Mr Wisely might have been likely to say to him, Jackie had certainly not foreseen anything of this sort.

'My drop? What – light in money, you mean? It can't have been. I mean – I ain't saying you's wrong, or nothing, but I'm ever so careful with the figures and everything, Mr Wisely. I ain't great with it, that side of things – why I always gets Jonny to check it over. How much you reckon it were shy? I mean – I'll make it up here and now, Mr Wisely, out my own pocket. I got twenty here . . .'

'Alas alas, dear boy. We are not discussing a matter of twenty pounds. The amount in question runs to hundreds.'

Jackie was dumbfounded.

'*Ay*? Hundreds? Nah. It ain't possible. I gone over and over it. Always does. I tell you it ain't *possible*, Mr Wisely. Here – I hope you don't think I'm—'

'No no no no *no* – of course not, of course not. Shall we, on this occasion, simply mark it down to a passing flaw in the accounting process, and leave it so?'

'Well . . . yeh. But listen, I hope you don't think I'm—'

'As I have sought to reassure you, my dear Jackie, the thought had not so much as occurred to me. The other matter, however, might, had it not been spotted, have given rise to rather graver consequences for us all. I refer to one of the certificates drawn up and signed by our own Dr Wheat.'

'Yeh? What he done wrong?'

'It was stated on the form that the young man in question was deaf in both ears. It transpired, however, that the said young man had been tutored in the art of appearing quite blind. You do see how embarrassing this might have been?'

'Yeh. I does. Blimey.'

'Mm. And you see, Jackie, Dr Wheat is your responsibility, is he not? I have heard from a little bird that he might be a trifle over-fond of the grape and the grain. Is there any truth in this, Jackie?'

'Well . . . he do like a drink. Which one of us don't, ay?'

'There is a drink,' said Mr Wisely, raising up his glass of champagne as if it were the chalice at a service, 'and then there is a *drink*. Do I make myself plain?'

'Yeh. Yeh. Sorry, Mr Wisely. I'll keep an eye. Won't happen again.'

'But you do see, Jackie, why I am reluctant to add to your burdens? You have now to keep an eye upon the sordid question of money, and then on the good doctor. And you seek also now to keep the same eye, is it, upon your poor one-legged brother . . . ? Too much to ask of you, surely? But no – no no:

I know you too well to persist with my protestation. For you will not let it lie, will you Jackie? You have a great sentiment for your brother, and I applaud it. So we shall try him. But you must, Jackie, accept full responsibility for all of his actions. That must be quite clear.'

Jackie released his pent-up breath, and rushed across to the sofa where Mr Wisely was elegantly sprawling.

'Oh *thank* you, Mr Wisely. Thank you thank you thank you. I can't tell you what this means to me – and him, it'll be just what he's after.'

'Do sit, Jackie. I don't care for your *looming* in such a way.'

'Yeh right. I will. And you don't have to worry about him, I gives you my word, Mr Wisely. I'll learn him up, like, and he'll come out Trojan.'

'I have no doubt of it,' said Mr Wisely, patting Jackie's knee and leaving his hand there, idling. 'It would be too much for me to bear if ever we were to have a falling-out, you know. Too much for me to bear. You are quite my favourite – you are aware of this? Our friend Jonathan Leakey I have no doubt whatever is most thoroughly jealous, but there – how is one to govern the heart? It is a simple fact. But Mr Leakey, of course . . .'

Jackie looked down at Nigel Wisely's hand, still caressing his knee.

'Yeh . . . ?'

'Mr Leakey, he does simply *everything* for me. So loyal. So thoroughly . . . obedient. And you, Jackie? Would you too? Do *everything* for me, I wonder?'

'Well . . . yeh. Course. Within reason . . .'

Nigel Wisely laughed quite joyously, and clapped his hands.

'I really must tease you no longer, my dear boy. It was just too naughty of me. Off you go now, Jackie. It was refreshing, our little discussion. Will you be availing yourself of the myriad distractions upon the upper floors . . . ?'

Jackie was on his feet, and grinning now.

'Wouldn't mind, matter of fact. Been hell of a day.'

And to be truthful to you, that were the other reason – apart from Alfie – why I gone over. I don't know what it were about that day, but I needed a seeing-to, yeh – and what's more, I needed it fast.

'Oh,' said Molly, flatly. 'It's you.'

'Not the best sort of a welcome I ever had,' said Jackie, breezily, as he threw shut the door. 'But yeh. It's me.'

And it's funny – I tried one or two of the other girls, I ain't denying, and they're lovely girls the lot of them, la cream de the cream, but it's Molly what I always comes back to. She ain't all soft soap and willing like what the rest of them is. She don't want to do it, and I like that. She hate me when I does it to her, and I like that a lot. What happens is – and it's always the same – she get down on her knees in front of me and then them bright red sticky lips of hers is doing all the business and she keep that up for a good while, she do, and since I told her, she's all over with the hands and all – lovely feeling, that is – and then when I had enough of all of that, she spread herself face down on the table over there, look, and I rams up her from the back for hardly more than a couple seconds, and then I finishes it, hard. Her choice, all of that, and it's only just lately I twig what it's all about. It's because that way, she don't have to go and look me in the face. Funny girl. Wouldn't never have her shaving me though, like what some of the others does – she'd slit my throat (as soon as look at me). And then I goes to the lav. You don't go pulling no chains in that house, no – it's all levers, low down like. Very jazzy. Yeh – so like I says to Mr Wisely, it were hell of a day, that one were. But that were then and this is now – and tonight, me and Alfie: we's going to be bandits.

He took to it all real good, he did, that little brother of mine, you know. And never mind all of that flannel I were flogging to

Mr Wisely – I did have my doubts, course I did, because he always been straight as a die, Alfie has . . . well of course we all was, once. I were myself. Hard to think it, now. Well when I told it to him, Alfie, he were . . . what do they say? Took aback, I think it is. Reckon he thought I were joking when I come to fill him in on a little of what it is I gets up to. Only did tell him a little, mind, else I could have lost him. And we got him a leg. Ain't the one I set my heart on – there's such a shortage, they're telling me, all of that: it's needed for the lads at the front. Oh yeh, I says to them – and where you think this poor little bleeder lost his bloody leg, then? Ay? You reckon, what – he just left it in the Odeon when he go to the Gents halfway through the bleeding cartoon? You's looking at a hero, son, and don't you bleeding forget it neither. And I got money: how much you want? Anyway, it weren't no good. Proper fake legs, you can't get the real thing nowhere. I got something for him, ain't too bad, but anyone's about when he hitch up his trousers and they's in for a hell of a shock, I can tell you: all bits of metal, like one of them lamps in a office what you can bend up and down. And it's a bit too long, and all: he lurch about a bit – pains me to watch it. Anyway – best we could do, and he says he's happy, Alfie, he's a golden boy, he really is. Don't never complain about nothing. And he never did, you know, tell me how he gets to be all shot up in the first place – just said he never felt nothing till he were dragged up on the boat, and then he just kind of seed his leg there, hanging off, sort of style. Got a bit weepy for his mates, he did – the lads what never made it. And yeh, he did say to me I never should of went, Jackie – I should of heard what you was saying to me – but I let it lie. Well – you don't want to be rubbing the salt in, does you? Ay? All I says is, well look Alfie, you's back ain't you? Ay? Safe and sound. More or less. And you got your big brother to look after you now, ain't you? So it's all of it tickety boo, my son. And I has to say to him quite regular – Alfie, you thanks me just one more time, one more time mind, and I'll clock you as I stand here, you mark my bleeding words. And Mary, she been wonderful. Like a mother to him. Like what she used to be to me, matter of fact. Love that girl, just love her. But of course . . . well, like everything bleeding else, it just ain't the same no more. Yeh. And then in them first few days he were going to me yeh but listen, Jackie – you says she gone away, Jeanie, but where she gone, ay? Why she go? That, son, I says to him, I couldn't tell you. But maybe, Alfie, she just weren't the one for you, ay? I mean to say – you wants a woman to stand by you, don't you? Ay? You don't want her pushing off, first sign of a bit of trouble, does you? Ay? Stands to reason. What you got to get for yourself, Alfie, are a little girl the likes of my Mary, that's what you want, son. Ain't too many of them about, I ain't denying: could be, I got the only one. Anyways – wherever it is she gone, your Jeanie, she'll be back, won't she? Ay? Then you and her, you can have a little chat. Yeh – that's what I told him. Won't never bleeding happen, though: I seen to that.

So anyway, we gets him all kitted out, like. Harry the Stitch, he done him proud like what I knew he would. Got him some lovely shirts and ties from Hilditch & Key down Jermyn Street, only they don't know nothing about it yet. And there's this cobbler what Jonny know, and he fix this wossname on the metal foot of his leg so's he can change all the boots about, like, and so when he's all dickied up and just standing there, well – you'd never hardly know that nothing had happened to the poor little bleeder. Yeh – and talking of Jonny, he weren't that pleased, I can't deny, when he get wind of Alfie coming in with us. I don't fancy it, Jackie, the idea of going out on no job with him, no offence, is what he says to me. I ain't *asking* you to Jonny, am I? Ay? All depends what sort of job it is, don't it? With Alfie, I keeps it simple – I ain't a mug. You and me, Jonny, we'll still be doing the business, just the two of us, like: all depends on the job, don't

479

it? Ay? (Blimey – this game, the people you got to keep sweet: telling you).

And I did. I were true to my word. Kept it all nice and simple, where Alfie was concerned. One night, we was off to a crematorium up North London, you can believe it. Bloke there, you pass him a couple notes, he heave off the lids of the coffins before they all gets fired, see? And it's quality stuff and all – oak, a lot of it. So we sell a ton of it to this little one-eyed chippie up Peckham. There's many a nest of tables or a kiddy's cot what once had a brass plaque on it with the name of the dearly departed. Point is – weren't going to do him no good, were it? Life is for the living – and day to day, that's all we's doing. Another time, we liberates a bit of cosmetics what was going to the Wrens. Couldn't hardly believe it, when I heard. What – here we is getting pounded to bleeding bits by the bloody Jerries, the whole of London like a grimy hole – factories going flat-out night and day getting all the guns and the planes to all them poor sodding soldiers, and what? We's going to send all this face paint to a pack of girls in blue what is sat behind a bloody desk? To do with morale, they says. Yeh well – price you can get for all this stuff in town – and it were good stuff and all, Coty the most of it – there's one or two Wrens what's just going to have to wear a bag over their heads for a couple days, that's all. Do you know what a tub of face powder is going to fetch you? Twenty-five bob. I ain't kidding. Lipstick, you can go a quid. Now granted, that ain't nothing compared with your Scotch – and that's what we's up to tonight. Four pound, five pound a bottle, people'll pay for the real McCoy. Because there's a lot of bad hooch about – you got to go careful, you don't want to end up blinded. Blimey – a *empty* bottle of Haig or Bell's or one of them is going to get you half a dollar; what they put in it, you don't want to think about. But five pound, ay? Before the war, man would have to slave his guts out for a whole bleeding week for that sort of money:

I know – I done it myself. And, stupid mug what I were – I reckoned I were doing pretty nicely on it, and all. Yeh well – you lives, you learns. The trouble with Scotch is, well – bulky, heavy, and you got to move it real quick. But this job, well – shouldn't be too bad. It were Jonny what got the tip-off. Nice little consignment to a Foreign Office safe house – not too much, twenty cases, nice little van full: in and out, two minutes, sweet as you like. Jonny, he says he'd do it hisself only he got to get a gang of Mr Wisely's women round the Dorchester sharpish on account of there's some general or admiral or one of them in town. So this whisky, he already bunged this geezer a pony to make sure he forget to lock the door, like, but it ain't going to keep another day now, is it? Stands to reason. So what it is is, it's me and Alfie, and I got old Victor on to it and all – good for hefting, he are, and he drive a real treat, even in the pitch bloody dark. So that's on for right now: tonight, yeh – we's going to be bandits.

⊙

This is the night when I must go mad. I am sitting in this accursed basement – alone, of course alone – shuddering from the whine and thudding of the constant and unstoppable bombing all around me, hugging my arms and rocking to and fro – wild-eyed, I must be, and near deranged with an agonising concern for the people I love. My fingers are scorched and orange from Craven As I had not noticed burning down, and under the nails is still the caking of the black and mingled blood of others that I can no longer be rid of, no matter that I scrub and scrub at them, until I bleed myself. For two days and nights I have heard not a single word from Jackie. He told me he had some business to attend to

481

with Alfie, and that is the last I know. He had barely left me when the siren went up, and I suppose since then there have been all-clears and sirens again and again. I seem to have been cowering down here for just ever, sick inside at the crumping of bombs, alarmed into near-insanity as an explosion shatters so close to me, and the whole house trembles. Yesterday . . . the day before? Maybe both days, I don't know, I was upstairs, alone – of course alone – and aborting three, was it four maybe, foetuses (more, yet more, premature death) and then I scurry back down here at the drone of yet more hundreds and hundreds of planes, each determined to kill us all, every single one of us. Which they must be so close to achieving. There can be no London left out there. I cannot bear to look. But there can be no London left out there, not now, no city could sustain it. And I was alone with the girls who needed rid of their sin – some of them tearful, others very frightened, more and more of them quite as casually accepting as they might be at a dentist – because Sheila, Sheila too, I just have not seen her. Was it the evening before last? God, I can't remember. She pecked my cheek, I gave her steak for Romeo and Vincent and a pound of Black Magic and she said she would see me in the morning. Would that be yesterday morning? Or another morning even earlier than that? Anyway, she has not come. And nor has Jackie. And nor has anyone, to tell me a word. I cannot wonder what has happened to them. I simply cannot.

I don't think I have been eating – although I see there a plate with a few dried-up bits of something on it, so presumably then I ate that, whatever it was. I make tea. And I smoke Craven A. I thought I had enough of a supply, courtesy of Jackie, to last me for years, and they've nearly all gone. Oh my *God* . . . !! That one . . . that bomb was just so close, oh my God, who now, screaming, has just been blown to pieces? The next one, surely, is destined for me. And I'm not even sure I can really care. What has happened to Jackie? What has happened to Sheila? Where *are* they? Why haven't they come back to me?

I was thinking of Jeremy, and how I used to yearn for him. The Rose & Crown, that was hit just a few nights ago. It was not destroyed, but the floors gave way into the cellar, and one of Sally's children was obliterated – the other still is hanging on, the last I heard. Sally said she would defy all of Hitler's bombs, just so's they could be a family again. And now look. So many round here are bombed out now: there's homeless everywhere. And Jeremy? Well he's somewhere, presumably, and presumably safe. All we can do is presume, and sometimes it keeps us sane, and at times like now it can send us wild.

I was all set to tell him, Jackie, what it is I do. When he suddenly appeared like that, it shook me badly. Just five minutes earlier and he surely would have walked in on me, a frenzied girl her legs flung wide, and I up to my elbows in all of her blood. The smell of it, blood, it haunts me for ever – I doubt it will ever leave me. And so I thought I must tell him, and somehow manage whatever his reaction may be. Were it not for all the money he earns, after all, I would hardly be free to pursue my mission. But now I don't know if ever I shall see him again, and so really, you know, it hardly seems to matter. It's strange how it should be that that is how things have become. When everything in the world is hanging in the balance, it sometimes hardly seems to even matter.

The bombing now, it's quite sporadic, so I assume that it must be near dawn. That is when they leave us to dazedly survey the latest great swathes of wanton destruction, to pick among the pieces, and maybe find our dead, or if not that, then possibly a still usable hallstand, a bedstead not too mangled. Soon the all-clear will go up, and those of us who have survived yet another terrible night of it will somehow confront the day and struggle on through – and then the night, it is upon us again, and the bombers return.

And after, when I tried my best to piece it all together, I think what must have happened is that the all-clear did sound, as I had expected it to do, and I heaved myself out of that blasted airless basement – and so very very tired I now was feeling, my feet that heavy on every tread of the stairs – and I was so determined not to look out of any window (though still in that damp and steely dawn, I must somehow have managed it anyway, for there was all the rubble and the splintered rafters heaped in front of a smoking hole on the other side of the road) – and then I may have made more tea and I know I thought of bathing, but the very idea was dulled by the shadow of all the effort that that would entail, and so in the end I just must have fallen on to the bed and sunk into the dead of sleep. This is, yes, what must have happened, because I only stirred when the first noise came, but disturbance was dragging me – and then I was propelled into a still groggy wakefulness as the door of the room was suddenly battered inwards and the headlong rush of him made me yelp and hold out my arms as the momentum of his hurtled entry had him staggering badly, his eyes so wide and rolling as he fell on me like a deadweight.

'Jackie! Oh my God, let me look at you! Oh Jackie, Jackie – you look so—! What happened? What has happened to you? Oh my God – I thought I'd never see you again, I thought you were—! Oh Jackie you look so *ill*. And your clothes! And you're cut, look – oh tell me you're all right. Is there something wrong? What has happened? I'll get you some . . . oh Jackie, are you awake? Are you injured? I'll get you some water, get you some brandy. Talk to me, Jackie – tell me what happened. Is there something *wrong* . . . ? Are you in *trouble* . . . ?'

Jackie rolled over on to his back and did his best to focus upon Mary's agitated face that was dancing about and jittering in and out of his bleary field of vision. His dark-rimmed eyes stared out fearfully from a face made gaunt by ash, darker streaks the tracks of tears. The bristles across his cheekbone were clogged with dried-on blood, his hair thickly coated in a greenish slime. His suit was just shredded, as if by blades or the fangs of rabid dogs. He held up his grimed and bloodied fingers, skinned and raw.

'Yeh ...' he just about managed. 'Something wrong ... *Trouble* ...'

It weren't never meant to be. Can't barely take it in, all of what's gone on. I been hoping I dreamed it, but I never. When it all got going, there weren't nothing to it. First off, just before it get dark, I had to go and see a bloke. My old barber Toni, as it happens – a little matter of he ain't been paying up. And I already fixed it with Victor how he were to pick up Alfie, where and when we was all going to get together and see about the Scotch. So round at Toni's, window of his shop were all plastered with bits of paper what he writ all over. 'This is a British business. Proprietor born in London. Son in British Army.' Still hadn't stopped his glass getting kicked in though, had it? Red and white pole there, someone painted on a black swastika and it dripped down all over, look.

'Jackie,' said Toni. 'I knew you would come. You can see how it has been for me. Ever since that madman Mussolini, ever since he went in with the Nazis, all my friends, my neighbours – they think I am the enemy. I'm so hurt. It's terrible. No one comes any more. I fear for my life.'

'Yeh,' said Jackie, reclining in the barber's chair and lighting up a Turkish. 'That's *your* problem. Mine, see, is that you ain't paid the rent. Nor the interest on the rent. That's my side of it, see. And it's Mr Robertson. Got it?'

Toni was imploring, his open and upturned palms extended towards Jackie as he batted his forearms up and down constantly in an effort to convey to him his need to be understood, his helplessness, and maybe also the sheer desperation.

'But Jackie! Mr Robertson – a thousand apologies. Mr Robertson – what can I do? What would you have me do?'

Jackie gave him the blanked-out fish-eye.

'You got any money?'

'No! Well – little. But—!'

'Give it me.'

'No but *listen* to me, Jackie! It's all I—!'

'Yeh yeh – I know. It's all you got in the whole wide world. Give it me. And you call me Jackie just one more bleeding time and you're in for a headache, I am not kidding you. Now, Toni – get the money. And give it me.'

Toni heaved his shoulders and let them slump down into defeat. He fished some money out of his jacket and passed it over to Jackie. Jackie fanned out the notes, and Toni shrank back when he looked at him.

'What's this, Toni? Ay? I got the date wrong, have I? This April the first, is it, and you're having a bit of a leg-pull?'

Toni sighed in resignation, and also fear.

'It's all I've got. I swear it you. It's all I've got.'

'Mm. You know what? Looking at this dead-and-alive little hole what you got here, I pretty much believe you, Toni old son. I mean – you *do* got more, course you do – I yet to meet the bloke what ain't got more than what he says he got, yeh. Stands to reason. But I reckon with you, it'd be a question of shaking you upside down, see what coppers roll out of you.'

Toni nodded in misery.

'It's true. I have enough for maybe food tomorrow. Maybe the next day. Don't take it from me, Jackie. I beg of you.'

Jackie stood up quickly and dropped his butt on to the floor, swivelling his boot into it, hard.

'Ain't going to, son. What I's going to take off of you, Toni, is the keys. Right now. You's out, mate. Out on your ear. You want to chuck a few bits in a suitcase, I give you half hour. And then, son, you is out. And no – it ain't no good you *crying*. No good just standing there and weeping like you was a little *girl*, is it Toni? War on, son – got to face up to it. Your Musso's fault. And anyway, bright side is – all you Eyeties, all being rounded up, ain't you? Alien – that's what you is, son. Alien.'

Because yeh – I knowed all this on account of old Jonny Midnight, he got another little scam going, just at the moment – invented it hisself, so you got to give the lad credit. He and someone, they goes round the house of your enemy aliens, flash at them a load of bogus old junk on a bit of paper, and you gets them all in a van – you going to be interned, is what you tell them, no time for no luggage, and you drives them all off into Surrey or somewhere, and then you dumps them in a field. And then you gets yourself back to all their empty houses and, well – Christmas Day, ain't it? He's a fly one, Jonny, and like I says – you got to give it to him.

So I hangs about, has a few fags, while Toni, he mope about a bit until he see I mean it, and then he start to get all his bits and bobs together – still sobbing away, he were, thanking God his father weren't alive to see this day, as if your bleeding father's got anything to do with any part of it, one way or the other – and it were mostly his scissors and his clippers what he were going for, razors and strops, couple them little looking-glasses with the handles on so's you can have a butcher's at the back of your bonce . . . whole load of photographs he dug out . . . like I says, just his bits and bobs. He says to me, the chairs – the barber's chairs: can I please take them, Mr Robertson? They cost me so much. Well yeh, I says – you reckon you can heave them up on your back, son, then you's welcome to them, course you is, Toni. They're bolted to the floor, he go – all weepy again – and they weighs a ton and I got no transport. Yeh well, I says: it's a tough old world – maybe you ain't noticed. And no I *didn't* feel bloody sorry for him – why bleeding should I? He ain't nothing to me.

Just another bloke. London's full of them, blokes. I don't care. I just don't care. Why do people go on wanting me to care about what ain't got nothing to do with me? Ay? It's like the other night – London up in flames, it were, never seen nothing like it, and the next morning all anyone were going is ooh ain't it *marvellous* they didn't get St Paul's? Well why? Ay? Only a bleeding church. How many of them moaning minnies even stepped inside of it? Ay? It's a church – big church, granted, but when all's said and done, it only an old bleeding church. It go and get bombed, well come the end of the war – if there going to be an end to the war, before we's all of us dead and buried – well they'll go and build a bloody great *new* church, won't they? What's the bleeding difference? Like now – one Eyetie barber out of work. So? Plenty more, ain't there? They's all over – so what's the bleeding *difference*?

So I gets Toni out in the street, takes his keys off of him, and he look at me all sort of doleful like he one of them puppies what you're going to get on a birthday card with a bow on. Jackie, he says – now I'm finished, could you just give me back a couple of pound? Cheeky blighter. No, I says – I'm already well out of pocket, ain't I? On account of you. And it's Mr *Robertson*, you bleeding Wop – go on, get out my sight before I goes and clocks you one. So he shamble off, silly sod, and it coming down a bit of a pea-souper, I'm any judge, so I reckon I'll get myself over Whitechapel sharpish, meet up with Victor and litle Alfie.

And yeh I were right, because by the time I gets there it were a good old fog, and what with the blackout and all I nearly slams right into the van before I even seed it. But you don't never mind fog, not in this game.

'Wotcha, Alfie. All right are you, Victor my son? Perishing, ain't it? Anyone want a fag? What I reckon – we just stay tight for a bit, give it a half-hour maybe, and then we takes the van round the corner where I said, all right Victor? Then you, Alfie, you do all of the usual, yeh? Keep the motor running and your eyes well peeled – not that you going to see nothing, night like this – and Victor and me, we'll get the business done real quick and then we'll be gone, sweet as you like. Go round and have a few with poor old Len in what's left of that boozer of his, dear oh dear. That's one Jerry pilot I'd like a little word with – bombing my bleeding local without a by your leave, bloody cheek. Clear then is it, lads? Fit are you, Alfie? Ay? Good boy. Right then: won't be long.'

Forty minutes later – Jackie left it a bit, safe side – Victor eased the van around the corner at little more than a walking pace, the engine barely purring, and down into the side street that Jackie had only seen before in daylight; now, the darkness was total.

'Good,' he approved. 'Don't want no one breaking the black-out, do we? Right now, Alfie – you slip yourself into the driving seat, there's a good lad. All set, Victor? Torch? Gloves? Right then.'

Jackie and Victor edged their way down the narrow lane, their rubber-bound torches pointed down at their feet. Most of the lenses had been obscured by strips of black insulating tape, the glimmer of light deliberately narrow and faint. Jackie felt his way along the wall with the flat of one hand and then found he was groping just air as he stumbled over the crunch of shattered brick.

'Looks like the neighbours got hit quite recent,' he whispered to Victor. 'Door ain't much further.'

Victor said nothing, which was another reason Jackie had taken to working with him. Some of the other lads – practically non-stop they was: nerves, could be. Not Jonny, of course – he's a real old pro, Jonny Midnight.

'Got it . . .' hissed Jackie, as his hands slid up and down the door frame, and Victor held his torch right up close to the dull brass handle. 'Now then . . .' breathed Jackie, turning it gently,

'let's see if our bent little pen-pusher done as he were told . . .
yeh: lovely. Right – in we go, Victor.'

The two of them stepped in quickly, leaving the door ajar.
They stood very still in what turned out to be a cold and musty
corridor, piled with boxes. After registering nothing but utter
silence for twenty seconds longer, Jackie eased his foot across
the concrete floor, idling it around until the toe of his boot was
gently nudging one of the cartons.

'This ain't our stuff . . . I were told about this – junk, this is.
Ours in a little room here, somewhere. Come on, Victor – can't
be far. Oh here – I reckon this is it. Give us a bit of light here, will
you? Yeh – there it is. White Horse. That's a nice change. Usually
Haig, ain't it? I'll take the first one, will I? Yeh – and you do the
business with the light, all right?'

Jackie totted up the number of cases – twenty exactly, the info
was good – and hoisted up the top one as Victor kept the pale
slits of light from both torches trained on to the floor, always
keeping it steady and just inches in front of Jackie's fast-moving
feet. Back at the van, Victor quickly had the rear doors unlocked
and Jackie noiselessly slid in the first case of whisky.

'Going to take a while,' grunted Victor. 'Doing it this way.'

Jackie nodded. 'I know what you mean. Yeh.'

He signalled to Alfie to wind down the window on the
driver's side.

'How's it been, Alfie?'

'Quiet as the tomb. Everything going all right?'

'Oh yeh – pushover, this one. Just going to take a bit of time,
way we's going.'

Victor cleared his throat. 'I can take a couple cases at the
one time,' he was husking, 'but if Alfie were doing the torches,
we could get it cleared in no time, Jackie. Three or four cases a
trip, like.'

'I don't mind, Jackie,' said Alfie.

'Mm . . . Yeh I know, Alfie, I know – see, thing is, Victor – I don't like leaving the van. That's the bit what I don't like.'

'Dead round here,' muttered Victor. 'We'll be away in five minutes.'

'Yeh . . . yeh well you're right there . . .' agreed Jackie. And then he made the decision. 'All right then, Alfie – out you gets. Lock her up, mind, and get a hold of them torches there, there's a good lad.'

The three of them rapidly got back into the building, and Jackie felt proud of the way Alfie seemed instinctively to know where exactly the two tepid beams from the torches should fall – because he'd not done this sort of work before, Alfie, never really been much more than a lookout – but still it pained him, Jackie, to hear with each step the unevenness of his little brother's footsteps, the click of the nails in one boot coming down sharply, a pause, and then the other one, much more lightly, like a metallic hiccup, then jerkily repeated. Back in the little office, Victor was as good as his word and he easily hoicked up the two cases and held them fast in his meaty arms, and Jackie, of course, did exactly the same. The light from Alfie's torches steered him away from the scatterings of rubble from the torn-open neighbouring building, but it was hard for Jackie to see anything at all past the bulk of the boxes, skimming his chin, and the weight on his arms seemed close now to breaking them. He was panting and his arms adored it as he set down each case into the back of the van.

'Right,' he said. 'Get them doors locked, Alfie. Four more trips and I reckon we's done. Gawd – it is quiet round here, ain't it? Like a ghost town. Bleeding nippy, though. Come on then, lads – let's get it done, ay? Work up a bit of a sweat.'

On the return journey, Alfie brought with him an old army haversack that someone had slung into the back of the van, and while Jackie and Victor heaved up their two cases, Alfie ripped open another and managed to cram eight bottles of whisky into it, and they clinked quite merrily as he shrugged it across his shoulders. Initiative, that is, thought Jackie, as his arms went on protesting under this latest grim deadweight: should've made him an officer, they should, not a bleeding squaddie – then, most likely, he'd have two legs to show for it and a chestful of medals.

He was openly wheezing, Jackie, by the time they got back to the van, and was wondering if he could get away with a little bit of a sit-down on the tailgate before they went back in for the next bleeding load, but he yelled out in shock as the stark white brightness of the flashlight struck him full in the face, and he felt the tight grip on his arms as he was aware of only the roar from Victor and the clatter of the two torches as they hit the pavement.

'Evening, lads,' came the deep and cocky voice from somewhere at the back of the blinding light that Jackie shied away from as he violently struggled with whatever two bastards were gripping him hard at each side. 'Taking a little stroll, are we? A bit of night air, is it?'

More flickering torchlight was now brought into play and Jackie's stomach convulsed at the winking glint from the lines of silver buttons on the jostling blue uniforms as the tussle of policemen was putting all its strength into keeping firm hold of the three captured villains. Jackie was sweating, his eyes now more used to the light and darting from a white-faced and terrified Alfie, shaking his head as they pinioned him, and then to the bullishly impassive mask of Victor, just waiting for the word. Jackie consciously relaxed the muscles in his tethered arms as he squinted at the jeering face of the sergeant in charge, whose eyes were alive with amusement, and he was licking his lips as he savoured this very sweet moment.

'And what might be in these boxes then, I wonder. Gas masks, could it be? Alms for the needy? Bit of shopping for the weekend?'

'Take a look,' said Jackie, affably. 'Could be your lucky day. You and your boys here, you might like a little slice of it.'

'Oh *dear* . . .' lamented the sergeant, quite theatrically, tutting away and wagging his head. 'As if you weren't in enough trouble. Attempted bribery on the top of it. Oh dear oh dear oh dear . . .'

'Well,' smiled Jackie, 'can't blame a bloke for trying, can you? Ay? All right if I have a fag?'

'Forget it, mate. The only thing that's coming out of your pockets, the three of you, is your identity cards. See what we got here, shall we? So you just do that, lads – and nothing else, we're watching you. Be careful. You do something foolish and my constables' truncheons will see to it that you spend the rest of your days in a wheelchair, I am not kidding you.'

'OK, then . . .' laughed Jackie. 'Fair cop. That's what they call this, ain't it? Ain't it, Harry?' he called out to Victor.

'Yeh, Dave,' grunted Victor. 'Fair cop.'

Jackie winked at Alfie, whose eyes were beseeching him. 'We had it I'm afraid, Wilf.'

'Cut the chat,' snapped the sergeant. 'Let's just see those cards, shall we Dave?'

At the nod from Jackie, Victor doubled forward and lashed back hard with the heel of his boot and roaringly brought out his arms as if he were bursting his way out of a barrel's confine-ment and the two men holding him were staggering as he cast them aside and Jackie had the flick-knife out and open and he played the blade in front of the ring of wary and backed-up policemen, slashing a semicircle into the air and barking at them to let go of Wilf and the sergeant was bellowing at his men to take them! Get them! Mash them up – go on men – *get* them! And Jackie had Alfie by the shoulder of his coat and then they were running, Victor pounding hard behind them, and Alfie was howling in pain at the jarring sent up by each sharp

493

clatter of his metal leg and foot as it was repeatedly slammed down into the black and retreating street, and still was lurching alongside Jackie – Jackie screaming into his ear to be faster, be faster Alfie, because they're coming, the bastards, they's right close behind us Alfie and you got to, you got to – you got to run *faster*! Victor now had Alfie by the scruff of his collar and was half-lifting him up off the ground as the shouts and torch-beams of the policemen behind them were shivering into Jackie's awareness as he blindly trampled his way onwards into the sheer black wall of the night. Alfie's chest was heaving and the hoarseness and baying was that of an exhausted and hunted wild animal, frightened and near to death – and suddenly Jackie was fending off another blow from the club out of nowhere that had winged and dazed him and Victor's fist was connecting with bone as a man yelled out and went down hard and Jackie could feel Alfie being tugged right away from him and he spun right round and lashed out madly with his feet and fists and Victor now was roaring at him that he had to run for Christ's sake, just get running, there's far too many of them, we just got to run – and Jackie was screaming out for Alfie – the boy now was gone from him – and he threw off a man in the dark who had had him around the neck, and now here was Victor, breathing heavily and getting his arm around and under him and propelling him forward and the two of them were spinning on now into the dread of night, Jackie spitting out and gulping and crying tears that burned him as he called out forlornly and with a terrible desperation the one name Alfie, again and again and again, until he could do no more than just gasp and weep as the staccato echo of their wild and thudding feet was everything that existed in the depth and blackness of all they blundered into. Jackie then was dizzied and lost all control of his skittering feet and he spun around in a drunken arc of his own momentum before crashing awkwardly to the ground with shocking impact and only as he sprawled there was he aware that he had hit his head and Victor now had hold of fistfuls of his clothes and was hauling him up and screaming that they had to keep going, they couldn't stop now, and Jackie just wheezed and tried to be rid of him and was croaking that he couldn't, he couldn't, he was finished, he was done – and the tumble of heavy boots, he could hear it coming on, and then he had to draw in sharply what breath was left to him at the sudden shock of the deep and lowering moan of the air-raid siren as it climbed its way to its terrible warning before subsiding, and then it rose up again. Victor manhandled Jackie up on to his feet and then just ran with him, the steel-tipped toes of Jackie's boots sparking and scudding hard along the wet and cobbled street – and then doors were opening all around them, the long faint chinks of light striping the street briefly, before they shut down. Suddenly there was a huddle of people all around, shunting them forward – they were caught up in their mass, and only dimly did Jackie now discern the just barely there and opaque glow of the Underground station, and now the two of them were jostled along by the wall of shoulders about them, and they mutely shuffled on into the dark and stale confines of the overflowing entrance, and as the jammed surge forward was slowed right down into no more than a discontented struggle, Jackie sucked in breath as deep as his lungs could take it and leaned against Victor, who still held him upright and was rhythmically panting, his face near crimson, and all over glazed with the prickle of sweat.

The huddle of people was largely silent and bowed into resignation under the weight of the constant undulation of the hovering siren, only the mothers there venturing to soothe a half-awake and cantankerous child with reassuring murmurs, or else warn a livelier one to stay close by and hold her hand and keep in sight and not run off. Jackie was craning back his neck, ducking around between the heads and shoulders to see if he could make out the agitated bobbing of a policeman's helmet, the urgently brandished truncheon, but there was only the usual subfusc welter of tweed peaked caps, grey and brown trilbies, women's slouch felts and jaunty berets and plenty of loosely knotted headscarves nearly concealing a battlement of curlers. He nodded a tentative OK up to Victor, who blinked his eyes once in tacit acknowledgement.

'Ticket. Where's your ticket? I got to have a ticket.'

Jackie looked narrowly at the bony, grey and beaten man wearing half a uniform, his moustache just falling like whitened reeds over the dead thin line of his mouth. For no reason whatever, it occurred to Jackie that here had once been a young and fit and gallant soldier from the 14–18 war, charged with derring-do and the unquenchable will to engage in battle for the glory of King and country. And look at him now, in his land of heroes.

'We ain't queuing for the one-and-nines in the Gaumont, you know.'

'Don't be funny,' sighed the man. 'You're holding everyone up. Bombs'll be coming down in a minute. You booked a place or haven't you? You can't just come in willy-nilly.'

Jackie rolled up his eyes and fished out a folded pound note from his jacket pocket and jerked it towards him. The man seemed amazed and hurt as he gazed up at Jackie.

'Hoy no!' And his voice was cracking under the depth of feeling. 'No – none of that. No no. Ticket. That's what I want. Else you're out.'

There were the beginnings of angry and fearful mutterings coming from behind as the insistency of the crush became more heightened and the odd child now was crying. Then they all could hear the rapping of the guns and the first sporadic crumping of distant devastation.

'Yeh?' hissed Jackie. 'Well how about this, then?'

The man looked down at Jackie's hand, and his mouth hung open as he stepped aside. A rush of people carried Jackie and Victor forward and the inspector just stood there with his head hung low, seemingly disinclined now to check another ticket. As the crowd bore him onward, Jackie smoothly and with just two fingers folded back the blade, and deftly pocketed it.

'I reckon, Jackie,' – and Victor had to say it quite loudly over the rumble of so many hundreds of feet tumbling down the first of the staircases – 'I reckon we could be all right. How's the head?'

Jackie touched his temple, his fingers just probing the raised and hardening abrasion. His mind, though, as he walked on blindly amid the surge of people, was jagged white and electric. Because what Victor's maybe not understood here is that it ain't a question of the state of my head nor whether or not we was going to get nicked – all that could matter is that they gone and got a hold of my Alfie, the bastards, they must've done, and it's my fault, this is, and it all just got to be dealt with, dealt with fast (and I don't bleeding know how).

When they emerged from the last of the arched and serpentine passageways, the shoulder of Jackie's coat slipping along the length of the oxblood tiling, snagging and tearing on the sharp and bronze-bound corner of the enamelled roundel, dusting off a flaking of soot from a tattered and disregarded poster extolling the qualities of Sanatogen Tonic Wine, he was forced to remember why he never did use it, not even in peacetime, the Underground railway, the Tube is what they call it – couldn't never abide it, no, not even the idea, of being just a grubby burrower among the dark and echoing tunnels so very deep under the throb of the city, throat and eyes stung by the hot and dead breath of unseen demons, lurking in the twist of the black beyond.

I heard that people come down here – all over London, in their tens of thousands, and I can't never understand it, why they does such a thing. The way I sees it, at least in an Anderson, you got a chance of getting out. Down here, well . . . if where we come goes and gets clobbered, then we's buried in a hole, could be for ever. They doesn't think of that, all this mob. And look at them – look at what we got: some of them, you'd swear they live down here, look. Mum, Dad and a fair few kids. Thought we got rid of all of them? The kids. Bleeding mattresses all about, little – what are they? Little, I don't know . . . what you bung under a kettle, light it, gas like – burner thing. All them. Old woman down the end, got an accordion on, she has. She start playing it, I'll bleeding deck her, I can tell you. Hundreds and hundreds of people, everywhere you look – all bundled up and just waiting, like when you see all them bales of old clothes put out for the rag-and-bone. Like they's dead already. And I daresay there's some of Jonny's boys down here somewhere, working their way down the line – a dip here, a snatch there, could be a three-card-trick.

So anyways, me and Victor, I reckon we just squat down here in the corner, like – hope the bleeding raid ain't going to be like last night, when it never packed it in until it were light. I don't like it down here, I'm telling you – my mouth, it gone all dry. My head where I hit it, that's going a bit – it's my eyes, though – it's them what's hurting the most. Like I need to cry, or something, just to keep the buggers rolling about. Teared my trousers at the knee there, look. Must look a right bleeding sight.

What gone wrong? Ay? What happened there, then? Should've been sweet as sugar, this one. So what gone wrong? How bad is it, and what's I going to do? No good asking Victor. He's a good lad, I ain't denying – big bloke, muscle, won't never let you down, got me out of it, don't keep yapping – but he ain't no thinker. He ain't no planner. He do what he told, which is what you want. Only, I don't know what to tell him, do I? So I got to work it out. Alfie. That's the number one. I got to assume they got him. Now see, they might still reckon his name are Wilf – because he won't be so stupid, Alfie, as to be toting his ID about with him, least I bleeding hopes not anyway. So that might hold them for a little bit, but not too long. It's his leg, see. They'll see it's recent, that, and they'll start digging, the bastards, like what they always does. And you'd think, wouldn't you – war on, coppers'd have better things to think about. But no – if they can get in your bloody way, you can depend on it they'll do it. Now the terrible thing is, because I never got round to the paperwork, Alfie, what he is official like, is a deserter. Never mind they already had a leg out of it – they'll have all what's bleeding left of him now, they will. One young bloke I heard of – never got to me soon enough, else I could've sorted him – MPs pick him up, judge give him six year hard labour. Six year. And never mind my Alfie can't hardly walk proper, they'll still have him out there breaking rocks, sweating his guts out, till he ain't a young man no more. Well I can't have that. I got to think. Now the other thing is . . . Mr Wisely. He ain't going to be pleased, it got to be faced. Not only we lost the Scotch, we lost the bleeding van. And he'll put it down to Alfie, he will, and it didn't have nothing to do with him, did it? Coppers show up out the blue, what you going to do? Ay? There ain't nothing. And what's going to happen to the booze, then? What you think? Down their throats, ain't it? In the name of the law.

Victor, look – he nodded off. Here we is, sitting on a concrete platform, and that bleeding old biddy, she only started up on her squeeze box, ain't she? And someone over here, they's frying up bread and dripping, I do not believe it. And Victor – he nodded off. Yeh well. Nice for some. Truth is, though, I don't got to think it out. Not really. I knows what I got to do. Knowed it the moment I lost him. What I got to do is save my Alfie. So come tomorrow, I gets myself round there. I got to go and talk to the cops.

●

It was God alone knows what time in the early, raw and mud-grey morning when Jackie became aware of a general stirring amid the slumped and trussed-up masses, bundled deep into their warren. His throat was so parched by the stale and flinty air that when he went to rouse the still-sleeping Victor, no sound came – just a husked-out hacking that he soon abandoned. He felt lame as he clambered to his feet, and mutely set to sullenly plodding along behind the shuffle-footed straggle of pale and sleepless yawning citizens, none of whom seemed gratified by the one more day of half-life that had been doggedly exacted from their nightly tormentors. Even what light there was in the cold and rubble-strewn street outside, as the knots of sleepwalkers peeled away, their sluggish eyes only slowly assessing and struggling to come to terms with yet another newly ravaged and distorted landscape – even this pitiful and greenish light had Jackie shading his eyes with a sheltering forearm, his hat long gone from him, he vaguely realised, as the drizzle was sprinkling his head and face, mottling the lashes over his tired and squinted eyes.

'Victor . . .' he croaked out – and Victor, rubbing his face, and with his other hand seeing to a muffler, nodded curtly in response. 'What we need first is a drink . . . And a fag – I run out of fags. Smoking all night. Then I got to think what I got to do. We'll make for the Rose & Crown, I reckon. Hell of a walk.

Maybe a bus come along. Blimey – take a look at this, will you? Street. Half gone. Can't even pick out the road what we was running down . . .'

Eventually they did, they got there, more than twenty minutes frittered at one point along the way when Jackie became so completely disoriented by the total obliteration of buildings on a crossroads that he stood at its centre and stared at the possibilities before leading them both in quite the wrong direction, only picking up the trail again when he spotted a landmark still standing. No bus did come along – a taxi did, that cruised towards them, its flag alight, the elderly driver glancing incuriously at Jackie's energetic attempts to attract his attention, maybe aware of Victor's low and throaty two-fingered whistle, while he motored along and past them and on into the distance amid a hail of fury and abuse from Jackie as he stood on a corner, his lips flecked with spittle, and flinging his fists into the rain around him.

'We must look a right pair,' he grunted. 'Come on then, Victor my son. Shanks's pony. Can't be too far now, can it? Christ, I bleeding well hope not. I'm just about done in, I am.'

The Rose & Crown didn't look too different, not from the outside, although there was corrugated iron and a sagging and wet green tarpaulin where one of the doors used to be. All the acid-etched windows had survived intact, though, and the swinging sign still hung there, because the bomb – this is what Len had said – fell straight through the roof leaving just a small hole through all of the floors before exploding with thunder directly under the cellar where it had embedded itself. And that, Len had sighed – passing an unsteady hand across his tired and flickering eyes and wagging his head in disbelief and an endless sorrow – that is how the two boys came to get it. Sally, she went near mad. Even now, she's broke into pieces. She don't talk no more. I try to get through to her, but it ain't no good. The second boy, Robert . . . he passed away, other night. She won't never be the same.

'Oh it's you, Jackie. Come on in. Blimey – you do look rough.'

'Ta, Len. You doesn't look too bright yourself, lad. You ain't met Victor, has you? Victor, this here is Len. Gaffer. Give us a couple very large Scotches, will you Len? And what fags you got?'

'Just about down to the last bottle, Jackie. You got any more coming, have you?'

Jackie slumped into a chair, and sighed.

'Bit of a sore point as it happens, Len. But yeh – maybe I can sort you out. Get that down you, Victor. Earned it, son.'

Len put a large glass of whisky in front of Jackie.

'Bit early, ain't it? Even for you, Jackie.'

'Yeh well,' said Jackie, gulping it, 'hell of a night. What about them fags then, ay Len?'

'Might do you ten Player's. It's getting harder and harder.'

'Yeh,' nodded Jackie, quite miserably, 'it bleeding is.'

He glanced around at the scatter of men slouched against the bar, or else sitting and staring into the precious dregs of all they had left.

'You open then, Len? What time is it?'

Len shrugged his shoulders. 'Don't seem to matter nowadays. I don't sleep no more – don't reckon none of us does – so I just lets people in, if they fancy it. Don't have too much to sell them. All the ale went up. Lost the lot.'

'Jesus . . . this bleeding war, ay? I don't mind telling you, Len – you getting this, is you Victor? I's just saying, this bleeding war, I had enough of it. I used to quite enjoy it, if I'm honest. But now . . . well, I just had enough of it.'

Jackie accepted the light from Len, and sucked in deep the length of the Player's from the packet of ten that Len had just slid out from under the counter. Jackie glanced about him as he languorously expelled the long blue force of the funnel of smoke.

'Here . . .' he said slowly, his eyes narrowing as he nodded in the direction of a big man crouched over the bar. 'I know him, don't I . . . ?'

Len idled his eyes across to where Jackie was meaning.

'Could be. Comes in, time to time.'

Jackie's eyes were bright as he set down his glass.

'Yeh I *do* know him – and I just remembered how I come to. Well well well. Victor – come with me, my son. Like to introduce you to an old acquaintance of mine. We'll just walk over, will we? Yeh. Hallo!' he greeted the man at the bar. 'All right, are we?'

The man's large head was revolving slowly, his eyes still dull as they locked on to Jackie.

'It's just I observed, see, you's nursing a drop of Gawd knows what there, and I were just wondering whether you might be interested in a half bottle Dewar's.'

The man was hissing through his teeth.

'Nothing I'd like better,' he grunted. 'Can't afford it from you boys.'

'It's cheap!' Jackie protested, his eyes so wide and sincere. 'Ten bob. Can't say fairer.'

Now the man was looking at him hard.

'Ten bob? Never. Must be rotgut for ten bob.'

'McCoy, son. Telling you. Dewar's. Check the seal – check the label. Just got to be shot of it, that's all.'

The man's eyes were blinking at Jackie, and then he looked down into the brownish lees of what he had been drinking.

'All right then – you're on. Ten bob. Let's have a look at it.'

'Well now be *serious*, my old mate! I ain't got it *here*, has I? What you take me for? Ay? It's in the motor. Just outside. You come with us, bring your ten bob, and you can have yourself a nice little drink. How about that? Ay? Can't say fairer.'

The man nodded briskly, pushed aside his glass, and strode over to the door. He towered over even Victor. Outside, down the little alley where Len had his old banger of a Morris up on bricks, Jackie led Victor and beckoned the man to follow. They stopped under the awning over the bench where Len kept his tools.

'Just under the bench, mate. Have a feel about. Matter of fact – you maybe doesn't remember, but we met before.'

The man was stooped low, his hands ferreting about beneath the flap of sacking.

'Yeh?' he grunted. 'Don't recall. I can't find no bottle . . .'

'Well it's there, I'm telling you. Try the other side. Yeh – while ago now,' Jackie continued, quite conversationally, while he caught Victor's eye and pointed to something at the side of the bench. 'In this very pub, as it happens. I were with a couple of mates.'

'There's no bloody bottle down here,' muttered the disgruntled man. 'What's going on? You got the Scotch or ain't you?'

'Try at the very back. Yeh – two mates I were with. And one of them, you didn't take kindly to the way he were talking. Thought he were talking too posh. Come back to you, do it?'

The man was still, and then he withdrew his head from under the curtain, and made to get up. Victor pressed down hard into his shoulders as the man began to struggle, and he hissed at Jackie to be quick for Christ's sake, because he's like an ox, this one.

'And *then* . . .' smiled Jackie, raising high above his head the jointed car-jack, 'you fucking fisted me right on the head. Like *this*, you *bastard!*' he roared, bringing down the jack square and heavily on to the back of the man's head. He was bellowing and staggered down on to his knees and Jackie was wild-eyed and spitting out any sort of vileness that flew into his head and he kicked out wildly at the sprawling man, whose limbs now were barely jerking. Jackie was panting hard as he threw aside the jack, and it clanged along the ground.

'No, Victor – leave him. Don't want him dead. Just a little lesson. Don't reckon he'll bother us no more. Let's go in and have another one with Len, and after that I got to be off. Important business.' Jackie was grinning as he clapped an impassive Victor across his shoulders. 'My my, Victor – I do feel better for that, I must say. Braced, are what I feel. Quite the new man. I'll see you inside then, will I?'

Yeh. And it were remembering Dickie, see, what give me the idea. Because it hadn't left my mind, nor nothing – the only thing I got to do is to get my Alfie safe. There ain't nothing more. But I got a big problem. Anyone else – anyone else but Alfie, and all I got to do is get in touch with Mr Wisely, he square it, and the lad's away. But he wouldn't do it, not for Alfie he wouldn't. He didn't want him in – and after this little lot, he won't want him back neither. And yeh I *know* it weren't Alfie's fault, I know that, I do know that – of course I bleeding know that . . . but it ain't how the boss are going to see it. In other words, Mr Wisely – he'd be happy to see my little brother rot in the clink for the rest of his natural. So it's down to me, this. But see – I goes over in person and, well . . . that sergeant, he going to have me behind bars before you can say Jack Wossname, ain't he? Ay? And then there's the two of us in the hole, and that ain't going to help my Alfie. So then I gets to reckoning, well – what if Dickie, what if he go along instead, ay? Doctor, after all. Speaks proper. He could say . . . I don't know . . . that Alfie, after his injury and all the shock of it and that – that he don't know what he doing. Something like that. And even if they don't let him go (which yeh – they won't, the bastards) well then if it got to come to trial, Dickie can talk to the beak, can't he? Better than what I can, even if I could show my face. So yeh – it ain't a plan, but it's all I got. So first thing, I reckon, is to get myself round to Dickie's.

So I done that, and what I sees there is this bit of brown paper stuck on the door with all his scrawl all over it: big pencil letters – Sorry, No Surgery Today. Yeh. And by the look of the way the writing's all over the bleeding shop, I maybe reckon I knows why, drunk old sot what he is.

'Who's there . . . ?! Go away!' came the slurred and panicked echo, rumbling through the panels of the door.

'Don't be stupid, Dickie!' shouted back Jackie, once again pummelling hard on the door and vainly rattling at the handle. 'It's me, ain't it? Jackie. Open up, for Christ's sake. What's wrong with you? It's Jackie, Dickie!'

There was a pause, and then Dickie came back with a heightened apprehension.

'Jackie . . . ? That you? That really you . . . ?'

'*Course* it's—! Come on – open the bloody door. What's got into you, Dickie? As if I didn't know. Best part of a crate, sounds like . . .'

Two bolts slid back, and Dickie's defeated and red-rimmed eyes were peering with anxiety around the just ajar door. Jackie barged his way in, and slammed it shut behind him.

'Bleeding rigmarole . . .' Jackie was huffing, as he threw himself into the rickety chair. And then he gazed about him. 'Gawd Almighty, Dickie . . . what has you been up to this time? Ay? Place look like a horse and cart just come through it. Come over here, son – let's be having you. Blimey – I thought *I* were looking rough. You been to bed yet? How many bottles you done? All this lot . . .' said Jackie, the toe of his boot clinking among the empties spinning around the floor 'this aren't just *today*? Not possible – even for you, Dickie.'

Dickie tottered over and fell into the other chair, his head just swinging about like a broken flower-head at the very end of its flat and sappy stem.

'Last night . . . today . . . don't know. Can't think. Oh God, Jackie – you've got to help me, old man . . . !'

Jackie was struck by the tone, and he looked at Dickie directly. The sheer white terror and utter disbelief in his dulled-over, bulbous and bloodshot eyes were so much more than merely drunken remorse, or fear over a fit of the shakes.

'Here . . .' said Jackie slowly, reaching his hand across the desk just to stop the constant jerking of Dickie's own. 'What you been up to . . . ? What's going on, Dickie? You can tell me. Look – I'll pour you a little drink, all right? Settle your nerves. Then you can tell me.'

Dickie shook his head wretchedly, and more tears were squeezed from out of his eyes. 'Isn't any more. Would've drunk it. Then maybe I'd be dead, bit of luck. Tried to get in to the drugs cabinet. Couldn't find the key. That's why the room's so wrecked. Tore it apart, you see . . . looking for the key. Went to rip it off the wall. Couldn't. Oh God. Oh *God*, Jackie . . . I just . . . oh *God*. Oh my *Christ*, Jackie . . . !'

Jackie was up now, and very uneasy. He walked around the desk, and patted Dickie's back.

'Now now, Dickie. You get calm, ay? You settle down. Then you tell me all about it. Can't be that bad.'

Dickie looked up sharply and focused on quite the wrong thing, and then he found Jackie's face and latched on to it with a passion.

'*Is!* It's worse than bad. I can't speak. But I must. I'll tell you, shall I Jackie? Yes? And you'll help me, will you? Say you will, old man. No one else can. You will, won't you Jackie? Tell me you will.'

'Course I will, Dickie. You knows I will. Now tell me what's going on. Start at the beginning, ay?'

Dickie nodded, and knotted together his fingers. He closed his eyes in deep concentration, and tried his hardest to remember just the sequence of the thing. The beginning, yes. The way it started: how it all came about . . . Yesterday. Surgery. I'd done that, pretty sure. Think I had. Well I must have, must have – of course I did, I must have. And then I was just sitting here at my desk, having a drink . . . oh yes, and I was trying hard to remember quite what it was I'd arranged with Sheila, because honestly you know, these days, I say a thing, and the next bally moment, well – gone. Can't remember. Useless. But I knew we'd arranged something, anyhow – we were going to eat, but whether here or over at Sheila's or in some sort of a café or something, I really couldn't have said. So I had a couple more, you know, the way you do when you're just loafing about, sort of thing, and then Sheila, she just sort of appeared, you know. Don't actually recall her ringing the bell or me going to answer the door, or anything . . . she just sort of all of a sudden was there, you know, and I was pretty relieved, on the whole – meant I could stop trying to remember where it was I was meant to be (here, evidently) and much more to the point, I didn't actually have to change and go off somewhere. Because after a day of surgery and hardly any sleep the night before – the drink, of course – I'm really pretty far gone, you know, come the evening. And washing, changing, catching a bus . . . all such a beastly effort. Well everything is, of course, these days. Going to bed. Shelter. Getting up. All such a beastly effort.

'You'd forgotten, hadn't you Dickie? You look ghastly.'

'No no no – not a bit. Of course I hadn't, Sheila old thing. What do you take me for? I'm sorry I look ghastly . . . Forgotten? No no. I'm *here*, aren't I?'

Sheila smiled indulgently and set down the wicker basket she was hefting on her hip.

'Just about,' she sniffed. 'And where's the wine? You haven't drunk it, have you?'

Dickie looked momentarily startled, before he recovered himself.

'The wine. No of course I haven't drunk it . . . just had a Scotch or so, that's all. What, er – what wine would that be, in fact? Sheila?'

'You see! You *have* forgotten. I don't know about you just lately, Dickie. Your mind's like a—'

'Oh God I *know* – it's awful. Sieve. You're quite right. But I do *have* some wine, pretty sure – upstairs somewhere. Red affair. Château something or other, you know.'

'Well good. Because I've brought everything else. There's cold beef – well, cold chunks of steak, really, but it'll be jolly good. Lettuce, bread, real butter, radishes . . . tin of peaches, bit of a treat, and a box of chox. Yum. Most of it courtesy of Mary, I have to say. So it'll be a lovely indoor picnic. Where shall we set it up? Not in here. Shall we go upstairs? Is the fire going? No, I don't suppose it is.'

Dickie drank Scotch and was answering her happily as he poured out more.

'Upstairs is splendid – splendid idea. Just go and get it all cosy, shall I? Bedroom's best – little gas fire, don't you know.'

Sheila regarded him with some hesitation.

'Mm . . . well all right then, Dickie . . . but you won't, will you? You must promise me you won't start up all of your malarkey. Promise me, Dickie.'

Dickie drank Scotch and was answering her quite miserably as he poured out more.

'Oh gosh, Sheila . . . it's not – *malarkey*, is it? Hey? It's just a – chap, you know, needing to express his affection for a chapess, sort of thing. All perfectly *natural*, after all . . .'

'Yes yes yes – I've heard all that, haven't I Dickie? It's just not natural to me, that's all. So are you going to promise me or aren't you?'

Mm. Yes . . . so it's all fairly clear to me up to that point, anyway. But the *rest* . . . ! Oh God. Anyway. We didn't. Go upstairs. Some reason. Why would that be, I wonder . . . ? Don't know. Can't think. Oh yes – I know, of course I know. Bally siren, wasn't it? Another, yet another blasted air raid. We must have known it was coming, the way it's been just lately – night after night after night. Anyway – that was it. That was why.

So next thing we know, we're both of us back down in the Anderson.

'Oh *God*, Dickie – just look at it! It's worse than ever. You said you were going to clean it all out. It's six inches deep! Oh God, Dickie – how can we enjoy a picnic when we're up to our knees in *mud*? It's really too bad.'

'. . . exaggerate . . . not up to our *knees*, is it? Hey? And we've got our wellingtons, and everything.'

'Not the point,' huffed Sheila, lighting the kerosene lamp and then clearing a space on one of the metal-framed bunks down there, spreading out a gingham cloth. 'Did you remember a corkscrew? Bet you didn't.'

Dickie lined up the three bottles of Scotch, one of them nearly done. He slowly shook his head.

'It's worse,' he admitted. 'I didn't remember the wine. Oh Lord. I can nip back upstairs and get it, though. Two secs.'

'You'll do no such thing. Listen: bombs are already dropping. Oh my *God*, Dickie, Dickie . . . ! That one was quite close. Oh it's just so horrible, this. Sitting in a tin can and just *waiting* . . . Oh well. Come on. Let's eat something, shall we? I'm starving.'

Mm. Yes . . . so it's all fairly clear to me up to that point, anyway. And then . . . I think I might have dozed off, you know. Did eat something, possibly. Not sure. Drank a lot, that's for definite. Bombing was hard – non-stop. Clearly we were in for a night of it. So I think I sort of lay on one of the bunks, you know, and just – well, as I say, dozed off, sort of thing, Must have, because – yes, I remember, my chin, my chin hit something, must have slipped off the bunk, hit something or other, and the lamp, that was out. Candles, though – Sheila, I suppose . . . she must have lit them, some point. Had one hell of a head. Bombs still coming down. One of them rattled the whole place so badly that a couple of plates were knocked off the ledge. Anyway. Had a drink. Finished off another bottle. And Sheila, she was sleeping. On the other bunk. Blanket over her. Looked lovely, to my eye. The sort of curve of her, you know. As she just sort of lay there.

'Sheila . . . ? Hallo . . . ? You awake? Sheila? It's Dickie. God, you feel so warm . . . Sheila . . . ? You awake?'

She started, suddenly – looking about her wide-eyed and assembling her senses. Then she was pushing at the deadweight slump of Dickie that was now sprawled across her – pummelling at his chest and gulping in bursts her annoyance and frustration.

'Dickie! Get – *off*. Get off me, Dickie. You're completely drunk. Take your hand away. Get *off* me, damn you! You promised. You promised me, Dickie!'

Dickie tried to hold her down, his wet lips nuzzling at the nape of her neck – so blood-hot – and his big dead hands were clambering around her.

'S'all right, Sheila my love . . . just . . . just let me . . .'

'Dickie get *off* me – I'm telling you for the last time. Get—!'

And Dickie's eyes clouded with anger as he drew back his arm and swung it across her face and then to cancel the look of hurt and alarm there, to dull the white candlelights alive in her eyes, he swept back his fist and hit her with it, hard. Then he roared out his self-loathing amid the thudding of bombs and the clang of the shelter and rolled away from her and staggered down heavily on to one knee into the cold and murky water and his head was reeling as he pulled himself up and fell back into his bunk and tugged out the cork from the bottle of whisky and his throat was jerking like a piston as the burn of Scotch pulsated within him. And then his leaden head slumped over and he closed his eyes and tumbled into a spangled and jerky unconsciousness.

⊙

Dickie was hugging Jackie's shoulder and weeping softly as he hauled open the door of the Anderson shelter. Jackie elbowed him aside, crouched down low and shone in a torch. There was a rumple of blankets and a mud-streaked gingham cloth, strewn with bits of lettuce and a crushed-in box of chocolates. Two empty whisky bottles were bobbing about in the tea-coloured water – and there too, face down, was all that could be seen of Sheila, a hump of wet tweed, the clogged and sopping tangle of her hair, so still, its tendrils lacing the surface.

Jackie's heart was thudding within him as he breathed out once, and heavily.

'*Jesus*, Dickie . . . !'

Dickie, behind him, gasped. His eyes were rolling as his rocking head was scanning the sky.

'She's . . . dead . . .' he just about managed.

'I can bloody see that. *Christ*, Dickie . . . !'

'I didn't *mean* to,' babbled Dickie, clawing Jackie's arms. 'I mean, God – I *loved* her, Jackie. I just . . . I only . . . I mean I only . . . oh God. And then she just must have . . . oh my God. Oh my *God*, Jackie – what can I *do* . . . ?!'

Jackie stood up slowly, and cranked the door shut.

'You got a key for this thing? Yeh? Well lock it. Now look, I got to go now, Dickie – no no, don't worry, don't worry, I'm coming back – I'll be back, I promise you Dickie. It's just I got important business. Yeh. Thought you was going to be able to help me out there, but you ain't. No – you ain't. Now listen. You listening, Dickie? When it get dark, bung her into something. You got something? Bag? Sack? Something? Well find something – and then you locks it up again. And make sure she got her handbag with all her doings in it. Come night-time, I'll be back. And then we gets rid of her. Somewhere she won't be noticed. All right? Answer me, Dickie. Look – it ain't no good just blubbing and shaking about like that, is it? Ay? Got to get you out of this, ain't we? I say – *ain't* we? Yeh. Right then. So pull yourself bleeding together. And no more fucking booze, got it? I means it, Dickie. I can't do this lot on my own, and I ain't going to bring in no one else. That's for your sake. Got me? So it just you and me, Dickie. And you got to be fit. See? Yeh? You better see, that's all. Your neck, Dickie – it's your neck, mate, they finds her here. Right then. I'll be off. You just do like I said. Got it? Dickie? Yeh? Right. And then I'll be back.'

Well what I reckoned was, the best thing was not to go thinking about it. Not none of it. Dead on my feet, I were – and worried, yeh, near out my mind. If it weren't for Alfie, I never would've left him, Dickie, not in the state he were in. Liable to do all sorts. Because I need him, Dickie – lifeline, he are. Can't go losing him. So yeh – I would've, I would've stayed with him, maybe feeding him a little bit of drink, time to time, save him from going mad. And I'll have to remember that – bring him back a flattie, keep him even, because elsewise he'll be flapping like a flag, come night-time.

And when I gets there, the police station – well, I hadn't planned too much. Had just the one card to play, but it weren't too strong. What I did know is, I had to get to see that sergeant. There were something about him, couldn't finger it. Anyways, I needn't have worried on account of as soon as I walks through the door, there he are, the bastard, bold as day, behind the thing what they got there, counter, yakking away to another of them.

'Well well well well *well* . . .' he goes, and he's grinning. 'What do we have here? Dave, isn't it? If I'm not mistaken.'

'I need to talk to you,' said Jackie, flatly. He had just noticed again the tear at the knee of his trousers – must've been when he came a cropper, running blindly into the night to get away from this lot.

'Well there is a happy coincidence. Because I was just this minute saying to my constable – wasn't I, Constable? I think

Constable Peakie will vouch. Just saying, I'd very much like a little word with that Dave character – isn't that so, Constable? Indeed. And who the next minute should walk through my door? Some days just seem blessed, don't they? My name, by the bye, is Sergeant Eales. Further particulars from your good self will no doubt be forthcoming as our interview progresses. Step into my office, would you? Most kind. Most kind, I'm sure.'

Jackie walked into the small and dismal room as Sergeant Eales stood with his back against the open door. He sat on the straight-backed chair on the other side of the dark oak desk. A green-shaded lamp, two black telephones and a rusting wire tray piled high with lemon-coloured forms, stapled into batches. On the wall behind hung crookedly a calendar, and Jackie recognised the rose-covered cottage from a magazine that Mary had shown to him, some time. It was where the bint of that bald old geezer holed up hundreds of years back, him what wrote all of the tosh.

'First off,' said Jackie, as the sergeant settled himself into the swivel chair opposite him. 'I got to know. Bloke you hauled in last night. You book him, or what?'

Sergeant Eales was smiling.

'Cigarette?'

'I'll have one of my own.'

'Mm. Very smart case. Gold. Expensive. Crime been good to you, has it Dave? And Turkish cigarettes as well. Mind if I try one?'

'Help yourself. Well? Has you or ain't you?'

Sergeant Eales lit his cigarette and cocked his head to one side as he slowly exhaled the column of smoke.

'Mm. Different. Very pleasant. Sorry, Dave – you were saying . . . ?'

Jackie was fired by anger, but somehow he forced himself to go on sitting there, to not leap over that desk and strangle the bastard, to continue to speak in as disinterested a tone as he could muster.

'The bloke. Last night. Book him, did you?'

'Oh I remember. Your young friend. Your accomplice in larceny. Wilf, isn't it? If that is his name. And if, Dave, you are really called Dave. Something we'll have to go into, isn't it? But since you ask – no, the paperwork is yet to be done. Pressure of time. All go.'

'So where is he, then? Where you got him?'

'Did I say I got him?'

'Well . . . ?'

'Mm. Yes I have. Since you ask.'

Jackie leaned across the desk and looked at the sergeant intently.

'Well look. what'll it take to just let him walk?'

'My my my my *my*. You are full of surprises, aren't you Dave? Last night it was Scotch, and now it's money you're offering me. It'll be up to the judge, won't it? Whether he walks.'

'Yeh but it's just you and me here, ain't it? Ay?'

Sergeant Eales eyed the cigarette between his fingers.

'What is it that you are proposing?'

'Hundred. Cash, of course. No questions asked.'

The sergeant nodded slowly and lowered his eyelids.

'Hundred, ay? Lot of money. Man such as myself, humble servant of the Crown, have to toil for many months, money like that. Tell me, Dave – what's it to you? Ay? Who is this bloke, you'd give all that money for? Relation is he, maybe?'

'Nah. Nothing like that. Just a young bloke what's had a bad break, that's all. You seen his leg.'

'Or the absence of same. Yes I did.'

'Well? Yes or no?'

Sergeant Eales picked up a wad of lemon forms, and let them drop back.

515

'Hundred, ay . . . ?'

'Hundred. Cash. Right now, and then it's done.'

'Mm. Well . . . I could see that as part payment. I maybe could, between these four walls, agree to the hundred being the first part of the payment.'

'First part? How much you think you going to get off of me? I ain't no mug, you know. I knows the going rate, and hundred, that's way over – and you knows it and all. So what you on about?'

'I think . . . I'll have a Woodbine now. They're nice, those Turkish. I'm not saying I didn't enjoy it. But for now, I reckon I'll just settle for a Woodbine. Want one, Dave?'

Jackie was sweating and his stomach was cramped. He was maybe hungry, or sick.

'Never mind Woodbines. What you want?'

'Well – since you ask me, Dave, I'll tell you. What I want is – a name. Not your name – not now. And not the name of some other little Jack the Lad either. I mean the man at the top. Your sort, you Flash Harrys, they're all over London. Like maggots. Like flies on a dung heap. Parasites, you are. You know that? We're all fighting a war, and you're just busy helping yourselves. Spivs. Aren't you? Hey? Fair makes me ill to think of it. So what I want to know, Dave, is who's running it all? Hey?'

Jackie shook his head in defiance.

'Got to be *joking*. What you take me for? Even if there are a name, which there ain't, you really reckon I give it you? I ain't no grass, mate. I'm offering you money – just take it, and me and the lad's out of here.'

'The hundred?'

'*Yeh*, the hundred. Keep bleeding saying it, don't I? What's wrong with you? Look – here it is. Nice clean fivers. Twenty of them. Feast your eyes, son. When you see money like that? And it's yours – you just got to take it.'

Sergeant Eales reached for the large white notes, and idly riffled through them. And then he folded them and tucked them into the top pocket of his tunic, buttoning it securely and adjusting the chain on his whistle.

'Right . . .' breathed Jackie. 'So we's on. Where is he?'

'*Part* payment, Dave . . .'

Jackie was standing now, and his eyes were blazing.

'*Look*, you bent bleeding lousy copper – what's it to you? Just another hoodlum. Let him go – you got the money.'

'I *will*, Dave. Course I will. Cut down on paperwork, won't it? *I* don't want him. Like you say – just another hoodlum. Another maggot. One more fly on the dung heap . . .'

'Yeh yeh – all right. You done all that. What you after?'

'Told you, Dave. A name. The name. Then he can walk, your chum. Otherwise, it could go hard on him. Breaking rocks, marching up and down . . . Some places, you know, they still got a treadmill. I know. Amazing to think it. Medieval, you might say. But they got them, and they wouldn't think twice about putting him on it, either. Leg or no leg. Twelve hours at a time, what I hear. Dear oh dear. And if I was to tell the magistrate that he roughed up two of my constables . . .'

'He never roughed up *nobody* – what you talking about?'

'Beside the point, Dave. You're not listening. I said if I told the magistrate that he *had* . . . well, could be ten years, the way they're going now. Very hard they are, just lately.'

Jackie sat down heavily, and chewed on his lip. His head was heavy and spinning and his limbs felt milky and weak. He knew it was true, what the bastard was saying: that was the bleeding trouble.

'Look, Dave – listen to me, there's a good boy. I know you hate me. I know you want to kill me, right this moment as you're sitting there. And maybe in your place, I'd be feeling the same, who can say? But you've got to see it from my point of view. Got to cover myself, haven't I? Hey? Everyone here, they've seen him, haven't they? Your young friend. So I have to be able to justify my turning that key in the lock and setting him free. You see? And the only thing that would justify it is a name. The name. So like I say, if I was sitting where you are, Dave, I'd no doubt be bitter. But you see – I'm not. Am I? I'm sitting here. Aren't I? And you're sitting over there. So you're going to have to decide, aren't you? Which of them's more important. Simple as that.'

Jackie licked his lips and looked about him.

'Pony. Another pony. It's all I got . . .'

'No no, Dave. Don't want more money. Mustn't be greedy, must we? Hundred's plenty. More than generous. No, Dave – I'm rather afraid it's name or nothing. Take your time. No rush. Sure you won't change your mind about having a Woodbine . . . ?'

Jackie's head hung low as he stared down at his hands as they knotted and unknotted, and the void between his legs. And then he muttered.

'Sorry, Dave? Didn't quite catch that . . . ?'

'What guarantee I got? How I know you going to keep your word. You're bent – we know that. So why should I believe you?'

'Mm. I appreciate your dilemma. All I can do is promise you that when you give me the name, I press this button here on my telephone and Constable Peakie goes down to the cells and brings up your boy and then we wave the two of you goodbye. Unless you'd both like to stay for a cup of tea, of course. Always welcome. But yes, I can see how you might not believe me . . .'

Jackie stared at him wretchedly. And then he looked down and was muttering again.

'No sorry, Dave – still a little bit incoherent. What is it you're saying?'

Jackie looked him in the eye.

'Wisely . . .'

'I'm sorry? What is wisely . . . ?'

'The name, you cloth-head. It's Wisely. Nigel Wisely. Up West. That's all I got. Now get him up here like what you said.'

Sergeant Eales nodded thoughtfully.

'Up West . . . big place, up West. Bit more specific, do you think you can be . . . ?'

Jackie sighed and picked up a pencil from the desk and wrote an address on a scrap of paper. The sergeant slid it towards him.

'Mm. Most salubrious. Lovely area. Nice for some. Well well. Thank you, Dave. You have done the right thing. I commend you.'

'Yeh yeh – never mind all that. Press it.'

'Sorry? Press it . . . ?'

'The—! The bleeding button on your bleeding telephone, you bastard. *Press* it.'

'Just about to, Dave. Just about to.'

The sergeant pressed a button close to the receiver and two policemen were immediately in the room and they had Jackie roughly by the arms and they hauled him to his feet as he spluttered out his shock and fury.

'That's it, lads,' said the sergeant with relish, coming around from behind the desk. 'Hold him fast, that's the way.'

'You *bastard* . . . !' Jackie howled into his face. 'You bleeding fucking *bastard* . . . !'

'Making a note of this, are you boys? Insulting a police officer. Profane language. He does pile it on, doesn't he?'

Jackie struggled fiercely as the policemen tightened their grip on him.

'And bribery!' he yelled. 'Tell them about the bribe you just took!'

'Bribe? Can't think what you mean. Right then – get him downstairs with the other one. You know, Dave – what you said earlier? Quite amusing. About you not being a mug? Wrong. I haven't ever met so big a mug as you before, sonny – and believe me, I've met a good few.'

The policemen shuffled Jackie into the hall, and he concentrated hard on willing all his muscles to relax, to unclench: he tried to go limp in their grasp.

'Even *more* amusing,' chuckled the sergeant, 'is the sort of mug you must have taken *me* for. I've now got two of you scum, you filthy little spivs – got the both of you in my lock-up now, haven't I? Hey? And what – you reckoned you were going to walk, did you? Just like that? Dear oh dear. One born every minute. And we've got an address to check up on, haven't we? I'll let you know how we get on. If it's false, well . . . you'll be behind bars for the rest of your natural, son. But if it's good, you rest assured, Dave, we'll see to telling this Mr Wisely just where it was we got the information. Right lads – get him out of here.'

Jackie grinned, and looked abashed.

'Yeh. You fair got me. I were stupid. You're clever you are, Sergeant Eales.'

'Good of you to say so, Dave. Give him a nice cup of tea when you get him locked up. He's not a bad lad, really.'

Jackie went on grinning as he eyed first the one policeman gripping him – young, scared, weak, distracted – and then the other – overweight and breathing heavily – and he nodded in so very docile a manner before bringing up his elbows and kicking back his heels, hard and with a ferocious determination as the young policeman screamed and bent down to his shin and Jackie was furiously wrestling his way away from the grasp of the other one as Sergeant Eales came doggedly forward and Jackie's hand was now scrabbling in his jacket as he sprinted for the double doors and he could hear the roaring and feel the breath of the two men behind him as he swept open one of the doors and turned and smashed it hard into the face of the burly policeman who spun away and fell to the floor as if he had been hit by a train and Jackie had now to beat away the hands of Sergeant Eales as he was clawing at his arms and only then could he wheel about and confront him with the knife and he thrust it forward repeatedly and with a scowling menace as his mouth barked out the direst warnings and all the time he was backing away, backing away, until the cold of the street struck him in the face and still the sergeant, he came on towards him and was telling him quietly not to be stupid and to put down the knife and to not make it any worse for himself than it already was and Jackie bellowed at him to keep away, to keep his distance, and still the sergeant kept on coming forward and then Jackie just lunged at him and heard the thud and sigh as he stuck the jutting-out blade deep into the man's shoulder and he turned and ran after seeing so fleetingly the tremor of fear, the blank astonishment in the sergeant's eyes as he sank on down to his knees, spitting gobbets of scarlet, and by the time he fell over to one side Jackie was cantering wildly down the length of an alleyway, his feet barely touching the rubbish-strewn pitch as he careered away and off into the distance and he cackled now madly as the pounding of his footsteps was ringing in his ears, and no he weren't no mug, no not him – I'm no mug, you stupid copper – I's Jack the Lad, I is, and I's away and I's gone, and it's you, you stupid bastard, it's you now what's down and just lying there on the ground, you bastard, bleeding all over my hundred quid.

☉

'One swig, Dickie. No more. I need you fit. It's dark now. We got to be moving.'

Dickie's eyes were wide, as if in the grip of a vision, as his white and shaking hands reach out towards the half bottle of Haig as if before him there was hovering the pale dove of peace

– something to be carefully enfolded, and which might so very easily flutter up, and disappear. It took both hands and intense concentration to steady the bottle and bring it to his lips which were juddering briefly before they latched on to the neck and then he was pulling with desperation and something approaching a pious devotion, as if at the fountainhead of a new and crystal future. Jackie then prised it away from him, one stiff cold finger at a time, and Dickie watched it go with a wistful sorrow, his throat still pounding and drily swallowing down the last hot memory. He passed the back of his hand across his mouth, and licked it.

'Thanks so much, Jackie old man. Needed it. Right. Right then. What do we do? Oh God, I simply can't believe it, that we're doing this.'

'Yeh well. What we do is, we gets her in the car – I put it right outside – and then we drives over to the docks. And then we waits.'

'Why there? Why not round here? And why wait? Bound to be a raid tonight.'

'Yeh I know. Whole point, ain't it? Look – I can't be doing with explaining it to you. Just do like I say, and then you're in the clear. All right? Right then. Where is she?'

Dickie sighed and rolled up his eyes to heaven.

'Next door. Oh God.'

Jackie opened the door and looked inside.

'Sheets. Are that the best you could do? Sheets? Couldn't you find a – I don't know – coal sack, or something? Potato sack? Something?'

Dickie shook his head and closed his eyes.

'Looked. Nothing. Sheets. All I had. Dried her, a bit. Deadweight, though.'

'Yeh well she would be. Right – have to bleeding do, then. So, Dickie – you able? What end you want?'

'Oh Christ, Jackie . . . you know I really don't know if I can—!'

'Yeh well – you cut that lot out for a start. You got to. You just got to. And that's the bleeding end of it. Here – you takes the feet.'

'Couldn't I first just have another little drink, Jackie? Just a drop?'

'No. Later. Come on. We losing time. Lift when I says. Got it? Right then. Now under your arm. That's it. That's the style. Blimey – she are a weight. Right now, Dickie – we's away.'

Jackie had been hoping that the Riley's boot would do for this, but it soon became clear that however he bent her up, she wasn't going to fit. It annoyed him and he was also rather surprised. Sheila, she'd never struck him as being that big a girl, but if it wasn't a knee, it was an elbow or a foot jutting out, and no matter how hard he slammed down the lid, it just wasn't going to go: she's stiff as a board, look.

'Right, Dickie – back seat. Nothing else for it. Out she come.'

Dickie was trembling badly, his incoherent muttering becoming drivel as he started up his weeping again, whether out of a fresh surge of remorse or the darkest fear or just the clutch of craving for alcohol, Jackie honestly couldn't have told you and nor did he bleeding care – he just wanted to get this job sorted and out of the way: he needed this day to be over and done.

Jackie drove very slowly, barely any road visible in the sullen soupy glow of his dim and blinkered lights. Dickie asked him at one point how on earth he could know where he was going, the night was that black, and Jackie replied that he was going by his nose. There was just enough moonlight to decipher the dull and pewter glisten of the river from the slab of enveloping coal, and Jackie parked close so that when he rolled down the window and was smacked by cold, he could hear it, the river, shivering and idly slapping at the wharves and embankments.

'God . . .' breathed Dickie. 'It's quiet. So black.'

Jackie lit a cigarette and inhaled it deeply.

'Be ready, Dickie. Hell are coming, son.'

Dickie whistled flatly through his teeth, and nodded morosely.

'Jackie . . . any chance of a . . . ?'

'I told you. Later. Just wait. When all this are over, you can drink the bloody lot, all I care.'

And then it came: the long and sonorous indolent moaning of the air-raid siren, and at once the tarry sky was crisscrossed with erections of cold white light – probing and shifting, each streaming shaft seeking out the very first fly-speck that will augur the swarm, the placid and relentless waves, the drone of enemy planes, each one solid with its own inferno.

'Christ, Jackie . . . we're right in the target zone. Are we just going to sit here . . . ?'

'We is, my son. We wait for the first strike. And if it's us, well . . . then it all don't matter no more. Do it? Just sit tight. Won't take long.'

Dickie was rocking his head from side to side, and then he was mewling.

'Oh God. Oh God, Jackie – I'm just no good at this. I'm scared. I'm not like you. I'm just so badly frightened. I've been frightened – out of my mind with fear ever since this bloody war started. I *live* in fear – I just can't do it any more, Jackie. Oh *please*, Jackie – please give me a drink. I can't tell you, old man, how much I need a drink . . . !'

The plocking and then staccato crack of the guns was muffled and intermittent and then there was a whistling in the sky that rose intolerably, before it just faded away, the droning above them constant and heavy. And then there was light from a thousand incendiaries, crackling into life in gutters and on parapets, over and all about them, yet more scattered and fizzing clusters spattering the Thames and making it gleam with a brief and molten radiance, before it swallowed them whole. The ferocious brightness of all the fires, high up and around them, threw into stark and theatrical silhouette the jagged angles and protrusions of gables and turrets, tiny jet and helmeted men jerkily alive and skimming the rooftops like a cast of miniature marionettes sent out to perform before so very furious a backdrop. In the steam of a lull, one could hear their cries.

'Right, Dickie . . .' breathed out Jackie. 'Soon, I reckon . . .'

The judder of guns and the pop and spray of the strings and ribboning of yellow incandescence from the litter of incendiaries was gaudily plastered over by the hissing and then the screech, the ear-splitting slicing through the fathoms of deep sea blackness suspended above them, and Dickie just yelled in panic as the screaming crescendo of a coming descent was just cut dead – and then he roared his terror and clutched at Jackie as the first great splintered crashings and then rumble of eruption rocked the car from side to side and fragments of brickwork were spattering down upon the roof and bonnet, and then they tumbled away as Dickie was cowering and hunching and whimpering badly.

'Right now, Dickie,' said Jackie sternly. 'This is it. We *go.*'

He ignored all of Dickie's protestations and hauled him out and on to the street – had him by the lapels of his coat and dragged him around to the side of the car while Dickie's eyes were just raking the sky, the dismal and eternal throb of the planes cut into viciously by the shriek of falling bombs and the burst of thunder as buildings bellied out and burst and then just tumbled down with outrage, protest and an angry roar into broken-backed and crumpled mountains. There was too much noise for Jackie to have any hope in this hell of making himself heard and so all he did when he had jerked open the back door of the car was to slap Dickie hard across the face and slap him again and then register the man's astonishment and his relative composure as Jackie urgently pointed to the slumped-over bundle and hunkered down now to humping it up on to the running board, and then he had his arms awkwardly around it. Dickie, through the stinging blindfold of all his tears, grabbed a hold of all that was trailing down and scraping amid all the rubble, and crying quite piteously and unstoppably, he crookedly stumbled over broken brick and splintered beams, to wherever Jackie's unseen back might lead him. His foot plunged down into an unsuspected gully and he lurched over sideways, nearly dropping his load, as the scream of bombs now was sending him crazy – and as he struggled up the crumbled-down hillock of a devastated homestead, he saw the frightened and lit-up eyes of all the windows in the wall alongside and heard the building wailing out to him as if a thousand stuck and terrified pigs were caught up inside it. The flash from another explosion lit up a caved-in pink and chintz-covered sofa and the dial on the wireless, smashed beneath it, still was glowing amber, and humming. Then Dickie was yelling out again as the bellow of an imminent implosion had him in its grip, and then on his hand he felt the touch of icy cold and rigid fingers, the sudden fierce light from another burst of fire momentarily capturing Sheila's stiff and greenish forearm, flopped out from among the tattered sheets that were splitting into pieces. Jackie now was signalling to him – his face had been gashed and it was streaked with black – and Dickie nodded quite deliriously as he mindlessly complied and set to doing whatever it was that Jackie was doing – laying down the body across the staved-in sofa and tearing away the remaining shreds of sheeting – and then he nearly lost all hope of reason as she lurched over drunkenly and her smooth, quite tranquil face was upturned and stark, her two white eyes so blankly curious, and asking him just to tell her why. Jackie was signalling again to him now – it was time to get out, to go back the way they came – and there was a ripped-away electric cable fizzing like fireworks, spitting its threats. Then Dickie tumbled over and screamed in pain and then he was screaming so much more loudly and the bombs were drowning him out and Jackie just stared into the cave of his strained and miming mouth as he dragged him out roughly from amongst the jagged collapse of broken joists and the choke of plaster that his feet had fallen down through and then another shrieking bomb just did for the building behind and Jackie threw up his arms to protect his head as well as he could as slates and splintered tiles now were flying like tremendous knives hurtled with fury by a maddened impi, ablaze with hatred and hell bent on vengeance. Jackie went on tugging and scrabbling until Dickie was out of it, his face creased up in a tight-lipped agony, and amid the grinding boom of warping metal from high above them, Jackie now was yelping out at the so sudden touch of a hand on his shoulder and he turned to the anxious man in the white steel helmet and he gestured to the grotesque sprawl of Sheila all over the sofa and shook his head with finality and a hopeless regret – and then there was a deafening lull in the howl and thunder – very briefly, only the crackle of burning and the creaking contortions of ruined buildings was all that could be heard – and then there was the muted screaming of people below – keening and hoarse and desperate pleading – and the man in the helmet fell to his knees and frantically began to pull away stone and fragmented timbers and beckoned to Jackie with urgency to come across and help him and Jackie got Dickie up and held him under the shoulders and they somehow managed to stumble away, while Dickie was shrieking at every step and the dumbfounded baying of the man in the helmet was obliterated again by a hideous rattle and then the drumming tremor of bursting brick, red-hot fragments scudding across their cheekbones, their faces and hands so badly scalded by a burning wind that had boiled up out of nowhere and they fell back down into what was left of the street and if

Jackie had not still been gripping him firmly with whatever strength was now left to him, Dickie surely would have given in and even sighed and passed away at the sight now laid before him of just the Riley's dusty nose protruding and askew from beneath a smoking landslide and as the shafts of torches were raking the wreckage of the buildings around them and the distant clang of a fire engine got closer now, and closer, Jackie spat out what ash and grit he could from deep inside his mouth and he ran and staggered and fell and clambered up again and all the while dragging beside or behind him the broken form of Dickie, Jackie screaming his exhortations to go, to go, to keep on *going*, Dickie, while Dickie screeched out his pain and protestations and neither one was hearing a single sound from the other, as all around the moan of tortured buildings and the thunder of their aggressors just smothered and covered them over. Jackie's eyes were now so seared by the blood-orange sky and the smarting of the red-hot smoke and steaming, his feet skewing uselessly in the rush of blackened water, sucked aside by the acrid pull of molten paint. The two spun away and on into blackness, seeking out the cooler alleyways, the precipitous walls aloof and powerless in the face of their coming demise. Jackie half-carried and hauled and kicked at Dickie until he just could do so no longer. The two fell on top of each other, slumped into the corner of a pitch-dark yard, the squawl of a cat as the galvanised bins were clangingly knocked sideways somehow so startling amid still the endless whine and terrible booming from the barrage of bombs that continued to fall. Jackie's chest was pumping with fury, gasping for life, and his bleeding fingers held on tight to his cold and peeling, roasted forehead. Dickie beside him could have been dead, but for the guttural and rackety wheezing, and then the sudden convulsion of yet more tears.

How much time had passed . . . ? Jackie could scarcely believe it when he kicked out and flinched, and sat up with a start. He must somehow, amid this inferno, have fallen asleep. He rubbed at his eyes and shied away from the continuing thunder. He managed to sit up a bit – humped and squirmed his way along the wall, shuffling and feeling around with his hands – and then he set his back against the roughness of the brick, the cold in his legs seeping up from the ground. They should, he thought, be further away, the two of them – much further away. The bombing still was vast and lush and relentless, the roar of spreading fires storming in his ears. But with the car gone, they hadn't a hope. Dickie, he might have bust a leg, or something. Either way, he's in no sort of a condition. Reckon we got to sit tight – not even think about it. If we gets it, we gets it. And soon as I'm a bit more able, I'll haul up old Dickie again, and then we'll scarper. Because this raid, it ain't going to stop – they won't pack it in, bleeding bastards: this one's on till dawn, like they all is, nowadays. Maybe . . . I don't know . . . they set up a firestorm like what they's aiming to do, then there won't be no London no more. How many nights like this one can we take? Ay? Got to be a limit. And come that time, well . . . then we's done for, I suppose. But up till then, I got to look out for myself. And Mary. And this silly sod Dickie, here. Yeh – but what about Alfie? Ay? What about my little kid brother, then? I ain't looked out for him, has I? Made a right pig's arse out of that one. He still in the clink, and there ain't nothing I can do about it now. I show my face, then it's me for the drop, and no bones about it. See . . . thing is, I ain't never been in such a hole. I ain't never been in a hole like this in all my born bleeding days. I got to dodge the police, yeh that's true – but that mob, they got a lot on their minds. Course, they don't at all take kindly to some bloke coming in to their station and sticking a knife in their sergeant on the way out, sort of style. Don't take kindly at all. So I got to lie low. But that ain't it. Nah. That ain't what's worrying me. I mean, I don't mean to say it *ain't* worrying me – course it is, only natural. But I tell you what's really on my mind. It's Mr Wisely. Yeh. I don't know if I were in my right mind, tell you the truth, when I ups and give that bastard his name and address. What were I thinking of? Well yeh – Alfie, of course: I were thinking of him. But any way you looks at it, it weren't clever – well were it? Ay? Because I just lost my job. Victor, he's a good lad, but he would've give Mr Wisely the lot by this time. Can't blame him. You got to look at what side your toast is buttered on, doesn't you? And what with the loss of the van and the loss of the Scotch and the loss of the motor, well . . . time's up for me, I reckon. I lost my job. And if word *do* get back to Mr Wisely that it were me what gone and turned grass on him, well . . . then I lost my life. Plain as day. You got to expect it, this line. Way it go.

I got to get back to my Mary. She'll maybe sort it out. Nah . . . I got to be real. Nothing here what she can sort. But she'll make me feel better, somehow she will. Yeh. I got to get back to my Mary. How's old Dickie doing . . . ? Just about breathing, poor old sod. Leg look bad – sticking out funny. Still – he's a doctor, ain't he? Maybe he can fix it. Got to get him home. Because I tell you – fix I'm in, he all I got left. His certificates, them's what's going to save us: ain't got nothing else. Poor old Dickie. Scared to death, he were. And he says to me – I ain't like you, Jackie, he says to me: I'm frightened. And what – he reckons I ain't? That it? Do me a favour. I'm frightened, son. I'm always frightened. And in the light of all what's been going on now, I'm bleeding terrified. Believe me. And I just been thinking . . . it just come into my mind. That ticket bloke – you know, down the Tube station after Victor and me gets away from them cops. The way he wouldn't take that quid off of me. I can't never forget. First straight bloke I met in years. And I wish I hadn't of, now – showed him the blade. He didn't want that. I shouldn't of done it. But there – lots I shouldn't of done, I suppose. Lost count of it all. And that bloke, that other bloke in the helmet back there. Once, I would of. Helped out, like. In like a shot, I'd of been. But now? Nah. Out for myself – got to be. I ain't no mug. What – me? No fear. I's Jack the Lad. Ain't I?

Do you know . . . the bombs, the fires, the crack of all the buildings . . . I can't hardly hear it no more. Funny, that. The way what you can get used to any old thing, it go on long enough. Forget, you does, how it all used to be before. Yeh. Well – reckon I'll rouse up old Dickie now. We got to get moving. Sitting ducks, we is, we stays here much longer. You waits around for trouble, then trouble, it going to find you, ain't it? Stands to reason. And also, I got to get back to my Mary. Ain't seen her, couple days. Frantic, she'll be, when she catch sight of the state I's in. What's wrong, she'll be going. Is there something *wrong*? She'll keep asking me that. Are you in *trouble*? . . . is the way she'll be going. And I'll be so bleeding grateful just to be back and with her again . . . because I loves her . . . I loves her so bleeding much, I does . . . and I won't want to say nothing, knowing me. But I'll have to, some time or other. And I'll just go to her yeh, something wrong . . . *Trouble*. And then the pair of us, we'll somehow sort it out. Yeh. Right. Haul up old Dickie. Going now. Yeh. I just got to get back to my Mary.

◉

4th March 1941
So much has happened, and so terribly quickly, and I never had the time to write it down. But I must now address myself to the task, because if this 'journal', or whatever one cares to call it, is to serve as any sort of record at all, then there are certain important things that simply have to be committed to paper. Although none of it, I suppose, is important at all – not in any sense an outsider might readily understand. Because

we each one of us now bear a tragedy of our own. Our whole lives, really, have become a seemingly endless tragedy that is unfolding daily. This just happens to be mine.

I have been looking at the last entry I made, and I got such a shock. I thought it was a matter of just a few weeks since I last wrote anything down, but I see it is so many months, and it is hard to believe. The biggest change, of course, has been in the way we live, Jackie and me. It all occurred the very day after he came home that night, all bloody and ragged – or was it nearer to dawn? He seemed half mad, and I was very frightened. He never did tell me what had really happened, and I didn't probe at all deeply – for his sake, at the beginning, and then for mine. I got him cleaned up and bandaged as best I could, and then he slept. He slept for so very long that I was getting rather worried – and when he did wake, he scolded me for having failed to rouse him earlier because, he said, there was much to do. We had to leave the flat. Immediately, he said. I didn't much mind about that, to be honest – it never really did feel like home, that place. It was rather above me, and Jackie, he was never there. The main thing on my mind, of course, was my 'consultancy', as I had begun to call it (although I am sure that no one else did). Now that it had come to moving, and so suddenly, I would finally have to tell him what it is that I do. I tried to do it in as casual a manner as I could, not at all knowing what his reaction might be. What I did not expect, though, was his instant enthusiasm – but of course, he had misunderstood the nature of my vocation. He said that he had decided to leave Mr Wisely's employ – that he would be better – more free, I think he said, out there on his own (doing whatever he does) but for a while there might be short-term difficulties with money, and so anything I could earn would be more than welcome. I then had to explain to him that I didn't do this for money, that it was a service, a donation to the war effort, a charity for young and misguided women. He said I was a 'mug', which I thought offensive. He said all that would have to change. A nominal fee would be in order, he said, and that I wouldn't have to trouble as to its application, as he himself could see to all that side of things. So now, in our new place, I continue to do what I do, but now I charge. I do not know how 'nominal' the fee is that Jackie has imposed, and nor do I care to. All I know is, I have never been busier. Imogen and I are rushed off our feet – the whole of London seems to know of Bloody Mary, it sometimes seems. She has been a godsend, Imogen. After I lost my beloved Sheila, I was quite at a loss as to what to do. I grieved for so long. And no one could tell me how she came to be in that house, so far from home. It's all such a mystery. Dickie, poor Dickie – he seems crazy, most of the time. I think he maybe drinks to excess. Or possibly it is simple grief that has done this to him. His practice, though, is ruined. He just seems to do the odd thing for Jackie, I'm sure I can't imagine what. Dear Sheila – it was days before she was officially certified as a victim of the bombing. Her funeral was horrible. There were dozens of them, all at the same time, and the coffin, it looked more like a tea chest, or something. Anyway – I had to have help, and so I called upon Lorna from the laundry, whom I hadn't seen for so very long (not knowing, of course, how she might react to the nature of my work). But it turned out that poor Lorna too now was dead. She had fallen into a crater during the blackout, and had broken her neck. Her sister Imogen told me this, her eyes just staring out with defiance. She is old beyond her years, and yet so very simple. When I asked her to help me, she agreed immediately. It was only later I discovered that she had no idea what was happening. She did not know how a woman might become pregnant, nor yet how she could be rid of

it. She seems quite impassive. On a particularly busy
afternoon, she said it was a bit like shelling peas. She is so
very strange. She said she understood now why they all
called me Bloody Mary, and that her only annoyance was that
it was so very hard to get it out from under her fingernails,
the blood, and her abiding disappointment appears to be that
no one to date has called her Bloody Imogen. I think that if I
had a badge made up for her, declaring her profession, she
would wear it with pride. I had to explain to her the illegality
of the situation, and she simply shrugged. I am not at all
sure that anyone any longer can grasp the concept of law, as
such. What I do I am convinced is right, but the authorities
proclaim it to be wrong. This war is wrong, the ultimate sin,
but it is those very same authorities who declared it, and
pursue the killing with unabated vigour. Well there. As Jackie
says, all we are doing, each of us, is simply earning a crust,
the best way we know.

We are now in three small rooms – an attic, really – in a
very poor and dark sort of a place. A back street, it is (suited
to my calling). We have very little. I don't really know where
the money goes. Jackie continues to have beautiful suits
tailored for himself – he says that it is important to maintain a
respectable front. Well I don't mind – I don't really need
much, I never have done. But the reason we lost simply
everything is really extraordinary. The very day after we
rented these rooms, we went back after dark to the old place
for our things – Jackie said we had to do it at night, I didn't
ask why – and we found it just devastated, razed to the
ground the evening before, a direct hit that penetrated deep
down into the basement, where God knows I would have
been cowering. Our three-legged table had miraculously
survived unscathed, amid all the ashes and rubble, and
nothing else at all. Although I did take a dusty and broken

umbrella as well. Jackie said I was mad to, but I wanted it. I didn't explain to him that it was the same umbrella he had been carrying that glorious summer's afternoon when first I met him – the one he had used to prod away a little boy's boat from among the reeds in the pond in the park. I doubt anyway that he would have remembered doing any such thing. So anyway, all of Jackie's remaining money was spent on clothes for the two of us – heaven knows where he found all the coupons – and a few bits of furniture. I didn't even miss my clothes, apart from an old coat with a half-belt and epaulettes and some tippets – sentimental value, of course. All the elegant, expensive and silky things that Jackie brought home – they were never really me. I got to hate dressing up in them – I always thought of it as dressing up – although Jackie hadn't asked me to, not for ages and ages. I had to equip the back room for my business, but really you need so very little, when it comes down to it. Water and buckets and towels. Tea and biscuits for afterwards. I pay a complicit sort of a binman, I suppose he is, to take away various canisters and bundles. We couldn't go on they way we were, always blocking up the drains. Sometimes Jackie will come home with something he has scrounged to eke out the rations, but it is all so very far removed from the way it used to be. When I think of all those prime cuts of steak that I used to give to Romeo and Vincent! I'd give anything for a slice of it now. I eat bread and jam, mostly. In poor Sheila's room, that's all I found – cupboards just bursting with all her greengage jam. That and Romeo and Vincent, starved to death, having clawed the soft furnishings to ribbons. But I bought a government pamphlet, and I have become really quite adept at making rather stodgy pies out of hardly anything at all. And fritters. And slightly heavy puddings from dried egg, a bit of stale bread, and yet more greengage jam.

I see my mother a little bit now, but only for the cruellest reason. Dad, he suffered a sort of seizure shortly before Christmas, no one quite knows for sure what it was, and the result of it is that he's paralysed all down one side, and it's really quite hard to make out what he's saying. She has to feed him, my mother, or else he spills it. She is, I suppose, as mellow as she'll ever be. She does not attack or ignore me any more, but her manner still is far from friendly. I forget, often, that she's my mother at all.

Which reminds me of Jeremy. For I – I too am a mother, and sometimes I forget that as well. After poor Sheila passed away, I realised that I didn't know exactly where he was. She forwarded all my silly letters and little gifts – it was she who occasionally saw him, told me of his progress, eternally promising to arrange for me to visit him, a thing I never did. So I have been making enquiries with the evacuation people, and they promise they will get in touch with me soon – although they did warn me that it would be wholly irresponsible to even consider bringing him back to London. A thing, in all honesty, that I no longer think of. Not particularly in view of his safety, my little Jeremy, and nor because Jackie, he would simply never hear of it. No. It's just that I no longer think of it.

A light day today – just three women. Seven tomorrow, though, so I'd better get an early night (not that there's ever much point). Jonathan Leakey came over in the afternoon, when Jackie was out. He does it more and more, just lately. I cut my hair earlier, not very well. Sheila always used to do it. I'm cooking something called mock goose and jam roly-poly this evening, and I've got a mountain of darning to do.

It been hard for a long time now – I ain't pretending otherwise. I mean, I'm earning a crust, don't get me wrong, but Easy

Street – I don't live there no more, that's for bleeding sure. All of that gone right out the window after that last little meet with Mr Wisely, like I knowed it had to. I didn't never expect to be seeing him again, after all what gone on, and no, I weren't too eager when Jonny, he give me the message. Look Jonny, I says to him, I don't know how much you knows, but if I goes and see him – he'll kill me, most likely. And Jonny, he says nah Jackie – he'll kill you if you doesn't. And then he go on to tell me it were a godsend when the coppers come round, on account of not only were Mr Wisely up in Scotland or somewhere, but Jonny, he were there like, and one of the rozzers, him and Jonny had a little understanding from way back, so it all got set aside. Yeh well, I were thinking – maybe that side of it's out the way, but them coppers, they still on the hunt for the bloke what knifed their sergeant, ain't they? It's always on my mind. I been ducking about now for so bleeding long – but I tries to change the way I looks, best I can. Grow my hair a bit, peak caps, moustache on and off. They don't got much to go on – just some geezer called Dave, are all they got on me. And the sarge, of course – he had that hundred nicker to explain away. But still – it don't make you easy. But all of that – ain't nothing to do with Jonny, so all he saying to me is, so listen to me Jackie, he going: I's the only one what know you grassed, but I understands it, see? I knows what your Alfie mean to you – your place, done the same, son. Now you know me, Jackie – I wouldn't never let you down. Because I'm telling you – Mr Wisely, he ever get a whiff of this and you's catsmeat, son – you do know that? Very large on loyalty, Mr Wisely is: you could say it's me what's keeping you alive, if you got me. Yeh right Jonny, I goes – well I owes you for that, son. But what he want to see me for, then? Jonny, he just give me his search me sort of a face and says I'd best find out for myself. So I thought yeh, all right then. So I gets myself over there, and no matter what Jonny told me, I were still right scared, I don't mind saying. And I were still all cut up and all from the Dickie and Sheila caper and grieving for my Alfie, and what they was going to do to him. So yeh, when I'm sat there in front of him, you could say I were rattled. He never offer me no champagne.

Mr Wisely was wearing a heavy silk and purple robe with wide and deep-quilted lapels; as he sat in an armchair, it skimmed the gleam of his small and dainty slippers. He continued to stare in silence. Jackie did his best not to be fidgety, and was careful not to talk. He felt himself flinch, though, when finally Mr Wisely began to speak.

'Mistakes, my dear Jackie. These, as I believe I have explained to you on more than just the single occasion as we have sat here together so very harmoniously in the past – these, Jackie, are not to be tolerated. Mistakes, Jackie, they breed yet more mistakes – and were I to allow such a condition to proliferate, well then all it is over which I preside would rapidly become no more at all than simply one gigantic *error*. You do see? But of course you do, dear boy. Of course you do.'

Mr Wisely rose and ambled across to Jackie. When he sat down next to him on the sofa, Jackie was aware of the sheen of his jawline and an essence that reminded him of something long ago. He would talk, he had decided, when and if he was asked a question, and not before.

'And shall I count the ways? My dear Jackie, I fear I must. Our friend Dr Wheat is far from reliable. I have recently been forced to charge a trusted colleague with checking and rechecking his every certificate. Your dear and enchanting little brother – a mistake, Jackie, as I believe I foretold. But there – you won me over with your impeccable charm. What was I to do? When one is quite bowled over, one permits oneself a certain laxity, a leeway that in all other circumstances would be debarred, with vigour. We have lost a van, Jackie, as you are aware, not to say twenty cases of excellent whisky. And Victor, one of my very best fellows, was placed in danger. And then there is the matter of accountancy, yet once more. Again I fear, Jackie, your last drop was low.'

'Oh here no!' Jackie was forced to blurt out, despite all his better intentions. 'Now wait just a minute now, Mr Wisely – all them other things, I grant you, I done wrong, and I'm sorry for it. Right sorry I am, Mr Wisely. But the drop – I must be going doolally then, because I count and count it – it were perfect, dead right, down to the last penny. Give you my word, Mr Wisely.'

'Which, once upon a time, was equal to the word of a king. But now, Jackie? I think not. Mistakes, you see – they breed yet more mistakes. And yours, dear boy, seem quite beyond control.'

Jackie would have protested further, but he sensed that there was something more to come. He sat very still and stared at a very large painting of fruit and flowers, aware only of the roaming hand exploring his thigh.

'You know, Jackie, do you not, that you teeter upon the brink of losing not merely your employ and concomitant income, but also your dwelling place, your motor car, and of course your prestige within the community . . . ?'

Jackie swallowed hard and licked his lips as Mr Wisely's hand grew ever bolder and he brought his face even closer to Jackie's ear. He had the scent, now: it was Eau de Paris.

'What, I wonder, would you be willing to do in order to save at the eleventh hour this very desperate situation? Would you do *anything* for me, Jackie? Would you? I asked you once before, and I recall your prevarication . . .'

Jackie was sweating as he swivelled round his head and regarded the man. His voice was dry and husky when he spoke.

'Yes . . .' he said.

'You would? Anything, Jackie? Anything in the whole wide world . . . ?'

Jackie nodded dumbly. 'Yes . . .' he said.

'I see. And upon this I have your word, do I?'

Jackie cleared his throat and glanced about him.

'Yes . . .' he said.

Mr Wisely stood up immediately and clapped his hands in open delight.

'And thrice he did say unto me: 'Yes'! How perfectly splendid, to witness at close quarters just how the web of corruption may entangle us all! But alas, your word is nothing. But no matter – I have derived enormous pleasure from seeing you dispense with the few fragmented atoms of what we lightly term your soul that still tenaciously loiter – and so very very easily. Go now, Jackie. We shall not encounter again. I shall request that Jonathan Leakey see to all the tiresome details with regard to your disestablishment. Not another word, if you please. Ah – Barnstaple. Mr Robertson, he is just leaving. I shall, of course, be conveying your heartfelt regrets to Miss Molly. Dear dear dear, Jackie – what a day you are having.'

Yeh: were, as it happens. And I never told him his motor were out by the docks, under a ton of bleeding rubble. And then the next night, his bleeding flat went and got it and all – smashed to bits, it were: we was lucky. It would've been lovely to get him on the blower and say to him oh dear dear dear, Mr Wisely – what a day you is having. Yeh well – I never thought of it serious: don't want to end up dead, does I? I ain't no mug. Why I says yes to the man – told him I'd do anything he want. And yeh – I thought about it after, I thought about it. All I can reckon is, it just as well he give me the boot. So anyway – whichever way you wanted to look at it, I were in a right hole. Not a hole like I would've been if Jonny gone and told Mr Wisely about all of that copper caper: six-feet hole that'd be, and not so much as a bunch of daisies on the top of it, I reckon. So I knowed right well that whatever were going to be happening next, I had to keep in touch with old Jonny Midnight, be right nice to the man. Because now he had a hold over me, and well he bleeding knowed it. Not what I likes, but what could I do?

Well I'm needing a job, so I starts asking around, sort of style. Went to Mr Prince, first off. Emerald cufflinks he had on him that day – ruby they is, in the normal way of things. Well how about it, Mr Prince? You was always saying you'd like to take me on – well here I is, ready and willing. But I should of knowed: word got round, like it always do. Bought me a drink, he did, and then he says he don't want to go treading on no corns, if I were getting his meaning. And I were, of course: Mr Wisely – he's a powerful man. He got respect. Better than that – he makes people afraid. And then he says to me, Mr Prince, he says, well sorry not to be able to oblige – and no hard feelings, ay Jackie boy? But I tell you what – why don't you have a little word with Slim Charlie: he might sort you out, you never know do you? Now Charlie Chance – Slim, they calls him on account of his second name, see? – he were way down the league, small-time, not even close to Mr Prince, let alone Mr Wisely. But I gone to see him – didn't have much of a choice. He laugh at me quite open. Swipe me! he go – what, me takes you on, after Mr Wisely show you the door? Swipe me! What do I look like to you, Jackie? Ay? Like I'm looking for trouble? No son, I'm sorry – it looks like to me you're on your own now, mate. And I thought to myself, yeh well all right then – if I got to be on my own, then I'll be on my bloody own, and I'll make a right good job of it, you bleeding see if I doesn't. Meantime, though, I were right relieved, weren't I? When Mary, she tell me all about this thing what she got going on the side: dark horse, ain't she? Ay? Never had no idea. She never let on. And I already heard about her, this Bloody Mary, on the streets, the way you does, you got your ear right down close to the ground – but I never twig it were *my* Mary what they was on about. Well how would I? Rather her than me, mind. All that gore? Turn my stomach. And then of course it turn out all she doing is being nice. Nice. Credit it? Just like my Mary, that is – giving it away. Some mumbo-jumbo she give me about all them poor little girls in lumber, and how she . . . what she say? How she call it? Can't hardly remember – but it were like how she were put on this earth to lend a hand, sort of style. Yeh, I goes – well that were then, Mary my love. Now – we needs the money. Only temporary, like, till I gets back on my feet again – but from now on, we taps them on the way in. Oh don't go looking at me like that! I'll only take a few bob off of them. Honest! Yeh well . . . I reckon the market could stand, ooh – fifteen, twenty quid easy. So I gets the word put out about the new address and the business, blimey – fairly flood in, it do. I reckon people is happier when they's shelling out. They gets funny, people, when you give them something for nothing, because the most of them, they ain't never had it before. Like with me and my mum and dad: nothing, they give me. Nothing, not never. Yeh well.

So I's in the money now, yeh? Well no I ain't. I ought to be, yeh – coining it in, Bloody Mary are: ain't enough hours in the day. But it weren't hardly no time before a problem come up – bleeding cops, they went and got wind of it. Were a mercy I were about at the time they come round – two of them, there was, keen young shavers – out for the arrest of Bloody Mary, you could smell it off of them. Well – it took all what I had to make them see reason, the little bastards. And it's just as well I learned all the score from the old days – it weren't enough they just goes away, oh no, not by a long chalk: I had to get all the papers, didn't I? Charge sheets, warrants, the whole bleeding caboodle. Reckon we safe now, but I'm telling you – fair cleaned me out. Never told Mary, nor nothing – she only would've worried. She maybe would've packed it all in, and I can't have that. Well can I? And then there's this other little problem, and all. Won't last too long though, on account of I'm working on a system. Once I crack it – and I'm nearly there – well then I'll be right back on Easy Street, won't I? Bigger than Mr Prince, I'll be – and one day, who knows? Maybe I'll have myself a right swanky mansion up

West like you-know-bleeding-who, with a miserable old bleeder what open the door, and all the upstairs right rammed with top-class floozies. Yeh well: one step at a time, ay? But see – thing is . . . and it's Sammy's fault really, I got into this. Little Sammy Punch – it's him what got me doing it. It's just there's this card game going on most nights – little room above the chippy. Rum bag of blokes, it is – there's a Greek what'd have your gizzard out soon as look at you . . . the rest of them, they ain't so bad. Stakes is high, though – and that were the attraction. Because don't get me wrong – I ain't no mug. Gambling, I always thought it were a right mug's game on account of what I knowed of it were all the Find The Lady and the three little nutshells and backing some broken-down old nag in the two-thirty what's been well nobbled before they even got the saddle on. But this here's different – poker, it is. Never heard of it. But I'm learning it, and I'm learning it fast. Now yeh, I does admit I drop a fortune, early on. Got to be expected, first off. But I had a couple little wins since then, nothing too much. But see – I got this system what I been working on, can't hardly fail. And when I cracked it – and I'm nearly there – well then, son, I put down my ante of so many hundred, and I ups and walks away with *thousands*, mate: *thousands*. Meantime though – bit strapped, if I'm honest. Now Sammy Punch, he work for the Family, the Firm we calls it. He's a weasel. And how it go is, if I had a little win, I sub him a bit. Then he give it me back with interest. Not too long ago, I were right flat broke. My gold cigarette case – the Dunhill? Had to flog it for tuppence-bleeding-ha'penny down that bastard Jew-boy pawnbroker. And the lighter. Back to the cheap ones now, what Mary give me that time. And it were about then when Sammy Punch, he come up to me – white as a wossname, he were. Look at this Jackie, he going – and what he's holding out to me is only his bleeding call-up papers. Every day I'm half expecting the same, if I'm honest, because Mr Wisely, he won't no more be keeping my name well out the frame, will he? Not no more he won't. Anyway, it were a bit of a godsend, as it happens, because I needed money pronto, and I still had old Dickie to do the business with all the certificates. Well . . . I say do the business, but dear oh dear, you don't want to see the state of him, not now you don't. The drinking, well – took a turn for the worse, what you wouldn't've thought he could've, would you? But see – I ain't dropping him round the cases of prime Scotch no more, is I? So he gets down him whatever he can. Rotgut gin, with all the bits floating about in it – Gawd knows where he get it. Then there's that stuff what a nurse go and rub on you before she stick the needle in – pints of that. Telling you – he'd have the paraffin out the heater as soon as look at it. Surgery's all gone, of course. Normal way of it, he'd be struck off – it's just they hasn't rumbled him yet. One of the beauties of this war – you can tuck a thing a bit out of sight; can be years before they twigs to it. Anyway – my point of view, I can't do without him. He got all the forms and the rubber stamps and you name it, so I can still be doing a little bit of business. Because I don't got too much on, to be honest with you. There's a peeping tom up the girls' hostel, most nights – he pay me not to grass on him. One of the last things Mr Wisely give me for Mary were this top-class crocodile handbag. I never give it her, though, because what I does, I'm in a tea room, right? And I spots a likely mark and I introduces myself to her, all polite like – why you needs a beautiful suit, shoes polished up all nice – and I opens up my cardboard box and lets her get a good butcher's inside, and most likely she near swooning with just the sight of it – because them young women, they gets dead funny over things like that. They'll be putting six month of coupons into a pair of stupid shoes, sewing little bits and bobs on all of their clothes . . . the more the war go on, the more they does it. Blimey – if I still had them lipsticks and bottles of Yardley's I could retire in style, mate, I am not joking. And a proper fur coat – your sable, your mink – you can get two, three *thousand* – no I am *not* kidding: price of a street. That's why the posh women, they doesn't dare wear them no more – it'd be stripped off of their back, broad daylight. Anyway – bint in the tea room, yeh? She clock the handbag, and I says I can lay my hands on some of them, you interested – get it you by nightfall. Only a tenner because I got to shift it, see? But I won't take the tenner off of you now, love – just give me the half of it, ay? Then we can settle up later. What colour you fancy? Red? Yeh – funny enough, so happen I do got a red one. Right then – see you here at six-thirty, if that suit you: she stuff the fiver into my hand, and I's away. Does I feel sorry for them? Nah. They don't want to be giving their hard-earned to a total stranger just for some bleeding old handbag – stands to reason. Don't they know there's a war on? I reckon what I does is, I gives them a lesson in life.

So like I say, it's all pretty small-time, I wouldn't want to pretend to you. If it wasn't for Bloody Mary, Lord love her, we'd be heading for Queer Street, you want the God's honest truth of it. Trouble is, I'm losing all that hand over fist. But I ain't worried. It's only temporary. Once I crack the system – and I nearly done it – then we's home and dry. Just a matter of time, really. Anyways – Sammy Punch, he were desperate for to get out of his call-up, see, so I says to him yeh okay then, Sammy boy, I'll see what I can do. Only, he says, it got to be fast on account of I's up before them, come Tuesday. Blimey, I goes – that *is* fast . . . but seeing as how it's yourself, Sammy my son, I think I can accommodate you. So we's looking at sixty for the green form and an extra score for putting it through so quick. He give me thirty on account, and we's all hunky-dory. I bungs all his details around to old Dickie – wake him up, slap him about a bit, remind him of his bleeding name, dear oh dear – and he do all of the business. What a sight he are now. That night way back when we was dumping Sheila, he must of broke his ankle, some point – I knowed there was something. Anyway, never got it fixed for could've been weeks, so he got a limp – permanent, I'd say. And he do stink, it got to be said. Don't never see to all that side of it. I bring him a bit of food, time to time. He still talk about her, Sheila, whether I's there or whether I ain't. Poor old Dickie – the war, it ain't been good to him. Weren't that long ago he were the toff with a future, the golden boy. Yeh – and my Alfie, he were looking rosy and all – and look at the pair of them now. One of them's close to a padded cell and the other one's a cripple what's stuck in the clink. Yeh well.

But now see, Sammy – he been a naughty boy. He got his certificate, bang on time, just like I tell him, and that were bleeding ages back, now. And I lost count of the number of times I been tapping him for the fifty what he into me for, and I had enough of it now, tell you the truth. There's a game on tonight and I got near two hundred off of Mary, but I needs more, see: I got to have the edge. Tonight, this could be the one where I walks away laughing – because the system, I might just have cracked it (I said I were nearly there). So I needs the extra fifty, and I decided. He going to give it me, Sammy Punch. No more of his bleeding nonsense. He going to give it me right now, and that's why I'm off to see him. I got it off of a little bird he'd be showing his face in the Rose & Crown a little bit later, our friend Sammy Punch, and so that's where I were headed. I wish it weren't tonight, in one way though. They's all saying there going to be a real heavy raid on, and I reckon they's right – and it never used to bother me, all of the bombing. I gone out in all sorts. But I reckon it were that one night, you know, it's that night what done it for me. When Dickie and me, we was dumping Sheila. Can't never forget it. And so now, the siren go up, I want to be all tucked up and safe in my Anderson, not playing for high stakes in the room above the chippy. And also . . . sounds funny, I suppose, the games we's into, the both of us, but of an evening these days in our ratty little attic, Mary and me, we's really very cosy. She'll do me my tea, get on with her darning. She like it, Mary, when we does a crossword together. Snug as two bugs in a rug, we is. Bit like how it were, before the whole world gone doolally. Because it ain't just Dickie and Alfie what gone wrong – and leave poor old Sheila right out of it. It's us and all – Bloody Mary, the back-street abortionist, and me, Jack the bleeding Lad, a villain on the run. How'd all that lot happen, then? When we wasn't looking. Because we was all normal, one time. And we can't be the only ones – just people what was living our lives. London – had to be full of them. And then . . . I don't know: something happened. All of this here. And see, it got so I don't want to be hunting for no Sammy Punch, and nor I don't want to be on an upper floor and a sitting duck for when the bombs come down. But I can't go on living like this. I got a taste for it, see, and I just got to get money again. And this are the only way I can think.

◉

And so I just sit here, and continue to wonder. Sitting and darn-ing, and asking myself all of these and other questions, to which, of course, I have no answers, none at all. In the little booklet I quite recently bought, it says that in order to darn a jacket, say, or a frock, I don't know what – you should unravel the threads, in order to get a perfect match, from seams and hems . . . but I've done all that already. There are no threads left, not anywhere, and that's the trouble, really. I am darning my darning. Soon the holes will be quite unstoppable. The bombs are coming down – a little bit distant tonight, but still you never know (they change direction all the time) – and Jackie is down in the shelter. When it became clear to him that I had no intention whatever of joining him there, you might have thought he would've come back up, but no. Well I'm pleased, because air raid or no air raid, it is peaceful up here, and I really need to think, now. To make a decision. Because can I? Can I go on loving the man, now I know that he's a killer? It's the hardest thing, this – of all the things he's done to me, it's this one, oh God yes, this one is just the very hardest to bear. After all that Jonathan Leakey told me this evening – well I just had to confront him, didn't I? Tell him I knew all about it. He denied it, my Jackie – denied it to my face. Hadn't seen him, Sammy Punch. Hadn't, then, hunted him down and slain him, like vermin. Wasn't even close to the vicinity in question. And I just stood there looking at him, while he went on doing it – even as his big and beautiful bastard eyes were imploring me to believe in all the love and sweetness that used to hang there behind them. And he didn't go out, as I had felt so sure he would. There is talk that it is gambling now, that that is the latest. It certainly would explain the utter lack of money. But I don't enquire. I never have done. All I want to know is less and less and less, but that, I suppose, will now never be.

It also says in the booklet that you should always use thread of the same material as the garment in question – wool for wool, silk for silk, cotton for cotton. Such utter harmony is indeed so very pleasant an idea, but how is one to bring it about, when no such resources are to hand? I don't, of course, tell Jackie of every occasion that Jonathan Leakey, that Jonny Midnight, comes to see me. Why do they call him that . . . ? Jonny Midnight. I can't remember. There must have been a reason, I suppose. Once upon a time. When there was a reason for everything, most of them gradually forgotten. Now we just do, and die. Sounds like a cowboy in an old Tom Mix film, Jonny Midnight. Anyway, he calls quite frequently, and always bearing gifts. Tinned loganberries it was tonight. And a nice piece of tongue. Well there. And always offering so very much more. Jackie would not care for it, if I told him, which is maybe why I don't. There was a crackle of guns, just now; the bombers, they must be moving closer.

It's a blessing, really, that I am just so tired. Well we all of us are, the whole of London. Grey and drawn and sleepless, numbed by the cold from queueing for hours for some or other scrap of something, so very unworthy. Stunned by disbelief. Darning our darning. One of the girls who came to see me rather recently, she told me that there is an air of aphrodisia abroad, I think this is the word – not at all how she put it, but a heady feeling of an arrogant lust, if I understood her correctly, that must inevitably lead to the condition I am put on this earth to relieve. Others, though, see it not quite so poetically: a bit of how d'you do to fill in the black and empty troughs of boredom, to alleviate loneliness, protect you from fear – or, more simply, because the boy, nice lad, just on leave for the weekend, told her he'd never done it before and he didn't want to go and get himself killed, not with never having done it before, and that anyway: nothing can happen, she had his word on it. It says in the booklet that a particularly neat and easy darn can be made on articles which are used only right side up by lightly tacking a scrap of net over the hole on the wrong side, and darning in and out of it. A scrap of net, I suppose, for safety's sake. This raid, I think, is on for the duration of the night. Beyond the blackout, the moon is white. And before Jonathan Leakey arrived, who should have come to see me this very afternoon but Molly, dear Molly, from so long ago. She still is so beautiful, but the strain is telling, even under all of the make-up and coiffure. Her eyes were red – she had clearly been crying. She said it wasn't a social call – she had heard of the reputation of Bloody Mary, and would trust none other. Odd, really. You would imagine that all these girls, they would hear of my monicker and turn and flee.

But no. I am, I can only conjecture, the lesser of very many evils. We didn't talk, not really. How could one speak of the old days? And anything to do with now is just always unsayable. To mend a ladder, it says in the booklet, one must catch the loop of the running stitch immediately. Well. In my very varied experience of young women nowadays – rich, you might call it – their legs are either smooth and perfect and encased in the finest new and pale silk stockings (such as Molly, for instance) or else they are chalk-white and stubbled, or stained unevenly with tealeaves misguidedly applied, spidery lines of wavering ink snaking their way up the backs, to the point where it no longer mattered. One imagines a pair of deluded and downtrodden slavies, gigglingly doing for one another.

Are we bad people? Is this what we have become? Or are we still good, though inevitably guilty? Before the war, all I was called was nice. Everyone thought how terribly nice I was – and I was, they were right, and I still am, God help me, I am nice. I *am* nice. At least I think so . . . it is so very hard to tell. And of course now I'm the other and bloody thing too. After all these years, you know, it gets so you're expecting a disaster the moment you're awake . . . and I suppose that today, with the news about Jackie from Jonathan Leakey, it has finally arrived: catastrophe has come to us. And as he says, Jonathan, about the murder of Sammy Punch, it is not as if the Firm is just going to leave things alone. I do not know what this 'Firm' is, I have to say, and as usual, I don't at all care to. But whoever they be, it's not as if it's *over*, is it? Not yet. My tea, you know, is cold, and I can't really face the rest of this sandwich, the greengage jam. Terrible noises are becoming ever louder, but I'll not leave my seat. And should a bomb come down and hit us directly – well then Jackie will be crushed and buried in the shelter, while I'll be up here, and shattered into pieces. And then that's the end of us – Jack the Lad and Bloody Mary. And who, I wonder, shall mourn? Who is there left to?

But can I? Can I go on loving the man now I know that he's a killer? Well . . . I think I have the answer to that one, at least. Now I do, yes. It says in the booklet that when you can't get a patch to match the cloth, you should make your mend as decorative as possible, and apply it with a fancy stitching. It is called *Make Do and Mend*, the booklet. Prepared for the Board of Trade by the Ministry of Information. Price threepence. Net.

⊙

I been thinking, see, and I don't like it, not a bit. It don't make no sense. Something funny's going on, I reckon, and I got to find out what it is. And it's Jonny what I got to see. The whole of last night down the shelter and half the bleeding day now I been going over and over it, and I can't see no way why he gone and done it. Mary, she ain't mentioned it again. I come upstairs for a bit of breakfast after the all-clear, and there she were asleep in the chair just like what I left her. How about a bit of breakfast, I goes to her, and she says yeh, course: we got bread, no butter, more of that – Gawd, I sick of the sight of it – jam, and there's oats, we got oats. So yeh, I says, I'll have a bowl of that. Put a few loganberries on it, will I? she asking. Any left, then? Course – else I wouldn't of offered. Yeh all right then, I goes – but here, doesn't *you* want them? I had, she says, like what she always do, so she give me them on my oats. But she didn't mention it again, all about Jonny coming over and saying to her what he did. Now I been going real easy with old Jonny – didn't want to go rubbing him up the wrong way now, did I? But this here is gone beyond: telling her it all, like that. So it's evening again now – just gone dark – and so it's him I got to see: Jonny Midnight.

Got lucky first time: here he is in the Rose & Crown, look – propping up the bar, usual little corner.

'Well well well, Jackie – this is nice. Still looking very dapper, I see. I were going to come looking for you, son, bit later on. But I might have knowed, ay? You'd be wanting a word. In the light of all what been going down. Drop of Scotch, Jackie? A time since you had it, I daresay.'

'Yeh Jonny – ta. Do with it, don't mind saying. Now listen here, Jonny—'

'No no no, Jackie. We don't want to talk in here, do we? It ain't the same nowadays, the old Rose & Crown. Walls has ears, ay? Get your drink down you – I got the car outside. What you say we has ourselves a bit of a spin? I can take you to a place what's really jumping. Good booze, classy girls, the lot. What you say?'

'Don't mind. I'm happy here, Jonny – but yeh, don't mind. You want us to have a turn in your little motor – yeh, don't mind a bit.'

Jonathan Leakey drained his glass and placed his hand on Jackie's shoulder.

'Humber,' he said. 'Nothing little about it. Right then – let's be off, ay?'

Jonathan Leakey drove slowly in the blackout, his face craned forward and over the wheel, squinting into the sulphurous glimmer from the covered-over headlamps.

'Fag, Jackie? Senior Service. Even I can't always get them, not nowadays. Hen's teeth. Or you still with the Turkish?'

'Turkish? Joking. Roll-ups, more often than not. Listen, Jonny – never mind all that. What I want to know is—'

'Yeh yeh, Jackie. I know. You got a lot of questions. And I promise you, son – I'll give you answers. Straight. I ever let you down?'

'Yeh – okay then, Jonny. Here – why you stopping? What's here? Middle of bleeding nowhere. Don't look jumping to me . . .'

'That's the beauty,' said Jonathan Leakey, climbing out of the car just as the sirens began to wail. 'Don't want to advertise it, do you. Bleeding Jerry – he early tonight . . .'

By the flickering light of Jonathan Leakey's torch, he led out the two of them over the rubble of a bomb site and into a blown-out doorway, shards of glass splintering and cracking beneath their boots.

'Why you stopped?' asked Jackie, having just stumbled into the back of him.

Jonathan Leakey turned and smiled.

'This is as far as we go. This, Jackie, is where we ends it.'

Jackie did his best to make out Jonny's features.

'Ends it? What you on about? Where the hell is we?'

'We is, Jackie – like what I were telling you – at the end. This is it. Here? Good a place as any, that's all it is. Now first off, you want to know why I gone and told your Mary that you went and done for Sammy Punch.'

'Yeh I bleeding does. I never even seed him, did I? I heard he were going to be in the Rose & Crown, but he never show, the little bastard.'

'No, Jackie. He never. That's on account of he were with me, see? Down by the railway. It were me what put it about he'd be in the Rose & Crown – and I told a lot of people you was looking for him and all. Going to sort him out once and for all, is what you was going to do. That's what I told them.'

'I don't get you, Jonny . . .'

'No? Dear oh dear. You don't get me, don't you? Well you will, son, believe me. You will soon, Jackie, promise you that. Now see, you wasn't the only one what Sammy Punch were in to. Owed Mr Wisely a bleeding fortune. But I keeps it quiet, see – not like you, Jackie boy. Everyone and his bleeding uncle knowed that Sammy was owing you, and that you was out to get him. But I got him first, see? Got my money off of him, but he puts up a bit of a struggle, see? So I done him. And that were that.'

Jackie's eyes were narrowed as he tried to understand. He could hear the bumping of bombs and the first great tumbling of imploded brickwork.

'Well . . . what you go and tell Mary that *I* done it for? She thinks I's a bleeding murderer now – and I ain't. I never has been.'

'I know, son. I know. I told you once, didn't I? That you wasn't the murdering sort. But me, Jackie – well I'm different. You got it yet? No. You ain't, has you? Well have a little think, Jackie boy. See, you just got too cosy with Mr Wisely, my way of reckoning. You was the golden boy – and it used to be me, see? So I gets to thinking, well – I were the bleeding Herbert what went and brung him in, so now I can get him out again. See?'

'Jonny . . . I ain't liking this. I ain't liking this, Jonny . . .'

'You won't like it a whole lot more in a minute, son. So listen. Them certificates of our good friend Dr Weak. What happened to them?'

Jackie was hearing the bombs, the thud of them, hearing the snap of gunfire, and listening intently, near to spellbound, to all that Jonny was telling him.

'What you mean – what happened to them?'

'When he give them to you, Jackie. What you do with them?'

'Ay? Well – I give them to you . . .'

'Correct. First prize. And I alters them. And then your weekly drop, with your tally on it. You give that to me and all, didn't you? So I nobbles it. Easy.'

Jackie stepped forward, his fists outstretched, his eyes alight.

'I ought to say, Jackie – I got a gun. Back, now. It's in my pocket, look. Trained on your groin. Yeh . . . I somehow thought you wouldn't be pleased. Now this gun of mine – I doesn't want to, Jackie, but I think you knows I will if I has to. Because me – I *is* the murdering sort, make no mistake, son. So – you wants the rest of it, does you?'

Jackie was stunned and seething, his eyes now making out the bulge in Jonny's coat pocket. Jonathan Leakey drew it out slowly, and it gleamed in the torchlight.

'You *bastard* . . . !' Jackie hissed at him. 'You fucking *bastard* . . . ! I thought you was my—'

'Mate? Yeh well – I were, one time. But it all changes, don't it? Just take a look around you, Jackie boy. All different now, ain't it? Whole new landscape. Now your little Alfie – I thought that were a godsend, if I'm honest. He'll mess up, I thought – one-legged little drip of a kid like that. *Steady!* Steady now, Jackie – remember I got a gun, ay? Keep it well in your mind. The way the bombs is getting closer, no one's ever going to hear. Ten minutes, you'd be buried, son. Right? Right. So . . . like I were saying – Alfie, I thought, he'll be the finisher. He'll mess up, and that for Mr Wisely will be the end of it. But he never, did he? Mess up. No. Nice little worker, all in all. So I has to do something. Think it odd, did you? When the coppers turns up at that little whisky job what I sets you up with? I knowed you and Victor would leg it, but Alfie, well . . . Worked like a charm, didn't it really? So then you was out on your ear – very good, I thought. But the *real* idea – the whole big idea – and remember, Jackie, you just remember the gun I got, now . . . the real idea was that when you gets chucked out by Mr Wisely, that Mary, she wouldn't want to know no more. Taste of the good life – wouldn't be keen on kissing it all goodbye, sort of style. Well I were wrong. Underestimated the girl, didn't I? Because . . . and don't never forget the gun now, Jackie . . . because it's her what I want. Always were. Right from the beginning. Only one I ever met what weren't a bleeding whore. Thought if I bided my time – here, Jackie, you get *back* now! You step right back, son, else I'll blow you all to bits, I ain't kidding you! Last warning you getting, son. Right then. So yeh – had to up the ante. Thought if she knowed you was a killer, like, well then she be off like a shot. I weaved her a wonderful tale – all sorts of detail. I maybe ought to be a writer, ay? But anyway – no. Yet again, I gone and underestimated her, didn't I? She's a wonder, really. So that, Jackie, is why we's here. It's *you* what's got to go off now. Leave me clear. Don't forget the gun now, will you lad? Yeh – reckon she'll be wanting a bit of comfort, Mary will, once you's away. Even more so, should think, when she gets to know about Molly, and all. Because what I done today is, I told the law it were you what sliced the sergeant, and it were you what done for Sammy Punch. Where to find him, and everything. They got all your details. The lot. And then I told the Firm, and all. Dear oh dear. They wasn't happy, not a bit. Yeh so – I think that's all of it . . . oh no, I near forgot. Mr Wisely. He now is aware that you grassed on him. Yeh – I'm afraid so. So what you got to do now, Jackie old lad – is run. You start running – see how far you can get. Just a question of which of them gets to you the first, really. I suppose you ought to pray it's the coppers, all in all . . . Still, no offence Jackie, ay?'

Jackie flinched as a bomb dropped quite close by, the roar of an avalanche of brick and tiles obliterating all of Jackie's wild and blaring rant as he stood there before him, red-eyed and the whole of him clenched into hatred.

'Look at you . . .' Jonathan Leakey was sneering, summing Jackie up with a contemptuous wave of the gun. 'And what? You really do think it, do you? You think you ain't a mug? Joke. You're the biggest mug what ever lived, son. Didn't see none of it, did you? Jack the *Lad* . . . ? Don't make me laugh.'

There was a screaming in the air, and then the blast was upon them in a thunder of explosive, and cascades of tumbling rubble. Jonathan Leakey was hurled over on to his side as he yelled out even as the gun was clattered from his hand. Jackie – batting away flying timbers and jagged daggers of slate from about his head and shoulders, his face so stung and burned by the pelting of stones – fell with all his weight on to Jonathan Leakey who was yelping in terror and kicking out madly in his scramble to be out from under him and Jackie didn't really know that he was beating the man's big and bloody head against the ground until he suddenly stopped doing it and he'd all gone quiet and there's a sort of gurgling from out of his throat, and the wet on his face, it's all coming out warm. Jackie fell across his chest in a rush of quite breathless exhaustion, and then he sat up again and shook all the brickdust and splinters from out of his burning hair and eyes and he saw only briefly the flash of the blade that was now in his hand, and he drove it downwards, burying it hard into Jonathan Leakey. He needed all the strength that was left to him to lever it back out again, and he flicked it shut. Jackie staggered to his feet, quite deafened by the great and savage arena of fire around him. Screwing tight his eyes and shielding his raw and boiling face with the fling of an arm, he was stopped in his need to be gone and away as the blaze continued its roaring and spat out vicious red-hot barbs and the licking was now lashing and it lunged for him then as he cried out in his desperation at the sheer and crackling, vast and soaring thundering walls of it – and then, crouching low and shrieking, he fled into the flames.

⊙

It was days before she heard anything. And then in the afternoon, a policeman called round. One hour earlier Mary had been scrubbing down an oilskin sheet, and was up to her elbows in a viscous solution of blood and chlorine. There wasn't much – his charred identity card, the burnt remains of his jacket and the rhodium-plated cigarette case with J.R. at its corner. She remembered that Christmas: they had laughed. Mary thanked the policeman, who woodenly uttered his condolences. She sat in her chair, mute and rocking gently, the pad of her thumb repeatedly caressing the indentations of the case's engraving. She remembered that Christmas. Her memory sang with the laughter throughout the hours of the night as the walls of the building shuddered and grumbled under the constant bombardment of yet another raid. When dawn came pale and cold around the edges of the blackout, she cried in silence.

What happened then

7th May 1945

Oh my goodness – the sheer and utter thrill of it! Here is the day we all despaired for so very many years of ever arriving, and now it is here. Tomorrow has been declared 'Victory in Europe Day' and is a national holiday. Mr Churchill is due to address us all in I'm fairly sure it's Piccadilly, but I'll know later on from the wireless. London, I think, will just go wild.

I had to stop, when I wrote the above, and just sit here and recover myself for a while. My hand was trembling holding the pen – it still is – and I am rather weepy and grinning, all at the same time. In common with everyone else, I suppose, I just simply can't believe that it is finally come. It has been so very hard. It is as if we are all emerging, blinking into the sunlight, after a hundred years of punishment in the deepest, blackest hole. Privations and hardships, everyone says that they are set to continue for a good long time yet – maybe even until 1950, it said in the *Mirror*, though I can hardly believe that. But we are no longer at *war*, that is the real thing. That evil man Hitler is dead. How could just one little man with a silly moustache come to cause the whole of the world to teeter upon the brink of utter devastation? To cause such suffering, and so much death. Well, I expect the historians will be telling and retelling it an awful lot better than me for many generations. Which is vital, really. The children of the future must never be allowed to forget, and nor must the greatness or horror of this terrible war be ever diminished. Maybe we truly have, this time, come through the war to end them all, for how could any war ever be longer or worse than this one? And what nation in the future would ever contemplate so dreadful a thing again?

I have decided to make this a good long entry in what has become a very haphazard and dilatory journal indeed, not much more than a ragbag (heaven knows what Mass Observation has made of it, not that they will have read a single word). In 1943 I wrote nothing at all, not a single word. I did in '42, of course, and mostly about Gary. '44 was agonising really, because it so often was seeming that peace might be at hand, but it never came, it never came. And then when London was on its knees, so ravaged and sad, all of us so downtrodden and shabby and quite utterly exhausted, then came the Doodlebugs, I don't know their real name, V something, and they were just the most terrifying weapon of all. They were sort of cruising rockets and you could hear them almost chugging along above you, and then the noise cut out completely, and that meant that it had started to fall and the whole of London was simply cowered into a collective and terrible silence, wondering and fearful lest this time it was for them. Our nerves were simply shredded, and it had become so hard just to find enough to eat and the basic necessities to keep yourself decent. Mr Arthur, the butcher, he told me he was plagued from morning till night by people wanting scraps for the dog when none of them, of course, even had one. If it hadn't been for Gary, I don't know what I should have done. Well the United States generally, really – I think that without them we might all have starved to death by now. Goodness, I couldn't remember the last time I had even *seen* a bottle of proper shampoo – what a treat. And somehow, Gary even managed to bring me some coal. All the evenings and nights I had sat up, huddled up in all my coats and scarves!

When the Americans entered the war, it did give us new hope – I suppose it was the turning point. Well it certainly was for me anyway, because otherwise I never would have met Gary, of course. Who would have thought it? The very first American I have ever encountered in the whole of my life, and now look at us. I have determined that when finally we are all living in Tennessee, I shall write this journal every single day. There will be so much new, so much to say. He has tried to paint me a picture of how it will be, but it's all so very hard to imagine. Thousands of acres his family has, apparently. A ranch with cows and horses and everything you can think of! He says I'll love it and that he'll make me so very happy, and I believe him. Still though the thought of it is all rather daunting. But there's nothing, now, to keep me here. London, it's just so raw – torn and empty. Ask anyone – there's much to be said for the Land of Plenty. Gary has only been back in London for a few days, four I think – I hadn't seen him for nearly a year, and all that time I have been so fearful of his getting injured, but he is back without a scratch and if anything is more handsome than I remember him. He was one of the first into Berlin, but he's hardly said anything about it. He was very good at writing, though – every single week he wrote me a letter, but sometimes there was a dreadful gap when I'd be worried sick, and then I'd get three in a bundle all at once. I wrote back whenever I could, but there was so little I could tell him. Not about my work, obviously – I was still doing it until fairly recently. And London had become just so awful, there was really nothing I could say about it. When he came back – a day earlier than I expected him and so of course my hair was in the most dreadful mess and I hadn't even begun to tidy up – I said to him I hope you haven't been consorting with French mam'selles and Italian signorinas and he laughed that laugh of his with all his shiny white teeth and he said that I was the only gal for him, in that lilting sort of cowboy voice he has. I love it. I'm a very lucky gal!

It really has been the most extraordinary week – I've barely slept. Rumours of the end of the war have been around for days – everyone glued to the wireless. And then Gary came back. He drove me up, the very same day, to go and collect Jeremy, my own little boy. I don't think ever in my life have I felt so very emotional, so drained, so dizzied by it all, as I did that day. Even now I am not sure quite what it is that I'm feeling, but I will try to write it down anyway. Maybe if I write it down, it will help me to understand. But just so much upheaval, it makes you spin, it truly does.

When we were quite close, I utterly panicked. I was beside myself. I clutched at Gary's arm and begged him to stop and to turn the car around, because I simply couldn't face this ordeal before me. It had been more than five years – five years! – since I had even laid eyes upon him, my own little boy. It was only the night before that I had woken up and realised with a terrible shock that of course he wouldn't know me. Gary was very good. He stopped the car and he stroked my arm as if I was a terrified little kitten or something, and I suppose that at the time that is quite how I must have appeared. We drove on. It's much nicer, Norfolk, than people give it credit for. It *is* flat, but pleasantly so. I could not remember when I had seen such greenery, seen such peace, and the air was so sweet. The war, it seemed to have happened in another country altogether. A pretty little red-brick farmhouse – smoke coiling up from out of the chimney. A huddle of people around the front door. My heart was beating wildly – I simply could not speak. When we got out of the car, Gary had to hold me up – my legs had just gone to jelly. An elderly man and a slightly younger woman – Mr and Mrs Grey, as I now know them to be – and five young children of varying ages. Five young children – that's all that I was aware of. And then I looked more closely – and oh my heavens, I was reeling – I must nearly have fainted! For there, peering up at me with his big brown handsome eyes, was the image of my Jackie. I gasped in shock and the tears were pouring down my face and I think I must have frightened him – this mad and weepy lady who had come to take him away – and he clung on fiercely to the arm and apron of poor Mrs Grey, who was sobbing quite silently, and smoothing down his hair (thick and dark, just like his father's). Mr Grey, he tried to be civil, but I could see he was so very upset. All the children, they looked beyond sad, nearly bereft. Gary had loaded the car with all sorts of presents for everyone – chocolates, tinned fruit and ham, toys, tobacco, a bottle of whisky and, for some reason, a selection of brightly coloured parasols, of all things, I never did get round to asking why. Mr Grey attempted a smile as he piled them up and set them all aside (the children seemed indifferent – in London, they would have gone wild with excitement). I thanked him and his wife from the bottom of my heart for all that they had done. They both just shook their heads. It was a pleasure, said Mrs Grey quietly: we all of us love him so, our little Jeremy – he's one of the family. Everyone was crying quite openly, and me more than any of them. It was terrible, then. Jeremy, he clung on to Mrs Grey and he began to scream, and Mr Grey tearfully tried to loosen his fingers as the other four children did their best to pull him away, wailing out loud that they didn't want Jeremy to go, that they loved him, and that he was their little brother. I died a thousand times – my agony was indescribable. When we got him into the car, Jeremy was still screaming and beating on the windows and Mrs Grey, she rushed forward, her arms outstretched, and Mr Grey was forced to restrain her. Jeremy continued to scream for nearly the whole of the journey, and I just wept and wept and shook my head. Gary drove on grimly.

Back at the flat, Jeremy, he just became impossible – repeatedly slamming doors and demanding to know who I was and why I had captured him! His accent is curious. Gary bribed him to be quiet with all sorts of sweets – or candies, as he calls them – and model aeroplanes and jeeps and so on, and eventually his voice was up to no more shouting and exhaustion took him over. In his case – oh heavens! – I found his little teddy bear Fluffy from all that time ago, but he said he was called Mr Brown, the bear, and that Fluffy was a stupid name. Golly wasn't there. The next morning was better, though – he seemed to like the flat and the room I had prepared for him (he certainly wouldn't have cared for the awful attic where I used to live, though) and he was amazed by the bustle in the streets. He's no Londoner – but we all of us must reacquaint ourselves with this wonderful city: just to see street lamps again, it makes you cry with joy. But he wanted to know when he could go back to his real mummy and daddy and I told him that I was his real mummy and he pointed to Gary and said is that my real daddy then? And I told him no. I think he's more confused than ever.

It will take an age, I quite see that. Gary has been just wonderful. He's taken him off somewhere this afternoon – why I have the peace to be writing all of this – and he's told me often that he has always loved children and cannot wait for us to be married so that he can have some of his own. But I know that he will always treat Jeremy as if he is one of them, his own. He is a good and kind man. I am looking forward to being a mother again. I have never forgotten that time when I could have been, and nor how that simply detestable experience so radically altered my life. And I never have been married (although I have told him that I am a widow, a war widow). And now it is all over, I feel what so many of us must do: I so want to begin again. I want everything from now on to be utterly *clean* – and if not how it all used to be before, then in a new and different way. Imogen, she took over my consultancy. The girls were in very good hands – I had taught her everything I knew – until, oh God, disaster struck. Everyone had come to think that she was Bloody Mary – it made her proud, and she made no move to correct them. I was pleased to pass on the title. I just wanted to be Mary again – there had been too much blood, too much. Imogen, though – I heard she had become boastful. Maybe why the police swooped down on her: dear God, if ever a poor child was caught red-handed. She is in prison, little Imogen, and will be for so very long a time. After she was sentenced, women beat upon the sides of the Black Maria, shouting abuse and terrible threats. How could they? Can they not see that it was women we were helping? It is men who have decided that ours was an illegal practice. All we did was help women – I cannot understand how they could not see that.

And how very sad that so many people cannot tomorrow celebrate the victory that rightfully belongs to everyone. My Dad, the gallant old soldier, he passed away more than a year ago now. Another seizure, stroke, I'm never quite sure what they call them, and that simply did for him. He should be in London tomorrow – and he will be, in my heart. My mother, what remains of her, has gone to live somewhere just outside of Brighton with an even older sister who I never knew existed. She never said goodbye, but she sent me a card with her address on it – the only thing she has ever written to me, in fact, apart from the scrawled-on old envelope that I came across while moving: 'I don't take things from spivs'. I tore it up. I keep on meaning to drop her a line. Maybe now I will. Alfie, he's still in jail, poor boy (and he never has told me even why he's there). It's shameful that they keep him, but at least he's been kept safe from all the bombing. I think they'll let him out, now the war is over. I visit him regularly, and he's in wonderful spirits. He says that when he's released, he wants to start afresh in Canada, which is where his cellmate hails from, apparently. Dear Alfie – he says he's not too sure though if Canada will be keen on taking on a peg-legged jailbird! His sense of humour in the circumstances is really quite a marvel. He's matured – opened up a good deal. Always cracking jokes. Not quite Jack the Lad, but you can see now very strongly the connection. My dear friend Sheila – she's been gone for so very long. I miss her bluffness, her good and simple kindness. I still have tons of her greengage jam. Dickie now is in an institution – he just simply lost his mind, in the end. Many have, they told me. Lunacy and suicide are two of the overlooked tragedies of the terrible war, and I know that there are many more. But there's a family trust fund or something, so it's quite a nice place where he is, poor Dickie. Len married Sally, which was lovely of him. They're going to get a brand-new pub out in Greenwich, if you please – but poor Sally, since she lost her boys, she's just shrunk into a shadow, really. But Len, he does all he can for her. Even Jonathan Leakey – he died as well, and I rather thought of him as utterly indestructible. He disappeared the very same night when my Jackie was killed, Len said, so I can only assume that they were out there together, engaged in one of their mysterious missions, into the night. I still never imagine the sorts of villainies they must both have got up to.

Jackie. Yes of *course*, Jackie. For how long did he fill my mind, both day and night? How long did it take me to come to terms with his passing, and have I yet managed to? I redoubled my efforts on the work front – it was that that kept me going, I'm sure of it – and spent just countless nights, alone and weeping, and always just waiting for him to walk in the door. At the beginning, I made him his tea, and then I threw it away when he didn't come, much as I often used to when still he was with me. Apart from a million memories, I have little of him. I keep my cigarettes – Chesterfield is what Gary now buys for me – in the case I gave him. I asked Gary too if he could find me a bottle of Eau de Paris, but what he bought was quite different, and I didn't put it on. Oh Jackie. I loved that man more than I treasured my very own life. Always I am reminded of him by some little thing. Just this morning there was a picture in the *Mirror* of that man who was his boss, Mr Wisely. Or Sir Nigel, as he is now: I think he must have got it for war work, or something of that order. But now through Jeremy, I shall be with my Jackie, and this time for ever. Tomorrow I shall be brimming over with all my memories of when the whole thing happened. And how it all began.

The sun shone down upon this quite miraculous scene from a clear and perfect, deep blue sky. And how very typical of good old England, Mary thought, that this is the very first day in nearly six whole years when the newspapers have been allowed to issue a weather forecast, and so of course they have got it quite hopelessly wrong. Cloudy and rain, they said, for later on – and just look at it! The most wonderful summer's afternoon, and it's only May. God is smiling down on us all, I can only think, as we bask in the rays of the sun and the justified glory of so very hard-won a victory. It's well into the seventies, I'm sure it must be, and all the thousands of people in uniform do look rather decidedly warm. I've just got on a quite new printed cotton tea dress – no mends or darns! – and a cute little bolero jacket (Gary, he said to me: that's cute, honey – he calls me honey) and I bought it just ages ago with all of my coupons and even some of Imogen's and I've kept it in tissue paper, just waiting for this day. Jeremy is wearing the sweetest little sailor suit (heaven only knows how Gary got hold of it) – it is only a little bit large, and oh my goodness, so many Royal Navy men have come up to him and saluted and so on and called him shipmate – quite delightful! An American sailor gave him some chewing gum, but I took it away from him afterwards. Gary chews gum – they all of them do – but I'm just terrified of Jeremy swallowing it because apparently you die if you do, or something. Gary has been telling me what all the different uniforms and decorations are – the Wrens of course I know, they're really very smart, and don't they know it – and there's the WAAFs and the ATS and regular nurses and Land Girls in their rather dashing jodhpurs . . . there are Poles, Free French, flying heroes from the Battle of Britain, just thousands of Tommies . . . and Gary says I mustn't get the GIs and the Canadians muddled up because they both get very offended. He looks so wonderful – he's in his very best uniform with all his captain's insignia and a lot of medals – he told me what they all are. And he's so very tall – I remember when first I saw him thinking goodness, that American soldier over there, he's so much taller than any man I've ever known. Looking back, it had all seemed meant, in a way, because I hadn't been even close to the West End since, well – before the war, must have been, and the only reason I was there was because the company in Coventry Street where I used to buy all the endless bales of towels that I was forever needing, they'd called to tell me that they could no longer deliver (their biggest customers, the owner Mr Perry had said to me one time, were the War Office, the hospitals and me; I have no idea whether or not he was being entirely serious). Anyway, I had a taxi very expensively puttering away at the kerbside and there I was, waiting for Mr Perry to pile up all the brown paper packages into the back while the cabbie was strapping yet more of them into that luggage bit they've got at the side, when I just happened to catch sight of this tall American soldier, ambling down the road with his so long legs, quite as if he were taking a stroll in the countryside. And of course I didn't mean to stare or anything, but I must have, I suppose, because to my enormous embarrassment he actually stopped and lifted his cap and started to talk to me! Well I'd heard about these Americans, but really! He said his name was Captain Gary Brooklyn, United States Army, and asked if he could help me in any way and I replied quite stiffly that everything was quite under control, thank you very much Captain – and then he asked me if I'd like to have a 'coke' with him in Rainbow Corner! I just goggled at him, largely I think because I could make not an atom of sense from a single word he had uttered (while loving, however, the way in which he said it). I just stuttered out something or other and made to get into the taxi and he gave me a card of some sort and said that he was there, in Rainbow Corner, every single afternoon from three until six and I said primly that I was sure that that must be very nice for him, and hastily signalled for the cabbie to drive away immediately. On the journey back, I was really rather flustered. So, I remember thinking, all the rumours are quite correct, then. They really are so very different from us, the Americans – so terribly forward. And certainly in my calling, business had increased dramatically – a thing I had barely thought possible – since the advent of the American army, and many of the foetuses I had recently had to dispose of were decidedly not utterly white, if you can understand what one is meaning. The United States army, I now know, actually segregates the coloured soldiers from the others – you certainly won't see one in Rainbow Corner – though young London girls seem all for integration. One did hear the most awful things – these girls, some as young as fourteen or fifteen, it's been rumoured, hanging around the US bases and Rainbow Corner (well certainly I've seen them there, though maybe not quite so young as that) ready and willing to consort with any GI at all, really, unless he is quite altogether too repellent, and simply because they have heard of all the money they earn and their apparently endless access to such things as girls in London have yearned and pined for for so many years – nylons mainly, but also scented soap and chocolates and even French champagne. Corruption again, you see – the war, it has corrupted so many of us. In the normal way of things, these girls would be at school, and virgins for another decade. The professional women, of course – the Piccadilly Warriors they were nicknamed, if you can believe it – they're apparently making an absolute mint. Gary told me later that the American government were blaming the huge rise in VD among the soldiers on the promiscuity of London women! Who would have thought it? But all of Gary's friends that I've met are just positively charming – officers, admittedly, but so easy-going, complimentary and always making jokes. I love their accents – it's as if they're film stars! The men in London largely loathe the 'Yanks', as they call them, for fairly understandable reasons – but there's no disguising the attractions of the GI for the Englishwoman, however . . . though still I was amazed to all of a sudden find myself among their number. I cannot deny that my brief encounter with Captain Gary Brooklyn had lodged in my mind – but it was Imogen who made me do it. I doubt very much I would have gone had it not been for Imogen's urging: if you don't take a break from the work then you'll die, Mary, she said to me – although she did so love it when I wasn't there, and then she was in sole command. Nonetheless, she might even have been right: I really was so desperately low at that time, so very tired, and yet just driven to work throughout the day and weep throughout the whole of the night. Such had become my life.

Rainbow Corner turned out to be a converted Lyons' Corner House, devoted to the pleasures of the American servicemen. I had never seen such a place in my life – it is just so vast, one cannot conceive. There can be a thousand couples jitterbugging away on the dance floor – Gary, he's very good at it and he taught me: he liked his music jazzy, he said, and I do, I do too. And 'coke' is short for Coca-Cola, a black and rather sweetish fizzy drink that I absolutely adore now. I've been there many times – the food is wonderful, compared with what I was used to, the portions quite gigantic. After some weeks, I was looking and feeling so very much better again, and many evenings I didn't cry at all. I could see he was falling in love with me – it alarmed me, though I did nothing to stop it. I had not considered a relationship with a man, not ever. I don't mean I had rejected the idea, it just had never occurred to me. I think women have this ability, you know, some women – to sort of place oneself into cold storage, as it were, for very many years or even the whole of one's life, if necessary, and come to view the prospect of a distant thawing and gradual resuscitation as unlikely in the extreme and yet somehow still, theoretically, just about possible. Well, in not very much time at all, really . . . I warmed to the man. Though still we have done no more than kiss. The thought of anything else I find sometimes just no more than strange, and then in other moods quite openly terrifying – though I daresay this will change once I am a wife, free of the grime of the past, and roaming a vast and brand-new landscape. It is quite incredible to me, you know, after so very long, when any thought of a future seemed to be utterly hopeless, foolish even, that so golden a prospect is now risen before me. And before every single one of us, it surely seems, on this simply glorious day, when all of London is so very happy, and smiling again – all now looking to the future.

'Oh my goodness, Gary – the crowds now! I've never seen so many people. Where are we? I used to know, but I've rather lost my bearings . . . Are you all right there, Jeremy? Keep hold of my hand, now.'

'Here, young feller,' said Gary, stooping down and sweeping up Jeremy in the one great movement that had Jeremy laughing in surprise and delight. 'You sit up there on my shoulders and you be sure you get the best view of Mr Churchill, yeah?'

'Oh *heavens*,' gasped Mary, clutching Gary's arm. 'Do you think we actually will? Get to see him? Oh I'd just *love* to. He's been such an inspiration.'

'Well honey, I guess the guy's got a pretty busy day, you know? But we're sure moving in the right direction, anyways.'

The crush of people was now enormous, but everyone was laughing and waving around their heads all the Monty berets and Union Jacks that hawkers were selling just everywhere, a lot of servicemen already rather drunk and swigging from bottles of ale – one knot of soldiers over there was now approaching all the women with crimson lips and with comic courtliness begging to be kissed – then proudly displaying the bright and smudgy imprints as the very highest trophy. Mary yelped out her delight as the huge and shifting crowd, with her wedged in there somewhere amongst it, surged and billowed around a corner, and there high above her was Nelson's Column, hundreds of pigeons wheeling about it, the fountains alive with drenched and cackling people, waving around their arms – there's one pretty girl now with lovely and bright blonde hair and she has hitched up her dress, oh my goodness, and two young sailors are reaching down from the very top of one of the fountains and she's wading across, look, and now she's got them by the hands and yes! Up she goes! There is much clapping and a roar of approval – and a Movietone camera, capturing the moment. Mary was thrilled for the wet and pretty, happy girl, though she could not help wondering how the sweet thing's father might react when he witnesses the entire escapade next weekend at the Odeon. Every parapet and plinth, the lampposts and balconies, are crawling with swarms of bright-eyed and energised Londoners, their faces near to cracking, sometimes, under the tugging strain of their grins of euphoria. And then there came a boom and crackling from all around them – a hesitation just palpable in the roaring of the crowd, the shudder of apprehension that was rippling through them, the flinch and impulse of so many years of wariness and alarm. Then a great and deafening shout went up – ear-splitting whistles and much applause – as the voice of Winston Churchill began to rumble around the Square from the dozens of speakers all about them. The noise from the crowd was so great that Mary was frantic to be missing nearly all of what this so wonderful man was saying to them and she was batting her hands up and down and shushing the people around her, near tearful in her frustration. And then she heard him say 'We may allow ourselves a brief period of rejoicing . . .' and amid the cheering, Gary laughed and hugged her shoulder – he may think, Mary reflected, that here is irony or something, for true British understatement he I don't think will ever understand.

Mary cried when the speech was over, and she was hardly alone. After that, it was up to the force of the press of the crowd, in which direction they next would be shunted. Rumours were eagerly passed among the masses that Churchill was going to appear on a balcony in Whitehall – others braying proudly that they had already seen him in the back of an open car on his way from Downing Street to join the King and Queen at the Palace:

he did his V-sign, they said – mimicking the gesture – he waved about his hat, and then his cigar. Jeremy seemed to be loving every moment, so far as a piteously grateful Mary could tell – she was glancing up at him constantly, his sturdy little legs each side of Gary's strong thick neck, waving his flag and shrieking and laughing, as Gary tightly held his ankles. I can't believe how big he's grown, my little Jeremy. We must, I've decided, keep up with Mr and Mrs Grey – they've done such a good job, and he never stops talking about them. Oh and *thank* you, Sheila – thank you for putting him there. I am, she thought, catching her breath, just at this moment so very terribly happy, I could actually die.

Gary's idea was to somehow manoeuvre themselves amid the throng towards Admiralty Arch, a vague intention of at least moving in the direction, anyway, of Buckingham Palace, though he did not say to Mary that he had no hope of their reaching it until way after nightfall. And soon enough, as they shuffled their way along among the hundreds of thousands of revellers, darkness came – though the sky was clear and purple, and still it felt to Mary so wonderfully warm. A distant roar from somewhere way on ahead that grew with the tumble of gathering thunder – more and more people were shouting and cheering from more than a mile away, and the wave of its contagion was rippling back towards them – it rolled over and then engulfed them. Word was passed around that Mr Churchill was up on the balcony of the Palace with the whole of the Royal Family and although even Gary from his eminence could still only distantly discern the gleam of gold on the finial of the pole and the flag that was fluttering, all of them cheered and stamped and clapped, quite as if they were as close as could be and were drinking in every last detail. And gradually, the crowd began to thin – at least to the extent where Mary could swing around her arms again – and more gangs of people peeled away now amid new and urgent, fevered gossip of all the pubs in danger of running out of beer. In the park there wound around the massive girth of an oak tree the longest conga line ever, the giggling girls and swaying men kicking out their legs at random moments and in every direction, some of them falling over and then quickly scrambling up again and rejoining the line. Mary signalled to a small patch of clearing at the base of a clump of plane trees, and they shouldered their way through yet another throng of tipsy people, doing the Lambeth Walk. The clang of a fire engine then made her jump and it clattered briefly into view and sped along its journey, panicked people scattering before it. The word was that at Hyde Park Corner a bonfire had been set up and an effigy of Hitler was being jeeringly burned, while squads of drunken Tommies hauled over park benches and hurled them on to the pyre. Mary was content to lean with the flat of her back against one of the trees, hugging her own arms and rubbing them up and down – closing her eyes and breathing in all the mingled aromas of roasting chestnuts, stale spilt ale and the sweet green tang of freshly-mown grass. She was shocked to hear the quite gruff bark of an elderly man not too distant concluding the sale of a prophylactic to a passing couple: five bob, he said – or two-and-a-tanner for a used one, well rinsed out. Gary was kneeling down on the grass a little way away and covering his eyes with his hands. Whenever he suddenly pulled them away and opened wide his mouth in a parody of surprise, Jeremy squealed with laughter, and then set to copying his antics. Oh look – oh bother. We had an ice cream earlier, all of us, and now I've gone and got a mark on the collar of my bolero jacket. How on *earth* did I manage to do that . . . ?

'Blimey, miss. Thought I'd gone and lost you.'

Mary started – was pulled out sharply from her state of distraction – and looked down enquiringly at the raggedy boy who had appeared at her side.

'What? I'm sorry . . . ?'

'Man want you to have this, miss,' said the boy, holding out an envelope.

Mary's eyebrows were raised in surprise as she took it from him.

'For me? Are you sure? Can it be from a distant admirer?' she smiled. 'Is it from Mr Churchill, do you suppose?'

'Ha! Not likely, miss. I don't know who it were, but he give me a bob, and I only just now catched up with you. Thought you was gone for good.'

'Oh. Well . . .' laughed Mary, as she opened the envelope and glanced down idly at the folded sheet inside. 'Thank you. Thank you very much indeed, young man.'

'Pleasure, miss,' grinned the ragamuffin, touching his forehead and scampering away.

Mary watched him go, and then she unfolded the paper, gasped once as her hand clamped hard across her mouth – she scarcely even glimpsed Gary's anxious flicker of concern as he strode now towards her, and then just blackness as her legs gave way beneath her, and she fell as if dead upon the ground.

◉

The sun shone weakly the next raw morning as she sat on the stump of a rotten elm tree amid the rutted earth and ravages of all that was left of what used to be once her little local park. No sign now of the pond around which she and Sheila and Molly had sat in the heat with baby Jeremy, and where a little lad one time had struggled to rescue his cigar-box boat from among the rushes. The skin around her hard and straining eyes felt to be stretched so tightly over her newly sharpened bones – she had since yesterday looked just mad and startled, she could only imagine, from the moment she had swum back into the world from out of the plunge of her swooning, gradually aware of Gary's large and looming eyes hovering above her. He was fanning her face with a piece of paper, and muttering noises.

'You OK now honey? You sit up? That's my girl. Easy, now. Day got too much for you, huh?'

Mary had stumbled to her feet, attempting a smile of reassurance to both Gary and Jeremy – wholly unconcerned, and dipping his hand into a crumpled-up bag of peppermint humbugs – though she felt she just must have appeared mad, and startled. She stood a little more steadily and smoothed down her dress, automatically mumbling her apologies for her silliness, her repeated insistences that she was perfectly fine. She reached quickly out to a tree, as she began to sway.

'We better start the long trek home, honey, you sure you're OK,' said Gary easily, swinging up Jeremy high on to his shoulders and putting one arm around Mary as they began to set off. A young woman was delightedly squealing and running away from a trio of soldiers, while a fourth of them was spewing up on to a gravel path, and moaning disconsolately. Gary shook out the sheet of paper as they ambled along, and he scanned it incuriously.

'So what we got us here . . . ? "Mary. Meet me at eight in the morning in the park. Please. Jackie". Who's Jackie?'

Mary trembled under the weight of his arm, and her knees felt weak. She sucked in breath, in order to speak.

'Oh just someone,' she managed to say. 'I used to work with her once. In a laundry. Long time ago.'

'Laundry, huh? Well I promise to you this, Mary honey – you won't never have to work in no laundry again, nor no place else. Look after you real good, I will honey. So help me God.'

The journey home seemed endless, Mary – aware of the heaviness of silence – having often to stutter out 'I'm sorry Gary,

I beg your pardon – what?' whenever she realised he had been speaking to her; and then later, she didn't trouble any more – just let him get on with whatever it was he felt he had to say: Jeremy's fast asleep, little feller; what a great day, huh? Sure do love you, honey.

And all through the night when Gary had finally (oh God, will he never go?) left her, she sat to the side of Jeremy's bed and just gazed at him, mesmerised by the languid fall of his long dark eyelashes, the untroubled murmur of his gentle breathing. Who, she asked herself fiercely, could be so unfeeling as to play such a joke on me? No . . . it is no joke, it cannot be: it is real. *Nonsense* – it's a hoax, pure and simple – and perpetrated by whom exactly, that's what I should like to know. I know: what it must be is the most awful coincidence – the note was intended for another, and that stupid little urchin, he had me confused, that's all. No – it was for me: it is real. This is happening. But it could not be, just couldn't. Three years have passed – such things are impossible. It is no more than a very distasteful joke, and that is the end of it – and of course I shall not go. But who could have done such a thing? I know no one. Not really. And so it must be true! But it cannot be . . . it *cannot* . . . But what if it is? What if it *is* . . . ?

She awoke soon after dawn, astounded to have slept – neck skewed sideways, and her arms cast over Jeremy. The second it took her to decide that it had all been just the most terrible dream – it lasted no more than a second. She telephoned the woman downstairs, babbled her apology for having woken her up and begged her, implored her to please please please, oh please God can you come up here right this instant and take care of Jeremy for me, will you, because there's somewhere, you see, that I just have to be.

And now she is here, and her cold and fluttering fingers are being held in the warmth of hands they remember, two big

578

thumbs sifting amid the softness of her palms as if in search of something embedded that they left there, long ago. When the first of her tears fell down, it was kneaded into the fleshy mix and whitened knuckles as they grasped at one another more urgently. She raised her eyes and looked again with an aching disbelief at the tan-skinned and full-bearded seaman who was crouching before her.

'I loves you, Mary . . . I ain't never missed nothing in my life like what I missed you . . .'

She looked at him with tear-filled eyes, and shook her head in wonder.

'*Why*, Jackie . . . ? How could you . . . ?'

'*Had* to, love – I had to. They was all of them after me – I come to you, that would've been the end of it for the both of us, telling you. Had to get out. But I wrote you, Mary love – I wrote you over and over, and you didn't never write me back.'

'Oh . . . I moved out of there straight away, the old place. Had to. But *who* was after you, Jackie? How did you—?'

'Don't matter. Not now it don't. This war – there's a lot of dead men walking. I change my name – had all the papers, stroke of luck. Few quid put aside, not a lot. Old Dickie, he clean me up a bit. I were burnt quite bad, Mary, you want the truth. Why I growed the beard, first off. You can still see the marks all down the side, look. Dickie – I told him to tell you I were all right, but he were in hell of a state, poor old sod. Never got word, then . . . ? Nah. Can't say I'm surprised. He all right, is he . . . ? Nah. Can't say I'm surprised about that neither. But I tell you, Mary . . . I'm the happiest bloke in the world right now – just sat here now with you. Ain't never loved no one else, you see Mary: not never. Not even a bit. It's always been you, Mary my love. Right from the first. You know that. And it's like that for you too – ain't it?'

Mary sucked down air, or else she felt she would have fainted. Her head was rocking from side to side and she was moaning

579

gently as her eyes were raking the sky above them. At last she managed to speak.

'How did you find me . . . ?'

Jackie chuckled at the memory.

'Weren't easy. Met a bloke what knowed a bloke what said he could track people down, like – even in wartime London: bleeding miracle. Took a bit. He done me a favour, and I done one for him, like.'

Despite just everything, Mary had to smile at that.

'Same old Jackie . . .'

And he pounced on this with an energy that made her shrink back.

'No! Wrong. Not the same old Jackie – leastwise, not the one I were when last you knowed me. I'm me again, Mary – the old Jackie. Straight up I am – you got to believe me. I can't hardly credit what it was I become. But I had time, see – time to sort it out in my head. In the Navy, I seed things different. Yeh. I always thought it were a mug's game, but it give me a right good feeling. The things I seen, Mary, you wouldn't hardly credit it.'

Mary just stared at him, her mouth hung open.

'Jackie . . . you're not really trying to tell me that this uniform is . . . *real*, are you? Oh my God – you almost had me believing you there for a minute. You're still doing it! You're lying and lying.'

Jackie's eyes were filled with passion, and he grabbed her hands more tightly.

'I ain't lying! This *is* real – course it's real. I joined up. Had to get out, see? I been on convoys in the Atlantic, most the time. I can prove it, Mary, you want me to.'

'Oh Jackie! You can prove *anything* . . . you always could. And the medals? I suppose they're real too, are they?'

Jackie glanced down at his chest and sniffed.

'Oh . . . yeh. But they ain't nothing. We all got them. Just for like being there. I ain't been no hero, nor nothing. We all got them. Here, Mary – have a fag, ay . . . ?'

He shuffled over to her a packet of Player's. She smiled as she took one.

'Looks like you,' she said. 'The sailor on the front. Looks like you.'

She rootled about in her handbag and took out the rhodium-plated cigarette case. Jackie laughed as he drew out the matching lighter, J.R. engraved at its corner.

'I wanted you to have that case, Mary – left it deliberate with all the doings. Hoped it'd get back to you. I hoped, maybe . . . you'd know I were still here, still about, sort of style.'

Mary now was dazed. She one minute was chatting quite easily with the man she had seemingly known since before she was born – and then she was stunned by the intrusion of a terrible and quite mad circumstance – a dead man, the emergence of an old and plastered-over thing from the long long ago. She had a *new* life, now . . . all this was gone and done. She had a *new* life now . . .

'I cried for you, Jackie . . . I cried and cried for you, night after night and day after day. You were my everything. All I had. But now . . . there is something else. I have something new. You were *gone*, Jackie – three years you were gone. It's too cruel of you just to . . . *arrive*. It's just . . . too cruel . . .'

Jackie looked down at the ground. When he raised his head again, his eyes were filled with a gentle fondness.

'I seed the lad . . . in the park yesterday, yeh? Grand, ain't he? Our Jeremy.'

'You were there? You were in the park?'

'Oh yeh. Following behind, like. I nearly come up to you – I were all meaning to. And then . . . well you know what I done. But he do look grand though, don't he? Ay? My son. Our boy. Don't he? Ay? Um . . . Mary? You listening, love, is you? Tell me,

Mary . . . who's the Yank? That's what you reckon's the new life then, is it? Some Yank?'

Mary bristled immediately.

'He is not, Jackie, just some 'Yank', as you call him. He is . . . important to me, Jackie. Important.'

Jackie nodded, quite slowly.

'You love him . . . ?'

'He's wonderful with Jeremy – quite wonderful. You should see him – well maybe you did. And he's *there*, Jackie – you, you were never *there*. I have . . . agreed to marry him. And you can't say, can you, that I am already married. To you. Because I'm not. I never have been. Because you never, ever, *asked*. So as I say – we are to be married, and then live in the United States. A wonderful future – you should be pleased for Jeremy, Jackie, if not for me. Having such an opportunity. Wide open spaces . . .'

Jackie nodded, quite slowly.

'You love him . . . ?'

Mary tutted out her frustration through the approach of more tears.

'It's not a question—! *Yes*, I love him. There. That what you want to hear? Is it Jackie? And it's going to be *clean*. Can you remember clean? I don't even know if *I* can. And it's what I want. Do you understand me, Jackie? I just want it all to be . . . clean again. I'm not, oh God – Bloody Mary any more—'

'And me! Nor me. I ain't a lad, not no more. Not me, Mary.'

'Oh Jackie you never *were*, were you? Jack the Lad. You were worse, much much worse than that. Have you forgotten? Because I haven't, Jackie. Sammy Punch . . . ?'

Jackie's face now was filled with hurt and anger.

'I never kill him! I told you at the time, Mary, and you should of believed me. I never kill Sammy Punch!'

Mary regarded him evenly.

'Jackie. Look at me. Look me in the eye, and tell me you are not a murderer.'

Jackie glanced away, and then he faced her.

'I never kill Sammy Punch! Look . . . God sake *listen* to me Mary, will you? I can't put things good in words, I never could, you knows that Mary. But just listen . . . I understand what you must of thought of me. And I understand . . . you thinks I'm dead and gone, well – you're a very good-looking woman, Mary. Beautiful, my eyes. So course, fullness of time, you going to be courting again. Stands to reason. No listen – hear me out, Mary, I begs of you. Now see – thing is, I'm *with* you, ain't I? Ay? I *is* you, Mary – and you's me and all. Always were. And Jeremy. Our little boy. Ain't he?'

Mary did her best to retain her composure. Her look was steely.

'I want more children, Jackie. I intend to have them.'

Jackie nodded rapidly, though she could see that his lips were quivering now.

'Yeh yeh – course you do. I knows you do. You always did – and I'm sorry for that, Mary. I swears I is. Thing is – you want more kids, well . . . I can *accommodate* you. See? But it *got* to be you and me, Mary. The two of us. Like it always were. Before. When we was . . .'

Mary nodded sadly.

'When were were just Jack and Mary. No, Jackie . . . it's just too easy. You think you can just . . . I don't know – arise from the dead, and just step back into my life as if nothing has happened. We've been through war, Jackie – hell on earth is what we've come through. And I've had enough. Don't look at me like that. Just listen. I owe it to Jeremy. He's not even a Londoner any more, Jackie – not like you and me. The countryside, it's all he knows – and . . . Jackie! Don't. Please don't cry, Jackie. I simply can't bear it if you cry . . . !'

Jackie did his best to dash away the rush of tears that had flooded up into his eyes, and now were rolling away down his face, caught and glistening like crystal beads on the bristle of his beard.

'Don't leave me, Mary . . . please don't leave me, Mary . . .'

'Jackie. Don't. I can't stand it . . .'

'Choose *me*, Mary. I begs of you, girl. Look at me, Mary – I's begging you now . . .'

'Jackie please! Don't *look* at me like that! I just can't . . .'

Jackie was on his knees beside her, his eyes distraught, and his hands so tightly entwined in hers.

'Don't . . . *leave* me, Mary. Please don't leave me . . . !'

Mary caught her breath at the sight of those big brown handsome eyes, liquid with tears. But she cannot believe a single word he says to her. He will not do this – he cannot come back and take away her future. She shook her head with violence. Her chest then gave in, and she kissed him with a fervour she could barely remember and he held on to her quite frantically, his mouth intent upon swallowing her whole, his arms so greedy and all over her. She pushed at his shoulders and when eventually she could pull herself away from him, she was flushed and gasping, aware of the throbbing in her heart. Jackie's face was heavy with devotion, wincing away from the needle of despair.

'Mary . . . I *loves* you. I *loves* you, Mary. I always love you, and I always will. I needs it, Mary, for us to be together. I needs it, Mary. I needs your love. Give it me, Mary. Oh please God, Mary – *give* it me . . . !'

Mary, suddenly, was calm. She had remembered when the whole thing happened . . . how it had all begun. And then she knew what just had to happen then. She smilingly touched his face and placed with care the cigarette case into his outstretched fingers, and he clasped it. His eyes were wet and beseeching, and her hands were covering his.

'Here, Jackie. Just take it. It's yours.'